THE
HOUSES IN BETWEEN

THE
HOUSES IN BETWEEN

A NOVEL

By HOWARD SPRING

HARPER & BROTHERS, PUBLISHERS
NEW YORK

For

DAVID and RUNA

With Love

Library of Congress catalog card number: 51-11956

AUTHOR'S FOREWORD

I SEE from some old letters that as long ago as 1940 I wrote to my agents asking them to obtain for me a copy of the music hall song containing the words: "You could see the Crystal Palace if it wasn't for the houses in between." The pathetic significance of the Crystal Palace had for long appealed to my imagination, and I wanted to make a novel out of the contrast between that fragile promise of peace and the dreadful realities of the years that followed. That the book, at last finished, is published in the year when the centenary of the Palace is being celebrated is accidental.

The idea remained in my head for a long time, came forward occasionally, and was put back again. I could not make up my mind what was the shape it should have. Then in 1947 I was invited to the birthday party of a lady who was ninety-nine years old. She was a spry old dear, clear-headed, and I talked to her of many things, and felt a sense of awe when I thought of the backward reach of her mind. She had been born before the idea of the Crystal Palace first entered Prince Albert's head! She was so old that she could have attended the opening at the age of three! And then I saw how the book must be written. It must be the personal record of someone old enough to have watched the fell progress of history from that day to this. But, even so, it remained unstarted until January of 1949.

As to the places of the book. The beautiful Cornish estate here called Tresant exists and is unchanged to this day, but its name is not Tresant, nor is the book's Porteven in fact called Porteven. I have never been into the house on the estate, and know nothing of it. So I have had to invent a house. The reader must take that, and the Gaylord family living in it, as fictitious. Indeed, every character of the book is fictitious. There is not anywhere on the estate which I here call Tresant a chapel such as that which is described as housing the Gaylord tombs. That chapel exists in all its moldering melancholy. I have scraped mildew from the tombs there. But it exists in another part of Cornwall, many miles away from "Tresant." For the purpose of the book, I have permitted chapel and estate a marriage of convenience.

H. S.

THE
HOUSES IN BETWEEN

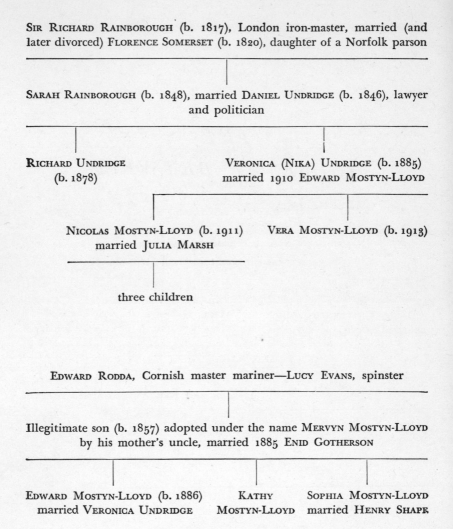

SIR RICHARD RAINBOROUGH (b. 1817), London iron-master, married (and later divorced) FLORENCE SOMERSET (b. 1820), daughter of a Norfolk parson

SARAH RAINBOROUGH (b. 1848), married DANIEL UNDRIDGE (b. 1846), lawyer and politician

RICHARD UNDRIDGE (b. 1878)

VERONICA (NIKA) UNDRIDGE (b. 1885) married 1910 EDWARD MOSTYN-LLOYD

NICOLAS MOSTYN-LLOYD (b. 1911) married JULIA MARSH

VERA MOSTYN-LLOYD (b. 1913)

three children

EDWARD RODDA, Cornish master mariner—LUCY EVANS, spinster

Illegitimate son (b. 1857) adopted under the name MERVYN MOSTYN-LLOYD by his mother's uncle, married 1885 ENID GOTHERSON

EDWARD MOSTYN-LLOYD (b. 1886) married VERONICA UNDRIDGE

KATHY MOSTYN-LLOYD

SOPHIA MOSTYN-LLOYD married HENRY SHAPE

CHARLES ORMISTON GAYLORD (b. 1815), 10th Baron Burnage, twice married

1st wife, LADY EDWINA SUDELEY

SALLY GAYLORD (b. 1847)

2nd wife, FLORENCE RAINBOROUGH, divorced by SIR RICHARD RAINBOROUGH

JUSTIN GAYLORD

FRANCIS UNDRIDGE, artist, married his model

DANIEL UNDRIDGE (b. 1846)   MARIE UNDRIDGE (b. 1856) married
married SARAH RAINBOROUGH   SEBASTIEN RIMMEL, shipowner of Bordeaux

---

JULIAN RIMMEL (b. 1877), art dealer of
London and New York, married MARTHE
GRONNET of Paris

PROLOGUE BY JULIAN RIMMEL

IF MY aunt, Sarah Undridge, had lived until today she would have been a hundred years old. I was at a small party given for her ninety-ninth birthday, and she was spry enough then. There was a sense of festivity. All of us who were present were ourselves "getting on," as they say. Certainly, more years were behind us than we could expect to find before us, and I suppose it was this, as much as anything, that made us all smile affectionately at old Sarah, sitting upright, thin as a lath and rather bloodless, in her winged chair, her pale blue watery eyes looking through the window at the May sunshine falling upon the grass and the flowers and the blossoming shrubs. She at any rate was defying the years as we all in our hearts wished to do. She was like a building standing erect in a bombed city. She was a symbol, giving us hope. A vast cake had been made, and there were ninety-nine candles upon it. We knew that she would never be able to blow them out, and so a small bellows had been bought for the occasion. The cake was placed on a table in front of her chair, and a few of us lit the candles with tapers. The sunshine fell strongly upon them, taking the substance from the flames. They wavered, pale and feeble, about their wicks, like so many infinitesimal ghosts, each struggling to detach itself from the mortal thread to which it had been too long attached. I placed the bellows in Sarah's transparent blue-veined hands, and it was pathetic to see how easily even she, herself so nearly a ghost, sent them—puff, puff, puff—flying into nothingness. A blue-gray fume lingered for a moment in the sunshine, and then was gone; and after that there was a strong bitter smell, earthy and astringent, as if all her years suddenly had condensed and coalesced, like a whole season of roses released from a phial of attar.

She did not complete her century. During some months after this she was up for a few hours every day, and she was able to read a little and to play dominoes. Then she took altogether to her bed. She read there, books in large print, and she liked someone to come in now and then for a bit of gossip. However, visitors tended more and more to find her sleeping. Waking out of one of these slumbers when I was there, she said with a smile that she had been sleeping to conserve her strength. "I find now," she said, "that if I'm to do it I must be very careful." She had set her mind, I think, on winning through to the hundred. "There will be a telegram from the King," she said. "One of the first things I remember in life is seeing the Queen, and it would be nice to get a telegram from her great-grandson."

I don't know whether it is a royal habit to send telegrams to all centenarians, but Sarah thought it was, and she looked forward to receiving hers. But the privy purse was spared that shilling. She died on New Year's Day of 1948. Someone had gone in to wish her a happy new year: she who had known so many years, happy and not so happy. Her tired body didn't want this one. She had been at moorings long enough. She had slipped the cable and gone. The new year had come in stormily down there at Tresant. All night long there had been a windy hullaballoo. The lawns were littered with debris of the trees, and one vast elm went down, ripping a great pit out of the earth in its gigantic death-fall. I wondered whether Sarah had been awake and aware of this elemental turmoil, whether she had heard that almighty crash and thought of the elms growing inside the frail glass walls of the Crystal Palace. That was where she had seen the Queen, amid sparkling fountains, with bands playing, and choirs singing, and aisles upon aisles of machines that were to unite the nations and bring in the golden age.

It was on the day after the Crystal Palace had been burned to the ground that I discovered how bright and clear in Sarah's memory that far-off day had remained. It hadn't meant much to me, that dis-appearance of the great glass building on Sydenham Hill, but I found her curiously agitated. She would talk of nothing else. "I was there," she said, "when they opened it. It's the first thing I remember with great clearness. It was on my birthday, you know, May the first. I was three."

She talked for a long time. She was then a lively old girl, still able to get about anywhere. She had a small flat in London, and stayed there all through the Second World War. After that, she retired finally to Tresant. It was in this flat that she talked to me that day about the Crystal Palace. It had become a symbol in her life. That she had been there at the opening lent the thing a vitality; but there was more to it than that. As she grew up, she went back again and again to that moment. She read all that had been said before the Palace was built, all that was said during its triumphal life in Hyde Park. She had seen the crystal dream, the shimmering bubble, blown to pieces. It was the palace of peace; all the nations were to meet there in understanding. "Can you think of anything lovelier," she asked, "than a palace of glass? Or anything more frail?"

"Give me that little box," she said, "there—on top of my bureau."

I brought the small red leather box and laid it on her lap. She opened it, and took out a bundle of tissue paper. From this she unwrapped a piece of china. It was a fragment of a common cup; the handle and a bit of the side; white china, with a segment of blue ring.

"There," she said, turning it over and over, "you would never guess what that is."

No, I could not guess what extraordinary emotions this relic aroused in the old woman's mind.

"Do you remember," she said, "how scared we all were in 1938? Well, we had reason to be. It was touch and go then. They dug trenches in Hyde Park. This was one of the things that were dug up. There was a lot of it—a lot of broken china. A lot of china was broken, you know, while the exhibition was on. You could get tea there, and people were careless. When it was over and the place was cleaned up, all the broken china was buried on the spot. And that's what they turned up when they were digging the trenches on the site of the Palace of Peace. Don't you think that extraordinary?"

I said that I did.

"It's more extraordinary than you think," Sarah said. "After that first grand opening day I often went to the exhibition. It was the thing, you know, because it was educational. The Prince of Wales, for one, was supposed to educate himself there. The Prince Consort demanded an essay on the wonders the boy had seen, and little Bertie, who was only ten, had a lot to say about Thugs. Don't ask me, my dear, why there was an exhibit about the habits of Thugs, but there was, and what is more it impressed itself deeply into the boy's essay. But Albert's idea was that salvation would come through people getting together round his machines, not round Thugs, and the poor child was given to understand that his tastes were shocking. However, I don't know so much about that. He was always interested in people, even Thugs, rather than in machines."

Sarah's maid brought in the tea, and when it had been poured out she said: "I was telling you about this piece of china. Well, my nannie, who was named, believe it or not, Mercy Kite, often took me on educational tours round the exhibition, but I never liked this much. What I liked was to see the thing from the outside, with the glass all glittering in the summer weather and the rows of flags at the top blowing out straight in the wind under the white clouds. However, having tea inside was always pleasant, and for some childish reason which I can't explain, the cups with the blue rings fascinated me. I thought them exquisite. One day I let one fall. I spilled tea all down myself, and Kite scolded me dreadfully. I cried and cried. She hustled me bawling out of the place, but my tears were not for my spoilt

3

frock or for her harsh words, but because I had broken one of the beautiful cups." She wrapped the fragment in its paper and put it back into the box. "I like to believe," she said, "that this is a bit of that very cup."

I hadn't known before how this matter obsessed her mind, but now she was well away. "There used to be an old song," she said, "one of those that the tradesmen's boys whistled. I don't remember much of it: just a line that said: 'You could see the Crystal Palace if it wasn't for the houses in between.' Well, I suppose you could—always —any time. But, unfortunately, they're always there—the houses in between. Now, let me give you some more tea. And put this box back on the bureau. I've chattered enough. Get out the dominoes."

I thought a lot about this conversation with my Aunt Sarah, about the irony, which she clearly perceived, of a palace of peace, so shining, so alluring, so terribly fragile. But, for her, it was always there, like St. Augustine's dear City of God, and anyone could see it—if it wasn't for the houses in between. All those houses, and all those people, grand houses and shabby houses, rich people and poor people, with all their feuds and rivalries, their hates and fears, allegiances, treacheries and dissents: yes, it would be easier to see the shining pavilions if it were not for all this in between.

"You know, my dear," Sarah said the next time I called upon her, "when you put my book into order I want you to call it *The Houses in Between*. I'm afraid the Palace has fallen into sad disrepute—just a place for cat shows and canary shows and letting off fireworks. Few people seem to realize that it's the supreme symbol of everything that's happened in the world from the time it was built till now. All the good intentions, all the terrible inability to do what ought to be done."

"What is all this about a book?" I asked.

"It's just the story of my life," she said modestly. She gave me a defiant grin. "It's not finished yet," she said, "because I'm not dead yet."

She had, it seemed, been writing the book for years. "Shockingly bad, I've no doubt," she said. "That's why I want you to go through it. Put it in order. Make it readable. You're clever at those things."

It was not till the war was over and she had retired finally to Tresant that she handed me the mass of manuscript. Remarkably little needed to be done with it. Here and there I have left things out; here and there a phrase has been sharpened. But this is Sarah's book, not mine: Sarah Undridge, who grew up as Sarah Rainborough.

May 1st, 1948

4

CHAPTER ONE

I

I REMEMBER that I was dancing up and down. "Shall I see the Queen?" I cried. "Shall I see the Queen's husband? Shall I see—?"

Mercy Kite, my nannie, said: "For goodness sake, Miss Sarah, stop hopping about and let me dress you, or you'll see nothing at all."

"Shall I see—?"

"Shall I see? Shall I see?" she mocked me. "From morning to night I hear nothing but 'Shall I see.' What d'you think the world is? A peep show arranged for your special benefit?"

"Shall I see Peace on Earth?"

"My!" said Mercy Kite. "Now you're asking!"

"I heard Papa say that the Exhibition meant peace on earth, good will to men."

"Your Papa says a lot," she answered grimly. "And he'll have something to say to me if the carriage is kept waiting. And it won't be Peace on Earth, either. Come on now. Give over hopping."

I gave over hopping, though I still wanted to hop. It was such a glorious day. After the early showers, the May sun was shining. I knew that the rain would have left wetness all over the surfaces of the Crystal Palace and that the sun would be making them sparkle. And it was my birthday, and I would be walking into the Exhibition with Papa on one side of me and Mama on the other. And the Queen would be there. I began to hop again. Mercy Kite took a handful of my long brown hair and gave it a pull. "*Will* you be quiet?" she hissed, "or shall I have to tell your Papa that it was impossible to get you ready in time?"

Tell your Papa. That sobered me, for Papa was awe and majesty.

Mama came into the schoolroom, a tall figure in white that shone and rustled. "Is Miss Sarah ready, Kite?"

"All but, Ma'am."

"You must hurry. It's almost time to go."

"Mama, shall I see—"

"You will see all that is to be seen, child," she said coolly. "Do what you can to help Kite to get you ready, and then come down at once." She rustled away.

5

When I reached the last turn of the banister, I saw Papa pacing up and down on the black and white squares of the hall. He had a long fair beard. What looked to me like a vast shining jewel dangled from a ribbon just below his waistcoat. Taking hold of this, he hauled a watch out of a pocket, looked at it, and tucked it back. Then he saw me, stepped to the open drawing-room door, and said, "She's here, Florence."

Mama came out, and Tetley, the footman, appeared, carrying Papa's tall hat. He opened the door, and there was the victoria already waiting, Ducat on the box. We got in, with me sitting between Papa and Mama, and Ducat looked over his shoulder to ask: "Where to, sir?"

"The Crystal Palace," Papa said; and we were off.

We were off; and I felt all tight and breathless inside. I could not speak. I could only look about me, and because I had for so long heard so much about this wonderful day I was amazed that everything did not look different from what it did. I had heard Papa telling Mama about "all the nations of the earth" having been invited and about the Prince's wish that the Great Exhibition should bring peace on earth, good will to men. And in church last Sunday the preacher, too, had talked about these same things: the coming together of the nations, and peace, and love.

Oh, I hardly know what I expected, silly child that I was: but as we sedately rolled through the shining air of that May day I should not have been surprised to see hordes of black and yellow men mingling with the white ones we knew so well, embracing and hugging and kissing, and maybe lifting their voices here and there in Christmas carols.

"The crowds are very well behaved," Papa said. "There was some fear of disturbances."

Certainly the crowds were well behaved. They gazed at us respectfully as we drove by; but I was disappointed to see not a black or brown or yellow face among them.

Still, it was a lovely day, and when we reached Hyde Park the very numbers of the people filled me with excitement. We drove through a lane of men and women, and on either hand, as far as we could see, there were thousands upon thousands upon thousands. Over them all now I could see the Crystal Palace rising up, flashing back the sunshine, and looking so light and airy that it would not have been surprising if all the flags straining and flickering and undulating on its roof had lifted it up and flown away with it into the sky.

I never lost that feeling about the palace, not that day nor on any of the other days when I entered it later. It seemed to my childish fancy a vast celestial vehicle, a crystal sky-ship, that had come to rest lightly on the earth, and might at any moment take off again and bear us upon some unimaginable voyage.

6

And now, as we entered, I saw that this great ship of glass was, inside, a garden. I had never imagined such flowers: tiers and banks and beds of them in the softest loveliest colors; and there were tiers and banks and beds of women whose clothes were of lovely colors, too; so that everywhere was color, on the ground and in delicate galleries; and there were palm trees, and an organ sending a wandering thread of music through everything; and there was a platform that Papa said was the dais. Great elm trees grew behind it, and in front of it a fountain was springing and glittering. And all this was inside the great glass ship. I looked up, and I could see the blue, and the white clouds racing across the happy May sky. I looked so long that at last the clouds seemed to be standing still and it was the sky-ship itself that was moving. We were off, bowling merrily beneath the sky: the elm trees and the fountain, the flower gardens and statues and the thousands upon thousands of people, and the music was going with us, and the twittering sparrows that didn't seem a bit alarmed but darted about in the elms. I was surprised to see them there, for I had heard Papa say that the Queen had been worried about them and wanted them all outside. For the life of me, I couldn't see why. But there it was, and the Duke of Wellington had told the Queen how to chase them all out. "Trust the Dook," Papa had said; and yet there the sparrows were.

"Mama," I said, "the Queen couldn't trust the Dook," and Mama said, "Don't keep craning your neck up, and don't chatter."

Then I was startled by a flourish of trumpets. It was sudden and unexpected; the sparrows seemed to leap into the air and then plunged themselves out of sight in the elms. "Ha!" I thought. "The Queen is coming, and they're afraid she'll see them."

Everybody was standing. The organ began to play "God Save the Queen," and a choir sang the words. It sounded small and lost because the palace was so big, but as soon as it was over there was noise enough, because everybody began to cheer and to wave handkerchiefs and papers.

Then I saw the Queen. She was dressed in pink and silver and she was walking with her husband. She held a little boy by the hand—a little boy dressed like a Highlander—and the Prince held a little girl. They went up onto the platform that Papa called the dais, and there they stood for a time, all four of them, with the people cheering like mad, and the fountain leaping in front of them, and the elm trees behind them, where the sparrows kept out of sight. I was glad of that, because the little boy looked the sort who would shoot at them with a catapult.

There was nothing so good after that: nothing so good as the moment when I saw the pink-and-silver Queen passing the shining

7

fountain, holding the little boy by the hand, with the sparrows hiding safely in the trees. There was some talking, and then a man in wonderful clothes prayed and said more about peace and all the nations of the earth. But the more they talked about the nations of the earth the more disappointed I was not to see all the exciting foreigners I had expected. There was one who came and bowed to the Queen, and Papa said it was a Chinese mandarin making obeisance. I knew that grand word, because Mercy Kite used to read to me out of the Bible, and once she read about the sheaves of corn making obeisance to Joseph's sheaf. I asked her what it meant, and she said it was going like this; and thereupon she tried a curtsy before me, but fell headlong to the schoolroom floor. The Chinese mandarin didn't do that, but, oh dear! how small a representative he seemed of the black and red, the brown and yellow and gold splendor I had expected from "all the nations of the earth."

I was very tired. It took us a long time to find the carriage, and I drowsed and nodded as we drove home. I was half aware of Papa approving of everything. "A splendid occasion." "The world has never seen anything like it." "The Prince is justified if ever man was."

"There were no black men, no brown men, no red men," I chanted drowsily.

"My dear child," said Papa, "surely you weren't expecting to see anything of the sort?"

"I expected to see all the ends of the earth in peace and good will."

"Well," said Papa, "so far as I'm concerned, the fewer foreigners we see over here the better I shall be pleased. The best guarantee of peace on earth is British trade. And that's what the Great Exhibition will promote."

I didn't know what he was talking about, and I said: "Mama, did you see the sparrows? I counted six. Why did the Queen want them all to be put out?"

Mama said severely: "It was necessary. You will understand such things in time."

In the schoolroom I repeated the question to Kite, and she said: "Well, duck, they might 'ave messed on yer 'at."

Now why, I wondered, couldn't Mama answer a simple question as simply as that?

2

I suppose at this time Papa was about thirty-five years old, but men in those days could, and did, look immensely venerable even before reaching that age. Papa had a long blond beard and cold penetrating blue eyes. He was one of the few men to own a private hansom cab,

8

and it was one of my morning delights to watch him set forth for his place of business in the City. The house was in Portman Square. Looking from the window of what was already called the schoolroom, though I had done no schooling, I would see the hansom coming from the mews, with Ducat, the coachman, perched up in his little seat. Tetley, the footman, would run from the house and stand waiting when the cab had come to a standstill at the curb. Presently, Papa would walk slowly out. He did everything slowly, with dignity. Tetley would fold back the apron of the cab, but, before getting in, Papa would turn and raise his tall hat, and I could imagine Mama standing at a window watching him. When he was in, Tetley would hand him a folded copy of the *Times*, and, if it were winter, wrap a bearskin rug round his knees. Ducat would open the trap and ask: "Where to, sir?" and Papa would say: "To the City." It was to be assumed, I suppose, that Papa might any morning decide to be driven to Buckingham Palace, the House of Commons, or goodness knows where. It was always: "To the City," but he expected to be asked, and what Papa expected was done. Away they went, the spokes of the yellow wheels twinkling in the sunshine if it were summertime, and, if it were winter, the lamps might be lit, for we had more fog then than we have now.

Except at the week ends, I saw little more of Papa than this, for he ate his luncheon at a club in the City, and though he was at home by five, my own day was ending then. They had a sameness, those days. Much of them was spent on the second floor of the house, which Kite and I had to ourselves. Kite was the person I knew most intimately. Papa and Mama came and went; Kite was always there. I don't know to this day whether she was wife, widow or spinster. She seemed very old, but I don't suppose she was; and she was cross, affectionate and reliable. Her crossness would sometimes give place to a dreadful sentimentality, though, at the time, there seemed to me nothing to dislike about these moods. Indeed, I approved them smugly. She took to calling me Rosie. "Why do you call me Rosie, Kite?" I demanded. "I am Miss Sarah." "Because you're a dear little Rosie Posy, a dear little Rosie Posy Rosebud," she said, hugging me to her and caressing my long brown hair, which, in other moods, she was apt to tug. I say I liked this mood, especially if it were on Mercy Kite at bedtime. It was agreeable to be tucked up feeling that I was a Rosie Posy Rosebud and that Mercy loved me.

She and I took breakfast together in the room that was called the schoolroom, looking out over the square. It was rather a poorly furnished place, but it was our own, and we made ourselves snug there, especially when the fire was lit and the curtains were drawn in the wintertime. We had a paraffin-oil lamp hanging from the ceiling

9

over a circular table covered with a red cloth. Mercy would sit with her elbows on the table and a book in front of her, and would read to me as I sat curled in a chair by the fireside. Sometimes Tetley would come lumping up the stairs and shoot coals from a bucket into our scuttle, and at six o'clock he would come and drag a zinc bath out of a cupboard on the landing. He would place this on the hearthrug and pour into it four buckets of water, two hot and two cold. This, I knew, was the end of my day. Soon I would be in my bed, in the small room adjoining the schoolroom. Kite's was next door. She would tuck me up, and if she were in a rosebud humor I would go quickly to sleep. If she were not, I would lie awake for a long time wondering whether Mama would come to say good night. I couldn't depend on it. Occasionally, when she came, she would be in full evening dress, with her white breasts showing, a spray of flowers on her shoulder, and with a beautiful smell wafting about her. Her skirts caressed the bare boards round my bed with a whispering sound. At such times, her clothes were almost always white and her flowers red. I would sleep then as though an angel had come to give me a blessing.

Looking back to that time—and I am looking now at a girl of six or seven—I see the old schoolroom as a safe and comfortable lair in which most of my life was spent and from which I made occasional sorties into the world. These sorties were well guarded. In the morning, if the weather were fine, I would be taken by Kite into the garden that filled the middle of the square. It was a poor sort of garden, but I had heard Mama say to Kite that we were "safe" there, and I suppose we were, for thick iron railings shut us in and no one ever came there except a few little girls walking round and round with their nannies, as I walked round and round with mine. The only one I knew was Sally Gaylord. Mercy Kite told me that she was the *Honorable* Sally Gaylord and that I might say "Good morning" to her, but that my Papa would not wish me to do more than that. I asked why, and Kite said: "Least said soonest mended. Those that ask no questions are told no lies." This made me wish to say more than "Good morning" to Sally Gaylord, but for a long time I did not. Of all of us who used the garden she was the only one who seemed to enjoy it. She never walked like the rest of us. She was forever rushing after a hoop, or skipping with a rope, or talking to her nannie in a loud excited voice, or even singing. She was dressed differently from the rest of us, too. We must have seemed, to the errand boys who went whistling outside the railings, a drab lot of little girls, except Sally, who always had a sprightliness in her clothes as well as in her manners. We did not see her in the winter. She appeared in May and disappeared when autumn was coming on, like the swallows. Kite said that her father, Lord Burnage, was in town only during the season. I was given to understand that there was something outrageous about Sally Gaylord, but I never understood what a dangerous girl she was till the morning when a butcher's boy, with a tray of meat on his head, went whistling past the railings and Sally, whistling like a blackbird, joined in the melody. The boy stopped walking but went on whistling, and there they stood, she inside the railings like a bird in a cage, he outside like a bird in freedom, whistling harmoniously. When they had finished, he waved his hand and said: "Wotcher!" and Sally waved back, grinning, and said: "Wotcher, boy!" Myself and two other girls standing by were dumfounded. We should not have been surprised if the boy had somehow leapt those high railings and come among us, and what we should have done then goodness knows; but he started whistling a new song and walked away, looking cheerful, just as Sally's nannie, who had been sitting on a seat some way off, talking to Kite, came running up. She took Sally by the arm and shook her. "Really!" she cried. "Really!" She seemed beyond words, and poor Kite, who had come bustling along to help repel the world, if that should be necessary, said: "Wherever does she get it from?" The nannie said sadly: "I've heard his Lordship whistling that tune. He encourages her." We went home that morning full of dark notions about Lord Burnage's household.

On fine afternoons, Mama usually drove in the Park, in the victoria. Occasionally she would take me with her. For such occasions I was dressed up in my best clothes and had to sit alongside Mama wearing my finest manners. No lolling, for one thing. She herself sat perfectly upright, a parasol over her, with hardly a movement except of the head. These were delightful and exciting occasions. So many grand people, such fine carriages of every sort, such splendid horses so well ridden. Now and then, as a carriage approached ours, Mama would say: "Bow," and as the carriages passed one another she would bow her head and I would bow mine. I noticed that occasionally she would say "Bow," and both she and I would do so, but there would be no answering bow; and in the same way people would bow to us, but we would not bow in return. I was aware in my childish way of a complex and difficult world, but it didn't worry me. It was all most enjoyable.

One afternoon, soon after Sally Gaylord had whistled in the garden, Mama and I, before driving into the Park, called at a house to pick up one of her friends. I was sandwiched between them in the victoria, with two parasols bobbing over my head. My companions were full of talk, which I didn't understand in the least, though occasionally Mama would murmur: "Somebody is growing up," or "Little pitchers have long ears," and things of that sort. There was all the customary bowing with a smile, bowing without a smile, and not bowing at all.

Presently, coming along on a fine roan horse, was a rider in the height of fashion, and, it seemed to me, of dazzling godlike looks. I was aware that my companions reacted as they had not done to anyone else in the Park that day. There was a sudden tautening of both of them. "Burnage," Mama said quietly; and her companion: "I suppose we cut him?" Mama answered, almost with a sigh: "I suppose so."

So this was Sally Gaylord's father. I looked at the approaching rider with great interest, expecting at any moment the command: "Bow." Lord Burnage smiled and raised his hat, and passed on, but there was no command. The two ladies looked rigidly at Ducat's shoulder-blades. I asked: "Mama, was that Sally Gaylord's Papa?"; and I was told coldly: "I do not know who it is."

3

Kite left me soon after this, and it was indeed an absurd affair that caused her going. I have told you about the paraffin lamp that hung over the table in the schoolroom, but I have not told you that the ceiling of that room had a certain amount of fanciful plaster decoration. In particular, there was in the middle a rollicking cherub who wore a wisp of gauze where that was obviously called for, but, in the manner of cherubs, nothing else. The large iron hook from which our lamp hung down on chains had been screwed plumb through this poor cherub's navel. There he floated above our cozy winter sessions, with this cruel weight tearing at him and causing me from time to time, when the matter engaged my attention, to writhe with sympathetic excruciation.

It was in the autumn following that summer when Sally Gaylord had whistled in the garden and my mother and her friend for some reason had not responded to Lord Burnage's salute. It was a dullish time. Sally had disappeared, and Mama no longer drove in the Park. The season was ended, and though that did not mean that Papa and Mama left town, as so many people did, it meant that she did not show herself in the afternoons among the undistinguished remnants who were left to keep London alive as best they might.

Well, there we were, Kite and I, that October evening, with tea finished, the fire burning, and the lamp lit. Kite was reading from a dog-eared book of fairy stories, all of them so well known to me that I could have gone on reciting at any place where she had chosen to leave off. I was bored; I don't think I was even hearing her. I was lolling back, in a way Mama would have reprimanded, in an old wicker chair, with my eyes on the ceiling. Presently they came to rest on the hook screwed into the cherub's navel. I broke rudely into the reading. "Kite, what is a belly button for?"

Poor Kite, who seemed half asleep, reading like an automaton, suddenly jerked wide awake. Her old-fashioned spectacles shot down to the end of her nose and she looked at me over them with absolute terror on her face.

"Now, Miss Sarah," she said, "don't you go asking me them sort of questions."

She was so startled and frightened that I was aware of having committed a first-class misdemeanor. This nettled me. Kite had so often said: "Ask no questions and you'll be told no lies," Mama had so often whispered: "Lady Jane is not such a child as she looks," and things of that sort, that I was suddenly oppressed by a sense of being kept outside a region full of fascinating information. I was now so incensed that I jumped out of my chair, went and stood before Kite, scowling and with clenched fists, and said: "You tell me, Kite! I've *got* a belly button. You tell me what it's for."

"You'll know all about them things when you grow up," she said. "You leave me alone now, Miss Sarah. It's not my place to tell you them things."

"Perhaps I'll die before I grow up," I answered. "Then I'll never know."

"You'll be none the worse for that," she assured me, beginning to recover firmness.

At this moment we heard Tetley's footsteps coming heavily along the passage, and he entered the room with a bucket of coals. My demon caused me to say: "If *you* won't tell me, Kite, I shall ask Tetley."

I recall Tetley as a cheerful good-looking youth with an impudent grin which he restrained only when being officially deferential to my parents. One day I chanced to be in the hall as Papa was going out, and there was all the usual how d'you do: Tetley brushing his shoulders, handing him his hat, opening the door, folding back the apron of the hansom. Then, when the hansom was gone and he came back into the hall, he saw me standing there and gave me a wink. It shook me to the core, as young moderns say. I had a feeling that Tetley had no right to wink at me, especially as the wink clearly said a lot of nonsense this was that accompanied the simple business of Papa walking out of the house, and I knew that I ought to feel outraged at his making any comment whatever on Papa's behavior. But I didn't: I felt pleased. An adult had taken me, with that brief grimace, completely into his confidence. This was something that had never happened before, and the sense of conspiracy was exhilarating.

And now, at this moment of tension with Mercy Kite, Tetley walked into the room, and there I was crying: "If *you* won't tell me, I shall ask Tetley."

He put the coals into the scuttle, made up the fire, and then asked: "What's up, Kitcy? What's she want to know?"

"You look after your own affairs," Mercy cried angrily. "You've no business to loiter here. You've done your job. Now go!"

"All right. All right," he said amiably. "I'm off," and picking up his bucket he made for the door. "Good night, Miss Sarah," he said.

I wouldn't let him go like that. I said: "She won't answer a simple question. She won't tell me what my belly button's for."

Mercy Kite flung her hands over her ears and looked horrified; but Tetley only grinned. With a hand on the china doorknob, he looked back and said: "Go on, Kitey. Tell 'er." Then we heard him going away along the passage.

There was silence for a moment, and then Kite moaned. "Oh Miss Sarah! To ask a man!"

This put a new twist to it, and I looked at her with interest and impatience. She continued to lament. "Oh, dear! This'll cost me my job. You see if it don't."

Now I flew into contrition. I didn't want Kite to lose her job because this would mean my losing Kite. I nuzzled into her, like a lamb into an old sheep, and I besought her not to think ill of me. "If I've asked something I oughtn't, don't tell me," I said; but now she too had swung into another direction. With an arm around me, she said: "If you *must* know, it's where you was hitched up to your Mama."

She left it at that, and, perplexed as I was by this reply, more confused than if I had been told nothing, I could not go on with the matter. I felt that, in some way I did not understand, I had done mischief enough. Soon afterward Tetley came up with the bath water; and, as I bathed, Kite and I were both constrained to avert our eyes from my belly button.

As I lay in bed that night, with the night light making a ghostly illumination, I puzzled over Kite's reply and *could* not see, to begin with, why one should be hitched up to one's Mama, or, if one had to be, how one could be hitched up by a flat bud in the middle of one's body, a flat bud in which the bath water settled like a drop of dew in a flower. And then Mama herself came rustling into the room. It was a going-out night. She was as usual in white, and as she rested on the edge of my bed I sat up and put my arms around her. She at once withdrew. "No, no, child," she said with a little laugh; "don't disarrange me."

She stood looking down at me in the ghost of candle shine, tall and white and glimmering. Her red flowers were almost black.

"I just came in to kiss you," she said. "I thought you would be asleep."

"I *can't* sleep," I answered. "I keep on thinking and thinking and thinking."

"What is worrying you, child? Tell me quickly. The carriage is waiting."

14

"I *can't understand*," I said emphatically, "how I could ever be hitched up to you by my belly button."

Well, the fat was in the fire then! Mama was a tall woman and she always dressed to emphasize her tallness. Now she seemed to grow before my eyes as she stood up from the bed, a white monument of offense and indignation. "*What* did you say?" she demanded. She was a tragic actress whose foundations had been rocked.

I was terrified. If, in the schoolroom, I had felt that I had gone too far with Kite, now I was overwhelmed with a sense of being a monster engaged in enormity. I shot down into the bed and pulled the clothes over my head. No use. Mama removed them firmly. "Sit up!" she commanded. I did so, quaking, and she repeated: "*What* did you say?"

In an almost inaudible squeak, I said: "Kite told me I was hitched up to you by my belly button."

And now poor Kite herself was dithering in the doorway. "Madam—" she stammered, and Mama almost hissed: "Leave the room!"

"Mama," I cried, "Mama, it wasn't Kite's fault. I plagued her. I pestered her. I asked her about it and she didn't want to tell me, and then Tetley came in . . ."

"Tetley!" Mama gasped, and I had an awful sense that every word I uttered was plunging me deeper and deeper into a morass from which there was no withdrawing.

Now Papa came into the room, all black and white, moving softly. "We mustn't keep the carriage waiting, Florence," he said. "What's this about Tetley? What's the fellow up to now?"

Mama ignored him. She concentrated her agonized glance upon me. "You were saying that then Tetley came in."

"Yes, Mama. I said to him that Kite wouldn't tell me, and he said that she should. So then I worried her again, and she said it was where I was hitched up to my Mama."

"Was Tetley there when she said that?"

"No, Mama. He made up the fire and went."

"Thank God!" she cried dramatically. "Thank God for that!"

She looked at me pityingly for a moment, as at someone snatched precariously from the mouth of disaster, then said more gently: "Lie down and try to go to sleep." She took Papa's arm and drew him out of the room. On the landing I heard her say to Kite: "Do not go into Miss Sarah's room again tonight."

Poor Kite! Only once more did she come into my room. In the morning a kitchenmaid brought up my breakfast, and soon afterward Papa came in, accompanied by a weeping Kite. She was dressed for going out, and I knew at once that she was going for good. I, too, began to weep.

For a moment Papa looked down at this pair of weepers; then he said:

15

"You see, Sarah, what your wickedness has done. You have driven Kite out of the house, and without a character. Tetley, too. Tetley is gone, and I have brought Kite here to receive your apology before she goes. You have done her a great wrong."

I flung myself into poor Kite's arms, and my weeping turned to howling. "Oh, Kite! I'm sorry. I didn't mean to do wrong."

"There, there!" she sniveled. "Poor little Rosie Posy. Of course you didn't. We've all got 'em, and we're all bound to wonder about 'em sooner or later."

Papa broke in sharply. "That will do, Kite. You were not brought here to discuss the matter but to receive Miss Sarah's apology."

Disaster made Kite bold. "Apology!" she said. "What is there to apologize about? I don't want the dear child's apology."

"Surely you do not suppose," Papa said coldly, "that what you want has anything to do with the matter? You are here now simply because a well-brought-up child should apologize when she has done harm to someone—even a servant. Well, Miss Sarah has said she's sorry, and now that's the end of the matter."

Kite gave me one convulsive squeeze and swept out of the room, a rather ridiculous bundle of rusty black. But I liked her immensely in that moment. At the door she paused and looked back at Papa. "You!" she said. Then she went, and he followed her.

The matter was never again referred to in my hearing. A few days later Mama came into the schoolroom where I was sadly glowering over the old fairy-tale book, and said: "This is Miss Whale. You are to begin lessons. Give Miss Whale your attention and respect."

I had stood up, as a good girl should, when Mama came into the room and addressed me, and now I looked sulkily at Miss Whale, still full of resentment because of Kite's disappearance and my loneliness. One look at her brought a smile to my face. "She looks more like Miss Minnow to me," I said saucily.

"That will do," Mama reproved me. "Miss Whale is to put up with no nonsense."

I didn't mind how sharply she spoke, for when I smiled and made that silly remark Miss Whale caught my eye and smiled back. There was something in the smile that took me even more completely into her confidence than Tetley's wink had taken me into his.

Miss Whale's Christian name was Margaret, but when, years afterward, I ceased to call her Miss Whale, she liked to be called Maggie. She was the only child of a country schoolmaster, and, when she was left alone in the world by his death, she had for a long time been his cook, housekeeper and companion, for her mother had died when she was a child. She had learned from him something of Latin and much of French, as well as of English literature, which was her deepest passion.

She was orphaned at seventeen, possessed of a few hundred pounds that her father had managed to save. She went to a school in France and stayed there as long as her money lasted, taking drawing and music lessons. She was nineteen when she came to us in Portman Square.

4

Although I felt at first glance a liking for Miss Whale, it must not be supposed that I was anxious to show it. When a tall young stranger wearing footman's uniform came up the stairs carrying her trunk, this was a reminder that all my settled world was in confusion. I saw so little of my parents, and what contacts I had with them were so formal, that to me Tetley and Kite were far more important than they as human beings. I looked with no sort of favor on this new young man, his face red with effort, as he lowered the trunk to the floor. "Who are you?" I asked.

"Stott, Miss . . ."

"Miss Sarah," my new governess said.

"I'm Stott, Miss Sarah."

"Very well, Stott. Please take Miss Whale's trunk into her bedroom."

I was imperious because I was sad and afraid. I was afraid that never could people like Stott and Miss Whale mean much to me. When he was gone, Miss Whale said: "Now show me everything."

"There's nothing to show," I said, hugging my sulks.

"What! Nothing at all?" she cried gaily.

"Only three rooms," I conceded.

"Well, let's have a look at them, shall we?"

We looked at the three rooms, and she was enthusiastic about them all. "How fortunate!" she said. "They all look out on the square! And how beautiful the square is today! Look at those trees!"

It was, indeed, a lovely day, autumn's best. The plane trees in the square were golden. The sky was blue. A few four-wheelers and hansom cabs were moving round the railings, raising a gentle dust. "I shall love this," Miss Whale said. "I had a room looking into a square in France. But it was tiny. Not so big as any one of these three. And the square wasn't so big as this, either, or so tidy. A little higgledy-piggledy square, with one tree in the middle, and the old women used to sit there under striped umbrellas, selling chickens and fruit and vegetables. I'll show you a picture of it. Come and see."

She reached out for my hand, but I withheld it. I followed her into her bedroom and she unstrapped the trunk. She unearthed a large portfolio full of water-color drawings. They were not very good, but

I didn't know that. They were bright and cheerful. "There. That's the one. Don't you think it's a lovely little square?"

"Yes," I said grudgingly. I passionately desired to have it, but would not say so.

"We'll put some of them up in the schoolroom," she said.

The schoolroom walls were covered by a plain light-brown varnished paper, so old that it had taken on a velvet texture. There were no pictures. Miss Whale selected a dozen drawings and gave them to me, with a box of drawing pins. "Now," she said. "You put them up where you'd like them to be while I unpack." She gave me some narrow strips of gray paper and a pair of scissors. "You can cut out frames and put them round the pictures."

"Kite never allowed me to have scissors," I said.

"Didn't you *want* to have them, all the same?"

"Yes."

"Well, now you've got them."

"What if I cut myself?"

"It'll teach you to be careful, and perhaps you won't cut yourself next time."

I didn't cut myself. I made the picture frames, dragged a chair here and there, and affixed the pictures to the walls. It took me a long time, and Miss Whale came out of her room as I was finishing. By now, I was more ready to be kind to her. "I think they're lovely," I said.

"Well, they make a bit of color, and soon we shall have the books."

I was not much interested in the books, because I knew nothing about books. The battered volume of fairy tales was lying on the window seat. It was the only book I had. My parents' ideas concerning education for girls were odd, though perhaps not so odd for the time. If it had not been for the scandalous affair of the belly button, goodness knows how long I should have gone on having no companionship but Kite's and no book but this one. Yet I had learned to read from it. Nobody taught me. I don't know how or when I learned, but learn I did, somehow, from that old book. Kite could not write, and I could not write. Miss Whale certainly had a virgin page to work upon. When she said that we should soon have the books, I was, however, polite enough to ask her what books she meant, for polite manners at least had been drilled into me.

"Oh, all sorts of books," she cried gaily. "Why, good gracious, we *must* have *books*," as though life without books were utterly unthinkable. "There's an old wooden trunk of mine stuffed with them, wandering about somewhere between here and France. It will arrive sooner or later. Then we shall want textbooks to read, exercise books to write in, pens, ink, rubbers, rulers, pencils, drawing books, crayons, water colors and brushes, some music books—oh, there's no end to the fun we shall have! Mr. Rainborough has given me permission to buy all we shall need. We shall go out this afternoon and make a start."

She had an enthusiastic way of making such things sound like an adventure; and I felt a great longing to be off at once. I even suggested this, but at that moment there was a knocking and banging on the stairs and Miss Whale cried: "That'll be the bookcase. Mr. Rainborough took the measurements and promised to have it sent round this morning."

She ran to open the door, and Stott and a man in a green baize apron sweated and grunted into the room. The bookcase was set against the wall opposite the fireplace. It was open-shelved, of white-painted wood. What with that and the water colors on the walls the room already looked different. Miss Whale's enthusiasm conveyed itself to me. I felt on the verge of great and exciting events. "Now," she said, "I think all we need do this morning is go out and buy ourselves some flowers."

Books, paintings, flowers! Never before had we had flowers in the schoolroom. That was altogether a day to be remembered. For one thing, although the sunshine of the morning and early afternoon had been warm, the air was nippy by teatime and Miss Whale said we had better have a fire. "But we can't," I explained to her. "It's not the first of November."

Fires in the schoolroom had been governed, like everything else in the house, by rules against which there was no appeal. The first fire was lit on November the first and the last on March the thirty-first. If the thirtieth of October were a freezing day, that would make no difference: there would be no fire. And if on the last day of March a warm sun asserted itself, that would make no difference either: there would be a fire. I had once heard Papa say, though he was not much given to figures of speech, that Rules and Regulations were like railway lines: life couldn't run punctually without them. And so there was a place for everything—including, I suppose, the people Mama didn't bow to—and everything was in its place; and a time for everything, including the lighting of schoolroom fires, and everything was done on time.

And now, when I reminded Miss Whale that to light a fire was an impossibility, she merely laughed and rang the bell. Ten minutes later, the new footman Stott had done what was necessary, and Miss Whale and I were sitting by the fire with our tea on a low table between us. It was cozy and enjoyable. The curtains had been drawn, the pictures brightened the walls, the bronze chrysanthemums we had bought in the morning were in an earthenware pot on the table, the new bookcase already had some furnishing, and there we were with the kindling wood crackling and the coals already spurting out their little gassy geysers. We needed only to pull our petticoats up over our knees to be two old cronies having the time of their lives.

Yet there was a sense of sin, not only on account of this unseasonable but so welcome warmth but also because we were not sitting up to the table. From time to time, when Mama was "receiving," I would be called down to the drawing room to bow to the guests and receive a few words from them. They sat here and there, straight upright, it is true, in their chairs, balancing saucers and plates dexterously on rigid fingers, but they *did not* sit up to the table. I, however, in the schoolroom, must always do so. It was a Rule and Regulation that I must acquire a Straight Back, and Kite would be on me like a shot if I committed the sin of Lolling.

So there I was, in a most confused if delighted frame of mind, shamelessly Lolling in a wicker chair in front of this unruly and irregular fire.

"You are seven—are you not, Sarah?" Miss Whale asked—not *Miss Sarah*, mark you, which was again something different.

"Yes, Miss Whale. I was seven on the first of May."

"At what time have you been in the habit of going to bed?"

"At six o'clock."

"It had better be seven for some time," she said, "and soon we shall make it eight."

I looked at Miss Whale, sitting there tranquilly sipping her tea, and all of a sudden a tremendous thought entered my mind. She was not afraid of Papa and Mama! Poor Kite had been in constant fear of them. The cry that she had uttered, "This'll cost me my job!" was still in my mind. That was the hold they had over her, and everything she did was with a view to preventing the exercise of their power. And I knew that I, also, was afraid of them. Oh, it was lovely when Mama, smelling like a bunch of mimosa, came in and leaned over my bed and kissed me good night, or when, say on my birthday or at Christmastime, Papa was smiling and even perhaps cracked a little joke as he handed me a present. Because of these things, my fear was not like Kite's: it rested on a vague and undefined knowledge that there were limits to our communion, that there was a grown-up world and a little girl's world, that they and I were not *really* at one. And now, in defiance of Rules and Regulations that said I should go to bed at six, here was Miss Whale announcing: "We shall make it eight."

When the tea things had been taken away, she said: "Your Mama tells me you have learned to read. Now let me hear you." She brought the fairy-tale book and I began to read. It was the first time I had ever read aloud, for Kite, too, had been a great one for making Rules and Regulations, and one of these was that she should read to me, never that I should read to her. However, Miss Whale praised me, though mine must have been a stumbling effort; and between then and my going to bed she talked to me about France. She laid a large map of the country on the table—not one of those repulsive varnished maps printed on linen and furnished with rollers, but a jolly colored thing on cartridge-paper that she had drawn herself. She talked of her life in the country, and of the people she knew, and of the markets, the rivers, the vineyards she had visited during her holidays, and of concerts and theaters she had attended. I began to think of France as a place where men and women lived and went about their affairs much as they did in England, and no doubt that is what Miss Whale intended me to do.

The bath came up at seven instead of six, and I stood waiting for Miss Whale to undress me and bath me. But she didn't. She said it was high time I learned to do without a nannie and to look after myself.

And so I did, with a fearful joy; and when I was in bed I fell asleep much quicker than I was used to do. I felt safe and happy; safe somehow deep down in me. I suppose, without knowing it, I was aware for the first time in my life of being a person, not an appendage.

CHAPTER TWO

I

ON NEW YEAR'S morning of 1856, when I was seven years old, Mama came into the schoolroom as Miss Whale and I were sitting down to breakfast. It was most unusual for her to appear so early, and I at once asked myself whether some misdemeanor of mine had brought her there. But she was smiling. She was in a good mood. Indeed, she looked gay and more than usually beautiful. She was younger than to my childish mind she seemed. She was then only twenty-eight.

Miss Whale surprised me by saying, as we rose: "Good morning, my lady."

Mama's smile deepened. She blushed with pleasure. "You have seen the newspapers?"

"Yes, my lady. Allow me to congratulate you."

"Have you said anything to Miss Sarah?"

"No. I thought you'd like to be the first to do so."

Mama said to me: "My dear, the Queen has honored your Papa with a knighthood. I should like you to come down now and congratulate him. Say to him: 'Good morning, Sir Richard. I congratulate you.' Can you remember that?"

"You must congratulate your Mama, too," said Miss Whale. "She is Lady Rainborough."

I said: "Congratulations, Mama," but I was rather wooden. I hadn't the least idea what had happened.

However, I went down to the breakfast room and curtseyed to Papa. "Good morning, Sir Richard. I congratulate you."

He was all smiles, like Mama. He took me under the arms, lifted me up, and kissed me. "Thank you, Sarah," he said. "Now you must stay and have breakfast with me and her ladyship."

It was a dark morning. Candles were burning in silver candlesticks on the table. My legs dangled. I looked at the mellow light falling on the radiant faces of my parents. Never had I known them so gay. "You were excessively naughty, Richard," Mama said, "to keep me in the dark. You must have known for some time."

He said gaily: "Well, my lady, I was able to make a guess a long time ago, and, as you say, I have known for some time."

"And you leave me to make the discovery from the newspapers. Really, Sir Richard! What if I had not wanted a title? You men may refuse. Do we women have no option?"

"Only to love, honor and obey. I command you to be Lady Rainborough, and like an obedient wife you have no option save to say 'Yes, Sir Richard.' "

I was perplexed. I had never before seen them in this rallying, bantering mood; but then, really, I saw them little.

Already I seemed to be forgotten. "Papa," I cried, "why did the Queen make you a knight?"

My mind was full of Walter Scott. A knight, to me, was a man of valiant action and beautiful courtesy, a man who went about on a splendid horse, wearing ladies' favors, clanking in armor, topped with a plumed helmet, fighting in wars or playing fiercely at tourneys.

Both Papa and Mama looked a little surprised at my question. It was Mama who answered. "Without the help of your Papa, my dear, we might not have won the war. That is what the Queen remembered."

"Well, thank God that is all over and done with," Papa said piously, wiping his lips with his napkin; and there was no time to ask more, for Stott appeared and announced: "The hansom is waiting, Sir Richard."

Papa came round the table and kissed me again. "This is a special day," he said. "You are excused from your lessons."

"But, Papa, I *love* my lessons."

"Very well, but don't become a little monster. We don't want a bluestocking in the family. Just learn to be good and beautiful, like your mama."

2

I knew that every day Papa went to the City, but I had no idea what the City was or what he did there. I had never been to the City, and

I don't think Mama had, either. There was a man's place, and there was a woman's place, and there was a child's place. They were marked off from one another by frontiers that were not crossed. There was also a butler's place, a cook's place, and a footman's place. It was a commendation to say of anybody that he "knew his place." There were, of course, people who didn't know their place, and they had to be "taught." I had heard Papa say more than once in recent years that it was time the Russians were taught their place; and now they had been taught. The war was over, and but for Papa's help, Mama has said, we might not have won it. This puzzled me, because Papa had not been to the war. Miss Nightingale had: everyone knew that: and so had the men to whom Miss Whale gave pennies when we were out walking: men with one arm or one leg, tootling on penny whistles or just sitting against the railings of Hyde Park with caps on the pavement alongside them. I had heard the words Inkerman and Sebastopol; I had heard of the charge of the gallant Six Hundred, and that thrilled me more than most of the things I knew about the Crimean War, because Lord Burnage had been one of these six hundred heroes charging the Russian guns at Balaclava. But really, to a girl brought up like me, the war had meant almost nothing. And now to my amazement I learned that Papa had helped to win it.

This is as good a place as any to tell some things that I did not learn till much later, and they begin with John Rainborough. He was born in the cottage of a farm laborer earning ten shillings a week. It is surprising that my Papa attached so much importance to everybody knowing his place because this grandfather of his appears to have never known his. Although his writing did not amount to much more than signing his name, and his reading was on a similar scale, he was, from his earliest days, restless and ambitious. There is a gap in his story that no one has been able to fill. He went to sea at the age of fifteen and returned, rich, when he was thirty-five. He had been, for all that time, in the East Indies. That is all that is known. One can only surmise what happened. He was too poor to have gone into the employment of the East India Company which was scooping the cream off that rich territory and which, in theory, had the exclusive right to trade. But theory didn't cover all that was then happening in the Indies. It was a time and a place favorable to adventurers, whether the adventure was blessed as trade or diverged into more unscrupulous courses. That John Rainborough chose to leave these twenty years open to conjecture can mean just what you want it to mean.

What is certain is that, having landed in London and, soon after, married a wealthy girl, he traveled to his native place in the Northeast of Yorkshire, and established himself there as a landowner whose properties ran into the Cleveland hills. His son developed the iron in these properties, and it was with this iron that Papa was concerned in the City. It was with this iron that he "helped to win the war" and earned a knighthood. It was an iron age. Iron was going down in railway tracks all over the country. It was going into bridges and machines of every sort and shape. There was iron everywhere, except at our house in Portman Square. We never heard iron mentioned, and I only once in my life, many years later, saw the distant hills from which the iron came. All that we had and all that we were had followed upon twenty years of mysterious work in the East Indies about which nobody knew anything or thought it discreet to inquire.

3

Do my parents seem shadowy, half-realized figures? I cannot help it. That is how they were. Stott, the footman, who had succeeded Tetley after the dreadful affair of my belly button so long (as it seemed) ago, was now familiar to me; so were Ducat the coachman and Threllfall the butler; and so, of course, doubly so, was my dear Miss Whale. But now I began to know my parents a little better. I was permitted to take breakfast with them once a week, and, since Rules and Regulations were still important, this was always on the same day: Wednesday. I recall a radiant Wednesday morning in May of that year when Papa became Sir Richard Rainborough. I said good-by to Miss Whale in the schoolroom, as I always did on these occasions, as though I were going from her for weeks or years, and I ran down to the breakfast room. It was at the back of the house, which I thought a pity on such a lovely day, but at least I could look out on to a little whitewashed paved courtyard with a green door and with a few box trees trained into curious shapes, growing in green tubs. I was the first to arrive as usual, and I began to turn over the letters alongside Papa's place at the table. It pleased me to read the name, Sir Richard Rainborough, again and again, in all sorts of handwritings, on all sorts of envelopes: white, blue, gray. It gave me a sense of importance. There was one envelope that I seized on eagerly: it was so much more imposing than any of the others, and more beautiful, too. It was a large square parchment envelope, cream colored, addressed to Sir Richard and Lady Rainborough. A crimson crest was embossed upon the back. I carried it to the window for examination. It excited me deeply. I should have liked, I felt, to receive lots of letters in envelopes like this. What a person that would make me! There was a helm on the crest, and a gauntlet, and a dagger, and there were the words *Fiat voluntas mea*. Now what on earth could that mean? I must ask Miss Whale. But would I ever

24

remember these outlandish words? I resolved to write them down. Papa's *Times* lay folded by his letters. I opened it, tore a strip from the edge of a page, and with a stump of pencil which I carried with me I copied the strange words. I tucked this out of sight, and was taking the letter to put it on Papa's pile when Mama came into the room. Her coming arrested me with the letter in my hand. "Good morning, Mama," I said.

"Good morning, Sarah. I see you have received a letter."

"Oh, no, Mama. It's a lovely looking letter, but I'm afraid it's not for me. It's addressed to you and Papa."

"Then what are you doing with it?" she asked sharply.

"I was looking at the crest on the back."

"But, my dear child, you could not have seen the crest on the back unless you had turned the letter over. Are you in the habit of prying into Papa's correspondence?"

I stood there with the letter in my hand, horribly shaken. It's always like this, I thought. I'm expected to know without being told. No one has ever said that I mustn't touch the letters, and now I'm wicked because I've done it. I don't want to have breakfast with them. I'd rather have breakfast with Miss Whale. If I do wrong she tells me nicely, and she tells me why.

"I asked you, Sarah, are you in the habit—"

"No, Mama," I broke in. "It was just this morning."

"Doesn't Miss Whale tell you not to reply till the person who is speaking to you has finished speaking?"

Oh, it was intolerable! And I felt it was not really anything to do with me at all. It was to do with this letter. Mama couldn't help seeing the crest, the writing, as I turned it in my hand. "Put it down," she said, and I did so.

I attempted to soothe her. "It is for Papa *and* you," I said. "May I not give it to you, Mama?"

Then she held out her hand, and I gave her the letter. She turned it over and over, and she blushed and looked uneasy. "I should not dream," she said at last, "of opening a letter addressed to me and Papa, so long as he is here to open it himself. And never—please, Sarah"—she was almost placating now, which threw me into greater confusion than ever—"never touch letters addressed to other people. One doesn't do such things."

Papa came in then, and breakfast began. After a few moments, he said to Mama, as he invariably did: "Will you excuse me, my dear, if I glance at my correspondence?" Without waiting for an answer, he took up an ivory paper-knife, which was always laid alongside his letters, and slit them open one by one. It was his habit to do this: to open all the letters before reading any. He laid them in a pile, and so the exciting letter, which had been on the top, went to the bottom. With Mama's eye upon me, I pretended to be uninterested, but I could hardly wait for him to come to this letter. He made no comment on any of the others, but when he came to this one he said: "For both of us, I see," and then, turning it over and glancing at the crest: "From Burnage."

Immediately, my excitement was redoubled. Lord Burnage and Sally Gaylord were romantic figures in my eyes. I always remembered my first sight of him, riding his horse in Hyde Park, looking so handsome and gallant, and I remembered how Mama and her companion had become flustered by his approach and then had not returned his salutation. On getting home, I had asked Mercy Kite what it meant to "cut" a person, and she answered: "Oh, it means they want to know you but you don't want to know them, and cutting 'em is letting 'em know it."

"But why should you do that?"

"Now don't start worryin' me with your whys. I'm not the one for whys and wherefores, and well you know it. I just tell you what's so, and why it's so is other folks' business. Still, there's plenty in this world as is not all they should be or all they appear to be. And the less you have to do with such the better. There's no harm in telling you that."

All this innuendo did no more, as one might expect, than put a luminous halo round Lord Burnage, and this was not diminished later when he went away to the war. So now, when Papa casually said: "From Burnage," I kept my eyes to my plate but pricked up my ears. Papa read the letter. "He invites us to accompany him to the Derby next week," he said. "He'll be driving down a four-in-hand."

I looked at Mama. She appeared to be not excited by what seemed to me a tremendous moment. She was reading one of her own letters, and looked up to say casually: "Shall you go?"

Papa seemed to be giving the matter deep thought. It was a way of his. If you asked: "Shall I pass you the marmalade, Papa?" he would consider the question before saying: "Yes—thank you—I think so."

And now when Mama said: "Shall you go?" and turned at once, without waiting for his answer, to her letter, he sat back holding the crested envelope in one hand and thoughtfully stroking his beard with the other. At last he said: "Yes, if it would amuse you, my dear."

Mama merely fluttered a passing look at him as she said: "Very well, Richard. Let us go then. It would be rather fun."

Oh, how deeply then I felt excluded from the world in which grownup people went their wonderful ways! Could anything ever happen in my life that would have the wonder of this: to be driving behind

26

four lovely horses with Lord Burnage? I fell into a reverie. I was bowling along under a blue sky with a horn blowing and sixteen iron hoofs thundering and the hedges unwinding a ragged green ribbon splotched here and there with a burst of creamy hawthorn. And then Papa was saying in his most hollow voice that always made me feel cold in the stomach: "Florence, I *will not* have the *Times* opened until I have opened it myself."

"I haven't touched the *Times*, Richard. I came into the room only just before you did yourself."

"*Somebody* has touched the *Times*," Papa insisted. "Threllfall knows how it should be placed upon the table, and it certainly is not in that condition now."

He picked up the paper and petulantly rustled open the pages. "Good God!" he cried. "It has been *torn!*"

I had not realized what sins I was committing that morning: first in handling the letters, then in opening the paper, and finally in tearing a strip from it. But now it was clear from Papa's angry look that to tear the *Times* was as serious an offense as to tear up the British constitution. "Who has done this?" he demanded, and holding the paper out at a trembling arm's length he inflicted upon it worse disfigurements than mine, squeezing its middle in his fist as though it were something he would strangle.

Inside me, I was cold with fear, but I said as firmly as I could: "I did not know, Papa, that I must not touch the newspaper. I have seen Stott use it to light a fire, and I didn't know. . . ."

"What are you taught?" he asked angrily. "God knows what I spend upon your education, and you do not understand the most elementary things."

Oh, dear! It seems so absurd, so pitiful, now, when a newspaper is no longer the morning's installment of God's truth about the stock markets or anything else, to be revealed first to the Head of the Family, and permitted by his will and good pleasure to percolate in due season down to lower strata of life. But it was serious then. I had, in deed and in truth, done something very black in Papa's eyes, and I suffered as acutely as he no doubt thought I should. To open the newspaper was his prerogative, and in striking innocently at that I had struck at the bases on which to him, I suppose, the family rested. All the same, there was a sneaking ray of joy amid my misery. He was so angry that he did not ask me *why* I had torn the paper. He got up and left the room, carrying the paper with him. "I must speak to Miss Whale," he said at the door.

When he had left for the City I returned to the schoolroom expecting to be greeted as a pretty black sheep by a Miss Whale herself reduced to despondency. But she was cheerful. She was putting tulips into the vase on the bookcase and she turned to me with a smile. "Well, let that be a lesson to you, Sarah," she said lightly. "Leave the *Times* alone. What on earth did you want with the *Times* of all things?"

I began to take the infection of her happy mood. "I wanted to make a note. There was a letter with a lovely crest and a motto and I wanted to ask you what the motto meant, and I had no paper to copy it on to, so I tore a piece off the *Times*."

"So you've been fiddling with the letters, too. Sir Richard didn't seem to know about that."

"I just looked at them."

"Well, don't do it any more. Letters are very private things."

"Yes, Miss Whale. But why shouldn't I open the *Times*?"

"Well, after all, your Papa pays for the *Times*. It's his paper, and if he wishes to have the pleasure of being the first to look at it, he has a perfect right to do so. So you will respect that in future, won't you?"

"Yes, Miss Whale."

"Good. Now let me see this motto."

I produced my crumpled fragment and smoothed it out on the table. *Fiat voluntas mea.*

"H'm," said Miss Whale. "It means *My will be done*. Pretty arrogant and self-satisfied, I must say."

CHAPTER THREE

I

IT WAS an exciting time in the square. Everything had just got on to tiptoe for the leap into summer. The green of the leaves of trees and shrubs was still tender; the railings had been repainted, and the whirr of the lawn-mower was accompanied by the smell of cut grass. All the houses were smiling in their new paint, most of it white, and every window was underlined with a broad brush stroke made by lobelias, marguerites and geraniums in green boxes. The air was clear, for London. The thousands and thousands of fires that had burned through the winter were burning no longer; only the fires in kitchens were kept going.

Walking with Miss Whale, I felt sorry for the girls moving sedately along the path in the garden with their nannies. It was a long time since I had walked in there. Miss Whale didn't like what she called that silly senseless treadmill. What was surprising this afternoon was that two of the girls were being almost boisterous. They were throwing

28

a ball to one another, throwing it hard and high, and here it came, sailing over the railings, dropping into the middle of the road, bouncing then onto the steps of Lord Burnage's house. I ran to gather it and throw it back, and, as I stooped with my behind in the air and toward the door, the doors opened and I received a mild tap on the stern. I straightened, turned, and found myself face to face with Lord Burnage. "You should bow *toward* me," he said.

I did not see him. *What* I saw I can hardly say, for so much rushed so quickly into my mind. I had not encountered him since he was back from the war, and it was the legend of the war that colored my vision. Somehow, in that war, to my childish mind, it was always winter. And now I looked at him through a haze of fierce gray Russians, appearing and disappearing in a gray welter of snow. Florence Nightingale was moving through the wintry dither, carrying a lamp and bending down now and then to cast a pitying glance at a heap of rags hardly to be distinguished from the snowdrift on which it was pillowed. Then horsemen were lining up file upon file, six hundred of them. Still the snow fell as they moved off at a foot pace that increased to a canter, and disappeared at a gallop into the white waving curtain. Now there was a terrific banging of cannon, and the whiteness was lit with crimson flashes, and in my head the lines were beating that I had read so often:

> Storm'd at with shot and shell,
> Boldly they rode and well,
> Into the jaws of Death,
> Into the mouth of Hell
> Rode the Six Hundred.

Oh, it was all so vivid and so terrible that suddenly the bright May morning was not there, and I myself was in the snow, listening to the hard breathing of men and horses, the frantic creak of leather, the snow-dumbed beat of hoofs, the whistle of sabers. The cannonballs came hurtling red-hot out of the mouth of Hell, and I heard the high screams of horses and the harsh sobs of men. And then I myself, standing there idiotically with the painted ball in one hand, was myself sobbing, sobbing, as though my heart would break, and I had run up and thrown myself upon Lord Burnage and was crying on his chest.

I cannot imagine what he thought. He put an arm round me, and it was most comforting. He let me cry, and when at last the crying stopped and I pulled away I could have died to see his footman still standing at the open door and Miss Whale, for the first time since I had known her, looking aghast, as though something had happened

29

beyond her ability to handle. Only Lord Burnage was undisturbed. "Well," he said, "at last the sun breaks through." He took out a large handkerchief, wiped my tears, and then held it to my nose. "Blow," he said. I blew, and he said: "Good! Now see if you can sniff without bubbling." I could. Then he handed the handkerchief to the footman who ran in and presently returned with another. "You see," said Lord Burnage, "you have increased my laundry bill for the week. I think you should tell me how this comes about. But first of all, allow me."

He took the ball from my hand, gave a tremendous swinging throw that sent it rocketing against blue sky and down into the garden. He turned to Miss Whale. "Now," he said, "if you are going my way, perhaps I may have the pleasure of your company? I am Lord Burnage. If I am not mistaken, this water cart is Sir Richard Rainborough's daughter? As the summer dust increases, we must find her municipal employment. Well, where are you walking to?"

"We are just walking," said Miss Whale.

"Excellent, excellent. All these aims and objectives and purposes! Just walking. That is how I like it myself."

"But you must not allow us to disturb you, sir. And I must apologize for Miss Sarah's behavior. I don't know what came over her."

"I expect I frightened her when I tapped her with my cane. But really it was only a little tap. Are you so easily frightened or hurt as all that, Sarah?"

"No, sir," I stammered. "It wasn't your cane. It was the Russians."

We had been walking all this time and had come into Oxford Street, and there on the pavement Lord Burnage came to a halt and looked at me with surprise. "The Russians? What on earth has it to do with the Russians?"

It all came tumbling out of me. In my confused childish way I tried to tell him of the imagination that had overwhelmed me: the Russians, the shot and shell, the blinding snow, and the gallant Six Hundred. He listened in silence, tall and straight, looking down at me as we stood outside a shop window. "Well, well!" he said. "That man Tennyson! We shall never live him down. But, my dear Miss Sarah, it wasn't a bit like that, you know. There was no snow at all. Not that day. It was nice October weather. Still, it was kind of you to cry about me. But you mustn't do it any more. Let us enjoy this lovely May morning. We shall cross over into Bond Street."

He took my hand in his, which was long and thin but had a hard grip. We crossed the road and sauntered down Bond Street. Now and then we stopped to gaze into shop windows, and in the mirrors I could observe him, straight and spare and made to seem even taller

30

than he was by the tall silk hat he was wearing. His face was dark and thin and clean-shaven.

"I do not think, Miss—?"

"Miss Whale, my lord."

"I do not think, Miss Whale, I have ever walked from one end of Bond Street to another without spending money. Indeed, I do not think one should. After all, it's rather a special sort of street, don't you agree? If we want a street like this—and I do—we must help to keep it up. The least we can do this afternoon is to enter this highly extravagant looking sweetshop. When I was at school I could buy all the sweets I wanted at a penny the quarter pound. Today, I do not think we shall be so fortunate."

"Indeed, my lord," Miss Whale began to protest, "I do not think—"

He cut her short. "I am sure," he said, "Miss Sarah could not disagree with you more. Is that not so, Sarah?" Giving me no time to answer, he opened the door and we went before him into the shop.

It was like Ali Baba's cave: glittering with jeweled confections of every color: white, nut-studded nougat, brown chocolates topped with little violet coronets, marzipan veined with pink and green and yellow like marvelous edible marble, Edinburgh rock in spirals of pale mustard, sage green, rose and amethyst. And all this—and much else—was displayed on silver trays and in crystal bottles amid a carpeted hush that made the shopgirls seem like acolytes in a cathedral of appetites. On the counter there were pyramids of boxes, immense ones at the base, rising in diminishing sizes, and all of alluring colors tied round with ribbons of pale blue or crimson that a courtier could have worn across his chest and looked the holder of a famous order. It was with one of these, one of the biggest, that we finally left the shop. Beautiful as it was, it must be wrapped in exquisite paper of white with pale green satin stripes and then tied round with red silken cord. Lord Burnage smiled when we were in the street again. "Definitely not a penny for a quarter pound," he said.

He bade us good-by when we had crossed over Piccadilly and come into St. James's Street. "Now, Miss Sarah," he said, "no more tears for me. If you want to think of me at all, think of me with a smile and wish me luck. Will you do that?"

"Oh, yes, sir," I cried.

"I shall need it," he said, bending suddenly and kissing me; and then he ran lightly up the steps of a club.

Indeed, indeed, I thought, I shall wish him luck in whatever he wants; and to Miss Whale I said: "Do you know, Whaley, I have never walked down Bond Street with Papa?"

As I lay in bed that night it occurred to me that there were many things I had never done with Papa. This idea had not come to me before, and now, when it *did* come to me, it was in a way that confused and troubled me, because I was certain that I would rather do things with Lord Burnage. This, I say, troubled me. Papa, after all, was the center of my world. I had always been given to understand that, and I had accepted it as something not to be questioned. And now I was questioning it. I did something I had never done before. I got out of bed and went into the schoolroom.

It had never occurred to me to wonder what Miss Whale did with herself when she was alone. Padding along on bare feet, I opened the door and came silently upon her. The curtains were drawn and the light from the paraffin lamp, hanging from the cherub's navel, fell upon the table and upon Miss Whale's bent head. The smooth black hair was drawn away from the white parting line that ran from her forehead to the top of her skull. She was writing, and she was so absorbed in this that I was able to stare at the white line for some moments before she raised her eyes and saw me. I was able to see that she was not writing upon letter paper but upon large sheets that I didn't know then to be called quarto. A little pile of them was stacked at her right hand, and scattered on the table were a few random sheets that she seemed to have just written. When at last her eyes rose from the paper and looked at me, there were a few seconds in which she did not appear to see me. Then she seemed to come to herself with a little start, and she said: "Good gracious, Sarah, I thought you were asleep hours ago."

"I couldn't sleep," I said. "I've been worrying about my sins."

"You'd better not add a cold to them. Get back at once and do your worrying between warm sheets. I'll come and talk to you."

However, I lingered long enough to see her sweep all the sheets of paper together, lock them into a drawer, and drop the key into her purse. I was wearing nothing but a pink flannelette nightdress, and when she had put her papers away she took me by the arm and said: "Come along now. If you must walk about at night, put on slippers and a dressing gown. It would be a nice thing if you started a cold and couldn't see the party setting off for the Derby."

This had been promised as a treat. Miss Whale and I were to be in Hyde Park, where Lord Burnage's party would assemble, and see them drive away. Now, suddenly, I did not want to do this. I got back into bed, which was still warm, and said: "I don't want to see them set off. I *will not* see them set off."

"But, Sarah darling, you so much wanted to go! You have so much been looking forward to meeting Miss Gaylord." She pulled up the white-painted wooden chair and sat by my bedside.

Meeting Sally Gaylord had been part of the promised treat. She, too, was to see the Derby party set out, and then she was to return with me and Whaley and spend the day with us.

Miss Whale reached her plump little hand under the bedclothes and grasped mine warmly. "Now," she said. "Let's hear all about it. Everything."

"I *love* Lord Burnage," I cried hotly, "and I can't *bear* to see him drive away with a lot of other people. If I can't go with him I'd rather not be there at all. And I *know* it's wicked, but I love him more than I love Papa. So now!"

Whaley said nothing for a long time. She just held my hand comfortingly. At last she got up and began to walk quietly to and fro. "H'm!" she said. "We should all be in a pretty mess, shouldn't we, if we carried on as you want to do! Lord Burnage buys you a box of chocolates, which is something Papa never does, and so you love him more than Papa."

"Oh, no! It's not that!"

"One moment. I know it's not *only* that. That's just what's brought it all into your head. Lord Burnage leads a life that seems to you fine and romantic. He is in London only during the season. Then he disappears into the country. When he is here, you see him riding beautifully in the Park, which is something Papa never does. He can drive a four-in-hand, and Papa never does anything so splendid. Papa spends hours and hours every day in a dull place called the City, and Lord Burnage never does anything so commonplace. Most wonderful of all, Lord Burnage goes off to fight in the war, and that's a brave thing to do, but no braver than for all the poor men we see with no arms or legs begging in the streets, and you don't get romantic about them. However, perhaps some of them, too, belonged to the gallant Six Hundred. They weren't all officers, you know, and they weren't all lords. And what's more, Lord Burnage went because he had to, not because he wanted to. He may have wanted to. I don't know. But he had to. He's a professional soldier. He does what his job demands. And so does your Papa. Your Papa has to earn his living, and yours too, and Lady Rainborough's. That's why he has to go to the City every day and can't run out of London as soon as the precious season ends. There have been Lord Burnages for centuries, and they've piled up a lot of money. All that a Lord Burnage has to do today is spend it. He doesn't even have to conserve it. His lawyers and agents do that for him. Another thing they've piled up is a lot of land. All that Lord Burnage need worry about is living in the lovely house on it and

33

shooting pheasants and hunting foxes, or whatever it is he does down there. I don't know. Mind you, I'm not speaking about your Lord Burnage. I'm speaking about *any* Lord Burnage, and I'm telling you they have an easy time with plenty of space for being romantic, while your Papa has to mind his P's and Q's in a difficult business. So don't be a silly little goose, stuffing your head with the idea that because one man has all the time there is and can walk little girls through Bond Street and buy them boxes of chocolates, while another man has to be out earning his living, the first man is better than the second. He may be, but if he is it has nothing to do with all the advantages that have come to him without his having had to do a single thing about it. Now, then. That's the sermon. Have I made myself clear?"

"You've given me a lot to think about."

Miss Whale laughed. "I'll bet I have. But don't do too much thinking tonight. Go to sleep."

3

Sally Gaylord was a year older than I, which is to say that she was eight on that first day of our acquaintance. As I have said, I had met her before and exchanged "Good mornings," but now I was to spend a whole day in her company. The prospect excited me.

It was a beautiful morning, fresh and dewy, when Miss Whale and I arrived at the rendezvous in Hyde Park. We were sent off very early, because Ducat had to drive the hansom back to bring Papa and Mama. I suppose no one today can imagine what the Park was like then, when motorcars were not only unknown but even undreamed of. And especially this was so on a Derby Day, for the Park was a great place for the assembling of parties who were to drive to Epsom. We found it full of the rolling and flashing of wheels, the creak of harness, the thudding of hooves, the blowing-out of great red nostrils, the proud arching of knees, and the resilient pressure upon the tan of insteps that seemed too delicate and slender for the weight they carried. Occasionally a high-spirited neighing or whinnying broke like a trumpet upon the air, to be mocked by a donkey's bray, for the costers were there, shimmering in pearly buttons, with women whose hat feathers flaunted like cheeky back-chat made visible. There was all this, and there were shouting happy crowds, and the may trees were in bloom.

My hand closed tight upon Whaley's when I saw the wagonette coming, with Lord Burnage in the driver's seat. I had to fight hard against an upsurge of my old sorrow, but I had promised Whaley to be good, and I was good.

The wagonette was newly varnished. The brass hubs twinkled in the sunshine. The horses were four splendid dapple-grays, and as they came to a stand I saw that the blinkers were furnished with little silver shields, and on each of these was engraved the crest that had been on the letter I had so wickedly removed from Papa's morning pile. All my thought was for Lord Burnage, but now I know that, without consciously taking it in, I took in every smallest detail of the wonderful moment. I have only to close my eyes to see again the yellowish spume upon the bits, and the forefeet fastidiously scraping at the earth, the flickering of long plushy ears, the flash of buckles, and the huge velvet eye of one of the leaders as he turned his head toward me and I looked down the dark slot between his head and the blinker. It was as exciting and unexpected and pleasurable as the sudden glimpse a man may be afforded by an indiscreet *décolletage*.

Lord Burnage handed the ribbons to a groom and climbed down. I was aware of the stock about his neck, the gold fox-head pinned into it, the tall gray hat, the gloves, the red carnation at his buttonhole. He raised his hat to Miss Whale and then bent down and kissed me. "Well," he said, "have you been wishing me luck?" It was a whisper, and I whispered back: "Yes, sir."

There were already a lady and gentleman in the wagonette, as well as Sally Gaylord. Sally got out, came to me and Miss Whale, and said: "Hallo! I've got to spend the day with you."

"It will give us great pleasure," Whaley replied.

"Good," said Sally. "I'm glad someone's going to be pleased."

"Miss Whale," Lord Burnage said, "you may as well know first as last that this child says what she thinks. She . . ." He stopped abruptly. The hansom containing Papa and Mama drew up, and he went with extraordinary alacrity to greet them. We seemed to be forgotten in a moment. Mama, I thought, had never looked more beautiful. Papa waved his hand to me and Miss Whale, but Mama did not appear even to see us. Lord Burnage helped her into the wagonette, saying, as he did so, something that caused her to laugh. How gay her laugh sounded! Several people who were standing by looked up when they heard it and their faces brightened. That's the sort of laugh it was: infectious, like all happy things.

4

We watched them drive away, and the morning was suddenly emptier. My heart was going with them, so that, although we lingered there for some time, I was not seeing much of what was happening about me. I was recalled to the moment by a voice saying: "Well, Sally, how you are growing!"

A curricle drawn by two roan horses had stopped near us. A man and a woman sat in it. The man seemed to me to be immensely old, but I know now that he cannot have been more than fifty. I didn't then know the word raffish. Had I known it, that is the word I should have used to describe his appearance. The woman appeared to be about as old as my mother, and she was as beautiful. As Mama's laugh had caused faces to brighten round her, so my face, lugubrious now that the wagonette was out of sight, brightened as I looked at this lovely woman speaking so graciously to Sally Gaylord. "Why!" she cried, "you're becoming quite a little person!"

Sally's conduct surprised me. She was anything but pleased. Indeed, she seemed intensely embarrassed. She looked at the woman from under her lashes and then turned to Miss Whale. "If you please," she said, "shall we be going now?"

"Certainly," cried Miss Whale, whose quick sense divined some awkwardness in this moment, and giving a hand to each of us, she led us to the hansom, which was near by. As we turned away, the man in the curricle gave a great roar of laughter. "Cut, by God!" he said. "The chit has cut you dead, Edwina! Let that be a lesson to you."

The hansom moved slowly away through the thronging traffic. It was not till we were out of the Park that Sally said. "That was my Mama and the Duke of Fallowshire. She is his Duchess."

5

I was surprised to find that there was such a person as Mrs. Ducat, and goodness knows how long I should have been in discovering this if it had not been for Sally Gaylord. Ducat was—well, just Ducat. He appeared punctually with the hansom or the victoria, and when his services had been rendered he disappeared into what I knew simply as the mews. Thus he knew his place and kept it, and I kept mine. I had never entered the mews.

Having made the remark about her Mama and the Duke of Fallow-shire, Sally brushed them both off the surface of her mind. They did not seem to interest her deeply. She began to look about her, to make remarks on anything she saw, to laugh, to point. Yes—actually to point! "Don't point!" How it had been driven into me as one of the laws! Don't point. Sit still. Speak when you are spoken to.

It was obvious that Sally Gaylord was not a well-brought-up girl as I had been led to understand those words. She was a quicksilver creature, alert and impulsive. She bounced up and down on the seat. She thrust an arm through Miss Whale's, who was sitting between us, and cried: "What a lovely morning!" Then she stood up, balancing herself by holding Whaley's shoulder, and rapped with her fist on the glass trap-door in the roof. Ducat opened it and looked through. "What's this horse's name?" Sally demanded.

Good gracious, I thought, what next! It had never occurred to me that our horse had a name. We never so much as spoke of the horse but always of the carriage. We'll have the hansom. We'll have the victoria.

A shy grin spread over Ducat's face, as though he were pleased that someone took an interest in the horse. "Rascal, miss," he said, looking a little shamefaced, and closed the shutter.

"I do like to know horses' names," Sally said. "Down at Tresant my father's horses have their names on brass plates over their mangers. I polish them myself. Once you've got them bright you don't need to use metal polish. Spit will do, if you do them regularly."

I cast a sidelong look at Miss Whale. Surely even she, tolerant and easy-going she, would reprove such language as this! She merely asked comfortably: "Where is Tresant?"

"Oh, in Heaven!" Sally cried, bouncing vigorously. "You can't believe what it's like at Tresant. Why we ever come to London I can't imagine. It's just a habit, and a very silly one too, this coming up for the season. Just when everything's glorious down there. Can you imagine," she demanded, looking at us quite fiercely, with her black brows meeting, "can you imagine anything sillier than to spend the winter in the country and then come to a horrible town just when everything begins to be beautiful?"

"I must say," Miss Whale agreed, "that I should prefer it the other way myself."

"Well, there it is," Sally said with comic resignation. "When one is young, one must put up with things as they are."

"Yes, indeed," said Whaley. "And sometimes when one is old."

The hansom stopped at our front door, and Sally cried: "Let us go on to the mews and see Rascal put into his stable."

I think there must have been a momentary flicker of doubt, of hesitation, even in Miss Whale's mind. But "All right," she said. "Let us do that." She pushed up the trap and said: "Ducat, drive on into the mews. The young ladies would like to see the stables."

This was one of the oddest moments of my life till then. It could hardly have been odder if Miss Whale had said: "Drive on to Timbuktu." A few hundred yards would bring us to the mews, but to traverse them would be to traverse all that dire and hidden territory where lurked the creatures who stood between me and what, in Mercy Kite's day, had been called my "safety." It is a literal fact that at the prospect my heart began to hammer on my ribs. Sally Gaylord's composure was something I could not understand.

Suddenly, we were shut out from the spacious streets. We had driven under an archway into a cobbled yard, drained by a gutter

37

flowing down the middle. On either hand were two-storied buildings. There were double doors on the ground floor, belonging to stables. Outside wooden stairs led to rooms above, and in these I saw that people lived, for here a man, there a woman or child, stood at a doorway. At one of these doorways a woman was nursing a baby, and she called down to Ducat: "Alf! It's through!" She had not seen that we were in the hansom. As we climbed out she gave an exclamation of surprise, almost dismay, and disappeared.

Well, there we stood in a powerful smell of horses' dung and urine, and with the occasional sound of a hoof thudding a stable floor or of nostrils blowing into a manger. Through an open door I saw a groom, his shirt sleeves rolled up, his braces hanging down his flanks, hissing over a curry comb. It was altogether a commonplace but not to me a customary scene; I found it stimulating and romantic.

Sally jerked her head toward the door through which the woman had disappeared. "That your wife?" she asked.

"Yes," said Ducat.

"What's her name?"

Again the rather sheepish, half-pleased, half-embarrassed grin spread on Ducat's face. "Jenny, miss."

"What's come through?"

"I expect it's the baby's tooth, miss. Been worrying her something cruel."

Sally nodded her head sagely. "They do," she said.

The woman named Jenny now came down the stairs and Sally said: "Good morning. I'm glad the baby's tooth's through."

Ducat stripped off his coat with the silver buttons, another coat that he wore under that, and handed these, with his hat, to his wife. She at once ran upstairs with them. Ducat began slowly to roll his sleeves above his elbows. A smudgy design in reds and blues was tattooed on his right forearm. I had never seen him like this before, never seen him without buttoned coat and official hat—never seen him with a wife and child; indeed, I had never seen him. He slapped the horse on the flank. "Come on, Rascal, old boy." Nor had I ever seen Rascal, old boy. I had seen "the horse."

When Rascal was out of the shafts, Sally, without invitation, began to take off his harness. I could only stand there, holding Miss Whale's hand, marveling. I marveled at the way in which the mews had suddenly emptied of everybody except those who had some work to do. When we arrived, a few children were running here and there on the cobbles, a few women were looking out of upper doors or windows. Now they had all silently withdrawn. Our presence seemed to have an extraordinary power of repulsion. It was like a magnet in reverse, driving things away.

38

I marveled, too, at Sally's ease. She was whistling. She deftly undid buckles, lifted the collar off Rascal's neck. He, too, seemed now different. Like Ducat, he was stripped down; he was pure horse. The blinkers gone, I could see his eyes. He looked altogether another creature, and he had a name. Sally took a fistful of his mane. "Which is his stable?" she asked.

Ducat ran and opened a door. Sally led Rascal toward it, slapped him on the behind and shouted: "In, boy." He went in with a clatter, Ducat after him; and Sally turned to us with a grin. "I'd like to see Mrs. Ducat's baby," she said. "But I don't think we ought to today. It would be intrusive."

"Well," said Whaley, "let's go and have breakfast."

6

When we had eaten breakfast the question arose of how we were to spend the day. "If you would like that," Sally said, "you could see our house. I asked my father if you might, and he said Yes—if you cared to."

We accepted this invitation, and were soon walking through the door near which, a few days earlier, I had run into Lord Burnage. I had never given much thought to houses. There were people like us who had houses like ours, and there were people like Ducat who naturally had houses of a different sort. These, I had discovered, were lofts over stables; and though I had always considered Lord Burnage to belong to the "people like us" I was now to find that his house, except in its outward appearance, was not like ours. The Rainboroughs had been rich for a few generations, and for all that time their energies had been directed to making themselves richer. For the first time I was in a house belonging to people whose ancestors for centuries had not had to bother about making money. They had had to think of nothing but spending it beautifully.

Sally was accustomed to being a guide. I have only a confused memory of the tour we made, with her chattering about Holbeins and Van Dycks, Romneys and Gainsboroughs, Lelys and Opies. I remember a luscious half-nude girl painted by Etty, and on the opposite wall a Burnage of Restoration days looking straight across at her with veiled watchful eyes and a smile that could well be of appreciation. "Those two always make me laugh," said Sally. "They say he was a caution." And there was a Gaylord—not yet a Burnage—a Sir Thomas Gaylord of Elizabethan times, handsome and melancholy—of whom Sally casually remarked: "They say he was the Queen's lover, but that's never been proved."

39

I didn't know what a lover in this sense was, nor, I imagine, did Sally; but the words sounded splendid and romantic. I remembered the Queen at the opening of the Crystal Palace. Lots and lots of men must love a woman like that.

The pictures, I must say, didn't mean much to me, because I knew nothing about painting and had never heard so much as the names of these painters. What I was more impressed with was the spaciousness of a house no bigger than our own. All the Victorian knickknackery that had ever been devised had come to rest with us. Here it seemed as though each century washed up a few things of perfection and that nothing else was permitted to remain.

We finished the tour at the top of the house. Here, as I in ours, Sally had her quarters, and in this one particular, the Victorian rule was observed. The stairs were oil-clothed, the room was bleak, bleaker than mine, for Whaley had made a difference. A couple of old rugs, worn down to their basic fabric, were on the floor; a plain deal table was in the middle of the room, and a plain woman was sitting in a wicker chair. She rose when we entered and curtseyed to me. Sally introduced her as Mademoiselle Lapage, her governess. She had nothing to say for herself. She was very correct, very silent, saying only to Whaley, as we left: "You will return Miss Sally at four? Yes? It is understood by his lordship."

We returned Sally at four, and what we did in the meantime I don't clearly remember. Some time thereafter Sally and I were doing so many things together. After the early morning, that first day is blurred.

7

Things came into focus again late that night. I have learned since of what happened up to the moment when I saw something for myself. Lord Burnage drove the wagonette back from Epsom and dropped his passengers here and there till none were left but Papa and Mama. Finally they pulled up outside our house, the three got down, and the coachman began to drive away the wagonette. Lord Burnage, Papa and Mama were standing near the edge of the pavement, and as the coachman pulled the horses round, the door into the wagonette at the back, which had been insecurely fastened, flew open and struck Mama. It was not much of a blow and merely bruised her arm, but it caused her to start back suddenly. She tripped on her long skirt and fell. It was this that did the damage. The men stooped to raise her, each holding an arm, but when she got her feet to the ground, she gave a groan and would have fallen again but for their support. One of her legs was broken.

Threllfall by this time had opened the door, and Papa shouted to him: "Send Stott across at once to Dr. Mackenzie. No! I'll go myself. I'll bring him back with me."

Dr. Mackenzie's house was not two minutes' walk away, and my father relinquished Mama to Lord Burnage and started to run, which was in itself an extraordinary sight. Lord Burnage said: "Put an arm round my neck." He lifted Mama bodily and carried her into the house.

I had not slept since going to bed. The excitements of the day tended to keep me awake, and, too, I was hoping that, late though it was, Mama would come up and tell me something of her adventures. I heard the wagonette stop outside the house, got out of bed, and went to the window. I heard Mama's cry and the perturbed voices of the men, and then I saw that extraordinary spectacle of Papa running, now a shadow, now clear in the light of a lamp. I was afraid. Something terrible was happening. . . . Mama was dying. . . . I pulled on a dressing gown and went swiftly downstairs. As I reached the last turn of the stairs I saw Threllfall come out of the drawing room and hurry toward the kitchen quarters, shouting some order to a housemaid. The drawing-room door was wide open, but I did not go in. I stopped my hasty course just in time. What I saw made my heart beat wildly. Mama had been laid on a sofa. A shaded standard lamp showered a soft light upon her, but I could not see her face, and she could not see me, for Lord Burnage, with his back to me, was between us. He was bending over her, holding her hand to his lips. The shock of seeing them in that posture overwhelmed me. The very vagueness of my thoughts added to my consternation. I turned and fled noiselessly on my bare feet to the first landing, and stood trembling there till Papa came breathlessly in with the doctor. "Calm, calm, Sir Richard, if you please," Dr. Mackenzie was saying. "I expect there's nothing here that a week or two won't cure."

CHAPTER FOUR

I

I WISH I had clearer memories of my father, and happier ones. But happier is not exactly the word I want. He dulled me, rather than made me unhappy. A day could be shining like silver, and some word of his, some gesture, would come upon it like breath upon a shining silver cup. When he was gone, this cloudy tarnish would dissolve, and there would be a shining again. Our visit to the Crystal

41

Palace at Sydenham comes to my mind. That was three years after I had seen the Queen open the first palace in Hyde Park.

Oh, what a disappointing day that was! The palace was not the same at all. I think now that it was far more beautiful, with its curved roofs and new shape, but it was not the *same*, and I had wanted to repeat something that was happy in my memory. There was a brass band, and a huge chorus. Cheers for the Queen boomed through the building, but this time it was not she, it was her Prince, who took my eye.

"Papa, why is the Prince sad?"

We were driving home, and I was deflated. His answer made little sense to me: how could it to a child, and one who led such a life as mine? "I expect it's because he realizes that all this Crystal Palace business is stuff and nonsense. A Palace of Peace! And here we are at war with the Russians already! The man's got his head in the clouds. A pity the Queen ever married him. She should have married some decent Englishman with his feet on the ground. I'm told the feller's always trying to stick his nose into state affairs."

He went on and on: about the war taxes which would ruin everybody, about twelve workmen who had been killed in the rebuilding of the Palace at Sydenham—"a warning, if ever there was one," he said, but I could not see why—and it all passed over my head without meaning a thing. I knew only that a day from which I had expected much joy had turned gray and comfortless; and the crown was put on it all when Mama greeted us in the hall, and he said: "Well, I hope young madam is satisfied with wasting my day at a time when there are plenty of serious things to be thought about, God knows." With that, he stumped straight away to a room he used for working in at home. Mama, seeing me disconsolate, gave me one of her rare kisses and said: "We must excuse Papa. Just now he has so much on his mind, what with the war and one thing and another."

2

I say it made no sense to me at the time, that grumbling monologue as we drove home from Sydenham. But now that I look back upon it I find in it the seeds of the disaster that came upon my parents' marriage. Papa had no use for a man with "his head in the clouds," which meant to him, alas! as to so many, a man who didn't have his heart in a ledger. "A decent Englishman with his feet on the ground" could tread no holier ground than Threadneedle Street and the region thereabout. I don't suppose there is any reason why he should have concerned himself with affairs as exclusively as he did. He could have

42

left a lot to underlings. But he never learned the wisdom of the great Pierpont Morgan's remark: "I can do a year's work in nine months, but not in twelve." He could have afforded a house in the country or by the sea, but he never had one. He did not hunt or shoot or fish, and he disliked dancing. The occasions to which he took Mama out were City dinners and functions of that sort. Each summer he rented the same house at Broadstairs, and we went there for a fortnight. It seems to me to have been, for a man of his great wealth, an incredible life to lead. In its way, it was admirable: it had a stern rectitude according to its own lights. But I cannot now recapture the surprise, the consternation, that assailed my young heart when I saw Mama lying on the sofa and Lord Burnage bending over her, kissing her hand.

3

I continued on one day of each week to take breakfast downstairs. For a time, though, it was with Papa only: Mama remained in her bedroom. When at last she was able to rejoin us, things were not as they had been before. There never had been cordiality, but at least there had been a perfect decorum, a punctilious observance of rules that kept things moving sweetly. Now I was aware of a constant grittiness and even an occasional jolt. To give an example: there was a morning when the grapes upon the table looked especially tempting and I asked if I might have some. I knew that they had been sent by Lord Burnage. Ever since Mama's accident he had been sending things: flowers and fruit and huge ribboned boxes of sweets like the one he had bought for me in Bond Street; and every day he would appear in person at the door to ask how Mama was and to leave his greetings to her. Other people sent their footmen to inquire.

Now when I asked Papa if he would be so kind as to pass me the grapes, he looked at me in that maddening way he had of seeming to bring all his mental faculties to bear upon the simplest request, and said presently: "The grapes . . . Yes, the grapes. Well, Sarah, the grapes are not mine. They are your mother's. She may or may not wish you to have some of them. But I imagine Lord Burnage intended them for her personal consumption. Would you not say so, Florence?"

Mama was reading a letter and did not answer. He pressed her: "Would you not say so, Florence? These grapes, my dear. Sarah is asking if she may have some. Do you think Lord Burnage would like his favors to be shared? Some men don't."

Mama pushed the plate of grapes across the table to me, got up, and stood for a moment looking at him. I was amazed by that look.

It was a glare, and there was loathing in it. However, Papa did not see it. He, too, was reading a letter. Mama walked out of the room. I felt that she would have *flung* out, as they say, but she was still a little lame.

I was not asked to the breakfast room again that summer; but on a day in early autumn Whaley was summoned to take breakfast with Papa. Mama was not present, and my own breakfast was served in the schoolroom, though I ate nothing, so shaken was I by a sense of crisis. I stood at the window, watching the familiar sights: the man sweeping up the yellow plane-tree leaves in the garden, the cabs and hansoms, the window-repair man with sheets of glass strapped to a frame on his back, the chimney sweep pushing his little cart loaded with gollywog-headed brushes. They all moved by in the silent air under the pale blue autumn sky; and then Papa's hansom came to the curb, and I watched to see it start for the City. But it did not. It drove to Lord Burnage's house, which I could clearly see, for it was on the side of the square that ran at right angles to ours. Lord Burnage came out, so promptly that it seemed he must have been waiting. He got into the hansom alongside Papa, and they drove away together.

At that moment Miss Whale came into the schoolroom, looking very grave. She did not speak for some time; then she said: "How would you like to go away for a holiday, Sarah?"

"But we've had our holiday," I cried, thinking of Broadstairs.

"Yes, but it's possible to have more than one holiday in a year. This will be a longer one. I don't know how long. Sir Richard wishes me to take you away till—well, till we are recalled."

"But when do we go?"

"This afternoon. We shall travel to Folkestone today. Tomorrow we shall cross over to Boulogne."

4

But Boulogne was not our destination. Our destination was the sweet township of Montreuil, standing, surrounded by ramparts, on its hill above the swift rushing of the Canche. What a business it had been! Never before in my life had I been so swept about, so lifted into a mounting transport of excitement. We had started to pack as soon as Whaley had said we were to be off, with me demanding all the time: Why? Why? Why? Why are we going, Whaley? Why are we going so suddenly, Whaley? Why are we going to France?

Whaley was reserved, and that was something new for her; but I gathered that there were urgent reasons why I should be out of the way. "It was Sir Richard who suggested France, and when I spoke of the Undridges he thought that would be just the thing. Boulogne,

44

after all, is almost within sight of England, and Montreuil is only a stone's throw behind it."

"Who are the Undridges?"

"Don't sit on that trunk. You're hindering me. And if there are any books you want to take you'd better get them out of the shelves. The Undridges are people I used to know when I lived in France. I've kept in touch with them, and they're always urging me to come and stay with them at Montreuil. The school I was at was near there, and Mr. Undridge used to come in to give drawing lessons. He's an artist. His wife took the English class. They have one little boy named Daniel. I suppose he's about twelve now."

The morning passed in this excited sort of chattering, in scrambling packing, and in a scrambling luncheon. After that, Whaley took me to the drawing-room door and gently pushed me in. I was dressed for the journey, and already a hired four-wheeler cab was at the door and the trunks were being put on top of it. Mama was lying on a sofa, resting her leg. She reached out a hand as I approached and drew me to her. I had never seen her face so expressionless. She was to flash and sparkle again, but now she was frozen. She kissed me very coldly. "Be a good child," she said. "I have every confidence in Miss Whale. Remember that for some time now you will be entirely in her charge. You must give her strict obedience."

I said dutifully: "Yes, Mama," and added impulsively: "Of course I will. I *love* Whaley."

She looked at me for a moment with sad speculation, and then said: "Well, that doesn't always make life easier."

She seemed to be seeking something to say, something that *ought* to be said, but she couldn't find it; and as I stood there restlessly, moving from foot to foot, wishing for nothing but to be done with the moment and off on my adventure, so childishly unaware of the so much greater adventure before which she was poised and perhaps daunted, she said: "Very well, then; off with you!" and, as I could see through the window the last trunk going up on to the cab, I turned ungraciously enough and hurried off to join Whaley at the front door.

After that it was a dazzle of new exciting experience that remains in my mind without cohesion or sequence: an experience of sailors and railwaymen, of sun glitter on a mid-Channel sea, of foreign chatter and foreign food, and Whaley cleaving her way through all this like a prow. I suppose even in those days getting to Montreuil was not much of an adventure; but to my circumscribed young mind it seemed one of the first magnitude, and I drew such a breath of relief as a crusader might have done on reaching Jerusalem when Whaley put me into bed at the Hotel de France and said: "Well, we've arrived. Tomorrow we shall look up the Undridges."

I am sorry to say that Daniel Undridge was wearing a suit of black velvet and a white lace collar. Even a woman of my age, who recalls such dress as customary, can hardly restrain, now, a smile at this absurd recollection. What I myself was wearing I do not remember, and happily no photograph survives to remind me. I can imagine pantaloons drooping to the tops of my boots, finishing off in a few inches of lace.

It was afternoon—late afternoon—and I shall never forget it, not a moment of it: the very quality of the light seemed different from any I had known. There in the garden enclosed by high whitewashed walls it had almost a color, an autumn color, and the air was utterly still. We had been walking, Miss Whale and I, down a narrow cobbled street—a lane was all you could truly call it—with long stretches of white wall on either hand, and here and there the butt end of a house. Miss Whale pushed open a little green door cut through a bigger door, and we went in and there was the house: low and white, glimmering in the autumnal air that all day long had been warm and hazy and now, with the sun's declension, made things seem almost insubstantial.

It looked a haphazard house, a chalky oblong, with green trellis on the walls supporting jasmine and red roses. The scent of these flowers was in the air, heavy as though it had been accumulating there all summer long between the high walls. A French window was open, and on the lawn in front of this the Undridges sat on green-painted iron chairs.

"Whaley, tell me something about the Undridges," I had demanded that morning, and Whaley, remembering as she did from time to time that to teach me French was part of her duty, replied with a laugh: "*Onde, onduler, Undridge. La vraie fonction d'un Undridge est d'onduler*. Which is to say, my dear Sarah, that an Undridge undulates."

The three Undridges rose as we approached, and flowed toward us. I saw at once what Whaley had meant. Mrs. Undridge was the most wavelike of the three, for her skirt made it possible to forget that she had legs. Even her feet were invisible. She was a beautiful woman according to the conception of the Pre-Raphaelites: tall, slender, a little goitrous, with a pale face out of which shone deep blue eyes. The lustrous silks that enveloped her rustled as she came toward me as though skating on invisible ice. One could see that Mr. Undridge had legs. They were encased in pepper-and-salt trousers. His black coat was loose and flowing; the bow of broad black silk at his neck was loose and flowing; the black sombrero, which he took from his head as he held Whaley's hand, had been brooding a moment before like a small dark cloud upon his careless hair. He did not flow like a wave, as his wife did, but like a leopard. His light eyes were curiously feral; and his pointed beard and pointed nose seemed made for ferreting things out. The boy Daniel, as I have said, was in velvet and lace. He was slim and graceful, all flowing lines, and his long dark hair fell down one side of his face in a waving wing that looked as though it were brushed every hour.

Mr. Undridge brought two more green iron chairs and an iron table, and Mrs. Undridge flowed through the French windows and came out with the things for tea. I remember that all the words were uttered that would be uttered on such an occasion. "Now, have a *real* cup of tea, Maggie." (This was to Miss Whale.) "I expect you're dying for a *real* cup of tea. That's one thing the French don't even begin to understand—how to make a *real* cup of tea."

"But they beat us at coffee," said Mr. Undridge.

"Yes," his wife conceded, "they can make a *real* cup of coffee, and we can't touch them at pastries. Daniel, manners! The pastries for Miss Rainborough."

Daniel swiftly placed upon his plate the two most appealing of the pastries and handed me the dish with what was left, while his mother rattled on: "And, of course, so far as vegetables are concerned we don't *begin* to understand them in England."

"The English don't begin to understand wine, either," said Mr. Undridge.

"Oh, that!" said Mrs. Undridge, and laughed a little silvery laugh which announced clearly enough that the English taste in wine was something which one indeed did not begin to understand.

Whaley, sipping her tea, conceded that it was a real English cup, and inquired about Mr. Undridge's work, his pictures. This, too, alas! appeared to be something that the English didn't begin to understand.

As they talked, Daniel sat and looked from one to another with his grave, almost adult face. From time to time his long thin hand would go up, scratching and ruffling in the wing of hair, and his mother would say: "Darling, your hair is so pretty. Don't disarrange it. Have you not a comb?" and Daniel would take a comb from his pocket and, still not speaking, but maintaining that odd intent listeningness, he would draw it slowly through and through, sleeking the wing.

In all this, I had been so much ignored that I was startled when Mrs. Undridge suddenly began: "Miss Rainborough—"

"No one would object," said Whaley, "if you called her Sarah."

"Well, Sarah, then. I expect you would like to look round the garden. Daniel, take Sarah to the pond."

I might have been a mare who was to be led off for a drink, or a puppy condemned to have a brick tied round its neck and to be hurled into the water, so abrupt was this command. Everybody got up. The

47

girl Berthe appeared, a stout, good-humored-looking creature, who began to clear away the tea things while Mr. and Mrs. Undridge and Whaley walked into the house. Daniel stood there at my side till everyone was gone. Then suddenly he gave a savage kick at the light iron table, sending it sprawling, and with both hands worked madly at his hair till it stood on end in wild disorder all over his head. From under this disheveled thatch he made a grimace at me, and, seizing my hand, he said: "Now we'll see the damned pond, if you want to."

We set off down a paved path between lawns, and as we went Daniel chanted, in a voice too low to be heard in the house, "The damned pond, the blasted pond, the bloody pond," looking sideways at me to see if I were shocked. I was: I had never heard such language before except in casual street snatches from the lips of cabbies and costers: but nothing would have induced me to let Daniel Undridge know that his words had any effect on me whatever.

The pond was beautiful. It was circular, with a stone edge that was crusted with moss and lichens. Round this was paving, and then a flower bed, full now of late autumn color. Outside this again was a hedge of clipped yew. It was a magic enclosure, secret, bloomy with dusk, cool with the drip of water over the edge of a basin. "Well," said Daniel, "here's the blasted pond. How do you like it?"

Now this was the first time I had ever been alone with a boy. It was not often that I had been alone with anybody, except first Kite and then Whaley. Sometimes I was taken to parties where boys were present, and there were boys at the dancing classes. But they were sad and repressed little boys. This was something altogether different and I thought: If this is what boys are like when they are left on their own, then I don't mind if I'm never with a boy again.

Daniel stood looking down into the pond, his hands in his pockets, his toe detaching from the stone rim a bright orange disc of lichen.

"Why do you swear?" I asked righteously.

He didn't answer, but went on industriously hacking at the lichen. "It takes years for those things to grow," he said.

"It was very pretty, and now you've destroyed it."

"*He* thinks they're wonderful. 'Don't you think this patina of lichen is really rather remarkable? It's such accidental beauties that move the heart more than all our contrived effects.' "

I realized that he was mimicking his father. "Don't you like your Papa?" I asked.

Again he did not answer, but, thrusting his ten fingers violently into his hair he heaved it about till it looked like a wrecked cornstook. He turned round and made a dreadful face at me, pulling down the skin round his eyes with his fingers, flattening his nose, and putting out his tongue. "How's that for an accidental beauty?" he demanded.

48

"I think you're a dreadful boy," I said.

This seemed to please him. He said: "I am—*bloody* dreadful. But *they* don't know it. I'm revolting. I could say things not fit for your ears." I had nothing to say to that, and he went on: "Another thing I could do. I could muck up this blasted suit and say you did it. You'd get into an awful row."

This, I thought, thinking of Mama, and the bowing, and the not bowing, is the sort of person one would "cut" in the Park; but I didn't want to cut Daniel Undridge. I wanted to dare him. "You wouldn't do that," I said. "I dare you."

He leaned down and thrust his hand into the pond and scooped a handful of green slime off its inner wall. He slabbed it like a trowelful of mortar on to the front of his black velvet coat, and with both hands smeared it up and down till, what with his reeking hands and wild hair and filthy coat, he looked disgusting. He rubbed his slimy hands all over his face, and now indeed he looked as utterly revolting as he had claimed to be. He produced another of his celebrated grimaces, this time contriving to go cockeyed. "Now," he said, "now let him paint me sitting on the edge of the pond. I'm sick of sitting on the edge of the blasted pond."

I looked at him in consternation. "You're going to say that I did *that* to you?"

"Yes," he said darkly. "I wouldn't like to be in your shoes."

He began to move toward the gap cut in the yew hedge, and now indeed I was troubled: not at what the Undridges would say: I didn't care a bit about that: but at what Whaley would think of me, for I did deeply value her good opinion. At this moment Whaley herself, moving unheard over the turf, appeared in the gap, and Daniel ran slap into her. She recoiled at the sight and threw up her hands. "Good gracious, Daniel! Whatever have you been doing with yourself?"

Daniel hung his head, silent for a time, then pointed at me. "Why did you bring her?" he demanded. "She's horrid. She mucked me up. She smeared me all over."

Now I waited for Whaley's wrath to strike me, but she only said: "Sit down for a moment, Daniel," and he obediently sat on the warm stone edge of the pond. Whaley looked from one to the other of us, and then said: "You're a bigger fool than I thought, Daniel."

"I'm a blasted big boy," he glowered, "and very intelligent."

"Yes," said Whaley, "you're so intelligent that you want me to believe that Sarah did this to you. You're mucked up from head to foot, and *she* did it. Look at her. She did it without getting a spot of dirt on her clothes or a drop of water on her hands. Or has she had time to go in and take a bath and change?"

Daniel still glowered, but now had nothing to say. "Well then," said

49

Miss Whale, "what are you going to tell your father and mother? You'll have to explain yourself somehow. Won't you?"

"S'pose so," said Daniel, now completely miserable.

"Well," Whale demanded briskly. "Have you got any ideas?"

But the deflated Daniel had none. I thought that in another moment he would begin to whimper. "We could say he fell into the pond," I offered, and now he shot me a look almost of gratitude; but Whaley came down coldly: "He looks awful, but he doesn't look bad enough for that. If he's going to say he's been in the pond, then he'll have to go into the pond. And as I see nothing else for it, in he goes."

With that, she put a foot under his knees, gave a heave, and over he went backward. She stooped down, took him by the scruff of the neck, and had him out almost as soon as he was in.

"Now," said Whaley as Daniel stood there dripping dismally, "any explaining that's to be done you can do for yourself. You got into the mess, and we've done our best to get you out. I've said *au revoir* for Sarah to your parents, and now we're off. *A demain*."

With that, she took me by the hand and off we marched, past the house where a pale light or two was appearing on the chalky face, through the green door into the cobbled lane, and so across the Grande Place to the Hotel de France, where, but not till then, Whaley exploded briefly: "The little horror!"

6

The Hotel de France was set back in a little bay off the Place, and it had a balconied courtyard. It was delightful to leap out of bed and run onto the balcony and see horses stamping on the cobbles below and smell the morning incense of coffee and new bread. After breakfast we wandered into the Place where old countrywomen had set up their stalls beneath the trees, and the autumn sun shone on apples and pears, cabbages, onions, carrots, all sorts of things that composed themselves into a score of glowing pictures, and there was a chatter of conversation unintelligible to me, and a squawking and quacking of hens and ducks, and rough ponies that had drawn the country carts were tied to the trees. The Undridge's Berthe, with a big wicker basket on either arm, was chaffering and haggling from stall to stall, and Whaley said: "She'll think it a great triumph if the complete morning's shopping gets done at two sous less than she's asked."

I had forgotten the Undridges, so charmed was I by the autumn morning that smelled of dewy cobwebs and by the shifting colored scene, but Berthe recalled them to my mind, and I asked: "Why do the Undridges live in France?"

"Well," Whaley answered, "people can please themselves where they live, can't they? They like France. For one thing, they're not well off and they find it a cheap place to live in, and for another they were not happy in England."

"Why were they not happy?" I persisted, and Whaley said: "Oh, there were many reasons. Have you ever heard of Dante Gabriel Rossetti?"

I hadn't, and Whaley was too sensible to confuse my mind with a lot of names and "movements" which would have meant nothing to me then. "Mr. Undridge quarreled with him," she said. "There was a lot of unpleasantness one way and another, and the Undridges cleared out."

It all came to me bit by bit later on, and it was simple enough, Rossetti being what he was and Mr. Undridge what *he* was. They were very sure of themselves, those young Pre-Raphaelite painters, happy in rebellion, rejoicing in being contumeliously spoken of, scornful of the older men. Undridge was in that set, hobnobbing with Millais and Rossetti, Ford Madox Brown and all the others. His wife had been a model for most of them. She had been the mother of Jesus and a beggar maid, a Greek girl holding a pitcher on her head and a big-eyed emigrant looking her last on England. But Undridge was not as good a painter as the rest: in fact, he was not a good painter at all. Rossetti tolerated him so long as he was safe for a pound now and a fiver later on; but Undridge was a poor man, and the first row came when he refused to lend Rossetti any more money. Thereupon, in the presence of Millais, Rossetti told him what he thought of his pictures, and slapped him across the face with a smoked herring. And this was the absurd reason why the Undridges had for years now been living in France. There, nourishing his injured self-esteem, Francis Undridge became more self-consciously a "painter" than ever, in dress, in talk, in everything but success. His wife was only too eager to play up to him, and Daniel had to. Francis painted one picture that became widely known. It was of the pond in the garden at Montreuil. Daniel, in black velvet and lace, his wing of hair immaculate, sat on the pond's edge, gazing at his image in the water. The picture was called "Reflection," and it was bought by a firm of brass-polish manufacturers. It was to be seen on every hoarding throughout a few decades, inscribed: "For perfect Reflections use Easyrub Metal Polish." Thereafter, poor Daniel was painted again and again, in many poses, on the edge of the pond; and if I had had any adult sense of all this on that afternoon of our first meeting I should not, I suppose, have thought him such a terrible little boy.

7

"I thought we were going to *live* with the Undridges," I said to Whaley as we watched Berthe moving off with her loaded baskets.

"Well," she said, "I hope we shall live in the Undridges' house, but they won't be there."

There was none of this nonsense about passports and papers and money-changing and all the rest of it in those days. Miss Whale had discussed with Papa what was best to be done with me in a moment of crisis. She had remembered the Undridges. They were always hard up, they would be glad to have paying guests; and so, that very same day off we had gone. But during the talk in the drawing room, while Daniel was acting like an idiot child by the pond, she learned that our unheralded arrival had come at a moment when the Undridges were themselves poised for flight. Mr. Undridge had accepted the direction of English studies in a school at Bordeaux and would be off in a day or two. However, his lease of this house in Montreuil did not expire until the coming spring, and if Miss Whale and I cared to live there, that would put a bit of rent into his pocket. Berthe would look after us, and if Daniel could stay there, too, that would be most convenient to the Undridges while they were finding their feet in Bordeaux. It remained now only for Whaley to communicate all this to Papa. His consent came promptly. Poor man! Little I knew what bitter business was occupying his mind and how pleased he was to fall in with any scheme that kept me out of the way and in good hands.

And so within a week the Undridges went, we left the attractive balcony rooms in the Hotel de France, and Miss Whale and I settled down with Berthe and Daniel in the long white house. We stayed there throughout the autumn and winter and far into the next spring, but I must not delay in recollection of that happy time. For me and Daniel, it was such a time as we had not known before. We were both released from trammels; we lived so democratic a life that I am sure Papa and Mama would have been horrified had they known about it. To them, the dreadful thing would have been that a servant—not a governess, to whom certain privileges were accorded, but a kitchen servant—was admitted to our companionship. We wandered everywhere together, the four of us, and as autumn gave place to winter those wanderings were especially lovely. Round the ramparts of the little town, down into the flat marsh country through which the Canche flowed, into cottages where we bought cider and into wayside pubs where we sat on benches and watched our eggs and potatoes frying on the stove, flower-pot shaped, with one little red glowing eye. Daniel and I were allowed to sip the rough hot red wine that Whaley and Berthe drank from tumblers with their eggs and chips and slices of coarse bread cut from loaves shaped like batons. There would be farmers and agricultural laborers sitting around, smoking and spitting, and talking the lingo that I never was any good at; and then there would be the walk home along the poplar-bordered roads, sometimes with the moon rising, sometimes with frost making the bright stars crack and tingle; and so we would come to our own fireside and the hanging lamp, and Berthe knitting in a corner, Whaley writing at a little desk, and Daniel and I bent over a book under the light. How reasonable a little boy he seemed now! He wore old clothes and brushed his hair when he felt like it, not that there was now much of it to bother about, for he had celebrated his parents' departure by giving himself the crop of his life. But he didn't swear or pull faces. All through that time Miss Whale gave me nothing that could be called a lesson, but I see now that her educational system was in full swing, and that, as I had so little time to spend in France, she was determined that I should see and know the bit of France I was in rather than sit and listen to rigmaroles *about* France. But she said nothing of this to me, and all too soon the morning came when she announced: "Well, that is that, Sarah. Back to England now as soon as we can settle things here."

It was a lovely May morning, the first on which we had breakfasted out of doors. We were sitting at one of the little green iron tables, very quietly, so as not to disturb the chaffinches that were hopping after crumbs thrown on the path. And there Whaley sat, holding the letter in her hand as she made this announcement, and I saw with a flutter of the heart that the envelope was of a kind I knew. "Is the letter from Lord Burnage?" I asked. Daniel had gone into the house. She and I were alone. She looked at me for some time without speaking, weighing the letter in her hand, and then said: "No, Sarah, it is not from Lord Burnage. It is from Lady Burnage. That is, your Mama. She and Lord Burnage are now married."

CHAPTER FIVE

I

I CANNOT say much about my sensations on hearing the news that Miss Whale had given me. They were confused and perplexed. How Mama, who had been Lady Rainborough, had now become Lady Burnage was something I had to accept as best I could. Even Whaley did not venture to explain to a ten-year-old child of those times what was meant by divorce. But here I may as well say something of what I gradually learned as the years passed, and so have done with the matter.

Lord Burnage was twice involved in divorce cases, first as what we call the aggrieved party, when his wife left him for the Duke of Fallowshire, and then as the offending party, when he met my mother. I must even write the strange phrase, which sounds like something out

53

of a Ouida novel, that he resigned from his regiment, but in those days men did such things for such reasons. Also, Lord Burnage never again sat in the House of Lords.

So the affair had a considerable effect upon his life, and no less upon the life of my father. He must have had some generous feelings, for there is no doubt that if he had wished to do so he could have had "the custody of the child," and when I read that old cliché and realize, withered wretch that I now am, that I was the child in question, I am forever grateful that he let me go. Still, without wishing to diminish him, I must recognize that the chances are he was acting in the way he found most convenient to himself. He never had been a "family man." His business affairs absorbed him wholly, and to have the custody of a child while deprived of the companionship of a wife no doubt seemed to him nothing but an expensive shackle. Anyway, he left the house in Portman Square and set himself up in Albany with a manservant. Let me not end this note upon him with a disparaging twist. He could, out of spite, have separated me from my mother, and he did not do so. He was never a man to lift up the heart, but he seems, in this, to have been just, according to his lights.

Well, so much for those tedious and dolorous details. They did not affect me then. All I realized was that a strange heart-stirring thing had happened. Mama was Lord Burnage's wife and I would live with them and Sally Gaylord. "Won't you love it?" I cried to Whaley, and she answered soberly: "I? What has it to do with me?"

"But you will be there! You will be with us all at Tresant."

"That remains to be seen," said Whaley. "No doubt Miss Gaylord has her own governess and perhaps you'll share."

It was a cloud over the morning. I was glum and not easy to be comforted. "Cheer up, Sarah," Whaley cried. "After all, I've got to leave you some day."

"I know that," I said. "But that shouldn't be till my character is formed. I heard Papa say so to Mama. That is what you are for: to Form my Character. When you've done that, I shall be strong enough to do without you, and you can go."

"Yes," Whaley answered. "That's a joyful thing for me to look forward to, isn't it?"

2

I was sorry to leave Daniel Undridge. His parents had been written to and told that Whaley and I would be leaving Montreuil any day, and Mr. Undridge had replied that Daniel should remain with Berthe until he could himself come to take him to Bordeaux. Almost a week had passed, and we still awaited instructions about the journey to

54

Tresant, and then a gloriously unexpected thing happened. Lord Burnage and Sally Gaylord stooped through our little wicket gate and were among us as we sat at tea! They had come to take us home.

From that moment Daniel's conduct made me ashamed. I had felt so proud of his improved manners that it was a shock to find he hadn't a word to say to our visitors. They sat down at our little green tables; Berthe brought cups, and Whaley poured out the tea. There was such a chatter as you may imagine as Lord Burnage outlined the plans for our journey: a chatter from everybody except Daniel. He sat and glowered.

"And how does this young man feel about his journey to Bordeaux?" Lord Burnage asked, for we had told him of Daniel's coming departure. Daniel frowned darkly, ruffled his hair which had begun to grow again, and answered: *"Je ne comprends pas l'Anglais."*

"Eh bien," said Lord Burnage. *"Parlons alors en Français. Ce voyage à Bordeaux. Vous serez content, sans doute, de revoir vos parents?"*

"I don't understand French," Daniel replied.

Whaley was shocked and said: "Daniel, would you like to take Miss Gaylord to see the pond?"

I leapt up in alarm. "I'll take her," I said, and as we went, Daniel got up and followed us. He *followed* us all the way to the pond. He was never *with* us: he lagged a few yards behind, and when Sally and I stood looking down at the water that was waking up like everything else into spring life, he remained, removed from us, his hands in his pockets, his shoe kicking sulkily at a stone. Sally turned round and looked at him. "What's the matter with you?" she demanded sharply.

Then, indeed, Daniel put the last touch to my shame and horror. He raised his head, looked Sally straight in the face, and said: "Mind your own bloody business."

I expected Sally to be shocked, but she only laughed. "Well," she said, "he's human at least. He talks like a stableboy."

Daniel's reply was what I expected. He fluffed up his hair, put out his tongue, and made a frightful face. Sally laughed again. "I could do that," she said. "But I shan't. I think one looks such a blasted idiot."

This unexpected use of a word out of his own forbidden repertory shook Daniel and left him defenseless. Seeing this, Sally said imperiously: "Come here, boy. No one's going to eat you."

Then Daniel shuffled up and stood between us, looking down at the pond. Sally put her arm through his and said nothing, but I could *feel*, standing apart though we were, that Daniel was becoming quiet and content. We remained there for a time, watching the light sparkle on the water, listening to the splash from the little fountain into the basin and from the brimming basin's edge into the pond. We didn't speak a single word till Sally at last said: "Well, now we've seen the pond, as ordered. Let us go back." She unhooked Daniel's arm and we all walked back to the house. Many, many years later I was to remember that small strange incident, that power to tranquillize that Sally so early showed herself to possess; though then, with so much else, the direction of the surprising career that was to be hers was hidden from me.

3

I remember many odds and ends out of those last days we spent in Montreuil. Whaley at lunch in the Hotel de France, where Lord Burnage and Sally were staying, beginning anxiously: "It would be a convenience, my lord, if my engagement to look after Miss Rainborough is to end, if I could know promptly whether . . ." and Lord Burnage's laugh as he answered: "It has never been our tradition, Miss Whale, to throw people into the streets." Our tradition . . . It sounded splendid. I liked it.

A book that I have still of beautiful parchment writing-paper, bound in blue leather, with my name in gold on the cover. "I expect, my dear," said Lord Burnage, "you will want to keep a record of the journey we are about to make. Here's a book for the purpose."

Daniel Undridge and Berthe scurrying through the market stalls on the Grande Place that morning when we set out. Trunks were being piled on top of a huge rollicking old coach that Lord Burnage had hired from Boulogne, with two horses to pull it. Lord Burnage preferred to ride. He came out of the hotel, slapping his leg with his crop. Daniel pulled off his cap, and Lord Burnage, towering above him, tapped him familiarly on the shoulder with the crop. "You're a good boy," he said, "but you must learn to know it. Don't think the whole world is trying to get you down. Can you remember that?"

"Yes, sir."

"Very well. Good-by now. Perhaps we shall meet again."

They shook hands, and I saw a gold coin slipped from palm to palm and Daniel's look of astonishment. There was a little gold brooch for Berthe, and then, as everything was ready and the riding horse was led up, Lord Burnage said to Daniel: "Now you'd better say good-by to the girls. You can kiss 'em if you like." So Sally and I were saluted by Daniel, not with a kiss but with a pressure of cheek to cheek, first on one side, then the other, in the French fashion. And then we climbed into the coach, where Whaley had already taken her place, Lord Burnage mounted his horse, and off we went amid the excited *brouhaha* of the market people who did not every day see an English lord setting out from the Hotel de France.

Off we went, through the *octroi* barrier, down the long straight, tree-

56

bordered road that we had so often followed to the Café de l'Agriculture and our feasts of chips and sips of hot red wine, southward, as
my blue book tells me, though little enough I wrote in it then save
names, to Abbeville, Amiens and Paris, and westward to Chartres, Le
Mans, Rennes and Brest. It was the ending of a wonderful time.

It is all so long ago, and, as I say, the blue book does not help much.
Not even dates are in it. But though it is not written in the book, it is
written in me, and nothing but death can cross it out. I am old and tired
and lonely. They are all dead now, those who bowled with me then
along the roads of France; but in this bitter and so different day I still
occasionally start out of a doze in which once more I am a child in a
beautiful world, and the coach is rolling into Brest, and Sally, leaning
out of the window, is shouting to Lord Burnage, who is riding ahead:
"Papa! Papa! There's Captain Rodda!"

4

Lord Burnage had not seen Captain Rodda, nor had he heard Sally's
cry. He went on at a sedate jog trot down the street, and I saw the
captain break into a run and follow him. It was something to see Eddy
Rodda running. He was a mountain of a man, but he moved as grace-
fully as the horse he was following, for his great size was splendidly
proportioned. His dark blue trousers were tucked into leather boots that
came above his knees. A dark blue jersey clothed his vast torso, and on
his head was a knitted cap in rings of red and white. The top of it was
finished off in a red tassel that dangled down his cheek. Seeing him
even as I did then, with his back to me and on the run, I was aware of
his black beard, for it was long and fine and blew behind him. It was
not till we met later face to face that I saw the wild blue of his eyes
and the buzzard beak. When we got out of the coach at our hotel, Lord
Burnage's horse was already being led away, and he and Captain Rodda
stood together, talking. I had always thought of Lord Burnage as a tall
man, but now he looked small. Rodda overtopped him by inches and
was in every way built on bigger lines. His hands hanging down at his
sides, I noticed, were like sledge hammers, and all about him the air
was filled with a pungent smell from the fish oil that kept his big boots
supple. There was another smell about him which I did not recognize.
He had been waiting for Lord Burnage for some days, and there had
been nothing for him to do, for his boat, the *Sally Gaylord*, was at
moorings, with his son, Wesley Rodda, aboard. It was dangerous for
Captain Rodda to have nothing to do, and the odor that mingled with
the fish oil was of red wine, cognac, and any other drink that he had
been able to come by. Something of the geniality that this had imparted

57

was in the grin of welcome that he turned upon Sally. It set his white teeth flashing out of the ambush of his beard. He looked like a corsair in a good mood that could not be trusted to last. His huge hand engulfed the one she at once extended to him. "Well, midear," he exclaimed. "The little ole boat's ready any time you are."

5

The next morning Whaley and I sat on one of the Brest quays watching Wesley Rodda take the luggage aboard the *Sally Gaylord*. The trunks had all been dumped down there on the quay; the ship lay at moorings out in the harbor; and Wesley sculled from her to the land, standing up in the dinghy, and then, with a bit more luggage, would row back and put the stuff aboard. Occasionally he would smile shyly at me and Whaley, but he had nothing of his father's geniality. Or of his father's physique. He was, I suppose, about twenty years old then, small, clean-shaved, and rather pale. There was an almost effeminate wistful beauty about his face, and he had a clear tenor voice which that morning he would raise in song as soon as he was away from us and out on the water. He sang:

> *What shall we offer our good Lord,*
> *Poor nothings! for His boundless grace?*
> *Fain would we His great name record,*
> *And worthily set forth His praise.*

It went to a good tune, and Whaley sang it, too. As Wesley drew near for the third or fourth time she said to him: "I like those Methodist hymns."

"Ay," said the young man quietly. "That one's by Spangenberg, translated by John Wesley."

"I didn't know that. But I like it, and I like the tune. My father was a local preacher."

"So's mine," said Wesley surprisingly. "But it was Mother wanted me called Wesley."

He seemed to feel he had said enough, humped another couple of trunks down to the dinghy, and rowed away singing:

> *O Thou who camest from above*
> *The pure celestial fire to impart,*
> *Kindle a flame of sacred love*
> *On the mean altar of my heart.*

58

He was dressed like his father, save that he had not a dramatic and self-conscious cap, and, though he smelled of fish, there was no added ingredient of alcohol. The sun shone. The well-tended blue dinghy moved sweetly over the calm harbor water. The gulls were swooping and calling, and Whaley said: "It will all be very strange for you, Sarah, but I think you'll be in a happy place."

I had given little enough thought to the sort of place it was to be. Day by day, ever since our hurried departure to Folkestone, I had taken the hours as they came, especially the magical hours of this journey now ended on the quays of Brest. "It will be strange," I said to Whaley now, "to see boats instead of cabs and men like Captain Rodda instead of chimney sweeps."

"Don't expect," she answered, "to see too many men like him. I imagine he's not the sort of man you'll find in great numbers anywhere. It would be rather overpowering if he were."

There was only one trunk left on the quay, the biggest of all, and Wesley was once more sculling in to the stone steps above which we were sitting, when Captain Rodda came strolling along with two French girls, one hanging onto either arm. I am sure this was one of those moments when Mercy Kite would have whisked me out of sight, to some place where I was "safe," and the world's contagion could not touch me. Nor would Mama, whom I could *not* think of as Lady Burnage, have approved my witnessing this scene, common enough though it was in any port. But Whaley stayed where she was. There was a small square stone-built hut with a slate roof and a couple of life belts hanging to the outer walls and a rough bench where one could sit, leaning back against the stone. There we were, on this bench, and there we stayed, as Captain Rodda and his girls approached, he talking in his loud voice with many "midears" and with many squeezings of their arms to his sides, they chattering in excited French of which I understood little. Wesley had tied the dinghy and come up the steps. He stood near us, watching his father approach, and I could feel his shame that we should witness this scene. He was blushing hotly, and to hide his confusion he turned to the great leather trunk that was too much for his strength. "Leave it! Leave it!" Captain Rodda bellowed: and disengaging himself from the girls he gave each a resounding kiss and a hearty slap on the bottom and shouted: "Off with you now, midears!" But they stood about, crying, "Monny! Monny!" The captain was not to be moved. He had done with them, and that was that. "*Allez!*" he roared. "No more monny. *Trèz* greedy. *Allez!*" and seeing us sitting there he gave us a wink that invited us to admire his skill in handling a situation of this sort. Wesley was still fiddling with the trunk, so that he might hide his shamed face. "Leave it alone," Captain Rodda ordered, and advancing upon it, he picked it up in his great

59

hands, swung it to his shoulder, and walked down the steps to the boat. It was he who took the oars that looked immense to me but to him seemed feather-light. "Now, Wesley boy," he shouted as the boat skimmed over the water, "what about a good ole hymn? What about *O for a heart . . .* ?" And over the sparkling water of Brest harbor we heard, what we were so often to hear, Eddy Rodda's voice raised in sacred song. It was moving and magnificent:

> *O for a heart to praise my God,*
> *A heart from sin set free,*
> *A heart that always feels Thy blood*
> *So freely spilt for me.*

The sun shone on the blue dinghy and sparkled on the oared water. It lit him up, woolen tasseled cap, great beard, and massive chest from which the shoulders made child's play of the oars. And out of that chest the song soared beautifully, lifting our hearts, with Wesley's tenor threading a grace through it. The *Sally Gaylord* was not far out: they were still singing as they climbed aboard; and leaning on the bulwarks they attacked the last verse:

> *Thy nature, gracious Lord, impart;*
> *Come quickly from above,*
> *Write Thy new name upon my heart,*
> *Thy new, best name of Love.*

Then they stood for a moment side by side looking over the water, before Captain Rodda slapped his son on the shoulder and shouted: "Praise the Lord, me ole lover. Forget not all His benefits," swung down into the dinghy and threw the trunk aboard like a draper's parcel.

6

It was like Lord Burnage to have arranged that we should go home by sea and that Captain Rodda should be at Brest to meet us. Even Sally hadn't known that this was to happen. But he liked to arrange charming and surprising occasions, though, of course, this could have been anything but charming for me and Whaley. He and Sally knew what to expect in a rough little working boat: experience had taught them that it would take a lot to make them sick; but we others were without any knowledge of the sea, save for my one cross-Channel journey and two or three that Whaley had made. And these had been in ships built for the purpose, not in such pitifully small craft as the *Sally Gay-*

lord appeared to our unaccustomed eyes. However, there we were, embarked, and the boat riding merrily beneath us, lying over on her side in what seemed to me at first a dangerous and desperate fashion. But by the end of an hour this became normal, and also it became clear that if nothing worse than this happened we were not going to be sick. The wind was light but steady. We sailed due west for a couple of hours, and then she was put around to the north. "She's heading straight for Cornwall now," Sally said, "straight for Tresant."

The nighttime remains in my mind. It was romantic to see the sailing lights rigged as the red west darkened and the dark east went black, and the stars came out. Captain Rodda handed the tiller to Lord Burnage and went into the cabin to brew tea for our last meal of the day. All we needed to eat had been brought aboard at Brest in a hamper. We went into the cabin to eat, leaving Wesley in the cockpit, and then there was some argument about our dispositions for the night. There were two berths in the cabin, and Lord Burnage wanted me and Whaley to sleep in them, but I had no wish to sleep at all. I had never sat up all night, and it seemed to me that this would be a fine chance to do so. Lord Burnage humored me, while swearing that I would sleep where I sat; and so at about ten o'clock Whaley and Sally turned in. I took my place on the cockpit seat beside Wesley, and Lord Burnage and Captain Rodda, rolling themselves in blankets, lay down on the deck with sailcloth beneath their heads. I, too, had a blanket wrapped round me. It was dark and cold. Forward, a vertical slit of light where the cabin door had not been completely slid to. Overhead, the sway of the mast across the stars. All around, the kiss and lisp and crisp whisper of water hissing by. Almost at my feet, the dark huddle of the two men on the deck, with presently a loud snoring from Captain Rodda, and from Lord Burnage a persistent muted snore like a cat's purring.

"So you be goin' to live at Tresant," Wesley suddenly spoke softly.

The quiet and the darkness made me answer on the same low conspiring note. "Yes. Lord Burnage is my new Papa."

"Tidd'n sense to talk like that," said Wesley with deep conviction. "Our Father which art in Heaven don' give us more'n one father here below. Not but what his lordship was in a sore situation. Her ladyship hated Tresant a'most as much as he loved it. 'Er didd'n like our wild ways hereabouts an' the roarin' o' wind an' sea in winter. An' so 'er couldn't get along with 'e. That's the bottom of it, midear, an' a sore situation it was, as everybody knowed long afore they parted. I've see'd your mother, her new ladyship, an' a beautiful woman she be, but as fer you having a new papa I don' 'old wi' that, an' I don' see God's blessin' on it."

There was nothing I could say. It was cold and dark, and Wesley, with one arm draped over the tiller, held me with the other close against

61

his warmth. The hiss and lisp of the hidden water went by, and far away the lights of another ship looked very lonely.

"I've prayed God's blessin' on it," said Wesley, "but 'e do give me no sign. Cleave to one another. One flesh. That's the word of the Lord, an' that do make divorce an abomination. Yet his lordship is not a son of Belial. He do feed the hungry an' help the oppressed. Very confusin', Miss, this world be to me."

A sigh came from him, a perplexed and weary sigh. Captain Rodda rolled over with a grunt, settled down, and snored again.

"Very confusin'," said Wesley, "the mixture there be in men, wi' God holdin' their right hand an' the Devil their left. There be my father, rollin' now in sleep, as I've seen 'im rollin' in drink, an' yet I've 'eard 'im powerful in prayer an' liftin' the heart wi' 'is discourse. An' us can't 'elp lovin' 'e, my mother an' I, as if 'e was the truest man God ever made, as indeed off'n enough 'e do appear to be. There's no fathomin' it, midear. There's no knowin' what our heavenly Father's up to when 'E makes a man."

Should I have hated him? Much that he said meant nothing. Divorce was a word that had no clear sense for me, and I had never, anyhow, associated it with Mama and Lord Burnage. All I knew was that she was his new wife, that he was my new Papa, and this had seemed to me a happy state of things. Yet here, in the dark and the cold—it was becoming very cold—with the sea that had been sparkling all day now black, mysterious, menacing, I was hearing that somehow something abominable had happened, something on which God's blessing could not fall. Should I have hated him? Anyway, I did not. The happy and wonderful resilience of childhood let it all drift off my mind, and I was conscious of little save his arm around me, his warmth, and a simple puzzled goodness that was in him. Soon I was asleep, a sleep in which I felt the cold and heard the slap of water, and knew the comfort and safety that his presence gave me.

I woke with a start, as a dash of cold water struck my face. The wind had freshened and had thrown a spatter of sea inboard. There was still an arm about me, but so soundly had I slept that I only now perceived that this was Captain Rodda's arm, not Wesley's. "Well, midear," he said, "you been 'aving forty winks."

I liked the comforting feel of his arm, the rumble of his voice. I drew my blanket closer about me and snuggled into him. The sails were deep-bellied in the lively wind; the water soughed past us urgently."

"So you be 'er new ladyship's lil' daughter?" said Captain Rodda, and I hoped I was not going to hear anything more about divorce and abomination and the displeasure of the Lord. There was no need for anxiety. "Well, a blessin' it be, I reckon, for his lordship. 'Er never belonged to be in a place like this, that other one as wanted to walk the woods in a golden gown. All very well that be for the streets of paradise when we get our 'arps and crowns, but Porteven's not paradise, though I wouldn't change the one for the other. You'll see, midear, when you get there, an' that won't be long wi' this lively lil' wind. Just a few houses it be, an' a stink o' fish, an' tannin' when the new nets spread to dry, an' gorse forever bloomin' on the cliffs. When gorse is out o' season kissin's out o' reason, they do say, an' thank God there's gorse all the year round."

He chuckled, and said: "God's blessin's on it, midear, an' these eyes o' mine would weep blood to see a fine man like his lordship denied a second chance."

I still could not—well, I suppose I must use the modern word and say "condition" myself to hearing the "lower classes" discussing so freely, and with me myself, those who belonged to my class. So I said abruptly: "I think this is a lovely ship you have, Captain Rodda."

"She ain't mine, me ole dear," he said, "she's his lordship's. But she's mine an' Wesley's as much as makes no diff'rence. All trim she be now, but you should see 'er when we're after pilchards. Up to our knees they be, flappin' an' gaspin', an' still the nets comin' in fit to bust. There's times, as now, when his lordship wants 'er, but she's a workin' girl is this li'l ship most o' the year 'round."

The smell of the pilchards was on him, rising from his boots even upon that sharp wind-cleaned air, and now he took a flask from his pocket and swigged, and I caught the other smell that was characteristic of him.

"That's a comfort," he said, smacking his lips, "and it's a comfort, too, to have the warrant of the Apostle to the Gentiles. 'Be no longer a drinker of water but use a little wine for thy stomach's sake,' he says to son Timothy, an' I reckon a mouthful o' brandy can go in as included in the reckonin'."

"Tell me about Tresant," I said.

"No. I didn' ought to do that. Tresant's his lordship's affair an' he'll want to tell you 'isself. You tell me something. What's that boy Wesley been sayin' to you?"

Now here was a facer that I could do nothing with. Divorce and damnation and father rolling drunk in the gutter. No, I couldn't tell him about that. "He says you're a local preacher. What's a local preacher?"

He cocked an eye up at the sails, tightened a sheet, and settled himself again comfortably.

"Well, that's goin' into history, midear. Ole John Wesley was a powerful man of God, an' he converted so many souls he didn' know what to do wi' 'em. There they'd be, over in Gwennap Pit and other places round about, crowded in so deep they'd be like pilchards in this

63

boat when we'd had a good haul. And there ole John'd be, upon the edge of the pit, lookin' down on all those poor sinners crowded beneath 'im, like as if he might be perched up there on the gun'le of this boat, lookin' down on the pilchards. A mighty rider 'e was, goin' everywhere on his ole nag, and the mobs with stones an' dead tomcats an' the magistrates wi' warrants couldn' stop 'im. Trot, trot, he goes from one end of England to another, a reg'lar angel on horseback. Well, 'e comes, let us say, to the edge of this ole pit an' looks down on all them sinners, and they looks up at 'im, standin' up against the sky. There 'e is, ole John, just come off his horse, an' wearin' white bands under 'is collar, an' a Bible under 'is arm, and his white hair shinin'. Like a gleamin' apparition 'e must've been to all them ole sinners down in the pit. Then 'e begins to speak, and maybe 'e says: 'Let's begin now wi' one of my brother Charles's li'l ole hymns.' Maybe it's 'Depth of Mercy':

> Depth of mercy! Can there be
> Mercy still reserved for me?
> Can my God His wrath forbear?
> Me, the chief of sinners, spare?

"Now up this comes out of the pit, 'cause there's a good tune to that ole hymn, and John stands there lookin' down at that pitful of sinners and knows 'e's got 'em in the 'ollow of 'is 'and. All that singin' comes floatin' up to 'im, an' they're singin' well, because if you're not a great saint it's something to think you're the chief of sinners, even if you're not that by a long chalk, because a man likes to think 'e's something special one way or the other, even when you couldn't tell 'im from his next-door neighbor any more than you could tell one rib from another in the backbone of a pilchard. So thinkin' of their terrible sins, which not one in a hundred of 'em 'ud ever commit, they begin to weep an' choke and think 'God could never 'ave mercy on the likes o' we, monumental sinners as we are,' and ole John is pleased an' thinks again: 'Ah! they're weepin'! Now they're in the 'ollow of my 'and.' Then he prays God to spare these terrible sinners, an' down in that ole pit there's silence, broken only by a groan or a cry an' p'raps in the mornin' air the whinnyin' of John's ole nag, tied to a post somewhere, a faithful servant of the Lord if ever there was one. Well, then John 'olds up 'is 'and, an' a great silence comes as they all look up at him standin' above 'em on the edge of the pit, an' p'raps the sun strikes through a cloud and light comes round him, so that he looks like a bein' lit up by the light of God.

"Ay, me ole lover, I've stood in that li'l pit on a spring mornin' an' I've seen it all like that. No one 'ud be surprised to see angels come slidin' down that beam of light that lies tender on the ole man's shoulder, an' the curlews are callin', an' when the curlews call 'tis like as if you 'eard the sound of souls bound in love to this ole earth, yet longin' for release into the love o' God. Terrible wistful they be, the curlews. You'll 'ear 'em plenty at Tresant, but upalong I reckon you don't know what they are.

"Well, ole John begins to preach an' pours the brimstone of Hell down into that pit. They listen in terror, an' they shout an' groan an' cry. They throw themselves on the ground and they writhe and wriggle as if already they felt ole Nick's fork takin' a purchase between their shoulder blades. An' then there's mercy. John's voice changes. He's layin' balm on their burns, the balm of the Love o' God. 'E's showin' 'em the signpost, an' that there's an arm pointin' to Heaven as well as one pointin' to Hell. Now 'e's pleadin' with 'em to make the great decision, and Alleluiahs an' Praise the Lords rise up out of the pit. Cries of joy, me ole lover, instead of groans of despair. There's a great harvest for ole John, the fisher of men. The nets break. But off 'e must go. The nag's waitin' an' the world's his parish, an' off he must go. Like ole Paul, he was. 'And when it came to pass that we were parted from them and had set sail we came with a straight course unto Cos, and the next day unto Rhodes, and from thence into Patara; and having found a ship crossing over into Phoenicia we went aboard and set sail. And when we had come in sight of Cyprus, leaving it on the left hand, we sailed into Syria and landed at Tyre.'

"That's how it was with Paul, ding-dongin' about the Mediterranean in search of souls, and that's how it was with ole John, except that he stayed in one land and used a nag instead of a ship. But for both of 'em there was the same problem, and that was finding them as 'ud look after the souls they saved. An' they solved it in the same way, midear. There couldn't be paid parsons 'ere, there an' everywhere; so when all the men an' women who found God began to build chapels to worship Him in, they 'ad to put up with their own mates for preachin' an' ex-poundin' the Word. An' that's what local preachers are, midear, to this day. There's no paid parson in Porteven, but Wesley an' I an' one or two others carry on the work o' the Lord."

"Thank you, Captain Rodda," I said, feeling this to be a terse and inadequate reply to his oration.

"Now you go to sleep," he commanded. "Tomorrow all things will be new to you. You'll be runnin' here and there an' seein' this an' that, an' that do wear you out body an' soul, so it do."

He pulled me closer into his side, and I was ready enough to go to sleep. The motion of the boat, the cold touch of the wind, the sound of the sea sliding alongside, all drowsed me and I shut my eyes. I always liked, when I settled down to sleep, to take hold of some thing or some words for my thoughts to move around, and now I took hold of this: "Tomorrow all things will be new to you." Oh, let it be a beautiful day,

65

I prayed. I know that it's May, but even in May the days can be wet and the sun not come at all. Let it be a beautiful day, with sun, and everything not only new but shining—not just *different*, but *new*.

I was awakened by a gentle tapping of fingers on my forehead. I opened my eyes, and it was light. Lord Burnage was sitting by me. It was light, not daylight but dawnlight. He spoke quietly: "I wonder whether you've ever seen that before, Sarah?"

No; I never had, and it was wonderful to see. Away on our right hand the sky was pale, and as I watched, the clouds—small flaky clouds—turned from gray to silver and from silver to rose. The burning edge of the sun appeared, and all the sea between us and him suddenly danced with light. He climbed swiftly, and it was day: it was tomorrow when all things would be new, but now tomorrow was today. I looked up at the sails which had been dark all night and now were a rich brownish red. They shone. Everything shone. There was no land to be seen behind us or before us: nothing but shining water, and the sun which had burned the few clouds out of the sky, and the little shining ship hurrying home.

It was good to be warm again. The sun fell on my face and my hands and seemed to pierce even through the blanket that wrapped me. Lord Burnage said: "Would you like me to rouse Sally? She's had a good night's sleep, and it wouldn't hurt you to turn in for an hour or two. I don't want to hand you over to your mother worn to a shadow."

I begged to be allowed to stay where I was. "I want to see the land when it first appears. And you won't be handing me over," I said. "You'll be keeping me. I shall have you *and* Mama. Do you know what Captain Rodda said to me?"

"I wouldn't like to guess, my dear. That old pirate's capable of saying anything. He could write the Psalms or the Decameron."

"What's the Dec—the what you said?"

"It's a book of wicked enjoyable stories."

"Can a wicked thing be enjoyable? Papa once said to me that I'd never be happy if I was wicked."

"I'm not going to discuss that with you, Sarah," he said firmly. "Perhaps we'll talk it over in twenty years' time. What did Captain Rodda say?"

"He said that today all things would be new for me."

He looked at me tenderly. "Yes. You won't find that the life we live in Cornwall is much like what you've been used to. I hope you will be very happy."

I looked at him in amazement. How could he doubt it? Did he not know that I loved him? Could a wicked thing be enjoyable? Was it wicked, this feeling in me: that it was not to meet Mama at Tresant, but to be with him there, that held all the promise of joy? But I wrapped

66

this up in my heart, and I said: "What is Captain Rodda captain of? Just this little ship?"

"He's been captain of bigger ships than this." And Lord Burnage told me something of Captain Rodda, and the years as they passed filled in other things for me: things that a child could not have been told. Porteven was a village of inshore fishermen, and Eddy Rodda was the son of one of these: a small, timorous devout Methodist, who must have begun soon to wonder whether God had singled him out as another Job, so many were the tribulations heaped on him through his son. At fourteen Eddy Rodda was roistering. He was already bigger than his father, a wild and wayward handsome lad, strong as a horse and obstinate as a mule. At fifteen he began to drink and to chase the girls, and at sixteen he laid the father of one of these flat in the bar parlor of the Richard Grenville, the Tresant pub. That was a night I often heard talked of: a winter night with a southwest gale tearing into Porteven, filling the streets with a briny drench, rocking the chimneys and wrenching the slates from the roofs. And there was this boy with his legs in the long sea boots stretched to the fire, comfortably drinking in the Richard Grenville, speaking to no one, placid as a young ox in a pasture, when the inn door burst open and the wind howled into the house, making the light of the oil lamps jump and the lamps swing under the wooden ceiling. And there is this man Richards, a grocer, but strong, burly, kicking the door shut behind him and advancing with this wretched girl of his shoved before him, she soaked to the skin and draggle-haired, for a wave had caught them as they scuttered along from his shop which is among the buildings huddling under the cliff that flanks the quay. He pushes her before him, under the yellow light of the lamps, where the tobacco smoke is settling down again after its wild dispersal, and there he holds her by the arm, saying nothing, but glaring at young Eddy Rodda. Everyone is very quiet, for everyone knows what this confrontation means, and you can hear the *hu-hu-u* of the wind shrieking down the street, and the shake of the building, and the sudden splash as though someone had thrown a bucket of water at the window.

Eddy Rodda looked at Richards and smiled. Then he spat into the brass spittoon at his feet, drained his tankard and got up. He put on his oilskin that was hanging on a hook, pulled on his sou'wester, and moved to the door. Still no one spoke, but Richards stepped in front of him, laid a detaining hand on him. Eddy shook him off, and then Richards struck. They say that no one had ever struck Rodda before, not his parents, certainly not the village boys over whom he had lorded it from the first. They say that he stopped, turned as if amazed, and that his eyes were terrible. Richards himself stepped away from that look, and pushed the girl behind him, down onto the bench where Rodda

67

had been sitting. Eddy struck him under the chin. He crashed onto the sanded flag-stones, bringing down a table. There was a tinkle of breaking glass, a wild whoosh of rain on the window, a wild cry of wind in the street, and a wild scream from the girl who rushed to her father, shouting that he was dead.

He looked dead enough, with blood trickling from a gash in his forehead and moving sluggishly among the sand on the floor. Eddy Rodda picked up from the bar a jug of water that stood there for diluting whisky, and chucked it hard into Richards's face. Richards opened his eyes, and then Eddy, without a word to the girl or the men standing there, threw him over his shoulder and marched with him into the roaring storm. Mary Richards followed. She was a slip of a thing, miserable-looking that night as a drowned cat. She trailed twenty yards behind, and stopped when Eddy called at Doctor Curnow's. He rang the bell, pushed open the door, and yelled above the yelling storm: "I've knocked old Richards out an' I'm takin' 'im 'ome. Better tell the doctor to come an' 'ave a look at 'im."

Then off he went again, with Richards hanging like a sodden sack over his shoulder, moaning now and then. The girl followed. The night was as black as Hell's mouth; even in the inner harbor, shut by a sluice gate from the main impact of the storm, the boats were pitching furiously. Mary Richards saw the dark figure, compounded of two figures, staggering ahead of her, turn the corner toward the row of houses under the cliff. She, too, made the turn, and here the full weight of wind and water hit her, roaring in from the open sea. Her sodden clothes whipped about her, and the waves, beating up over the granite edging of the harbor, flew round her in icy spray higher than herself. She had to battle with the weather to move forward at all. Head down, she bored as if against the pressure of a mighty hand, and now and then this pressure was too great for her and drove her backward. The gleam of lamps in the windows of the houses drew her on. They were comforting; but it seemed miraculous that they were not blown out, for now the gale had reached its height. It seemed miraculous that anything—anything at all, whether frail lights or solid buildings—could withstand its strength. There was nothing but blackness weltering with hissing white, and off it this giant wind racing and yelling toward the shore.

Mary's head had been down. She had lost sight of the figure weaving and staggering ahead of her, and now, to get her breath, she sidled into the doorway of the first of the houses and held on to the door knob. She looked ahead, and at that moment it came: the crash that all the wild circumstances of the nights seemed to make inevitable. She saw Rodda hurled to the ground and her father roll a little away from him. Neither of them moved. A wave, shattered

68

on the harbor wall, smacked down, soaking them where they lay.

Then she beat with her fists on the door to which she was clinging, and people came out, and they picked up Rodda and Richards from among the debris of the wind-wrecked chimney and carried them both into Richards's house.

Eddy Rodda was already walking about when Doctor Curnow came. He had only been bruised and winded. Richards was dead. These were the important questions asked at the inquest, and the answers.

The Coroner: Then in your opinion, Doctor Curnow, death was caused by a brick striking this man's head, fracturing the skull, and causing bone splinters to penetrate the brain?

Doctor Curnow: Yes, sir. That is so.

The Coroner: But there were other injuries to the head—on the other side of the head—and we have heard evidence as to how they were caused. Were these other injuries serious?

Doctor Curnow: Very.

The Coroner: Had the deceased not been struck by the brick from the chimney, do you think it likely that we might, even so, still be holding this inquest?

Doctor Curnow: That is a difficult question to answer, sir.

The Coroner: Still, will you try to answer it, doctor? Might these injuries that were first caused have proved, in themselves, fatal?

Doctor Curnow: They were very grave.

The Coroner: I understand your reluctance, doctor, but I must press you to be frank.

Dr. Curnow: I think they would have proved fatal within a few hours.

The Coroner: There is one other question that I must put to you. Did these prior injuries, in your opinion, contribute in any way to this man's death? I mean, did they, for example, weaken the skull, so that the blow from the brick had, so to speak, already a bit of a start in its fatal work when it struck Richards's head?

Doctor Curnow: No, sir. There was, if I may put it so, a considerable area of sound skull between the two injuries. Death was due entirely to the second injury.

The Coroner: I am glad you have been able to give that answer with assurance. Otherwise, as this court will see, a grave charge would have lain against Edward Rodda. As it is, that young man finds himself in an extraordinary situation—one I have not known the like of in my long experience as a coroner; one, indeed, that I don't think can ever have been matched. A man whom he has, as the evidence shows, brutally struck would, in the doctor's opinion, have died within a few hours from the injuries inflicted. I invite Edward

Rodda to consider the gravity of the situation in which, in that case, he would have found himself. But Richards, on the doctor's evidence, did not, in fact, die from those injuries. In all seriousness and in all solemnity I say that it seems as though the hand of Providence intervened to save Rodda from the consequences of his own wickedness. Let him take this to heart. It is unlikely that a second miracle will save one who fails to learn the lesson of the first.

"Accidental death," was the verdict.

Reading all this in the faded columns of a local newspaper, I could picture clearly enough the rather drab scene, staged in the bleak room of the local Sunday school, hear the sententious words of the coroner, see the lusty young giant, Eddy Rodda, looking about him as puzzled as a young bull in a pen on a railway station. It is the day after that wild fatal night: a day of such warm winter sunshine as can come to Cornwall. The sea is murmuring. The golden gorse, here and there along the cliffs, is shining in small radiant bosses. They say that when the inquest was ended, Rodda came out of the schoolroom and lingered in the roadway, channeled by last night's storm, till Mary Richards appeared. He spoke to her, tried to take her arm, but she broke away and hurried, weeping, toward the house and shop where she would now be alone, for her mother was dead and she was an only child. Rodda went before her, walking quickly, looking back now and then, and when Mary reached the door of the shop he had passed it by a hundred yards and was standing as though waiting. As last night she had stood clutching the door knob of a neighbor's house, so now she stood clutching her own, torn by a terrible indecision; then suddenly she went quickly after Rodda. They went on together, turned left and eastward, walking along the cliffs. There are paths here and there going steeply down to the sands, which were golden that day—a day of unexpected loveliness, which they call in winter, in those parts, a day lent—and watchers, who, you may be sure, were soon concealed among the heather and gorse of the cliff tops, saw those two, remote diminished figures, walking side by side, up and down, on the sand, and presently arm in arm. Life was born anew out of passion and sudden death.

Mary Richards was fifteen then, and Eddy Rodda married her when she was twenty-five. Wesley was their only child. It would be a happy and romantic thing to record that Eddy became a new man after that night's work. He did not, but he became a man rarely seen in Porteven. Mary ran the little shop, prospering on the sympathy of her neighbors, and the Porteven postmistress could be relied on to make known when she received a letter from foreign parts. They came two or three times a year, those letters, and from the stamps, as noted by the postmistress, Porteven was able to trace the Odyssey: to the Mediterranean and India, to China and Japan, to Hawaii and Valparaiso, round the Horn to North America: and presently Porteven was able to say: "He'll soon be home."

It was a bearded turbulent man who reappeared in Porteven. "Drinking like a fish and swearing like a trooper," said Dr. Curnow. The doctor was an oldish man now, and some trivial occasion—I forget what—had brought him to Tresant.

"I was only a youngster," he said, "when Richards died, just come to Porteven—my first year there. It had been nothing but mumps an' measles till that night, so I'm not likely to forget it, or my sight of Rodda when he came back. I suppose I was the first person to see him—swaggering along the road with a sailor's bag on his shoulder, an' that damn great black beard of his. He'd be about twenty then."

So it went, voyage after voyage, till Rodda was captain of a schooner trading to the Mediterranean, and he and Mary Richards were married. For a time all went well, and then his homecomings became scandalous again. And then he was home for good. His ship was run upon a reef in the Adriatic; she and her cargo were a total loss, and there was loss of life, too. Captain Rodda, the court of inquiry learned, was hauled from his cabin at the critical moment, but could not stand on his feet. After that, Eddy Rodda became an inshore fisherman at Porteven, like his father, who was now dead. One autumn night Lord Burnage, who had a taste for such adventures, went out on the night's fishing with Rodda and his son, then a boy of seventeen. These outings with the fleet, from which Lord Burnage, in blue jersey and sea boots, would return smelling like a fisherman, were among the things that the first Lady Burnage disliked. She detested all such things, could not understand why Burnage was happier on a fishing boat in Cornwall than in a London drawing room. That autumn night, the wind died and a fog came up, blanketing them as they lay idly flapping, and out of the fog came a steamer that cut the fishing smack in two and then went on. All three of the men were good swimmers, but Lord Burnage could not do much swimming, for he had received a paralyzing blow on the leg. Till dawn came, and a wind thinned the mist, and another smack came to their rescue, Eddy and Wesley supported Lord Burnage with the help of a drifting spar; and that is why, when we crossed from Brest to Cornwall, it was in this ship which belonged to Lord Burnage, but which the Roddas were permitted to use as though it were their own.

7

I was a miserable child when I at last reached Tresant. With the dawn the wind dropped. Miss Whale and Sally Gaylord came out

71

of the cabin, and Wesley Rodda went in to light a stove and make tea. We ate breakfast with the sails drooping like the broken wings they were, and the mast lurching to and fro across a small arc of sky. I stopped looking at it: it made me feel so queer. Soon I had to rush to the side.

However, until that wind so treacherously died, we had made good progress toward the Cornish shore, and, though I didn't know it, we were still making a *little* progress, so that in the early afternoon, Sally shouted "Land!" I was too ill to be interested. The slate-gray blur that my aching eyes could just make out looked remote and utterly inaccessible.

Wesley announced: "There's a puff comin'," and the puff came and lasted for an hour. By then, the blur was indubitable land, with discernible houses, fields and hedges. But we were becalmed again, the mast again at its sickening swaying. By now I felt that I had no stomach left to be sick from, nothing to be sick *with*, but I was succeeding in stirring up a bilious sediment that nauseated every inch of my being. Lord Burnage ordered Captain Rodda and Wesley to unlash the dinghy from the cabin top and put it overboard. "I'll have to leave you to it," he said to the captain. "Bring the luggage on to Tresant as soon as you can."

It was a long way to row, but that is how I came for the first time into the little harbor of Porteven: Lord Burnage at the oars, my miserable head in Whaley's lap, and Sally holding my icy hand. I was carried up the granite steps, and Sally, who seemed fully at home here, hustled me into a shop, where I sat down, and looked through the window at gulls swooping and screaming over fish offal on the other side of the harbor. Their screeching sawed into my aching head, and all the time I was in the little shop, smelling of lamp oil and onions and candles and cough drops, I felt as I am sure the first Lady Burnage must often have felt: that this was a dreadful place.

Then we were driving along a road in a closed carriage that Lord Burnage had brought from some baiting stable, and Sally was exclaiming, calling my attention to daffodils and bluebells and heaven knows what. But I was not aware of them; I was not even aware when we had turned into the long drive to the house, except that Sally shouted, excited: "It's Robber!" as a vast dog joined our cavalcade, almost killing me with barks of joyous welcome, running with us all the way to the house, splitting my skull. This huge creature's legs on my shoulders and his tongue on my face, a bustle of unprepared servants, a journey upstairs in Lord Burnage's arms, the warm bed that received my shivering body, and my mother's fingertips spreading eau de cologne on my forehead: this is all I remember of my first coming to dear Tresant. Whaley drew the curtains and tiptoed out. In the shadowed room the bed was still a boat, with all the dizzying discomfort of a boat betrayed by its ally the wind, but now it was a warm boat, and the warmth slowly seeped through me, and from very far away I heard Sally's voice saying: "Quiet, Robber! Not another sound!" I smiled happily, and slept.

CHAPTER SIX

1

THE bar and the road to it are always for me the loveliest things at Tresant. On the morning after our arrival I walked that road for the first of the many times that I have walked it. This writing is being done wherever I chance to be: sometimes at Tresant, sometimes in London; and if I am in London and grow weary—as, God knows, I often do now—I can lie back and shut my eyes and loiter along that lovely way. The woods and the lake, the bar and the sea: I can go back to them for refreshment in any weather. I can see the swans upon the summer water and hear the curlews in winter at their desolate piping. The bluebells in the springtime woods, and here and there white wood anemones, cool under the new-fledged wings of the beech trees; the noble pines whose roots writhe up out of the ground and down in again, wrestling for a grip in fissures of rock. The June solemnity, when down the rides one sees the blue of the burning day like daylight seen through the open door of a church. Autumn, and beechnuts and acorns dropping upon the crisp red leaves with a sound that is small till you listen to the silence and hear it again and again, when it becomes terrible and obsessive, the footfall of stealthy ruin, the falling apart of one more year; and winter, when you come out from the woods and suddenly there is the bar, and the wild sea beyond it, with the wind driving you backward and the long Atlantic rollers pounding in and smashing furiously upon the sand.

2

When I awoke I felt well but hollow. I got out of bed and pulled aside the curtains. Beneath me was the graveled circle on which last night we had drawn up at the front door. I wondered if I should have a glimpse of the sea. I hadn't, for Tresant stands with its back to the sea, sheltering under a wooded hill that hides the water and breaks up the Atlantic winds. Beyond the gravel was a lawn that ended in an iron railing, and beyond that was a meadow threaded by a small stream. On the far side of the meadow the land rose slightly and was wooded. There was nothing more that I could see.

The sound of my moving about must have been heard, for the door opened and a maid came in with a breakfast tray. I got back into bed and she placed it across my knees. I asked if Miss Whale were up, and was told that she and everybody else had been up for hours. It was ten o'clock. They were all gone out. They were gone to the bar, and if I felt well enough, would I please join them.

When I was out of doors I was glad to be alone. I had been told how to get to the bar, and as soon as I was beyond the front door, in the May sunshine, I stood still with a thought suddenly in my mind. This was the first time I had been told how to get anywhere! Till now, I had been *taken*. The way I had been told to go was across fields, and along a lake, and through woods, and all this certainly would never have been "safe" for me in Papa's eyes! And now it was with a shock of pleasure that I had a sense of shackles loosened and of enormously enlarged possibility. Suddenly I began to run and sing.

All the way to the bar I made a rushing and a dawdling of it on that May morning: a joyful rushing because of the sunshine and the way the rooks were cawing and a cuckoo was shouting and the black-birds and the graybirds, as they call the thrushes down there, were scuttering among the bushes with bursts of song. Dawdling when sudden enchantment held me. I came to the lake, and I must tell you how the lake is. Years ago, I imagine, it was an arm of the sea. It is long and narrow, and at its southern end the bar rises up, a vast ridge of sand, and shuts it in from the salt water, and every raging storm that tries to break that barrier down only throws out of its own furious throat more and more sand and pebbles that raise the bar still higher.

So there now that lake of pure water is, running north from the sea, with dense woods on its rocky rising western bank and pasture sloping more gradually down on the east. When it has run north for a mile it broadens out toward the west, toward Tresant, and it was here, when I first came on this broad water, that my flighty running stopped and I stood enchanted, looking at what is still to me the place where all my heart is.

I was looking through trees that stood in a small meadow, and be-tween the smooth gray boles—for these were beeches—shone the water on which the sunshine lay in flecks and sparkles. There were rafts of water-lily leaves that would in time support a freight of creamy lilies and red lilies, but the year was not yet ready for that. A punt

74

was moving across the water, lazily paddled by a man who sat in it smoking a pipe; and as I watched, it came to rest on the far shore where there was a wooden jetty and a boat house. The man got out and walked into a cottage that stood beyond a lawn, and it seemed to me that nowhere in the world would you find a place of more peace than that cottage, with the lake water in front of it and the trees close about it. A pennant of blue smoke hung over a chimney.

How small and set about my life had been till then! I was a child of the fortunate class, but I had seen nothing but a few London streets and parks, the sea at Broadstairs, and a corner of France that had been exciting enough but had shown me nothing like this. And the great joy of it was that I was alone. I felt as though I had suddenly become responsible enough to be entrusted with the whole world.

The way I had been told to go turned to the right, which is to the south, and now I was on a path that had the rising woods on the right, and on the left the rocky western bank of the lake. Trees found root-hold there, and you could look through them, down to the water. It is like that all the way to the bar: the woods and the path and the rocky, tree-grown abrupt declivity to the lake. I want to make it clear, once and for all, and I never saw it more sharply than on that first morning. The woods were full of bluebells; they were an azure misty lake, and because the trees were not fully clothed the sun was coming through, lighting them up and turning to shining pewter the trunks of the beeches that rose out of them. The beech leaves had not yet shed the husks out of which they had been born, and the silvery down of childhood was on them. This path along which I had been loitering had been hewn here and there through reddish rock, and splendid pines were there, the trunks rough like crocodile hide, and the roots fantastic, gripping for anchorage. Some had fallen, and the soil had been heaved and torn in a great area round about, and terrifying that must have been for many creatures of earth and air, like the death of a mighty one on whom many simple lives had depended.

But I must not go on about the woods and walks of Tresant: about the rafty nest on which that day I saw a swan sitting, or about the badgers that later, when I had come to know the place well, I saw grunting along the path. It is all so much to me that I could become tiresome to those who do not know it.

For a mile that path runs between wood and water, and halfway along it that day I stopped, spellbound by a small sinuous creature that looked at me for a moment and then rippled out of sight. I know now that it was a stoat, but I did not know that then. To my right the rock rose up rather sharply at this spot, pine-fringed, and on the level of the path a few bushes grew. It was into these that the little creature had disappeared, and I ran forward, hoping to see it again, and began to draw the bushes apart. I saw that behind them there was a hole in the rock, shaped like a door; and, fascinated as any child would be at the thought of a cave, I was preparing to look farther when there was a rustling in the mat of pine needles over my head. Looking up, I was surprised to see Captain Rodda, wearing his tasseled cap, gazing calmly down at me. He had one arm hooked round a pine trunk, the other was stroking his beard. We looked at one another in silence for a moment, and then he shouted cheerfully: "Good morning, midear. How be the ole stomach this mornin'? Settled, I hope."

"Yes, thank you, Captain Rodda," I answered politely, but a little startled by this unexpected appearance, by this sense of having been watched when I had thought myself alone. He scrambled down, and came to my side in a rush of shale.

"I saw a little animal," I said. And added innocently: "I think it was a squirrel."

"I saw un," he said. "That weren't no ole squirrel. That were a stot. Vicious things they be. Don't 'e ever go pokin' about after stots, midear. Leave the bushes alone. Don't 'e go pokin' into the ole bushes."

I said nothing about the hole in the rock, and he seemed anxious to be gone from that place. He began to walk in the direction of the bar, and I trotted at his side. We hadn't gone far when the woods began to peter out and the rock faces to be clothed with cascades of mesembryanthemum, the noon flower, dark green fleshy leaves and starry blossoms of rose and creamy yellow. We began to hear the breakers. Ahead of us, sitting on a wall, were Whaley and Sally Gaylord. I ran to join them, and there, visible from where we sat, was the sea.

It is a superb prospect from that spot. Facing the wall is a rough bank clothed with heather, bracken and sea pinks. Below the wall is a drop down to the lake, shallow here, so that you see the herons' feet as they wade and the dark shadows that are fishes, now poised, now darting. Closing in the lake is the ridge, the bar, a quarter of a mile of shining sand; and then the sea, reaching away beyond the limits of sight.

3

Captain Rodda came up and invited us all to take a cup of tea in his cottage. "And where have *you* suddenly risen from?" Sally asked him. "Miss Whale and I have been dawdling here for an hour or more. We didn't see you go by."

"I climbed up back an' came down through the ole woods," the captain answered easily. "Come on now, midears. I could do with a cup myself."

We had not far to go to reach the cottage, but that little distance made an enormous difference to the prospect. The path ended in a gate, and Eddy's cottage was just there. It was, in fact, one of the lodges to the Tresant estate: a forthright little building of stone, all its corners reinforced with granite. It was as strong and stony and uncompromising as the cottage by the lake was gentle and romantic: that cottage at which I had looked earlier and which, I learned in time, was another lodge entrance to Tresant. Eddy's cottage, perched on the very edge of the cliff, was surrounded by a wall as utilitarian as itself.

" 'Er needs to be strong," he said with a grin, pulling off his tasseled cap and scratching his head; and indeed you could see that, for now the prospect had opened out, and east, west and south was nothing but the sea. The cliff path ran ahead of us to Porteven, which we could see, a mile away, clustered round its harbor. Those were the nearest habitations, and it could be terrible in the winter, I thought, here in this stone eyrie leaning out into all the winds of the world.

"Ay," said Eddy Rodda, his fingers combing his black beard, "she looks fine an' cozy now, the ole sea, fine an' cozy"; and Sally said: "But not so fine and cozy when the lifeboat goes out. Captain Rodda is cox'n of the lifeboat," she added for our enlightenment. "My father and Wesley are in the crew."

More and more surprising. More and more *different,* this life in which I could still feel the splash of being so suddenly dropped. Imagine my Papa in a lifeboat! No, no; you couldn't. But you *could* imagine Lord Burnage, and the great oars lifting and dipping, and the boat plunging and climbing, and the wild gray rags of a disordered night hurrying across the sky. You could imagine that, but not easily that morning, as Captain Rodda repeated: "Ay, fine an' cozy now," and then, pulling himself up: "Well, come on in, mideurs."

If I had at that time known the story of Captain Rodda and the death of Richards the grocer—but I did not—I should not have found it easy to recognize in Mrs. Rodda the "slip of a girl" who had been Mary Richards. Mrs. Rodda was short: short in speech, short in body, short of breath. She was a heavy, rolling, female creature, as broad as she was long, florid in the face, and gray-haired. She brought tea into the front room, put the tray onto a bamboo table, gave a bob in our direction, and went out. Through a window, we could see Wesley Rodda mending wicker lobster pots: how ignorant I was! I didn't know they were lobster pots till Sally told me: and his father talking to him. I had all this life to learn, not only about such things as lobster pots but about rooms like this. I had never been in such a room before. It had no sense of being used. The furniture was upholstered in slippy pricky horsehair; the top of the harmonium was decorated with large pearly shells; on the mantelpiece was a small porcelain pulpit with John Wesley perched in it, and a book of Wesleyan hymns stood on the music bracket of the harmonium. The only picture in the room was over the mantelpiece: a steel engraving showing John Wesley preaching on the edge of Gwennap Pit. It was not difficult to see that here was the inspiration of the discourse Captain Rodda had given me. It was all in the picture: the preacher's white bands and uplifted angelic face, the sunlight piercing the clouds and falling upon the anguished eyes and locked fingers of trembling sinners; even the old horse was standing by, ready to jog along with the principal actor to his next stand.

We sipped our tea and ate our saffron cake, and Whaley said: "I wonder whether we might have the window open?" The little room was stuffy with unused air.

"Not without asking Mrs. Rodda's permission," said Sally, who went through and knocked at the kitchen door. Mrs. Rodda, wiping her hands on an apron of sacking, came back and opened the window with difficulty and reluctance. Then surprisingly (to me) she said: "Would you like a tune, Miss Sally?"

"Yes," said Sally. "I'm sure we all would, if we're not hindering you."

The ungainly woman sat down at the instrument, rubbed her hands once or twice on her sack-covered thighs, and began to play. At the first sound of the music Captain Rodda came to the window and pulled it further down. His wife had conceded only a meager slit. But now there was space enough for Eddy Rodda's laughing face to come into the room. Mrs. Rodda sang as she played, and not only the captain, leaning through the window, but Wesley also, sitting on a bench with a lobster pot on the ground before him, chimed in. And now I saw an odd thing, odder even than this sudden offer to sit down and inflict a hymn on us. Because you didn't have to know the Roddas long to realize that there was nothing odd about that at all. They were a singing family; they loved singing; and the only things they knew to sing were hymns. No; the really odd and moving thing was to observe Mary Rodda's face. The stolid flesh seemed to soften. She was a tender woman. All the time she sang, her eyes were on Rodda leaning through the window, and his on her. It seemed as though the handsome corsair hypnotized her, and as she quavered

Thine is the power; behold I sit
In willing bonds before Thy feet,

you would have been hard put to it to say whether she was singing to him or to her God.

"Well, me ole lover," Captain Rodda cried when the hymn was done, "'an'some that was, 'an'some." And he added: "Speaking one to another in psalms and hymns and spiritual songs, singing and making melody with your heart to the Lord. Eh, Wesley, boy?"

Wesley did not answer. He had dropped the lobster pot and walked to the low wall beyond which was the cliff path to Porteven. Beyond the wall we could see a girl's head and shoulders and a huddle of shawl out of which a baby's face appeared. And now another transformation came over the countenance of Mary Rodda. It became red and congested, as though she were going to have a fit. Captain Rodda had disappeared. He must have gone into the house by a back door. Mrs. Rodda was shouting through the window: "You go back where you belong, Lucy Evans. Go on now. You don't belong to be 'ere! I won't 'ave you hangin' about!"

She was shaking her fist and trembling. Miss Whale hastily gathered me and Sally, an arm round each. "We must be off," she said. And without a word to Mrs. Rodda, who seemed to have forgotten our presence, we went. When we were on the path, we could see the girl and the bundled child moving toward Porteven, still pursued by Mrs. Rodda's voice; but, voice or no voice, we saw Wesley leap the wall and go after them.

Sally said: "Poor Lucy Evans. Everyone shouts after her. She's not married and she's got a baby."

4

I am afraid that most people today, if they heard this remark from a girl of ten, would think it unusually mature and, perhaps, "not quite nice." Sally said what she had to say about Lucy Evans simply and sensibly, and all her conversation, I think, would sound "grown-up" to a contemporary parent.

Nothing more was said then concerning Lucy Evans. We walked out of the Roddas' house, and in front of us was a scrambling pathway down to the bar. We strolled on the sand and to the edge of the water that always there comes in with a roll, never with the pussy purring that you find on some beaches. "Fine and cozy" she looked that day, as Eddy Rodda had said; but Sally talked to us of the winter fury, told us how ships had been driven ashore here and bodies washed up.

"Have you ever known nights when his lordship has been out in the lifeboat?" Whaley asked.

"Oh, yes," said Sally, "not many, but enough. I can't sleep then. The hill and the wood shelter Tresant, so that when the worst

79

winds are blowing out here, it's calm enough in there. But that's no good, because you *know* what it's like outside, and once you *know,* you can't put your head under a sheet and go to sleep, can you? You'd feel such a worm. That is why I despise my Mama."

This, evidently, was something Miss Whale did not wish to discuss. "Well," she said, "shall we walk on a little, or should we be getting back to the house?"

"Oh," Sally cried, refusing to be sidetracked, "I know I shouldn't talk about such things, but you might as well know how I feel."

And then she let out something that had evidently been simmering in her heart for a long time. She told of a night of storm and of how Lord Burnage had gone to Porteven, as he did when it was likely that the boat would go out. Later a messenger came to say that distress signals had been seen and that the boat was gone. Sally went to bed at her usual time, but she did not sleep, for her imagination pictured the little boat, so unlike a powered lifeboat of today—the little open boat, depending on nothing but arms at the oars, the oil-skinned crew slashed by the wind and with the rain and sea spray rattling onto them. "There was only one thing," Sally said, "that made me a bit happier than I should otherwise have been, and that was that Mama was up and would look after him when he came home. But presently I heard her go to bed."

Sally couldn't believe it. She got out of her own bed and crept to her mother's door. "She always said her prayers, and she had a peculiar habit. She said them aloud. I asked her about it once, and she laughed and said it was so that God could hear better. I could hear her prayers that night. They were all askings, and I loathed her. There wasn't a word about my father or Captain Rodda or Wesley. It was all bless me and give me. So I knelt down right against the door, and I prayed in a loud voice, and I asked God to bless any men whose ship might be in danger and to help the lifeboat men to save them and bring them safely home."

The next thing Sally knew was that the door had opened and Lady Burnage stood there, holding a candle, with her hair down to her waist and her eyes hard with anger. "What is this?" she cried. "Have you come to insult me?"

Sally was speechless with rage and misery. Her mother took her by the arm, marched her to her own room, and commanded her to get into bed. Then she went out and locked the door. "It was that," said Sally, "that finished it forever between her and me. She would not wait up for him herself, and she tried to stop me from doing it, too."

Sally sat on her bed and heard a clock on the landing strike ten. She opened the window and got out. There was a tree growing up to the window, and its branches were as easy to manage as the rungs

80

of a ladder. There was nothing romantic in her first impulse. Since she couldn't get downstairs by opening her door, she would reach the ground and get in through the front. That was all she had in mind. But as soon as she was down, she saw that this would not do. Servants would be waiting up. She would be marched to bed again. Nor was it possible for her to clothe herself properly to meet such a night as this, for her oilskins were in a cupboard downstairs, and she could not reach them without being seen. The southwest wind did not reach in here with much force, but the rain was falling heavily, and already, while she was pondering her situation, it was soaking her light clothes. Presently it stopped, and through the clouds that began to break up she could see the moon lurching about the sky. She decided to walk to Porteven.

You can make that journey either by going along the lake and through the woods to Eddy Rodda's lodge and then for a mile along the cliffs, or by leaving the grounds of Tresant in the opposite direction and following the high road. To a town child like me, either way, alone at night, would have been terrifying; but Sally knew every yard of road and every field and tree and every person living in that district, so that, for her, there was no emotional disturbance arising from the physical facts of the situation. But there was intense emotional disturbance arising from the conflict which had suddenly blown up with her mother, especially as this concerned her almost idolatrous feeling for her father. It was a child outwardly unconcerned but with a terrible premature turmoil in her heart who hurried along the road, exposed to the wind now, with the trees lashing over her head and the stormy sky opening and shutting its doors upon the moon.

And that, when she found him, he and those who had gone out with him had failed: this was what made the matter more terrible to her than it would otherwise have been. For it was a downcast beaten man she met being driven home by Dr. Curnow. When she was halfway to Porteven she saw the gig lamps twinkling toward her, and got into the middle of the road so that the gig stopped and Dr. Curnow shouted: "Good God, child! What are you up to?"

She got in and gave a cry when she saw her father leaning back exhausted, a bandage round his head, his eyes closed. He put an arm round her and drew her onto his lap and murmured: "God, Sal, you're soaked," but seemed unable to say more.

When they reached the house and the servants were gaping at this appearance out of the night of a child they had thought to be sleeping, Dr. Curnow said: "Now, Sally, get off to bed. Tomorrow will do for any explanations," and obediently she went, leaving her father sitting in a chair by the fire in the hall. She learned afterward how wind and water had beaten the lifeboat back time after time as it struggled to reach the little ship dragging at her anchor, with the waves pounding over her, sweeping men from the deck before their eyes, carrying away spars and finally the mainmast. They could do nothing, and at last they saw her go under, and a wash of rubbish—hencoops and barrels and broken gear—came tossing on the waves toward them. It was some fag end of this stuff, carried on the hissing water, that struck Lord Burnage on the forehead, stunning him.

She learned this afterward, but that night, just as she was opening her bedroom door, the turned key being still in the lock, her mother came out from her room, aroused by a servant. Sally and her mother looked at one another for a moment, but neither spoke. "I think," Sally said to me years later, "that each of us knew in her own way that there was nothing to be said, nothing at all. It was a crossroads moment. What had happened showed that she had made up her mind to go one way and I the other. The Duke of Fallowshire came down for the shooting the next week."

5

We were on the western end of the bar. It ran eastward, a long level stretch that ended in green rising land. "There they are!" Sally cried, and in the distance we saw two riders coming toward us. It is a moment framing one of those pictures that do not fade: the morning of late May with the sun strengthening, the sea on our right tumbling in noisily but not angrily, the sand rolling away like an enormous golden carpet to where the land rose up in sage-green cliff tops marching eastward to the Lizard. Coming toward us were the two mounted figures, the horses trotting sedately, then breaking into a canter that rose to a gallop, so that, when they pulled up before us, both they and their riders were breathing heavily. Lord Burnage leapt to the ground, and Sally took the reins of his horse as he helped my mother to dismount. She was flushed and laughing. I had never seen her look so handsome or so happy. She had never spoken much to me of her own girlhood, but I knew she had had a country upbringing, that she had done much riding, and that my father's dislike of it had been one of her sorrows. In more ways than one, at Tresant she must have found her youth again. Children are not often aware of what their parents look like, but that morning I saw that my mother was a most beautiful woman.

She put me from her when she had kissed me, and held me at arm's length, looking at me. There was something almost shy in her manner, as though she wondered how I would take to her after the disrupting things that had happened; almost—God forgive me if anything in my

82

conduct made such an idea necessary—almost as though she were asking me to forgive her.

She turned to Lord Burnage, and, child though I was, I could not help seeing how his face and hers brightened as their glances met. "Well, Harry," she said, "is she all right? Are you satisfied that I haven't brought you a monster?"

Lord Burnage laughed. "We shall do our best with her," he said. "She doesn't look bad stuff to start working on. She and I got on pretty well from the start, didn't we, Miss Whale?"

"She certainly made a profit out of the meeting," said Whaley; and I blushed to think how shamelessly that morning in Bond Street I had accepted all that his good nature offered.

"Well," said Lord Burnage, "I made a profit, too," and again his eyes met Mama's. I did not feel now that I was with him as intimately as I had been during the journey through France. I had been moved aside a little, and I felt that this was a shadow over the group talking so happily on the sand. I asked abruptly: "What am I to call you, sir? I cannot call you Lord Burnage?"

He laughed immensely at that. "Why not?" he teased me. "It's an excellent name. It has done for better men than I. What's wrong with it?"

"Well," I said, "I didn't call Papa Sir Richard Rainborough."

It was a mistake to mention Papa. I saw that at once. The smile went off Lord Burnage's face and off Mama's. Sally said: "I *hate* Papas and Mamas. I positively *hate* them. From now on I shall call you two Father and Mother, and I think Sarah had better do the same."

"How does that suit Sarah?" Lord Burnage asked. It suited me so well that for the rest of this narrative Father must be understood to mean Lord Burnage, not Sir Richard Rainborough.

6

My father and mother, then, put their horses to the path that climbed from the beach to Eddy Rodda's cottage and went before us at a walking pace through the wood. Sally was running ahead of me and Whaley, answering the whistle of a blackbird, swinging on branches of trees that grew out of the rocky declivity toward the lake. "Mind you don't fall in," Miss Whale shouted; and Sally shouted back: "What would it matter? I can swim. I have swum right across this lake, but I prefer the sea."

"It wouldn't be nice to get your clothes wet through," Whaley warned her; and she shouted back: "I could change them. It's not as though

I ever caught cold. You ask Dr. Curnow. He says I'm a tough little devil."

Then she was reaching up into a half-greened hazel, to show us the nest of a thrush or blackbird. She lifted out the eggs: the blue with black spots, the green mottled with brown: and this was something I had never seen before. I begged to be allowed to hold them. "You won't find *those* in Portman Square!" Sally said decisively. "Oh, the dirty old sooty laurels! I'm glad I shan't see them this year."

"Is his lordship remaining here all through the summer?" Whaley asked; and Sally said: "No, but we are. Father and mother will be going soon—almost at once."

She skipped away after a red squirrel, leaving us to digest this unexpected news. When we overtook her, she had reached the point whence you look across the lake to the cottage standing on the lawn beyond the boathouse. "How lovely that is!" Whaley cried.

Sally said: "It'll be going begging soon. I wonder whom Father will put in there?"

"Oh, does it belong to Father?" I cried, anxious to have this new name in my mouth.

"Yes, indeed," said Sally. "The estate goes right away beyond that for a mile or so." She looked ponderingly at the cottage, shining so happily in the noon light; and then—what a surprising girl she was!— she said seriously: "Look, you two. You mustn't think everything is what it seems. You'll soon learn that down here. That's why Captain Rodda laughs at the sea when she's fine an' cozy. He knows too much about the sea to be taken in. There have been some horrible things in that cottage. Mr. and Mrs. Bennetts lived there, and now he's alone. She died in agony."

It had taken Mrs. Bennetts more than a year to die. Sally used to read to her as she lay in bed. "Old Bennetts can't read a word," she said. "There he is." Out of the cottage came the man I had seen paddling the punt, looking, I thought, so blissfully content in the sweet May weather. "He used to sit on one side of the bed," said Sally, "and I on the other. Anything out of the Bible Mrs. Bennetts liked. I'd open it anywhere and start off at the first thing my eyes fell on. She liked it all: the tower of Babel or the New Testament or the long lists of people who begat other people, as Captain Rodda begat Lucy Evans's baby."

"Really—Sally!" Whaley cried; and then, primly remembering her place, "*Miss* Sally, I should say."

"Call me what you like," said Sally. "But everyone knows about Eddy Rodda and Lucy Evans." What gardeners and stableboys talked about was not lost on Sally.

We began to walk on, and Sally told us how, as her readings went on week by week and month by month, Mrs. Bennetts's groans became

84

worse, her agony more apparent, until at last Dr. Curnow had forbidden the readings, "so that," said Sally, as though she had missed something, "I wasn't with her when she died."

Bennetts had lived alone in the lodge since then, and now, it seemed, his brother's wife had died, too. The brother had a small farm, and Bennetts intended to join him there, "and so," Sally explained, "the place will be going begging."

7

I have told how, when we were living in Portman Square, I got out of bed one night and went into the schoolroom to consult Miss Whale about something that was on my mind. I found her bowed over the table, writing away on large sheets of paper. It had never occurred to me that this had anything to do with the profoundest side of Whaley's life; but a new light fell upon it that afternoon of my first day at Tresant. Sally, Whaley and I were summoned to attend my father in the library, and he invited us all to sit down. "There is a lot that we must discuss," he said, as we sank into our chairs. "But first of all, there is a letter here for you, Miss Whale."

He took a letter from his desk and handed it to her, and no one could fail to see the animation, the excitement, of her face when she looked at it. This indeed was so remarkable that Father said: "If you would care to read your letter at once, Miss Whale, pray do so."

Making an apology, Whaley tore open the letter with a trembling hand, read hastily, and cried "Oh!" in a small astonished voice, which caused my father to say: "I trust you have no bad news?"

Whaley had risen, and was now visibly trembling with excitement. "Indeed, no, my lord," she said. "It is wonderful news—incredible."

We all looked at her in some surprise, and she sank back into her chair and said in a breathless rush. "I can hardly believe it! Mr. Dickens is going to use one of my stories in *Household Words*."

"Well," said my father, "but that is splendid. I had no idea that you were an author."

Having made her first announcement, Whaley seemed unable to say more. She just sat there, with the letter shaking in her hand, and Father said: "I am sure you must be congratulated. No writer could have a more celebrated editor. I have met Mr. Dickens at Miss Burdett-Coutts's." He added with a smile. "His waistcoat repelled me. Rather florid."

Whaley rallied at that and burst out: "It would be a sad thing, sir, if so great a man were judged by his little vanities."

"Indeed it would," Father soothed her. "Forgive me. Don't think I am unaware that Mr. Dickens is a very great man."

Oh, he is, he is! I was thinking; for to me it seemed almost as wonderful as it must have done to Whaley that the letter she held in her hand was from the man whose books had for so long been beloved by her and me. She had read them all to me, and I had read some for myself; we had laughed and cried over them together; and now I could not resist saying: "Please let me see." Whaley handed me the letter and I looked at the bottom, and there, heavily underscored with a line that came to and fro beneath itself again and again, I read "Charles Dickens." I looked at Whaley in awe and wonder.

"He asks for more," she said quietly, as if this too could not be true.

"That is excellent," said Father. "But this, I fear, may alter all I intended to say. This is a great chance for you, Miss Whale, and no doubt you will wish to leave us—to go to London where you can be in touch with people who will be of advantage to you."

But, happily, this did not seem to be what Whaley wanted at all. "Oh dear, no, sir!" she cried. "I was brought up in the country, and I am happier in the country than in town. All I have ever tried to write has been concerned with the country and will continue to be so."

"All the same," said my father, "you may want to leave us. With the encouragement you now have, you may want to give time to writing, and you can hardly do that if you continue to have the care of these two young people. I'm afraid it's going to be a bigger task than ever, for Lady Burnage and I will soon be leaving for London and you'll have the whole responsibility on your shoulders."

Whaley said that she had all the time she needed for her writing and that she would be glad to stay.

"Very well, then. We shall have to find time later to discuss the curriculum"; and to me and Sally, with a smile, "the curriculum meaning the work to be done. And now, if you two will leave us, there are a few things I want to speak of with Miss Whale."

It was the question of Lucy Evans, above all, that he wanted to discuss, and the ins and outs of this question, as I learned them later, were simple enough. Her father was a cavalryman who served with Lord Burnage in the Crimea and became a groom at Tresant when the war was over. A little bow-legged timid man was Evans, and his wife a tall dour woman who seemed the better man of the two. Evans died, and the woman, left with a growing girl, was given work in the sculleries at Tresant, the cottage where she had lived having been taken from her by the landlord. This scullery work was all she could find to do, and she didn't want to do even that. She soon took herself off, and, having nowhere else to live, seized a decaying shack in a field on the outskirts of Porteven and installed herself there with the girl. There was argument for a long time with the owner of the field, but now, having been there for some years, Mrs. Evans had established squatter's

86

rights and no one disturbed her. She was forever tinkering the place up with a plank stolen here or a bit of sheet iron found there, and she wandered the beaches after southerly storms, gathering wreckage. She became a handy, defiant and self-sufficient creature, well able to fend for herself. She had built a fireplace and chimney in one end of the shack. She and Lucy were to be seen with the gleaners after the harvests and working the autumn hedgerows for fruits and berries with which Mrs. Evans made jams and wines. It was said that the pot never lacked a hare or a rabbit, or even a pheasant. She was as good a poacher as any in the district. She never passed a tatter of wool left by a sheep in a hedge without gathering it. She carded it and spun it, dyed it with dyes made from vegetables, and knitted herself clothes. Leading this life, she became a lean hard creature, living to herself, and she was treated with caution and respect. The woman of this mechanized age, even most village women, would have died where Betty Evans lived with a flourish.

Betty adored her child Lucy. Lucy was her triumph. Living as she did, fending for herself, she would show them that she could bring up a child with the best. Lucy was good-looking, shy as a wild creature, for she was rarely permitted to go even into Porteven. Mrs. Evans could read and write, and she taught the girl to do so. The ambition flowered in her mind to "make something" of Lucy. When Lucy grew up, she, too, would "show them." On shiny nights when Betty was abroad, she locked the girl in the shack with a book and a candle.

On one of the rare occasions when Mrs. Evans and Lucy were in Porteven, they were seen by Wesley Rodda, then a boy of eighteen or nineteen. Like everyone else in the place, he knew who they were, understood the almost witchlike reputation of the mother and the mysterious evasiveness of the girl. He made a shy gesture toward his hat, and Lucy Evans smiled at him. Girls were not in the habit of smiling at Wesley. He was known already as a local preacher in the Wesleyan chapel, as a teetotaler, and altogether a grave reserved person. He was surprised when Lucy smiled. It was the sort of thing that didn't belong to happen to him. He followed the pair for a time with his heart in a turmoil; and suddenly the lean brown woman stopped, faced round to him, and stared him out of countenance. She simply said: "Be off with you!" and he slunk away. There were standers-by, and they laughed, and Wesley wished he could disappear beneath the earth. But he heard —he heard for days thereafter—Lucy's gentle voice saying: "Hush, mother! That's no way to speak."

He took to wandering out toward the shack, and he saw that it was a comely enough place that had improved with the years. There was even, in front of it, a flower bed marked out in white stones, and daffodils were bending in it before an April wind. He did not see Betty or

Lucy, but he was sure that Lucy had made the flower bed and planted the daffodils.

On the Sunday after that, Wesley was the preacher in the Methodist chapel. Lucy was in the small congregation. He could hardly speak for the emotions that were in his heart. It was his habit, when the service was over, to stand in the porch and shake hands with the people as they left, saying a word to each. He shook hands with Lucy, and they smiled again at one another, and he asked: "Did you plant the daffodils?"

"Yes," she said. That was all they said; but to Wesley it was as though they had exchanged lovers' vows.

8

Lucy was able to attend the chapel service because her mother was out. The girl had promised to stay at home, and for the first time she broke her word. Poor Wesley did not know that she had smiled at him because he was Eddy Rodda's son, or that she attended the service because, having seen the son's name announced as preacher on the notice board, she thought the father would be there, too. For she was under the spell which, years ago, after the inquest on Richards the grocer, had drawn his daughter to follow Eddy along the cliffs.

Not long before this, Betty Evans and Lucy had been on the sands under the Roddas' lodge, gathering driftwood after a storm. At least, Betty was gathering it and Lucy was enjoying the beauty of the spring morning. The task of "making something" of Lucy, which had become an obsession with Betty, the one thing to which all her life was directed, did not involve making the girl do hard work. Lucy's hands were white and as soft as her voice. It was Mrs. Evans who lugged together the chunks of wood, stained with tar, spiked with rusty nails, splintered and wounding. Mrs. Evans's hands were like her face: tough and leathery. She piled her burden, passed round it a rope she had brought for the purpose, and began to haul it up onto her back.

"That's no job for a 'ansome woman."

Captain Rodda came out from a cleft of the rocks whence he had been watching them, and laid his hand on the burden. To Lucy's surprise, her mother did not tell him to be off.

"A woman like you don't belong to be carrying great chunks of stuff like that." He swung the burden up as if it had been a child's satchel.

Mrs. Evans said nothing, but still she did not repel him. They dawdled along the beach together. Lucy was extraordinarily happy. To have a third party with them broke up the unnatural feeling of isolation in which she normally lived and which had begun to oppress her. Her heart expanded. Her surprise at her mother's acceptance of Captain Rodda would not have been so great had she known that on a shiny night in the winter Betty and Eddy had come face to face in the Tresant woods. They had been skirmishing round one another for a long time, each supposing the other to be a keeper, and, finally, they had laughed together in relief. They had hunted as a pair after that throughout the winter, and Betty Evans discovered that she was not altogether the mannish creature which she supposed the years had made of her. To be alone with Eddy Rodda in the woods soon taught her that.

And so they moved toward Porteven, and presently Rodda dropped his burden and said: "There's a fine ole log comin' in. Wait a minute now. We must get'n."

In his long sea boots he waded into the water and hauled the wood ashore. He held it up triumphantly. "Mahogany that is! Now you won't want to be burnin' that, midear. A couple of fine ole shelves or a chimney piece that'll make. You let me come an' see to that. I'll fix'n."

But now Betty Evans pulled herself back into her customary reticence. "No," she said. "We never have anyone about our place. We don't like it, do we, Lucy? We like to be alone."

Directly appealed to in this way, the girl was at a loss. She liked this handsome swaggerer with the black beard and flashing teeth and the tasseled cap drooping over his ear. She had heard of Captain Rodda. Even to her retired existence some rumor of his legend had penetrated. In a community of fishermen whose farthest beat was the coast of Brittany, he stood alone as one who had sailed the seas of the world. She tossed out of her hand the yellow shells she had been gathering and looked at her mother. Betty had hoisted the roped wood onto her shoulder. They were near Porteven. She was not going to be seen walking through the village with Captain Rodda. "I don't like to be alone. Not all the time," Lucy said.

That was as far as she dared to go. Betty looked at her and pondered. When she had made something of Lucy the girl would have to leave her. She would have to meet people sooner or later. And what was to be done with her, anyway? Betty's notions about launching a girl into a career were vague. Captain Rodda had the reputation of being a man of the world. Perhaps he could help. Perhaps the time had come to end this seclusion. "Very well," she said grudgingly. With that they parted, Betty trudging with her load in one direction, the captain bearing his mahogany log in the other. For a moment Lucy stood still, looking from one to the other; then hastened after Betty.

9

To reach the shack in which the Evanses lived, you turned down a lane that was rarely used except by farm carts and climbed through a gap in the hedge. Mrs. Evans made that gap—a small gap then, just enough to push herself through—when she took possession. It had gradually grown wider, though the farmer who owned the land stopped it up now and then in the beginning with lopped branches. Mrs. Evans pulled them out, and at last the farmer gave up the struggle, and the gap widened, but there had never been a straight run in or a gate. You had to climb over the bank.

Late that same day, Eddy Rodda did so, carrying his mahogany log. He might easily have brought a few tools at the same time, but he thought it would be better to have an excuse for coming again. There was no one in the shack, so he dumped the log under the hedge and looked about him. He had learned in the course of this winter to have a high opinion of Betty Evans's self-sufficiency, and what he saw now confirmed this. He smiled to see how in the course of the years she had stealthily extended her territory, so that not only the shack but the whole of this corner of the field had become virtually hers. She had been crafty enough not to make any enclosure, but she had pushed out a vegetable bed here, a row of bush fruit there, till the place had a prosperous cared-for appearance, as though the occupants did not lack. The trees that made the right angle of hedge in which the shack nestled were hawthorns. They were in bloom, filling the air with fragrance. Looking over the roofs of Porteven, you could see the blue water stretching itself lazily in the sun.

Eddy Rodda smiled and approved it all. He was enough of a buccaneer himself to enjoy the spectacle of this piece of land that had been insidiously stolen. The winter was over, but nevertheless the woodpile in the hedge corner was full. That was good, too. Mrs. Evans was evidently not one to let things run down.

He turned up again the next day with his tools and found the women at home. He was asked in, and his was the first foot that had crossed that threshold since the shack had been Betty Evans's home. It was one large room, whitewashed throughout, walls and ceiling alike. The floor was of neatly laid bricks, and where these had come from, a few at a time in the quiet of winter nights, was Betty's business. Bricks composed the hearth and the chimney, too. Bits of old tarpaulin kept the roof watertight. Betty never passed a bit of old tarpaulin whether it was derelict or, not being derelict, privily accessible. Rodda noted the wooden shutters for the window, the heavy wooden bar that could be dropped to secure the door. It could be snug enough here at nights. A paraffin lamp swung from the ceiling. The furniture had come out of the cottage from which Mrs. Evans had been ejected long ago: a dresser with its china, a table, a couple of kitchen chairs, a settle by the fire, a double bed screened by curtains of clean sacking. For washing, there was a tin bath hanging on hooks near the woodpile, outside.

Rodda was as happy as a schoolboy. It was a beautiful day and he was in the company of women. Also, he exulted at having broken down the taboo. He—he alone—ever since these women had been here, was permitted to enter and be at home. His masculinity was pleased. It had been successful again. It had empowered him where everyone else had failed. It had given him standing with the two feared, discussed and avoided women. He sawed and planed and chiseled, whistling and singing. Little was said. Mrs. Evans worked on her vegetable plot; Lucy sat on a bench fixed to the outside wall of the shack, sewing, smiling with quiet happiness, looking out to sea. "A fair picture she be, that li'l maid," Rodda thought. He had not before noticed how attractive Lucy was.

He purposely left his job unfinished, and he was there again the next day. He fixed the chimney shelf, and this time stayed to tea. Lucy, unbidden, had prepared it. Her mother was annoyed, but kept her feelings to herself. She tried to re-establish her position by thanking Eddy for what he had done and asking "How much will that be?"

He laughed boisterously, filled his pipe, and settled down comfortably between the two women on the outside bench. He didn't even bother to answer. He laughed, and smoked contentedly as the blackbirds sang in the hawthorns and the peewits gave their broken-hearted cries, drooping on the wing, running in the field. "This is a good ole life," he said, and lazily contemplated the smoke of a steamer moving down channel.

When at last he got up, he said: "There's a lot needs doin' here, midears. You want a li'l table here in front of the bench, for one thing. It's daft carrying out this great monster."

And he came and knocked up a table, and brought gravel for the paths between the vegetable beds, and addressed himself to the question of water supply. There were about ten yards of land between the back of the shack and the hedge that divided this field from the next, and under the hedge ran a trickle of water that did not earn the name of stream. But it was pure, and didn't fail, and it had been enough for the women's needs. Now Rodda must excavate, must bank up with big smooth stones, and there at last was a pool, as big and deep as a bath, with the trickle running in at one end and out at the other. It was certainly a convenience to be able to dip the largest vessel and have done with it.

It was while the acquaintanceship of Rodda and the two women was at this stage that Wesley Rodda met them in Porteven and was rebuffed by Betty. Betty wanted no more people hanging round her home, certainly not young men like Wesley Rodda. It was not in Porteven that Lucy was to meet young men. She did not know that Lucy was already lost.

Lucy would always remember May and June of that year. It had been raining off and on and one May day, toward the end of the afternoon, Eddy Rodda appeared between the showers, and it seemed to her that it was because of him that the weather cleared. He always had an excuse for coming, and this time it was a chicken run. The day darkened again and the rain came back, and he went with the women into the shack for shelter. This time the rain stayed. "I could run for it," he offered, having no intention of doing anything of the sort, and knowing that to be wet to the skin had never harmed him. No; this was comfortable, and here he meant to stay, especially now that Mrs. Evans had fastened the shutters, dropped the bar across the door, and lit the lamp. It was cozy with the fire blazing, blue and green and orange flames spurting from the salty driftwood, and Betty busy with a frying pan. The smell of the cooking fish, the rattle of the rain on the tarpaulin, the clatter of cups and plates and cutlery as Lucy laid the supper table: this was all most agreeable, and the sight of that mantel shelf and the other things that his own hands had made gave him a satisfactory proprietorial feeling. He leaned back on the settee, smoking his pipe, expansively at home. The firelight and lamplight fell on the dull gold of his earrings. They were circles, big enough to pass a small egg through. He had pulled off his woolen cap. The triumph of being intimately here where no other men had been lit him up. Virility seemed to pour out of him. Lucy was disturbingly and deliciously aware of it.

The meal was ready and they sat down, the two women on one side and Rodda on the other. The table was narrow and presently Eddy's knee touched Lucy's. It was accidental, but fateful. He was aware, looking at the girl whose face was so close to his, that the brief contact both alarmed and excited her; and what had begun by accident he now pursued with intent. It fascinated him to play this game under Betty's very eyes. Before long, Lucy's knees, gripped tight together, were fast between his, and he knew, as he always knew such things, that she was enchanted to have it so.

The rain continued to drum upon the roof; the lamplight fell gently onto the table, and Rodda, excited by a triumph that he had not looked for, talked and talked. There was no one in Porteven who could talk like Eddy Rodda, no one who had seen the world, East and West, as he had, not even Lord Burnage, and he could carry himself away as readily as he carried his hearers. That is why he was successful as a local preacher. Fifty years later, he would probably have talked politics on a street corner; but then the chapel and the pub were the only places that gave a man a chance; and so Eddy talked in both. He could describe the Mediterranean shipwrecks of St. Paul in terms of his own experiences so that one almost lived for a moment inside the pages of the New Testament. He was the wonder and the bafflement of the Porteven Methodists. They were aware of his reputation, but he could disarm them by accepting it. To hear him preach from some such text as "Sinners, of whom I am chief" was to suspend judgment. It was not that Eddy Rodda was a hypocrite. Far from it. Concerning himself, he could weep tears of blood and feel everyone of them welling out of his heart; but there were tides in him that were irresistible, and that he did not want to resist.

Betty Evans, no less than Lucy, listened fascinated when the table had been cleared and they had drawn up to the fire and he began his saga. But it was to Lucy he was now addressing himself, consciously using everything that experience told him would be of service in this case; and it was Lucy who, when the two women were stretched side by side on the bed, did not sleep but, fearful lest tossing should disturb her mother, perhaps awaken suspicion in her mind, lay rigid upon her back, looking at the unseen ceiling and beyond it the sky full of stars, as she had seen them when, the night having cleared, Rodda went at last, and, as he climbed the gap in the hedge, had seemed a huge shape on the sky, with those stars blazing about him.

That was what Lucy would always remember of May month; and of June she would remember hay harvest, and the burning sun and the red poppies and white dog daisies lying in the swathes as the scythes hissed and rasped and a thousand small things scurried and scuttered from the swinging blades. She stood by the fieldgate as the mowers moved slowly forward, and her imagination was filled with the thought of mice and voles that had lived foolish happy lives, making homes under the wind-stirred, flower-starred canopies that had seemed secure and that now were tumbling about them. She had seen a nest of harvest mice after a scythe had passed through it, and now she turned, with a sudden imaginative apprehension of life's callous inevitability, and looked seaward. The sea was sleeping. Even more than the land, it was deceptive. Now it looked like an immense silken sheet of blue on which one might rest, lulled in security, but devils of rage and fury could rise out of it to shatter and destroy.

Of late, she was full of sweet unhappy thoughts like these, and her body was tormented with strange unknown desires. She turned to take a last look at the reapers and began to walk to the shack. Her mother had learned to swing a scythe with the best. Tall and leather-browned by the midsummer sun, with a scarlet rag tied about her hair, she moved among the men, taciturn and forbidding. It had been a surprise when she asked for this work, and it had been given to her reluctantly. But new ideas were moving in her mind. Hitherto, she had been content by crafty ways to keep body and soul together for herself and Lucy. Now this was not enough. To make something of Lucy, she began to understand, would call for money, and so from now on she would put herself in the way of earning it. She reproached herself that already she had left this late. The girl was seventeen, and Betty was quick to perceive symptoms of restlessness.

The restless girl wandered between the June-high hedges, fragrant with eglantine and lit with pearl-pink dog roses. Campion and ragged robin on either hand gave color amid the yeasty froth of meadowsweet; and on one side, making the June green richer, slid the trickle of water that soon passed under the hedge, through a little culvert of stones, to fall with hardly a sound into the brimming sunken trough that Eddy Rodda had made.

Now, in this high moment of the summer, it was an enchanting place. The end of the hut, with the door in it, the right angle of the two hedges, made it recluse and cool. The dog roses grew freely in that angle, lifting waywardly against the blue sky, and ferns, lusty in the damp, fringed the pool's edge. The broiling sun had no power here, and a few clumps of late primroses bloomed in the mossy shadowed bank.

Lucy stood looking down into the pool. The slight flow set her image wavering in the crystal water. The pool was so newly made that no sediment had yet been carried in to hide the white stones that covered the bottom. They gleamed invitingly, and the girl was overcome by a desire to lie in the cool stillness of the water. Never in her life, so far as she could remember, had she immersed herself. Once a week, the tin bath that hung to the outside wall of the shack was dragged within, water was heated, and she and Betty bathed. But you could not lie down in the tin bath; and the pagan thought of lying down in cold water seized upon her now. It was part of the sweet distress that Eddy Rodda was inflicting upon her. She wanted to go naked into his pool.

It was the noon of the day and of the year. The reapers were half a mile away; no one ever came down this byway; and the angle of the hedge made the bathing place as secluded as a room. It was but a pace or two from the door to the water, along a flagged pathway, and when her naked feet touched the unwarmed flags and the air of the sunless enclosure flowed around her body she paused for a moment, shivering slightly, her arms folded about her breast. She stood thus, wrapped in her own embrace, her heart beating heavily at her hardihood, thinking of embraces more warm and carnal. Looking up, she could see the sky, cloudless, unbounded, with the untrammeled gulls soaring in the blue gulfs, free as she felt not free, and she longed for life to lift her up, to take her out of her enclosure.

Rodda lifted her up. She lay upon the water, almost swooning when she saw that he was there, stricken with shame, but so beaten down by joy and terror that she could do nothing. As she had seen him huge against the stars, so now he was huge against the blue-white dazzle of the sky. He bestrid one end of the pool, a foot planted on either side; then she saw him bend, his great beard coming down toward her face. She was more helpless than a mouse with the scythe advancing. She could not scuttle away, and she did not want to. Rodda's earrings were like golden moons falling out of the sky toward her. There was just a moment when she was aware of the face, not laughing as she had been accustomed to see it laugh, but grimly set, and of the dog roses making a fantastic halo about it, and of the sky at which she seemed to be looking through a tilted tunnel; and then she felt his arms plunged down into the water, his fingers feeling beneath her body, his great strength lifting her out of the pool. She lay upon his chest, dripping; her head sank upon his shoulder and her eyes closed. He carried her into the house.

CHAPTER SEVEN

I

THAT day when Maggie Whale received the letter from Charles Dickens, Sally and I left her to discuss certain matters with Father: matters that concerned the future of a number of people: me and Sally, Lucy Evans and her son, whom she regrettably insisted on naming Merlin. Lucy and her child were, in a sense, not my father's concern. They did not live on his land and had no legal claim or claim of custom upon him. But he was never a man to confine his good-doing to the narrowest limits that could be thought of; and there were two reasons why he showed an especial interest in Lucy Evans. One was his old comradeship with her father, and the other was his liking for that picturesque villain Captain Rodda. By the time it burst upon my notice—that is, by the morning when I saw Lucy with her child outside the lodge, and Rodda slinking from sight, and Mrs. Rodda shouting abuse, and Wesley hot in pursuit—the situation was indeed one to call for a kindly intervention.

I was to know Lucy so well and to hear, in the days to come, so much of this story from her, that I have no difficulty in seeing her that morning flying along the cliff path from the lodge to Porteven with the child bundled in her arms, no difficulty in understanding the turmoil in the mind of this young person, till then singularly sheltered and apart from the normal stress of life, now thrown with one sudden and tremendous impact upon its lively reality. She was deserted, save by the young pursuer whom she did not want. She had, up to this very moment, persuaded herself that, could she but meet Eddy Rodda, her situation would somehow disentangle itself. When it was evident that she was with child he had ceased to appear at the shack, and what was evident to him was soon evident to Mrs. Evans also. That was a dreadful night. Betty had been away all day. She returned in the evening carrying a long parcel, which she made a mystery of, refusing to open it. She put it aside, and she and the girl sat down to their supper. Betty was in an exceptionally good mood, gay and talkative. They had not had a night like this for a long time, for all through that summer she had found work here and there, intent on earning the money that would help Lucy to become something.

Now, with supper over, she began to speak. She told Lucy of her ambitions, and the girl saw her mother for the first time not as a reserved, isolated person but as a member of a family. She learned of a sister who had been a barmaid. Betty was amusing and informative on the wonderful openings a barmaid had. She met all sorts, some of them real gents, and with a girl who knew what she was up to, that could lead to something good. With her sister, it had led to marriage with a commercial traveler in drapery goods, a man with his head screwed on right, who had, ten years ago, managed to start his own draper's shop in Swansea.

It was to Lucy wonderful, miraculous. Relatives who owned a draper's shop! She could hardly conceive such grandeur, and her mother chuckled at the greater surprise she had up her sleeve. Mostyn Lloyd—that was the draper's magnificent name—was a warm careful man. Swansea was not big enough for him. London was what he had always wanted. And now it had come. He was to open a London shop!

Betty, usually taciturn, talked and talked. She had been storing up too much for too long. All through this summer, ever since the thought had come to her that something practical must now be done about Lucy, she had been worming her way into the citadel. Her first letter to Meg Mostyn Lloyd had not been warmly answered, but that it was answered at all encouraged her to go on. Gradually some of the old friendliness had come back, and now this! It was not tremendous, but it seemed so to Betty. The Mostyn Lloyds had no children. When they were settled in London they would be willing to have Lucy with them to see how she shaped. Mostyn Lloyd himself condescended to write, because he didn't want any misunderstanding. Lucy must do as she was told. She must be willing to work in the shop or in the home if this were required. It might have sounded to anyone else like bargaining for the services of a cheap servant, but not to Betty. She was satisfied that Lucy, once established, would be irresistible. Already she was seeing her as the heiress in that childless home.

And now, the supper being cleared away, and the shack locked up for the night, and the lamp lit, she at last unwrapped her parcel. It had cost her all that her hard labor had earned that year. She had tramped to the neighboring town and back to get these things, and now she spread them on the table, running her leathery hand over them lovingly: the bonnet and the dress, the petticoats and stockings, the shoes, gloves and underclothing. There was even an absurd frivolous parasol. Meg Mostyn Lloyd should see that Betty's life had not been in vain.

"Put them on!" she cried eagerly.

Lucy put them on. She stood there under the lamp in all those frills and furbelows, pulling the violet gloves up her white forearms while her mother, laughing with delight, tied the bonnet strings beneath her chin in a fetching bow. She stood back and looked at the girl. If Porteven could see her now! She'd show 'em! She handed her the parasol. "Put it up!"

Lucy was in a daze at what was happening to her. It had been a long lonely day, very hot, and now, with all the air shut out, and the fire burning, because it had been necessary to cook the supper, and with the smell of the frying-pan fat in her nostrils, she felt suddenly vertiginous and queasy.

"Put it up!" her mother repeated.

Lucy dully opened the parasol and sloped it back over her right shoulder. And there she was: the product, complete at last, that her mother had worked so hard to attain. But she saw that mother, standing on the other side of the room and looking at her with an artist's ecstasy, only as a shape that quivered like the grass on the cliff or the sand on the shore when a day was over-hot. The parasol slipped from her hand. She clutched the edge of the table and her stomach heaved. A little vomit dribbled down her chin on to her flounces.

Betty was rooted to the ground for a moment by her consternation. Then she leapt with fury in her eyes. She picked up the frivolous parasol and folded it, and beat Lucy with it about the head and shoulders. "My God!" she cried. "You little bitch you! You dirty little bitch!"

2

The woman's fury lasted only for a moment. It was a fury engendered not so much by the girl's mischance as by Betty's own personal sense of frustration. She felt as though someone had put a foot through a picture at the very moment when she had known that it was to be hung on the line. There was jealousy in it, too. Betty did not need to be told who

97

was responsible for this. And there was self-condemnation at the final failure of a vigilance that had endured so long. All these emotions, rushing into the void where her cozy dream had lived, clashed in an awful but brief commotion and fell in blow after blow upon Lucy's body.

The girl had sunk to the floor, annihilated by this onslaught, as much destroyed as some image that had lived in a niche might be had its worshiper turned suddenly upon it, and it been sentient. Betty herself sank into a chair, breathing hard, recovering a stony composure, looking at the white-faced creature groveling among the stylish flounces. Then, saying nothing, she undressed and got into bed. She heard the swish and crackle of the silks falling off the girl, and presently Lucy crept in beside her. They lay apart, and neither slept.

There were no more blows or reproaches, nothing but a sullen and obstinate dedication such as a hard-faced wardress might give to a fragile prisoner. There was only one thing to remind Lucy of that terrible night. Waking from uneasy sleep early in the morning, she found that her mother had left the bed. The window had been flung up and the early sun was streaming in. Lucy walked weakly to the window and looked out, and there was her mother touching a match to the clothes that had been gathered from the floor. The girl saw the blue flounced skirt, the white petticoats, the violet gloves, the many-colored flowers in the gay streamered bonnet making a bright splash on the edge of the field. Evidently the things had been saturated in paraffin, for at the touch of the match they flamed furiously and Betty's dream danced skyward like a sudden flight of fiery birds. To Lucy it was as terrible a moment as any. She crawled, chilled, back into bed and did not stir till her mother was at her side, a hand on her shoulder. "Here's a cup o' tea."

She took up from that moment all her old service, but she did it with a grim and obvious resolution, a self-accusing persistence, that were more destroying than recrimination would have been. Rodda, we may be sure, kept his mouth shut, and Betty saw to it that no one else came near the shack. She was forever encountering Wesley, wandering sheepishly in the precincts, and frightening him with her gruff "Be off with you." She herself, when the moment came, delivered the child, and still no news of what had happened reached anyone in Porteven. It was at three o'clock on a mad March morning, with the wind rushing off the sea, over the roofs of Porteven, and shaking the timbers of the shack, that the child was born; and with the first flat light of day, the wind having died, Lucy lay in a great stillness and heard the crying of lambs coming out of the fields. It was so weak and forlorn and defenseless a crying that Lucy stirred in the bed and pulled the child to her, and her mother, who had been huddled over the fire, got up and said gruffly: "Oh, you're awake, are you? It's a boy."

The weather remained cold and still, and at intervals throughout the day Lucy could hear, coming from the enclosure where Rodda had made the bath, the sound of hammering: sharp, persistent, and somehow terrifying, as though a coffin were being made out there. As the daylight was dying, Betty dragged through the door an ungainly rude cradle on rockers that she had made from driftwood. She put it near the hearth and the firelight filled it and she sat down looking at it, testing the rockers with a gentle motion of her calloused hand, and suddenly dissolved in tears.

Lucy looked at her from the bed, full of love for her and full of sorrow, and said, rallying her, "Mother, don't cry. It's better than I thought. I thought it was a coffin."

Betty got up, wiping her eyes with her sack apron. "Well," she said dourly, "when you know all, there's not much to choose between them."

And after all, thought Lucy, three weeks later, things might be worse. There are three of us now instead of two, and that seems to be all that's happened. Indeed, in many ways life was lovely. She had made a good recovery and the child was lusty. March had stepped over into April and there were ravishing blue and white days with the larks singing and the leaf buds green on the hawthorns. True, her mother's oppressive taciturnity continued. She did all that needed to be done, never stirring far from the shack. She knitted and sewed for the child. There was a different collection of things to be assembled now from those that had flamed in the field. There was still the question of the moment that could not forever be avoided: the moment when this child must be seen by the world. Lucy did not know it, but that was a moment her mother did not intend to face. Betty had intended to show Porteven what such a woman as she could make of a daughter. Well, that was done with: she did not intend to show a fallen idol. And so, on the morning when the child was a month old, Lucy awoke to find that her mother was absent. She was not at first alarmed by this, but when she got out of bed she saw on the table a cocoa tin that she had known all her life. Use had rubbed it to a high shine. It was Betty's money box. Where it was hidden Lucy did not know. It appeared at moments of crisis, when Betty would count her savings to see whether she could do this or that. Then it would disappear again into some secret place. Now there it was, placed where she was intended to see it, and she pulled off the lid, aware that she was frightened by the significance of the box appearing in this way. She shook out onto the table three gold sovereigns, a few shillings, a lot of pence and ha'pence. There was nothing else, no message, except the obvious message of this gesture. "Well, here you are. This is the last I can do for you."

The proud woman had no use for failure, and she did not intend to stand by and endure the knowledge that the people she had always flouted were laughing in their sleeves. She was well able to look after herself, and now Lucy could learn to do the same. All this Lucy well understood, standing by the table with the worn tin box in her hand and the coins scattered beneath her tears.

3

"I don't want you to come till I'm properly settled in," Whaley had said. Old Man Bennetts was gone from the lodge by the lake and here Maggie Whale was establishing herself, with Lucy Evans for her maid and young Merlin spending most of his time lying in the sun on a blanket on the lawn. This was how Father had dealt with Lucy's problem. The girl was quite unfit to live like her mother by her own resources. Since Betty's disappearance, things with her had gone from bad to worse. She was living on the charity of Dr. Curnow and a few neighbors and making constant raids, with the child in her arms, toward Eddy Rodda's lodge. Eddy always managed to disappear, and Wesley, whose infatuation had been deepened by the girl's misfortune, would follow her along the cliff and through the village, providing a public entertainment that Father thought had better come to an end.

When I saw Lucy on my first morning at Tresant, there had been nothing but a back retreating before Mrs. Rodda's vituperation. Now I was able to look at her closely. Sally and I, informed that the time for beginning lessons had arrived, walked to Maggie Whale's lodge on a June morning. It was customary to Sally, but to me all new. When we got there, I could not but stand and stare. The footpath to the big house ran in front of the cottage garden, and on the other side of this footpath was the lawn that sloped down to the boathouse, with the lake, here at its widest, reaching away to the low hills on the other side. The water lilies were out now, growing so densely that they made islands colored with red and creamy flowers, resting like cups upon the dark green saucers of leaves stained with burgundy-crimson.

We turned at Whaley's voice, and there she was coming through the granite porch of the cottage. "Well," she asked, "don't you think I'm lucky to have a place like this?"

She was. We stood for a moment in her small garden. There was no sound that was not enchanting: the June drone of insects, the calling of birds. Across the water we could see men swinging their scythes in a field on the hill.

"Come in," Whaley said.

We went into the cool solid cottage. Whaley had turned the room on the right of the entrance passage into her workroom. It was white-washed and had little in it save her books, a table with a writing chair, and an easy chair by the fireplace. The curtains were of bright chintz. Over the fireplace was the only picture in the room: a portrait of a woman painted in pale colors.

"That's Mrs. Undridge!" I exclaimed.

"Yes," said Whaley. "It reached me the other day: a present from the Undridges for having looked after Daniel last winter. I don't as a rule like Mr. Undridge's pictures, but this is not bad."

Certainly, it was not bad at all. "There's a letter from them," Maggie Whale added. "They apologize for landing the boy on us, but explain that Mrs. Undridge was expecting a baby when we descended on them. I don't see why they couldn't have told me at the time. Anyhow, they thought it would be a good idea to have Daniel out of the way till things settled down again. Now he has a sister named Marie."

Well, it was that morning that I took stock of Lucy Evans. Maggie Whale must have been a remarkable person in many ways. At that time it was almost unthinkable that one should employ a servant without dressing her up in uniform. But this girl was not in uniform, nor did Whaley ever, so far as I know, call her a servant. She said to me that morning: "Sarah, this is Lucy Evans who is sharing the lodge with me. That's her son out there kicking on the grass. We call him Merlin, and he's certainly a wizard."

I found myself shaking hands with a cowlike girl wearing such clothes as any girl might wear in summer in the country. When I call Lucy cowlike I am not being rude but complimentary. After all, Hera was called oxeyed; and the sort of cow Lucy made me think of was one of those slim beautifully-colored Guernseys whose eyes are enormous, trustful and velvety. Lucy was utter docility and placidity.

Maggie couldn't have charge of any young person, in any capacity, without applying her own methods of education, adapted to the case. "What on earth could I have done with Lucy," she said later, "except be a friend to her? She was so helpless. All her life long her mother had been her servant. She was the most pampered little thing you ever met. And then the bottom fell out of it all. She was in a dreadful state when she came to me. To have treated her like a menial, ordering her to do things she had never done in her life, would have made her sullen and useless. At the same time, I had no intention of going on as that fool of a woman had done and treating her like a doll. So we did everything together, the cleaning and the cooking and our little bit of gardening, and all the rest of it. We always had meals together. The only thing is," Maggie grinned, "that I never helped with the feeding of Master Merlin, and Lucy never helped with the writing."

All through that summer, down at Tresant we went about in a
bunch: Whaley, Lucy, Sally and I, with Merlin in a pram that we
took turns to push, and Sally and I became accustomed to seeing Lucy,
sitting under a hedge or on a log by the lake, bare her breast and feed
the child. We would watch fascinated and count it a privilege to be
permitted, when he was full, to wipe away the milky dew that hung
on the wet bud of his mouth. Merlin gave little trouble. He was as
placid as his mother. Or, with a meal in a hamper, we would all
get into the punt and paddle about among the water lilies, and eat
our meal on the shore of some small bay of the lake, with the child
lying on a blanket and Lucy languidly fanning the flies from his face
with a burdock leaf. Then I would take my swimming lesson from
Sally, who was like a fish in the water.

There were lessons given in Maggie Whale's own fashion. Our
habit was to eat breakfast at the house and then to walk to Maggie's
cottage. We would get there at about ten, and from then till one o'clock
we would have lessons either in the cottage or on the lawn by the boathouse. We read and drew and wrote little essays and chattered, either
in English or bad French, though in time we got to read French well
enough; but the main thing, as I remember it, was that we learned to
like to read. Once you have done that, it is as though you had learned
to like walking. All territories are open to you.

Lucy Evans joined us in our lessons. She could read and write as
well as we could. It was she, of all people, who introduced Malory
into our reading. She had a battered copy of the *Morte d'Arthur*
that her mother had given her, and where Betty Evans had picked
that up goodness knows. From it Lucy had taken the name Merlin
for her son. I remember clearly a morning when the summer was
fully advanced—it must have been in August—and we were sprawled
on the lawn, with the child among us, passing the book from hand
to hand and reading in turns. Suddenly, Lucy was gone. Without a
word, picking up the baby, she fled into the lodge. It was my turn
to read. Lying on my stomach, with my hands cupping my chin,
and the book on the grass before me, I was at once kicking my heels
in the air and reading, when Whaley rose to her feet, saying: "Just
a moment, Sarah." I stopped and got up, and then I saw that Lucy
and the child were gone. And coming toward us, looking pale and
worried, swinging a straw frail in his hand, was Wesley Rodda.

We all knew that there was trouble in the Rodda household. On
Saturdays and Sundays there were no lessons, and Sally and I, on our
ponies or afoot, wandered the countryside. Some time before this

apparition of Wesley at Maggie's lodge, we had been walking in the country behind Porteven when Sally proposed that we should go and look at the shack where Lucy had for so long lived. We wandered down the lane, climbed through the gap in the hedge, and to our surprise ran into Wesley Rodda. He was sitting moodily on the bench outside the shack, gazing at the glittering sea. Even to us two children, there was something so smitten and dejected in his air, his hands hanging between his knees, his shoulders bowed, that we felt a surge of pity, and Sally cried: "Hallo, Wesley! What's the matter with you?"

He heaved himself up with a sigh and denied what was obvious. "Matter, Miss Sally? Why, there be nothing the matter. A bit lonesome p'raps, here all by myself."

We thought he was speaking of the passing loneliness of the day and place; but he went on: "Well, what about a cup o' tea, seein' you're here? I'll have it ready in a minute."

He flung open the door of the shack, and Sally cried: "But you're not *living* here, Wesley?"

"Ay, that I be," he said emphatically. "Blessed is the man that walketh not in the way of the ungodly. I'll walk with him no longer. No, not I."

That was how we learned that Wesley was not living with his parents, and the rest of it soon came to our ears. Poor Mrs. Rodda, distraught between her two men, was now with the one, now the other, cooking and cleaning, trying to mend a situation that had passed beyond repair. When the fishing boat *Sally Gaylord* went out, Eddy and Wesley were still her crew, but they said in Porteven that, beyond what was necessary to the task in hand, those two spoke never a word to one another. When they came in they would part, one to walk to the lodge, one to the shack, and sometimes Mrs. Rodda would be there to meet them, and she would be distracted, not knowing which way to go.

Miss Whale went, rather hurriedly I thought, to meet our unexpected visitor. "Good morning, Wesley," she cried. "A bit off your beat, aren't you?"

He opened the frail he was carrying. "Good morning, Miss," he said. "I thought maybe you could do with a bit o' fresh fish. Caught'n myself. A good ole bass."

He had paused where she had met him, and there was a sense that she was blocking the way. "Why, thank you," she cried. "It's most kind of you. Sarah, will you take this into the kitchen and bring back the frail?"

I did so, and there was no sign of Lucy and the child anywhere in the house. When I returned with the frail the situation was uneasy. Neither Maggie nor Wesley had anything to say. They were just silently confronting one another. She gave him the frail and then took his arm and began to walk in the direction from which he had come. He allowed himself to be led off like a good but disappointed and rather sullen child. When they were out of earshot, I could see that Whaley was talking to him earnestly, still holding his arm and keeping him moving. Then she loosed him, and stood watching till his sad lonely figure was out of sight. She came back, and her voice trembled a little as she said: "Now, you two. Amuse yourselves for a bit," and she almost ran into the cottage. The perspicacious Sally said: "She'll be back when she's had her cry out."

5

From time to time we had news from my father and mother in London; then they went on to stay with friends in Scotland; and soon now they would be back in Tresant. "We shall, I fear, miss being with you on your birthday," Father wrote to Sally, "but we shall try to make up for that when we return, and I hope that you and Sarah will contrive to give yourselves a good time."

We gave ourselves a very different time from any that he could have expected.

It was on a Saturday in September that Sally and I were riding our ponies along that path through the wood and beside the lake which I had followed on my first morning at Tresant. Tomorrow would be her birthday. She was putting on a good pretense of being reconciled to Father's absence, but this was the first time, save for those years when he was in the Crimea, that they had spent the birthday apart. She decreed that there must be no celebration of any sort until his return: then we would have a retrospective birthday party.

And so as we rode through the wood we were keeping this matter out of our minds. It was one of the still days that come at that season. Everything had ceased to grow but had not yet begun to fall. The sky's blue was hazed and milky and the lake was untroubled by a ripple. We ambled along, making for the bar, where Sally would gallop and I potter; and then we were suddenly thrown into our adventure by a coincidence. At the very spot where, on my first walk there, I had seen a stoat run across the path, we saw one run that morning. It disappeared into the self-same bushes at the foot of the shaly cliff, and instantly my mind went back to that other occasion. I pulled up my pony and said: "I wonder whether that's the same stot?" Sally and I liked using these patois words.

"The same as what?" she asked.

I told her of that day's happening. "And when I began to poke about in the bushes, I looked up, and there was Captain Rodda: up there on top, among the pine trees. You remember? We came on together and found you and Whaley sitting on the wall."

"Yes. We'd been there a long time, and I wondered how Captain Rodda had got past without being seen. He's not supposed to be in the woods, you know, but he seems to think he can do as he likes."

"Everything was strange to me then," I said, "and I may have been mistaken; but I had a feeling that he didn't like me poking into those bushes. He came sliding down from the trees and almost carried me off."

"He's capable of anything," said Sally. "I've heard Father say so: 'That old pirate is capable of anything.'"

We had dismounted and tied the ponies to trees. "Let's have a look," Sally suggested. "It wouldn't surprise me to find him up to something."

She parted the thick growth of hazel and pushed through. "Hold back the bushes," she called over her shoulder. I did so, and Sally squirmed farther forward. "There's a hole—a cave of sorts," she said. I let the bushes fall behind me and followed her.

We could get easily enough through the hole, but a big man like Captain Eddy would have had to crouch. We found ourselves in a rock passage. It was dark, and we could tell what was about us only by touch. This revealed a ceiling just above our heads and rock walls about a yard apart. I was rather frightened in there in the dark, but I pressed on behind Sally, who went forward for about a dozen yards and then said: "I can't feel the roof any more, or the sides. It's a sort of rock chamber."

It was: not large, but, as we discovered, exploring with our hands, roughly circular. Presently Sally's foot kicked something and there was a clinking sound. She bent down and said "Bottles!" While she was doing this I stepped past her in the darkness, still feeling the walls, and moved into another passage like the one we had come through. "We can get out here, I think," I said, glad enough at the thought; and Sally said: "All right. Lead on. I'm bringing a bottle."

We emerged into the woods, pushing aside a thick curtain of ivy and old man's beard. Standing away and looking back at it, you would never guess what lay behind, for it made a small part of a cascade of this stuff falling down the side of a low acclivity a hundred yards along.

Sally sat down, holding the bottle, and began to laugh. "The old fox!" she said. "A bolt-hole either end! What a marvelous place!"

"But what's it for?" I asked innocently.

"To dodge the revenue men," she said and laughed again. "Father's a magistrate. Wouldn't it be fun to blow the gaff and have Eddy Rodda up before him for smuggling?"

Now I began to understand. I had heard of smugglers.

"But we couldn't get him," said Sally. "We couldn't prove a thing unless we saw him at it. And I wouldn't say anything anyway. But I'm sure Father guesses what he's up to. I remember a time when Eddy came back from France and Father said: 'What makes the fish so much better over there, Eddy?' and Eddy grinned and said: 'They smell better, my lord, and keep a bit of heart in you on cold nights.'" She fondled the bottle and added: "And so they do. Do you remember the hot red wine we used to drink with Whaley at Montreuil?"

Yes, I did; but what I didn't know, or Sally either, was that Whaley had seen to it that our "wine" was warm water, mildly colored. We both allowed our minds to dwell on those agreeable outings to the Café de l'Agriculture, with the hot food and the warm drink and the stove blinking its red eye; and suddenly Sally said: "Let's have a birthday party in the cave tomorrow! Just the two of us. We'll bring a lantern and something to eat. There'll be plenty to drink."

Alas! how true that was!

6

We took a basket into the fruit garden and picked pears and peaches from the espaliered walls. We scrounged cakes from the kitchen, and surreptitiously acquired two cups. We snatched a lantern from the stables and we set off. It was about four o'clock.

There was no reason why we should not have said that we were going to have a picnic in a cave that we had discovered, but somehow the adventure began in this spirit of furtiveness that changed to bravado once we were well away and walking along the path through the wood. There Sally began to sing in a loud voice some lines she had found goodness knows where:

> Belly and back go bare, go bare,
>   Hand and foot go cold,
> So long as I have good wine enough,
>   Whether it be new or old.

"We are going to fall into terrible temptation," she announced. "It will be Whaley's fault. She should never have given us a love of liquor."

She was running ahead, swinging the lantern, and I plodded behind, carrying the heavier basket. She looked back and urged me on. "Come along!" she cried. "We are going to carouse, and you must learn my song. I never liked a dolorous drinker."

However, I did not find it easy to come up to her reckless mood. It was not so long ago that I had been living in Portman Square, with every moment of my life supervised, every word I uttered watched. I couldn't take so easily to singing aloud in the woods about bare bellies. I remembered how my curiosity about belly buttons had produced a tremendous storm. And, incidentally, had produced Whaley, too. "Don't you think," I shouted, "we should have let Miss Whale know where we were going?"

Sally waited for me to catch up. "Miss Whale," she said, "is no doubt glad to see the back of us now and then. After all, she has her own life to think of. Perhaps she's writing a story for Mr. Dickens."

We were soon in the cavern. Sally struck a match and lit the candle in the lantern. We were able now to see just what the place came to, and for one thing we saw that we needn't have brought a lantern at all. There was one hanging from a hook in the roof. Sally lit that, too.

It was a roughly circular chamber, high enough for a man to stand upright in, and a big man, standing in the middle, could almost have touched the walls on either side. It was perfectly dry, but cold. It contained nothing but the lantern, a lot of corked bottles, and a small wooden keg with a spigot. Sally looked around her with satisfaction. "The smuggler's lair!" she exclaimed. "Well, we must make ourselves comfortable. We shall need something to lie on. Come with me."

She went out through the passage that led into the woods. The bracken was still green. We pulled up armfuls of it and carried it in. A summer storm had torn some branches from the pines, and these, too, we took into the cavern. They would only just go through the narrow passage. We hauled, and they swished behind us like peacocks' tails. With these laid against the wall and the bracken piled on them, we could recline—"like odalisques," said the imaginative Sally.

We laid on the floor in front of us the paper in which our provisions were wrapped and spread out the feast. "It is rather cold," said Sally. "We must warm ourselves with wine."

We did not know that brandy was the only wine in this cache. It was fortunate—or was it disastrous?—that some of the brandy was in the wooden keg, for we had not thought of bringing a corkscrew, and anyway I doubt if either of us would have had the strength to pull a cork out of a bottle. But there it was. Nothing need be done but turn the tap of the spigot. Sally did so and filled our cups to the brim. We sat there side by side, each holding a cup and Sally's eyes were dancing. "Your very good health, my dear sister," she said, with a grave inclination of the head, and we both drank.

We drank as though what we held was cold spring water on a thirsty day, and with one accord we put the cups down on the floor and looked at one another. Our throats were burning; we gasped.

"This is strong wine," said Sally, "stronger than we had in Montreuil."

She had come late to Montreuil. She had joined in only one of our expeditions to the Café de l'Agriculture. I, who had known them all, agreed that it was strong wine. Whaley had never given us anything like this.

"It must be a vintage wine," Sally proposed judiciously. "We must treat it with respect."

Our sensible inclination was to treat it with complete disavowal, to leave it there in the cups, but this was a birthday party and valor overcame discretion. We ate our fruit and cake, and as we ate we occasionally moistened our lips with a discreet sip. Taken that way, it was not so repulsive; and presently Sally began to giggle. "This is excellent tipple," she said. "I must ask Captain Rodda to give me the name of his wine merchant."

We had eaten all the food. I was not feeling cold now, and the cavern, with these branchy couches and the soft light of the lanterns, was even cozy. It seemed an excellent place for a sleep, and I wanted to sleep. Sally had become remote, and I hardly knew what she was talking about as she proposed that we should presently walk in to Porteven and attend evening service at the Methodist Chapel. She said she had never been there, but that no doubt we should meet Captain Eddy. We should be able to thank him for his hospitality.

And go there we did. That was the utterly disastrous end of this altogether disastrous afternoon. We didn't go at once. The desire for sleep was too much for me. Those discreet sips had mounted up, and, added to our first indiscreet swig, they had me lying full length, watching Sally lie down beside me; and presently I was in an unreal, uneasy sleep in which I could hear her muttering and feel her stirring restlessly at my side.

When I came to, one of the lanterns had burned out. The cavern was rather dark and I felt cold. My head ached. Sally was sitting up, rubbing her eyes and yawning. I felt dreadful and she looked dreadful. I even began to cry. "Let's go home. I want to go to bed."

Sally was in a terrible dogged mood. "Go if you want to," she said. "I'm going to Porteven."

The idea of going there appeared to obsess her. She said nothing more but scrambled through one of the passageways. I followed, unable to face the thought of going home alone. We were on the pathway where I had seen the stoat running. The evening was darkening toward sunset, and when we came onto the cliff path that led to Porteven all the western sky was a smother of mauves and lilacs and the dusk was marching over the water. It was a gorgeous and melancholy moment, and it made me feel so small and sick and lonely that I began to cry again. Sally was going ahead of me with a strange tottering walk that I was aware was afflicting me too. Presently she was approaching the doors of the repellent little gray-painted chapel. I hurried to catch up with her, and to hurry made me feel sicker than ever. I caught at her arm, and we went in together.

The sleep that the brandy had put on us had made us very late. The service was ending, and that means that for more than an hour the place had been filled with people. In Porteven and thereabout at that time Methodist chapels *were* filled. All these people had made the place hot, and the burning of oil lamps had made it hotter, and as I went in I was struck by a blast of fetid air that made my stomach heave anew. I rediscovered all the sensations that had bedeviled the end of my voyage in the *Sally Gaylord*. The noise didn't help. The congregation was singing the final hymn:

> *We think ourselves sincere;*
> *But show us, Lord, is every one*
> *Thy real worshipper?*

and this was a verse that Sally liked afterward to declaim, with great emphasis on "re-al worship*peer*."

At the time, it was no laughing matter. Wesley Rodda was in the pulpit, the light of a lamp that hung above his head falling upon his pale uplifted face. Mrs. Rodda was pedaling away sturdily at the harmonium, and Eddy was there as large as life, his earrings swinging and a hearty braying mouth open in the midst of his beard. These were the only three I knew, but Sally must have known them all, and they her. At our entrance heads were turned and I was aware of astonished looks as the fact became known that the Honorable Sally Gaylord and her stepsister had favored the chapel with their presence. Our appearance must have deepened the astonishment. We were disheveled and glassy-eyed. Moreover, Sally all this time had been carrying the kitchen basket and a lantern.

We stood between the wall and the rearmost pitch-pine seats. There was no room anywhere to sit down. When the hymn was ended, Wesley pronounced the benediction, the door behind us was thrown open, and people began to stream out. I was jostled by the crowd, and this jostling was my final undoing. I was revoltingly sick on the chapel floor.

I was not aware of much then except misery and shame till Captain Rodda put his arms round me and carried me through the door. This opened upon the street, and there amid a staring interested crowd I was sick again, and Sally was being sympathetically sick at my side. She was using the kitchen basket, as a sick but good-mannered horse might use his nose bag. It must have been a great evening for Porteven, and what would have happened to us I don't know if Dr. Curnow had not chanced to pass by. He was a bachelor and his house was but a stone's throw away. He gave us one glance, then picked up Sally and moved off with her, Eddy Rodda following with me. Five minutes later we were lying side by side in a large bed warmed by bricks wrapped in flannel, our stomachs already feeling soothed by something the doctor had given us to drink. I think it must have been opiate as well as sedative, for we were soon asleep.

CHAPTER EIGHT

1

I REMEMBER how Father, when we left Montreuil, gave a brooch to our maidservant, whom he had not seen before and was not likely to see again; and I remember how, when he came home that autumn, he brought for Lucy's child a rattle of ivory and silver. There was something for each of us: for Whaley splendid sheets of quarto paper; for Sally a workbasket, silken lined, which she loved with a passion as great as her apparent resolve never to use it; for me a useless lovely bauble, a silver-gilt bird with ruby eyes; for Lucy attractive materials that she could make into clothes. And then, when I thought that that was all, out came Merlin's rattle. Who else would have remembered little Merlin? Oh, how I loved him! Lucy's face was radiant as she jangled the pretty silver bells.

All these presents were unpacked in Whaley's cottage. On the day after his return, Father had walked down there with Sally and me. Mother had not come. She looked beautiful and happy, but from this time of her return she did not go out much, and not at all in the afternoons. She rested. Sally said: "I expect she's going to have a baby."

Whaley had prepared tea, and after that there was the unpacking ceremony, and then the four of us sat on the lawn by the lake. It was late autumn, but still warm enough.

And now the dread story of our drunkenness came out. It was like Whaley, I thought, to lose no time and to tell of the whole matter frankly and simply. When she had finished, Father said to Sally: "Where did you find this stuff?"

This was something we had told no one. Dr. Curnow had asked us and Whaley had asked us, but we had held our tongues. However, we had decided between ourselves that, if Father asked us, we would tell. And now Sally did so.

All that Father said then was: "We will go into the matter tomorrow. Sally and Sarah, say nothing of this to your mother. Miss Whale, please be at the house at ten in the morning."

I remembered that he was a magistrate; he was magisterial now, and we were all subdued. He was calm but cold, and we would have preferred a fiery outburst. The joys of the present-giving evaporated.

It was a subdued column of three that trailed behind him on the following morning. He must have been thinking things over, for he stopped and asked when we came up with him: "You say you brought away the lantern that was in the cave. Where is it now?"

We didn't know. Sally didn't remember taking it with her when we went to Dr. Curnow's. "A pity," he grumbled and strode ahead again.

Certainly, it had not returned to the cave. We saw that as soon as we got there. Father hung up the lantern he had brought. The one we had picked up in the stables was hanging from its hook, and that was all that the cave contained. The bottles were gone, and so were the branchy beds we had lain on. Sally and I exclaimed in surprise, and for the first time since hearing our story he smiled. "You didn't think, did you," he asked, "that the old fox would have done nothing in all this time?"

I can imagine what the magisterial mind was thinking. No bottles; no lantern; no evidence. Of course, these two children could swear to the bottles and to the *kind* of lantern, and there are plenty of people who know that a lantern of that kind belongs to Eddy Rodda. But I certainly don't intend to ask these two to give evidence in a public court, and even if Eddy were convicted, he would merely find another hiding place. Besides, he might have added to himself with a grin, I've bought the stuff from Rodda myself. Cornishmen never took a harsh view of a smuggler.

So we put out the lantern and went back to the pathway beside the lake and wandered on in the direction of Eddy's lodge. We met him there, gazing out to sea; and he and Father exchanged polite greetings. Eddy hoped that his lordship had enjoyed his stay in London and that her ladyship was well; and Father inquired about Mrs. Rodda and Wesley. Then we began to walk back the way we had come and Father kept Eddy in conversation, so that he had to walk with us. When we were near my stot hole, Father shouted to us children, who had gone ahead: "Here, you two! Here's something I brought from London for you."

We looked back and saw him tossing a rubber ball from hand to hand. This surprised us: it was such a childish thing, not at all the sort of gift he would bring; but he shouted: "Here you are!" and threw the ball. It didn't reach us, but went into the bushes that hid the passage. We ran to retrieve it, but he shouted: "You'll scratch yourselves there. Let me get it," and a moment later he was calling over his shoulder: "Hallo! There's quite a passageway here!"

And that is how all of us, including Eddy, found ourselves in the cave. Eddy struck a match and exclaimed coolly: "Looks as if someone uses this li'l ole place. Here's a lantern." And then, with amazement: "One o' your lordship's, too, by the look of 'n. Now who's up to what, I wonder?"

Father looked around him. "Another way out here," he said, and made his way through. "It leads into the woods," he reported, returning presently.

He and Rodda looked at one another without a blink. "It would be a handy place for a smuggler," Father said.

Rodda glanced appraisingly round. "Made for it," he admitted. "But I can't imagine," he added with grave deference, "that anyone knowing your lordship would do such a thing on your lordship's land."

"No," Father answered. "Of course, there's no evidence at all that it's used for such a purpose, but, if it is, I suppose the offender comes from far afield. Anyway, when you're about the woods at night you might keep your eyes open."

"Me about the woods at night! Your lordship!"

"My dear Rodda," said Father blandly, "I'm suggesting nothing except that you might be in the habit of taking an occasional moonlight stroll like the rest of us."

"I spend nights enough on the water. When I'm ashore there's my ole bed an' I like to get into'n."

"That's a sensible fellow. I wish everybody was as wise."

We said good-by to Eddy on the path, and as we walked homeward Father said: "Well, we've frightened him off that, but he'll find another place. I'm afraid that's all it comes to." He added presently: "Now, Sally and Sarah, run ahead. I wish to speak privately with Miss Whale."

The consequence of this talk was that our solitary week-end rides and rambles came to an end. A groom was always behind us when we rode and Whaley with us when we walked. Whether the desperate affair ever reached Mother's ears I do not know. She said nothing about it.

2

However, Porteven said a great deal about it, following a sermon by Wesley Rodda. Wesley, like everyone else, knew who was the father of Lucy Evans's child. The little scene on the quay at Brest was enough to show anyone how Wesley suffered at sight of his father's ways, and now that those ways so poignantly involved himself he sat in his hut overlooking Porteven, brooding upon Eddy's sins like a prophet brooding over the wickedness of all mankind. He had always been considered queer; now he became *exalté*. His slow-moving mind remembered the lantern which he had seen in Sally's hand and ponderously in time connected it with the smuggling operations which he knew his father engaged in. How could he not know, seeing that the stuff came aboard under his eyes? But that was all he would have to do with it. The Scriptures warned him that strong drink was raging, and he would not touch it.

Once he was convinced that Eddy was concerned in this new outrage, all that he had suffered on account of Lucy Evans swelled like a flood behind his determination to denounce his father; and he did so in a sermon on the text: "Whoso shall cause one of these little ones to stumble, it is profitable for him that a great millstone should be hanged about his neck and that he should be sunk in the depth of the sea."

We learned of this from the young groom who rode with us, a devout attendant at the Porteven chapel. Even Wesley in the mood that held him could not bring himself to mention his father by name, but no one doubted what was in the young preacher's mind or that the little ones who had been caused to stumble were Lucy Evans, Sally and myself.

What Eddy Rodda's thoughts were on hearing himself denounced, I cannot say, but what happened a little later made it clear that at any rate the sermon did not "convert" him. He never was a smuggler on the grand scale—on the scale of those who made a business of it and accumulated large profits. But he could not resist the temptation to buy brandy cheap—a few dozen bottles now and then taken aboard a mile or so off the French coast—and to sell it here and there about Porteven. And so it happened when that autumn passed into winter. It was still dark when the *Sally Gaylord* approached the harbor. But she did not sail into it. She made for the long beach to the east, and Eddy paddled quietly ashore in the dinghy. He concealed his bottles in a cleft of the rocks which he had always used for this purpose. It would serve till he could remove them to a safer, more permanent hiding place. But that was something he had not yet found. He rowed back to the ship. The tide was rising. By the time it was light no trace of his footprints would be left on the sand. He made out to sea then, and innocently sailed into harbor with the dawn.

That was a Saturday morning. In the course of the day Eddy had decided where to hide the bottles. The simplicity of the idea must have amused him. The next night he was missing from the Methodist chapel. Wesley was "planned," as the Methodists say, to preach at a chapel a few miles away, and so the coast was clear. Captain Rodda placed his bottles in the bath that he had dug for Betty Evans, the bath from which he had lifted Lucy, and he covered them with a layer of gravel. By the morning, you would see nothing but the clear water lying upon the pebbles.

You see, there was nothing romantic about Captain Rodda's smuggling. It did not make a story of mules struggling up cliff paths, curses and shots in the night, and all the rest of it. It was not a business: it was the outcome of a normal human inclination to diddle Authority and to make a bit of pocket money while doing so. But it had unfortunate consequences all the same.

The next day was clear and sunny: the sort of day when Wesley's hermit life was not so bad. There was no need to pity him: he was a person with an inclination to solitude. He came out in mid-morning to fill a kettle at the bath and stood there listening to the lisp of the water over the sill and watching the play of light on the gravel. His eye was caught by a blue flash among the white and yellow stones. For a moment he thought nothing of this; then suddenly he knew what it was. He had seen it often enough: a big turquoise from the barbaric earrings that his father habitually wore. He took a stick and tried to flick it out of the water, but succeeded only in sinking it deeper. He went indoors, put on his long sea boots, and rolled his shirt sleeves above his elbows. Then he came back and stepped into the pool. He thrust down his hand, searching among the gravel, and, disturbing this, he disclosed a bottle. Soon he had them all out, and the turquoise, too.

If he had been able to take a rational view of the matter, it would have been better for him; but his mind became obsessed by his own interpretation of what had happened. This was his father's revenge for the sermon he had preached. The brandy had been "planted" on him, and no doubt the revenue officials would be privily informed where to find it. All alone up there in the shack above the village, he must have spent a morbid day, going over and over in his mind the events that had begun on the morning when Lucy Evans smiled on him in Porteven and that had now reached this dreadful end.

He emptied most of the brandy into a ditch, but two bottles he kept as a token of his discovery. That night he carried them down to Eddy's lodge, laid them on the doorstep, and smashed them with a stone. He placed the turquoise amid the splintered glass, and returned to his shack satisfied, no doubt, that he had well expressed his view of a villain.

Poor Eddy! Anyone less villainous, but more full of human folly and bombast, I have never known. But from then the breach was final. Wesley never again sailed in the *Sally Gaylord*.

3

It was all moving to an end as the winter came on, but this was still hidden from us. There was a day when, for those parts, the weather was harsh and cold. The woods were leafless and the lake was leaden. We walked with Whaley into Porteven. It was a favorite walk of ours: by the road to the village, back along the cliffs to Eddy Rodda's lodge, and home through the woods by the lake. All Porteven was busy with the pilchards. They lay in salted mounds upon the quay: rectangular heaps shaped like the clamps of root crops that you see on a farm. We had been upon the cliffs, Sally and I, when the huer had raised his cry, and we had watched the seine boats go out into the sea where the fish boiled and bubbled in their millions, making a turbulence like the wake of a great ship. The nets went down and drew them to the surface, and then there was such a bailing and dipping with buckets and baskets that, when the boats came ashore, their gunwales were wallowing almost at water level and they were solid with the scaly suffocated mass of the fish. These were shoveled out upon the quay and the women and children, working furiously among the screaming maddening gulls, piled them, layered with salt, into the masses we now saw. The piles had been thatched, but now that the pilchards were well pickled the thatch had been taken away and all hands were engaged in stowing the fish into baskets. There were stones like the ones that curlers use when they play upon the ice, and these, suspended by ropes to levers, pressed the fish into the baskets.

A cold wind blowing off the sea sneaked in here, and Whaley did not allow us to linger long, but we were there long enough to observe Eddy Rodda working at one end of the clamp and Wesley at the other. You may be sure it was not chance that had separated them. They did not so much as look at one another. The men and women were singing as they worked, and as usual it was a hymn. Eddy and Wesley were singing with the rest, Wesley with a grave concentration, Eddy with bravado and self-display. We watched for a while, and were then about to move off when one of the men cried to Sally: "Well, my little maid, be 'e sober today?"

Some of the people laughed, some looked ashamed, and among them all there was a sudden hold of the breath. Something had been put into words that had not been named before, at any rate not to

115

us and not, I am sure, to Eddy Rodda. But it was not Eddy, it was Wesley, who reacted as sharply as though the man had struck him. He walked to the middle of the line, stuck out his chin aggressively toward this man, and said: "You don't belong to talk like that to the maiden."

I don't think the fellow had meant any harm. It had been a carelessly spoken word, and he seemed surprised to find it taken so much amiss. Especially it must have been surprising to see the gentle Wesley thrusting out his jaw like a prizefighter—surprising and irresistible, for the man drew back a few feet and gave Wesley a blow that landed him flat upon the salty mound of fish. It was not much of a blow: Wesley was not hurt: he got up and began to walk back to his place at the end of the clamp. But the effect upon Captain Rodda was astounding. He stood for a moment as though he could not believe what he had seen; then he launched his great weight forward and fell upon the man. His fist went into the man's mouth like a hammer, and a spatter of blood stained the gray-white pile of pilchards. Eddy did not give a chance of recovery. His attack was so swift and surprising that no one intervened. He smacked blow after blow into the man's face till I felt sick to see the bloody mess it was in. Miss Whale was audibly groaning. She took my hand and Sally's and began to tug us away. I was nauseated by the bloodshed and ready enough to go, but Sally broke loose and ran into the melée. While everyone else stood paralyzed by this orgy of violence in which (it seems to me now) Eddy was releasing his own self-loathing, she took him by the sleeve and shouted in a sharp imperious voice: "Rodda! Stop this! Stop it at once!"

And he did. The sound of her voice recalled him from whatever privy madhouse he was loose in. His hands dropped to his sides, the knuckles red. He looked down at them, then rubbed them on his jersey. The man he had battered walked away. Eddy went back to his place at the end of the clamp and looked down the line of workers to his son. "You all right, Wesley?" he asked. Wesley did not answer. The work began again, but now there was no singing. As we moved off with Whaley through that gray lowering afternoon, we could feel the tension behind us pressing on our backs. I, at least, was glad to go, to reach the cliff path where the wind met us, wholesome off the miles of toppling water.

4

Sally left us and went down a zigzag track that led from the cliff to the beach. We could see her down there, keeping pace with our own progress, but close to the sea. The wind was southerly, so that it was behind the rising tide, and the rollers came in piling up into bottle-green concavities, crested with tossing gray. They towered and curled and fell with a smashing reverberation. But before they fell the wind caught the crests and tore them off the waves and blew them inshore in mist and spindrift. Sally was enveloped in this gray curtain. She ran through it blithely as the little sandpipers run, scrounging their food on the edge of a rising sea.

We were approaching Rodda's lodge, and the thunder of the water on the bar beyond it reached us. It was like the booming of guns. We ran down the path near the lodge, with the wind snatching at our clothes, and Sally joined us there as we stood with the incessant blow making us breathless, looking out upon the majestic confusion. Our clothes pressed upon us in front, streamed out behind, so that we leaned upon the weather like figureheads. "It's worsening," Sally shouted above the uproar, and if it could get worse than this then, I thought, it would be bad indeed. In the foreground were these perpetually smashing rollers that made the earth tremble beneath our feet and that ran back with a hiss and rattle of pebbles that were everlastingly caught up again and hurled ashore by the next wave. Farther out, the sea was a somber heaving tumult and the spume upon it seemed to unite it in one menace with the torn and streaming gray rags of the sky. The evening was coming quickly on. A wild distraught pallor in the west was all that spoke of sunset, and here and there a gull plunged and swerved, making the wind almost visible.

Sally's face was aglow. "When this starts," she shouted, "it usually goes on for days. Isn't it gorgeous?"

To the east, where the land sloped up gradually out of the bar, the darkness was taking hold. Indeed, you could not now see that land's beginning: you could see only grayness merging into blackness, and out of this, as if putting aside a curtain and so coming into sight, appeared my father riding upon his horse Peter, who had carried him at Balaclava. One would have said the weather had seized upon his spirit, as it had upon Sally's; he rode madly. That hard-beaten sand was a wonderful place for such exercise, and he came down upon us in a pounding gallop, that made my romantic heart beat wildly as I thought that thus, with hundreds of others, he and this horse had charged through a Russian valley to its narrowing throat stopped with guns. And the sound of these waves might be the sound of guns, this tattered sky the smoking wrack of battle. He gave a great shout as he went past us with a creak of leather, a panting of the horse's breath, a streaming of its tail. Then he came more slowly back, passed us without a word, and turned Peter's head toward the water.

Sally now was almost literally dancing with excitement. "Watch this!" she shouted. "It's wonderful!"

"He's never going into the sea!" Whaley cried.

"Oh, yes!" Sally said. "He often does. He likes to think that Peter will do *anything* for him."

Now the horse was going in a slow canter toward the water, moving straight into the wind, tossing his head up and down, and the wind was tossing the mane, and the tail was a wonderful streamed conclusion of the line of neck and back that flowed as if the wind had drawn it. His ears were pricked forward, and the wind brought back to us the snorting of his flared nostrils. In that wide solitude there was something profound and elemental in the moment as the man leaned on the neck of the gray horse, soothing and whispering to him, and the horse slowly approached the gray sea. For now all was gray. The green had been dredged out of the hollows of the waves. They were black, and only their torn cockscombs had a livid whiteness that flung itself despairingly above the thunder on the bar.

Whaley and I caught our breath when at last Peter's proud feet went into the water. In a moment he was among the breakers and I did not see how he could survive what was happening there. It was as though all the Atlantic were boiling in rage at the affront, pushing the waves forward in endless echelons to sweep this puny invader back whence he had come. My heart contracted with fear, for the gray horse and the gray sea were hard to disentangle and the immense undulation held valleys in which horse and rider from time to time disappeared.

A man went past us, and I saw that it was Captain Rodda. He ran down to the water's edge and stood there amid the wreckage of shattered waves, peering seaward. There was nothing he could do, but it comforted me to see him there. I felt sure—and feel sure now— that had that struggling unity of man and horse toppled and over- turned he would have thrown himself into the waves and tried to beat a way to them, hopeless and forlorn though the effort might be. But there was no call for that. Incredibly and unconquerably, they were returning; as they were lifted up to a wave's summit it was com- forting now to see Peter's head and not his rump. The three of us ran then and joined Captain Rodda among the spindrift's drenching, reckoning nothing of this in the relief that warmed us. Man and horse were heavily panting. Captain Rodda shouted: "You're mad, Burnage!" and Father answered with a laugh: "It's a moment for brandy, Rodda. I must be off home."

He leaned down and picked up Sally, swung her onto the saddle in front of him and cantered off. Rodda went, too, without a word to us; and, following after, clutching Maggie's hand, I felt as desolate as on that day when I was left behind in Hyde Park and he had dis- appeared into the May morning driving the four-in-hand. "Of course he would pick up Sally. Why should he pick up *you?*" I asked myself reasonably as we walked through the dark woods. But I wished all the same that he had picked up me.

5

Sally was right. The weather worsened. For the first time in my life I understood the power of wind and water. The boats remained locked in Porteven harbor. Life there was half suspended, as though a devil were raging and nothing could be done until it pleased him to depart. Even in Tresant, with the shoulder of the cliff and the woods between us and the sea, the wind that rushed shoreward was frightening, to me at any rate, screaming and sobbing high above the roofs as if mortified at being unable to reach us. Trees crashed in the woods, and as I lay awake listening to the insensate commotion it would sometimes be threaded by the crying of the curlews. This has always seemed to me the most disembodied cry in nature, the cry of loneliness itself, beautiful, forlorn, and inhuman; and, child though I was, it stirred in me vague but disturbing visions of a world in which men were done with, and the seas raged upon uninhabited and desolate shores, shores without footprints, the dead moon gleaming and the curlews crying.

I hardly slept through those nights when the storm raged. Even today, however far inland I may be, the cry of the wind is the one thing that will keep me awake at night, my imagination breasting through it, as Peter breasted through the waves, back to its source above the hills and hollows of a troubled sea. Because out on the sea are the boats, and men in them: the men who have been caught too far from a landfall and lie under the stress with their salty eyelids straining for the first wan blink of day. If you have lived by the sea, if you have ever had men on the sea, you cannot be cozy when the winds and tides unite in rage.

My mother knew the effect the weather was having upon me, and one night, to my joy, she came into my room, with a dressing gown tied about her, and carrying a lamp. She shut the door quietly, put the lamp on a table, and sat upon the edge of my bed. Oh, it was blessedness, as on those evenings in Mercy Kite's time when she would come in dressed for some grand occasion and say good night to me. She placed a hand upon my forehead and said: "You feel hot, darling. Can't you sleep?"

"No," I said, seizing her hand and holding it close; "I can't sleep with this going on, but when it's over I shall sleep like a log, night after night."

We remained quiet for a while, listening to the shrieking of the wind. Even in here, my windows rattled like teeth in a head whose throat is seized and shaken. She began to stroke my hand, and suddenly she asked: "Are you happy?"

"Oh, how can you ask?" I cried; and she said: "Well, I feel rather responsible. I turned your life upside down, didn't I? One is always snatching after one's own happiness without thinking much about other people."

She seemed to be talking as much to herself as to me; and I said: "I've been happier at Tresant than anywhere else in the world."

She smiled at that, and said: "Poor darling! What do you know of the world?" and I cried impulsively: "Oh, I don't know and I don't care what else there is in the world. I know I *couldn't* be happier than I am now."

The lamplight was falling on her face. I thought she looked more tranquil and content than I had ever seen her. "Wouldn't you be happier if you had a brother?" she asked.

"I would do my best to be happier," I said sturdily, "but it would be difficult."

"You're a quaint creature, Sarah. I want you to know that you will have a brother—very soon now."

"He will only be my half brother," I said, "and Sally's half brother"; and my Father, who had come in and heard this last exchange, said: "Well, that will be splendid. You'll have a whole brother between you."

He stroked Mother's hair and said: "You're pretty certain, aren't you, that it'll be a boy?"

"Oh, yes," she answered. "I have no doubt at all about that."

"Very well, then," he said. "We'll call him Justin. Now come to bed."

"In a moment. I must try and get Sarah to sleep."

He kissed me and her and went; and for some time she sat there, stroking my forehead, fondling my hand, and crooning a song to me. It was something she had never done before, and it soothed me and I slept. When I woke the wind had ceased to howl. The countryside was quiet, as if recovering from a fever.

6

This respite did not last long. It was on a Monday morning that I awoke to find the world so still; in the middle of the week the wind began to blow in occasional fitful gusts; and by the week's end the frantic madness was there again. Our few days of grace were lovely. Such deep agitation had been imparted to the sea that it continued to roll and swing tremendously; but the lake calmed and reflected the pale blue winter sky, and in the woods there was silence. The great trees were stripped down to bone; but not black bone, for they harbored many living things. Lichens of sage-green, red and yellow starred the trunks, and where the branches sprang from the trunks saw-edged ferns sprouted in the crotches and even found sometimes a roothold along the lines of the branches themselves, feathering them from end to end. The ivy was looped about the trees in lustrous swags, and the sun, coming through, lit all this up, shining over the copper floor of dead bracken, onto the pewter beech boles, the white satin of birches, and the prehistoric-looking red alligator-hide of the pines. Here and there—and this was December—we found already a violet or two, and flowers of the winter heliotrope filled the air with their sweetness.

It was never dead in the woods: always this violent jostle of life was going on there; on the hazels already you could see the tight-fisted catkins that soon would be swinging in the air, gold-dusted with pollen.

We wandered that way, and past Eddy Rodda's lodge that had stood through the storm, as through so many, unprotected by so much as a twig or sapling. Up there, perched on its crag above the sea, it must have taken a terrible buffetting. It looked like a little fortress, part of the rock itself, gaunt and impregnable. Sally called to make a formal inquiry of Mrs. Rodda about how they had fared. She was always precise and punctilious in such matters. Eddy was not at home. Mrs. Rodda said he was gone in to Porteven, to repair the roof of Wesley's shack, which had been torn off in the gale.

We walked on, the three of us—for Sally and I were not allowed to wander without Whaley since the affair of the brandy—and we came to the shack and found a number of neighbors come to lend Wesley a hand. He must have had a wretched time, for the roof went early in the gale, but he had stayed there in his obstinate way, sheltering in a corner covered with tarpaulin, unable to sleep and seeing his few possessions drenched by the rain squalls that fell out of the cracks of the wind. He looked pale and exhausted, but his place was almost shipshape again by the time we got there, for he was liked and nobody seemed to have arrived without a plank or two, a saw and some nails, or other contribution to his rehousing. The work being almost done, the men stood there in the thin afternoon sunshine and talked of the gale and of chimney pots and roofs damaged in Porteven and of windows blown in.

" 'Er'll come back, too," one ancient prophesied. "Us 'aven't seen the last o' she," and this seemed to be the opinion of them all; and I heard the hope expressed that ships wouldn't be taken in by this lull and put to sea. "That'll be a dirty ole time if we 'ave to go out after 'n," said the ancient; and Sally told me he was a member of the lifeboat crew. It was hard to believe, so venerable he looked, as if a pipe in the chimney corner would be as much as he could handle.

Soon they all went save Eddy Rodda and Wesley. Eddy was occupying himself on the roof, standing on a short ladder, though obviously now there was nothing more to be done. Wesley looked at him without a word, then went inside. We peeped in and saw that already he had a fire in the grate. Some feel of comfort was creeping back into the place, though it still steamed with damp. Wesley put on the kettle and invited us to have a cup of tea. Over our heads we could hear the slow, sad, unnecessary hammering. Sally looked up, and, following her gaze, Wesley looked too; and instinctively Maggie Whale and I raised our eyes. It was as though we were all looking through the new planks, looking at the man on the roof. Sally said: "We will stay if you ask Captain Rodda."

Wesley's face darkened, and he turned toward the fire, saying nothing, showing us an obstinate back. His arm was along the mantelpiece that Eddy had put there for Betty Evans, and his face rested on his arm. He kicked morosely at a log.

We filed out in silence. Captain Rodda had climbed down from the roof and with the light ladder on his shoulder was already walking away toward Porteven and the cliff path to his lodge. We watched him for a moment, then set off in the other direction, going home by the road.

7

The wintry gleam in the woods was like the sweet smile of sanity between two bouts of raging madness. On the Thursday night as I was falling asleep I was aware of the wind making a fitful whimper, and in the morning it was blowing steadily. Doctor Curnow came riding out to see Mother, and I heard him and my father discussing the weather and prophesying that a gale would blow up. "It'll be here by tonight," Father said. "I shall be at Porteven in case I'm wanted."

"I don't advise it," the doctor answered. "You'd better stay here. This is where you may be wanted."

Father looked at him sharply. "Are you trying to tell me something disagreeable?"

"No. It's a matter of prudence, that's all."

"It's a matter of prudence for all the crew. Fortunately for anybody in trouble, they're not a prudent lot."

Doctor Curnow said stubbornly: "If the boat goes out tonight, you won't go with it if I can stop you." He mounted his horse and said:

"Let's hope it won't be necessary for anyone. I don't like the look of it. It's getting worse every moment. It'll be a filthy night."

The light went quickly that day. By four o'clock it was almost dark and the wind had risen to the force of a gale. A servant who had been in to Porteven came back with the news that a schooner had been sighted far out to sea, but driving in diagonally before the wind which was out of the southwest, and evidently in difficulty. The lifeboat crew was standing by. My father went out, and Sally and I followed him to the stables. They were beautifully "lew," as the Cornish say, meaning cozily sheltered. It was difficult in there to believe in the pandemonium on the other side of the hill. A few lanterns were burning and there was warmth and the comforting smell of the animals and the sound of their lazy stirring. A groom was hissing over his work with a curry comb. "Saddle Peter," Father said.

While this was being done, he pulled on sea boots and an oil-skin and put a sou'wester on his head. In this improbable riding kit, he walked out of the stables, mounted Peter the Great, and rode away. It was then about six o'clock. Rain had begun to fall heavily.

We went back toward the house, and as we approached it we could see away to the right a bobbing gleam close to the ground, which meant that someone was carrying a lantern along the path from Whaley's lodge. We waited to see who this might be, and it was Maggie herself, accompanied by Lucy Evans, who was carrying Merlin in a shawl covered over by a waterproof cape. When we were inside the house the candlelight showed us Lucy pale and distraught. There was a strange atmosphere in the house, as if everyone were torn two ways. It was known that Father had ridden away on Peter, and no one needed to be told why he was gone; and this attracted thought to the schooner which by now was becoming a terrible element in the lives of us all. In our imaginations we could see her, though from the shore now she would be invisible, so dark had it become; and we could see the men in her and the driven rain sweeping into their faces, and the torn ashen sky pressing down upon them, and the wind-maddened sea rising up above their heads and crashing down upon their decks and pouring in cascades over their gunwales. And all this was important to us because we knew that in Porteven Eddy Rodda and Wesley, and Lord Burnage and that little shriveled man who had been piping outside Wesley's shack: these and others would be waiting for Captain Rodda to decide when the moment had come.

All this, then, was tearing us one way as we loitered in the hall where a fire was burning and a gentle candle shine seemed odd and incongruous, for we could hear the storm increasing in fury, uttering every imaginable sort of daunting sound: shrieks and bellowings, poundings and long-drawn shuddering sobs. You would have said that the upper air was possessed not by one phenomenon but by an army of warring creatures, some powerful and aggressive, some weak and persecuted, but all yelling, crying, triumphing and despairing after their kinds. It was this that had brought Maggie to the house with the girl and child. So overwrought, she said, had Lucy Evans become, thinking of what even at this moment perhaps was beginning to happen, that she had decided to bring the girl here where she would at any rate have the consolation of numerous company. Lucy was now gone through to the kitchen.

My mother had not risen from her bed that day, and that is what was tearing us all the other way. Amid the tumult was a feeling that this should be a time of quiet, of expectancy, a time to listen for newborn cries, not for these maniac noises which suggested that aerial cities were being bombarded and were hurtling down in ruin. Dr. Curnow had been twice to the house that day; but I heard comments on the significance of old Mother Trenoweth's not having been brought in. Nothing, then, was expected that night. This ancient dame had helped Sally into the world, and most of the young people of Porteven, too.

It was impossible to settle down. We lingered in the hall for a time and then went upstairs to a room that Sally and I shared as a sitting room. It was a small and rather bare cell, but we were fond of it, and it was pleasing enough with the fire burning. We did our best to act as though this was a night like any other. Whaley had recently had leave to go to London. She had done what seemed miraculous to us two girls: written a whole book. It had been sent to Mr. Dickens and he had wished to meet her and discuss it with her, and it was soon to be published in his magazine. So there we sat with the gale howling and no light in the room save the light flickering from the fire upon Maggie's skirt as she sat in our only easy chair and we on the floor at her feet. Mr. Dickens had invited her to dinner, and she told us all about the glittering occasion, and the famous people who were there, and the candles rising out of artificial flowers and the general—"Well, my dears, I hate to say it, but I can only call it the general feeling of slightly vulgar show. I was glad to get back."

In the little room it seemed a long way off. We tried to be interested and Whaley tried to interest us; but she couldn't banish the present reality. Her words faltered as an exceptional shriek rose on the air, died away into a momentary silence, and was followed by a sudden hammering on the front door. We all started to our feet and with one accord ran downstairs. News—news—any news of what was happening in Porteven and out there where the schooner was fighting for life: this was what we really wanted, not chat about Mr. Dickens's artificial flowers. Perhaps now we should have it.

Over the front door of Tresant at that time there was a wall bracket supporting a glass frame within which an oil lamp was contained. It was at any time an insufficient arrangement, and that night, as we stood just within the door that had been opened, it confused rather than lighted what we looked upon, for the wind had the little smoky flame dancing. The foliage of the jasmine that grew around the door framed a great depth of howling darkness, and in the foreground such fugitive gleams as there were fell upon the rain-glistened flanks of Dr. Curnow's pony and the spokes of his gig wheels. The gig's headlamps made two cones of light through which the rods of the rain whipped and shone. A veering wind gust threw a splash into our faces. The reality of what was outside seemed to come into the house.

Dr. Curnow was helping someone out of the gig, and presently they stood there on the gravel, fitfully illuminated, both of them cloaked and caped and hooded, bulky awkward figures in the wind and the rain. A groom had appeared, and the doctor asked him to take charge of the pony and gig. Then he came in with Mrs. Trenoweth, and we gratefully banged the door. Mrs. Trenoweth was taken through to the kitchen and the doctor shed his cocoon. Whaley asked if he wished to see her ladyship, and he said not at once, but he thought it well to be on hand. Possibly he would stay through the night.

Somehow, we all felt happier. He was in the nature of reinforcements coming to a beleaguered garrison; and almost gaily we led him to our little room. We had sandwiches sent up, with wine for him and Whaley and tea for me and Sally, and we installed him in the chair and grouped ourselves on the floor about him.

"Where is his lordship?" Whaley asked; and the doctor answered: "I don't know. He has promised me not to go out with the boat, but what else he may decide to do I can't say."

He said that the lifeboat had not gone out when he left Porteven. The schooner had sent up a rocket or two from which it could be gauged that she was being borne irresistibly shoreward; she would no doubt put down anchors when the moment came, but they were not likely to hold in such weather as this; and if she went ashore Eddy Rodda had calculated it would be on the bar. But Eddy wouldn't wait for that. When she was near enough, he would order the boat out to her. Perhaps by this time he had done so.

It was now eight o'clock, and I at any rate was beginning to feel as though I had been physically buffeted for hours. The roaring of the wind over the house had reached a monotonous intensity, as though an unending railway train were rushing through the air. Outside our window we could hear an elm thrashing its arms and groaning as if a great force were trying to lift its roots out of the ground. I asked the doctor if he thought the storm had reached its height, and he said he doubted it.

"There's one thing," he said to Whaley; "if the boat goes out it may end this ridiculous business between the Roddas. They'll be in the same boat once more, and that may knock some sense into their heads."

"Have you seen them tonight?" Whaley asked; and he said: "Yes, they're there with the others. The old man's praying for a look of recognition, and Wesley's praying God not to let him fall into the temptation of knowing his father. P'raps God'll have a word to say to him on the judgment of sinners before this night's over."

We talked for an hour or so, and then Dr. Curnow said he'd like to see her ladyship, and he went away with Maggie Whale. They were no sooner out of the room than overhead there was a shriek so prolonged and harrowing that Sally and I both stood suddenly still and looked at one another with frightened eyes. It was only the wind, but the wind in a mood that made us both feel little and forlorn. "I'm going out," Sally said. "I can't stand this any longer. I'm going out and I'm going down to the bar. I must see what's happening. Will you come?"

"Yes," I said.

When Maggie came back she said that Mother was restless, disturbed by the wind, and a little feverish. She was asking for Father, and Dr. Curnow was having his work cut out reassuring her that there was no fear of his going out with the lifeboat. But for this, I doubt whether Maggie would have allowed us to leave the house. As it was, she at once said that she would come with us and try to persuade Father to return to the house.

9

It was inky black out of doors, but all three of us knew the way so well that we could almost have walked it blindfold. But the lantern Whaley had brought was useful, for once we got into the woods we found the pathway littered with the debris of the storm, and here and there considerable branches blocked our way. On the left, there were several places where the declivity to the lake was sheer, and what with one thing and another our progress was slower than I had ever known it. Mercifully, the rain had stopped, but the wind rushing among the trees caused them to send down drenching showers.

Till now, it had been the many-voiced wind and the petulant hiss and slap of rain that constituted the noise of the storm, but we had not gone far into the woods before a new and direful note came booming to our ears: the roaring of the sea, and this was the thing itself, the danger, the devourer. All else was but the "effects" of the mighty spectacle to which we now drew near.

Standing by Eddy Rodda's lodge, with the pitiful lantern gleam lighting the pebbles at our feet, we looked out into a chaos of wind and water. South, east and west of us, as far as we would have been able to see had there been a ray of light to see by, was the ocean, and that we could see little increased rather than diminished the sense of being surrounded by irresistible destructive power. With Whaley's arms about us, Sally and I leaned back against the strong low wall that separated the lodge from the cliff path—rather than leaned we were pasted back upon it—and peered through the spume that was whirling about us. All we could see down there at the cliff foot was a tumult of blackness made visible only by the gray tossing of tormented water. This grayness thinned into invisibility not far from the shore, but imagination marched on where eyesight ended and summoned up a notion of pandemonium endlessly triumphing. If, within the walls of Tresant, the power of the wind had been able to daunt the mind, here it was a physical thing that stunned us by its violence. I was to know many a storm on that coast in the long years before me, but never again such a one as that. I shall never forget the violent discord of the wind's voices threaded by the majestic regularity of the rollers' thunder on the bar.

We were not alone. Rodda's opinion that if the schooner came ashore it would be in this maelstrom beneath us, had brought people walking the mile along the cliff, and they were gathered in anxious groups, women as well as men, and even a few children. Some men had already passed us, taking the path that slanted away from our feet down to the bar. The instinct that draws people as near as possible to disaster, whether to help or wonder, caused others to follow them, and soon all who came staggering aslant the wind took that way. Presently a few who came at a run shouted to us as they passed that the boat had put out from Porteven. Almost at the same moment a flare on the water, a wind-torn transient gleam, told us where the ship was. She was close in, but once the light vanished she could not be seen. However, that flash in the dark held a world of horror for me, because it had shown me a man waving the torch and so had populated that dreadful wilderness. I felt Maggie's grip tighten round our waists and heard her gasp. Sally said: "Her mainmast is gone."

Behind us, the lights were on in the lodge. Every window that faced the sea was lit, as though in some forlorn hope that the house could become a heartening beacon; and it was perhaps in the same hope that men and women now came climbing back from the bar to tear up the furze that grew along the cliff and take this down again. Here and there I had seen in the summer days the bones of old dinghies and even of bigger boats bleaching on the sand; and one of the men shouted to us that once the fire was started these would make lasting fuel. We saw presently the dry furze crackle into flames that streamed inland with the sparks blowing off them like a fiery spindrift. The fire grew and grew till it was a vast beacon and the people till then invisible on the bar could now be seen moving in the ruddy ambiance. They looked small and ineffective and disheartening, as though they had invented a game to dissipate despair.

Sally shouted through the wind that we had better go into the lodge, to see what was being done, and there we found three or four women besides Mrs. Rodda. They had come from Porteven, and, like their men, they needed no telling about what had to be done on an occasion like this. Rodda's was the only house near the spot where the ship would strike, if strike she had to, and it was there that men would have to be tended if, happily, there were any to tend. These women had brought blankets, and everything was being done to see that blessed warmth was present. In all the rooms fires were lit. I remembered the only other time I had been in that house, and the bleak respectability of the parlor into which we had been shown. Now the room was transformed with light and fire. On the hearthrug blankets were warming, and bricks to go into improvised beds were heating on the hearths. There were but two beds in the Rodda house, but half a dozen of these improvised beds had been laid out on the floors of the rooms. Kettles were boiling in the kitchen, and on the tables were bottles of brandy and glasses. With the grown-up gravity that she had on occasion, Sally inspected all this; but she said nothing. There was nothing to be said. The women, having done all that they could do, were silent and tight-lipped with anxiety. I learned afterward that every one of them had a husband or son in the lifeboat crew. Normally, such an assembly would have been unthinkable without knitting needles and a busy teapot. We left them unconcerned about their own comforts, sitting in the kitchen, their hands in their laps, waiting.

We went out again into the undiminished tumult of the night. Down on the bar the fire was burning now with a red steady heat, and the crowd about it seemed to have increased. We watched men and women converging upon it, carrying armfuls of fuel and heaving them upon the blaze. Then we heard a new sound: a horse's footsteps coming slowly from the direction of Porteven.

I should not have liked to walk the footpath through the wind and darkness of that night; and it seemed to me superhuman that my father should have ridden it. But I was ignorant of horses, especially of such horses as Peter who now loomed upon our sight. Oh, how my heart lifted up at this addition to our company, and not least because an unconfessed fear was blown away. I had been in dread all through this time lest, after all, Father had taken his place in the boat.

It would not have surprised me if he had been angry on finding us out in such a night, if he had ordered Whaley to take us home at once. But at a moment when so much that was terrible had to be accepted as matter of fact, I suppose our presence seemed a small thing. When Peter came to a stand, making no movement save a tossing up and down of the head that caused the bit to jingle, and a scraping of the hoof upon the gravel, how welcome and sane these small sounds were in the whirling madness about us! The smell of horse and leather was lovelier at that moment than the smell of roses in June.

Father said that he had ridden slowly along the cliff hoping to keep pace with the lifeboat, but that he had no idea how it had fared: there had been not a glimpse of it in the darkness. "And if they get anybody off," he said, "they'll have to get back to harbor at Porteven. It would be difficult enough to beach a boat here on a summer afternoon. In this, it would be death."

"Then why," Maggie asked, "are they preparing beds in Captain Rodda's?"

I could see him, a dark mass against the hurrying rags of the sky upon which his gaze rested anxiously. "Because," he answered after a moment, "these women have the sense to be ready for the worst. If they are washed ashore down there, God help them."

And now, I thought, she will tell him that the doctor is at Tresant, and he will go, and perhaps take us with him; and I hardly knew whether I should feel glad or sorry to be out of that racked and tortured night. But at that moment another flare lit the spot where the schooner was laboring, and even to my ignorant eyes it was clear that she was much nearer the shore than when we saw her last.

"My God!" Father shouted, "she's done for! It's all over with her!" and he put Peter to the sloping path and disappeared toward the bar.

Still we remained where we were, buffeted back against the wall, and presently we saw him moving on his horse among the people round the fire. It seemed a fearful and infernal bivouac as we looked down upon it from the cliff.

And now this night began to disclose its supreme disaster. Aware that whatever was to happen was nearing its climax, we three at last followed the footsteps of all the others and descended the path. We could feel the sand of the bar shaking beneath our feet as the rollers came in with hammer blow after blow, and we staggered diagonally into the wind, making for the fire. Everyone was grouped on the seaward side of it, for the bellows of the wind blew licking tongues of flame and showers of sparks landward. The fire had by now reached a mighty size, and at the moment when we joined the crowd half a dozen men arrived bearing on their shoulders the skeleton of a boat that they had dug out of the sand, and with one united heave they tossed it into the heart of the

129

flames. As the hulk sank into the embers the sparks flew upward and the fire seized the gaunt salty ribs and blue and orange lights flickered upon what seemed the setting for a Viking's funeral.

As we gazed at this moving spectacle a cry was blown to us from the sea's edge. We all turned that way, and a man who had been patrolling there among the spume and spindrift came staggering toward us bearing a burden upon his shoulders. It was a light and pitiful burden when he laid it down by the fire. It was that old man whom we had heard talking in the winter sunshine by Wesley's shack. His face was blue and pinched and in one hand he grasped a hank of seaweed. Silence fell as everyone stood there looking down upon him, silence so far as human noises went, but the wind screamed and the sea thundered and the flames whipped and crackled. And amid these noises was this great stillness in which everyone looked down at the dead man and thought of the other men in the boat from which he had been swept.

So here was the Viking's funeral, here was the first score in the battle. There was nothing to be done for him. My father said: "Put him up here," and he was laid across the saddle. Peter moved away, and the women at Rodda's lodge were given their first charge, beyond their skill and compassion.

This was but the opening of the night's disaster. When the old man's body had been carried away everyone turned again toward the sea, and there broke out upon it, at the point where we suspected the schooner to be, a smoky light which grew before our eyes. It was not this time the light of a waved torch. It was a red dusky flame from which black smoke rose, and this flame seemed to flow as though it were water, so that for the first time we could clearly see the ship and the men in her.

We learned afterward what had happened. A ship's boy had been told to do what he had done before: to tie rags to the end of a pole, soak them in paraffin, and wave them aloft, lighted. But the agitation of the ship was so great, and this child who was making his first voyage was trembling so with terror, that he upset the keg of paraffin. The oil ran swiftly over the surface of the water that was washing from one end of the ship to the other, and the torch which the boy had already lighted set it aflame.

All of us on the beach moved under one impulse as near as we dared to the sea's edge, drawn by the fascination of this spectacle. The ship, now luridly visible, lurching to the crests of the waves, rushing down into the valleys, was so sodden and waterlogged that she was in no danger of taking fire, but the whole surface of the water in her, washing about as she wallowed beam-on to the seas, was curling with flame. She was perhaps a couple of hundred yards from where we stood.

Suddenly a woman screeched, pointing an arm into the wind. "The lifeboat!" and there she was, visible for the first time since she had left the harbor at Porteven. The light from the schooner was enough to show her to us, poised on the top of a wave, and we saw the bent backs and the great straining oars, and then she was gone again down into the trough.

My father had returned and was standing with us, holding Peter by the bridle. The salt water was blown upon us like heavy rain and the wind had reached its last violence. We were upon the supreme and awful moment of the night. My father groaned in the extremity of his feeling. "Oh, go back! Go back!" he was crying quietly; and a man who was standing by said, "Ay, my lord. They're too late to do anything for'n now. She'll strike any minute, an' if they get into that ole mess, they'll never put 'er about."

The schooner struck. We saw that she was no longer moving with the sea. She was fast upon the outer edge of the bar and the rollers fell upon her, washing the fire out of her, so that flickers of light sped toward us but went out before they reached this extremity where the furious sea made its last smash and rolled back in white hissing sheets full of the noise of pebbles rubbing together. A small wan light made it still possible to see the men aboard. There appeared to be seven or eight of them, and as the great rollers passed over her we saw these become fewer. One man deliberately threw himself upon the back of one of the monsters rushing shoreward in the hope that it would carry him to safety. But it seemed as though nothing could survive this seething, hissing, pounding confusion where land and water met. It would beat the life out of the strongest, and the undertow was as powerful as a millrace.

Nevertheless, the crowd about us now began to break up, men and women scattering along the shore on the forlorn chance that a helping hand might pull some wretch to safety. But they were all arrested in their tracks by a scream the like of which I had not heard before. It was the woman who had cried "The lifeboat!" but this time she had no words, only this yell of despair, for what she had glimpsed, with an eyesight sharpened by the agony of having both son and husband in the boat, was an upturned keel.

Some last flicker of light from the schooner had shown her this, and the rest of the tragedy passed in darkness. There was nothing for it now but to scan the shore, and presently I saw tossed up and as quickly snatched back again an oar which I guessed belonged to the lifeboat.

All along the beach now people were ranging in independent parties, and a few of these passed us, making for the path to Rodda's lodge, carrying a man, whether dead or alive we had not time then to discover. My father, Maggie Whale, Sally and I stayed where we were. One place was as good or as bad as another. Peter was restless, snorting and pawing, and Father was stroking his neck and whispering comforting words to him.

Suddenly, on the water in front of us there was a great cry. With one accord we moved nearer to the smashing sea so that we stood in the backwash of the waves and I could feel the pebbles bruising my legs and strong fingers trying to drag me seaward. We strained our eyes into the chaos, but could see nothing. The cry came again, and this time I knew whose voice that was. It did not need my father's agitated words: "By God! It's Eddy Rodda."

For a moment we saw him, a dark blob on the white breaking water. My father dropped Peter's bridle, which Sally caught, and moved forward. But the backwash swept the dark figure out of sight, and Father, submerged to the waist, staggered back as another roller roared in. It overturned him, and he wallowed to our feet. He remained on hands and knees for a time, shaking his head, then got slowly up."He was holding someone," he said. "Wesley, I should think."

He walked back up the beach, and we followed, Sally leading the horse, till we were clear of the lacy edges of the water. I have said that when he set out that night he was wearing sea boots and an oilskin. Without a word to us, he now took these off and leapt into the saddle. The toes of those great boots would not fit into stirrups. Till now, he had been riding with legs dangling. He leaned over Peter's neck and talked to him and turned his head toward the water. We were all breathless, knowing what he was going to do, and my heart went as cold as my body, and that was numb and sodden.

The men we had seen carrying a body up to the lodge now returned, and they stayed with us, following as we went behind the horse down toward the water. On the edge, Father stopped, turned in the saddle, and shouted to them: "Stand by for a moment. Rodda's out there. I'm going to get him."

I could not believe that this was happening. I saw him lean forward and heard him say: "Peter, old boy! Peter! We can do it!" and the lovely horse, with the wind streaming his tail toward us, the white water breaking over his fetlocks, suddenly neighed: a great sound of defiance and confidence; and Father shouted: "I see them!"

Then they were in the water. We all crowded as near as we dared, but we could see little. But Peter was not swept back. We could vaguely see the commotion of his thrashing through the water. And then he was out of sight, and the hearts of all of us stood still as we looked upon nothing but the welter, the chaos, that rushed upon us and was sucked away from us everlastingly.

How long this endured I do not know, but it seemed as though eternity had passed before, rising above a towering wave, we saw Peter's head. He swept toward us down a glissade of water and then we lost him again. Again he was up, but now the undertow was strong, and our hearts panted to communicate our puny strength to his mighty strength as he strained against the hands of the sea that were pulling him backward. Whaley was sobbing, and Sally shouted: "Peter! Peter! Come, come!" but he seemed to be beating against a wall, and the men with us groaned. One horse against the sea. It didn't seem possible. But now the specially high wave that comes at intervals roared in, and Peter, taking the chance, thrashed forward, and suddenly his height increased, and we knew he was standing. He shuddered, shook himself, and walked toward us.

Then the men rushed forward and seized the burden that my father was towing with one hand. It was a man whose arms were tight clasped about another man. They hauled them ashore, and my father reeled in the saddle now that his task was done. He fell sideways, and Peter dragged him slowly, head-down, through the thinning foam. Sally seized the bridle and held Peter still, murmuring praise to him while my father kicked his foot out of the stirrup. And even as he lay there doing this, exhausted but triumphant, a wave lifted aloft an oar and hurled it shoreward. It was like a spear thrown by a defeated and envious enemy. He was just rising when the butt struck him in the middle of the back. He fell again, tried again to rise, but could not. A groan of pain broke from him, and there in the white edges of the water he laid his face upon his hands.

10

The news of what was happening at Porteven had spread to villages round about, and two or three doctors had come in to give help if it should be needed. While the disaster was in its last stages these had assembled at Rodda's lodge, and one of them had come down to the water's edge. He had arrived in time to see my father lying in the water, and the oar strike his spine, and to guess the significance of that groan of pain as he tried to rise.

"Don't lift him!" he shouted; and picking up Father's oilskin from the beach he laid it in the water near him and gently rolled him upon it. Then, with the help of one of the men, he carefully drew him up out of the reach of the water, close to where the fire was burning.

Captain Rodda and Wesley were carried there, too, and as the three lay side by side it was impossible to say whether any one of them was alive or dead. They lay in the ruddy light with closed eyes; their sodden clothes began to steam in the heat.

The doctor called to some men who were coming down from the lodge: "Take these two away, and see if you can make some sort of stretcher. Bring it back here."

Sally bent down and kissed her father's forehead. Then she said: "There's nothing I can do for him. I'll take Peter home." She sprang into the saddle.

"Say nothing of this at Tresant," Whaley warned her.

In the fire glow I saw Sally look at her with a contempt that said: "What do you take me for? As if I should!"

And, indeed, at Tresant there was no need to add this to the tragedy that already existed. Justin Gaylord came into the world that night: a child whose mother died in giving him birth and whose father never rode or walked again.

CHAPTER NINE

I

IT WAS a little wicker contraption, pulled by a donkey. There Father would be, looking as keen as ever, without a gray hair on him, so that a stranger might think he had got into the donkey cart for fun. And there would be Eddy Rodda, leading the donkey, and every time they went out you would see them stop by the railings of the paddock where Peter the Great was at pasture. Up he would trot, whinnying his welcome, and his head would come over the rail to nuzzle a nose into Father's palm. It was enough to break your heart. No one ever rode Peter again, but he was there for a long time to bring joy to the eyes, running in the paddock, perfect, beautiful.

It was Rodda, not Father, who had put on the badges of age. His hair and beard were streaked with gray and he had given up his earrings. No one would call him picturesque, a corsair, any more. He was just a man on the wrong side of middle age, quickly showing it. There were eight dead men that night, and four of them were out of his boat, and one of them was his son. The direction of his life took a new course. He no longer attended the Methodist chapel, nor did the Porteven pubs see him again. And the odd thing is that toward this new and gentle Rodda there sprang up a great loathing in Mrs. Rodda's heart. The man she had known, the man she had followed soon after he had dealt a blow that might have killed her father, the showy alluring braggart, died suddenly, and in his place she saw only the man who did not bring her son home alive that night. For the rest of that winter the lodge was a little hell. You could not pass it without hearing the woman's shrill berating voice, without seeing Eddy bowed and submissive like a rock taking a lashing from a wave. That he did not answer her, but sat without a word pulling on his pipe, made her the more furious. So mad she was that even in our presence she could not cease. I recall a day when Sally insisted, to my distress and Maggie's, on making a call as we were passing by. Mrs. Rodda invited us to take tea, though why I could not imagine, unless to have an audience for her spleen. The cups and plates were rattled angrily onto the table, and though, with us there, she did not speak to Eddy, it was evident that all this suppressed fury was addressed to him.

At last he spoke in a new quiet voice, expressing what he felt, though he had not been spoken to. "Do 'e think I don't miss 'im, midear, as much as you do! Do 'e think my 'eart's not broken?"

At that she turned upon him. "Miss 'im—you!" she shouted. "For the last months of 'is life you drove 'im away from 'is mother's love—you with your whoring. Heart! You never had a heart—and neither have I now. All that kept my heart alive is dead an' gone, an' seems to me the sooner I go after it the better."

Go after it she did. She was the ninth to die because of that night's storm; and after she was taken from the tide Rodda and my father came closer together, the one with a body and the other with a mind damaged beyond repair.

2

At Father's house in Portman Square there had been the usual retinue of menservants. These were all dismissed and the house was shut up. At Tresant there had never been menservants indoors till Eddy Rodda came, and he was never a manservant in the usual sense. After his wife's funeral, his coming to the house seemed not to be arranged: it just happened. I don't suppose there was discussion about wages or hours of service or anything of that sort. My father could not walk or stand without sticks. When he was not sitting or lying, he needed a strong arm, and Eddy was there to give it. Indoors, they spent most of their time in the comfortable room called the library. Father's bed was moved in there; Eddy put him into it at nights and in the mornings lifted him out and dressed him. There was a small room opening off this, and there Eddy's own bed was put. Gradually, his status in the household increased and became defined. He ceased to be Eddy or even "the captain" to the servants. Again and again, if a servant consulted Father about this or that, you would hear him say: "Speak to Mr. Rodda about it."

What I remember as remarkable is the tranquillity that settled upon Tresant as the spring came on. The poignancy of the sudden and terrible blows that had fallen upon us passed away. No gaiety came back, but neither did agony persist. I wouldn't say that Father was like the king who "never smiled again," but a kindly gravity hung about him and Rodda that I cannot forget. Father continued to look after the affairs of

135

the estate. In the donkey cart he visited almost every part of it daily, his back cushioned into an enormous pillow of swan's-down. In the evenings he taught Rodda to play chess, which became a great consolation to them, and sometimes he asked me or Sally to read to him. But he was never much interested in the adventures of fiction, and it was for our company rather than our reading that he asked us.

A young woman whose surname I forget, if I ever knew it, had charge of the Honorable Justin Gaylord. She was brought over from Porteven by Dr. Curnow, and everybody called her Amy. She was one of the victims of the storm that had changed the course of so many lives. Her child had died soon after its birth, and her husband, the man whose face Rodda had smashed that day we watched the work on the pilchards, was drowned when the lifeboat capsized. And so one might have expected Amy to suckle Justin on bitter milk, but she was as comfortable as a young cow. Experiences that would turn most women I know today into shivering wrecks left her at any rate outwardly as unperturbed as though to go on placidly living was all that mattered, and this she did.

3

Spring, which comes early, is the loveliest time at Tresant, and it was on one of the loveliest of spring days, following that disastrous winter, that Sally and I were lying on rugs spread on the lawn in front of Maggie's cottage. The lake sparkled; the beeches were downy with green; daffodils trumpeted everywhere. We were waiting for Maggie to start our morning lessons, when we saw a small procession coming toward us from Tresant. Ebenezer the donkey ambled along, drawing the wicker cart with Father in it. Rodda walked alongside, holding Ebenezer by one ear. It was he who had named the beast, and I was glad of that because it showed that some vestige of his droll spirit remained. There is a verse of a Methodist hymn that says:

> *Here I raise my Ebenezer,*
> *Hither by Thine help I'm come;*
> *And I hope, by Thy good pleasure,*
> *Safely to arrive at home.*

And indeed with Ebenezer pulling the cart there could be no more than a hope in his good pleasure, for he was a stolid and plodding person who certainly covered any required distance, but all in his own good time and pleasure. Sometimes he was called Ben, and Maggie called him Sudden Sneezer, for he had a bad habit of taking you unaware as you held a carrot or lump of sugar to his nose.

Well, there they came through the balmy morning, and just behind them was Amy pushing a perambulator that we knew contained Justin.

"One of these days," Father had said, "Justin will have to learn something about the estate."

He was all seriousness, and here, at four months old, was Justin Gaylord going the rounds of the property he was some day to command. Maggie came out of the cottage as the procession drew to a stand near the gate. Sally and I leaned over the perambulator, looking at the pink sleeping face of our half brother, Maggie's prospective landlord, who didn't seem at all interested in property or tenants. As he slept, his mouth made sucking motions. Near where Sally and I had been lying on the lawn, Merlin was kicking and crowing on a blanket. Eddy Rodda left Ebenezer standing and walked over to look down on his son. I could see Maggie watching him, and perhaps she was thinking it was as well that Lucy Evans had gone into the neighboring town to do some shopping. Rodda knelt on the grass, his great bulk hanging over the child, and put a finger gently into the curled fist, pressing it open. Merlin seized the finger, and Rodda softly waggled the little rosy fist to and fro. Merlin was just over a year old. This was the first time Rodda had seen his son: the son whose begetting began his woe. Now he had no other son and no wife. This scrap kicking on the mat, opening candid eyes to the pale blue sky, was all that was left to him of his own flesh. "Hey!" he said, waggling the little fist, and his voice trembled. "Hey, me ole dear!"

Father said in a quiet voice to Whaley: "Good God! I'd forgotten that. I forgot you had Rodda's son here."

"It's not so easy for us to forget, sir," Maggie answered.

"No. No, I suppose not. What's to be done?"

"Done?" said Maggie. "Ought we to do anything? Isn't this something between him and Lucy Evans? What's it to do with us?"

He sighed and shifted his back uneasily on the pillows. "Rodda!" he shouted.

Eddy got awkwardly to his feet and joined us. Neither he nor Father said anything about the child. "Unstrap that parcel," Father said.

It was a flat square parcel strapped to the back of the donkey cart. "Have you any room for a picture on your walls?" Father asked Whaley; and she said with a laugh: "Plenty, sir. There's so much because I'm rather particular about the pictures I hang."

"Yes, yes," he said, "I understand that. You have taste. You are becoming a famous woman, too. I don't know why you bother with us down here."

"So long as you want me, sir, and the children need me, I am very happy here," she said.

"Will you oblige me by hanging this picture? I don't want it to be

137

where I am likely to see it. I haven't opened the packing. I haven't looked at it, but perhaps my son will want it some day. We must be moving on, Rodda."

When they were out of sight, Maggie took up the parcel which was leaning against the garden railing. "Well," she said, "let's go in and solve the mystery."

This is what it was all about. When Father and Mother had been in London during the summer, he had had her portrait painted by G. F. Watts. It had been left behind for the painter to put in some finishing touches, and these had taken a long time. But now here it was at last, and I know that my father never set eyes on it. We hung it in Maggie's workroom. She always called it "his lordship's dear ghost."

4

The coming of this child to Lucy Evans, the disappearance of Lucy's mother almost at once thereafter, and then the deaths of Mrs. Rodda and Wesley, and the obvious attachment of Eddy to the child: this seemed a situation made for a romantic conclusion, for Lucy's marriage to Rodda, followed by a comfortable life as an old man's darling. But we were in for nothing of that sort. After the terrible upheaval of the storm, which cleared so much out of all our lives, we were in for a long season of tranquillity and almost tedious growth. When everything was uncertain in Lucy's life, when reality broke so cruelly into the cloister wherein her mother had kept her, she had rushed madly about, pursuing Rodda, the god who had given her enlightenment and in whom alone, she foolishly thought, she would find the harborage she needed for herself and her child. But she had learned that he was not the only harbor. With Maggie Whale she had found something she had not known before: a companionship free alike of pampering and passion, an opportunity to satisfy the need to learn which was latent in her, and a home where her child was obviously growing in strength and beauty. She was able during the summer that followed to receive calmly the infrequent moments that saw Rodda at the lodge. He had never acknowledged himself to be Merlin's father, and it was too late for him now. Lucy acted as though he were any casual visitor showing an interest in a growing child.

The time is coming when I shall have to write of how we left Tresant: Maggie, Lucy and I; but before I come to that I must say something of a matter that I would rather not write of at all. Still, I must do it, or this will be merely a romantic record of moments when things went well, and they didn't continue to go well between me and Father.

It was in the second winter after the death of my mother that I was reading to him in the library. I was then halfway through my twelfth year. Only the two of us were there. Some affair in Porteven had kept Rodda out, and Sally had gone to a party for children in a house a few miles away. I was to have gone, too, but a miserable headache came upon me in the course of the afternoon and I begged to be excused. I watched Sally being driven away in a closed carriage as the evening was coming down, and then went up to the den we shared on the first floor. My headache was worse and I did not light a lamp, for the last thing I wished to do was read. I sat back in the fireshine with my eyes closed, trying to go to sleep, but soon I was interrupted by a maidservant who said: "Would you please see his lordship in the library, Miss Sarah?"

He was sitting on one side of the fireplace, and on the other was a chair with a standard lamp alongside it. He asked me to sit there and read to him. I took up *Monte Cristo*, which Sally and I had been reading to him in turns, but I had not read long before he said: "What rubbish this is! Couldn't we have something more intelligent?"

I looked up in surprise. The lamplight didn't reach him, but the light of the pine logs burning in the great fireplace undulated duskily across his face, which was frowning and was marked, too, by deep lines that I thought must be of pain. At once the plague of my own headache passed from my thoughts, and I asked: "Are you in pain? Can I arrange your cushions?"

"No!" he snapped, and I remembered too late how he hated any allusion to his imperfection. He added: "It's just this nonsense you're reading. I'm not a schoolboy."

I was terribly upset, not so much by his words as by his manner, and the pain above my eyes came on with throbbing force. "What shall I read?" I asked weakly.

"Don't bother," he said. "Don't read anything. Why are you not gone with Sally?"

"I have a headache, sir," I answered. "I get them often now, and this one's very bad."

It was a little cry for sympathy, but I got none. "You should ride like Sally," he said. "It's dreadful to see a great girl like you jogging along like a sack on that pony of yours. No wonder you get headaches. You're losing your looks. You must shake yourself up. Ah, Rodda! See to these cushions. They feel like iron bars." Eddy was mercifully back. He dealt with the cushions, pulled up a little table, and got out the chessmen. I lingered there miserably till Father said: "I think it would be a good idea if you went straight to bed and tried to have a long sleep. Had you better see Dr. Curnow?"

"It will be gone by the morning," I said, and crept unhappily away.

But I had to see Dr. Curnow after all. The next afternoon I said to Sally: "Don't you think it's time I tried to ride something a bit more spirited than old McFlimsy? It must be dreadful to see a great girl like me jogging along like a sack."

Sally laughed. "Why worry?" she asked. "He gets you where you want to go. You've got no way with horses, that's what it comes to. You're a bit afraid of 'em, aren't you?"

"Yes. A little bit."

"Well, then. The beggars know it, and take advantage of it. But there's no need to let that upset you. If I felt about horses as you do, I'd keep away from 'em. After all, horse-riding isn't the only thing on earth. How's the headache?"

"Not so bad, but I see spots dancing."

"Keep off the drink," she laughed. "And keep off the horses. You're very well as you are."

But I was not to be laughed out of it, and Sally agreed that I should try my luck on her Macaire. She rode McFlimsy, and it was astonishing to me to see what she could do even with him. But with Macaire I could do nothing. He fretted and fumed and had his own way all the time. And as our ride was coming to an end it was evident to me that his way included getting rid of me. I was grimly determined not to allow this, and as we drew near to the stables I had the more reason for making a good show. There was Rodda standing by Ebenezer, and there was Father in the wicker cart, watching us critically. It was at this moment, just as we came up to them, that Ebenezer lifted his silly great head and let out a bray of derision, his rubber lips drawn horribly back over his huge yellow teeth. Macaire hated it, as though Ebenezer had cried: "You—the great Macaire, letting that sack stay on your back! Ha, ha!" And he threw me unceremoniously to the cobbles.

My right arm was broken, and when Dr. Curnow came to set it, Sally told him about my spots and headaches. And so the plain child (as I was to find my mother had called me in her letter which I found so many years later) became plainer still, an unsightly object crawling about with her arm in a sling and spectacles on her nose. "You were spotty, too, at that time," Whaley said when I recalled the moment. "Believe me, my dear, you were no one's dream of fair women." I was aware of this, and unhappy, and I suppose this made me plainer still.

I can look back now on this experience with an adult's intelligence; but then I could only endure it with the unthinking passion of a child. There were several incidents like the one in the library, and almost all of them arose out of my poor eyesight. I suspect now that Dr. Curnow's knowledge of ophthalmic affairs was not great and that the spectacles he provided for me could have been better. They helped me to see things more clearly, though I had a habit of *peering*, which Whaley tells me was distressing; but they did little to stop my headaches, and the headaches made me morose, and the consequence was that, when unobserved, I would take the spectacles off. But my eyes having become used to them, I found that, without them, my sight was worse than ever: so dim that I took alarm and persuaded myself that blindness was only a matter of time. But I said nothing of this to anyone. I found a ghoulish pleasure in suffering silently, telling myself that when it was too late, and I was groping through life with outstretched hands or tapping with a stick, *they* would be sorry.

And *they*, of course, if I had been adult enough to realize this, was Father, and no one else. It was his approbation I craved, his coldness that chilled me to the heart. There was the affair of that dog Robber, whom I have mentioned only once: the dog that appeared, barking frantically, on the day when we reached Tresant after traveling from Montreuil. With seasickness and the strangeness of everything, I was then almost praying for death, and this dog's assaulting gladness of welcome felled me like blows. I suppose the first meeting with Robber conditioned to some extent my view of him always. He was one of several dogs that roamed about the place, and he was the sudden, unpredictable member of the fraternity, apt to appear out of nowhere with a rush, his tongue lolling like a red steaming shoehorn, grinning with harmless mischief, announcing with stupendous *joie de vivre* that God was in his heaven and that if you didn't consider all to be well with the world you were a pretty liverish type.

I was walking alone near the house one day when this bringer of good tidings came like a black thunderbolt out of a thicket of rhododendrons. My spectacles were in my hand. I hated them. They were not curing my headaches and they were making me look a fright. So I had taken them off, and what I saw was simply a black swirl rushing upon me. I tried to push him off when he stood against me, grinning into my face, and my struggles must have persuaded him that I was out to share his fun. He retreated for a dozen yards, crouched with all four feet splayed on the gravel, then charged between my legs, bringing me down. He stood over me, raining frantic barks into my face. My spectacles fell out of my hand, and my head was aching from the noise and agitation. My hands were powerless against him, and suddenly I became furious with him for making me so sorry a sight. We were right under the windows of the library, and I knew that my father and Rodda were sitting there, looking out. There was a flower bed under the window, edged with loose stones, fairly big. My hand found one of these, hardly knowing what it was doing, and I brought it down with a good whack on Robber's head. At once he realized that this was not play. He retreated, uttering lamentable howls as though I had broken every bone in his body. I struggled to my feet, looked down for my spectacles, and saw that I was standing on them. Both lenses were broken. I began to cry.

In the midst of this, I heard Father's voice calling through the open window. He was not speaking to me. He was calling "Robber! Robber! Come, boy!"

And presently that inimitable actor came, crouching along as though the life had been all but beaten out of him, his eyes turned up to show pathetic whites, evidence of a broken heart. He went slowly through the window, stood with his forepaws on Father's knees, and wept. Father pulled his ears, fondled his head, and crooned to him: "Poor old boy! Poor old boy, then! Did they hurt him? Didn't they understand him?"

Oh, I could have wrung the wretched creature's neck! Not a word for me, except in so far as these words were clearly disapproving of what I had done. It was not even noticed that my spectacles were gone. I walked blindly away, and the blurred world about me was full of my hate.

7

I said that I had mislaid my spectacles, and Maggie, Sally and I spent a long time searching for them in Tresant and in the cottage. When we had wasted a morning thus, a gardener's boy raked up the frames while tidying the gravel. Dr. Curnow put new lenses into them, and these were like the old ones. So I lost them again, and I became notorious as a loser of spectacles. Sometimes I would lose them where they could be found; sometimes I would drop them into the lake or throw them into a hedge. These deceptions made me miserable, and my misery made my health bad, so that my spots became worse and I was given brimstone and treacle, which I detested. But I took it in as exhibitionist a way as possible in order to call attention to myself. If I couldn't be anything else, at least I could be, or try to be, an "interesting" invalid, a groping owl of a child, making much of her fear of dogs and horses. If I couldn't be loved, let me be detested.

In the autumn everything changed. I have said nothing about our neighbors at Tresant, but one of them, Colonel Edwardes, was the means of ending this unhappy interlude. He rode over one day and told Father that he was about to leave for Devonshire where he would be staying for a month with a relative. He was taking his son and daughter, who were at the same age as Sally and I, and he would be glad to add us two to the party, if Father would consent. This consent was given at once, but then, to my surprise, Maggie Whale said: "I don't think, sir, that Miss Sarah should go. Her health is not up to it."

For the first time in my life I felt furious with Whaley. In my heart I was calling her an interfering old cat, a busybody who should have the sense to keep out when she wasn't wanted. But she was firm. Father and Colonel Edwardes suggested that the change might be just what I wanted; and Father, in particular, insisted on this so strongly that my unbalanced mind made another wild swerve, and in utter misery I cried: "I see you want to get rid of me!" The eyebrows of the two men went up, and Whaley hurried me out of the room.

During the next few days Whaley said nothing of this outburst; but then, when Sally was gone and we were walking through the autumn woods, she sat down on a log and, when I sat beside her, she put an arm about me. That was unusual. She was not given to gestures of affection. I tried to draw peevishly away, but she kept hold of me and said quietly: "Be still. Try and be *still* for a moment."

She was still herself, and the still afternoon was disturbed by nothing but the occasional fall of a leaf, and the blue sky hung over the motionless water. On the edge of the water old long-shanks heron stood dozing with hunched gray shoulders. My tremors, my resistance, melted. I seemed to merge into Whaley's comfort, and I slept with her stillness and the stillness of the day possessing me.

I felt better when I woke, and the first thing she said to me was: "We shall be leaving for London tomorrow. Lucy and Merlin will be coming with us."

The news pleased me, but I restrained an impulse to shout for joy. I couldn't so easily give up a part I had learned to play so well. "But I'm not fit to travel," I said. "London's farther than Devonshire, and you said yourself that my health wasn't up to going there."

"Well," she said, "if you'd rather be at Tresant all on your own . . . Lucy and I will be going anyway."

"Yes, I *am* fit to go," I cried eagerly; and she said: "Of course you are. I don't know what you've been playing at all the year."

I was all defensive indignation again. "Playing—!" I began hotly, and she interrupted me. "Yes, Sarah, playing. That's why I didn't

143

want you to go to Devonshire, especially when I saw how much you would have liked to go. It's just as well for you to learn that if you pretend you must take the consequences of pretending. If you pretend to be so ill that you can't even ride a pony, well, you can hardly expect to go rushing off on a holiday tour, can you?"

I hung my head sulkily, and she went on, as we began to walk homeward: "You must be sensible about this, Sarah. I've seen you hiding your spectacles and pretending to have lost them—"

"You *saw*! And never said a word?"

"I'm saying my word now—once for all. I've been very unhappy to see you *making* yourself ill by all sorts of tricks. That's one reason why we're going to London. I don't suppose I should have stopped you from going to Devonshire if I hadn't got that in store. I want you to have your eyes seen to properly. I don't imagine there's much the matter with them, but Dr. Curnow is perhaps not the best man for the job. So I've arranged this with his lordship. He's very anxious that everything should be done for you that can be done."

"Nonsense," I said rudely. "He despises me."

She looked at me sadly. "Sarah, you've got a lot to learn and unlearn," she said. "But don't let us go into that now. Except that I must say this. When you think people despise you, it's not a good idea to act as though you wanted them to. And you have been acting, you know, all through the summer."

I hadn't known it till Whaley's cool words told me. I had been deceiving myself as effectively as, I hoped, I was deceiving other people. But now I knew, and this was the beginning of my cure.

8

The affair of my eyesight can now be dismissed. Whaley was right. There was not much the matter with me, but the little that was wrong was being worsened by ignorant treatment. I was given new spectacles that made me see with wonderful clearness; my headaches went; and I was cheered by the news that in a few years' time I would not need spectacles at all. And so it turned out to be. My health improved, and I became a not exciting-looking young woman, but still not one who needed to hide behind doors.

It is of Maggie Whale and Lucy Evans that I wish to write now, not of myself. Maggie's novel that had been appearing as a serial story in Mr. Dickens's magazine was now to be published as a book. It was not the first book she had had published, but the publishers were sure it was going to be a successful one, and Maggie wanted to be in London on publication day. The publishers were right.

Soon everyone was talking about *Cornelia Constantine,* and from that moment Maggie never looked back, as they say. She was one of the recognized literary persons of her generation, not of the first rank, but in the class, if I must find a comparison, of Rhoda Broughton. And, so far as I understand such matters, that is not bad.

This, however, is to go ahead, and at the moment I must keep to what happened during our London visit, from which Lucy Evans and Merlin did not return.

It was strange to be again in Portman Square. We could have stayed in an hotel, but Father had asked Maggie to live in the house, to see that the place should have an airing, and to report to him on the condition of things. "I don't suppose I shall ever be there again," he said, "but Justin will."

One or two servants were hired for the month we were there. You could do improbable things like that in those days. Sheets were taken off furniture in a few rooms, fires were lit, and we settled down. Father had not done this thing by halves once he had determined to do it at all, so that we were empowered even to hire a nursemaid for Merlin. Father wanted Lucy to be able to enjoy the holiday like me and Maggie.

Lucy was a handsome young woman. It was a fortunate day for her when she fell in with Maggie Whale. They had been together now for three years, and this tall, self-possessed, good-looking girl was something very different from the distraught and hag-ridden creature we had seen running from Rodda's cottage soon after our arrival at Tresant. All that had happened to her then was still part of her. It was in her as a gravity, a sweet seriousness, that went well with her tall fair beauty and blue eyes. It gave a depth of attraction to her rare smiles. The surroundings in Portman Square did not daunt her. She had become a favorite with my father, and often, when he invited Maggie to take tea with him, he would ask her to bring Lucy. I remember that it was after one of these occasions, just before we set out for London, that he said: "I'm not qualified, Miss Whale, to speak to you about your books, but you've certainly one work of art to your credit, and that's Lucy Evans."

Beginning as her servant, Lucy was now Maggie's companion and secretary. She made, in her clear beautiful handwriting, fair copies of Maggie's muddled sprawl of manuscript and helped her in many other ways. I often thought with envy of those two in the quiet lamp-lit cottage by the lake on winter nights when I was in Tresant, tortured by a headache. There was a serenity about them.

We were all in a happy mood one night toward the end of our first week in Portman Square. Maggie and I had already made several visits to an oculist in Harley Street, and I had received my first

145

hints of her coming fame from the way in which he spoke to her as to a person of distinction, and that afternoon we had heard his happy prognostication that I had nothing at all to worry about. We had eaten our evening meal, I was wearing my new, comfortable and miraculous spectacles, I had noted in the mirror that a spot on my chin was clearing up, and altogether, for all of us, it was a cheerful moment there by the drawing-room fire. A maid brought in a letter which had come for Maggie by a late post, and when she had read it she said with a laugh: "Well! I've never heard of such a thing in my life!"

The letter had been addressed to Maggie at her publishers' office and thence readdressed. She read it aloud:

Dear Madam.—I am the first draper in London to have the idea of opening a book department. I am sure that drapers' shops of the future will become veritable emporiums, catering for varied sides of human existence, happy meeting-places, where all the world and his wife may come, to dine, to browse among books, to buy anything from new socks for the children to a dining-room suite that would not be discreditable in Haddon Hall or Chatsworth. The day of the old-fashioned draper's shop is over. The drapery will remain, excellent as ever, for British fabrics are not likely to decline from their proud pre-eminence as the finest in the world, but these will be only one element in a multifarious attractiveness that will make the great emporiums the same thing to London that the bazaars are to the East, minus, we hope, the discomforts—e.g. smells and overcrowding—inseparable, I understand, from life in Oriental climes.

But to return to the point. The opening of my book department, widely advertised, coincides with the publication on Wednesday next of your novel *Cornelia Constantine*. I have risked the purchase of no less than 100 (one hundred) copies of this book, and I propose to give it a dominant display at my opening. Now, madam, to the muttons. There is a laudable desire implanted in the breast of the reading public to see in person the men and women whose great works make British Literature second, in my humble opinion, to none in the world, and those who gratify this desire strike a blow for British Literature and for themselves. Can we—you and I, madam—come to an understanding by which such a blow can be struck? If you were there in person at the opening of my book department, and if I were able to announce that you would have the condescension to append your signature to each and every copy of *Cornelia Constantine* purchased (and paid for) on the opening day, would not this be something of mutual satisfaction and advantage? At any rate, madam, I trust you will give this somewhat unorthodox proposal your earnest consideration and communicate your decision to me. It might even be possible to pay a fee for your attendance—say £5 5s. (five guineas).

I am, madam, your obedient servant, Mostyn Lloyd.

"Well," said Whaley, "what do you think of that? What a horrid vulgar little man he sounds."

"What shall you do about it?" Lucy asked.

"Really! What can one do about it? I could never look my publisher in the face again."

"Still, I wish you would go," Lucy persisted quietly.

"Whatever for? I'm not interested in building up this little horror's emporium."

"I am," Lucy answered. "He's married to my mother's sister."

Whaley and I looked at her in surprise. This was news! Admirably as Lucy had developed while living with Whaley, it was impossible not to think of her as in some sort an outcast, a person who had come near to disaster from which only an almost miraculous intervention had saved her. To learn now that she was closely related to people who, whatever else they might be, were probably well-to-do financially, was an eye-opener. She told us of the letters that had passed between her mother and Meg Mostyn Lloyd, and added: "I should have liked to go there then. But they would probably have put upon me. If I went now I would have a better chance of holding my own. I ought not to stand in Merlin's way."

"Well!" said Whaley. "You calculating creature! Could you put up with a horrid little man capable of writing a letter like that?"

"He's not little," Lucy answered. "He's tall and not bad-looking."

"How do you know that?"

"I spied him out in the shop when you were in Harley Street today. Another thing is this. If I had gone when my mother wanted me to, that would have been when he was just starting here in London. Now he's had a few years to get on his feet, and believe me, he *has* got on his feet, if the shop's anything to go by."

"A veritable emporium, I suppose?" Whaley mocked.

"A wonderful shop," said Lucy. "I expect he'll be easier in temper now that something of his struggle is over."

"Well! Of all the cold-blooded little hussies!"

"I'm thinking of Merlin."

Maggie took up the letter from the table and weighed it in her hand. "So!" she said. "We shall have to think about this windy bombast after all. What do you suggest, Lucy?"

Lucy was serious and unsmiling. "I can only tell you what I should *like* you to do," she said. "If you think me unpardonable, say so. I shall understand well enough."

She got up and took a turn or two about the room, a tall lovely girl, with a little frown of concentration on her forehead. She paused, looking down at her shoes, near Maggie. "I should like this," she said, choosing her words with care. "You will write to Mr. Mostyn Lloyd, accepting his invitation. And you will do this not in an off-hand condescending way, but rather flattering him, making him think well of himself. Of course, this address, and Lord Burnage's crest on the notepaper, will do that to begin with, but you will refer to the things he says in his letter about the future of shops like his, and you will agree with them, and put him in a good humor. Because, after all, he's probably right, however ridiculously he has expressed himself. You see, his way of expressing himself is in shops, and his shop is not ridiculous."

She paused, and walked again, then went on: "Well, it shouldn't be difficult for you to be agreeable to him when you meet, and you could find an opportunity to ask him and his wife to visit you here. I don't suppose he's ever been in a house like this, unless to measure for carpets or curtains. He will be flattered, and so will his wife. You could ask a few people—the sort that he wouldn't have much chance to meet otherwise. Of course, they'll ask us to their place, wherever it is, and we'll go, and it shouldn't be impossible to discover accidentally that Mrs. Mostyn Lloyd is the aunt I should have gone to a few years ago."

She stood with her back to the fire, prodding the rug with her toe. "Of course," she said, "Merlin is the difficulty there." She looked up defiantly. "This is where we shall all have to tell some lies."

Still Whaley said nothing, and Lucy went on: "My mother died suddenly. I knew nothing of the plans she was making for me. All I knew was that she had a sister married to Mr. Mostyn Lloyd who had just opened a shop in London, but I didn't want to intrude on someone I had never met. Being left alone in the world, I married a young local fisherman. He was drowned in the lifeboat disaster, and there was I with Merlin on my hands. Lord Burnage came to my help, for my father had been his servant in the Crimea, and here we are, over the awkward part, back in the truth again. Then I lived with you, and owe everything to you—and that, indeed, is the truth, God knows," Lucy ended abruptly, kneeling before Maggie and kissing the hands that lay idly in her lap.

Maggie rose from her chair, leaving Lucy kneeling there. "Don't wheedle," she said. "You seem to have thought it out very unsentimentally so far. Don't let us be sentimental now."

After a moment she said: "You'd have to have a new name if

you pretend to be married. That's always awkward. One instinctively uses the old one."

Lucy got up. "Why shouldn't my husband have had the same name as myself? Cornish villages are full of people having the same name. I would simply have to be Mrs. Evans instead of Miss Evans. There *was* a young Evans drowned from the boat that night."

Maggie shuddered at this realism. "And suppose your mother turns up?"

"She will not turn up," Lucy answered. "There is no need to go into that, but I know that my mother is dead."

"Well, we shall have to think about it. It's not a thing to undertake lightly."

"Don't undertake it at all if you don't want to," Lucy said. "I'm thinking of Merlin."

"I'm thinking of myself," Whaley answered. "It will be lonely in my cottage. Well, we'd better be off to bed."

9

Mostyn Lloyd has long been dead, but his name remains so valuable that no one would dream of changing it. There it still is today, reigning in Oxford Street over acres of plate glass, emblazoned with window boxes, crowned with flags fluttering above story that was added to story as simple shop became veritable emporium.

As Lucy had said, Mostyn Lloyd was tall and not bad-looking. He came to tea, bringing his wife with him, and what is more, he came in a brougham. No grass ever grew under Mostyn Lloyd's feet, and one of his sayings, which I was to hear later, was: "You must not only *be* prosperous: you must be seen to be prosperous," and this was a rule that he applied to himself, his wife, and his shop.

Lucy's plan of campaign was working. Whaley went alone to the opening of the book department and came back rather exhausted but satisfied that she had done her part well. She had even made a little speech, something she had not done before, but Mostyn Lloyd had called for it suddenly and she had, as she said, "managed somehow." She had then had tea with him in his office, which she said was "quite a little drawing room," and there she had met Meg Mostyn Lloyd. Over the tea cups she had invited them both to Portman Square, but she had not obliged Lucy by asking anyone to meet them.

And now here they were, sitting by our fire, Mostyn Lloyd in a frock coat with shiny satin lapels, dark, forceful-looking, but yet with a smile that broke out again and again, reducing his eyes to sparkling points decorated with attractive fans of wrinkles. As I got to know him better, I was to find that it was with the wheedling of those eyes and the soft intonation of his Welsh voice that he preferred to get his way, but get it he would, and if not by guile then by brutal directness that appeared when the smile was wiped off his face and the eyes became points of iron.

Mrs. Lloyd—or, as she never failed to call herself, Mrs. Mostyn Lloyd—was a stout florid woman, dressed to kill. In the firelight of our rather dusky room she scintillated. Did she but turn her neck or a wrist, did she but heave her bosom, the gleam caught fire from bangles and spangles, bugles and sequins, the links of gold chains or the facets of cut stones. Remembering her sister, the tanned and down-to-the-bone mother of Lucy Evans, I marveled at this amorphous heliograph, flashing in all directions its messages of luxury.

Whaley presented me to the visitors. "This," she said, "is Lord Burnage's stepdaughter," and Mostyn Lloyd, who, I suppose, had looked up his Debrett, said: "Ah! The Honorable Miss Gaylord, eh?"

"No, no," said Whaley. "Sarah is his lordship's *step*daughter. I'm afraid she's not honorable at all. Her mother was Lord Burnage's second wife. Sarah is plain Miss Rainborough. Sir Richard Rainborough is her father."

I was afraid I might be letting the side down by not being honorable; but when he heard who I was Mostyn Lloyd looked at me keenly and said: "Ah—Rainborough—iron, eh?" That I was iron seemed deeply satisfying to him.

"And this," Whaley said, "is Mrs. Evans. I hope you will meet her son some day. I think you'll like him, Mrs. Mostyn Lloyd. He's a dear child, but, alas! fatherless. Lord Burnage is deeply interested in both Lucy—that's Mrs. Evans—and her son. What I should ever do without Lucy I don't know. She is my invaluable secretary."

Lucy shook hands with her aunt, who said: "You poor child! You're so young to be a widow."

Lucy poured a cup of tea and took it to her. "Have you any children, Mrs. Mostyn Lloyd?" she asked.

The lady heaved and scintillated. "Alas! no," she said. "Sometimes Mr. Mostyn Lloyd and I regret it, but perhaps it's a mercy—an uncovenanted mercy—for I am far from well."

"Mrs. Mostyn Lloyd," her husband explained, "is in danger—"

"In imminent danger," his wife murmured.

"—in imminent danger of a nervous breakdown. You may say that she lives on the verge of a nervous breakdown, but her resolution of spirit has never allowed her to go over it."

Lucy handed him his tea. He sipped it, looking meanwhile at his wife, as though at any moment she might slide the fatal inch over the verge.

"The last thing I wish to do," he said, "is to praise Mrs. Mostyn Lloyd before strangers—although I hope that even already we need not consider one another altogether in that light. But in her delicate state of health Mrs. Mostyn Lloyd manages to maintain a medium—"

"A happy medium," his wife supplied.

"—yes, a happy medium between good health and surrender."

"Abject surrender."

"Yes, one might put it that way: between good health and abject sur render. Mrs. Mostyn Lloyd always has a knack of finding the right word."

"It is fortunate, Mr. Mostyn Lloyd," said Whaley, "that you are able to supply all the comforts necessary in such a condition."

"Yes, indeed," he said, not without complaisance. "If Mrs. Mostyn Lloyd has been a wife in a million, I have not been too bad as a husband. She is able to take life quietly, not getting up till lunchtime and having her forty winks after lunch and perhaps in the evening. Like that, she holds her own."

They did not stay long, and before going they invited us to take tea with them at Kensington on the following Sunday. When Whaley came back from watching them drive off in the brougham, she said with a laugh: "Well, a tyro—the *veriest* tyro—could see that Mrs. Mostyn Lloyd is having the time of her life. I should think she's as fit as a fiddle, apart from having too much fat, and I'm afraid that's a disease she's not treating very wisely."

Lucy was silent, thoughtful. "Well," Whaley challenged her, "tell us what you think."

"I think it would be most interesting to know what they're talking about now. She's giving nothing away, that woman."

"What is there to give away?" Whaley asked.

"Well, you mentioned the name of Lord Burnage, and that gave her a chance, if she had wanted to take it. She could have said that her sister was married to the man who had been his lordship's servant in the Crimea. But she took care not to say it."

"In her place, would you have said it?"

"No."

"Very well, then. Have patience. Are you regretting the whole thing? Are you repelled by the woman?"

"So far, there's nothing to regret, is there?" Lucy said noncommittally. "And it's Merlin I'm thinking about."

10

We drove in a hired cab to Kensington, to the secluded square of Georgian houses where the Mostyn Lloyds lived. It was a four-wheeler, because we needed space. A letter had come from Mrs. Mostyn Lloyd, saying that she understood Mrs. Evans's son was with us in Portman Square and that she would be pleased to have an opportunity of seeing him.

"Whatever for?" Lucy asked.

"I wonder," Maggie said darkly. "Perhaps this is an omen—a happy omen."

It was a beautiful day of late autumn, and already when we reached the square the blue dusk was deepening among the trees and here and there a light burned in a window. Inside the Mostyn Lloyds' house we lost this calm and graciousness of the exterior. We walked into a stifle of plush and brocade, a jumble on the floors and on the walls, a rich and heterogeneous mess which, nevertheless, was an expression not of a depraved taste peculiar to the Mostyn Lloyds, but of what most people then thought the appropriate way to furnish a house.

At any rate we could not complain of our welcome. Mr. Mostyn Lloyd himself came bustling out into the hall to greet us. He chucked Merlin under the chin, crying, "So this is your fine young fellow, eh?" and went upstairs to show the nursemaid (whom we had brought with us) the room where Master Merlin, as he promptly called him, was to have tea and amuse himself with toys till Mrs. Mostyn Lloyd should be ready to see him. We waited for him to come down, and he bowed us into the drawing room where his wife was flashing and sparkling in the firelight. Maggie inquired concerning her health, and we gathered that, having but half an hour ago awakened from her afternoon sleep, she was fortified to resist for a little longer the push over the verge on which she trembled.

It was a happy party. Mostyn Lloyd was in a good humor, because his book department was promising to be successful, and he was generous enough to give Maggie her share of credit for this. I was pleased to see that he was deferential to her, not condescending; and, indeed, child though I still was, I had become aware that during this past fortnight Maggie had increased as a person of consequence. On most days Lucy and I took either luncheon or dinner alone, and some times both, Maggie having been invited to places where she met all sorts of celebrated people. So I thought it was no more than her due that Mostyn Lloyd should say: "Mrs. Mostyn Lloyd and I think it very gracious of you, Miss Whale, that you should spare us a moment from your Tennysons and Thackerays and all the rest of them."

Maggie smiled. "I'm just the new thing, Mr. Mostyn Lloyd," she said. "I expect it'll be a different tale in a few years' time."

We were alone with him in the drawing room. His wife had risen a few moments before and said to Lucy: "Now, Mrs. Evans, shall we have a look at the boy?" and when Whaley and I rose too, she added: "No. Just me and Mrs. Evans."

Mostyn Lloyd would not hear of our going home in a hired cab. He had his own brougham brought round to the door and personally saw us off with as much attention as though we were ducal customers driving away from his doors in Oxford Street. Lucy was very quiet, and she continued to be quiet all through our evening meal. Afterward, as we sat round the fire, she said: "Well, I'd better tell you what happened."

II

Merlin was an attractive child. Maggie rather than Lucy had been responsible for his upbringing, and Maggie's ideas knew nothing of swaddling, coddling and cosseting. The boy had become strong and well set up, and he would answer intelligently when spoken to. But conversation rarely began from his side. Having been reared in a place where he met few adults and no children, he had a reserve which I for one liked.

Mrs. Mostyn Lloyd climbed the stairs with a resolution strange for an invalid. She took Lucy to a large room on the first floor. A fire was burning behind a guard. The maid got up from a comfortable chair, and Merlin, who had been taught his manners, rose from the floor on which he had been kneeling.

"Merlin," said Lucy, "this is Mrs. Mostyn Lloyd, who has given you all these lovely things to play with."

Merlin said: "Good afternoon, ma'am. I'm making our house."

Mrs. Mostyn Lloyd sat in the chair the maid had left, and said: "Would you like to explain it to me?"

There were piles of wooden blocks on the carpet, and Merlin had used them not to build with, but to draw a plan. On one side was the ground floor, on the other were the upper rooms. "This is the passage," he said. "You come in here from the lawn by the lake. Where this brick is missing, that's a door, and you go through that into Miss Whale's room, where she writes books, so you've got to be quiet when she's in there. Mama says so, but Miss Whale says she could write whatever row was going on."

He went through all the rooms of his house, and Mrs. Mostyn Lloyd listened attentively. When he had finished she thanked him and asked: "Can you read, Merlin?"

"Yes, ma'am."

She gave him a child's book which he read with gusto.

"Can you write?"

"No, ma'am. Miss Whale says I must start soon."

The nursemaid and Merlin were then packed off into another room. Mrs. Mostyn Lloyd sat still for a moment, examining her rings, and then asked abruptly: "Did you know your mother was dead?"

Lucy, who had so vehemently assured Whaley that she knew her mother, was dead, in fact knew nothing of the sort: that had been a piece of invention. So now, completely taken aback by this sudden question, she blurted: "No, ma'am."

Mrs. Mostyn Lloyd said: "There's no need to call me ma'am. You can call me Aunt. I am your aunt, am I not?"

Lucy answered, on the verge of tears: "Yes."

"Very well, then. Don't treat me as if I were a fool."

After a while she said: "I used to wonder why your mother suddenly stopped writing to me a few years ago, when we were arranging for you to come and live with me and my husband. However, there it was. If you don't want to write, you needn't, I thought; and I had plenty of other things to occupy my mind because we'd just come to London and it was touch-and-go between us and the workhouse. Or so I thought. Fortunately, my husband is not one to make mistakes. Maybe your mother was a better woman than I am. In many ways she was. I was always a soft lazy slut—"

"Oh, ma'am!" Lucy cried.

"Now, you shut up and listen to me. Let me be myself for once. I do enough pretending. You'll have a bellyfull of it if you come here."

"Come here? But, Aunt—"

"I said if. There's a lot of pros and cons. My sister had guts, which is more than I ever had, but life's a rum do, and it was for her to marry a soft creature like Evans and for me to marry Mr. Mostyn Lloyd. If my sister became a bit peculiar at last, that was because she knew she'd bungled herself into one mistake after another, and I suppose in the end she thought: To the devil with all of 'em. I'll be on my own. When those letters stopped, I didn't think I'd ever see her again, but I did—about six months ago.

"She was dying in a workhouse infirmary not far from London. They found one of those old letters of mine still among her things, and I hope she kept it because she had a bit of a soft feeling for me. I'm dead certain she didn't keep it because she ever intended to turn up on me. She wasn't that sort. Anyway, they sent for me, and Mr. Mostyn Lloyd went with me and took her out of that place, and she died you might say in luxury—in the lap of luxury."

Lucy was crying, and there was plenty in memory from which tears might spring: the lean brown woman bending over her as the lambs were crying in the cold dawn, the London finery blazing in the garden patch, the cocoa tin with its pitiful hoard.

"Well," said her aunt. "I don't say you've got nothing to cry for.

You've got plenty. I heard it all in the three days I was with her before she died. Her heart was set on you, and you broke her heart. Don't think you're any surprise to me, or your son either. She told me all of it, but she didn't know what luck you'd had. She'd wanted to go back and have a look at you many a time, but she was too proud to do it, or as obstinate as a mule. Have it any way you like. She thought you'd end up in a desperate mess, but you were lucky to find this Miss Whale.

"Mind you, *she's* no surprise to us, either. I don't need to ask you any questions. I know everything. My sister would have eaten her poor old worn-out boots before she'd have come to me to ask for a thing. Of that I'm certain. But being that they fetched me to her, and she being too weak to be resolute any more, she told me everything and begged me to look after you. I promised her that I would, and I don't mind telling you this: that I made that promise to comfort her last hours and with no intention of carrying it out if it didn't suit me and Mr. Mostyn Lloyd to do so. Now stop crying, for God's sake. Try and have a bit of the guts your mother had."

Lucy dried her eyes and looked with wonder and a new respect at this woman whom she had hoped to impose on, but who seemed to know every move of the game. She flopped like a jelly in her chair, but Lucy felt a tough core beneath that surface.

"How did you know?" Lucy asked. "I mean about Miss Whale —and—and everything?"

"Why, by going and finding out. There's no difficulty about that. I can tell you this: if you'd turned out to be a half-baked slut with a dirty brat there's not much, if anything, that would have been done for you. But the report was eminently satisfactory."

"Report?"

"Yes, report—from Mr. Mostyn Lloyd's solicitor. He was down there for a week, living in a pub at Porteven. I tell you, there's nothing about you we don't know. And I congratulate you on having the sense to wear a wedding ring and call yourself a widow. I'd have done the same if I'd been in the same fix, but I'd like to see the man who could have fixed me without providing the wedding ring first."

She allowed herself a chuckle, and her little black-currant eyes glistened with a worldly knowledge that, Lucy realized now, she should have given her credit for. She felt like a chicken that had thought it was stalking a fox.

"My God!" said this new-found Auntie Meg, "you should think yourself lucky. If you had come to us at the time when we first moved to London you'd have had to work—my, you would! There wasn't much rest in those days, and there wasn't this house and a staff of servants. So bear that in mind and treat your uncle with respect.

You had a mother in a thousand and I don't suppose you ever knew it; and you've got an uncle in a thousand, and that's something I'd advise you to remember. Your auntie doesn't amount to much, but don't try any tricks with her."

She chuckled again, and the small black eyes caught the fire gleam companionably with the bangles and necklaces.

"There are some people," she said, "that things work out for, and Mr. Mostyn Lloyd is one of 'em. 'Meg,' he says, 'one of these days you're going to marry me. You can't help it.' And one of those days I married him, though no one would have called him much of a catch. And 'Meg,' he says, 'we're going to start a shop in Swansea,' and we started a shop in Swansea, and I stood on my hind legs behind the counter till the thing was a flaming success and I'd got varicose veins for life. That's what's the matter with me, my dear, varicose veins, though it's not a genteel thing to have or to talk about, so we don't mention it. And then he says 'Meg, what about London? What about Oxford Street?' and a year ago he says 'What about Kensington?' and here we are."

Lucy looked at her in fascination, the monumental complaisance, the unending watchfulness of the lizard eyes. She marveled at her own innocence in thinking that this was prey her silly wiles could trap.

"Well," said Auntie Meg, "it worked out as far as you were concerned, too. 'Meg, what about getting that girl and her boy to London?' says Mr. Mostyn Lloyd, and you walk right in. It's uncanny," she said, "it's positively uncanny, the way things work out for Mr. Mostyn Lloyd. He knew that Miss Whale would be in London for this book of hers, and so he asks her to his shop—a first step, you might say, toward knowing you and seeing what you're like. Then she asks us to tea, and there you are, handed up on a plate for us to look at, though we had no idea that you had come to London with Miss Whale. However, now you're here, you might as well stay."

At last, though almost smothered by the oily flow of Aunt Meg's conviction that she could mold all as she desired, Lucy ventured to cry: "But, Aunt, you haven't even asked me! How can you be sure that I'll want to come?"

"Asked you!" cried Auntie Meg. "Didn't I promise my sister? And what do you mean—*want* to come? *Don't* you want to come? D'you think Miss Whale will stay puttering about down there much longer? And what are you going to do then? Look at you! Why, I can read you like a book. Spoiled, always spoiled—that's you. First by your mother and then by Miss Whale, for which you can thank your Maker, for you were pretty near the rocks, from what I've heard. But you're one of the lucky ones: always someone there when you want 'em. And this time it's me. There'll never be any children in this house—not from me, anyway. That's a sore point and a sad point, and from now on we'll shut up about it. But there it is, and it happens to be another rock for you to step on just when you're going to need one. So don't talk nonsense about wanting to come. What's to become of that boy of yours? You've got him to think about, haven't you?"

Overborne, Lucy murmured: "Yes, Auntie."

"Very well, then. That's settled. And keep that ring. Don't forget you're a widow. There's one other thing. Mr. Mostyn Lloyd and I don't like this name Merlin. We've decided to change it to Mervyn. It's a very small change, and the child won't know the difference."

"But, Auntie—"

"That's all, then. Mr. Mostyn Lloyd and I think you're a nice lady-like girl, and Mervyn is an attractive child, and intelligent. Intelligent enough to thank you for what you're doing when he grows up. Not that he need ever know. What d'you think your husband could have been?"

"Oh, Aunt, I've never thought of such a thing!" Lucy lied.

"That's good, because you won't have anything to forget. Mr. Mostyn Lloyd and I thought a gentleman farmer. That could mean anything or nothing, which is an advantage in a way. Does that suit you?"

"Very well, Aunt."

"The brougham will take you home, and as soon as you are ready to come to us it will bring you. Don't bother about clothes or anything else. We will amuse ourselves with some shopping."

"Yes, Aunt. It will be amusing to ransack Mr. Mostyn Lloyd's shop."

"He would like you to call him Uncle Tom. He asked me to tell you that. We will do the shopping in Bond Street."

CHAPTER TEN

I

I LEFT Tresant when I was sixteen years old, and had no reason to think that I should ever after that be more than a visitor there. But things rarely turn out as we think they will, and now here I am in Tresant, writing away at this record, which I have put together in many places, and there seems little likelihood that at my age I shall ever leave the place again. But who knows? If my long life has taught me anything it is to allow for the unforeseen. If I had to choose a family motto, it would not be the defiant *Fiat voluntas mea* of the Gaylords, but *Who knows?*

I must skip hastily over the few years that followed the time when Maggie and I returned from London, leaving Lucy Evans and the new-named Mervyn at the Mostyn Lloyds'. My health improved, and I gave up spectacles forever, or at any rate till I took to a lorgnette as a stage property. But that was pretty late. It still helps me to outstare people whom I find offensive.

I came to realize the importance of not wanting to be like other people or to do what other people did. Much as I continued to like and admire Sally, I let her go her way, and I went mine. It didn't seem to me any longer a matter of shame or regret that horses and I were not made for one another. I gave up riding even McFlimsy, and I went on my feet wherever I wanted to go. I was so sick of pretense. The discovery that Whaley *knew* I had been acting all through my time of wretchedness filled me with a sudden and salutary shame, and I sought a cure in being my plain and unexciting self.

I suppose the impact of this new unpretending Sarah Rainborough must have been more pleasing to other people than any effect I had made in the past. Anyway, I remember those last few years at Tresant as peaceable and unworried. My father accepted me and we got on well together. A girl's affections tend to shift and veer, and I did not feel for him at that time the almost passionate regard which had possessed me when a child. Maggie Whale—the Margaret Whale of respected title pages—became the center of my life. The good-humored friendliness I had always felt for her deepened into a secret passion, common enough among young girls for young women.

It was just before our return from London that I became aware of this. Lucy and Mervyn had said good-by that afternoon and had been driven off in Mr. Mostyn Lloyd's carriage. In the morning Whaley and I would start for Cornwall. That night she went out to dinner, and no one was in the house but myself and a few servants. I was afflicted by my loneliness and went to bed early, but I could not sleep, and presently I became aware that what I was waiting for was the sound of Maggie's returning cab.

It must have been hard on midnight when I heard the wheels, and then her footstep on the stair, and I sank down into the bed and pulled the sheets about my ears, ready now for blissful sleep. The door opened, and I sat up to see her framed in the doorway, holding a lighted candle in a candlestick. She came in and put this down on the bedside table, and, leaning over me, kissed me. "I just wanted to see that you were all right," she said. "I thought you might be lonely."

A kiss from Maggie was so unusual that I felt my heart beating excitedly, and I flung my arms round her neck and returned the kiss warmly.

"Why! You fierce little bear!" she laughed. "What a hug!"

She pressed me back into the bed and tucked the clothes round me and went out quietly. I at once sank down into the blissful sleep I had been waiting for.

2

In the early spring after our return I moved into the lodge and became Maggie's secretary-companion. It was a wonderful situation for a child: it made me older than my years, as they say, but it gave me a long time of intense happiness. Our attachments to Tresant were slender but cordial. Every day we took at least one meal there, and we endured much chaffing from my father who would berate Sally for her idle life and call upon her to profit from observing the ways of the world's workers. I imagine he thought of my conduct as freakish and not likely to last, and I must indeed have been an earnest little oddity, deserving to raise a smile, and I am glad he found something to smile at.

"How is our secretary today, Miss Whale?"

"Excellent, sir. Soon she will be indispensable. But what shall I do when she has to be dispensed with? One of these days, I suppose, she will fall in love and want to get married."

"That I never shall," I declared fiercely. "I shall never leave you."

"One meets no one in Cornwall," said Sally gravely, "whom one could *begin* to think of marrying."

Father looked at her quizzically. "Falling in love," he said, "is one of those things that don't seem to have a beginning. That's why it's called falling. You're there, all of a sudden."

He was silent for a while, looking at me earnestly. Then he said: "Sarah, you're oddly unlike your Mama."

I was still wearing spectacles, and I suppose I had an intent owlish look, and certainly I could not guess what process of thought or feeling had led to his remark. "No," I said flatly. "I'm afraid I shall never be like Mama."

"But you're a good girl," he said. And back into his bantering: "I hope you pay her well, Miss Whale."

"Oh, no, sir," she answered blithely. "I know from experience that governesses, secretaries, and such like are cheap as dirt. And so I grind her face."

This was an edged remark, and it may have rankled in Father's mind. Be that as it may, he turned up that afternoon, with Eddy Rodda leading the Sudden Sneezer. Rodda was told to come back in an hour's time, and during that hour Father and Maggie had a long talk which she afterward retailed to me. He could not understand, he said, why she bothered to go on with her work as a governess now that there was no need for her to do so; and she answered that it was because she was happy with the girls, had the mornings on her hands, and would like to finish a job she had begun. Father raised two objections. First, he did not think it was fitting that a distinguished woman should work as a governess, to which Maggie answered in her forthright way that it was a pity so many parents who should know better were willing to entrust their girls to undistinguished women with no qualifications for the work they were expected to do. Secondly, Father thought the time had come when the girls should go away to be "finished," and to that Maggie had nothing to say except that it was a matter for him to decide.

"But I want your advice," he insisted; and Maggie said that though she knew little of the sort of schools he had in mind, she felt that Miss Sally was more likely than Miss Sarah to benefit from whatever one of them might have to give.

"I don't want to feel," he said, "that I am making any difference in my treatment of the girls."

"But that is just what you ought to feel," she objected. "Different girls benefit from different things, and I should be happy if Sarah were left where she is. It would be best for her."

"But you. You don't want to hang about in this Godforsaken backwater. What reason is there for it any longer?"

"I imagine, sir," she said, "that if anyone else called this a God-forsaken backwater, you would have a ready answer."

"Yes, that's true. But is it the best place for *you*—your objects in life being what they are?"

"I have never had any object in life except to live each day as contentedly as I could, and happily if possible. People with objects in life are great bores, and often great dangers to others. No, sir; believe me, I am content here and shall be pleased if you will permit me to stay a little longer. But I'm afraid I'm quite unscrupulous. If ever the time comes when it seems to me good to go, I shall—well, just go."

Soon after this, Sally went off to school in Sussex, and our odd life at Tresant began: Father and Rodda in the house, Maggie and I in the lodge.

3

Whenever I write the word December it has two meanings for me. It can mean London with the fog thickening, darkness come by half past three in the afternoon, and muffins by the fire, with the curtains drawn. Or it can mean Tresant where there may be a sea mist indeed, but no lung-choking fog, and already the first camellias are incredibly blooming and the garden of the lodge is heavy with the scent of wintersweet.

It was such a day. Maggie and I had just got back to the lodge after walking through the woods by the lake and we had gathered a handful of honeysuckle twigs tufted with green tender leaves. Before going in, we went to the sheltered small garden at the back to see the camellias. We should soon have them in red and pink, and white shot and streaked and mottled with pink or red; but these first arrivals were pure white with golden stamens clustered at the heart. We stood there looking at these wondrous flowers shining against their large dark-green glistening leaves, when we heard Rodda's voice shouting: "Anyone in?"

We found him at the front door, and he said without ceremony: "His lordship sent me to say the Prince Consort is dead."

No one spoke for a while, and then Eddy said: "Well, the ole scythe had to come for 'e, as for anyone else, I suppose. He was a German, they do say."

Yes, his time had to come, but this sudden announcement of it shook me deeply. Not because the Prince Consort meant anything to me in himself, but because he was a figure in a memory of splendor. Through the fading light of the December afternoon my imagination flew back to the bright May weather and the lines of flags streaming against the clouds over the flashing crystal of the Palace. I was holding my father's hand and my mother was with me as we entered the Palace of Peace, and soon my father would become a knight because we were at peace no longer and he controlled the iron so important when we were at war. But no one yet knew anything of this, and the organs were filling the place with rivers of music that flowed among gardens of flowers. It was only of the moment that I had been conscious then and that I was conscious of now as it re-created itself in my memory: the Prince walking amid all this splendor, holding a little girl by the hand, and the Queen holding a little boy. She was in pink and silver, and now she would be in black.

I suppose it was only for seconds that I was thus transported, but so completely that it was almost with a shock that I came back to see Maggie twisting a white camellia in her fingers and to hear her saying tritely: "Thank his lordship for letting us know. Will you stay and have some tea?"

"Thank you, Miss, I will. It's not ofen I get off on the razzle nowadays."

"Come in, then," Maggie invited with a laugh. "Miss Sarah and I always drink tea most razzlingly. We'll be delighted to share our orgies."

Rodda went through to the kitchen and put on the kettle, while I laid out the crockery on the table and Maggie cut the bread and buttered it. The evening had now deepened. I drew the curtains and poked up our fire. It was the moment I hugged secretly to my breast: the moment when the day outside was done with and darkness inhabited the wide spaces that cut me and Maggie off, shut us up in our intimacy, folded us round in a silence that nothing would break save an owl's tremolo or a heron's harsh sudden cry or the reedy bubbling of the curlews. Sometimes, at full moon, I would go outside the door to rejoice in *seeing* the great space that was our secrecy's shield: the reeds standing up in the moon-washed lake, the folded swans rocking there like huge white fantastic flowers, the dark solid woods, the silvery canopy overhead; and through the night would come the far-off Atlantic rumor, the everlasting, intervaled noise of the bar: surge and silence, surge and silence. The very punt, lying black and still as a coffin on the water, seemed to have its life. I used to wonder what it would be like to be the punt, sleeping there so quietly all night and waking with the early sun a-glitter on its dew. I knew, in those days, how Coleridge felt when he wrote of "the silly buckets on the deck." Everything was wonderful to me, except, that afternoon, to have Eddy Rodda lingering with us. We had finished tea, and he had insisted on doing the washing up, and then he filled his pipe and settled himself in an armchair.

"I suppose now," he said, not looking at us but staring straight into the fire, "you wouldn't ever be hearing what happened to that young woman Lucy Evans?"

Maggie Whale was not one to give a powder when the moment needed surgery. "Oh, yes," she said, "I hear from her every week."

"She don't ever send a message for folks in these parts?"

"No. I would hardly expect that, would you? She sends her respects now and then to his lordship, but there's no one else, is there, that she has any reason to remember with gratitude?"

"She never remembers an old man like me, now?"

"If she does, she doesn't say so."

" 'Er being upalong among all they foreigners—that don't seem right to me."

"You have no need for anxiety, Captain Rodda," she assured him, "and neither, happily, has she. The foreigners she is with are looking after her well enough."

"I'd like to have that out of 'er own mouth," he said, "if so be you'd let me 'ave 'er address some day."

Maggie got up, threw a log on to the fire, and remained standing on the hearthrug, looking down at him. However, she couldn't look down far, even when she was standing and he sitting. Already I was as tall as she. But she had a look of dumpy obstinate resolution as she said: "Captain Rodda, so long as Lucy was here and able to make her own resolutions, I didn't feel that the situation between you two had anything to do with me. Indeed, I once told his lordship himself that it was something for you and her to settle. But now that she *has* chosen, now that she has gone out of this district and seems to have no wish to see anyone in it again, you may depend upon it you won't get her address out of me. So please don't mention Lucy to me again."

He was taken aback by her vehemence and seemed a bit shame-faced. "It don't seem right," he mumbled, " 'er among all they foreigners, unprotected."

"We know how well she was protected here among her own people," said Maggie, driving her dagger home. "And now, that will do."

This was so clearly a dismissal that Captain Rodda rose, and when he was gone I said: "You were rather hard on him, Maggie."

"Hard? I was trembling for fear that he'd answer me back. But it's time to put a stop to his nonsense."

4

Throughout this time which I am trying to deal with quickly Maggie and I made several visits to London. These were years of wild financial speculation, especially in railways. That strange man Joseph Paxton, who had begun his life as a gardener and reached its peak, so far as the public went, with the designing of the Crystal Palace, was up to the neck in the railway mania long before his great national day in 1851; and many thousands of people, for better or worse, were scrambling along the same trail after easy money. For Captain Henry Grimshaw it was a ruinous trail. He was the son of a Lancashire industrialist, not of an important one, but a man who had been able to buy his son a commission in the Army. This, the old man hoped, would give the boy a social leg-up in the world. But young Henry was a romantic; he married one of his father's weavers in a runaway match. His time in the Army was not happy thereafter, but he stuck it out, obtained his captaincy, and soon afterward retired. His father's death at about this same time left him reasonably well provided for. He bought a charming house in St. John's Wood. There was a walled garden with a pond in it, over which a nude marble lady leaned, dropping one hand down to tickle the goldfish swimming among the water lilies, and using the other to ensure that their goggling eyes should receive no affront to modesty. There was a seat under an ancient mulberry tree, and over a trellis on the back of the house a wistaria in springtime draped its mauve festoons.

Here Captain Grimshaw and his still attractive but childless Annie might have been happy together for a long time had not the railway-investment bug bitten him deeply. He was a man with neither sense nor experience in financial affairs, and the marble lady looked down with faultless modesty and unconcern while the goldfish nibbled the hairs of his ears and mustache during the few hours that passed before he was lifted out of the pond at seven o'clock on a sleety winter morning.

This was why Annie Grimshaw, with a considerable house on her hands and no more than five pounds a week for income, was pleased to have so quiet and occasional a lodger as Maggie Whale. The time would come, Maggie knew, when she would settle down here at 24, Pembroke Road. Till then, it was pleasant to use the place during her increasingly frequent visits to London. She disliked hotels. She was already a well-to-do woman, and was to be a rich one, and she could afford to deal generously with Mrs. Grimshaw.

Here, then, we stayed when we came to town. Overlooking the garden from the first floor, Maggie had a large sitting room, a bathroom, which was something you did not often find in those days, and two bedrooms. Mrs. Grimshaw did the cooking, and Glory Jane, over whom for the moment I shall draw a decent veil, did everything else.

5

In the summer preceding that December day when Captain Rodda came with news that the Prince Consort was dead we had a strange encounter. We took the *Observer,* and it was from this newspaper that I had cut a few paragraphs just a year before Rodda's call. I still have my old scrapbooks and can give you the very words that interested me. "At last," they begin, "we have the iron frigate," and that is why they engaged my attention. Iron was a word that spoke to one who was still a Rainborough, despite all that had happened to her; and when I continued to read: "It is gratifying to find that the Thames Ironworks Company have, after repeated disappointments, at length advanced so far with the work as to admit of the hull of the new frigate being launched, even in an unfinished state. Iron-plated ships have now become a necessity for naval warfare"—why, then it seemed that this was indeed my concern, for the Thames Ironworks Company was one I had heard Sir Richard speak of, though he spoke rarely enough of iron when at home in Portman Square. But I recalled a morning when I had stood at the front door watching him leave. Ducat leaned his face over the open trap in the roof of the hansom and asked as usual: "Where to, sir?" and I waited for the usual reply "To the City." But instead, the reply was: "The Thames Ironworks," and the breach of custom stuck it in my mind.

164

Another thing was this. I remembered Mama saying to me that Papa was knighted because he had helped to win the war, and now here again was iron—"a necessity for naval warfare." I said nothing to Maggie of the muddled perturbed thoughts that these paragraphs stirred up in me, but I pasted the cutting into the book, and when we were in London during the following summer I asked her if we might take a boat on to the Thames to see the new iron ship.

There are many reasons why I recall that day, and chief among them is the strange—or at any rate unexpected—encounter that I have spoken of. There was no Victoria Embankment then: some years were to pass before the building of it began: and it was in an altogether different scene from what you look on today that Maggie and I hired a boat at Blackfriars and were pulled downstream to the busy part of the river where sailing ships still abounded. It was a scene that no one would look on much longer: the sails would go and the river would be squeezed between granite walls and iron would float and funnels belch and ships' sirens moan on winter nights through the Thames fog. It was a moment of transition for many things and many people, and for me among them, though I did not know it.

We looked at the *Warrior* frigate, with what emotions I cannot recollect, and were being rowed back to Blackfriars through a lovely afternoon of light breeze and slowly-moving cloud. The tide was rising, so that our boatman had little to do but dip his paddles easily and let the incoming North Sea or German Ocean do the rest. Looking forward toward Blackfriars, Maggie and I could see a boat coming toward us, rowed against the tide by two boys who were making heavy weather of it. Their boat was a clumsy tub, and they seemed unaccustomed to rowing, and the tide made hard work for them. Again and again they caught a crab, rocking their craft, but nevertheless shouting with laughter. They were having a good time, but their antics caused Maggie some anxiety. "Do you think," she timidly said to our villainous-looking boatman, "that you'd better watch out for this boat coming toward us?"

He spat over the side, gave one contemptuous look over his shoulder, and said: "Let 'em look out for themselves. Didn't oughter be on the river."

But there they were, indubitably on the river, and indubitably they were going to smack into us. They did so, their bow giving a glancing blow to our beam forward. Both the tubs were so sturdy that no harm was done; but a volley of black oaths from our boat poured into a volley of laughter and French chatter from theirs. For our boatman this was conclusive. "There y'are," he scowled. "Bleed'n' foreigners. Didn' oughter be on the river. Bleed'n' foreigners didn' oughter be anywhere. They mucked things up good an' proper in India," he added, with a feeling reference to the Mutiny of a few years before, in which Captain Grim-

165

shaw had seen service, "an' they comes to England an' takes the very bread out of a decent Englishman's mouth." He had rested a fist like a ham on the gunwale of the other boat, and both were drifting upstream on the tide. He spat into the brown eddy, the frothy swirl, and again summed up all men of whatever color who had the misfortune not to speak the tongue that he handled with such range and grace. "Bleed'n' foreigners. They didn' oughter live."

One of the boys in the other boat was seized by a new spasm of laughter. He addressed himself to our boatman. "Cheese it, Charley. And cheer up. You'll soon be dead."

"Oh, English are yer?"

"Not 'arf. Sorry I banged into your bleed'n' boat. However, no damage done."

His coat was lying on one of the thwarts. His shirt sleeves were rolled above his elbows, and his arm was alongside the boatman's as each held the other's gunwhale. They were richly in contrast: one hairy as an ape's, knotted with muscle, blue, red and green with a complication of tattoo work; the other slim and silky, brown as a baked biscuit. Maggie was looking intently at the owner of this arm, and now she said: "Good heavens! Aren't you Daniel Undridge?"

He laughed again. He was full of laughter. "Have you only just tumbled to it?" he asked. "I knew you at once. I expect I've changed a lot." To the boy with him he said: "Sebastien, this is Miss Whale, and, I think, Miss Sarah Rainborough."

Sebastien said: "Rainbor? Plees? Spik more slow," and our boatman growled with satisfaction: "Ah! Bleed'n' foreigner."

We were at the Blackfriars steps. Daniel paid the man who was waiting there to take his boat and then turned to ours. He slipped half a crown into his hand. "That'll pay for a lick of paint. So long, Charley. Keep the bleed'n' old flag flying."

"Any more o' your lip an' I'll knock yer bleed'n' block orf," said the man. "English or no English, you don't belong round 'ere." But the half crown left his words without venom.

We set off toward the Strand, and Daniel introduced his companion as Sebastien Rimmel. He was a boy about as old as Daniel, and his English was small, though he and Daniel, we learned, had been in London since the spring. Mr. and Mrs. Undridge were still in Bordeaux. Sebastien was the son of the headmaster of the school at which they worked, and this was the second time that Daniel had brought him to London for the improvement of his English. They lodged in Chelsea with a widowed sister of Mrs. Undridge.

All this we gathered as we walked toward Ludgate Circus, Daniel chattering away, happily bilingual, now to us and now to Sebastien. Maggie invited them to visit us at St. John's Wood, but they were not able to do so. They had to return to France in a day or two, and they had engagements that would take up all their time.

"I see you again when next—not?" said Sebastien, whose encounters with English sentences, indomitable, polite, had nevertheless a memory of the Laocoön; and off they went, laughing, through the hot summer street.

"I thought them a couple of very nice boys," said Maggie when we were back in St. John's Wood. "Daniel has improved beyond belief."

I thought so, too.

6

Our big sitting room, looking onto the garden and the gardens of other houses, was cool and green. It had been frightful, for the tastes of Annie Grimshaw and the late captain were by nature florid and, by acquisition during residence in India, Oriental. Seeing that she hoped to live here for a long time, Maggie had ruthlessly demanded a clean sweep. No end of voluptuous shawls had been swept away with the intricately carved ebony chairs they draped. Ebony and ivory elephants had trumpeted their last, an elephant's foot that held the coal and a tiger skin complete with snarling teeth and glaring eyes had been sent about their business. Brass trays, candlesticks shaped like hooded cobras, a miniature Taj Mahal beneath a glass dome, a sinister weapon that Mrs. Grimshaw called a tulwar: all these and much else were now heaven knows where, and we didn't care as long as they were not with us.

"If I am to have my being here," said Maggie, "it's going to be *my* being," and her ideas flew flat in the face of everything that was then considered modish and elegant. The fireplace happened to be of attractive white marble in the manner of Adam, and that was left where it was. All else was stripped and scraped down to the bone, and then the walls were painted a pale mat green and all the woodwork a gleaming white enamel. We were staying at an hotel in London when things had reached this stage, and we went along "for to see and to admire." Mrs. Grimshaw entered the room with us and sniffed disapprovingly. She had ladylike airs, but now and then she fell back on the accent of her origins. "Cold," she pronounced. "The Captain and I became accustomed to warmth. I couldn't live in a room like that."

"Perhaps you'll like it better when there's a bit of furniture in it," said Maggie.

"The Captain insisted on the best," said Mr. Grimshaw. "Out East, he had the entry to palaces."

"Well," Maggie laughed, "we're out west now, and this is no palace. It's just a working woman's office."

"It could be rendered habitable with a touch here and there," Mrs. Grimshaw conceded, casting her eye round as if in search of a hook from which she might hang a swag of crimson velvet. "Out East, one had unlimited choice of the richest fabrics."

"What I want," said Maggie, "is a bit of simple furniture."

Mrs. Grimshaw sighed. "If that's all," she said, as though washing her hands of the matter, "you might care to make an inspection of the stuff in t'attic."

Maggie's ears pricked up. Stuff in attics interested her. "What stuff is that?" she asked.

"Rubbish, I daresay. It was there when the Captain and I returned from Out East. The family from whom the Captain purchased the residence had it put in t'attics when they refurnished. They didn't want it any more. So we consented to their leaving it where it was. Naturally, it didn't appeal to us."

The stuff from the attics was about us as we sat at tea that June afternoon. There was a Hepplewhite dining table, six Hepplewhite shield-backed chairs with leather seats now gleaming like honey, a knee-hole writing desk and a few occasional tables, including one with a "pie-frill" edge and three greyhound feet. These things, and a comfortable divan which she had found elsewhere, were all Maggie needed, save for the breast-high bookshelves along one wall. She considered it a fortunate day when the wind of a changing fashion relegated "this stuff to t'attic," as Mrs. Grimshaw said. Mrs. Grimshaw was not vanquished all at once. She fought a rearguard action whose last shot was when, one day, she put her head round the door and cooed: "Not even t'tulwar? Over t'mantelpiece?"

"Not even the tulwar over the mantelpiece," said Maggie firmly.

7

Glory Jane, wearing her cap and apron, came in with the tea tray. On a trim demure creature those adornments—not of her, mark you, but of her employer's status—could look appropriate, even charming. Whenever I think back about Glory Jane, I remember the "dames" I saw later in pantomime. All that they wore was right for them in the character of someone dressed as someone—and something—else. Considered as adornment for themselves, it had a sense of wrongness, and this odd combination of being at once right and wrong made the rightness of a dame. Glory Jane had the same effect upon my mind. That flaming carroty hair looked as if at any moment it would set fire to the wisp of goffered muslin; upon that superb torso the apron hung with the sense of a fig leaf upon primeval Eve. She produced prodigiously the feeling of masquerade, and yet, because of her drollery, of rightness. To hear Mrs. Grimshaw chiding Glory Jane because her cap was not straight was to feel as though, Out East, she was using a fly whisk to an elephant.

It is the custom in the North, whence Mrs. Grimshaw came, to use two Christian names, to speak of John Willie or Sarah Ann; and Mrs. Grimshaw spoke of Glory Jane in this sense, refusing to surrender her conviction that Jane could not be a surname. But a surname it was, and Mrs. Jane, Glory Jane's mother, lived a changeful life, swaying from a condition of being what her daughter called "with Jesus" to one of being "on the razzle." During the few hours which, once a week, Glory Jane had off, she would go to Bermondsey, where her widowed parent lived in one room, curious about the condition in which she would find her. Her report, which she made with a relishing lack of reticence, was full of admiration for her protean parent. We gathered that life would be dull for Glory Jane if Mrs. Jane's character became fixed. "Like a music 'all she is. You never know what the curtain'll go up on next." A creamy chuckle would bubble in the classic white column of her throat.

Glory Jane's confidences to us were liable to be interrupted by Mrs. Grimshaw's voice from the foot of the stair. "Glory Jane! No gossiping. Leave the tray and come down. I don't like the look of the brasses."

But Glory Jane was not to be hurried. She would fall into her conspiratorial mood, always presaged by the laying of a finger to her lips and a fall of voice as she began: "Listen." She was a Sybil, about to utter.

"Listen! 'Er! What do I care for 'er! I 'aven't told you this before. This is rich. D'you know what she's got on her dressing table? Not the late captain—oh dear no! A bloomin' Rajer! Now what's 'e there for? That's all I want to know. What's 'e *there* for? What comes back to 'er when she gazes on 'is dusky Nibs in the silence of the night? Not the late captain, take it from me. There's strange doings Out East. Concubinage. Ever 'eard of concubinage?"

"You'd better be off, Glory Jane. Mrs. Grimshaw's getting impatient."

" 'Is dusky 'Ighness's concubine. Take it from me. That's what she was. You can trust them cakes. Made 'em myself, same as I do everything else in this 'ouse. So she don't like the look of the brasses, eh? I'll brasses 'er one of these days. She oughter know something about brass. I'll Rajer 'er!"

"Listen!" she began another time. "This is rich. I 'aven't told you this before. This is 'ow I got my name. They was a fair scream from all I've 'eard—my old man and the old woman. Absolutely barmy about one another. A regular love match. Razzling round drinking every penny 'e earned. 'E denied 'er nothing. An' then when she was great with me an' nearly gone 'er full time, 'e was smashed flat by a great chunk o' wood down at the docks. Mahogany, I always 'eard it was. Anyway, it done 'im in all right, and what with me comin' and 'im goin' the old woman was crazy. She went absolutely over to Jesus. Not a drop passed 'er lips, and when I come nothing'd satisfy 'er but I must be christened. So she got old Alf Higginbottom the marine-store dealer to stand godfather an' old Granny Popplewell the midwife for godmother. So off they go, an' on the way to church old Alf says: 'Well, what about one, seein' it's a great day an' a bit early?' 'Well,' says the old woman, 'only one, mind you, Alf. I know what you are.' 'I'm not a camel anyway,' says Alf. 'I can't cross a desert on 'arf a pint.' 'Well, mind what you're up to,' says the old woman, 'because this is a great day in the annals of my child.' Old Granny Popplewell says nothing, but already she was wipin' 'er mustache as if she was comin' out instead of goin' in. She 'ardly ever knew which. Anyway, they took a cab afterward, because they was a bit on the late side, but they could all stand up, and everything went as merry as a marriage bell till the parson asked my name. And, believe it or not, the daft coots 'ad never thought of it. But the old woman was excited by the occasion, an' she cried 'Glory be!' 'What does the B. stand for?' asked the parson, and Ma yelled again: 'Glory be!' Then he turns to old Alf Higginbottom and asks, very polite because he knew Alf, being the sort of shepherd who knows his flock, whether inside the fold or out: 'What does the B. stand for, Mr. Higginbottom?' And old Alf, who had reached the sullen stage, having 'ad to refuse one on the 'ouse, it being late, says: ''Ow the 'ell should I know? Call it Glory Bloody Jane.' So the parson says sharply: 'That's enough lip from you, Mr. Higginbottom, in these sacred precincts,' and he brings the ceremony quickly to an end and writes me down Glory Bee Jane. I know that's the truth of it because I 'eard old Alf tell the tale many times, an' I've got a copy of the certificate with Glory Bee on it as plain as a pikestaff."

That day when we came back from looking at the iron warship on the river, Glory Jane put down the tray, strolled to the window, and gazed for a moment upon the marble lady in the garden. "Look at 'er," she said. "I wonder what *she* thinks about, all by 'erself in the moonlight? Something that wouldn't 'arf bring a blush to a virgin cheek, I bet."

I am afraid that Maggie enjoyed Glory Jane. She rarely cut her off and sent her about her business. "Well," she said, "I fear that's something we shall never know."

"And 'er downstairs—what did she put it there for? That's a question if you like. Just a little reminder, if you ask me, of good old days posing for the Rajer in the Tage Mee-all. No wonder the poor old captain done 'imself in. Though p'raps it was a twinge of conscience with 'im, too. No doubt 'e 'ad 'is memories."

"Glory Jane!" It was Mrs. Grimshaw's voice. "Don't stand about gossiping. You haven't polished the sacred cow."

"Sacred cows, temple bells and Budders," said Glory Jane. "You wouldn't believe the brass polish we get through in this place in a week. Oh, well, enjoy the cake, Miss Whale. I made it meself, and if it tastes of blacking don't blame me."

8

Well, this was in the summer before the Prince Consort died, and Maggie and I were in London again during the summer that followed. I was then fifteen years old, and more mature than the mere number of my years would suggest. I had met a lot of people during our visits to London. Maggie disliked social visiting, but she had to do some of it and she usually managed to have me invited, too, as a buffer. We had even been down to Gadshill in Kent to spend a week end with Mr. Charles Dickens, for whose new magazine *All the Year Round* Maggie was writing. We went down by rail, and were met at the little Kentish station by an Irish jaunting car, and at the house by two enormous dogs, a St. Bernard and a bloodhound, and at supper by Mr. Dickens who was very volatile and talkative and walked us off our legs through the Kentish countryside when the meal was over. All this although he was suffering acutely from neuralgia and was writing *Great Expectations*. Later that year, he sent me a copy of the book, bound in Russian leather decorated with gold, and inscribed to "Sarah Rainborough, Margaret Whale's mute, devoted, efficient, grim companion and factotum," which tells clearly enough of the rather frightened condition in which I had passed the week end. Still, such encounters shaped me and gradually gave me confidence; and, finding myself everywhere looked upon as Maggie's "companion and factotum," I began to take that position seriously, and at last I was, in fact, just that, doing for wages what I had for a time done from devotion. But the devotion was none the less. However, I sometimes wondered what Sir Richard and Lady Rainborough would have thought had they known that the situation was reversed: that I was now Maggie's servant, not she mine. I think they would have been unhappy to know that I had earned my keep. That was certainly not what they were paying their money for. I had even gone so far as to make myself a shorthand writer.

9

Since Lucy Evans went away, we had heard from her now and then, but her letters became fewer, and for some time we had not received one. I occasionally suggested to Maggie that we should call at the Mostyn Lloyds' to see how Lucy was getting on, or that we should invite her to visit us in St. John's Wood. But Maggie said: "No, no. She's had a big jump to make, and I think she'll have a better chance of landing on her feet if we leave her to herself. Let her come to us when she wants to."

It was on that afternoon when we met Daniel Undridge and Sebastien Rimmel that we received Lucy's letter. She congratulated Maggie on her new book, made a few intelligent comments on it, and said that she proposed to call upon us the day after next, unless she heard that this would be inconvenient. Maggie was pleased. She liked Lucy and she had had a lot to do with making her what she was, and from this letter it appeared that this was a sensible person, able to express herself well.

We didn't see her arrive, because our windows looked onto the back, but Glory Jane did. She was in our bedroom at the front of the house when the carriage drew up, and she rushed in at once to announce: "Carriage folk! That'll be for you, Miss Whale. There's never the likes of that for 'er."

"I expect Mrs. Grimshaw would like you to answer the bell," Maggie said in mild reproof; and Glory Jane said: "Well, 'oo else? She's out—this bein' a Thursday afternoon. And where do she go to on a Thursday, reg'lar as clockwork and all dressed up? That's something I'd like to know. She's gettin' on, but she's still got a kick in 'er, I bet. She always come back looking contented. Suspicious I call that."

She went, adjusting the cap that was like a marguerite perched on a sunflower, and I said: "I wonder what she thinks and says about us?"

"She never thinks about anything," Maggie answered. "What she says is another matter, but hardly an important one."

Our room caught the sun of the summer afternoon, and Lucy was well able to bear its scrutiny. Her tall fairness was draped in a blue so pale that it almost merged into smoke-gray. She seemed to be wrapped in a film of this infinitely soft muslin from head to foot. Flounces of it rippled down her body and flowed behind her in a trail. Her hat, her parasol, her gloves, were all a smoky blue-gray.

"I must say, Lucy," said Maggie, taking her hand affectionately and looking her up and down, "that someone has taught you how to dress. Is it Mrs. Mostyn Lloyd? Frankly, I should not have thought she had the taste."

Lucy sat upon the divan. The dress spread its skirts in a soft subsiding billow round her feet. She looked down at it not without satisfaction, then smoothed her gloved hand gently over her knees. "No," she said, "not Auntie Meg. For one thing, she never gets out now. She never leaves her bed. Uncle Tom chooses my clothes."

Glory Jane came in with the tray. She looked with reverence at the apparition, placed the tray on the table before it as if making an offering, and backed out of the room.

Maggie poured out the tea. "So Mrs. Mostyn Lloyd is not well?" she asked.

"She is and she isn't," Lucy answered. "It must be six months ago now that she took to her bed, and she won't have a doctor. It was very sudden. Uncle Tom and I had been to hear Sims Reeves sing. He likes taking me out. It wasn't as though Auntie hadn't been asked. She had, but she said she thought I ought to be at home more, looking after Mervyn. Naturally, we thought that was nonsense, seeing that he'd be asleep and that there were servants in the house. So Uncle Tom and I went together. He's so fond of singing. The Welsh are."

She drew her fingers out of one glove and turned it back over her wrist. "Well," she said, taking a cup of tea, "it was perhaps unfortunate that Uncle Tom decided on that night of all nights to eat supper out. We went to Rule's. There were two or three famous actors there, and Uncle Tom became rather excited about the whole thing and we stayed late. We went home in a hansom and he was a bit gay. Auntie Meg said he was drunk, but I'm sure he wasn't. He was only singing Sims Reeves's songs. She'd got supper waiting, and she'd been up rather a long time, of course, and when she found we didn't want anything she went off to bed at once in a huff. She didn't get up the next day, and she hasn't been up since."

She had now completely pulled off one glove and was drawing it through the other, looking down at it absently. Then, suddenly looking up into our faces, she said: "Well, there it is," and gave a little laugh. Her face was fair and frank and candid.

There was a silence that I felt to be rather creepy for a moment or two; and I broke it by asking: "How is Mervyn?"—our little Merlin, who had kicked on the lawn by the lake, and whom Sally and I used to watch with interest as he sucked at Lucy's breast. Captain Rodda's little Merlin.

"Oh, progressing famously," she said. "Uncle Tom wants to adopt him altogether. He says you can have a name changed by something he calls deed poll. He knows all about such things. And then Mervyn would be Mervyn Mostyn Lloyd. You see, Uncle Tom having no children of his own, and not wanting the name of the firm to die out, that would be excellent all round."

"How does Mrs. Mostyn Lloyd like the idea?" Maggie asked.

"Oh, we haven't discussed it with her yet."

"Do you think she would like me to make a call?"

Lucy considered the point, nibbling a cake with her delicious teeth. "Perhaps not just at the moment," she said at last. "Let's wait a bit and

173

see how things go with her—shall we? But I thought you'd like to know how I was getting on."

"And how *are* you getting on?" Maggie asked, refilling Lucy's cup.

"Oh, but haven't I been telling you? Excellently, don't you think?"

When the carriage returned, we went down to see her off. She looked lovely, leaning back in the victoria with the hood down and the parasol shading her face. She waved one smoke-blue hand as the carriage moved off.

"Listen!" said Glory Jane, who was removing the tray when we came up. "*Some* man's going to be lucky. That's what I *call* a cut off the joint."

10

I had not seen much of Sally since her going to school. During her holidays Maggie and I as likely as not spent part of our time in London, and when we were at Tresant there was always the chance that she would be away, staying with some schoolfellow's relatives. Sometimes she brought a girl to stay with her, and they would be off all day, riding and swimming, or, in the wintertime, attending dances and parties at neighboring houses. A series of suave and self-possessed young creatures thus came and went, and I was rather shy with them all, thinking that they must consider me a dowdy little owl. Sally wrote to me regularly, and for some time I had been hearing a lot about Dolly Dewhirst, a new girl at the school. I could not doubt that Dolly Dewhirst was having a success with Sally.

When Maggie and I returned to Cornwall at the end of that summer I was not surprised to find that Dolly Dewhirst was staying at Tresant. She and Sally were out when we went up to the house to pay our respects to my father, but we had hardly got back to the lodge when we saw the two girls rushing toward us in tearing high spirits. High spirits were natural where Dolly Dewhirst was. She was short and rather fat, dark, with sparkling eyes, and gave an immediate impression of having both her feet solidly on the ground. "This is Dolly!" Sally shouted as she approached; and added: "We're both expelled. Did Father tell you?"

He had not told us, and I must say I was surprised at the cheerfulness of the pair of them.

"Come in and tell us about it," said Maggie.

We learned in the course of the next hour a lot more than the immediate cause of the girls' expulsion.

Dolly Dewhirst's father was a wealthy Bradford wool manufacturer. The family lived in an old stone house among the beech woods of

Cottingley, a few miles outside the city. They kept regal state, as a wool king's family should. Mr. Dewhirst was a Member of Parliament and altogether a person of consequence. Dolly began to take an interest in her father's workers through a freak chance. Long before we met her, she had been driven in to Bradford on a winter's night to attend a children's party. Mr. Dewhirst, who had affairs of his own in the town, arranged to call for her and take her home at ten o'clock. He was a little late and found the party broken up and Dolly's host rather worried. She was ill; he had had her put to bed, and had sent for a doctor.

Mr. Dewhirst went up to the bedroom, where a fire was burning and a shaded lamp diffused a soft light. The child was lying in bed, groaning quietly, and his heart was sick. He was always overanxious about her. He had known deathbeds: his wife's, his son's. Dolly was all that he had left.

The doctor came. It was nothing to worry about, he said. The child had eaten something that disagreed with her. He gave her an emetic. She would be all right, he said, after a good sleep.

Her host now urged Mr. Dewhirst to go home. Dolly could stay there for the night and be called for on the morrow. But Mr. Dewhirst had been in the panic that any illness of Dolly's brought on. She had been snatched from the jaws of death: he would sit up with her. "Then Ah'll sit up with thee," said Midgley, an up-and-coming man proud of his working-class origins. "Ah'll not 'ave thee mopin' there alone for hours on end."

So they sat in a room adjoining the bedroom and talked and smoked Midgley's cigars and drank his whisky till, at five in the morning, they heard Dolly's voice. They went into the bedroom. She was sitting up in bed, smiling, and the smile, to Dewhirst, was like a light shining out of heaven. "Take me home," Dolly said.

They tried to dissuade her. She must stay in bed till daylight and have breakfast and go home at a sensible hour. But she would have none of it: with a child's obstinacy she kept on repeating: "Take me home."

So Dewhirst took her home. Midgley went down to the kitchen and warmed some beef tea for her and roused Dewhirst's coachman who was snoring in a chair by the stove. The horse had been put into the stable, and the coachman went out, shivering and cursing into the raw Yorkshire morning through which a few feathers of snow were fluttering. Fortified by her hot drink and wrapped in a cloak, Dolly was carried by her father to the carriage. She sat on his knee; a bearskin rug was wrapped round them both. "Now go to sleep," he said. "You'll soon be in your own bed."

But she did not want to sleep: this was an adventure such as she had never had before. The town was dark and dumb; out of the purple-black sky the snow was falling more quickly, and through it the carriage lamps drove two spears of dusky light. The horse's hooves made hardly any sound, for the snow was settling. It was entrancing to be moving through this silence and to imagine, in the warmth here under the bearskin and within her father's arms, how cold it must be out there in the street.

And then, suddenly, the silence was broken by the donging of bells. "Oh, are the churches going to open?" she cried, and her father gave a laugh of merriment. "No, no," he said. "Not the churches—the mills. They open at six."

They were bowling along the level road that would take them to Cottingley, and now, on the hills on one side and in the valley on the other, she saw large blocks of light splotching the darkness. The mills! Then she was aware that the darkness was not uninhabited. Vaguely she could see figures hurrying through the snow: men, women and children. She was surprised by their numbers, but presently they thinned out and soon there were only a few, and these began to run.

"Look!" she cried. "They're running!"

"So would you run," said her father, "if it was near six o'clock and you had to be there on the stroke or lost some of your pay."

"Me!" she said; and suddenly, in imagination, she was out there, running through the snow with the other children, and she shivered.

"But I don't have to," she said.

"No. You're one of the lucky ones."

"Why am I one of the lucky ones?"

"Because you've got a father who worked hard when he was a young man."

"Do these people work hard?"

"Well, some do and some don't."

"And those that do—their children are the lucky ones and don't go to the mill?"

"Now, Dolly, count your blessings and don't argue."

The sound of the bells stopped. It was six o'clock. But still an occasional figure came sprinting through the darkness, was seen for a moment as the light of the carriage lamps caught it and then was gone. They were oddly remote. Out there in the cold and the darkness, with the snow falling, they seemed to belong to a world that had nothing at all to do with this enclosed warm world of a bearskin rug and a father's arms. She remembered how, in a night of the summer before this, she was driving home with her father, after it was dark, from a visit to friends in the country, and the light of the carriage lamps picked up a creature shuffling across the road ahead of them. "Look! A badger!" her father said. She was thrilled by the sight, but more by the thought of the strange nocturnal life of such creatures: creatures outside any contact, remote, living in an unknown world.

And these creatures now, sprinting through the darkness that lay outside this comfortable moving cubicle: they were equally beyond her contact and understanding.

Her father's voice broke up her thoughts. "It must be delightful, this early morning walk to work in the summertime. Everything fresh. The sun just up. Sometimes I envy these people."

At that moment the lamps lit up what must surely, she thought, be the last of this not now so enviable breed. He was not like some of the others, running like a hare. Rather, in the light he seemed to flutter like a moth, weaving to and fro on the pavement as though he were half asleep. And then suddenly he fell. She watched to see him rise, and he didn't, and the carriage went by—steady, jog trot. It was that, more than anything, when she came to think about it, that horrified her: the indifference, the lordly calm, with which they bowled by, leaving that bundle lying in the snow.

It was her uncontrollable loud outcry, mingled of pity and horror, that caused her father to stop the carriage. "Stay where you are," he said. "I'll look at him."

But no sooner was he out than she was out after him, the rug draped over her thin party clothes. The keenness of the air made her draw in her breath sharply. It was a bitter morning.

Here, on either side of the road, were high stone walls enclosing the gardens of big houses. Under one of the walls the boy lay as still as an old newspaper that the wind had drifted there or a wornout discarded coat. Mr. Dewhirst spoke sharply to him, but there was no answer, and he said irritably: "What on earth are we to do? You'll catch your death if you stand about in this weather."

"We must take him home," Dolly said. She bent down and put a hand to the boy's cheek. It was thin and cold and white. He looked about eight years old.

"Get back into the carriage. Remember, you've been ill."

"He looks a lot iller than I ever was," said Dolly. "He looks as if he's ill because he's hungry. I was ill because I was a greedy little pig and ate too much."

The coachman had brought the horse round and drawn up the carriage near them.

"Hurry," said Dolly. "He's dying." She truly felt that this was so. She was terribly afraid. She got into the carriage. Her father picked up the child and followed. "Hold him as you did me," Dolly ordered, and she threw the bearskin over the child as he lay in her father's arms.

The servants were up when they got home, and Dolly enjoyed the bustle and alarm. The child had revived in the warmth, but was as frightened as a frozen bird that recovers to find itself in a room. He seemed unable to utter a word. The housekeeper gave him a warm drink, stripped the damp rags off him, and put him into a warm bed, and presently reported that he was asleep.

"And so should you be, Miss Dolly," she said when Mr. Dewhirst had given her an account of the night's proceedings. It was Dolly he was worrying about, not the waif. "You'd better have Dr. Kershaw along in the morning to have a look at her," he said. "And while he's here he can have a look at the boy. I shall take an hour's sleep now. I've got to catch the early train to London."

Dolly went up to bed. The reluctant morning was beginning to appear. The snow was still falling. She saw through her window that the lawn was a level white and that the dark shelves of the cedar were weighted with snow. A fire had been lit in her room, and she got into bed thinking excitedly that when her father was gone she would have a long talk with the boy.

11

The boy was gone. Dolly did not see him again. While she was still sleeping Dr. Kershaw came and looked at her and put a hand on her forehead and a finger on her pulse and listened gravely while the housekeeper told of her sickness. "Let her go on sleeping," he said, and promised to send a draught. And then the housekeeper told him about the boy and they went along to have a look at him and the boy was not there. A ladder left leaning against the window sill by a gardener who had been cleaning the window and a track of clogs through the snow: this was all they found, and it was enough to explain the manner of the wild creature's flight. When Dolly looked at the footprints later, they seemed to her as fugitive and inconsequential as a sparrow's. Dr. Kershaw laughed. "Doesn't seem much the matter with *him*," he said. "A bit of a fainting fit, I suppose. They're as tough as old boots. Well, you shall have Miss Dolly's medicine within an hour. Keep the fire going in her room. Keep her warm."

If she had not seen him at all, or if she had seen him again, it might have been different; but the way in which the boy had streaked across Dolly's life was as if he had been fire and had indelibly seared his passage. It was a long time before she got him out of her head, and he was never out for good. He was a recurring image, a symbol shooting out of darkness, disappearing into it again, so that at last the darkness itself was the thing that fascinated her, he its momentary messenger and embodiment. As she grew she pondered and read, and, what was more difficult, she made personal investigations into the lives of the mill workers. Her father was unhappy about her tendencies—"Count your blessings, Dolly, and don't argue"—but he passed for a liberal man and

178

he was delighted to have the honor of being host to John Ruskin who came to lecture in Bradford. It chanced that that night, having introduced his famous guest to the audience, he had to leave to keep another engagement, and so Dolly, who was in a profoundly moved and exalted condition because of the address she had listened to, drove home alone with Mr. Ruskin and had an hour's conversation with him before her father's return. First the transient boy and now the transient man. But as the boy came back to her imagination, so Ruskin came back in a number of letters and in advice about reading. Mr. Dewhirst couldn't understand the girl. He so earnestly wanted to be proud of her, but he could only be shocked. She was sixteen when she said to him one morning at breakfast: "Do you think wage conditions have anything to do with the prostitution that is so common among Bradford mill girls?"

He didn't know what to do. To think that Dolly should have heard such a word horrified him. That she should so calmly use it, as though she understood what it meant, created a situation which, he felt, must at last be firmly dealt with. And this was why Dolly was sent to a school that turned out perfect young ladies. They turned *her* out, anyway, pretty quickly.

12

Dolly and Sally took to one another at once. There was a day soon after Dolly arrived at the school when a few of the girls, including these two, were out walking with a mistress, and a drunken man came lurching along the road. The mistress at once called the young ladies' attention to the ·beauty of a pair of wood pigeons which, although she did not know it, were publicly making love with a charming lack of self-consciousness. Sally, who knew all about the ways of birds and beasts, began to laugh, and Dolly rounded on her sharply. "There's nothing funny about drunkenness," she said. "It's simply an attempt to escape from intolerable social conditions."

The drunk ambled by, ogling the girls; the wood pigeons flew away; Sally and Dolly, loitering behind the others, tagged along the road.

"You do talk rot," Sally said. She had by now heard a lot about Dolly's social theories and had proudly been shown letters from Mr. Ruskin. "People get drunk because they like drinking. I've seen lords as drunk as bricklayers, and bricklayers as drunk as lords. I've seen the Duke of Fallowshire, who married my Mama, lying under the table. Would you call his social conditions intolerable?"

"Yes," said Dolly firmly. "I certainly would."

"Well," Sally replied practically, "you can take it from me that he certainly wouldn't. The poor get tight on beer and the rich on Mr. Ruskin's sherry."

Dolly's dusky cheeks flamed. Her idol had been touched. She stopped in her tracks and looked incredulously at her companion. "What on earth are you talking about?"

"Mr. Ruskin's sherry. You don't mean to say you've never heard of it?" Dolly had not heard of it, and said so.

"Then let me tell you that Mr. Ruskin's father is a sherry salesman and that Mr. Ruskin's money comes from his father. And another thing: you're always going on about the wonders of William Morris's workshops. Where did *he* get his money from? 'No wages without work.' Dolly Dewhirst's motto. I'll tell you one thing: John Ruskin and William Morris have jolly good reason to say 'Count your blessings and don't argue.' "

Dolly had derisively related her father's phrase; she hated now to find it twisted against her.

"Well," she said, "you haven't told me about William Morris's money."

"Oh, that. Well, William's father was owed a bit of money. The poor chap who owed it couldn't pay, so he asked Mr. Morris if he'd accept some shares in a mining company instead. They weren't worth much, but old Morris agreed. Then they suddenly became valuable. Mind you, not through any work that Morris did. There was no 'wages for work' about it. He just suddenly found that there was two hundred thousand pounds in his pocket. When he took them over, the shares were worth two hundred and seventy-two pounds. I call that a good slice of wages without work."

"How can you possibly know of such things?"

"I know all right," said Sally, who had, in fact, learned these things from Maggie Whale.

"Well," Dolly said defiantly, "if it is as you say, I should call it a jolly good job that money, however it was come by, should fall into such hands."

"So should I," Sally agreed. "But that's another matter. It's not what you were talking about. All I'm trying to do is make you see that you're not going to reform the world with a few catchwords, a lack of information, and a plentiful misunderstanding of what men and women are up to. If you have a vision of a world full of saintly poor and devilish rich you won't get far, because all that most people want is to exchange their saintly poverty for devilish riches. We shall begin to get somewhere when it's the other way about."

So they were accustomed to argue, half bantering, half earnest, and altogether double-dutch to the rest of the girls, who didn't have much to do with them. They were considered an odd pair; and shocking though the effect was on the mind of the headmistress, the scholars themselves were certainly not surprised by the Food for the Fosters episode.

The Fosters lived in a lodge at the gates of the estate in which the school stood. Dolly had a mania for what she called "case histories" and Sally found this amusing. She had never known "cases." She had known men and women, and was content with that. She always addressed Foster, the school gardener, as Frank; and she persisted in this when reproved and told that, if she addressed him at all, he should be called Foster. In Dolly's "Case Book" he was "Foster, F., gardener," and it was noted that he was forty years old, had a wife—"Foster, Gertrude"—and three children aged ten, six and three. It was further noted that "Foster, John, ten," had "a tubercular tendency," that "Foster, Daisy, six" was "richitic," and that "Foster, Alexander, three" was "insufficiently clothed in cutdowns." Sally, invited to read the "Case Book," learned further that the cottage was damp, that cooking arrangements were primitive, that the parents and children all occupied the same bedroom—"although Foster, John, is approaching the age of puberty"—and that "Foster, F.," was paid a pound a week. "Foster, Gertrude" was "pregnant, though in poor physical condition."

Sally would have said, with no urge to write it down, that Frank Foster's cottage was a disgrace, that his family were a wretched-looking lot, and that poor Mrs. Foster was unfortunately going to have another baby, though how she fed the ones she had goodness only knew.

Sally, Dolly and a girl named Monica, whom they didn't like, were walking on the school drive near the lodge one day and found the three Foster children playing there. They were no ornament to their charming surroundings, and they had transgressed by marking out a hopscotch pitch on the sacred gravel. Monica went by with a twitch of annoyance, and said in the hearing of the children: "They look half-starved. Why don't they keep in their own place? Foster has orders to see that they don't play on the drive."

"Whoever had this place before it became a school was very thoughtful for his dogs," said Dolly. "Have you noticed the excellent kennels?"

"Oh, yes—absolutely first-rate," said Monica.

"It is so wasteful to have them out of use," Dolly said. "They would make a splendid place for the young Fosters to run in. For one thing, they're well drained, which is more than you can say for the lodge."

It was soon after this that Dolly's "Case Book" disappeared. Monica was the natural suspect, but this was not proved. All that Dolly knew was that a blistering interview took place in the headmistress's study. There was the book on the table, and there in the book were words like "pregnant," phrases like "the age of puberty." The woman lost her head and castigated Dolly as a foul-thinking evil thing, dangerous to the purity of the school. Dolly, usually loquacious enough, had nothing to say. What was the use? She was told that she must go. It was late on a Saturday—too late for the immediate expulsion on which the headmistress had determined, and tomorrow was Sunday, so that wouldn't do, either. Dolly left the study under sentence to depart on Monday morning. The necessary telegrams were sent at once.

She wasn't disturbed by this. She had a mind that gloried in martyrdom. But Sally minded. The stupidity of the affair made her mad, and she knew that Dolly, in her own obstinate crack-brained way, was right. Practically, she saw that foul little cottage as the cause of it all. She knew that her father would have trodden it underfoot like a fungus. And so she was heartily on Dolly's side, ripe to join in Dolly's plan for a final gesture.

This took place at midday dinnertime on the Sunday. When the plates were before them—beef, cabbage, potatoes—they stood up and each swiftly pinned to the back of the other a notice which they had kept concealed: FOOD FOR THE FOSTERS. While this surprise move held everyone spellbound, they picked up their plates and marched out of the room.

They had left the house before the headmistress unfroze and sprang up at the high table. "After them," she commanded the mistresses around her. "Girls, remain seated."

But the girls were soon crowding at the windows, shouting with excitement as they watched the pursuit. Dolly and Sally, hampered by having to keep the plates level, were soon outdistanced by mistresses who turned to face them on the path. There was an unseemly scuffle. The headmistress's Sunday dress was drenched with gravy. Palpitating strenuously, she seized a plate in each hand, wrenched them away, and hurled two good dinners inelegantly slap in the face of a pink pearl rhododendron. The games mistress pluckily ripped the notices from the girls' backs, impaling her right thumb deeply upon a pin. Dolly and Sally were a nine-days' wonder, and Foster, F., was sacked.

CHAPTER ELEVEN

I

IN 1873, when I was twenty-five years old, I was waiting at 24 Pembroke Road, St. John's Wood, for Maggie to arrive from Eton with my half brother, Justin Gaylord. It was a day of late summer, very hot, and I went to sit under the mulberry tree in the garden. Here, I could be seen from the kitchen window, and I was no sooner seated than Annie Grimshaw came fussing out. "It's so hot, Miss Rainborough! Could I bring you a nice, long, cool drink?"

Poor Annie! She had become terribly anxious to please. You couldn't move without her being there to offer a service of one kind or another. Things had gone from bad to worse with her. The mania that had destroyed her husband had possessed her, too. It was a year or so before this that she had come up to our room, looking more dead than alive, and had poured her sorrows into Whaley's ears. "You being so clever, writing them books," she sobbed, "I'm sure you can tell me how to get out o' t' mess."

Yes, she actually sobbed; her face was all blubbered over with tears; and Maggie said: "Sit down now. Let me get you some tea."

It was Glory Jane's afternoon out. Whaley came back with the tea, and when Mrs. Grimshaw was more composed she began to cross question her, in an effort to make some sense of her confused outpouring. But this only set her off again. "It's all turned out so different from what I imagined it was goin' to be when I married the captain," she sobbed. "You wouldn't believe, Miss Whale, what it was to me. I was just a silly thing—a weaver—"

Maggie headed her off this romantic retrospection, and gradually the facts became as clear as they were simple. Annie Grimshaw had been speculating with the little she had, and, when that was gone, she had made a desperate effort to retrieve her situation by borrowing money. It was the old tale of fools the world over. She had got into the hands of one of those villains whose interest charges soon turn a mole-hill of debt into a mountain, and now she literally didn't know what she owed or what she was to do. Her life had indeed "turned out different," as lives have a habit of doing. "But you, being so clever . . ." she hopelessly appealed to Maggie again.

"I'm afraid, Mrs. Grimshaw," Maggie said, "that if I have any cleverness at all where money is concerned, it shows itself simply in my never touching things I don't understand. I leave all such matters to a lawyer. I think we ought to let him clear this up for you."

Mrs. Grimshaw agreed to this, and Daniel Undridge, who had been called to the bar, combed out the tangle. There wasn't much left for poor Annie Grimshaw. She owned the freehold of the house and had to sell it. Maggie bought it, and with the purchase price Annie scraped clear. She remained in the house as cook-housekeeper and seemed happier than we had ever known her. She was a woman unfitted for any responsibility, even the small responsibility of owning a house. Now that she had nothing but a job and a wage she perked up, but her relief at shedding her worries would manifest itself in little rushes upon me and Maggie—can I do this?—can I do that?"

After this turn of circumstance, she got on well with Glory Jane. There were no sacred cows, temple bells and Budders to bother about now, and Glory Jane took her to her heart like a private accepting a

183

sergeant who has been reduced to the ranks. Mrs. Grimshaw had even been to Bermondsey to meet "my old woman." "Listen! You wouldn't believe this. She sang a song—all in Lancashire. Laugh! We nearly died! You wouldn't'a' thought she 'ad it in her."

2

Justin would be sixteen in the coming December. It was a strange relationship, this of being a half sister, especially as we saw so little of one another. I had been in London all through his growing up, so that, when I met him during long-spaced visits to Tresant, he had always had time to make a big jump in development, and this kept him perpetually interesting. He was turning out to be what his father wanted him to be, and I was glad of that because Sally and I, I thought, must be considered disappointments. There had never been any opposition to the ways we had chosen, but I was certain that Father—as Lord Burnage had the more firmly become now that his son was so real a person to me and my half brother—I was certain that he would have liked us, and Sally especially, to choose something different. Occasionally I felt a pang of self-reproach when I thought of him, alone at Tresant now that Justin was at school, sitting at the chess table with Eddy Rodda or trailing round the estate drawn by the still surviving obstinate Ebenezer. I would not have blamed him if at such moments he had considered us deserters.

When Sally went home, long ago now, after her expulsion from school, he was unperturbed, not sorry to have her with him again. She and Dolly Dewhirst remained for about a fortnight, and then they went to Dolly's home near Bradford. Things there were not so cordial. Mr. Dewhirst did not take the expulsion with the amused indifference of Lord Burnage. Each of them had received a letter from the headmistress. Father, who had heard the whole story from Sally, and seemed not displeased that a Gaylord had known how to make a gesture, merely remarked to Maggie: "The woman must be living in a fool's paradise if she thinks people will put up with conditions like that," and nothing more was ever heard from him on the matter.

Mr. Dewhirst was not able to look at it so calmly. If Dolly was going to get worked up about living conditions, he thought, then, by heck, she'll find plenty to get excited about in Bradford, with its back-to-back houses, one earth closet to a row of them, and all the rest of it. His workers were not his friends and neighbors, as Lord Burnage's were, and he didn't see any sense in pretending they were. If Midgley could make a do of it after beginning as a half-timer, then that showed

184

that "the system" worked all right for people with go and guts. There was a chance to climb, and if the chance was slender that was simply the way in which the unfit were weeded out and the right people got to the top of the ladder. The chance was there. That was the thing; and so long as it was there he didn't see that anyone had much to grumble about.

It was hard for him to be patient when, at the end of one of his discourses, Dolly exclaimed, as if she had not heard a word he had been saying: "I must get my Case Book back from that woman. It's my property and she has no right to keep it."

Mr. Dewhirst had heard about the Case Book. The headmistress had informed him of its scandalous contents.

"I'd like you to write a letter to her," Dolly said, "demanding back my property. That book's full of valuable information."

Mr. Dewhirst was firm. He would have no hand in the matter, so the next day Dolly and Sally had the joy of driving in privately to Bradford and consulting a solicitor. They didn't know a solicitor, and it was fun looking on the office fronts for a solicitor's brass plate. They found one, and went giggling up the stairs, a little frightened, a little amused, very much in earnest. It was carrying on the Food-for-the-Fosters campaign, even though Foster and his family were now worse off for food than ever. But they didn't know that.

It was a very young solicitor, in a very new office, with new furniture and new shining deed boxes that didn't yet have names painted on them and contained very few deeds. He had a fair young mustache and a new frock coat and didn't look at all how they thought a solicitor should look. Nor did the two shy blushing girls look like what he imagined when he thought of the magic word "clients."

There was only one client's chair, so he put one of them into it and the other into his own chair. He sat on the edge of the desk and the smoky autumn sun sent a ray through the window to smolder on the Turkey carpet that was second-hand and that he intended to put into his clerk's room when he could afford a new carpet and a clerk. He wondered whether he ought to offer them sherry and a biscuit, as old-established solicitors did with old-established clients? He remembered that there was only one bottle, and decided that they were too young. It was, for all of them, a tentative situation as they sat there in the ray of sunshine, listening to the clop of hooves and the grind of iron-clad wheels as horses drew lorries over the stone setts of the street without.

Dolly did the talking, and Sally admired the way in which, once she was launched, she told the whole story clearly and consecutively. "So, as the book is my property, I hope you'll be able to get it back for me," she concluded.

The young man jumped down from the desk and considered her attentively, the rounded glowing face beneath the beaver hat, the beaver muff in which the hands were hidden. There was a winy tang of autumn already here in the North.

"I think you have an excellent case," he said. "I shall write today, and I should have an answer by the day after tomorrow. I'll communicate with you then."

"No. Please don't do that," said Dolly, rising. "We'll call again to hear how you've got on." She didn't want to have her father asking about her letters. The young man was pleased by the thought that they would call again.

When they did so, he had a fire lit in the office and there were bronze chrysanthemums in a vase on the desk and he had bought a third chair and a decanter in which the sherry stood on a tray with three glasses. He was sorry when they both declined it, Dolly remarking that she considered strong drink a national curse.

"Well," said the young man, "I'm afraid our reply is not satisfactory."

He took up a letter from his desk and read: "Sir—In reply to your letter of yesterday's date, I have to say that it is impossible to return the document you write about as this has been destroyed. In view of the indecent nature of the contents, I put the book into the fire. Yours faithfully."

"Well," cried Dolly, her litigious blood alight, "what impudence! You will please write to her again. We can get her on two counts. Tell her that we are prepared to proceed against her," she said, feeling as if she were the Lord Chancellor himself, "for destruction of someone else's property and for defamation of character. It *is* defamation, isn't it, to say that I have written indecencies?"

"It might be held," said the young solicitor, "that the occasion was privileged."

"Well, try it on," Dolly commanded. "Put the fear of the Lord into her." Her face glowed righteously and she was wearing a new hat.

"I shall leave no stone unturned," said the young man.

"The only stone I'd leave unturned," said Dolly wrathfully, "would be her tombstone. I'd fasten that down with rivets. We'll see you on Monday."

On Monday the solicitor handed Dolly her Case Book. "Here it is. It came without an accompanying letter." He had had time to read it through and he looked at Dolly with deepened and amused interest.

"Thank you," said Dolly. "You see! The old liar . . . I expect we frightened her out of her wits. A law case would have done the school no good. I don't suppose law cases do anybody much good, do they, except lawyers?"

He was pleased with her candor. "You're a bit of an abolitionist, aren't you?" he twitted her.

"An abolitionist?"

"Yes. You want to abolish all sorts of things."

"Oh, rather!"

"Well, don't try to abolish the law. I assure you it would be a bad idea. I'll send my bill."

"Couldn't I pay now?" She was clutching her purse.

"Oh, no! You must give me time for invention."

He never did send her a bill, and though he told himself that this was no way to conduct business, he knew that this was precisely the way in which this piece of business should be conducted. He had no regrets; and when his deed boxes were filling and he had a clerk and a new carpet and didn't have to bother about the price of sherry, he sometimes thought of the two girls and the tang of the autumn mornings, and on such days he forgot to reprove the office boy for whistling as he worked.

3

Well, this had all happened a long time before I sat there under the mulberry tree waiting for Justin and Maggie. This had happened, and many things had happened, especially to Sally. That visit to Dolly's home in the North had been an eye-opener. Sally had been in the North before, but only in the North of great houses and grouse moors and shooting parties. She knew something of the limestone dales and clean rivers, the spreading prospect where bracken stained the purple miles with umber, under the pale autumn skies. But now, with Dolly for teacher, she learned to look at a new North where rivers became sewers fouled with the excrement of industry and hills that had been lovely were afforested with stony lanes and streets and cul-de-sacs, crowded with houses standing back to back, with never anywhere a space permitted in which a green shoot might raise its head. She, who had known fishermen and farmers living, God knows, a hard enough life beneath the rage of wind and weather, here met people who seemed to her of another breed, inhabitants of another world, an iron world that rang in the sound of their clogs upon the stone-bound streets, and in the grind of lorry wheels, and in the altogether different and, to her, more terrifying rage of whirling machines.

Dolly, passionate evangelist, spared her none of it. When Sally returned to Cornwall, she was alight with the same enthusiasm that burned in Dolly Dewhirst, and this was the deeper because of the peace and serenity of her Cornish life. Walking in the woods, listening to the bar's roaring, watching the swans upon the lake, she would be shaken by an awful sense of the two worlds, and she did not think there could be any happiness for anyone so long as they lay, as they did, with a chasm of ignorance and indifference dividing them.

4

Annie Grimshaw shouted from the kitchen window: "I can hear them arriving, Miss Rainborough," and I went through the house to the front door. Justin climbed out of the four-wheeler and held the door open for Maggie, and when she was out there came a third person whom I had not expected. He was a tall boy whose face was familiar, and yet I could not fix it. Justin came forward and gave me his hand and said: "This is a friend of mine from school, Mostyn Lloyd. We gave him a lift."

Yes, of course, Mervyn Mostyn Lloyd. Merlin Evans. Merlin Rodda, if it came to that. I wondered how much lingered in his memory. Did he remember the lake and the lawn, the reeds, the punt, the curlews calling, and the moss on the trees in the cool corridors of the woods?"

"Mervyn," Justin said, "this is my sister, but she hasn't my name. Sarah Rainborough. She's a half sister."

Mervyn shook hands with me. His hand was long and firm and cool. His dark eyes smiled into mine. He had none of his mother's fairness. He turned away to pay the cabman and Justin went in with his suitcase. Maggie whispered to me: "Not a word. We don't know him."

The last time we had seen Mervyn was on that far-off day when he and Lucy had driven in the cab from Portman Square to live with the Mostyn Lloyds. We had seen nothing of him in his growing time. He was now sixteen. The only other fact that we knew about the situation was that Meg Mostyn Lloyd was dead. Her husband had become sufficiently well known for the newspapers to take some slight notice of the fact, and we saw this announcement about a year after Lucy had come to us, a vision in smoky blue. It had been a disappointment to Glory Jane that the visit was not repeated. To us, also. We felt no ill will toward Lucy: we wished her well. Maggie, alert and interested where any sort of human conduct was concerned, said to me one day: "Lucy is the sort of girl who will survive fire, flood and earthquake. She'll only have to stand at the top of a ladder and ten firemen will rush to save her. There'll always be someone to give her a place in the boat or to turn over a hundred tons of rubble to find her."

"She looks so fragile and helpless," I said.

Maggie laughed. "I know. She's the sort of flower that will always inspire someone to build a greenhouse round it. As soon as her mother was gone, all Porteven was surging to help her. Eddy Rodda would have looked after her. So would Wesley. But she didn't choose either of them. She clung to me."

"That was wise of her," I said.

"You needn't tell me that. Lucy's instinct is faultless. I was the rock till the Mostyn Lloyds appeared. D'you remember? 'I'm thinking of Merlin.' I imagine she believed it, too. I wonder what Mrs. Mostyn Lloyd thought of her at last? At the beginning, I've no doubt she looked on Lucy as a poor timid cowering beastie. Ah well. She lived and learned like the rest of us, poor woman."

5

We had tea in the garden. It was soon obvious that Justin had a worshiping regard for Mervyn, who was the elder by about nine months. For one thing, we gathered, Justin was not much good at games. He wanted to be. It was not that games bored him as they did me. It was that he could not, try as he would, catch the knack that separated the earnest trier from the brilliant player. Mervyn had this knack. Moreover, there had been a day when a boat collision on the river threw Justin into the water, and Mervyn hauled him out. "I'd have been drowned sure as eggs," Justin said.

Mervyn laughed. "In that ditch? With a dozen men about?"

"Anyway, it was you who got me out."

"You should get Sally to teach you to swim properly," I said. "She swims like a trout."

"Sally!" he said. "A lot Sally cares nowadays about things like swimming. She's hardly ever at Tresant. She's always slumming around somewhere with Miss Dewhirst. But wait till I get Mervyn down to Tresant! When I get him onto a horse I'll show him a thing or two."

And so he would, I thought. He had his father's love of horses.

"Is Mervyn going to Tresant?" Maggie asked carefully.

"Well, there's nothing definite arranged yet. But it'll have to come one of these days. He's a Cornishman, too, you know, though his name sounds Welsh."

"It's rather a bogus name," Mervyn explained easily. "It's not my name at all—not my birth name, that is. My mother is Mrs. Evans. She was married to a gentleman farmer in North Cornwall."

Maggie gave me a meaning glance which said: "*North* Cornwall, eh?"

"When he died," said Mervyn, "—oh, before I can remember— Mother came to live with her aunt, who was married to Mr. Mostyn Lloyd. Perhaps you've heard of him?" he asked diffidently.

"Yes, indeed," said Maggie, "and I'm sure we shall hear more. He must be a remarkable man."

"He's been very decent to me, anyway," said Mervyn. "Mother was pretty hard up, you know, and he looked after us both. He had my name changed by deed poll, and while he was at it he had a hyphen put between Mostyn and Lloyd. He uses the hyphen himself now, though he's not really entitled to do so." He laughed merrily, showing white teeth. "He's full of little vanities, but a good chap. When his wife died—that is, Mother's aunt—Mother took over the management of the household."

He went off soon afterward in a cab, and we returned to sit in the coolness of the garden. Justin was anxious that we should approve of his friend. "What do you think of Mervyn?" he asked bluntly.

"A very handsome boy," said Maggie.

"Oh—that. Well, I suppose he is in a way. But I mean what do you *think* of him."

"You mustn't rush me, Justin," Maggie laughed. "I'm becoming too old to fall into a devotion in one hour."

"Well, I'll tell you what I think of him," said Justin. "I knocked a chap's tooth out for Mervyn's sake. Knocked it right down his silly throat."

Justin was so little bellicose that this interested us. He went on: "It was a little snot whose father's just been made a baronet. We were playing cricket and he got a smack on the hand from a bat that swiped round when he was wicket-keeping. His knuckles began to bleed, and someone said: 'Bind it up with a handkerchief.' So he shouted out: 'Mostyn-Lloyd, could you sell me a few handkerchiefs?' Mervyn joked it off. 'Certainly,' he said. 'I'm always out to turn an honest penny. Would you like the family crest embroidered on them? Or is it too new to have been registered yet?' Well, that wasn't a bad answer, but I thought it needed a different sort of answer, so I smacked him in the teeth and said: 'I don't allow little snots like you to insult my friends.'"

"What part of Cornwall does he come from?" Maggie asked.

"Some region I don't know. Somewhere in the North. He was very young when he left there and he doesn't remember much. He talks of woods, and a bank where pink flowers grew—sea pinks, I imagine. It might be anywhere."

"So he won't be going down to Tresant this holiday?"

"No. He's going with his mother to the South of France."

190

Justin was not going on to Cornwall for a day or two. He had arranged to meet Mervyn in the morning and to spend the day watching a county cricket match.

"I think," said Maggie, "that, with them both out of the way, this afternoon would be a good time to call on Lucy. Would you care to come?"

I would, indeed. We drove over, and found at the outset that things had changed at the house in the pleasant Kensington Square. I remembered how, when we first called so long ago, Mostyn Lloyd himself had come to the door to welcome cordially the rising author. The only servants we saw then were a few girls. Now the door was opened by a footman, and later, when tea was brought to the drawing room, it was brought by a butler. After the free and easy life of Tresant, this was a severe throw-back to the starch and ceremony of Sir Richard in Portman Square.

In the crowded drawing room, Lucy might have been Madame Récamier. She sat on a Récamier couch in a Récamier attitude and, I must admit, with Récamier beauty. I suppose she was then in her early thirties—thirty-two or -three; she looked absurdly young to have a tall son like Mervyn.

We talked for a while of this and that, and Maggie frankly congratulated her on her beauty. She smiled, accepting the compliment without embarrassment. It was one, I imagine, often paid to her. "It is rather a nuisance, in a way, being so beautiful," she said. "So many people want to paint one. Mr. Mostyn-Lloyd has permitted Millais to do so, but no one else."

The portrait hung over the mantelpiece, and Maggie and I stepped across the room to admire it. The mantelpiece was crammed with that sort of bric-a-brac which we always summed up as "sacred cows," but among these sacred cows was an object that caught my eye by its incongruity. It was the sort of common tin in which you would buy sixpennyworth of cocoa, but it was gleaming as such tins rarely do, as though it were polished with the other sacred cows every day. It was a thing so unusual in that setting that I picked it up, and Lucy, who was watching us from her couch, said: "Bring it to me."

I placed it in her hands and she turned it over thoughtfully. Maggie and I sat down, and Lucy said: "Let me tell you what this is. You two know so much about me that there's no sense in pretending to you."

She told us then the story of the cocoa tin, which I have already related: the story of that morning when she woke to find her mother gone and this tin on the table in the hut above Porteven, and in it the few coins that her mother had saved.

She handed me the tin. "Will you please put it back?" she said. "It is one of the features of the room and my visitors would miss it. 'You *must* see Mrs. Evans's cocoa tin,' they say to any newcomer. My cocoa tin is a great joke—part of my legend as a sentimental young woman. It belongs to my childhood. I used to keep beads and pretty pebbles and shells in it. That is the story. Do you think I am a sentimental young woman, Miss Whale?"

"I think you're as hard as nails," Maggie said emphatically.

Lucy smiled, as if more pleased with this than with the compliment on her beauty. "That is a secret," she said, "that only you and I share. I've got a dreadful reputation as a—oh, I don't know—a piece of Dresden, a dog rose—something of that sort. Even Mr. Mostyn-Lloyd sees me more or less like that. He knows the true story of that cocoa tin, of course, and thinks it's wonderfully dutiful of me to cling to the only relic I have of my mother. But I know I can't bluff you, Miss Whale."

"You'd better not try," Maggie said gruffly.

"I shan't. You know as well as I do that I keep the thing as a warning. You will find in it, if you care to look, exactly the sum of money that was in it that morning. Not much to face the world on."

Maggie switched away from the subject. "I was sorry," she said, "to read of Mrs. Mostyn-Lloyd's death."

"It was a happy release," said Lucy. "She was in great pain. She was very worried, too. I spent a lot of time at her bedside and I *know* she was worried, though she said nothing to me."

"What was worrying her?" I asked.

"Oh, the whole problem of her life with her husband. It's not easy, you know, when a man moves ahead, and his wife can't keep up."

"I thought they were managing well enough, from the little I saw of them together," said Maggie.

"Yes, but you saw *so* little."

"Lucy," said Maggie rather sharply, "—and allow me to call you Lucy though you, for heaven knows what reason, call me Miss Whale —don't deceive yourself. You *are* deceiving yourself, you know, and it's the first bit of self-deception I've ever found in you."

A flush spread over Lucy's cheek. "What do you mean?"

"I mean that those two got on together like a house on fire, and would have continued to do so if you hadn't come along."

"But I *did* come along. And I came along innocently enough. It was Mervyn I was thinking of. And then that woman thought she was going to run me. You'd never believe the bullying I had to put up with."

192

"I can believe it well enough," said Maggie. "And I could have told her she was a fool to try it. All I'm saying now is: Don't deceive yourself. You're certainly not deceiving me."

Lucy shot her a glance from under lowered eyelids. "You don't much approve of me nowadays, do you, Maggie?"

"I'm not going to say that I approve of you or that I don't. Who am I to approve and disapprove? But don't try to bluff me."

Lucy changed the subject. "So Mervyn was at your place yesterday?"

"Yes. That's why we called."

"I know that."

"Why *North* Cornwall?" I asked.

"Because Mervyn doesn't remember enough about it to know whether it was North or South. I shall certainly never go back there, but he may take a sentimental fancy to do so some day, and he may as well go browsing round in the wrong place."

"Lucy," said Maggie, "I have a great admiration for your intelligence, but I think that this time you've made a mistake. Justin and Mervyn are friends. Some day they'll go down to Tresant together. I think Mervyn is far less likely to run into unpleasantness if he knows the truth. When he knows it, he can go on being a North Cornishman if he wants to, but I think the decision should be his."

Lucy considered this for a long time. "Why do you think the decision should be his?" she asked at last.

"Because," said Maggie, "if this thing came out while he was at Tresant, he would be in an awkward situation. He might find it hard to forgive you, even though he would no doubt pretend to do so. Don't forget, I'm fond of the boy. He grew up in my house, and I think I know something about him. You can take it from me that when he gets down to Tresant, as he will, all sorts of things will touch his memory. He'll know where he is all right."

For the first time that afternoon Lucy was a little flustered. "What a bore it is that Lord Burnage's boy went to Eton!" she said. "Mervyn was there first."

Maggie burst into frank laughter. "Don't you believe it!" she cried. "Justin was there before he was born, so to speak. The Gaylords always go there."

Lucy ceased to be Madame Récamier. She got up and walked about the room, tall, silver-birch-like. "Advise me, Maggie," she said at last.

"I have done so. But tell me one thing. How many people at Porteven knew that your mother's sister was Mrs. Mostyn-Lloyd?"

"None. I am certain of that."

"Then there is no one down there to whom the name will mean anything. The only danger is in Mervyn's own memory and the questions it might lead him to ask. That is what you have to guard against."

"Lord Burnage, of course, knows the name."

"You needn't worry about Lord Burnage. You can rely on him as you can on me."

At that, Lucy turned to her impulsively and took her hand. "I *know* I can rely on you," she said. "I always could. Don't think that I forget, or ever shall forget, what I owe to you—and what Mervyn owes, too."

Maggie smiled. "It's certainly nice," she said, "to have people one can rely on. But don't get into the habit, Lucy, of giving yourself *only* to people who can be cushions or pillows. It might leave you lonely in the end. There's only this to add: Let Mr. Mostyn-Lloyd know what you are doing and why you are doing it."

"Oh, I shall be able to make him see sense."

"I'm sure of that," Maggie twinkled, looking her coolly up and down. "And don't forget that when Mervyn goes to Tresant he'll meet Eddy Rodda. There's no reason why he should know who Eddy Rodda is. I see nothing against Mervyn's father being dead."

Lucy nodded.

"Would you like me to write to Lord Burnage?"

"Do, please, Maggie. You would do it so much better than I."

"Ah well," Maggie laughed. "Each to his aptitude. There are fields in which I couldn't hope to compete with you."

7

We saw Justin onto the train at Paddington and got back to find a letter from Mervyn.

"Dear Miss Whale—I shall be off to France with Mama next week, but do you think we could have a meeting in the meantime? I should be greatly pleased if you and Miss Rainborough could be my guests at Lord's on Thursday. Yours very truly, Mervyn Mostyn-Lloyd."

"I've never been to a cricket match in my life," I said.

"Nor have I," said Maggie, "but I think we'd better go."

And go we did. It was a beautiful morning when Mervyn called for us in the Mostyn-Lloyd carriage, and it was beautiful to sit there with the cool green grass before our eyes, the clouds moving without menace over the blue sky, the white figures running to and fro. The game didn't mean much to me or Maggie, and we both had a feeling that, though Mervyn was obviously understanding and enjoying what he saw, it wasn't in order that we should watch cricket that he had brought us there. He sat between us, a handsome boy that we were not displeased to be seen with, and I am sure that Maggie's mind, like my own, was busy with memories of those early days that so much had since happened to obscure for him. The moment would come, we knew, when he would begin to talk about them.

It came in the luncheon interval. We sat on warm grass and Mervyn opened the luncheon basket that he had carried from the carriage. "I chose this luncheon myself," he said, smiling. "I hope you approve." It was all right, if a little standardized: cold chicken, cold veal-and-ham pie, green salad, a fruit salad with cream, and a bottle of some white wine. When we were halfway through, he said: "Do you know, Miss Whale, what this reminds me of?"

"Cold chicken and salad," Maggie twitted him, "must remind anyone of a thousand picnic lunches."

He laughed. "True enough. I apologize for being unimaginative. But I'm not thinking of any particular luncheon. This just reminds me of lounging on a lawn, with food spread on a cloth on the grass. But instead of that green cricket-pitch I see water, and a flat sort of boat, and reeds standing up along the edge."

Well, there it was.

Maggie said: "How wise of your mother to tell you."

"I wish," he said, "that my grandmother had lived. I liked all that I heard about her. She sounds to me to have been a splendid person."

"I never knew her," Maggie answered. "She had gone just before we went to Tresant for the first time. When I say gone, I mean she had deserted you and your mother. I don't think that was a splendid thing to do."

"No, I suppose not. I don't know any perfect people, do you?"

"That's a wise question to come from the mouth of someone as young as you," Maggie answered. "So long as you learn not to *dislike* people because they're imperfect. It's folk who are always grizzling for a perfect world and perfect people who are miserable in this world and unjust to the sort of people most of us have to put up with. That is why I can't admire your grandmother as much as you do. She seems to have expected your mother to live up to her own ideas of perfection, and because she didn't, off she went and left her in the ditch. And she did this at the very moment when your mother needed her as never before. Fallen idols cause a lot of trouble in the world. It's better to have no idols at all—to realize that you have to get along with fellow sinners."

Mervyn smiled. "Miss Whale," he said severely, "I shall not ask any more wise questions if they loose such torrents upon me."

I think we both loved that smile, at once diffident and mischievous.

"I apologize," said Maggie, resting a hand upon his, pressed upon the grass, carrying his weight.

"It's no good," he said, "for you to tell me to have no idols. It's no good, and too late. I have an idol already. I idolize my mother."

"You could do worse," Maggie assured him.

"She was terribly afraid that what she had to tell me was going to make me—oh, I don't know—hate her, despise her. 'Pon my soul! What a notion! After all, there have been plenty of illegitimate children in the world," he added with blushing defiance, "and some of them have become famous—great men in history."

He knelt on the grass, assembling the things into the luncheon basket. "Not that anything like that is in my line. I shall go into the shop and be glad to do it." He paused and looked up at Maggie from his hands and knees. "One thing I wanted to ask you," he said. "Should I tell Justin about this?"

"You must decide that for yourself. His sister knows—Sally Gaylord. And so does Lord Burnage, his father. So far as I am aware, those are the only people who do know, apart from Sarah here and myself, and your mother and Mr. Mostyn-Lloyd."

"Very well, then. I'll tell him. I should hate to have such a secret from him. Now, tell me about Tresant."

We were glad to leave the other matter and to talk about Tresant.

"I remember a day," he said, "when there were two men—one with a beard and one sitting in a donkey carriage. I remember the donkey best."

"That would be Justin's father and his servant, Captain Rodda," Maggie explained.

"I know that Justin's father can't walk."

"You'll meet him and Captain Rodda if you go down to Tresant. Lord Burnage has to go about in the donkey cart because his spine was injured years ago."

"Justin has told me about that."

"It happened on the day Justin was born," I explained. "He's never seen his father walk. I have."

"I think we'll leave this game now," he said. "I fear it bores you, and, of course, I dragged you out here only to talk to you, as you've guessed."

"It's been a lovely day," I said. "Thank you, Mervyn."

And, indeed, I thought, this has been a lovely day that has dispelled some threatening clouds, both for Mervyn and Lucy.

"There's only one thing," he said shyly, "that I must make myself say somehow or other. Mama is very fond of you, Miss Whale, but," with a laugh, "a little bit frightened of you. But I think that's only because she's terribly anxious for your good opinion. And I can understand that. That's what I must say. She's told me a lot about you, and so I'm just trying to say thank you, for her and me."

Maggie blinked in the bright sunshine. "Nonsense," she said roughly. "I'm just an old pedagogue. I can't help trying to make people grow up."

8

Before I began to write this morning I was looking at a photograph taken in those days. It shows the sort of person I was when I married Daniel Undridge: the sort of person who, as they say, would pass with a push in a donkey show, neither short nor tall, neither stout nor thin, neither handsome nor repulsive, neither well-dressed nor dowdy: an almost anonymous young woman in her middle twenties, wearing a chain round her neck, to which we must presume is attached a watch that is pushed out of sight somewhere in the region vaguely called the bosom. The face is neither smiling nor scowling, but its gaze appears to be fixed on something that pleases it. I was looking at Maggie.

Well, that was Sarah Rainborough, who had begun to think more than was good for her about Daniel Undridge, who was all that she was not. He was tall, handsome, well-dressed and amiable, amusing to talk to, serious and ambitious where his work was concerned. After that fleeting encounter on the day when we went to see the iron warship, we met Daniel every summer. He came over from France with young Sebastien Rimmel to stay with his aunt in Chelsea; and as, by now, Maggie and I were permanently in London we always arranged a few meetings. We met his aunt at her house in Cheyne Row—a different person from her younger sister, Daniel's mother: a vigilant, salty old creature, very well-to-do. Her husband had been a member of a famous firm of solicitors. She was childless and very close with her money, except where Daniel was concerned. It was obvious at our first visit that she lived the year through for the couple of months when he would be with her. A recluse at other times, then she became what our Glory Jane would have called "a reg'lar razzler." Concerts and plays, outings in the country and on the river, dinner parties in her own house: the sere old girl blossomed annually into all such diversions when Daniel's sun arose. It was she who paid the bills when he went to Balliol; and it was while he was ending his last year there that she suddenly died. It was a strange death. She had written asking Maggie and me to dinner, and would we be there at half past six? It was an unusually early hour, and we found that she had brought us there at that time

197

for a consultation about the dinner table—she who was accustomed, when alone, to dine off a poached egg, a piece of toast, and a cup of tea. But this was Daniel's homecoming dinner from Balliol, and we must celebrate his Double First. Should it be the Spode or the Worcester, the Waterford glass or the glass she had bought in Vienna? A dozen tablecloths were paraded to be chosen from, and the flowers that had been arranged were all taken out of the room and arranged anew.

When at last things pleased her, she sat down to wait for the sound of the cab wheels and Daniel's knock. Her old veined hands, I noticed, were trembling in her lap. It was a hot evening. I asked her if she would like the window open or whether I could get her anything to drink. She said: "Pour me a little brandy, my dear," and as I was doing so at the sideboard she fanned herself with her handkerchief. I placed the glass in her hand, and when she had drunk a little she said: "Don't *hover*! I am all right." After a moment she added: "And if I'm not, take care of Daniel. Remember, I shall be watching you, from one place or another."

I was so taken aback that I could only gasp: "Mrs. Gemstone . . . !"

"You can pretend to yourself, if you like," she said grimly, "but you can't to me. You're head over heels in love with him, whether you know it or not."

I did, alas! know it, but I did not think anyone else did, and I was sure Daniel didn't. To have my secret torn out of me in that ruthless way, and held up in public by this old woman who was now looking like death itself, undermined me terribly, and my whole body trembled as her hands were trembling.

"Come here," she said. "If you can't stand, kneel down."

I knelt at her feet and felt her withered hands in my hair. "There, there!" she said. "See what I've done now! Come, child. This won't do tonight of all nights."

I looked up into her face and she managed a twisted grin which, no doubt, she intended to be a reassuring smile. It was wiped off her wrinkled features by a sudden shocking spasm of pain.

"Maggie!" I shrieked. But Maggie had seen it and got her arms round her, preventing her from falling. We laid her on the floor with a cushion under her head and sent a maid for a doctor. She was dead before he arrived.

CHAPTER TWELVE

I

MRS. GEMSTONE, unlike Grimshaw, was a woman who could be trusted with money. That is to say, she at least knew how to make money grow, though I suppose ideally the person to be trusted with money is one who knows how to spend it intelligently rather than one who merely nurses it. However, I mustn't complain about Mrs. Gemstone, because her way of living turned out to my advantage and Daniel's. It was not exactly a miser's way, for, as I have said, she was capable of extravagance and generosity; but for the most part she lived near the bone, investing her money and recording in an amusing diary that I have read the state of her financial health at the end of each year. There was only one year when she found herself worse off than she had been twelve months before; and she chides herself sharply. "This will never do! We must do better than this." And so she did, so that she was able to write next time: "My recent follies, thank God, have not brought the consequences they so richly deserved. The situation now is better than it has ever been." Another entry reads: "Zebedee Cogan asked for new grates. I laughed and said: 'Why not pigeon cotes and white pigeons to go with 'em while you're about it?'" I couldn't make head or tail of this mysterious sentence when I first read it during the time when Daniel, Maggie and I were going through the old woman's papers after her death. Neither could they.

She had left Daniel this house and all her money. He still had some years of hard work ahead before he could be called to the bar, and so he let the house. "I shall probably live here if ever I marry," he said. "I don't want to be bothered with the place in the meantime." It was a week or so after the funeral, a melancholy affair at which no one had been present save us three. Mrs. Undridge did not come. She had never got on well with her sister, and after the two of them had married the split widened to a breach, and the breach developed into hostility. Mr. Gemstone, I gathered, had despised Mr. Undridge. Being himself as sharp a child of Mammon as his wife, he said disparaging things about Mr. Undridge's fiddling life. A Leighton or a Millais was Mr. Gemstone's idea of a painter: someone whose canvases were ordered by the acre for millionaires' walls. Poor Undridge, half painter, half teacher, wholly incapable of making money that could be planted and allowed to grow, was to him a disgraceful and inefficient son of the *sauve qui peut* society in which he lived. It seemed to the Gemstones a sad thing that Providence should entrust two children to the Undridges and none to them, who clearly were better endowed with the qualities necessary to improve British stock. It was this which made the resentment between the two sisters so sharp that Mrs. Undridge hardly referred to her sister in answering Daniel's letter which gave news of her death.

"The surprising thing to me," said Maggie, "is that your mother permitted you to visit your aunt in the first place."

"She didn't," Daniel said. "The first time Sebastien and I were sent over, we were fixed up in a dreadful boarding house in Blooms-bury. We had the most gloomy and oppressive time. And so the second time we came—that was the time we nearly sank you on the river—I said to Sebastien: 'Let's go and have a look at my aunt. I hear she's terrible, but no terrors can exceed the ones we are now enduring.' So off we went. You will agree," he laughed, "for you saw us then, that we were boys with delightful manners, and we put on all our charm. The old girl didn't know what to make of us. She was, to say the least, on guard, but we wore her down. Once we had really made her believe that we had come on our own, that we hadn't been sent, she softened, and when I hinted that I would get into hot water if it were known that I had called at all—why, then she was conquered."

He paused, filling his pipe, with gestures that seemed to me robustly masculine, enchanting. "It was all rather distressing," he said. "I was only a boy, and I'd done this thing thoughtlessly; but even to one as young as I was then it was soon pretty obvious that I was being used in a rather unpleasant game. The old girl knew that her sister wouldn't want me to be there, and so she angled for me. It was she who suggested that to be with her would be pleasanter than to be in Bloomsbury. So Sebastien and I brought our luggage along, and then she began to give us generous pocket money. I didn't tumble to what was happening till there was no going back on this; and by then the deuce of it was that I had got to like the old thing in an odd way, and she liked me."

"I don't think you need let it worry you," Maggie said. "Family feuds are loathesome, and you did break it down in part."

"I did that all right, but what made me unhappy was that my people's poverty was involved in it. Even to send me to that wretched boarding house was a drain on them, and they couldn't resist accepting what my aunt could do for me. They would have resisted all right if only themselves were concerned, but they knew what I wanted—Oxford and the bar—and they knew jolly well that they could never give it to me and that she could. And so there was this unhappy situation: they allowing me to accept everything, but resentfully, and with no falling off of the bitterness on their side. They never wrote to her or she to them."

He rubbed his hair all ways, with a sudden wanton gesture that reminded me of the naughty boy by the pond in the Montreuil garden. He looked unhappy. "I don't see that I could have acted differently," he said. "After all, so far as Aunt and I were concerned, we did build something up. I'm sure she was happier in these last years, and we came to know one another and there were some qualities in her that I could respect. I don't think, honestly, it was all take and no give on my part. And now all this money . . ."

"Don't let it worry you," Maggie repeated. "There's no need for all this self-justification. I've never known a family quarrel yet where two-pennorth of pride-sinking on either side wouldn't put things right. If your mother couldn't manage that, why should you break your heart about it?"

He laughed. "Thank you, Miss Whale. You put confidence into me, as you used to do with hot red wine at the Café de l'Agriculture."

I looked at him, standing there laughing in that room full of the jumble of Mrs. Gemstone's papers; and I longed to tell him of how Sally and I, too, had one day at Tresant remembered the hot red wine, and tried to recreate its joys, and got drunk on Captain Rodda's firewater. I longed to tell him that, and to tell him everything, and to say: "Now tell *me*. What have *you* been doing in all these years?" But he went on to say that he would let this house. He wouldn't sell it because "I shall probably live here if ever I marry."

I turned heavily again to the task, untied another hank of red tape.

2

Since Daniel did not intend to live in the house in Cheyne Row, he went into lodgings, and these seemed to me to be a drearily long way off. They were in Chancery Lane. He was a hard-working person and wanted to be in the very heart of legal activity. Throughout the next few years Maggie and I saw him only occasionally. From time to time he would send us a polite and formal note asking us to go to the theater with him and to take supper afterward in a chop house, and we all three spent an occasional week end walking in the country. One of these walks took us to the top of Leith Hill, and as we sat there looking at the shimmer of summer blue over the country beneath us, he said: "I have news that I've been expecting for some time. Old Sebastien is engaged to my sister."

Old Sebastien was about his own age. We hadn't seen him for some time. Daniel's sister must be much younger. I remembered that she was born at Bordeaux during the winter we spent at Montreuil. She couldn't yet be twenty. And here was I, becoming hoary and hopeless, a mere confidante, the sort of person to whom a handsome young man would tell his domestic news. I felt envious of Daniel's sister whom I had never seen. "They intend to marry quite soon," he said, "probably next spring. I shall have to go over to Bordeaux."

Sebastien had been for a long time now in a shipping house in Bordeaux. He was doing well, Daniel said, and could afford to take a bride. "He never got on very well with his English," he laughed. "Marie will be able to help him with the firm's English correspondence."

So you see the sort of things we talked about at our suppers after the theater, during our walks, and on those rare occasions when he came and spent a lazy evening smoking his pipe at Maggie's house in St. John's Wood. On one of those evenings—a winter evening of bitter frost—we went down to the front door with him and watched him set out on his walk back to Chancery Lane—an alert, energetic figure striding away under the shining of the stars. He had talked about everything except the things I would have liked him to talk about: the theater and books and the ghastly little boy he had been at Montreuil and the last lap of work he was now on before being called to the bar. That was the only night I really lost control about him. I put up the chain on the front door, shot the bolt, and ran upstairs, leaving Maggie standing there without so much as a good night. In my bedroom, I sat in the bedside chair and wept. It was a return of the awful Tresant experience—the time of the spectacles and the feeling of abandonment. His last words were in my ears: "Well, au'voir, Sarah"—so casual, so friendly, so abominably *brotherly*. And I could have killed myself, not because of his casual friendliness but because of my own self-pity. It was a dangerous quality in me that I had long recognized and battled with, and that I thought I had overcome. I had only to turn my mind back to the day at Tresant when I realized that Maggie had been quietly watching my antics, and a blush of shame would burn all over me and fill me with self-contempt. But it didn't do so *that* night. It was an appalling back-sliding. I wallowed in my tears. And I was certain that Maggie knew what was happening behind my closed door, and that presently she would knock and come in and say the perfect comforting word.

She didn't. I heard her at last go to bed in the room next door, and that gave me a shock, because it made me realize what I had been longing for, that I had ceased to be my own master and was waiting like a dog for the pat of a friendly hand. Then, at last, shame did burn me up, and I had a feeling that that was what Maggie had intended. I got into bed with a crashing headache and hardly slept all night. I heard the shrill cries of the milkmen in the street and the rattle of carts and cans before I finally went off, and when I awoke it was midday. Someone had drawn my curtains. The room was shadowy. When I joined Maggie at luncheon she said: "Hello! I thought you'd better sleep on. Feeling better?"

"Yes, thank you."

"Good," said Maggie.

3

Sebastien Rimmel and Marie Undridge were married in the spring after that. Maggie accompanied Daniel to Bordeaux, and I remembered my duty and took this occasion to visit Father at Tresant. With shame I recalled that three years had passed since my last visit. My pre-occupation with Daniel, which caused me to feel that my own life was slipping by at alarming speed, made me sensitive to signs of age, and at Tresant they abounded. Now for the first time Father looked to me an old man. Pain had gained on him: it was burned into his eyes, it lay upon his forehead, it twisted his lips. In unguarded moments he was haggard. The poor Sudden Sneezer had sneezed his last and had been given honored burial, with a stone at his head, in the field where Peter the Great had long been lying. Another donkey now drew the cart. Eddy Rodda was still the guide and stay. In these three years he had changed more than anything or anybody at Tresant. His beard and hair were long and perfectly white and his eyes were of an almost disconcerting blue. He was thinner, but looked well, a hale and distinguished old philosopher who had long considered life and conquered it by accepting all that it could do. He wore a gray broadcloth suit and a white-spotted blue neckcloth.

There were no other visitors, and I wandered alone through the woods and along the bar, where the sea was quiet with summer. I took the cliff path to Porteven, where not a soul knew me, and climbed to the field where Lucy Evans and her mother had lived, and Wesley Rodda had lived after that. Nothing was left of the hut save a few rotting timbers. I lay in the grass where I could look over the roofs of the village out to the blue-silk summer sea that separated me from France, where Daniel was. My own personal feelings, and the feeling I had of all that I had known coming to an end at Tresant, filled me with melancholy but not with unhappiness. There was nothing I could do about my own situation or my father's, and at least one saved oneself from mental and spiritual exhaustion by not kicking against the goads. So, lying there and letting the summer day drift over me, watching the gulls high up, in lazy beauty navigating the casual airs, and squeezing my hands into scents of thyme and clover, I was in a good mood for Captain Rodda's arrival. The shadow fell across my face and, opening my eyes, which I had closed for a moment the better to disentangle the far sea murmur, I saw the broadcloth column at my head, the stick planted in the ground, Eddy leaning solidly upon it, his blue gaze on the sparkle of the horizon.

"Well, m'dear," he said after a moment, "I'm glad you've come to see us at last. It's lonesome for his lordship now all you young 'uns are careering about on your own affairs. Glad he is to see you do it. 'May I be damned, Rodda,' he says to me, 'if I try to tie any of 'em up to this ole carcass,' but all the same, believe you me, you bring him joy, though nowadays the poor soul don't find it easy to show it."

Neither of us spoke for a while. That spot was rustling with memory for both of us. It was here that Lucy Evans on a drear morning had picked up the cocoa tin, now so bright and shining in Kensington. It was here, on a summer day before that, that he had begotten her son. And it was here that I had seen him helping to hammer the shack into place for Wesley after a storm, and Wesley turning a cold back upon him.

"At times," he said, as if divining my thoughts, "I sit here and think of ancient days and ask God Almighty to forgive me my sins. And I know He's done it. I don't go to chapel no more an' I don't sing hymns, but I know, midear, that all's well now. The boy's a sign."

I looked up, startled, into his startling blue eyes. "The boy?" I said. "What boy?"

"Why," he said quite calmly, "my own boy, to be sure: the boy I got in sin an' iniquity on that very spot." He pointed with his stick to a tangle of nettles and docks growing among the shards of timber.

"But—" I began in a terrible fluster. He did not let me finish. His large hand clamped down on mine, pinning it to the earth. "Don't 'e fear, midear," he said. "Now stop trembling."

I *was* trembling, but some strength passed from his hand into mine, and spread through my body, and my trembling ceased at his command. He took away his hand. "That's better," he said.

He was in no hurry. He took out a pipe, filled it and lit it, looked thoughtfully for a moment at the little flame paled almost to invisibility in the blaring flame of the sunlight. The flame burned down to his horny fingers. He squeezed it out and dropped the fragment of match into the grass. He spoke slowly between heavy draws on the pipe to get it going: "I've known you a long time, midear. You'm a young maid, an' I'm an old man, an' there's many a thing as shouldn't be mentioned between such. But I've known you a long time, and I'm longing to say these things to some soul, an' I'm goin' to say 'em to you.

Tid'n right or wholesome to keep such things locked up in the breast."

He paused for a moment, plugging down the burning tobacco with a finger, then went on. "I suppose you an' Miss Whale, an' anyone else as is concerned in this, thinks it's all right for that boy to come down here with that fancy name Mostyn-Lloyd. That's all right, you say. No one's never heard tell of such a name down to Tresant. I daresay Lucy Evans thinks that's all right. Mostyn-Lloyd. Whoever would know such a name down in that Godforsaken old 'ole? Well, there's a lot Lucy Evans never knew. She never knew what a sinner I was or anything about the long talks I 'ad with her mother, lying in the woods under the summer moon."

It was then that Lucy's mother, so reserved with everyone else, had let herself go. Captain Rodda learned all about her sister, and her sister's husband, and the hopes for Lucy. "And so you see, midear, when the boy comes down 'ere with Mr. Justin, and they tell me this is Mr. Mostyn-Lloyd—why, me ole ticker gives a great lurch like a ship smacked on the fore-peak by a twelve-foot wave. I nearly foundered, an' I 'ad to think of some ole twaddling excuse to go out of the room. Well-dressed 'e was and 'ansome, not what 'e'd a' been if he stayed with his father, and talking like a Dook. But for all that, I'd a' know'd 'im. With that fancy name to remind me or without it, I'd 'a known 'im for my own boy—all that's left to me on earth. An' that's as true as the angels are singin' in 'eaven."

So now what? I wondered. What could I say about this to Maggie, whose advice to Lucy had caused it to happen? I was deeply distressed and began to tremble again, and again Eddy placed a hand over mine. With the other hand he knocked out his pipe against a stone. "Miss Sarah," he said, "I was once in Plymouth town, and in the theater there I saw just this thing: a young toff and an old down-and-outer who was the young toff's father, unbeknownst to the young toff." He chuckled as if at the recollection of a rich absurdity, and I was glad to hear that laugh. "Well, 'e reveals 'imself, this old down-an'-outer, and demands money, an' before the play's over 'e's well-nigh ruined this young toff who's about to marry a lord's daughter. So there's nothing to do but for the toff to arrange to have him killed off, but the lord's daughter 'ears of this an' says: 'Don't kill the pore ole man. I love you for yourself alone, with that ole codger or without 'im.' So they marries, and the ole man is there in church, with a white flower in 'is button 'ole and a silk 'at in 'is 'and. That's the only time I was ever in a theater. We laughed ourselves sick."

In a neighboring field the hay was being cut. I could hear the rasp of scythes, and the sigh as the grass and flowers lay down, and the to-and-fro of the whetstones upon blade edges as the reapers paused near the hedge where we sat. The air was full of the scent of that sacrifice.

Eddy Rodda had paused as if he, too, were absorbing the summer day, and then he went on, and he might have been St. Paul reaching a clinching line in a letter to the Thessalonians. "Now seein' that we are sons of God, we don't belong to act like that. If a man sin, let him accept the consequences thereof. I laughed then, but now I'm sorry for that ole man in the play, because there was no grace in 'is soul. Suppose now I was to find myself in France, or in China, or in some of the isles of the seas; an' someone says to me: 'There's your son, Eddy Rodda, that feller shoveling muck in the stableyard, that half-witted boy there, pulling a rickshaw, or that beachcomber gone to pot in the sun.' Now there'd be some reason for taking those sons of mine an' trying to raise them up, though there'd be little enough sense in that, either, for our actions go on, Miss Sarah, and the seed becomes the oak, or maybe a tree of thorns. However, you might say, m'dear, ' 'Ave a shot,' but the thing that 'as no sense at all would be to butt in when the son is not goin' down but up."

My heart gave a sigh of relief as his tedious argument drew to this satisfactory close. "No," I said, "I don't think there would be any sense in that."

"And yet," he said with a laugh, "it's a queer ole set-out, look at it this way or that. There's 'is lordship who certainly knows, and there's me who certainly knows, and we say nothing to one another but nod away over the chessboard while we 'ear the sound of our sons' voices comin' in through the window. An' that's why I'm tellin' you this, Miss Sarah, because it's not wholesome to 'ave things rottin' in the cellar. Now I've let in a bit o' light, seein' that you know I know; and if you think right to tell this to Miss Whale, do so, an' I'd be happy."

I did tell Maggie, and all she said was: "Well, there it is. We must hope for the best."

4

As the time approached when Daniel was to be called to the bar, the tenants of his house in Chelsea went, and he began the business of furnishing. He could well afford to live in such a house, even if his earnings as a barrister were small for a time. "And so," he said, "I might as well settle down here with a servant or two till I find me a wife."

The tenants had used Mrs. Gemstone's furniture, but not much of this was now kept. It was old and dowdy, and Daniel's piety, happily, did not run to the preservation and worship of sacred cows. The place was emptied, scrubbed from top to bottom, repainted inside and out, and then a few essential rooms were furnished. It was an amazing transformation. A house that had always oppressed and depressed me seemed to take wing in light and airiness. When Maggie and I walked with Daniel through the newly carpeted and curtained rooms, with a little lovely furniture in them and a summer breeze blowing in through the open windows, we congratulated him on what he had achieved.

"Oh, it's just a matter of *seeing*," he said rather complacently. "You must *see* the end of the matter before you begin and then work toward that."

"Don't be so stuffy and superior," Maggie chided him. "All that most people can see is thirty shillings a week coming in, and an old chest-of-drawers going for five bob at the shop on the corner. They have to make do with shifts and changes. There's nothing either virtuous or clever in furnishing a house beautifully when someone has given you both the house and money to play about in it."

He gave her an odd sidelong glance and then tumbled all his hair in disorder, as if wondering: "What have I done to offend old Maggie now?"

"And another thing," she said. "When a judge puts you in your place, as he doubtless will often have to, you won't be able to do that with a wig."

He recovered his good humor. "There are very attractive things to be done with wigs," he said. "I've been studying the question in the courts. I'm not sure that I shan't have red, white and blue ribbons plaited into the tail of mine. I shall probably ask Sarah to do it."

"It's about time you asked Sarah *something*," Maggie said, and stalked huffily out of the room.

At first the significance of her words did not strike me, and when, in a moment, they did, I was shattered. I could not believe that she would dare to say such a thing. My knees were water and I could no more look at Daniel than try to jump over the moon. I wished he would go, and leave me to endure alone that burning moment of shame. It is a moment I shall never forget. We were in the drawing room on the first floor and I was standing by the open window, watching the new rose chintz curtains blowing inward and threatening to disarrange a bowl of roses that stood there. As long as I live I shall remember the pattern of those curtains and the smell of the roses fighting with the odious smell of new paint. I could do nothing but tremble and wait to hear the sounds that would tell me he had followed Maggie, so that I might then sink into a chair and try to find some composure. But I didn't hear those sounds, nor the sound of his footsteps coming toward me, for the floor had been carpeted; and when he put his hand on my shoulder and began to turn me gently toward him I was utterly taken by surprise.

"You seem," he said, "to be the only one of us three who doesn't know that I am in love with you."

He looked at me half smiling, half sad. "It's not surprising," he said. "Why should you have guessed it? Why should you think it possible for me to be so presumptuous?"

"You? Presumptuous?" I could do no more than stammer that.

"Don't you think so?"

I shook my head mutely. The very muscles of my face were so trembling that I could not speak. It was with difficulty that I prevented my teeth from chattering.

He said nothing more, but took me closely in his arms. Tobacco, paint, roses: what an odd conglomerate, this moment that lives in me forever.

5

Sometimes there are days that begin with gray, and with little hope that anything else will be seen before sunset. Ah, well, we think, it might be worse. It might be raining cats and dogs. A raging wind might be throwing the trees down, or lightning setting the barns on fire. This placid, uninspiring, pewter day may not be gold or silver, but at any rate it is safe and harmless. And then, unexpectedly, the sun tears a hole through a cloud and looks down with shame on men who are prepared to find good in so drab and lifeless a compromise. His warmth withers the clouds. Dew sparkles; color glows. The day that was a dungeon becomes a temple with all its bells ringing. Bravery comes back to the humble creeping earth. The very snails put out their horns and march valiantly.

It was now as though all this had happened to me. "Sarah," Maggie said gravely a few nights later, "you mustn't become beautiful. You are in danger of doing so, and that would upset all my calculations."

"My mother was beautiful," I reminded Maggie; and at that she fell into a gravity and was silent for a time. Then she said: "I don't often think of your mother, but you make me think of her now. I remember the first time I saw her. There had been some trouble with an indiscreet old servant. Your mother was dreadfully agitated about it. She couldn't even bring herself to speak coherently, and so I never knew exactly what the trouble was. And I didn't care. I was looking at her and thinking how beautiful she was. It didn't seem fair. I'd known for a long time that I should have to get along without beauty, and that

208

I *would* too," she said with fierce emphasis, "but, all the same, looking at her, I wished the good God had spread things out a bit more evenly among women. It doesn't matter so much with men. Indeed, a beautiful man always gives me the shudders."

"But Daniel is beautiful!" I cried; and she said placidly: "Don't you believe it, my dear. I should have opposed the marriage if he had been. Well, when your mother was speaking to me I was wondering what paragon of female loveliness her child would turn out to be. And then I met you, and was profoundly relieved. Your scowling little visage made me feel much happier. Do you realize that that's getting on for twenty years ago?"

She was silent for a moment, and then "I shall have no one to live here when you're gone," she said suddenly. "I couldn't bear to. I suppose I shall have to find some person to come in daily and do what has to be done. But I cannot have anyone living here. I cannot. I cannot do it."

It was a long step from that moment when she had first come into the Portman Square schoolroom to now. We looked at one another with a sense of all those years lying between us, years when we had hardly for a moment been apart, and I knew how those years had been kind to me and forgiving in sending me this friend. I tried to say what was in my heart; but the moment could not be to my heart what it was to hers, for mine was welling with a new spring that diminished and almost destroyed my sense of loss. For her, there was only the loss. As long as her life lasted we were, thank God, to be very close to one another, but never again so close that we could say: Let us do this or that, and do it at once together without thought for anyone else in the world.

6

Daniel and I were married in London the next spring. We would have been married in Cornwall had my father been fit to be present, but he was not. But he begged us to spend our honeymoon in the lodge Maggie had lived in at Tresant, and we did so. My remembrance of the wedding is confused. The first clear picture is of waking up in the lodge and seeing Daniel, a dressing gown with slippers at one end of it and a head of tangled hair at the other, leaning out of the window. "It's not true," he was intoning. "It's not true. It can't be true."

I got out of bed, wrapped something round me, and joined him at the window, my arm about his shoulder. To me it was a loved familiar sight, but I looked at it with new-washed eyes and I could almost say with him that it couldn't be true. It was very early and there was not yet any sunlight; but there was a pallor that made things visible, and through this the night was rising up and making room for the day. It was rising off lawn and lake in clots and wreaths of mist that wavered and dispersed and coalesced but all the time thinned, going higher and higher into the air and leaving the surface of the water clear. And on the water the punt was lying against the little wooden landing stage, and three swans, startlingly white in all the gray about them, were standing upon the water on broad webs and shaking the sleep out of their wings. The silence was broken by nothing but the sound of those wings and a drowsy cheep and twitter that strengthened as the light strengthened and that bloomed here and there into the full-throated song of thrush and blackbird. I was aware not only of these things that I could see and hear but also of what was happening unseen: the badgers grunting and shuffling homeward to the banks in the wood and the red, sly foxes trotting warily to their earths.

Our window looked eastward, and the rim of the land that rose across the lake was sharpening, and soon it was drawn against light that showed us the beasts in the fields over there getting to their knees and to their legs. The sun itself at last looked over, and the scattered wisps and chiffons of the night hurried into the upper air like ghosts caught out at cockcrow. Now all the birds were singing, and the swans suddenly took off and flew toward us, beating low across our roof with a noise of majestic wings, and swift noiseless wings hurtled the swallows over the glittering surface of the water. The morning was awake.

I left Daniel standing there bemused, and went down to the kitchen and made coffee on an oil stove. I carried it up to the bedroom with some biscuits, and when we had eaten and drunk we dressed and went across the lawn, webbed with gossamer that flashed blue and red, and got into the punt. It had been late when we arrived last night, and Daniel had seen nothing of what he was seeing now; and as he sat there paddling the punt down toward the bar he kept on saying that this couldn't be true.

It was still only seven o'clock. The sun was comforting but not yet hot. Everything was dewy fresh: the wood of the boat, the fields rising to the east, the trees, tender with young green, to the west. The rocks that stood out of the water on the woodland side were still moist and gleaming, and, as we moved through the morning as silently as if through a dream, a heron rose here and there, transforming his gawky body into a vehicle of grace and skill and went before us on slow wing beats toward the bar.

The punt grated on the sand. We got out and pulled it up, then climbed the bar to look upon the huge prospect of sea and coast under the drench of morning light. To our left and to our right the land ran on beyond vision, not abruptly ending but melting tenderly into invisibility; and before us the sea did so, too, a sea that had not defined its horizon, but faded in a blue and silver haze.

With our arms about one another we stood there, small in an immensity of earth and air and sea. But our little selves will burst into the most magnificent that the world about us can do, and I found myself saying: "Do you know that not so long ago I spent the greater part of a night weeping because you had called on me and Maggie and talked of nothing but ordinary things?"

"Let's talk of ordinary things now," Daniel said. "Let's talk about you."

"Oh, darling," I cried, "do you find me terribly ordinary?"

He held me closer as we moved back toward the punt. "This morning," he said, "is full of things that make me cry: 'I can't believe it.' And the incredible fact above all others is that from now on you become an ordinary thing in my life. That gives me enough to be going on with."

7

We dined with Father and Eddy Rodda each day of the month we were in Cornwall. Father was getting out less and less, and Rodda was Mr. Rodda more than ever to everyone on the estate. "When I'm gone," Father said, "Eddy will look after things until Justin is ready to take over."

It would have been futile for me to cry out against the notion of his being "gone," for it was plain even to a less devoted eye than mine that this was something we must soon expect. He and I were alone in the library, where a log fire was burning, bright though the day was, and he lay near it on a couch with a rug over him.

"There are not enough weddings in this family," he said, managing a difficult smile. "I hoped we'd have had Sally packed off before this. Do you see much of her? How is she getting on? It seems odd to me, this life she's living."

I could not tell him enough about Sally. She was near his heart, but her life was far removed from his imagination. "I've never been in such a place," he said. "What is it like?"

It wasn't easy to make him see. Visiting Sally and Dolly Dewhirst in the Bermondsey settlement where they lived, I had found women and children who had never seen a field or a wood, a cow grazing or a horse doing anything but pull a dray. I had talked to them and tried to make them understand what a harvest field was like and how the sea looked in calm and storm, but their minds could find no point of reference. And so it was now when I tried to make Father see the settlement with its dreary sanitary rooms, smelling of carbolic soap and beeswax, and the streets about it with their mean, downtrodden houses and the strip of murky sky. His mind could hardly grasp the fact that even such houses as those were too big, too expensive, for the means of a single family, that one room might house a father and mother and children, for the purposes of living and eating and sleeping.

"It's beyond me," he said hopelessly. "Why Sally?"

Well, why anyone? Why not let them stew in their own juice? But I couldn't say that to him.

"That's a difficult question to answer," I said. "The only thing about it that's clear to me is that Sally and Dolly Dewhirst, though I don't think they know it, are not there for the same purpose. Sally is there because she's got an immense love of people. Dolly is there because she's got an immense loathing of conditions. I suppose that's what makes them a useful pair, but I sometimes wonder whether they won't split some day."

"It's all beyond me," he repeated; and I said: "I don't see why you should think so. Sally is just you all over again."

"Me?" he cried, really startled. "What the deuce have such goings on to do with me?"

"Don't belittle yourself," I urged him. "You may not know it, but you are a good man. You've lived in love and friendship with those about you, and that's what Sally's trying to do. She's found people who need her more than the people round here do. That's all. But her way of going about things comes out of the very air she's always breathed with you."

He growled that I was talking stuff and nonsense, and I dropped the matter, but I was glad I had said that to him.

8

Zebedee Cogan, whose name had occurred in a puzzling phrase of Mrs. Gemstone's diary, was now flesh and blood to us. At least, one had to assume that he possessed flesh and blood. Parchment over bone was all that was apparent. We had met him before our marriage. Daniel was at Maggie's house one evening and said: "I've had a letter from Zebedee Cogan—you remember: the man who asked for new grates."

" 'Why not pigeon cotes and white pigeons to go with 'em while you're about it?' " Maggie quoted.

"That's the chap. He'll be calling on me tomorrow at Cheyne Row. He's a rent collector whom my aunt used to employ. I'm slowly getting to the bottom of her complicated sources of income. There seems to be a lot of house property."

Daniel asked me to be at Cheyne Row so that we might meet Mr. Cogan together. He was to call at three the next afternoon, and at five minutes before that time, standing at the drawing-room window, we saw a little man walking up and down on the other side of the street. He looked up at the house, pulled a watch from his pocket, put it back, and continued to walk. "That obviously is Cogan," said Daniel, "waiting for the stroke of three. Zealous Zebedee. Conscientious Cogan."

He ran downstairs, opened the front door, and shouted: "Mr. Cogan!"

The little man looked up, then looked at his watch again, and seemed doubtful what to do.

"Come in!" Daniel shouted; and at that Mr. Cogan crossed the road, and a moment later he and Daniel joined me in the drawing room.

He cannot have been much more than five feet high. His face was thin and anxious and drooping. His mustache drooped; a lock of hair drooped over his forehead; lines dropped from nose to mouth. He was wearing a frock coat that shone with age. One of its satin lapels was decorated with the morsel of blue ribbon that announced abhorrence of intoxicating liquor. He laid a tattered black dispatch case on the table and said: "I'm sorry to intrude before my time, sir. Time, I know, is money."

"Then why waste it hovering about on the other side of the street?" Daniel demanded.

Mr. Cogan seemed surprised by this point of view. "*Your* time, sir," he said. "It's *your* time I must consider. I like to keep appointments to the second, sir. If Mrs. Gemstone had said three, I should not have liked to present myself at two-fifty-nine or three-one."

"I see," said Daniel. "I never found her so precise as all that."

"As the Heir, sir," said Mr. Cogan, breathing a reverence into the capital H, "you were privileged. With me, it was otherwise. I dared not presume."

There was a moment's silence, during which he seemed uneasy as if at the thought of time passing unused—Time, which was Money. He was sitting by the table with his small hand resting on the catch of the dispatch case, ready, it appeared, to spring it open and plunge into affairs at a second's notice. As Daniel did not encourage him to do so, but was, indeed, standing easily at the window, jingling some coins in his trouser pockets, Mr. Cogan gave a little cough and said: "I am expected to get through in half an hour, sir. Half an hour a month. Mrs. Gemstone never allowed me more."

Daniel was suddenly very annoyed. "Mrs. Gemstone is in her grave,"

213

he said sharply. "I don't propose to have my time measured out by her—or by you, either."

I fancied that the veriest ghost of a sigh—imagined rather than heard—floated from Mr. Cogan. It was perhaps absurd, but I had an idea that something had happened that he had been awaiting for a long time, but that he had never dared to hope *would* happen. Was it something that he had hoped to do himself, but that his small trembling heart could never rise to? Anyway, someone had answered Mrs. Gemstone back, and even though it was a dead Mrs. Gemstone, it seemed better than nothing. Mr. Cogan's hand on the fastening of the dispatch case relaxed.

"What about a glass of sherry?" Daniel asked.

Mr. Cogan's watery blue eye dropped to the blue tab on his lapel, hesitated there for a second; and then he said: "That is good of you, sir. Thank you kindly."

I brought the decanter and glasses and a barrel of biscuits. Mr. Cogan held his wine to the light, then passed it knowledgeably under his nose. "Your very best health," said Daniel. "Why the blue ribbon?"

"Your health, sir, and yours, madam. I wear it, sir, as an example. It was Mrs. Gemstone's idea. The rents were often sadly in arrears, and she thought this was due to indulgence in strong liquor. I was expected to say a word on this subject now and then, and the blue ribbon was there to give point to my remarks."

"Where do you collect these rents?" Daniel asked. "What sort of property is it?"

"Oh, most varied and heterogeneous," said Mr. Cogan, holding up his glass to the light again, as though seeing through it an enchanting picture of Mrs. Gemstone's property. He drained the glass and Daniel refilled it. Mr. Cogan drank again and a flush appeared on his parchment cheek.

"Well," said Daniel, "varied and heterogeneous. That's not very explicit."

Mr. Cogan leaned back, his legs thrust out, one hand resting easily on the table, the fingers of the other twirling his glass. "Oh, a widespread net, Mr. Undridge," he said. "I assumed that, as the Heir, you would know the meshes." Meshes was a difficult word for him. "Palatial property—none of my concern—paid quarterly by check. But all sorts. Detached, semidetached, desirable cottages all in neat rows, and undesirable bloody awful slums."

Daniel did not chide him, and Mr. Cogan seemed unaware that he had said anything that deserved reproof. He munched a biscuit and looked as though he would at any moment loosen his waistcoat. He glanced about the room with approval. "Speaking as man to man, Mr. Undridge," he said, "you have a nice little property here, and what's more you've spent a pretty penny on it. That's what got my goat in the old girl's day. Screwing it out of other houses—and, my God, I *had* to screw sometimes, Mr. Undridge, to say nothing of putting the bailiffs in and seeing their poor old bits an' pieces out on the pavement and the rain falling and the kids crying—well, there it was, an' me with the softest heart in the world looking to them like some bloody monster—why, I've *paid* the rent sometimes—me, out of my own pocket, put it in that bag there on the table an' paid it over to her and showed her the rent books all correct—and this house—that's what I'm getting at by a roundabout route if you'll pardon me—without a lick of paint or repapering from year's end to year's end, and she like some brown old spider sitting in the web, doling me out her half hour once a month. 'Time is money, Cogan, an' don't you waste mine,' and 'You'll have to do better than this, Cogan. I don't want evictions, I want rent.' Bah! That's what I say, Mr. Undridge—bah! What sort of a way of living is that? Though, speaking to the Heir, p'raps, I'm overstepping the mark. But somehow, sir, you unbutton me, and in this place I'm used to being all buttoned up."

Daniel approached again with the decanter, but Mr. Cogan resolutely placed a hand over his glass. "No, sir. Another drop and I should say too much. I have given you a hint and I must do no more."

"Tell me," said Daniel. "There were some houses that needed new stoves. You spoke to Mrs. Gemstone about them."

"Spoke! Why great sakes and man alive! I pleaded on bended knees. Three families in one of those houses and all using the same kitchen. Just a little oven alongside the fire for all of 'em, and the iron side was burnt through so that their bits of meat were all smoked up an' ruined. Pitiful to see, Mr. Undridge. An' she says: 'Stoves? Why not give 'em white pigeons?' Well, that stirred something in my heart, sir, and I goes home thinking: 'Why not? Well, why not?' I don't know whether you're acquainted with Chinese customs, sir, but they're a fanciful people. In my leisure moments, sir, I like to visit the Celestial Empire. I could have been happy as a mandarin. Yes, sir, a fanciful people. They tie flutes to pigeons' tails, and you can imagine the joy of that, sir—all those birds flying about making a heavenly music. Well, not more than half a glass, sir. Imagine that in Bermondsey! That'd give 'em something to live for! That, and new stoves. Good health, sir. I'm an imaginative man, and sometimes that don't do on my job. Why, sometimes I've seen those pigeons flying about, dyed all colors, playing the Hallelujah Chorus. But it was just a gibe to her—just a gibe."

He swigged his wine and pulled out his watch. "Why, good God, sir! It's four o'clock! We must get to business."

"Some other time, Mr. Cogan," Daniel said. "Say the day after tomorrow at three—or thereabouts."

In Cornwall they call a thrush a graybird, and Sally used to say that she felt at home in the settlement because it was in Graybird Court. There is something heartbreaking about the names of slum streets: the Paradise Rows and Angel Crescents and Laburnam Avenues: whispers of old grace, of ancient fancy, long dead with the hearts that first heard them. I often wondered about Graybird Court. Had some Cornish exile in these parts built it? Had there once been a graybird nesting here in a tree? There had been a tree, that was certain, for in the midst of the cobbles that paved the court there was an un-cobbled circle of hard-beaten earth in which could still be seen the wood of a tree trunk, flat with the ground, pounded into it by the passage of generations of feet. I liked to think that it had been a may tree, and that once, on spring mornings, there had been that green-and-white glory at the heart of the little court, with the song of the graybird pouring out of it and the hawthorn perfume heady under the blue sky.

You turned off an interminable gray gritty street, stinking with the smells of gasworks and a pickle factory and a fell-monger's and other industries that all seemed notable for arresting and offensive odors. Where there were not such things there were flyblown tobacconist and newspaper shops, dirty-looking little barbers' saloons, down-at-heel drapers', grocers' and nauseous butchers' shops, with bluebottle flies buzzing in the air and crawling over blood-stained viscera. I was to see that street in all seasons: in winter nights, with fog of gray or yellow heightening its sinister load upon my mind as the gas lamps bloomed murkily in the upper air and smudged a dismal light behind window panes; in cold mornings when the wind ran through it like a pack of snapping arctic wolves; in summer when it stewed and simmered and stank; and sometimes when the grace of spring alighted even here and a whisper came through from an awakening beautiful world and the sky was tender and merciful.

It was easy to miss the entrance to Graybird Court, unless you knew the landmarks. They were on the one hand a herbalist's shop with a window full of dusty poppy-heads and jars of desiccated roots and seeds, boxes of pills that promised vitality to men and the cure of all ills to women, and a pile of dumpy little books, each in an unbroken wrapper, labeled *The Works of Aristotle*; and on the other a bird fancier's that was enough to break the heart, for it trembled with imprisoned wings and was full of trills and chirpings and cadenzas, all coming from the tiniest imaginable cages and seeming haunted with memories of field and woodland. For these were linnets and larks and bullfinches, and I have seen there a nightingale that never sang. Goldfishes moved turgidly through slimy water. Usually a dead one or two floated in foul disintegration on the top. And there were cages of mice, furnished with wire treadmills, on which the tiny creatures furiously raced in an endeavor to escape from ennui. The place seemed to me a madhouse.

There was between these two shops a narrow passage cluttered with garbage. This was the only way in or out—that is, for you or me. But anyone who knew Graybird Court as Sally did, or Dolly Dewhirst, could show you another way. The court was a narrow oblong. The house which was the Settlement occupied almost the whole of the short side that faced you when you came in through the passage. Almost, but not quite, for on either hand, completing the line at that end, was a high wall about ten feet long. In the heyday of Graybird Court, the house had been the stylish center of things: probably the landlord lived there. He wanted the whole of that end; but the plan of the house didn't quite fill it, and these two walls were thrown out like wings, for no other purpose than to use the space, to complete the encirclement. And on either of these walls you would find foot- and finger-holds. You would sometimes see children practicing the ascent, going up and over as swiftly and skillfully as monkeys. Beyond the walls were dark lanes, leading away into a slummy labyrinth, and young hooligans, pursued at night by the police, used this way out.

Once darkness had fallen, there was no light in the court, except what fell from a window here and there, where an oil lamp burned, and from the windows of the Settlement, and from the window of Mr. Cogan, which faced the Settlement down the length of the oblong. Mr. Cogan lived over the passage through which you came into the court. One of his rooms looked into the lugubrious main street, the other into the court, and on the ledge of each of these windows was a green-painted box dedicated to gardening in the Chinese manner. I have seen Mr. Cogan of a summer's evening incredibly arrayed in a robe of Chinese inspiration, embroidered with dragons, and wearing upon his head a black velvet tasseled smoking cap, busy at his boxes which contained stunted shrubs and little wooden bridges crossing streams made of strips of glass. Upon the streams were lotus flowers made of wood shavings and glued upon the glass, and beneath this vitreous illusive water were goldfish carved out of match sticks, painted yellow.

The lotus flowers and the goldfish were delicate works, beyond the skill of Mr. Cogan's fingers. They had been made by the Young Lady of Graybird Court. You would see as you came into the court that outside one of the houses was a small table on which all sorts of fancy things were displayed. There were pincushions and aprons, boxes with sea shells glued upon them, tiny wooden toys, and much else of that sort, each with a price label upon it; and there was a lidless cigar box in which you might see a few coppers and sometimes a silver three-pennybit or a sixpence. All these things had been made by the Young Lady, who was so called to distinguish her from the Lady, her mother, who lived with her in one room on the first floor. The Young Lady was never seen: she lived in bed, a bundle of useless bones, and the Lady arranged the stall each morning, and took it in each night, together with whatever small harvest the cigar box contained.

"But isn't the money ever stolen? Or don't they take a six-penny thing and put in a penny?" I asked Sally, when first I looked at this pathetic unattended shop.

Sally was almost shocked by the question. "No, they don't," she said sharply. "Anybody who did wouldn't want to go on living here for long."

It was the Lady's rent that Mr. Cogan had more than once paid out of his own pocket; and the Young Lady made him lovely little offerings.

There was a pump in one corner of the court, for none of the houses had water, and there was an earth closet in another, though the bigger house that was the Settlement had its own. Well, that was Graybird Court, stewing behind the high street, and that was what helped to send Daniel to Balliol and to finance his studies for the bar.

CHAPTER THIRTEEN

I

DANIEL and I met Sally and Dolly Dewhirst at Paddington, and we traveled down to Cornwall together for the coming-of-age of Lord Burnage. My son Richard was seven months old. I was leaving him for the first time and felt badly about it.

Justin had been Lord Burnage now for two years. I hadn't been to Tresant since Father's death, or indeed for some time before it. He died suddenly. I did not attend the funeral. As the train pulled out of Paddington station into the gloom of the December morning, past lighted windows wan behind the day's fog, I could think of little but the changes I would find. Father and Eddy Rodda: Tresant without them was unthinkable.

The first hint of the changes to come reached me and Maggie Whale some time before this. Mervyn Mostyn-Lloyd was then up at Oxford, and Justin was a second lieutenant of infantry. He secured his commission a little time before his father died. Lieutenant Lord Burnage at the age of nineteen was a fine-looking man. Necessarily, he was not seeing as much of Mervyn as he had done when they were at Eton together, but their attachment was as warm as ever. In the university vacations they went down to Tresant, and Justin often stayed for a day or two at the Mostyn-Lloyd house in Kensington. The draper was proud to entertain his son's titled friend.

One morning, just after the Oxford long vacation had begun, Mervyn turned up at Maggie's house in St. John's Wood and invited her to attend a cricket match with him at Lord's. I don't know how he dared, for the morning was Maggie's work time, and she had told him so. She would have bitten anyone else's head off, but she had a weakness for this attractive youth. "Why?" she asked. "Where's Justin? I thought he was staying at your place for a few days? Why doesn't he go with you?"

"I asked him to come, but he says he can't. There's something he's got to swot at. So we arranged to separate till tonight when we're taking Mama to the theater. I didn't feel like going to the match on my own, so I said I'd run up to Hampstead to pay a promised call on a man from my college. But I no sooner get out than the idea bores me, and I *do* want to see this match. But you know what it is, sitting by yourself all day . . . *Do* come, Whaley."

"Well, you'll have to keep me in my old age," Maggie teased him. "I'm a working woman, you know. If I don't work I don't eat."

"All right," he promised. "That's a bargain. When it comes to me or the workhouse, you can choose whichever you think then the less intolerable. Shall we try and drag Sarah out?"

So they came along, and they dragged me out, and I was glad to go. There was no young Richard to think of then, and, with Daniel away all day, I sometimes found the time long.

By now the morning was well advanced. It was almost noon when we arrived at Lord's in a hired cab. There were a few other cabs in front of ours at the gate, and we sat where we were, waiting for these to discharge their passengers and drive away. It was with shock and foreboding that I saw Justin and Lucy Evans get out of one of them and go through the gate. Whaley did not see them: she was looking through the window on the other side of the cab, and I quickly pretended to be doing the same. But Mervyn had seen them. He said, with a quite successful pretense of casualness: "Look, Whaley. I deserve all you're going to say to me, and if you don't say something really bad and savage I shall be disappointed in you. But I've changed my mind again. I really must go and see that man in Hampstead."

"Well!" said Maggie. "You rob me of my day's work, which is my day's bread, and then drag in your wretched man from Hampstead! May he stew in Hades with the man from Porlock."

She tried to laugh it out with mock fierceness, but she was both annoyed and puzzled. "Get along then," she said. "At any rate you must find yourself another cab. I shall keep this one."

Mervyn picked up a cab which was dropping a fare and drove away. "Well, the day's wasted," said Maggie. "We'd better go into town and find luncheon somewhere."

2

There was something about the way in which Justin handed Lucy out of the cab that day at Lord's that told me he was in love with her. I was in love myself, and so I was sure I was not mistaken. There was nothing to be surprised at in such a situation. Lucy was very young when the child she called Merlin was born. She must now be in her middle thirties. She looked younger; indeed she looked younger than I. You could have taken her for a woman in her twenties, and a lovely one at that: fair, calm and self-possessed. No; there was nothing to be surprised at, but a good deal to fill the mind with anxiety.

Maggie's annoyance had not cleared up by the time we were having luncheon. "Whatever came over him?" she asked crossly. "These young creatures! They waste your life without a moment's thought."

I told her then what I had seen. She was so overcome that for once she had nothing to say, except in repentance for her own harsh words to Mervyn. "That poor boy," she said. "Oh, God! How we should guard our tongues! We never see so much as the crust of the hearts of people we speak to. We go over them like steamrollers when they would wince at thistledown."

How much Mervyn was affected by what he deduced from that glimpse at Lord's we discovered from Justin himself. He called upon me the next afternoon in Chelsea, full of tribulation. He and Mervyn had arranged to go down to Tresant within a few days. Now Mervyn had cried off. "Never heard such a rotten excuse in my life," Justin grumbled. "He went off to Hampstead yesterday to see a man, and when he gets back, would you believe it, he'd changed his mind about everything! He and this man are going off walking in Germany. All settled just like that in five minutes. He was to have come to the theater with me and Mrs. Evans. But he couldn't even do that. Had to pack at once, and he was off early this morning."

"And what happened about the theater? Did you and Mrs. Evans go?"

"Oh, rather! And we had supper out afterward."

"Well, at any rate you had pleasant company."

He looked at me sharply, but he was not to be drawn. "What about you?" he asked. "Could you come down to Cornwall? Could Dan spare you for a week or two?"

"I'm sure he couldn't. And even if he could I couldn't spare him. What about Sally?"

"Oh, Sally! Well, I did ask her, and she said there were plenty of people who needed a holiday more than she did. She could provide me with half a dozen children who would think Tresant was paradise. Imagine me arriving at Tresant with half a dozen brats from Bermondsey!"

I asked him if he had ever been in Bermondsey, and he said: "Good lord—no! That Dewhirst woman scares me to death, even when I meet her on my own ground."

"She wouldn't be so good to take out to supper?"

"No. She'd analyze the bill and present me with a report on the number of shoes and undervests we could have bought with the money."

"But Mrs. Evans would simply ask for another meringue."

However, he sidestepped Mrs. Evans once more. I told him that I knew Maggie Whale was just finishing a book. She would be through in a day or two, and I was sure she would want to take a holiday.

"What?" he said. "After writing a book? I shouldn't have thought that would take much out of anyone. It comes easy, don't it, if you've got the knack?"

He was so young, so innocent about so much, that I could have wept for him. "Believe me," I said, "Maggie needs a rest. Be a dear, and take her with you."

He talked for a time about not going at all, and I knew that since Father's death he had tended to dodge Tresant unless he could take agreeable company with him. He had not yet settled down to the idea that everything there now hung upon him. "Oh, Rodda will look after that," was too often on his lips.

"I think you should go," I persuaded him. "Eddy will be dying to take you round and give an account of himself."

He agreed at last to do this, and to take Maggie with him; and you may imagine Maggie's consternation a few days later, when she was awaiting him on the platform at Paddington, to see him coming, behind the porter with the luggage, in the company of Lucy Evans. It looked as though he was going to have his agreeable company after all. Lucy, Maggie told me, was a vision of delight, and Justin was exalted.

3

I learned of this unexpected development from a letter which Maggie wrote in the train and posted to me in the course of the journey. It was easy to gather from this letter that Maggie was shaken by apprehension and expected little rest or joy from her holiday. The letter left me, too, utterly wretched, full of sad expectations for both Mervyn and Justin. What neither Maggie nor I knew was that the small scene I had glimpsed at the entrance to Lord's was not the first in which Lucy and Justin had been engaged, that for some months now Lucy had been aware of Justin's feelings, and that, with that streak of hardness which we knew to underlie her silken appearance, she had made up her mind to end the situation one way or another.

There is no doubt, Maggie told me afterward, that as soon as the three of them reached the house, and Eddy received them in the hall, he recognized Lucy Evans, this woman he had not seen for nearly twenty years. In him the change was greater than in her. She would remember the virile creature whose earrings had glinted between her young eyes and the summer sunshine as he lifted her out of the pool and carried her naked into the hut. She saw a white-haired, white-bearded old man, dressed with drab respectability, with bowed shoulders and blue eyes a little rheumy. Maggie saw him start back as this lovely ghost rose out of his past, and recover himself with difficulty as Justin shook him by the hand and said with pride: "Eddy, this is Mrs. Evans— my friend Mostyn-Lloyd's mother. She'll be staying with us for a little while."

One of the maids took Maggie and Lucy to their rooms. Maggie's was at the back of the house, looking into the woods that sloped away upward. The evening was well advanced. A sunset flush was reddening the topmost platform of the trees, where the rooks were circling and calling, settling and rising again, making their customary restless approach to a night's rest; and, oh dear! Maggie thought, now indeed we shall see some birds coming home to roost. She was emotionally exhausted, what with the book she had just finished writing and the events of this day. She threw herself on the bed and fell asleep at once, and did not rise till the sound of the gong was rolling through the house. Then she dashed some cold water upon her face and went down in her travel-rumpled clothes.

Sometimes, when Father was alive, Eddy Rodda joined us at a meal. Sometimes he did not. Tresant at that time was attractively free of rules and regulations. On this night, Justin, Lucy and Maggie sat down to the table and Eddy hovered in the background. The meal was late and he had already eaten. It was by now dark, but it had been an exceptionally hot day, and the heat lingered in the air. The windows were flung up; a warm breeze stirred the flames of the candles that stood along the table. Lucy had changed into ice-blue silk that shimmered in the wavering light. She looked cool and rested, not a bit as though she had spent the day in stuffy travel. Justin had put on evening clothes, and that meant something in those days when short dinner jackets and soft shirts and collars were unthinkable. His chest was armored in starched linen down which sparkled diamond studs. A dusky red carnation was in his lapel. Rodda must have been thinking, as Maggie certainly was, that it was a long time since two people dressed like that had been seen in the Tresant dining room.

They were so beautiful, Lucy and Justin, Maggie told me, that she shivered in the warm room as the moths came fluttering in out of the darkness and danced around the candle flames. They were dining at a small table, and only this intimate oasis was lit. Rodda was in the shadows of the big room. Justin could not see him, but Maggie was faced toward him. She wished he would go away. There was no reason for him to stay: a maid was serving the meal; but he seemed fascinated by the ice-blue cold beauty of this woman whom he had once, he could not fail to remember, possessed utterly.

The meal was drawing to its close when Justin said: "Eddy, come out of the shadows. Come and sit down here and speak to me."

Rodda approached, and Justin pushed out a chair with his foot, and the old man sat down. He looked haggard. "Yes, Mr. Justin," he said. He had never learned to call Justin Lord Burnage.

"I shall want some riding," Justin said. "How is Jack Pudding?" This oddly named horse was his favorite mount at Tresant.

"Not very good, Mr. Justin," Eddy answered. "Seemed to me, as soon as I knew you'd be coming down, I'd better have a look at Jack, an' I did'n like'n. Lackadaisical 'e was, an' that fool of a new groom 'e 'ad'n said anything to me about'n. This was yesterday, an' Jack weren't no better this mornin'. So I sent off for Mr. Morrow, the new vet over to Porteven. He's got a very good reputation, Mr. Justin. 'E come over at once an' said 'e did'n like the look of'n. 'E gave Jack something, an' then 'e 'ad to go off. 'E's got work all over the county. Said 'e did'n know when 'e'd be back, but 'e'd come along 'owever late it were."

Eddy Rodda said all this in a spiritless voice, sitting there at that small table with the candles burning between him and Lucy Evans. His knees could have touched hers.

Justin was annoyed. He got up and began to walk about the room. "Well, that's a damned thing!" he said. "Now, of all times!" It was clear that he had looked forward to showing himself off on Jack Pudding.

"Well, p'raps it's nothing much," Eddy said. "We'll know soon, anyway. Mr. Morrow won't be long now."

Mr. Morrow, indeed, was announced at that moment, and Justin, with an apology to Maggie and Lucy, went to join him. In full fig as he was, the pair of them went off to the stables. Maggie saw them pass the open window, a groom with a lantern before them; then she got up and walked out into the warm dark night. There was no moon. She had not gone far, strolling slowly along the path that led to the lodge where she and I had known so many happy days, and where Lucy

Evans had watched Eddy Rodda's son kicking on the lawn in lusty babyhood, when Lucy joined her. Maggie was aware of her approach, as though, in a warm sea, a gust had come off an iceberg. She turned, and saw what Lucy was not aware of: that Rodda, too, was coming along the path. Soon the three of them were in a knot there, standing still, each waiting for one of the others to speak. Presently, Eddy said roughly to Lucy Evans: "What are you up to? Don't you know your place?"

Lucy said: "Yes. That is why I have come down here. I want Lord Burnage to know my place, too. There must be no misunderstandings."

Rodda's eyes had not been idle, looking out of the shadows of the dining room. "He's in love with you," he said.

"Yes."

She said it without pride or boastfulness: a statement of fact.

Rodda said brutally: "Well, then, you can give 'im what you gave me, an' leave it at that."

Maggie winced, but Lucy was unperturbed. "I couldn't do that," she said virtuously. "One's point of view about such things changes as one grows older. And the trouble is that Justin doesn't want that, either. He wants to marry me."

"He must be mad," said Rodda. "He knows you've got a son as old as he is himself—a bit older, in fact."

"Yes. Of course he knows that. But it doesn't make any difference. He wants me just the same."

Maggie asked: "Do you want to marry him?"

"I wouldn't dream of doing so."

"Then why can't you make that clear to him?"

Lucy cried impatiently: "Oh, for heaven's sake! Don't you know *anything* about such matters? Make it clear indeed! You try making it clear to someone who's crazy. It's not so easy as you think."

"What are you going to do?" Eddy asked.

"I'm going to give him such a shock that he'll drop me like a hot brick and leave me in peace. I'm going to tell him the truth, and I'm going to do it here, where you and Miss Whale can bear me out."

There was a long silence. Rodda said at last: "I wouldn't advise you to do that, Lucy Evans," and there was menace in his voice.

She said: "If you knew how he's pestered me these last few months, you'd realize that it's the only thing to do: tell him the whole truth in the presence of people who know it's the truth. Tell him my mother was a tramp, my son's a bastard, and that you're his father, Eddy Rodda." Her voice had taken on a shrill edge; for the first time she seemed to weaken in her self-possession. She said: "You don't know what I've had to put up with. I've had enough of it. I'm very happy with Mr. Mostyn-Lloyd. I don't want men. Men disgust me."

So that was out at last. She had known all about it too young, and in circumstances too violent and terrible. Rodda himself was to blame for that, but she did not throw it in his teeth.

("I think I understood most things about Lucy when she said that. I should have seen it before," Maggie said to me. "I felt a great pity for her.")

Maggie said: "Why don't you go away for a long holiday? Justin need not know where you are. If you like, I'll explain everything to him while you're away. Don't you think that would be less melodramatic?"

But Lucy had made up her mind. "I've come here to do it," she said, "and I shall do it. I've had enough, I tell you. I've got into the way of being too agreeable to him. It's hard not to. He asks me to go here and there, and I refuse, and he presses me, and then I consent. I've done too much of that sort of thing. I can't go on. I must stop it. Mervyn is beginning to notice things. He and I must stand on our own feet."

She turned with a rustle of her silks in the warm night and began to walk back toward the house. Rodda put himself in the path in front of her and stopped her. "Now you listen 'ere, Lucy Evans," he said. "We've 'ad all about what *you* can't stand and what *you're* goin' to do, an' all the rest of it. But you're not the only one in this: my son's in this. 'E don't know 'e's my son, and Mr. Justin don't know it, either: an' what's more, they're not goin' to know it. I've watched that boy, an' I've loved that boy, an' I'd 'ave put myself under 'is feet for a doormat if that'd 'ave done 'im any good. But I've always known the best thing I could do for 'im—the *only* thing—was to stand out of 'is light. I've done that now for year after year—just standing out of 'is light, because 'e's not goin' to feel the same in 'imself, an' Mr. Justin isn't goin' to feel the same to 'im, if they know 'e belongs to an ole good-for-nothing like Eddy Rodda. An' that's been 'ard work, that 'as. It's 'ard work to see your own flesh an' blood growin' up like a flower, an' you not darin' so much as to smell it. An' don't you lay a finger on that work I've been doin', Lucy Evans. We been a pair of sinners, you an' me; but there's no call for Mr. Justin's friend to suffer because of that."

He was moved by a deep complication of loyalties: to Tresant and to his son. This was not only his son: it was Justin's friend.

Lucy stepped past him and walked away without answering. He had made his long speech with confidence, as though feeling that it could not fail. Now, when she had gone some way, he cried after her brokenly: "I beg you . . . I'm an old man . . . It won't be long . . ." Still she did not answer.

Maggie took his arm and was surprised to find how shrunken it had become. He was trembling, and she sensed that he knew he was defeated.

It was a moment when something should have happened to comfort him, to re-establish his badly shocked sense that the world was a place he could get through without dishonor; but another blow now fell upon him. Ahead, moving from the stables toward the house, the light of a lantern was bobbing through the darkness. Maggie saw a man mount a horse and ride away, and she supposed that that was the vet going home, as indeed it was. As they drew near, the lantern illuminated Justin's white shirt front. He was standing alone outside the front door, and he shouted: "Is that you, Rodda?"

Soon all three joined him and found him in great agitation.

"How is Jack, Mr. Justin?" Eddy asked.

Justin did not directly reply, but asked angrily: "Where have you been? Why are you never on hand when you're wanted?"

Maggie took him by the sleeve and said soothingly: "What is it, Justin? What has happened? I took Captain Rodda for a little walk."

She was surprised to see that Justin was on the point of tears. His face was working like a child's who has suffered a loss that seems beyond repair. "He takes too many damned walks!" he broke out unreasonably, again as a stricken child might; but Rodda was so shaken by what had already happened that he was in no mood to hear more than the words themselves. "Why doesn't he keep an eye on things?" Justin demanded. "Why hasn't he been watching Jack Pudding? Strolling round the place like a lord—the damned useless old fool!"

Maggie knew then that Jack Pudding was either dead or condemned to die, and that this must have smitten Justin to the heart; but she knew also how smitten Rodda was, and she waited for the match to fall into the gunpowder.

"I am sorry, my lord," Eddy said—and it was the first time Maggie had heard him call Justin that—"but long as I knew your lordship's father an' *his* father before him, I've never been spoke to like that before. I'm not used to it, an' I can't hope to get used to it at my age."

The lantern light showed his white flowing beard and lit a spark in his eye. He looked suddenly mad, as though too much had crumbled beneath him too suddenly. "I must go," he said. "Things at Tresant are not what they were, an' they're likely to be worse. I'm better out of it."

Justin recovered his senses. "Come here, Rodda," he said; and when Eddy remained rooted where he was, he stepped forward a pace and put a hand on his shoulder. "Forgive me," he said. "I was talking like a fool. I am upset. Jack is dead." Again that fact caught him in the throat and he couldn't go on. He stood there looking very young and distressed, the lantern in one hand, the other on Eddy's shoulder. Eddy moved brusquely from beneath the hand and said: "You're quite right, my lord. I'm a damned useless ole fool. I'm no use to anyone no more. No one don't listen to me. No one don't take my advice. I don't under-

226

stand this world. I don't understand why people want to poke an' meddle with things that're best left alone. . . ." He went rambling on like that, becoming less and less coherent, and, still mumbling to himself, he walked away from them and round to the back of the house.

Maggie was full of an apprehension she could not define. The night had turned thick and sultry. She felt a threat in the air, but could not say from whom or to whom. Lucy had gone in. Maggie looked toward the heavy darkness at the side of the house in which Eddy had disappeared and said to Justin: "He is unhappy. Go after him and say something comforting."

But Eddy's words and abrupt departure had hurt the boy. He said: "So am I unhappy. I want comfort, too." As if to find it, he followed Lucy Evans into the house.

Maggie walked up and down on the gravel as the sky pulsed with lightning that did not bring the relief of thunder or rain. She thought of the Rodda she had met so long ago on the quayside at Brest: the sturdy picturesque swaggerer with the pair of French doxies hanging onto his arms; and she thought of the arm she had taken a few moments ago, so shrunk and withered. He hadn't much left, she thought, except his pride, and she had seen that knocked into the dust. It was a pity the blow had come from Justin, of all people. Eddy had been so proud of Justin, the boy who had never known a mother—was it that, Maggie wondered, that attracted him to his friend's mother?—and had never had a father competent to help him in the manifold affairs of growing up. Eddy had stood by him in his riding lessons, and had given him his sailing lessons, and had taught him the secrets of the woods, and later had proudly instructed him in the management of the estate. And all this devotion was complicated through the recent years by the presence of "Mr. Justin's friend." Hot though the night was, Maggie shivered. There was a menace that frightened her.

She went in, said good night to Justin and Lucy, and, in her bedroom, rang for a maid. "Will you see if Mr. Rodda is in?" she said. "Ask him if he could spare me a moment."

Eddy was not in, and this deepened her uneasiness. She wrote a note, asking him to see her when he returned. "Please put this somewhere in his room," she said, "where he can't help finding it as soon as he's back. Understand? It's important."

The girl took the note and said: "I expect he's grieving about that ole horse, Miss. I see'n with a lantern going to the stables."

Maggie sat in an easy chair to wait, watching the dark oblong of the window flush and flicker from time to time with pallid light. She was distressed to think of the old man looking down in the lantern light at the dead horse and chewing a trembling lip. All his fault, he would think—"the damned useless old fool."

It wouldn't be easy to assuage the throb of such a wound, but she must think of something to say—something that would have come better from Justin himself.

She heard Justin and Lucy go to their rooms soon after the clock over the stables had struck eleven; but Rodda did not come. She would not give up hope, did not undress, but threw herself clothed upon the bed. She was exhausted by the heat and by emotion and dozed fitfully. Then she fell sound asleep, and when she awoke it was dawn. The sun was not yet up, but her window was light and the air was cool. The flickering was gone from the sky and in the roof gutters starlings were giving their long whistles of surprise and admiration. Rodda had not come.

She slipped off the bed and put on her shoes, listening to the deep silence of the house. No one was stirring. She went down to the kitchen and made herself some coffee on an oil stove, ate a few biscuits, washed her face in cold water at the kitchen sink, and went out into the morning. She felt better. It was going to be a lovely day. The sun was now up; the sultry menace of the night had passed over; and, when they woke, Justin and Eddy would see things differently. Trying to persuade herself that this was what she thought, she walked toward the lake, following the path that went through the woods along its edge. The water lay down beneath her on the left, glittering in the sun that had risen over the low land beyond it. It was some time since she had been there, and she strode along rejoicing to find everything as it had been: the curlews rose from the water fringe and flew piping before her; the level light struck into the red corrugations of the pine-boles; the rabbits scuttered away, and the morning air was like a cool drink. She would walk as far as the bar, whose everlasting murmur she could hear as the background note to the transient calling of birds and the rustle of leaves and the rheumatic creak of hoary moss-grown limbs.

It is a path that at no point allows a long forward view. It twists and turns, so that Maggie was almost suddenly face to face with what, when she saw it, she realized she had come to seek. It was at that spot where, long ago, I had seen a stoat run across the path, and had prodded into the bushes that hid it, and, hearing Rodda's voice, had looked up to find him holding onto a pine trunk and looking down at me. But now he was not holding on to the trunk: he was hanging from a bough that reached out from it across the path, and Maggie approached him, she told me, with a curious absence of shock, with a sense of having known that something like this would happen from the moment when she urged Justin to speak to him, and he would not.

It was a great sadness, rather than horror, that filled her. The old man, who was always so neat about the house and in a boat, had taken off his collar and blue white-spotted neckcloth. The neckcloth was folded and placed on a flat stone, with the collar upon it. Even the collar stud had been removed from the neck of the shirt. It glinted in the morning light, at the center of the white circle of the collar.

But there was no glint now in Eddy Rodda's eye. It was as dull and lifeless as the gray eyes of the fishes that had flapped and kicked to death in the bottom of his boat, as he must have flapped and kicked here in the darkness, with no one to see, while the trees etched themselves on the recurrent pallor of the lightninged sky. His beard was drenched with dew, and he was so dead a thing that already from the point of his beard up to his shoulder a spider had draped the miracle of its web. It spread like a little net, and it had caught a shoal of dewdrops that trembled in a glister of blue and red. On the toe cap of one of his boots was a clot of horse dung, and Maggie's sadness overbroke in tears as she saw that and pondered on the old man standing in the stable, looking down at the dead horse, and feeling flow over him a sense of dereliction and uselessness so great that he took up the rope lying there with its dreadful suggestion of what he must do. She was still crying, crying uncontrollably now, when she got back to the house.

4

Lucy Evans returned alone to London. She insisted on leaving at once, with a cold resolution that surprised Justin, but not Maggie, who wondered what feeling—perhaps of responsibility for the old man's death?—drove her from the scene. Knowing nothing of what had passed between Lucy and Rodda, Justin was overwhelmed with a sense of guilt; and in this state of mind it was especially difficult for him to accept Lucy's desertion. So it appeared to him. "But I *need* you here," he said. "Now, more than ever, I want you to be with me."

Maggie was not sorry to see the stoniness with which Lucy went her own way. This, she thought, may perhaps be as good a means as any other of showing him a different Lucy from the one imagined by a lover. She stood outside the conflict between them, but was glad when Lucy won. She felt that the idol had rocked on the pedestal; and she said to Lucy, taking her aside at the last moment: "This dreadful business has helped you. Now take the advice I gave you last night and go out of the country for a time. Write to Mervyn in Germany. You'll find that he'll be ready to drop his friend like a shot and join you somewhere."

Maggie stayed with Justin. They attended the coroner's court together. The verdict was foregone: Edward Rodda had taken his own life during temporary insanity.

He was given a grand funeral. There was now nothing too much that Justin could do for him. He might have been the lord of the manor passing to his fathers. The coffin was placed in a farm cart and was drawn to the cemetery by two mighty farm horses, shining like silk in the summer weather. All the tenants of the estate walked behind the cart, and the members of the lifeboat crew, and many people from the country round about and from Porteven. Eddy Rodda for many years past had led a quiet and private life, but the manner of his death revived the legend of the corsair who was once the admiration and the dread of the community. There was talk again of how, when a mere boy, he had killed the father of the girl he later married, of his voyages, of the women he had put in the family way, of his robustious preaching and his smuggling. But most of all it was to that savage blow in the Porteven pub that minds went back: the blow that made so many people now say: "Ay, 'e dodged the noose that time, but the noose got 'im in the end, midear. Funny that, iddn' it? Looks as if it was meant."

Maggie felt no need to pass judgment on him one way or the other. Standing among them at the open grave, with Justin at her side, she was aware of nothing but the ruthless passage of time. She had known Rodda before Justin was born, and a lot of people had died since then: my mother, and Justin's father, and Mr. Dickens, who had helped her in the beginning. She was young when first she saw Eddy brazening it out under Wesley's eyes at Brest. And now she was middle-aged. At the graveside the people were singing "They fly, forgotten, as a dream dies at the opening day." Forgotten or remembered, she reflected, what does it matter? They fly. That is the thing. And then she cried—for Eddy and for herself, for poor Jack Pudding and for us all.

5

It was of these things, and things like these, that I was thinking as the train took us westward through the December weather toward Justin's coming-of-age. The four of us had a carriage to ourselves. Daniel was reading the *Times*, and presently he said quietly: "I don't like the look of things in South Africa."

Dolly Dewhirst said: "Why? What's happening there?"

Daniel jerked his shoulders impatiently. "I don't think your mind ever gets outside your Graybird Court," he said.

Dolly, I thought, had not improved with the years. Her words, about almost any matter, tended to be aggressive and dogmatic. "It's not *my* court," she said. "It's *your* court. And I don't need to take my mind out of it. I can stay there and see every sort of human misery."

"Very well," said Daniel. "It's my court. I can't help that. I've spent money on it and done all I could to make the houses fit to be lived in.

230

Indeed, I go on spending money on it—far more than I shall ever get out of it. And do what I will, the place is soon as bad as ever. The tenants knock it all to bits. Mr. Cogan could tell you that he's never had to find rent out of his own pocket since I've been the landlord. He finds it out of mine. How is Mr. Cogan, Sally?" he asked, cutting the conversation from under Dolly's feet.

"Deliciously Chinese," said Sally. "I shouldn't be surprised if he soon takes to eating his food with chopsticks. One can only hope he'll stop short at opium. Still, Mrs. Cogan will see to that."

It had been an extraordinary day—the day that Mr. Cogan became a bridegroom and the Young Lady of Graybird Court became Mrs. Cogan. God knows how he had done it, but Mr. Cogan had found a rickshaw—a rickshaw in some East End junk shop!—and it was this that first pushed into his head the notion that the Young Lady need not live so desolate a life as hers had been till then. He had been visiting the Lady and the Young Lady a good deal, admiring the cleverness with which the Young Lady could carve the smallest thing. The carving of minute things was a Chinese skill, and so he loved it. He would read to her as she worked, and he found bits of ivory for her in junk shops, and she was making a set of chessmen for him. The Young Lady was vaguely spoken of in the court as being "paralyzed from the waist down." She suffered, indeed, from what is now called infantile paralysis. The population of the court was migratory, but there were those who had lived there long enough to remember her being carried under the archway and up the stairs. That was five years ago. She had not come down since. She was now a girl of twenty.

Just before Mr. Cogan saw the rickshaw, the Lady died. A severe cold, and influenza, and pneumonia, and there it was. And then the Young Lady had no one but Mr. Cogan. When he saw the rickshaw he knew at once what he must do. He must see that the Young Lady was released from the prison she lived in. He bought the thing and trundled it home to the court, and as there was now a room vacant on a ground floor, he had the Young Lady removed into it. Now it was easy for him to pick her up, put her into the rickshaw, and take her about the streets.

I often saw that strange spectacle, and I never saw it without emotion: Zebedee Cogan standing in the shafts of his absurd contraption, come to a halt outside some shop window, while his passenger, who can hardly have weighed more than a pigeon, feasted her eyes on things long denied them: the squalid goldfish and hysterically racing mice in the pet shop, the flowers and fruit and vegetables. The very horses trudging along sturdily in front of drays would make her draw deep breaths of joy and wonder. "Oh!" she would say to me, if I stopped to speak to them, "it's wonderful to be *seeing* things again! Mr. Cogan has given me back my eyes."

There were days when Mr. Cogan's work would not permit him to take Dinah out. Dinah Morfe her name was, but she must have almost forgotten this, so long had she been the Young Lady. There were plenty of people in Graybird Court whose names were known to no one but Mr. Cogan. He learned them from the rent books. Old Snitchy, Billy Conk, Dot-and-Carry, were the sort of names that most people there were known by, and no one could say what else they had ever been called. When Mr. Cogan couldn't take Dinah out, there were plenty of people who would have done the job for him, but he could never bring himself to entrust Precious Freight to anyone but himself. (It was inevitable that she should become Precious Freight to Mr. Cogan. I need not go into that.) When she was alone, Sally or Dolly saw to her meals.

As the days drew out from spring to summer, the rickshaw went farther afield. Dinah's eyes again saw running water and ships upon it and trees breaking into leaf. "It's a good thing, sir," Mr. Cogan said to Daniel, one day when he had come to render his account at Chelsea, "it's a good thing that you have your back to the passenger in a rickshaw. She's so happy I can't bear to look at her for too long." By some public seat on an embankment of the river Mr. Cogan would bring the rickshaw to a halt, and while he sat there smoking his pipe Precious Freight would fill the pages of a notebook with the wings of ships and of birds, with leaves bursting against the sky, with the scrawny bodies of little boys venturing naked into the edges of the brown turbid river. Mr. Cogan one day diffidently produced one of these sketch books and showed it to Daniel. Daniel took it across to the window and looked at it for a long time. He gave it back with the simple remark: "Look after her well, Mr. Cogan. You're doing more than you think."

"I don't know how to say this, sir," said Mr. Cogan, methodically tucking the portfolio into his dispatch case with the rent books and ledger, "but I ought to look after her altogether. Do you see what I mean, sir?"

"Do you want to adopt her?"

"No, sir. I want to ask her to marry me."

I suppose amazement must have shown on Daniel's face and mine, for Zealous Zebedee blushed and stammered and could not look at us. "I don't see any future for her, sir," he said at last, "if she's left on her own. What is there in this world for the likes of her? We do what we can—*you* do what you can, and God bless you for it—but this is no world for the weak and lonely."

The lock of his dispatch case clicked in the silence; the silence stretched itself out; and Mr. Cogan broke it by saying: "I know there are plenty who would say it could be no marriage, with a girl like that. And in that sense it couldn't. That's something I've never dreamed of.

But there's more in love than that, sir. There's working your fingers to the bone, and there's thinking of someone else before you think of yourself, and knowing that there's nothing in the world to compare with what comes out of doing that. Well, sir," he said lamely, "that's how it is."

It was odd to hear Mr. Cogan talking of love and self-sacrifice in that room where he had so often been reminded that time was money and been cut off each month with a half hour's ration of the precious commodity. I said, for the sake of having *something* to say: "Mr. Cogan, we shall never cure you of hearing pigeons with whistles in their tails over Graybird Court."

Well, we didn't hear that, but the wedding night was remarkable enough. Mr. Cogan stretched ropes in a criss-cross from side to side and end to end of the court, and on these he hung Chinese lanterns, and when dusk came he lit all these and then carried down from the room over the entry the bride whom he had taken to and from the church in the rickshaw. All the neighbors had gathered, and the Settlement workers, and Daniel and I were there, too. Daniel had provided the feast. It was laid out on trestle tables that stretched from one end of the court to the other. The people brought out their own wooden chairs and sat where they liked, and Old Snitchy with a concertina and Billy Conk with a mouth organ kept music going all the time. It was a hot moonless night, and the lanterns were still, their candles burning steadily, throwing down a soft light that veiled the squalor of tattered curtains at the windows and battered dustbins at the doors. Daniel had seen to it that there was beer in plenty, and the people ate and drank and became noisily merry. Everyone was happy except Dolly Dewhirst, who was sitting next to me and who got up suddenly and hissed in my ear: "Oh, I find all this intolerable! I can't stand any more of it. I loathe palliatives. We're making all this"—she waved a hand wildly round the court—"we're making it seem tolerable. What we have to do is destroy it."

Sally had drunk two unaccustomed glasses of beer. She was smiling seraphically. She pushed Dolly back into her hard wooden chair and said: "For God's sake, Dolly, try to love people as well as to hate institutions."

But Dolly would have none of it. She went into the Settlement and sulked while the tables were dismantled and piled in a corner, and Billy Conk and Snitchy kept it up as the people danced and sang, and the lanterns at last burned low and guttered out. Then the sky was dark and we could see the stars shining over Graybird Court, and Mr. Cogan picked up his Precious Freight and carried her up his stairs as tenderly as if she had been an armful of gold.

CHAPTER FOURTEEN

I

I AM glad to remember that Mervyn was at the coming-of-age party. Since Eddy Rodda's suicide he and Justin had not met. Now he was down from Oxford, where he had scraped through with a degree but without distinction; and when we four arrived at Tresant, there he was. For the first time, he and Justin were meeting without any cloud or equivocation. Mervyn now knew that he was Eddy Rodda's son. Justin knew it, too; and they found that it made no difference whatever.

I need not say much about the details of that celebration. Such affairs do not differ much, and all went along the lines of the old plan. There was a reception of farmers and tenants, followed by a feast where the expected speeches were made and toasts drunk. We enjoyed ourselves enormously, despite Dolly Dewhirst's conviction that she was having a glimpse of the Feudal Age and that the Feudal Age was something no modern reforming mind should tolerate.

The next night there was a dinner party and dance to which the county gentry were invited. In all the time I had known Tresant there had not been such an occasion as that, and, as it happened, the house was never to see such an occasion again. Perhaps that is why I so vividly remember it. Ever since Justin's birth Tresant had been a quiet place with a crippled recluse for owner. Now I saw it as once it had been, and as Justin intended that it should be henceforth. He had been in conference with his solicitors in London and much money had been spent. The house in Portman Square that had been shrouded for so long was to be lived in again. A staff had been engaged there, and Justin brought the butler and footmen to Tresant for this celebration. The ballroom is the only really large room at Tresant, and here the curtains and decorations were new, the chandeliers had been taken down, washed, and rehung like clusters of shining icicles, the portraits had come back cleaned from London, glowing in colors that for years had been subdued.

You could almost feel the throb of the kitchens all through that gray December day on which the few of us who were staying in the house wished Justin "Many happy returns" at the breakfast table. And he *was* happy. The shadow of the obsession with Lucy Evans seemed to have lifted. He was full of the future. I wished Whaley could have been there to feel the new currents pouring through the house that she had never known as anything but sedate, to see the new brightness on the young face that, when she was last here, was so

234

clouded and troubled. There was a letter from her, and a present, and regrets that a writer of serials for a weekly paper was chained to a desk.

It was good to see Sally looking a grand lady again. In the Settlement one might think sometimes that she dressed in the left-offs of the inhabitants of Graybird Court. I wondered what they would make of her if they could see her now, standing with Justin under the chandelier, waiting to receive the guests. "Some girl you see tonight," she said with a laugh, "will no doubt be doing this soon, but I must hold the fort for her as well as I can."

She looked almost beautiful, though she never was that in any formal and conventional sense. But she was happy for Justin, happy, I am sure, to see him and Mervyn together again, and this gave her a sparkle. Her cheeks, after a few windy Cornish days, had lost their East End pallor. She was dressed in a soft stuff of rose-pink, and diamonds shone at her neck and on her wrists. The bracelets drew attention to her hands, which were rough, swollen and etched with dirt crackles. That was something you couldn't put right in a day or two. I could not resist going up to her and giving her a kiss, and then, standing back, I said with surprise: "Why, Sally, you have gray hairs!"

"Why, Sarah," she laughed, "so have you!"

I denied it hotly, and she called: "Daniel, will you come here and convince this wife of yours that time is not standing still?"

What fools we are, how unaccepting, when young! I did not wait for Daniel, but ran almost in panic to my bedroom, where the candles were still lit on the dressing table. I scrutinized my head as though expecting it to crumble into graveyard dust before my eyes! And there the gray hairs were: three or four, or five or six: what did it matter? They were not as many as on Sally's head, and hers were few enough, or I should have noticed them before; but they chilled me like premonitory snows. There were tears in my eyes when Daniel came in. He laughed them away soon enough, but I never after that thought of myself as a girl. It had been "natural" that Whaley should be quite gray, that my elders should die; but never before had I looked face-to-face steadily at my own mortality. Nowadays, I know, people say: "Old Sarah Undridge? Good Lord! Is she still alive? She must be one of the Immortals!" I didn't feel one that night.

"You recall Byron to my mind," Daniel said, standing with a hand on my bare shoulder and smiling over my head at my candlelit image in the glass. "There's a sound of revelry by night, but you insist on listening for the far-off noise of battle."

"He was writing about Waterloo," I said grimly. "The Duke of

Wellington was there, and I saw the Duke when the Queen opened the Crystal Palace. You make me feel older than ever."

"I don't care if you saw Hannibal crossing the Alps. Come along now. Dab something on your peepers and let's go down to meet the County. Doesn't the thought thrill you?"

"I'd give all the County if I could kiss young Richard good night at this moment," I said.

"Well, you can't. You'll have to make do with kissing me instead, and then come along and see what's being decanted from the tumbrils I hear rolling up."

2

I had purposely kept out of the renovated ballroom in order that Justin might have the pleasure of seeing it burst upon me in all its lighted splendor. Splendid indeed it was when at last we made our way in there after dinner. The dripping crystals of three chandeliers shone over our heads and upon the green and gold of the new brocade drawn across the windows, and upon the flowers to make whose colored banks the greenhouses had been rifled. The music of a waltz came in from a box of a room that opened off one end and had been built to house musicians who should be heard but not seen. Justin took me onto the floor, and Daniel took Sally, and, to my amusement, Mervyn took Dolly Dewhirst, who looked like a strict Israelite accredited to the House of Rimmon, and bowing the knee for purely diplomatic reasons. Mervyn told me that she hissed in his ear: "Looking for a few white hairs! It's looking for nits that takes up my time!"

I imagine that Dolly, clasped in the arms of this young male of the County or that, caused a good deal of consternation that night. As for Sally, her clothes, her jewels, her faultless behavior, must have been as puzzling as Dolly's intransigeance. Everybody was aware that she lived in a Settlement in the East End of London. But look at her now! Which was Sally Gaylord—that or this? Those who were acquainted with the family's history knew that the Gaylords had produced some queer women in their time—unmarried daughters who had gone abroad and lived among Turks and infidels. At any rate they were being British among foreigners. But the East End of London: that was another matter!

Thank goodness, they must have thought, Justin was all right. It was clear now that Tresant was safe: in the hands of one who understood his obligations and was determined to bring the place back to what it had been.

"This is how Tresant ought to be," Justin said. "Do you think I've done it well?"

It was his night and I warmed toward him. "You've done splendidly," I said.

He smiled. "It depends on how you look at it. I imagine it breaks Miss Dewhirst's heart. I have a theory about Miss Dewhirst's heart. It was made by James Watt, and it pumps ink, not blood. I had a long talk with her yesterday—or rather a long being-talked-to. Couldn't get out of it. She has the oddest theories. She thinks you can make people good by educating them. Look as us chaps from Eton. We're not a bad lot, and God knows we don't know B from a bull's foot."

Our waltz came to an end, and I found myself ensnared by a Colonel Hawkes, who was great with speech. It was ruining the night for him, he told me. "Never get let in for a speech, my dear," he said, patting my hand. "I tried to dodge it. Couldn't. They *would* have me do it. It's been buzzin' in my head for days. However, I think I've got it off now. Excuse me." And he strolled away, took a paper from his pocket, and studied it privily in a corner.

The dance went on till one o'clock, and I was tired out. I looked round for Colonel Hawkes, hoping that he would soon go into action. If oratory was to follow dancing, it was high time it began. Happily others seemed to share this opinion, for I heard a voice: "Come on, Hawkes. Time's gettin' on."

Then Colonel Hawkes cleared his throat with a sound that would have quelled mutiny. All eyes turned to him, and his eyes took a last furtive look at his paper. I sank into a chair: at least I could rest during the oration. Colonel Hawkes bellowed: "Well, we all wish Burnage well—very well. Very well indeed. I'm sure we do. Well, let's express it in the good old traditional manner—jolly good feller."

So I heaved myself out of the chair again and joined the others in singing that Justin was a jolly good fellow, which nobody could deny. Then Colonel Hawkes yelped: "Speech, Burnage!" and looked prodigiously relieved that his own ordeal was over and that someone else's was to begin.

Justin said: "Thank you all for coming tonight. I hope you've enjoyed yourselves at Tresant as much as I've enjoyed having you here. It's a start. I want Tresant to be what it couldn't be in my dear father's time. Of course, I don't mean just a lot of junketing like this. This sort of thing is all very well now and then, but there's a lot more than this to a house and an estate like Tresant. I just want you to know that I'm aware of that, and that when I get back I shall keep that well in mind. This is my place.

"I expect you wonder what I mean by when I get back. Well, there's a bit of trouble in Africa, you know. I didn't want to dim anyone's enjoyment tonight with talk about that, but I'm afraid I'm due to join in it.

While you're still sleeping off this happy night I shall be hurrying to London to join my regiment. Thank you all again, and *au revoir*."

We sat in our room, Daniel and I, for a long time, listening to what he called the tumbrils rolling away into the night. To me they sounded like—oh, like all the devilish things that have become steadily more devilish from that day to this: like gun teams, like ammunition columns, like all the chariots and juggernauts that have rolled through time. We heard them go, one by one, with creaking wheels and straining leather and crunching gravel, and there was a pawing of hooves accompanied by a voice that rang like a trumpet. "Well, good-by, Burnage. Remember your father was at Balaclava. Let's all be proud of you, my boy." That would be Colonel Hawkes, who had been at the relief of Lucknow.

I sat on the bed, too tired to speak, too overcome by this sudden and unexpected and, I felt, disastrous news. Daniel walked up and down, undressing in a distracted piecemeal fashion. He had thrown off his coat and was pulling at his tie. "Well," he said, "you were right. You heard it."

I looked at him, not understanding. "The sound of battle beyond the sound of revelry," he said. He leaned through the open window. Some servant put out the lights at the front of the house. Everything went dark; the last sounds of the departing guests were gone. We could hear shuffles along the carpeted corridor as people went to bed. Justin passed by whistling. "Good night, you two," he shouted. "Night, Sarah —Dan. Sleep well."

Daniel shut the window and pulled the curtains across and came and sat on the bed beside me. He put an arm round me and kissed me, comforting me in my speechless sorrow. Speech came presently, and I burst out: "What's it all *about*? These things go on happening and we—common people like me—we don't even know what they're about."

He was grave, and he did not try to slur the matter into insignificance. He never did, and I was thankful to him for that. "Well," he said, "at the moment, it's a matter of fighting against Zulus, and I should think that's a desperate business enough. But that's not the root of it. South Africa is a rich country, and there are Dutchmen in it and Englishmen. Black men, too. But at the moment—at the moment, mind you—the black men are only a buffer between these others. It's these others that are going to cause the trouble. One of these days the black men will have been dealt with—for the time being—and then the Dutchmen and the English will have to decide who's the boss."

We didn't sleep at all that night. There was a fire in the room and Daniel made it up and put new candles in the candlesticks, and we talked and talked. "You know that woman Grimshaw," I said, "who keeps house for Whaley. I remember her bursting out one day about the time when she married her employer's son. He was an army officer.

'Oh, I thought it was going to be wonderful!' she said, and it wasn't wonderful at all. It turned out gray and commonplace. It's like that for all of us—no, don't interrupt me, darling: I'm not talking about you and me. There's many a snug spot to be found in a howling gale, and we've found one. I know that all right. I'm talking about life as it seems to me to have been ever since I can remember anything."

"It's your misfortune," he said, "that your first memory is of one of humanity's great moments of optimism."

"I've bored you with it often enough, darling: the Crystal Palace, and the Queen's lovely dress, and the music and the fountains. I sometimes think it was a bit hard on me to receive such notions as came to me then."

Daniel pulled on a dressing gown and lit a pipe. "It wasn't only you, my dear. I suppose the Prince Consort bluffed even himself with his grand show of the New Jerusalem coming down from heaven and dwelling among pumps and pistons. Glory to God in the highest and on earth room for the expansion of the steam engine and of British exports in general."

"In two years we were at war with Russia—in two years! In six there was that awful business in India. In nine we started to build iron warships, and the *Observer*—I can see the lines before my eyes now—congratulated us on being 'for the present at least safe from the attack of our "good friends" across the Channel.' Then we just missed war with America. And now this! And you say this is only the beginning of something worse."

"It doesn't sound a good record, or a good outlook."

"What on earth's the matter with us all?" I cried desperately.

"You're not the first person to ask that, my darling, and I'm afraid you won't be the last. Lie down now. Get your head onto the pillow and try to sleep."

But I could not. We talked on and on, and when daylight came we went down and found Sally and Mervyn and Dolly prowling restlessly about. It looked as though there had been small sleep for anyone. Presently Justin joined us, and nothing at all was said to suggest that this was a different sort of breakfast from any other. Nothing was said, but everything was felt. Justin would not allow anyone to join him in the carriage that took him to the railway station. We waved him off at the front door, and it seemed to me odd that every one of us was dry-eyed except Dolly Dewhirst. We were all standing there, continuing to gaze at the path after the carriage had vanished round a bend, and suddenly she was not there with us.

It was Sally who asked: "Hallo! Where's Dolly?"

"Let her be," said Mervyn.

I thought then of Justin's joke about Dolly's clockwork heart, and more and more felt that I would never understand anything about men and women.

3

It is difficult to say exactly what relation Justin was to my little Richard. He was my half brother. My mother (whom he never knew) was his mother, but his father was not my father. He was some sort of uncle to Richard: a half uncle, if there is such a thing: and he and the child had once or twice looked at one another. However, it was convenient to call him Uncle Justin, and Richard, at seven, was very conscious of his Uncle Justin. Uncle Justin was a historic character to him, and he treasured all the relics he could get hold of. In a box in his nursery were a button from a uniform coat, an old hunting crop, an end of pencil that had been found in Justin's pocket, a bit that Jack Pudding had once champed upon, and things of that sort. Richard was conscious, indeed, of all the Gaylords, though he had no drop of their blood. His grandmother had been Lady Burnage, and that was enough for him. He could, and I knew that he did, build a shimmering edifice on that slight foundation. The bit had been in the mouth of a charger, and on this splendid horse Uncle Justin had rushed upon the Zulus, beating the horse forward with the riding crop. The chief of the Zulus, was also mounted upon a horse—a black one: Justin's was white. They met with a terrible clash, the black men and the white men standing still, withdrawn on either hand, to watch that encounter. Justin with his bare hands unhorsed the Zulu, who then traitorously thrust up from the ground with a spear, causing Justin's horse to rear and throw him. As he fell, the Zulu smashed him upon the head with a knobkerrie. The watching hosts assumed that he was dead and rushed together. The tide of battle swayed away from that spot and Justin came out of his swoon. Somehow, he managed to extricate the bit from the rest of the charger's equipment. He cut a button off his coat, and laid bit, button and riding crop upon the ground. Then he took out a pencil and scribbled a message with his dying hand: "Give these things as a sacred trust to my dear nephew Richard Undridge." He was found dead with the pencil grasped in his hand and a peaceful smile upon his face.

I didn't like these fantasies, and I more than once told Richard the truth about Justin's lamentable end. How could he, I asked, be on a horse when he was an infantryman? And to that Richard replied: "He borrowed it from a passing colonel." Did he not know that Justin had been one of those who formed the fatal square at Ulundi, where the might of the Zulus was finally broken seven months after we had watched Justin disappear down the drive at Tresant?

240

How then, he would ask, could he have Uncle Justin's last message? And he would produce that evidence, scrawled in pencil on a piece of paper that he had crushed and dirtied and horribly stained with blood by rubbing it across a joint of beef in the kitchen.

4

When he was seven and we were down at Tresant he said: "I have never seen the tombs of my ancestors."

I was rather tired of his obsession, and answered crossly: "Richard, how often have I to tell you that the Gaylords are no ancestors of yours?"

He looked at me sulkily and said: "You know very well, Mama, that my Grandmama was Lady Burnage and that her son was my Uncle Justin, Lord Burnage."

I tried once more to get it straight for him. Patiently I explained: "Your Grandmama married Lord Burnage after your mother was born. Therefore your mother was nothing whatever to do with the Gaylords, so far as blood goes. Is that clear?"

He knew all this. We had had it out before. "Yes, Mama," he said, "that is clear, but—"

"There's no but about it, Richard. Your mother was no Gaylord, and your father, as you well know, is the son of a poor man who tries to earn a living by teaching in a school and by painting."

We were at breakfast at a small table in a corner of the dining room. Gaylord portraits were on the walls around us, and among them hung the portrait of my mother that Justin's father had never been able to look upon and had entrusted to Maggie Whale. Justin had hung it here. Richard looked around him at the portraits, and his roving gaze came to a stand at this picture of his grandmother. I did not need to be told what he was thinking, and, to draw him away from these delusive thoughts, I asked: "Well, what shall we do this morning?"

"Visit the tombs of my ancestors," he said.

I saved myself from a petulant outburst by reflecting that Mr. Cogan, at any rate, would have approved so Chinese a spirit of devotion.

5

My father was an iron-master. If he must be clapped into a cliché, he was a hard-headed businessman who had a corner in a commodity that happened to be increasingly, even frantically, in demand. My beautiful mother was a daughter of a Norfolk canon of the Church of England, a man whose life began in a village draper's shop. His only other child, whom I never met, was an actress. My father had not permitted my mother to associate with her.

Mr. Undridge, Daniel's father, we know: a poor stick, if ever there was one, full of illusion about an importance he never possessed. Mrs. Undridge was a starving little dressmaker when he first met her and persuaded her to be his model and afterward his wife. The odd ebb and flow of English society, where talent, beauty, wealth, scruple and lack of it, are all waves that wash people hither and thither between trough and crest, had brought about the contacts of these men and women (and who knows what strange combinations before their time?) and the immediate outcome was this seven-year-old Richard Undridge who dreamed delusive dreams of "ancestors" stretching back in a fabulous line of unbroken splendor and rectitude.

I was proud of him. Certainly, if lordliness and looks have anything to do with one another, he might have been a young lord. He was thinner than I would have liked him to be, but he was well and wiry, and he had a rich dark beauty. The diverse elements had here coalesced into something fine and rare to look at. I think my mother handed him that; and so far as mind and spirit went he seemed an amalgam of his grandfather Rainborough's harsh practicality, which permitted nobody to fool him, streaked with his grandfather Undridge's ability to fool himself.

Of course, all this did not present itself to my mind as I thought of Richard then. I loved him and occasionally I was troubled about him: that was all. But there have been since then long long years for thinking of Richard and of many things.

6

"All right," I said, getting up from the table. "Let us go and see the tombs."

At once he was a new boy—vivacious, eager. He clutched my hand warmly as we set out.

It was a spring day, with clouds idling across the tender blue of the sky. Down there in Cornwall, though so much vegetation is earlier than elsewhere, the trees come to leaf later. They were now bursting with young green, and the air was full of bird song and the cries of lambs. The church is shut in by trees that grow to its very walls. In the tumbled grass outside, sown richly now with blue and white violets and the shining gold of celandine, the gravestones of the common people lean at all angles—some of crumbling stone, some of damson-blue slate so soft for carving that the cursive lettering and ornament of the local craftsmen flow beautifully upon it. The tombs of the Gaylords are within.

No one was there but we two—no one seems ever to be there—as the heavy oaken door groaned and we stepped inside. I sat on a bench near the door and allowed Richard to wander at will. I was at once afflicted with the feelings that always came to me in that place. The church itself was like a tomb. The glass in the windows was dim, and the light, falling through the besieging trees, undulated green and wan, as if the building were rocking delicately under water. Cold that had been imprisoned here for centuries seeped through the stones of the floor and chilled the air. You could smell the mold. You could see it and feel it. If you rubbed the tombs, the stone crumbled in your fingers and came away in green-gray dust. There was a bluish bloom on the wood of the altar rails, and the iron that enclosed some of the tombs was flaky and flecked with rust. It would not have been surprising to see fungus growing from the cracks of the stones, and once I did find there a toad, squatting contentedly at the foot of the lectern, whose eagle alone spread its brassy wings with a shining defiance of dissolution. Upon the altar hyacinths drooped their heavy blue-curled heads and exuded rather than exhaled a charnel smell that filled the church. Above all was the cold and the silence, not broken but deepened by the sough of a wind-stirred branch, the sudden wild scuttering cry of a bird, and the creak of Richard's shoes as he tiptoed in awe from tomb to tomb, reading the inscriptions.

I could never sit in that place without hearing, as if a voice were murmuring them, the lines:

> *Here, where the world is quiet;*
> *Here, where all trouble seems*
> *Dead winds' and spent waves' riot*
> *In doubtful dreams of dreams.*

"Swinburne! Huh! Chinless little runt! I used to meet him with Rossetti." So Daniel's father had said, as ever envious of fame.

Well, he may have been all that; but the used words stirred me, and I looked at Richard, enraptured, enmeshed in these so doubtful dreams of dreams, and I said, quite loudly, so that the words breaking on the silent air startled even myself: "Darling, hadn't we better be going? It's so cold."

He looked up at me reproachfully, a finger to his lips, and whispered: "S-sh!"

I got up and wandered to him where he was standing before a tomb of that Lord Burnage who had been "for fifteen years afflicted with the gout which he sustained with Christian fortitude," and of his lady who died in her thirtieth year "in childbed of her tenth son." They were all here, some in effigy with their wives alongside them and

243

little dogs nuzzling at their feet; some armored and grim; some in-effective-looking and pathetic, with beards sticking over their ruffs; all dead as doornails! And where they were not in effigy they were com-memorated on tablets that adorned the walls, inscribed with rigmaroles in Greek or Latin, which, if they were like the few that used plain English, represented every Gaylord who had ever lived to have been a model of Christian virtue, an example of physical valor, a faithful husband, a good father, a beloved friend, a benefactor of the poor and a pillar of the state. The women had all been chaste and pious and prolific; and the many children who had died young had been of a beauty and a promise which, if fulfilled, could hardly have failed to make England a paradise of piety and learning.

Well, there they were, and you could read how they had served Elizabeth and harbored Charles and fought with Marlborough by land and with Nelson on the sea. From the blotched marble and the tar-nished brass great names blazed forth: Minden and Trafalgar, Copen-hagen and Waterloo. But somehow to me they were all dreams of dreams except the tomb, with no effigy, but a few simple carved words, where *my* Lord Burnage, as I should always think of him, was sleeping after his twenty long unhappy years; and the new marble tablet on the wall above it which recorded Justin's death in Africa. I stood before these, with the pale green light pulsing upon them as the wind and the wings of birds stirred the branches of the trees; and then I could understand all these other memorials, and how each may have brought some solace to a heart new-smarting with loneliness and loss. God help us, I thought, we should need each a church to himself if all our sins and follies were to be recorded as well as the few starry deeds and aptitudes that shine against the cold immensity and darkness of our lives. Even if we do no more than sustain our gout with Christian fortitude, let us put that down. It is something.

"Well, darling, we'd better go."

"If you're cold, Mama, will you wait for me outside in the sunshine? I shan't be long."

I left him there, and as I went through the low porch I felt like risen Lazarus. The spring day exploded round my head in green and blue and white, and the air was whirring with the wings of birds hurrying to their nests, their beaks tufted with spoil for gaping mouths. The sunshine was warm; the cracked old bell in the church tower spoke without resonance of noon. I sat on a tombstone, rough with sage-green and yellow lichens, and my eyes fell upon a slate headstone. I had forgotten that he was there: Edward Rodda, master mariner. Simply that, with the date of his birth and of his death. A vase of daffodils was standing in front of the headstone, and I wondered who was remember-ing Eddy Rodda, and why. On the stone edging that defined the grave a blackbird alighted, cocked a bright eye at me, and, accepting my stillness, began to batter the shell off a snail. The yellow bill was a pincer holding the soft pulp of the body, the shining neck a lever, the stone an anvil, and the notes rang out, *tap, tap, tap,* sharp and clear amid the thronging life and death of the churchyard.

I got up and walked over the uneven grass and noticed what I had not seen before: that there was a leper-squint cut through the church wall. I put my eye to it, and the interior of the church came upon my sight framed like a dim old picture that needs cleaning. Richard was bending over one of the tombs. I could not for a moment make out what he was doing. Then I saw that he had an open pocketknife in his hand and that he was scraping away at the moldering stone, allowing the dust to fall into a small tin box.

I hated myself for having, even thus accidentally, overlooked him, and I hurried back to my tombstone seat. But the morning did not seem so bright, and my heart was beating with unaccustomed force. I didn't like this collecting of dust and ashes. God save the child from morbidity!

When he came out, he didn't look morbid. He had put the knife and the box into his pocket. His face was clear and open. As we were walking back to the house he said: "There's one thing, Mama, that you seem to have forgotten. My Grandmama was Uncle Justin's mother. So Uncle Justin and I have some of the same blood in our veins."

7

Julian Rimmel was six months older than Richard. I had not met the boy or his mother, who was my husband's sister Marie, but I was expecting them, and Marie's husband, Sebastien Rimmel, that afternoon. Sebastien, of course, I knew, or rather I had met. I could hardly claim to know the elusive boy who was with Daniel in England now and then when Maggie Whale and I first began to go to London. Daniel himself would be coming down with these three.

The winter before this had been most disagreeable in London. By the river at Chelsea we endured one fog after another, or it may have been one continuous fog that occasionally went north for a holiday in Manchester or Sheffield and then came back refreshed. Daniel was exceedingly busy, and upon his return from the Temple at night, he would, as often as not, when dinner was done, go to his study and work till bedtime. He liked me to sit there with him, so long as I kept quiet, and with Maggie I had had plenty of practice in that; and these were the happiest hours of that dismal season, sitting by the fire with a book in my hand as Daniel worked at the table over which a green-shaded lamp burned.

Just after Christmas came unexpected and tragic news. Daniel's father and mother were returning in a hackney carriage from a public dinner in Bordeaux when Mrs. Undridge collapsed and died. It was late at night, and in such weather as we had been suffering from in London. Mr. Undridge stopped the cab and got out into the brown coiling vapor of the street to direct the cabman to drive to a doctor's house. He then began to get back into the cab, and the driver, excited by what he had been told and unable to see clearly in that abominable weather, started off while Mr. Undridge's foot was still on the step. The sudden movement threw him into the road, and a vehicle which was coming up behind passed over his head. His cabman, unaware of this, arrived at the doctor's house unable to explain the absence of his living passenger and with Mrs. Undridge's corpse lolling on the seat.

And so Daniel had to make the dreary journey to Bordeaux in these more than dreary circumstances. He came back full of cold and cough, and was not well for the rest of the winter. As soon as the weather brightened, his doctor said, he must get out of London for a week or two; and that is why I had come down to Tresant with Richard to prepare the place. It was necessary now to make sure that rooms and beds would be in a condition to receive visitors, for Tresant was not what it had been.

8

Justin's death broke the tradition of the Gaylords. As far back as the family records went, male heir had succeeded male heir. They had been good or bad, public-spirited or recluse. They had gone abroad and fought in wars or they had stayed at home and looked after their cows and corn. Some had followed the fortunes of the Court and some had never stirred out of Cornwall. But whatever else they had done or left undone, they had begotten sons to succeed them. Perhaps Justin would have done this, too, if Eddy Rodda had not lain one day with Lucy Evans.

Tresant was now Sally's. It had fallen into her hands at the moment when Justin was waking it up out of its sleep. It began to go to sleep again: that is to say, in so far as it was a house built for elegant living. In so far as it was an agricultural estate, it was kept in perfect order, and, through Mr. Merriman, the agent, Sally was as strict as her father had been that not a decaying stone, a sagging gate, a loose tile or a choked ditch should be neglected. But the house in Portman Square was sold out of hand, the imposing staff that Justin had engaged for

246

its service was dismissed; and at Tresant the house got along as best it could with a man and wife to look after it.

"The fact is," said Sally, "I'm that odious thing, an absentee landlord."

She said it half playfully, half with some serious perturbation of spirit. We looked out through the windows of the Settlement upon Graybird Court that was a pit filled with sweltering heat in the noon of a summer day. Women sat on the doorsteps or on chairs they had dragged out; a few mongrels lay with panting tongues in a strip of shade; children listlessly hopped on one foot from square to square chalked upon the stone. Sally was the absentee landlord of Tresant. Daniel was the absentee landlord of this. But there was a difference. The Tresant estate, which included not only the house and the agricultural land but much invested money and valuable urban property, a lot of it in London, made Sally rich. Graybird Court was an unending drain on Daniel's pocket.

We were sitting in what was called the rest room. It was fairly large, furnished with comfortable wicker chairs, but the floor was of bare scrubbed boards, and the magazines on the tables placed here and there seemed to me rather forbiddingly "improving." Any woman in the court was at liberty to come here and relax, and there were a few cribs where babies could be left if their mothers had to go out shopping or working. The walls were of a pallid blue, as if they had been washed in skimmed milk.

Through the open door a shrill voice reached us. I recognized it as Dolly Dewhirst's. It had become more shrill, I thought, with the passage of the years. "Gaylord! There are at least half a dozen women sitting in the court. Shouldn't they be invited into the rest room?"

Sally gave me a smile. "Very well, Superintendent," she called, and we went out together into the court.

Dolly Dewhirst had been superintendent of the Settlement for a few months now, and she was a woman who could never take hold of anything without beginning at once to reform it. She had made it clear that slopping about with a vague and general good will would not do. The staff of the Settlement, she said, must take a lesson from the Jesuits. Results were achieved through discipline and a program. In the interests of discipline Christian names were no longer to be used. She would in future be addressed as Superintendent, and the rest of them would be Gaylord, Johnson and so forth. And they mustn't sit about waiting for wayfarers to come in: they must go out and bring them in.

Sally and I went into the court. A languid dog got up and sniffed at our heels. The languid children gave Sally shy smiles, and a little boy came up and asked: "Give us a penny, Miss?"

"You know how to earn a penny, don't you, Tom?" Sally asked; and Tom said: "Got no blackin', Miss."

"Well, you know what the Superintendent would say to that, don't you?"

Tom's face darkened. "That ole bitch!" he said and darted off into one of the houses.

"We're trying the system of Incentives and Rewards," Sally said, succeeding somehow in emphasizing the capital letters. "Little boys who keep their boots clean—when they've got any—get a penny a week, and if they've got no blacking—well, a lot can be done, the Superintendent says, with spit and a bit of sacking."

She sounded dispirited, which was something new for Sally. "Then there are the window boxes," she said.

They made so poor a show that I had not noticed them; but now, my interest being invited, I looked up and saw a box here and there on the ledges of the upper rooms. "But not one of them has a flower!" I cried; and Sally answered: "No. Flowers are not the idea. The people are to be taught the virtues of fresh vegetables."

I looked at the boxes again and saw that they contained a few wilting lettuces or sprigs of parsley. They were depressing beyond belief, all save a box which defiantly spilled down a cascade of nasturtiums in full flower.

"Mr. Cogan's breaking the rules," I said. "Look! A bee!"

And there, indeed, beneath Mr. Cogan's window, was a big furry bee, bumbling and fussing from flower to flower. Sally looked at it as if entranced. "I've never seen a bee in this place before!"

We stood there watching it, as pleased as though an archangel had decided to visit Graybird Court. In the silence of the noontide heat we could hear the busy whirr of its wings as it poised in front of the flowers before plunging in to lick up their honey. Into the rest of the court it seemed to bring the warm hale smell of clover fields, and it was, above all, so joyous, so unaware of the squalor it was invading. Even in Chelsea a bee was something. Here it had the shining quality of a miracle. As we continued to watch it, I was aware of a stealthy sound behind us, and, turning, I saw the child Tom creeping up, some sort of gun in his hand. "Look, Sal! What's he up to?"

"Put that thing down!" she shouted. "I've told you about it before. Put it down!"

But the boy did not obey. His sharp ratlike face looked resentful at the order, and I saw his finger press upon the trigger. It was an airgun, a mere toy that expelled a few pellets, and the sound of it was hardly audible, a soft *phut!* But by the one in a million chance a pellet found that minute target. We turned as the gun was fired, and the bee was lying on its back, a wing broken, its feet clawing at the air. Tom rushed in between us and stamped it to pulp. "That stings, that do—see?" he said. "Saved you from that, I did. Boots is clean enough for that—see? Gi's a penny."

Sally grabbed my arm. "Let's go back," she said. "I feel sick."

We went back into the rest room of the Settlement, and she collapsed into a chair. The small piece of ignorant barbarity seemed to have affected her out of reason. I guessed it was some last straw, some culmination.

"I'll get you a cup of tea, Sal," I said.

She was leaning back with her rough stained hands in the lap of her uniform skirt. She no longer wore any old clothes that came to hand. The skirt was of gray flannel with red piping defining the entrance to the pocket on the hip. The Superintendent's skirt was black, with blue piping.

When I returned with the tea Sally was not alone. A woman, who could hardly have been other than Tom's mother, was with her: a thin, undersized, gray old rat, snapping with yellow teeth. "I 'eard you shoutin' at our Tom. Won't 'ave it, see? We're not goin' to take orders from the likes of you. We got a right to do wot we like, see?"

She was walking up and down, arms akimbo. Sally had not risen from the chair. Her eyes were closed, and she let the woman rant. Tom's mother might not have existed, and was therefore infuriated. "You get up when you're bein' spoke to," she said. "You take a bit o' notice of a person, will you? Sittin' there like Godormity."

She stepped forward as if she would have seized Sally to drag her upright. I put down the tea cup and moved between them. "Miss Gaylord is not feeling very well," I said. "It's so hot."

"It's so Hot!" she mimicked, with a tremendous aspirate. "Godormity! 'Aven't we gotter put up with the 'eat? Year in, year out, in this bloody 'ole!"

"Well, so does Miss Gaylord."

"You keep yer mouth out of it," she rounded on me. "Who's talkin' to you? She can take 'er backside outter that chair an' talk to a person civil, can't she?"

"No. At the moment she can't. You'd better get out and leave her alone."

"Get out, is it? More orders! Orders from *you* now! Oo d'you think you bloody people are, comin' round 'ere with yer orders? Godormity! Oo *asked* you?"

Dolly Dewhirst came in. She had a pencil in her hand and she rat-tat-tatted on a table with it, like a chairman calling a meeting to order. "What is all this? What's going on? Mrs. Drummond, you speak first."

"More bloody orders! Mrs. Drummond, you speak first!" Again the mincing mimicry; but now without much confidence. Dolly Dewhirst gave her a cold look and said: "Yes, you speak first, and don't use that language to me. That's another order."

Mrs. Drummond looked at Dolly furtively, folding her skinny arms in a sacking apron. "Ain't goin' to tell you nothing—see?"

"All right. Then sit down and let's hear someone else. What is it all about, Gaylord?"

Sally opened her eyes and looked at her with a sort of weary wisdom, as if seeing her for the first time. "You wouldn't understand," she said.

"I can have a good try. That's what I'm here for: to get to the bottom of things. You and Mrs. Drummond have come to loggerheads. I want to know why, so that your relationship can be adjusted."

"Why do you call her Mrs. Drummond and me Gaylord?"

"Because you're a member of our team."

Sally said: "Quack, quack! You make me sick."

Even I, aware as I was that Sally had reached some crisis, was surprised by this. Mrs. Drummond was overjoyed and Dolly went white with anger.

Mrs. Drummond cried: "Quack, quack! Come on, duck, let's hear you again," and Dolly said: "Get up, Gaylord. Get up and apologize."

Sally's eyes were still closed. Dolly advanced upon her, even as Mrs. Drummond had done a moment before, and this time it was Mrs. Drummond who intervened. She stood in front of Sally, showing her yellow fangs, and said quietly: "You lay an 'and on 'er an' I'll gouge you."

Whatever else might be amiss with Dolly, she was physically afraid of no one. She stepped forward, put a hand on Mrs. Drummond's shoulder, and tried to sweep her aside. Like a flash the rat-teeth snapped upon her wrist, and the dirty wiry little witch with both hands seized Dolly's hair, pulling it into a disordered fall about her shoulders, and shaking her head back and forth, to and fro. "You keep yer 'ands orf 'er—see?" Mrs. Drummond panted. "Worth ten of you, she is. She treats us like 'uman beings, she do. I'll gouge yer. I warned yer!"

I could see that the dreadful little woman was indeed preparing to carry out this threat. Holding the hair with all her other fingers, she was drawing it inward and her thumbs were moving toward Dolly's eyes. I was in such horrid fascination that I could do nothing but stand as if watching a stoat with its teeth in a rabbit's neck.

The rumpus shook Sally out of her lethargy. She stood up, and a long acquaintance with the techniques of Graybird Court showed her what was threatened. She stepped forward and gave Mrs. Drummond such a stinger across the cheek that the sound rang in the room like a pistol shot. Mrs. Drummond's hands fell to her sides. She sank into a chair and began to blubber, with the sacking apron at her eyes. Sally gave both to her and to Dolly Dewhirst a look of unutterable loathing, and walked out of the room.

I followed her up the stairs to the attic where she slept. The energy that had surged into her blow had subsided again. She looked pale, ill and apathetic, but she did not sit down. She pulled an old carpet bag from under the bed and began to stuff her few possessions recklessly into it. I sat on the bed, with its harsh iron head and foot, and looked round the room which for many years now had afforded her all the privacy she knew. The boards were bare; the only furniture was the bed, a chest-of-drawers that could have been bought for five shillings in any junk shop, and a wooden kitchen chair. The walls were white-washed. A photograph of Justin was propped against half a dozen books on the chest-of-drawers, and standing next to it was a tin of insect powder. The books, I saw, were a Bible, the *Pilgrim's Progress*, some sermons by C. H. Spurgeon, and a couple of Maggie Whale's novels. As Sally kneeled on the boards, putting things into the bag, the top of her head was under my eyes, and the pitiless noon, which stewed and simmered in that little cell under the slates, showed me how gray she had become. It was no question now of seeing, as I had seen at Justin's coming-of-age party, a gray hair or two. She looked old. I knew that now she had come to the end of something, and I did not doubt that soon there would be a new beginning, but in what direction that would take her I could not guess. I could do nothing but remember Sally: the child who had whistled to the butcher's boy in Portman Square, who had pleased Ducat by asking the name of the horse, who had ridden and swum at Tresant and been drunk with me in Eddy Rodda's cave, and whose love for people had swung her so impetuously at first, and then so steadfastly, along Dolly Dewhirst's path. Of all the Gaylords I had read about or whom I had known, she was the one I loved the best. Now, with the uniform blouse and skirt stripped from her and thrown upon the bed, there she stood in her underclothes, an aging woman who did not look very clean. She spoke for the first time since we had come into the room. "There! That's gone, thank God! I don't like uniforms."

She pulled on a rusty black skirt and blouse, and said: "I have been happy in this little room." Then she kissed me and said: "I'm glad you were here at the end. I'm ready now; but would you mind going outside for a moment and waiting on the landing?"

I did so, and closed the door softly, and I did not need to be told why Sally wanted to be alone. She was on her knees by the hideous little bed, thanking God for the happiness she had known in that room and asking what now she must do. She was a Gaylord, and some day she would be laid with all the other Gaylords among the moldering tombs in the church where only the leaves and the birds broke the silence. But there would be no sanctification in that; and now, when this has indeed happened, the sweetness of Sally's life comes back to me most powerfully when I think of how I stood on the landing and she knelt within, alongside the bag containing the tin of insect powder.

CHAPTER FIFTEEN

I

I SHALL hand these pages over to Julian Rimmel when I have done with them, and I shan't feel that I am imposing on him. He owes me something. "You know, *ma chère tante*," he said to me not long ago, "it was my first visit to Tresant that determined the course of my life."

Julian is rather a dramatic person, given to utterances of that sort, not strictly true, but having a grain of truth that makes them difficult to disprove. Certainly, Tresant had a different effect on him from the one it had on me when I first knew it as a child.

When the Rimmels turned up with Daniel, they were an odd-looking trio. Sebastien was the only one I had met, and that was so infrequently and so long ago that I had forgotten what he looked like. He was now nearing forty and had become a stout, stolid, responsible-looking bourgeois with a close-cropped gray skull and a clipped gray mustache. I had gathered something about him from Daniel, and knew that by years of attention to business, with a careful eye on every sou and a stringency in household expenditure, he was now a part proprietor in the shipping house which he had entered as a youth. The opportunity to take this step had come some years ago, and Sebastien had boldly seized it by putting in every penny he had and borrowing more. It was the necessity to repay this loan that had been, ever since, the supreme economic fact of the Rimmel household. Marie remembered it when she went to buy vegetables in the market or a new pair of shoes for Julian, and she remembered it when she decided *not* to buy a new hat for herself or new sheets for the beds. There had been ten years of this struggle. It was over now, but the habits it had induced remained. One was always conscious of a financial watchfulness about the Rimmels, as though sous were something to be stolen upon carefully, lest, like a flock of quails, they should take wing and vanish. Daniel told me of an odd happening that showed their drift. Little though Mr. and Mrs. Undridge had left behind them when they so tragically died on the same night, that little was almost enough to kill the debt. But not quite. There were some personal belongings that the dead couple had left: a few bits of jewelry for Marie, Mr. Undridge's gold watch for Sebastien. They had made clear, while still alive, that they wished these things to be kept as mementoes. But they were thrown into the pool. They brought in the last necessary hundred pounds, and the Rimmels were clear. This was the moment they had talked of for years. They had always said it was to be celebrated: a theater followed by dinner out; perhaps, then, a holiday; but now that the moment was upon them they looked at one another and each knew that the other recoiled from the extravagance. There was no celebration. They sat at home and brooded contentedly upon their deliverance. Was it not clear, now that the debit account was dealt with, that prudence suggested the building up of a credit account before a plunge into self-indulgence?

All this, I thought, when I met them at the train, was in Marie's face. Though her parents had been English, she had never been out of France, and rarely out of Bordeaux. Her English was excellent, but it had a French accent, and she looked the middle-class French wife that she was: rather squat, dark, and with a shadow of *duvet* on her upper lip.

If these two, dressed in dowdy town clothes, which they continued to wear throughout the holiday, were out of place in the Cornish spring countryside, their son Julian contrasted with them as startlingly as did the flowering hedges and all the country sounds and scenes. I had never met a more flyaway-looking child. A pair of ballet shoes standing between two pairs of Lancashire clogs would not have looked more incongruous. Julian was tall for his age, thin and dark, with curling careless hair, restless and inquisitive, volleying *qu'est-ce que c'est's?* and *pourquoi's?* at everything through which his parents steadily plodded. I learned later that Sebastien Rimmel's father, who owned a small private school, had married a beautiful Jewess, perhaps because she was a good pianist and music teacher. Nothing of his mother's beauty and artistic finesse had become apparent in Sebastien, but it must have been slumbering there all the same, for here it was, blazing forth in Julian, who also was the grandson, as my Richard was, of old Undridge.

2

I have said that the first impact of Tresant upon me as a child was different from the impact upon Julian; and in nothing was this shown more than in his hanging about inside the house. For me, all the beauty had been in the woods and the fields. For Julian, the contents of the house had an endless fascination. Daniel had described to me the Rimmel home in Bordeaux, and I knew that it was as clean, beeswax-smelling, sanitary and repulsive as the waiting room of a hospital. Knowing what I do of Julian now, I can understand how all that must have been a dead weight on his spirit, and how, let loose in Tresant, his natural inclinations leapt up like Jack released from the box. And a Jack who had not, till then, known how wonderful the world outside the box was. The place subdued the boy's volubility. I would find him, grave and silent, looking at a piece of tapestry, running his hand over a carving, standing back and admiring the color that glowed in the Gaylord portraits, or, with a considering look, weighing some silver trifle in his hand. The place gave him plenty to look at. When Sally sold the house in Portman Square, all that had accumulated there was added to all that had accumulated here, so that the place was more like a store than a house.

Only a few rooms were lived in now, and Julian prowled through the rest of them where portraits and other pictures were hanging at times so closely that the frames were touching, and one had to edge one's way between Tudor tables and Jacobean chairs, Queen Anne tallboys and Chinese Chippendale mirrors. The place was a congested museum, and wherever he looked Julian found something to raise his musical murmur: *"Ah, c'est beau!"*

"Why don't you get out into the fresh air?" I would ask, in such French as I could master, and he would answer with an airy wave of the hand: *"Tout à l'heure, ma chère tante, tout à l'heure."*

3

Julian was about six months older than Richard. Daniel used to take the pair of them for long walks, and the consequence was that I spent a lot of time with Sebastien and Marie. I would have liked nothing better than to be off with the others, but these two were not given to exercise, and I could hardly desert them. However, the lake helped to make those occasions not too melancholy. Sebastien had the Frenchman's love of fishing in quiet waters. We would pack a luncheon basket, get into a punt and paddle away. Sebastien's concession to a holiday mood was a large floppy straw hat. Otherwise, he and Marie retained their solemn black. I think she was bored with the whole holiday, and pined all through it for the customary duties of her house in Bordeaux. She talked but little, and, in any case, if I did stir her occasionally to animation, Sebastien, gazing with a frown of concentration at the bobbing of his green and white float, was apt to hiss "P'st!" as though our talk could penetrate the water and scare the roach and tench. Sometimes he would strike sharply, bring up a hook lamentably free of prey, and thereupon direct at Marie a dark look which asked how a fisherman could prosper in a boat filled with chattering women. Marie would pass the look on to me, and I would subside into mere cargo, hardly venturing to breathe as we rocked over the clouds reflected in the blue water. Now and then a hapless mite of a fish would come up wriggling on the hook, and Sebastien's stout fingers would disengage it and lay it reverently on the fern leaves with which he had lined his creel. Marie would silently hand him the box of dough from which he would take a pinch, rebait the hook, and throw it into the water, permitting himself at last to speak. *"Enfin! Il y en a, tu vois!"* When we had thus assembled a sufficient luncheon for a fair-sized kitten, we would paddle to the bank, sit on the rocks under the pines, and eat our own.

It was not an exhilarating holiday for me, but it did give me some insight into the Rimmels' attitude to Julian. Sitting there with the light dappling us as it fell through the trees and flashing upon the water when a passing wind ruffled the surface and slapped little waves into the side of the punt, they would become almost eloquent on the subject of the boy. He was as dear to them as their debt had become throughout the years. They sometimes spoke of "our debt" as of a loved friend, late departed, a stern friend who had always been there to keep them on their toes and save them from folly. "And you recall, Sebastien, the day I was tempted by the brocade curtains at the sale of Madame Lafitte-Mory's effects? *Mon dieu!* That was a close thing!"

Julian, it seemed to me, was destined to take the place of "our debt." They did not appear to have a clear notion of what they wanted him to become or of his intrinsic possibilities, but vaguely they were resolved that only "the best" would do for him, and that they could get "the best" for him by saving hard. Thus they would at the same time be serving Julian and preventing their own footsteps from straying.

Exhausted by the eloquence this subject alone permitted him, and by the morning's exacting sport, Sebastien would extend himself upon the grass, place the straw hat over his face, and presently break into gentle snores. Now, if I ventured to speak, it was Marie's turn to emit a scarcely audible "P'st!" as she pointed to her recumbent lord. I would withdraw a little and fall into my own thoughts, and out of the corner of my eye I would see Marie, with her handkerchief ready to flap, watching for flies that should be impertinent enough to approach Sebastien too closely.

4

I called the other day at the Rimmel Galleries in Bond Street, and that will show you at once what Julian meant when he said that Tresant had determined his career. There were pits and caverns in Bond Street where shops had once been, and already spires of willow herb and mauve tassels of buddleia had come as an army of occupation from the wilderness, ready, given half a chance, to take over for good. There was not much in the gallery. Everything of value had been sent elsewhere; but enough of secondary worth was kept to support Julian's resolve that the war should not close so famous a place.

He still lived in his flat at the top of the building, and on the mantelpiece was the Hispano-Mauresque tile that I had given him so long ago. I didn't know then what it was, nor did he. It was just a tile thrown into a corner of one of the cluttered rooms, and he had picked it up and washed it, and been fascinated by the rich metallic luster. I wanted him to take away some small thing to remind him of a visit that he had found satisfying, so I gave him that.

To be seen out with Julian always made me feel proud; to be with him privately like this always gave me pleasure. His tall figure, his formal old-fashioned clothes and manners, the luster of his white hair and mustache and imperial, emphasized by the blackness of his eyebrows, the monocle swinging on watered silk, which he never used except to quiz at a pot or a picture: all these were "properties," and he used them like an actor of genius.

Julian went into his kitchen to make me some coffee. For the last few days, in this record I am compiling, I had been at the time of his first coming to Tresant, and I wanted to talk to him about that. When he came back and placed the coffee on the table he poured a spoonful of brandy into each cup. "This is something else that I have salved from the ruins, *my chère tante*," he said, and added regretfully, holding the bottle to the light: "But it doesn't last like other things that I have got my hands onto. It has been an odd life mine."

"Well, you've done what you wanted to."

"Yes, I suppose I have. Of course, I could be noble and say that I'd rather have painted one of Van Gogh's pictures and starved than have sold fifty of them at an enormous profit. That would just be an attitude. Still, it's odd to have nothing but taste, to go about the world smelling out lovely things that other people have made without having oneself as much skill as a village carpenter or signboard painter."

"You have the skill of recognition, which is a lot. And what do you mean by nothing but taste? God knows, this is an increasingly tasteless world. People with taste couldn't fall into the barbarism that is sinking us. If you can't make flags, at any rate it's something to keep 'em flying."

"You are always to be depended on for a comforting aphorism."

"Well, I return one comfort for another. You are a comforting person to me, you know. There aren't many now, comforting or otherwise."

"No. I'm beginning to find that out for myself. The leaves are getting thin on the trees."

"How old are you now, Julian?"

"*Ma chère tante,* permit me not to answer. It would be an impertinence to yourself."

"Not so impertinent as to suggest that I'm so old that my age mustn't even be hinted at. Anyway, there comes a point when one takes a pride in the very greatness of one's years. Tell me."

"I am sixty-five."

If Richard had lived, he would be about as old as that. "Then I expect every detail of your first visit to Tresant is gone from your memory," I said.

"Oh, no. A lot is gone, but what remains is very bright."

"How did you get on with Richard?"

It was long ago, and we had learned to be frank with one another. "I thought him *un peu barbare,*" he said. "Still, we got on well enough. *Le bon oncle* Daniel was usually with us. We only once came to a real clash."

"I never heard about that. Tell me."

"First let me refresh your coffee." He did so, and sacrificed a little more of the brandy. "I am seeing a man of the Normandy Resistance tonight. He has promised me a bottle of Armagnac. Well, now"—he sat down and lit a cigarette and considered for a moment the blue curl of smoke—"to make the little step back of six decades. It was a matter of a church door."

5

The good uncle Daniel couldn't always be with the boys. He had brought some work with him, and now and then they had to fend for themselves. Richard produced his Uncle Justin box and told the fabulous story of its contents, to which Julian gave a polite and unenthusiastic attention. Whether Richard's story was true or not he had no means of knowing, but the crumpled piece of bloody paper disgusted him, and the other things in the box seemed to him dull and meaningless. It must, in any case, have been a queer conversation, without Daniel as interpreter, for Richard had no French, and Julian's English, picked up from his mother, was reluctant and unreliable.

Disappointed of his effect, Richard said they had better get out and see the estate. They wandered here and there through the spring morning, and presently found themselves in the churchyard. As usual, it was windless, deserted, full of busy birds fluttering and singing in the trees that trailed their swags of gray ancient moss amid the vivid green of the year's leaves.

"You must come and see the tombs of my ancestors," said Richard; but Julian did not get farther than the church doors. They are still there, the same doors, almost sixty years after that spring morning when the two boys stood facing them, and how long they had been there before that I cannot say. Each wing of them was a solid slab of oak, a mere chunk of wood, but of an indescribable beauty as the repository of the centuries' weather. No one ever oiled or polished those doors. Since some smith attached to them the lovely ironwork they still wear and hung them in their place, nothing had happened to them but time, which had brought them to a harmony with the stone and with the ragged moss hanging upon the trees, like the battle colors in the church itself, hanging from their staffs drained of hue and gray as cobwebs. They were peasant doors, and had the wisdom and beauty of old peasant faces.

All this was in the doors for those who could feel it, and Julian was one of these. He had no knowledge of such matters, though that was to come; but already he had the feeling upon which knowledge was to operate, and these gray slabs of oak held him there after Richard had passed into the church. The sun that day was shining upon them. He laid his hand on the warm wood and on the iron of the great hinges, and decided that nothing he had seen at Tresant was the equal of this.

He stepped back and sat upon a tombstone, looking at the doors and waiting for Richard, who, when at last he came out, asked sulkily: "Don't you want to see our tombs?"

"No," said Julian, "I do not wish to go indoors at all."

"One of my ancestors was a crusader."

"*Ciel!* You and your ancestors!"

"Have you any ancestors?"

"It has been established that we spring from Adam and Eve, but the records in between are unfortunately lost."

"That only means you haven't got any."

"Oh, shut up!" Julian said rudely. "Look at that door! I've been looking at it for half an hour."

"What about it?"

"Don't you think it's lovely?"

Richard walked over to the door and gave it a kick. "Solid," he conceded.

"It certainly is. That'll be there when you're nothing but an ancestor yourself."

Richard took out his pocketknife and began scratching at the oak. With that toy he could not have done much, for the wood was as hard as iron, but Julian at once strode over to him and asked sharply: "What are you doing?"

"I'm going to carve my name."

"No. Please don't do that."

"Why shouldn't I?"

258

The hidden thought in Julian's mind was that it would be an offensive thing to do: an offense not against the church but against this incomparable piece of wood. But he didn't know what was moving him, and he could not express himself. He said lamely: "No. It would not be a good thing to do."

Richard laughed. "This knife's no good. I shall come tomorrow and bring a hammer and a small chisel."

"No. You mustn't."

The tone was peremptory; and it angered Richard. "I shall do as I please," he said. "I'd like to see you stop me."

Julian's mind, even in infancy, had a subtlety that Richard's never had. He apprehended that Richard's grand obsessions were a weakness through which he could be attacked, and he said: "It's a point of honor. I'll meet you in single combat."

That was something Richard could not resist. "All right," he said. "I'll fight you."

"And if I win you will not cut the door?"

"Honor bright," Richard promised.

There were no rules in that fight. It was not boxing and it was not wrestling. They simply took off their coats and there amid the headstones in the graveyard went for one another hammer and tongs, striking with fists and flat hands, seizing and gripping and swaying, panting hard at last, stumbling over the green mounds.

Julian, aged sixty-five, put a new cigarette into the ivory holder, held it in his long ivory fingers. "What little fools we were," he said. "As if a bit of carving on that door would have mattered one way or another! It might even have improved it, like the names carved on the wood at Eton. It gives a richer sense of time, n'est-ce pas? All those little people who have carved and died and rotted, and there the wood still is!

"Enfin! We were very serious! I had never fought before, and I hoped I would never fight again. But I found myself in Verdun. . . . Still . . . Back to those two silly children. There were jars of flowers on some of the graves, and daffodils growing on nearly all of them, and we thrashed and pounded through it like oxen, trampling the place to pieces. I won. Do not ask me why, ma chère tante. I am not a scientist of the ring. No doubt it was an accident. Richard stumbled and fell, and I hurled myself down on him and drove the breath out of him. I knelt on him till he gasped Pax! Then I got up. He was a long time getting his wind back, and while I waited, the birds that we had scared began to sing again. We hadn't scared the snails. I noticed one moving slowly over Eddy Rodda's headstone near which Richard was lying. It had drawn a silver line to emphasize that Eddy was a master mariner."

"And Richard kept his promise?"

"Oh, yes. Sometimes I wish he hadn't. You see, he so ardently wished to have his name carved near all those others that he had been considering in the church. That was the root of the thing. And I stopped him."

6

We all went back to London together, we three Undridges and the three Rimmels. They spent the night with us in Chelsea, and the next morning, after Daniel had gone to his chambers, I took them to the station. Marie made no bones about her joy at being en route for Bordeaux. Taciturn Sebastien, with his fisherman's creel slung over his broadcloth bourgeois suit, was no odder than many of the figures one sees on the Continental platform—odd only, I suppose, to our insular eyes. It was left to Julian to express, with voluble incomprehensibility, his thanks for the holiday, his joy in the visit, his hope that he might come again. I hoped so, too; but I was not sure that Marie would welcome it. Julian, she said, had become *presque fauve,* and she was evidently looking forward to a season of calming him down.

It was May Day, my birthday, and when the train was gone, Julian alone leaning out of the window to wave to the last, I got into a cab and was driven to St. John's Wood. It had been arranged that Maggie Whale should take me to a celebrating luncheon.

I was thirty-seven. That, I thought, is getting on. But even at the stupendous age of thirty-seven, one could take pleasure in that May morning, and, too, I was full of the sense of happy release with which even the most conscientious hostess says good-by to the most cherished guest. Laburnum and flowering cherry looked over the walls of the St. John's Wood gardens as the old horse clip-clopped along beneath the blue sky and the white astrakhan clouds. Chestnut trees were aflame with candles of red and cream, and the very cries of milkmen and butchers' boys seemed like joy bursting irresistibly forth.

There was no longer a Mrs. Grimshaw to share these earthly delights. She had been gathered to her captain, and Glory Jane, assisted by a female mite, looked after Maggie's home. Glory Jane, who read nothing, was enormously conscious of her prestige as controller of an author's establishment. I am doubtful whether I myself would have been permitted to see Whaley at that hour if it had not been arranged that she was to take the day off. Glory Jane opened the door and greeted me with a wink which I should have been disappointed not to receive. The red-headed Juno had shed much of her old exuberance, deferring thus to a growing sense of responsibility; but something of it survived in the greeting, customary to me as an old member of the household. "Well!

What a world! What goings-on in it! I wonder what *you've* been up to!" All this was in Glory Jane's management of her superb eye.

"She's upstairs," she said. "Miss Gaylord is with her. They're expecting you."

7

Well, this was a surprise. So at long last Sally had come out of retire ment. On that torrid day in the summer of the year before, when she had slapped Mrs. Drummond's face and left the Settlement without saying good-by to Dolly Dewhirst, we had walked through the East End streets, she carrying her bag, till we came to a district where a cab was to be found. I put her into it and took her home to Chelsea. She did not speak all the way, and I left her to her own thoughts, aware that whatever it was that now confronted her was something she must settle for herself. There was nothing I could do but be with her, ready to help in any way she might ask.

She stayed with us for a few days, spending most of the time in her own room, and then she thanked us for our hospitality and said she had arranged to go and stay for a while with Maggie Whale. I had recognized Maggie's handwriting on a letter that came for her that morning. She went the next day, and I was rather hurt and jealous, plagued with the notion that somehow we had failed Sally, that we had not been able to give her whatever it was she was seeking. But I got rid of these feelings. A household wherein were a husband, wife and child—a demanding child at that—certainly didn't give what Maggie could give. And what Maggie gave was abstention from work for a week and such overflowing of understanding as I could well imagine. She never told me what passed between her and Sally that week: simply that "I think she'll be all right."

That was after Sally had gone away. Even Maggie didn't know where she had gone to. "Don't worry about me. I'll be back all in good time— all in God's time, if you like to put it that way." That was all she said to Maggie. Throughout the rest of that summer and the autumn and the winter we had heard nothing of her. There was not so much as a postcard. And now here she was, looking remarkably well: lean, brown and vigorous. On the floor was the disreputable old bag that I had watched her pack in the Settlement. It was now even nearer to dissolution. It was held together by a piece of thin rope whose ends were frayed out in a way Captain Rodda would not have approved. He would have had them whipped at once. There was an inescapable air of vagabondage about Sally and the bag, as though they were both alighted for no more than a moment. She embraced me, and the inevitable question came to my lips: "Well, Sal! Where on earth have you been?"

"Andorra," she said, as though Andorra were Penge or Pinner.

To me it was nothing more than a name, and a fine high-sounding one at that; and I thought at once of those Gaylord ladies—the eighteenth century had produced two of them—who had disappeared as Sally had done, and had been heard of lording it in the Middle East, and had never come back to England. But Sally was back. That was something to be thankful for. "Where on earth is Andorra?" I asked.

"It's a little Catholic commune up in the Pyrenees," Sally explained. "I've had a bitterly cold winter there. I got there by an accident which was God's design."

For some time before leaving the Settlement Sally had occasionally spoken of God in this casual, almost familiar, way. I had seen it infuriate Dolly Dewhirst more than once. I recalled an occasion when something Sally had said led Dolly to answer sharply: "You might as well realize, Sally, once for all, that I'm a Rationalist. That means I use my brains. If this God of yours is responsible for giving me my brains then it's his fault, for a thing given is meant to be used. And my brains tell me this: a point of view that is concerned with some mythological paradise beyond the sky is of no use to me. I want people to have heaven here and now."

Sally laughed, and put a hand on Dolly's shoulder. "I know," she said. "Food for the Fosters. Don't be angry with me, Doll. I'm not being dogmatic. I'm only just beginning to think seriously about such things, and I'm beginning to wonder whether the Christian religion isn't the only thing that offers what you call a heaven here and now. I'm not sure," she said tenderly, and obviously afraid that she was going to hurt Dolly, "I'm not sure that your thinking about such matters isn't rather primitive. You've never got beyond 'a home for little children above the bright blue sky.'"

"And where have you got to?" Dolly asked truculently.

"Nowhere yet, I'm afraid. But I'm moving toward 'the kingdom of heaven is within you,' and that's here and now if anything is. 'Now is the acceptable time.' That's another thing that impresses me."

"You're impressed by any blarney that comes along," Dolly said, not without affection, for they had not yet reached the gulf that was finally to separate them.

"No, but seriously, Doll: paradise round the corner is never religion's promise. It's always the promise of the reformer. There are the Golden Agers, who tell us it was all in the past, and the England's green and pleasant landers, who tell us it's all in the future, if and when. There's always something: destroy capital, destroy the aristocracy, destroy the bourgeoisie. Abolish democracy. Abolish dictators. Give the people baths and parks; do away with bugs and landlords. Always a corner to turn, and then another. After this and after that. After electoral reform. After the night of the long knives. Oh, I'm as keen as you are to see all sorts of corners turned. But you seem to think we can create a perfect world, and that only when that's done can we say 'Heaven at last!' Well, I don't believe in perfect worlds. I only believe in working for 'em without any illusions. And in the meantime I take comfort in this thought: that the kingdom of heaven is here and now within us, imperfect though we are, like a park in a slum. And what slums we are!"

"Speak for yourself!" Dolly was still able to laugh. "But so far as all that goes, leave it to the Salvation Army. I'm quite prepared not to poach on their territory."

"All right," Sally answered. "That'll do for now, Doll. I must go and put a new poultice on Mrs. Drummond's arm."

"Why don't you show that hulking brute of a husband how to do it?"

"I have done, but he doesn't do it all the same." She permitted herself a last mischievous grin. "You should take him to hear Bradlaugh inviting God to strike him dead tonight. Perhaps a taste of Rationalism would show him the way."

8

Glory Jane came in with coffee and another wink which invited me to consider what Miss Gaylord had been up to, gallivanting about the earth.

"I just wanted to be alone," Sally said. "I didn't go to Andorra in the sense of taking a ticket and saying 'Andorra, please.' I'd never heard of the place, and who would? But there are names that fascinate me. It's like certain people that one had heard of or read about, and one feels if only one could meet them! Well, places affect me like that. Arles, Tarascon, Carcassonne. I felt these places could give me something, and they did. They gave me Andorra. It was while I was wandering about in those regions that I first heard Andorra mentioned. And at once I felt: I must go to Andorra! However, easier said than done!"

It was late summer. She had wandered with her battered bag through a lot of territory, walking, riding on country carts, staying at inns and cottages; and it was in a cottage at the foot of the Pyrenees that she first heard of Andorra. She was living with a peasant woman and her daughter who kept a few goats and cultivated a few stony acres. I could never have done a thing like that, but Sally could. Perhaps it was the greatest of her gifts that, to use the common inadequate phrase, people of all sorts "took to her." There was an outflowing of herself, something most beautiful and unpremeditated and unreserved, that people could not resist, for it was a living force, unaware of itself, like a spring at which you drank without question and without thanks.

263

The woman of the cottage was a widow. Her husband had died earlier in that year, but she was to be married again soon. She was only forty, but toughened and roughened by a life of labor, so that she was like briar root. She looked forward to her new marriage without enthusiasm, with nothing, it seemed, but a practical recognition that she would again have a strong arm on the land. Sometimes the husband-to-be came to the cottage, wearing a black suit and a bowler hat. He was a grim person with a drip of sad black mustache who hardly ever opened his mouth. But now and then he would whistle. Sally said she had never heard such whistling. The man was like a nightingale, and she would steal out of the cottage so that, in the still dusk, she might listen to that mellifluous outpouring without the distraction of seeing the clod from whom it flowed. Once started, he would go on and on. It was his love invitation. The two women would sit without a word, sewing and knitting in the lamplight. When Sally returned, they would perhaps play cards; and when the man went away at last they would hear his high requiem fading in the distances of the rocky valley. "Sometimes," Sally said, "I was so moved that I would go out again, and stand there while that extraordinary music echoed in the hills, and the sky was full of enormous stars, like lumps of blazing silver. It was enough to make you cry. But the women didn't seem to be affected. I would go back to find them discussing tomorrow's jobs."

It was here that Sally first heard of Andorra. The younger woman, who was barely twenty, was married to a man of Andorra. She had come from the mountain fastness to help her mother on the farm and to sew wedding garments. She was a beautiful needlewoman. Her husband would come down for the wedding and she would return with him.

Sally helped to gather the meager harvest, and stayed for the wedding. She met the younger woman's husband, whose resounding name was Fernando Calatrava. He was in his middle twenties, swarthily handsome. He came riding on a mule and imparting to it the air of an Arab stallion. He was very courteous and very cold to Sally, doing his best to dissuade her from her intention of going to Andorra. He told her it was a barbarous hole at the top of the mountains. You lived there—if you could be said to live—with vast doors of rock slammed round you, as it were bolted and barred. You stood on rock, and you looked up at rock, and there was nothing round you but rock even when you were at your own fireside, for the houses were rock piled on rock. A man needed to be an eagle to live in such a place, Fernando Calatrava said, or a fox or a bear. No human being would think of living there who was not, like himself, a fool from his cradle; and he said all this with such a fierce pride in Andorra, it was so obvious that he would be ready to knife anyone who said a word against the place, that Sally laughed, and then he smiled, and she knew she would go to Andorra, where Europe piled itself into a hump, to look down one way on France and the other on Spain.

Fernando was amused by the bridegroom, whom he called Monsieur Navet-Rossignol, and he advised his mother-in-law to gag him on the wedding night, lest all the valley have a musical commentary on the crescendo and diminuendo of his bliss.

That night Sally, with Fernando and his wife, were at an inn some miles away, for the newly married couple had returned to the cottage where, in the morning, they would begin to dig potatoes. It was necessary, Fernando said, for Sally to buy a mule, unless she had a fancy for walking up mountains. He chose the animal for her, and bargained hotly about the price; and when they had set off he was pleased to tell Sally that she knew how to ride a mule. It was a well-broken beast, and Sally, who had ridden thunderbolts, had nothing to do but sit on. But she was glad to rise in Fernando's estimation.

Fernando and his wife and Sally started at dawn and took turns to walk and to ride. They went up and up through the September morning, and they halted awhile to eat bread and cheese and onions, and they went up and up through the September afternoon. They halted again where there was no shred of grass or bush or tree. There was a solitude in which Sally saw eagles flying, and a desolation of tilted rocks through which they entered into a cave where they hobbled the mules and ate meagerly, and Fernando sang wild songs, and they wrapped themselves in cloaks and slept.

They were off again at dawn, coming quickly to the summit of the range, warmed by the sun that was opening the eyes of Greece and raising a milky fume from the Mediterranean; but here it fell on rocks and rocks and rocks over which the mules' hooves clicked and amid which the music of their bells tinkled and Fernando's voice sang in the bitter crystal of the air which vibrated to that attack like glass delicately struck.

When Fernando ceased to sing there was nothing but the rocky silence and eagles looking down upon it and the mules' feet tapping staccato through it; and presently a point from which one gazed down and saw water falling and water flowing and fields that looked like green handkerchiefs spread at a slant on the rocks; and it was all a long way off, and they went down and down and down, slipping and sliding among loose stones, and in good time some of the rocks down there were houses with smoke rising from them and a church and an inn, and the pocket handkerchiefs were oats and barley.

And this place, with its few hard people, where the sun of afternoon was now tilting the purple shadows eastward, was the place, at last made manifest, that had been a place in a dream for Sally, and here she stayed throughout what was left of that autumn and throughout the winter and the opening spring.

She gave the mule to Fernando, who was amazed by the generosity of the gift, and who would not have been able to believe—if she had been the person to tell him—that a few seconds' ticking of the clock in her agent's office would have bought the beast ten times over. Fernando would not have been able to believe it of the gray-haired tough woman in rusty clothes who rode a mule as well as he did himself; and Sally did not want to remember it, because it was to forget such things that she had come to this place.

All the same, it was a fortunate gift, for Fernando was a man of some consequence, a property owner, and but for that she would have been hard put to it to find a house, as she wished to do, in which she could stay for a long time. There was an empty cottage that he chanced to own: a cube of masonry perched by itself on a spur of rock, attained by an uphill goat scramble, and it had been built as if to withstand till judgment day. To swing back the iron-studded oak door and go in was to have the impression of entering a cave rather than a house, and the window slits had an air more of strategy than of common use. There was only this room and a small room behind it, where she slept; but this was all she needed. She had a table and a chair, a lamp and a few shelves; and for the bedroom Fernando made her a bed of leather thongs stretched on a frame of wood. There she slept wrapped in a cloak. She ate one meal a day at the inn, and for the rest lived mostly on bread and coffee. Outside her door, she could sit on the spur of rock and look across the village at the mountains, threaded with waterfalls, beyond which lay France and the Channel and England—Bermondsey and Tresant. Sitting there she had plenty of time to wonder why she had come: plenty of time then and in the long winter nights when the white moon hung over the white valley and in the silence you imagined the cold crackle of the stars.

The priest lived in a house not unlike her own, except that it had two bedrooms, one for his housekeeper who was also his sister. They were an odd pair. Father Miguel was a fat wise peasant, but the Señorita, as the village called her, had an air of worldly suavity. She called upon Sally, almost with the formality of an English county call upon a new neighbor, and greeted her in English. She stayed gossiping for a long time, and seemed as pleased to have someone to talk to as if she had been a spinster meeting in foreign parts one who had been a neighbor in Cranford.

Sally soon gathered the Señorita's story. She and her brother were peasants who had had to fend for themselves. The Church for Miguel, and for her the needle. The needle was the small weapon with which she had fought her way through the world. It had found her work, first outside and then inside the house of the British Ambassador in Madrid. Then she had become my lady's personal maid, and when my lord and my lady returned to England she went with them. She had been with my lady a long time then, and was indispensable, she said complacently. My lord was getting on in years and didn't take another post. They settled down in England, living now in London, now in the country, and constantly traveling and visiting. Then my lord died, and my lady, who was much younger than he, married again, and the indispensable Señorita went with her to her new home. And now, after twenty years of this, my lady herself was dead, and the Señorita had returned, just a year ago, to look after Miguel.

"You must miss that life, after so long," Sally said; and the Señorita answered calmly: "No, after so long it was this life that I missed. One must at last find time for one's soul."

Father Miguel's sister was little more than a child when she began her twenty years of work in an English household. She was still younger than Sally. She became Sally's invaluable interpreter, and, more than this, what might be called her guarantee. The strange woman who had come traveling out of nowhere with Fernando and Joconde Calatrava was looked on with suspicion and reserve until the Señorita went bail for her.

Sally got to know Father Miguel and to like his simplicity and shrewdness. He rarely read anything and was a bit of a glutton and was peevish if his tobacco ran out. It was this very love of his own fleshy comfort that made so impressive his joyful alacrity when called upon for the services of his office. There was a night of midwinter when she had accepted the Señorita's invitation to take supper with her and Father Miguel. It had snowed for days, and now the snow had stopped without bringing the calm cold weather that can be so beautiful in the mountains. The sky indeed was clear and full of icy stars, but there was a wolf-pack wind, snapping and snarling; and Sally hugged her cloak tight about her as she slithered down the goat track from her cottage to the road, which was not a road but only a foot track, and now was deep in snow that had a crackling surface. It wasn't far to the priest's house, but far enough for her to gauge the vicious bite of the wind and to be glad that she had not long to be out in it. The thin red curtains toward which she was making looked warm and she went with the alacrity of a belated traveler who sees the light of an unexpected lodging.

There was a good fire. Father Miguel was relaxed in an armchair, a pair of comfortable shapeless slippers on his feet. There was a smell of warm food, and, on Sally's appearance, Father Miguel tipped red wine into a saucepan and held it over the fire. Sally's thoughts flew back through the years to the Café de l'Agriculture on the road outside

Montreuil, where, with me and Whaley, she had seen wine mulled in this speedy simple fashion.

Father Miguel poured the wine as the Señorita came in with a steaming and odorous dish. His broad hairy nostrils flared and in the lamplight his face shone with greedy anticipation. Sally guessed that it was not often he and his sister thus let themselves go, and she was glad to provide the occasion for this primitive and undisguised joy in the flesh.

At that moment, there was a thudding, as with a heavy staff, upon the thick oak door, and the wild world was among them in the shape of a young man, crying and moaning, inarticulate with the immensity of what he had to tell. It was but a small landslide that had caused so great a grief—nothing but a few boulders hurled down a hillside by the shift of a weight of snow; something that could have been no more than a noise in the night without meaning and consequence. Except that the young man's wife was in its way, and the boulders had struck her, some in the back and some in the head and now she did not speak, Father, she did not move. She lay with her hands on her breast, and she was quiet. And the child was to have been born in a month, Father.

The dish of hot food was on the table, and the wine was smoking in thick earthenware mugs, and Father Miguel already, while the young man was hysterically telling his tale, was gathering together his holy things, ready to carry God through the knives of the wind and the clog of snow. He clapped the boy upon the shoulder, and he did not say any babbling meaningless words. He only said: "Drink this," and gave him a mug of hot wine; and then he took up his staff and said: "Let us go." But, himself, he drank no wine, and he went with an arm round the young man's shoulders into the wind that rushed through the door and set the lamp shadows leaping.

9

Sally didn't tell us all this in a continuous and considered story as we sat there on that May morning in Maggie's room. I picked up bits of it throughout months, and even years, and mainly during my calls on her in Bermondsey. For she went back to Bermondsey, though not to the Settlement. "I don't think Father Miguel was an outstanding person," she said to me once, "but I've found again and again that simple people can be more important in one's life than all the bigwigs and celebrities. You know, we tried the bigwig stuff in Graybird Court, and I don't think we did much that was worth doing."

Graybird Court was a long way behind by then. Sally must have

268

been sixty. She was small and wrinkled, not overclean, and all her fire had retreated to her remarkable eyes. I said that I couldn't recall much bigwiggery in connection with Graybird Court, and she answered: "It was the way we went about it. We were reformers, and, oh Sarah, how I've come to distrust reformers! So often reform is nothing but an attempt to turn people into what we are ourselves, so pleased we are with our own perfections. However odd people's shapes may be, we think our own tailor is the only one for them. And then, you know, reformers are often so full of hate. They hate everybody who disagrees with them, and they even come to hate the people who don't want to be reformed. I believe that toward the end Dolly Dewhirst hated almost everybody in Graybird Court."

She didn't often speak of Dolly now, and she hadn't seen her for years; but you couldn't fail to know what Dolly was doing, if you read the newspapers. She was a famous woman, and somewhere she had an office where she studied statistics and wrote reports and compiled endless "case histories," and she sat on committees and royal commissions and addressed public meetings, and all her admirers thought it was high time women were in Parliament, because when such women as Dolly Dewhirst were in Parliament questions arising out of strong drink and poverty and unemployment and horrible man-made wars and the subjection of women to brutal men would be answered once for all, and there would·be no more crying or pain, and the tears would be wiped away from all eyes.

"You were telling me about Father Miguel," I prompted Sally

"Oh, well, it was just that he accepted evil. He said to me once: 'You wouldn't need God if there weren't a Devil. You've got to choose whose side you're on, that's all.' 'There's more to it than that,' I said. 'One must *fight* on the side one chooses.' He gave me an impudent grin. He was an earthly little man with a low forehead and coarse black hair growing down almost to his eyes. 'Oh well,' he said, 'fight if you want to, but the better man will win in the long run, anyway. Don't expect it to be a short run, that's all.'"

"I was puzzled by him for a long time," Sally said. "Even now I blush sometimes when I remember that I once said to him: 'I expect you'd like me to join your Church.' I don't know what we'd been arguing about, but I said that petulantly. He was frankly amazed. He looked at me for a long time without speaking, then said: 'It is a matter for rejoicing when anyone is absorbed into the Body of Christ; but really, Niagara is not overconcerned about water drops. It's for the water drop to take the first steps. At the moment, my tendency would be to repel any notion of your joining the Church.'"

"How was he really important to you?" I asked Sally. I had often wanted to know that.

"I should say," she said, after considering the matter, "it was because he confirmed what I had thought out for myself." Her wise old eyes smiled. "We haven't much use for people who don't do that, have we? And quite rightly, too, because it's what we find, not what we're given, that matters. You see, he believed in the two kingdoms, existing here and now: the kingdom of heaven and the kingdom of the Devil. He didn't believe that we have to reform this and change that and build something else before we can enter into the kingdom of heaven. He believed that there it was, within you, and you just had to become aware of it; and he believed also that you could 'reform' everything and still have men living in hell. He had the sense to know that this was no argument against 'reform'—only an argument against illusion."

"And how did you go on from there?"

"Well, it seemed to me that what people call 'reform' is almost a matter of mathematics. It happens. There's not much anyone can do to speed it or stop it, although a lot of busy people live and become leaders on the pretense that it wouldn't happen without them. It's almost a mechanical process, like a repair job at the gasworks. But the reform of souls, causing people to pursue good rather than evil, is not mechanical. I don't think anything at all can be done about it by preaching or teaching or indeed *doing* anything. It's a matter of *being*. And it's not easy to *be* in that way. You've got to keep on filling your own lamp if you are to 'let your light so shine before men that they may *see*. . . .'"

"And so," I said with affectionate raillery, "you decided to come and shine in Bermondsey."

I did not expect that this would hurt her, but it did. She laid her head upon her arms on the table, covered with cracked American cloth, and her shoulders shook with her sobs. She had been here now in this little slum house where, do what you would, you could not control the bugs or keep yourself really clean, for hard on a quarter of a century. My chance remark must have made her face suddenly the implications of her life; but it was not with regret that she was weeping, not with a retracting of her dedication. It was simply that her own insufficiency appalled her. "Such darkness," she said at last, "and such a little light!"

CHAPTER SIXTEEN

I

WHEN Whaley took me out to luncheon on that birthday morning in 1885, when I was thirty-seven years old, we found Lucy Evans walking up and down in the entrance hall of the restaurant. She was dressed in some light-blue clinging stuff that whispered on the carpet as she moved, and, despite her age, she looked a desirable woman. What her age was I don't know. When I was first associated with her at Tresant, I used to think of her as a person nine or ten years older than I. She was, at any rate, on the "wrong side," as they say, of forty-five when we met her that day. She carried her slim height elegantly, and there was no gray in her pretty hair. Few of the men coming through the door from Regent Street failed to give her a second glance as they left their hats and sticks and went on into the restaurant. Her firm little chin, her blue eyes, her lovely complexion unmarked by a wrinkle, deserved those appraising and approving looks.

She was gracious to me and Whaley. There was no other word for it. We were commoners who once had had the luck to be presented to this princess; we had been held in the royal memory and were now recalled and acknowledged. Her slim hand in a blue silken glove was held out for us to touch.

Amazing woman! If, in these present days, I looked into the mauve shadows under her eyes, softened and made incredibly alluring by the dusk of her wide-brimmed hat, I should have thought that her beauty parlor was superlative; but no such thought could cross the mind then. I gave her my homage: she was brilliant, and hard as sapphire.

She looked at the clock on the wall of the entrance lobby and said: "I'm expecting Mervyn. He's rather late."

She sat down on one of the dove-gray sofas, sinking into a whisper of silks. She tapped the toe of her pretty shoe with the ferrule of her parasol. Now that she has come out of mourning, I thought, she has done it with a vengeance.

There had been, of course, no reason why her mourning should be so complete. After all, Mostyn Lloyd was the husband of her aunt, and that was not a close relationship, but upon his death, following a short illness, she had gone into mourning as if for a husband. It was, I imagine, the payment of a debt to one who had treated her so handsomely; for if she had indeed been Mostyn-Lloyd's lovely, devoted and adored wife he could not have done better by her. One way and another, everything was hers and Mervyn's. Now at last, after the long

271

strategy of her years, she had won and consolidated a position: she was not a dependent but a possessor.

All this, I felt, was in her attitude that morning; and when Mervyn came through the doors she rose like a queen mother, still looking absurdly young for the office, to receive the reigning prince.

Men had style in those days, and indeed for many days to come thereafter. Mervyn's formal striped trousers and black coat, his gray silk stock with a black pearl stuck into it, the silk hat he carried and the gray suede gloves upon his hands, the ivory-headed malacca beneath his arm: these all had an elegance that he sustained with his tall wiry figure, his frank smiling face, adorned with a clipped mustache. I had not seen him for some time, and it seemed to me that at twenty-eight Mervyn Mostyn-Lloyd was no discredit to the late Captain Eddy Rodda.

He affectionately touched his lips to his mother's cheek, ducking beneath her hat brim, and said: "You look marvelous, Mama," and he greeted me and Whaley with a warmth that cheered me by its sincerity. I was already old enough to be a connoisseur of attitudes, and in Mervyn's affection I found no reserve. After all, Maggie and I had done our best for him in the cottage by the lake at Tresant. It was good to feel that he remembered this.

But something was clearly missing from his day. He had cast a swift scrutinizing look round this anteroom, where not many people were waiting now, for the hour was getting on; and he said: "Mama, I hope you won't mind, but we shall take luncheon *à trois*. I've asked a girl to join us. I hoped she'd be here by now."

"Do I know her, darling?" Lucy asked with admirable calm.

"No, but you'll love her. Her name's Enid Gotherson."

"Excuse us, won't you? We must go in," I said, and as we went through the swing doors Maggie said: "Love her? I wonder. Lucy's looking so marvelous today that somehow I don't think motherly love will appeal to her."

Our table faced the door, and a few moments later we had our first glimpse of Enid Gotherson. She was a dainty little dark girl in dark red silk, and as the three of them edged toward their table I noticed that Mervyn's hand was resting under Enid's elbow and that once she turned and looked up into his face with a smile. I noticed, too, that in that room of mirrors Lucy was aware of this. That was about all I saw of them at the time, for potted palms and table flowers swallowed them into a jungle.

Toward the end of our meal the distinguished-looking Henry Rokeby strolled across to us. He was the head of the firm that published Maggie's novels, and he had been taking luncheon with George Meredith, who was now gone. "Let me sit down and drink my brandy and coffee with you, Mag," he said, and took a chair facing us. He lit a cigar and fondled Maggie's hand that was lying on the table. "When are you going to marry me?" he asked.

"I should hate to marry you," she laughed. "My life would be intolerably bleak without your weekly proposal."

He dropped her hand back casually onto the table and cupped his palms round a balloon glass that he rotated slowly under his nose. "Ah, well," he said, "brandy's the next best thing. I'd prefer you, but there it is. You're a full-blooded burgundy. I always see a woman as a wine. A lovely slim bottle of iced hock was sitting near me with a young man and little Miss Gotherson. Now there's a girl—sparkling Moselle."

"You know Miss Gotherson?"

"Oddly enough," he said, "I'm her godfather."

"Why is that odd, Harry?"

"Well, you know what a wicked man I am, Mag. That's why you won't marry me. And she's an angel."

"Heaven will be fun if all the angels are sparkling Moselle."

"She's my idea of an angel, anyway, though I daresay I'm theologically unreliable. She's a charming unselfish child."

"Tell me about her," Maggie commanded, pouring out the coffee.

"Old Jack Gotherson was up at Oxford with me. He was one of those men who used to make us terribly excited when we thought of their futures. He was president of the Union, he won the Newdigate. He went into the Foreign Office, and one would have expected him to become Permanent Under Secretary. I lost sight of him for a time, then I read in the papers of his marriage—some peer's younger daughter. The next thing I heard was that he'd left the F.O. because he wanted to write, and he's been writing ever since."

"I've never heard of him," said Maggie. "What does he write?"

"Nobody's heard of him," Henry Rokeby said, "except a few specialists. He's a terrific medievalist: books about the medieval Church, medieval domestic life, medieval washing bills and carpenters' accounts. I suppose someone reads it. He publishes through the University presses. God knows how he lives. Just gets along, I imagine. He never had any money, nor did his wife. She's been dead now for years, and Enid's the only child. They've got a small house in Bayswater. Enid's devoted to the old boy."

"And manages to remain sparkling Moselle."

"Yes. That's a good girl, believe me. Who's the boy with her? D'you know him?"

"Mervyn Mostyn-Lloyd. A sort of protégé of mine. The iced hock is his mother."

"Mostyn-Lloyd, eh. The draper's shop?"

"If you want to put it like that. We call it an emporium."

"You would. I buy my socks there."

273

"Never mind your socks, Harry. When you introduce domestic topics I never know where you'll stop."

"There are fourteen lady novelists on our lists, all unmarried, and not one of them will have me."

"It's important to them that you should confine your attention to business."

"They're just going," I said.

Lucy and Mervyn and Enid Gotherson passed near our table. Enid gave Henry Rokeby a smile and a wave of the hand. "Enid looks well," he said. "I wonder where she got the money to buy that dress? It looks to me like something acquired for a special occasion."

"She's a pretty little thing," Maggie said.

"And the boy knows how to dress and doesn't look a fool. How does a draper do it?"

"Eton and Oxford," Maggie said briefly.

"Good God! Is that necessary in order to sell me socks?"

"Oh, I don't know. Wasn't George Meredith's father a draper?"

Rokeby looked shocked. "Tut, tut, Mag. I thought George was keeping that dark."

"These things get about," she said. "I can't stand the handsome old snob."

2

Enid took to me as readily as I took to her, and she enlisted me as an ally against Mervyn's ardor. He wanted to marry at once; Enid, who was only twenty, did not wish to marry so long as her father needed her. Mervyn's idea that Dr. Gotherson should be supplied with a housekeeper and a secretary did not please her at all. It was to let me see for myself how much she was needed that she took me to the house in Bayswater. This was about a month after I had first seen her. June had come. We had taken luncheon with Mervyn in his rooms at the Mostyn-Lloyd premises, and then we set off to walk through the great heat to Bayswater. I would have liked to jump into a hansom, but Enid's economical upbringing was all against it, and I didn't want to undermine her admirable principles.

It was only to be expected that, as we walked round the head of the park, past the Marble Arch, she should chatter of Mervyn and how she had first met him. She had gone to Mostyn-Lloyd's to buy a few things that she needed. "Sometimes father sleeps in the afternoon," she said. "I don't like leaving him unless he's asleep or there's someone with him. We have no maid at all, except a woman who comes in in the mornings. That afternoon Colonel Slinn had called."

I asked her who that was, and she said that Colonel Slinn had written to her father during the winter before this, commenting on one of his books, and had presented himself soon after. "We see hardly a soul," Enid said, and added with a kind of desperate indignant loyalty: "It's a scandal how everybody neglects Daddy. He's a great man, and it's years since anyone of his own sort has been near him." I blushed for Henry Rokeby.

She didn't think much of Colonel Slinn, nor did her father. "Really, we wondered what he was up to—why he had bothered us at all," but he was a great talker about this and that, and Dr. Gotherson seemed to like hearing of a world different from his own, and so Colonel Slinn had become a visitor welcomed for his own peculiar contribution to the small family's amusement.

One day the colonel apologized because he would not be able to call for some time. He was to visit some friends in the North. "And by the way, Gotherson, you might let your father-in-law know I'll be in his parts. Would you do that, dear boy? I might have time to call."

That was the first time they realized that Colonel Slinn knew that Lord Avonmere was Gotherson's father-in-law. "He's very ancient," Enid said, "and as poor as a church mouse, but we wondered whether Colonel Slinn was just an utter snob, cultivating us for the chance of getting to know grandfather."

Grandfather was annoyed, and wrote what, I gathered, was one of his characteristic letters. Enid recited it with pleasure. "Jack—Who the devil is this fellow Slinn? What the devil is he colonel of? There's nothing here to steal, but you're a man of property compared with me, so watch your spoons."

On that afternoon when Enid first met Mervyn, the Colonel had called, debonair, full of chat about that charming old peer Lord Avonmere. "I could see that Daddy was grimly amused, so I thought it a good chance to step out and do my shopping. Colonel Slinn's silk hat was lying on the table in the hall. My bag was alongside it. I knew there were a couple of pounds in it, so off I went. The Colonel was telling Daddy about Turkey. He had been military attaché at our embassy there."

At Mostyn-Lloyd's Enid bought some handkerchiefs, a pair of gloves, and so forth. When it came to paying, there was no money in her bag. The poor child must have been in a great state of blushing confusion. The young lady in black who had been serving her switched from "Yes, madam," to "No, miss," and looked as though she suspected an attempt at kleptomania.

"But I'm *sure* there was money in my bag," Enid said helplessly; and, of course, she would be, and she would know whether it was one pound or two, and even whether it was sixpence or sixpence ha'penny.

It was at this moment that Mervyn came up and, seeing that something was jarring the smooth routine on which Mostyn-Lloyd's prided itself, he asked what was the matter. He asked with so sympathetic a smile that for Enid there was then nothing the matter at all. Mervyn handed two pounds to the young woman in black, who put the coins into a cylinder with the bill, and with expert nonchalance sent it winging an aerial way along a maze of wires whose terminus was a cash desk.

Enid, feeling herself in some sort still a suspect, hastily wrote her name and address on a piece of paper, protesting that she would return with payment in a day or two, and Mervyn, looking at what she had written, and looking with even more pleasure at her, asked: "Any relation of John Gotherson?"

It was exhilarating to Enid to find that her father, whom she was sure everyone should know, was known to this St. George who had so casually slain her dragon; and to Mervyn it seemed fortunate that one of Gotherson's books had been forced upon his none too eager attention by his tutor at Oxford. More fortunate still that he even remembered a little of what it was about. Altogether, it seemed that the cylinder containing six and sevenpence three farthings returned with inconsiderate haste. Mervyn pressed the change, wrapped in the bill, into Enid's protesting hand. "You may want to take a cab home," he said.

"But what *had* happened to the money? Did you never find out?"

No, said Enid, she had not found out. She had no idea what had happened.

3

The Gothersons lived in a small house in a street off the Bayswater Road. There was not a sizable room in the place, but the folding doors between the two main rooms on the ground floor had been taken away and thus a fairly large study was provided for Dr. Gotherson. It was into this study that I went with Enid on the June day when I first met her father, and it was unlike any study I had ever seen before. It was more like a pigeon cote than anything else. All round the walls from floor to ceiling was row after row of pigeonholes, and each pigeonhole was stuffed with little bundles of paper tied in red tape. In the midst of the double room was an enormous writing table, and this, too, was piled with little tied-up bundles. There was a writing chair at the table and an easy chair on a rug by the fireplace, and there was nothing else. I was not to know Dr. Gotherson for long before realizing that this room was the quintessence of a scholar's life. "Books!" he would cry. "Good lord, Mrs. Undridge, who wants books? What you want is the *stuffing* out of books. There's hardly a book in the world whose stuffing you can't rip out in ten pages." Or "The Bodleian!" he would say. "Why, good lord, Mrs. Undridge, the place is a nightmare! Foundering in miles of bog! Here are the footholds, the essential hard patches, that take you through."

The first thing I was aware of on that June day was the breadth of an enormous back. It was covered by a Jaeger dressing gown, stretched tight. Dr. Gotherson, looking out of the window, made me think of a bear on its hind legs. The bear had carpet slippers on its feet and a nimbus of tobacco smoke round its head. He turned, and padded heavily toward us, and held out a fat paw which crushed my hand unmercifully. There were piercing eyes in his flabby dew-lapped face, and his voice was thin and rather shrill. His round powerful skull was fluffed with babyish fair hair. It was not from him that Enid got her attractive dark looks.

"So you know Harry Rokeby?" he said. "Poor Harry! He was a promising chap at Oxford, but I'm afraid he'll never amount to anything now. How is he?"

I told him that he seemed very well, and Dr. Gotherson said: "I suffer a good deal of self-reproach about him. I don't want him to feel neglected. I ought to look him up, but I can't get about, you know, as I used to."

One didn't need to be a doctor to see that the less getting about he did the better for him. Even the slight effort of our conversation made him short of breath, and when I went he asked me to excuse him from rising.

"You'd better have a little sleep, Daddy," Enid said.

"Yes. I feel very tired in this heat. You tell Harry Rokeby, Mrs. Undridge, that I haven't forgotten him. Give him my apologies, and say I'll be looking him up one of these days. Good lord! It's three or four years since we met."

4

After that luncheon when Mervyn introduced Enid to his mother there had been an uneasy time. Maggie and I had called on Lucy a week or so later, and she had received us in bed. It was a beautiful bed. I felt the journey to Kensington was worth while to see that alone. The head was a great shell of dull white material that might be coral, with the ribs of the fluting picked out in gold. The blankets were sea-green, and here and there they broke into a foam of white lace where the edgings of the sheets appeared. Lucy was sitting up, her head resting on a foam-edged pillow that subsided into the cave of the shell: Undine, the sea nymph without a soul. She looked in excellent health. The room was filled with the pleasant airs of the spring day that gently stirred the lawn of the curtains, so that they seemed like fragile sails about to fill.

Maggie took Lucy's hand and asked with a laugh: "What's this— the embarkation for Cythera?"

For me, I was enchanted. It really did seem as though for two pins Lucy and her fantastic bark would rise from the carpet and sail out into the morning with a noise of flutes. Her eyes were extraordinary. "Violets dim," I thought, "but sweeter than the lids of Juno's eyes, or Cytherea's breath." I had never known, nor have I known since, a woman of that age so wrapped in the seductions of youth.

Lucy pouted at Maggie's question, which she did not understand. Her hand lay on a table at the bedside, gay with daffodils, and fruit in a bowl, and a few novels. "I feel exhausted—very run down," she said.

Maggie laughed again. "Then God help any man who sees you bursting with health."

At that, Lucy began to cry. "No man would look at me," she babbled, dabbing at her eyes with a few inches of scented lawn. "I am old, old. I've sacrificed the best years of my life, and in return I get nothing but ingratitude."

"Are you talking about Mervyn?" Maggie asked.

"He has thrown me aside," Lucy sobbed, "like an old glove."

We looked upon the old glove and exchanged amused glances. "Oh, yes," said Maggie, "we shall obviously have to dispose of you now in some church rummage sale, or pack you off to a home for waifs and strays." She plucked a few grapes from the dish and began to munch contentedly.

There was a tap at the door, and a maid came in with a glass on a tray, advancing over the carpet as reverently as if in a death chamber. "Madam's sedative," she murmured.

"Leave it," Lucy said languidly. "I haven't the strength to take it now."

The maid gave me and Maggie a look which dismissed us as inquisitors, torturers, tossed the pillows into foam behind Lucy's head, and went.

"Talking of sacrificing the best years of your life," said Maggie, removing a grapestone from her mouth, "you haven't done badly, you know."

Lucy looked at her reproachfully. "You are brutal," she said. "You don't understand me. I have never known love."

Maggie's strong teeth cracked a nut, and her brown fingers picked away the shell from the kernel. "No," she said, looking up at Lucy, "I don't think you have."

"I could have married Justin," said Lucy.

278

Well, so she could, but the remark shocked us both. We felt there was nothing to say. Disturbed by our silence, Lucy repeated defiantly: "I could have married Justin, and then Tresant would have been mine —not that crazy woman's."

And now the enchantment of all this luxurious folly dissolved, and I thought of how it would be on this lovely day in Sally's slum, and I got up, ready to go, looking down on Lucy Evans in her silken barge almost with hatred.

Maggie got up, too. She said to Lucy: "So you think it's a bad thing to have sacrificed the best years of your life?"

"Yes, I do."

"Well, then, have the common sense to see that Mervyn might think it a bad thing to make that sacrifice for you. He's a good boy. If you want to keep him, let him go."

Lucy said outrageously: "You don't know what you're talking about. You were never made for love."

"Let's go," I besought Maggie. I was afraid that that last remark would infuriate and disgust her. But all she did was to take an edge of the silk sheet in her fingers and ruffle it contemptuously. She let it drop. "Love!" she said, and brushed the feel of it off her fingers. After a moment she added: "I advise you to get up, Lucy. Mervyn is worth living for. He won't like this nonsense."

Downstairs, Lucy's butler came to open the door. "How did you find Madam?" he asked with professional gloom.

"I think she'll survive," Maggie said sharply; and to that he answered with a most unprofessional wink which said to Maggie: "We know our way about—you and I. They can't fool us."

Maggie regrettably returned this grimace of understanding.

5

It had been a long time, Enid said, since there was any sort of entertainment at the house in Bayswater, and she was as excited at having a few people in to tea as if she were organizing a dinner at the Mansion House. It was, as it happened, an occasion of significance, for it was at this tea party that Lucy Evans met Aloysius Slinn.

Daniel became a queen's counsel that year, and I was proud to arrive at Dr. Gotherson's house with Daniel Undridge, Q.C. We did not often get out together, and when we did it was to formal dinners where, almost always, Daniel was one of the speakers. He took his speeches seriously. He liked, when we were driving to such an occasion, to brood upon what he was going to say. It was always light and charming, thrown out with a spontaneous gaiety which belied the long preparation, and his hearers thought, no doubt, that I was a fortunate woman to share the private life of so delightful a person as appeared in these public locutions. Well, I was, of course; but I could not, and did not, expect them to understand that Daniel's growing preoccupation with public appearances, his increasing fame and wealth as a lawyer, the turning of his thoughts more and more to a political career, all meant my own passing into a deepening sense of being incidental, rather than central, in his affairs. To have him with me on an occasion like this that Enid had arranged—what one might call a trivial, tom-fool occasion—hardly ever happened now: and when I say that I was proud to arrive with the Q.C., I realize clearly enough what I mean: I mean that time, for me, had slid past the point when to be with Daniel—whether Q.C., tinker, tailor, sailor or beggarman—would in itself have been ecstasy.

It was a wet day. We took a hansom from his chambers, and, when we arrived, found Dr. Gotherson, Enid and Mervyn, Maggie and Colonel Slinn. Enid whispered to me that Colonel Slinn had not been invited. He had happened to drop in. I was glad of that, because I was anxious to meet this person of whom I had heard much that stirred my interest. He was flawlessly dressed. So, for that matter, was Mervyn, but there was a difference. I had a feeling that Slinn had put his clothes on as an actor puts on the clothes that belong to a part. Not that he didn't look well in them, and at home in them. He did, and I must leave unexplained, because I cannot explain it, this feeling of masquerade. He was tall, dark, handsome, with one feature of startling contradiction. His firm jaw, his rather severe lips, his well-made nose: all these, and his straight black eyebrows, were traditionally manly and military; but as I stood talking to him, Enid having presented him to me, I was fascinated by his eyes. They were the eyes of a woman, at once frightened and furtive. They were large, a doe's eyes, of a melancholy deep brown, and they did not look at you but slid round you, and edged away from you and beyond you, and seemed to be forever shiftily trying to look sideways, to keep aware of what was happening in all quarters, as though danger might anywhere appear. I felt suddenly a deep inexplicable pity for him, as if for a hunted creature, but I had somehow to reconcile this with the fact that he looked a hunter, too. He seemed to be at once the startled fawn with long-lashed houri eyes and the man with the gun, slipping stealthily from rock to rock.

The only person now expected was Lucy, and Colonel Slinn and I saw her arrive. We were standing together in the bay window, watching the silver lash of rain striking upon the road and rising up again to fill the air with steam that moved in sluggish whiteness. Through the open window came the smell that no one knows now, for roads are all hard rock: the smell of rain-laid dust. Colonel Slinn sniffed at it. I felt that he would be very sensitive to smells. "There is nothing," he said, in a voice which, like his eyes, denied his military bearing—a voice that I could not imagine shouting commands, for it was caressing like dark-brown velvet—"there is nothing so much as the smell of rain on dust that reminds me of my boyhood. And hawthorn. I remember sheltering under hawthorns, and watching the drops of rain on the white dust, all separate at first, and then running into a paste, and the smell of it, and the smell of the hawthorns. I was about ten, I should think."

"Where was that, Colonel?" I asked.

"Oh, it was in a remote English village," he said vaguely. "I lived there with my mother."

"Was your father dead?"

"Oh, no. But somehow, whenever I think of that time, I think of living with my mother. I suppose my father was about somewhere. Of course he was. Must have been."

We went on to talk of Enid and Mervyn, and I said: "How odd that they should meet in that way. If Enid hadn't lost her money they would probably not have met at all. She's certain the money was in her bag. What can have happened to it?"

"A pickpocket," he said decisively; and when I wondered that anyone could be as light-fingered as that, he said: "Oh, that's nothing. You'd be surprised at what these people can do."

One of his tricks was to be forever brushing his mustache upward with the index finger of his left hand. I couldn't help noticing how slim, yet strong, his fingers looked.

"Well," he said, "whoever relieved her of her cash did her a good turn. Financially, Mostyn-Lloyd must be a wonderful catch."

"Yes, he is, of course. But there's more to him than that, you know."

"Oh, no doubt, no doubt. But that's an aspect that appeals to me. All family pride and no investments—it's a bit hard to have to get along that way." He gave a rueful little laugh. "I'm told," he said, brushing away at his mustache, "that Mostyn-Lloyd is the son of an earlier marriage of his mother's and took the name by deed poll."

Now who on earth can have told you that, I wondered? Not Enid, I'll be bound.

"His mother must be a remarkable woman to have done so well for him. Do you know her?"

"Oh, yes. I've known her for years—ever since I was a child. Yes, she *is* a remarkable woman—in some ways."

"Tell me about her."

I thought he was becoming inquisitorial, and I looked full into his liquid eyes. My own eyes must have had a hint of hardness, perhaps of scorn at this direct assault, for his immediately wavered, and, as

Daniel was crossing the room toward us, they began the flickering that suggested a search for escape. "Daniel," I said, "I don't think Enid introduced you to Colonel Slinn. Colonel, this is my husband, Daniel Undridge."

Daniel had become rather stout and florid. His face had a look of genial good temper that led many a witness cheerfully toward the point where, his head cocked on one side, his hands under his tail, and the smile still on his face, he would let fall the fatal clinching question from which there was no escape. And when the cheese was taken, and the mousetrap gave its conclusive snip, he would still smile, tilt his wig down over his eyebrows, and ruffle his hair in that way he had as a boy. "Well, Mr. Jones, that being so, on your own admission, it surely follows . . . Don't you agree?" And Mr. Jones had nothing for it but to agree, damning in his heart that cheerful ingenuous countenance. I should have liked to watch an encounter between Daniel and Colonel Slinn, but all I was granted on that occasion was the awareness of the Colonel's antennæ delicately twitching toward this possibly dangerous newcomer. For at this moment we saw through the window Lucy's carriage stop at the gate.

"Well, Colonel," I said, "here is Mervyn's mother at last."

The rain was falling as heavily as ever, dancing on the carriage roof, gleaming on the coachman's cloak, and turning the brown horse black. "Good lord!" said the Colonel. "She'll be drowned!" He moved off at once in his lithe fashion, and a moment later appeared on the short garden path. Mervyn, too, had gone to meet his mother, but Colonel Slinn was before him. With an umbrella held over her, he escorted Lucy along the few yards of tiles as solicitously as though she were that lump of sugar of which Mercy Kite used to speak if we were caught in a shower when I was a child. "You'll get home solid, never fear. What d'you think you are—a lump of sugar?" And if she were in her sentimental mood, she would say: "Of course you are! You're old Kitey's Rosie Posy lump of sugar." But if I rejoiced in the rain and naughtily ran out from under her old green umbrella, as I often did, liking the cool splash of drops on my upturned face, she would grumble: "All right, get soaked through and through, and I'll stir you up with a spoon, and you'll disappear, and then I'll be rid of you for good an' all, you little nuisance."

Mervyn and Lucy and the Colonel had disappeared into the house, and Enid had gone out to the hall to meet her guest, and I stood at the window, my thoughts in this way oddly snatched back through the years; and then they were in the room and Colonel Slinn was saying in his brown velvet voice: "You are all right, ma'am? You have come to no harm?" as though he had swum through Niagara to save her from threatened death. She didn't answer him, and Dr.

Gotherson, who, even on this occasion, was not to be parted from his dressing gown and carpet slippers, took her hand and said to Slinn: "Good lord, Colonel, Mrs. Evans isn't sugar candy. How are you, ma'am? It's kind of you to come on such a day."

Lucy stood between the two of them, looking undecided whether to be sugar candy or a brave-hearted woman to whom a walk through the rain from carriage to house door was nothing—all in the day's work. Now that she was freed from her wrappings, she certainly looked sugar candy, for she was wearing silk of the delicious-colored stripes that, gleaming through bottles in shop windows, had set my mouth watering when I was a little girl. They were of pale green and white, these stripes, flowing down her from waist to feet. Above the waist, she was horizontal flounces of alternate green and white, and her large hat had a green virginal quality that would have made it unsurprising had birds begun suddenly to sing in it. Our Undine had become Primavera.

It was charming to observe her showing us how well she knew her place. If a couple of young people had been unseemly enough to engage themselves to marry, thus reminding her of the passage of the years, well, she would accept the part handed to her. She sat down next to Dr. Gotherson, who, though he cannot have been much older than she, if older at all, had an aura of wisdom and experience that made him venerable; and so she contrived, while being where a matron should be, to present the picture of a flowering convolvulus twined about a broken fragment of antiquity.

Two people who were enjoying themselves were Daniel and Maggie. Maggie's appreciation of a situation like this showed always in the sardonic twitch of her mouth; and Daniel, standing well apart from everyone, with a cherubic grin upon his face and a tuft of hair standing up on his head, had the look of innocence that I at any rate knew cloaked a wickedly penetrating insight. Mervyn and Enid seemed to be concerned with no one but themselves, and so it fell to Colonel Slinn to potter about with plates of sandwiches and cups of tea.

"Mrs. Evans, let me get you a hot cup, ma'am. I fear you may have contracted a chill."

"Nonsense," said old Gotherson. "Don't keep blathering about a drop of rain, Slinn. Mrs. Evans looks in excellent health. Good lord! I can't believe Mervyn is her son. She looks more like his sister, and I'm sure I look like Enid's grandfather."

Lucy turned her wide blue gaze from him to the Colonel, trying to fit into the conception of each. Daniel strolled across the room, holding a cup in his hand, and said: "I've just read an article in the *Cornhill*, Colonel, by an old soldier. He was in the medical service. He says it's a fact that exposure to weather isn't a harmful thing. He's known men get wet through day after day, and their clothes dry on them, and their health's none the worse. His theory is that fugging up causes more colds than wet weather. What d'you say? What's your own experience as a soldier?"

The Colonel looked at Dan's smiling face, and his eyes slid here and there, and he said: "Yes, I saw that article myself. It was by old—?"

But Daniel wasn't to be caught like that. He didn't supply the name, but went on smiling expectantly.

"Well, never mind him," he said, after a moment. "What was your own experience? Where did your campaigns take you?"

"Colonel," said Maggie, "*I'll* have another cup, please."

Slinn's liquid eyes warmed with gratitude as he took her cup; and I was glad to see Daniel stroll back to his corner. Another thing I saw was that Lucy followed his withdrawal with a look of venomous dislike. Presently she surrendered her seat beside Dr. Gotherson to Maggie Whale, who soon had him enthusiastically explaining the growth of his strange library. "But, my dear man," I heard her say, "what on earth do you do when you want to *read*? A book isn't just facts. An author communicates himself in all his odd incidental fancies and fribbles."

"Oh, you're talking like a mere novelist. I don't read books. I use 'em."

I left them at it, Maggie purple at those words 'a mere novelist,' which always enraged her; and sat down to talk to Mervyn. Dan had carried off Enid, and the Colonel was now free to do what obviously he had been wanting to do ever since her arrival, and that was hobnob with Lucy Evans.

The party remained disposed thus till we saw Lucy's carriage draw up at the gate. The rain had stopped, and a bit of blue sky peeped through the gray draggle of clouds. Lucy got up and said her good-bys. Then she turned to Slinn and said: "Can I drop you anywhere, Colonel?"

Slinn looked at his watch and said: "Five o'clock! Heavens! I have an appointment at my club at half past. Could you drop me there, Mrs. Evans? It would be an enormous convenience. The Garrick."

It was arranged, and we watched them drive off together. The hansom that Daniel had ordered soon arrived, and we went, too. "The Garrick," said Dan. "That's odd, isn't it? I've never seen him there, and I've been a member for seven years. Let me tell you what will happen. He'll thank her profusely, watch the carriage drive off, move toward the entrance, and then, when she's out of sight, go home to his attic in Long Acre, or somewhere, and relax with his stays off."

"Stays!" I cried. "Oh, Daniel, surely not?"

"Almost certainly," he said. "I'll bet he sags like a poached egg." After a moment he added: "It's incredible how people allow themselves to be sucked in through not doing a simple obvious thing."

"Who's being sucked in now?"

"The Gothersons. That chap's not a colonel, you know. If they had taken the elementary precaution of looking up the Army List they'd know that he's not in it at all."

"Did you think Lucy Evans was a bit taken by him?"

"She certainly gave me an ugly look when I tried to rattle him. He's the sort of man who might get away with it."

"With what?"

"With Mrs. Evans. He's got eyes that whimper for sympathy and a general cut of the jib that suggests a strong guiding mind. A lot of women find that an irresistible combination. And then, of course, Mrs. Evans is at a susceptible moment."

"Mrs. Evans is a pretty tough woman."

"No doubt, but remember this. Everything seemed arranged for her to settle down at last as head of an establishment that would include an obedient and dependent son. It was a bad moment for Mervyn to find a bride. Pretty soon Mrs. Evans will be stranded in that big house with a lot of time on her hands for getting into mischief. She's never been married. The state may appeal to her idle imagination. You know —an unconscious retort to Mervyn and Miss Gotherson. 'If you think I'm done for just because you've deserted me—well, you're mistaken.'"

I couldn't help laughing at all this. "You assess human problems very mathematically," I said.

"Well, I've got a mathematical mind."

"If she wants to get married, I should think she could find plenty of nice men. A lot of them used to go to the house when Mostyn-Lloyd was alive."

"She's not in an easy position. Her situation in the house was rather equivocal—don't you think?"

"I don't think she was ever more than Mostyn-Lloyd's housekeeper and adored ornament."

"Perhaps not. But you know what people are."

"So poor Lucy is condemned to be the victim of an adventurer?"

"I didn't say so. I don't think it's she who'll be the victim in the long run."

"Your heart bleeds for Colonel Slinn?"

"My heart never bleeds for anybody." He opened the window in the roof and directed the cabby to his chambers. "I shall be rather late," he said to me. "I've got a mountain of work to attack."

6

When we had dropped Daniel, I drove home feeling sad and depressed. I tried to dismiss my mood as unreasonable. How could I expect, I asked myself, that things should remain as they always had been? It was in the nature of life to change, and only a fool expected every change to be for the better. All the same, I thought wistfully of the days when Daniel brought his work home with him and sat with his papers under the green lamp while I read by the fireside. Of course, there was more work now, and there were books to be consulted and a whole paraphernalia of documents that one couldn't reasonably expect a man to carry to and from his home and chambers. Still, it wasn't always chambers, was it? Sometimes it was the Garrick, and I didn't know where else. And when we have had a talk, how often it was like the talk we had just had in the cab; a calm analysis of a situation that hadn't anything to do with either of us. And what a thing to say! "My heart never bleeds for anybody." There was a time when he would have turned to me at that and added: "Except for you." Perhaps it had never been true. I should have liked to hear it all the same.

The hint of blue that had declared itself when we were leaving the Gothersons' had spread and taken possession of the evening. There was a warm level light on everything and the rain-soaked trees looked cool and grateful. Window panes shone in sudden golden flashes, and the horse pulling my cab was wearing an absurd straw hat through which his ears poked skittishly. But none of it lightened my mood, and I thought of those days when Daniel was studying in London and I was living with Maggie and he would sometimes visit us of an evening and talk of everything except what I wanted to hear. I felt as though I were right back in that old unhappy time, and I recalled the night when he went away in his casual fashion and I ran to my room and wept the hours through. I didn't want to weep now; but, though the sun was shining, I felt as though I were wearing a gray mackintosh and walking in a drizzle down a gray street. I hoped that Mervyn and Enid would be very happy. It had come to that—hoping for other people.

7

I went up to Richard's room, intending to spend half an hour with him and the young woman who was to him what Maggie Whale had once been to me. I doubted, though, whether she had any of Maggie's quality; and I told myself for the hundredth time that it was absurd of me not to take Richard's lessons myself. I could do it much better than this frightened little thing who always stood up meekly when Daniel or I came into the room and who was, I feared, being given an unhappy time by Richard. Richard was precocious in speech and in reading and writing. This little Miss Mackenzie occasionally tripped

286

up over a word that he knew, and he never let her forget it. I remember a dreadful moment when I was in the schoolroom, listening to her as she read to him, and she came upon the sentence: "His cravat was awry." She was always as nervous as a cat when performing in my presence, and perhaps that was the reason for her pronouncing it: "His *crav*-at was *aw*-ry." Richard was what they call nowadays an exhibitionist. He immediately leapt from his chair, and began to run round the room, hooting with laughter, and singing: "His *crav*-at was *aw*-ry, so terribly *aw*-ry. I'm frightfully *saw*-ry his *crav*-at was *aw*-ry."

Little Miss Mackenzie sat with her hands folded on the book in her lap, her head bowed, showing me the straight white path traveling over the meek hill of her skull. She was utterly abject, and I saw a tear splash onto the book. What smote my heart as much as her plight was the child's indifference to it. He continued to parade and sing till I took him by the arm and hustled him out of the room. I talked to him severely, but I had done it before and did not expect much consequence. When I was alone in the drawing room that evening, Miss Mackenzie sent a message by one of the maids, asking if I could spare her a moment. She never had the courage simply to come to my door and knock and enter.

I was reading by the fireside, and when she came she hovered in the shadow just inside the door till I asked her to come forward, and then she stood uneasily till I told her to be seated. She had evidently been crying, and now she had come, I found, to ask me whether I thought she should resign her post. Before giving me time to reply, she went on to talk of her mother, a widow, who lived in Worcestershire, and existed barely. Of course, mother or no mother, I should have let her go. She was thoroughly bad for Richard; but, like a fool, moved by her woe, I merely urged her to try to handle him more resolutely. She said she would stay, and seemed both relieved and terrified by this outcome. But many times thereafter, despite my talking to him and despite what I had said to her, I heard Richard ask with a sly leer: "Is my *crav*-at *aw*-ry, Miss Mackenzie?"

When I went up to them that evening, they were playing draughts. I stood and watched them for a moment, and presently, after one of Miss Mackenzie's moves, Richard said irritably: "You did that deliberately. You *put* it there for me to take. You're trying to *make* me win. You're *humoring* me, and I can beat you any day without that."

He then spilled the pieces onto the floor, and Miss Mackenzie, looking terrified, began to grope after them.

"Leave them alone!" I said to her sharply. "Get up! Don't *crawl*!" I was furious.

She got up, and I ordered Richard to pick up the pieces. He did so, and put them in the box.

287

"Now," I said, "apologize to Miss Mackenzie."

"Oh, really, Mrs. Undridge, it's not at all necessary," she babbled. I felt I could have slain her. "Allow *me* to know what is necessary," I said. "Richard!"

He sulked for a moment, then drawled: "I'm *saw*-ry."

It was such a calculated insult, to her and to me, that, for the first and last time in my life, I struck him: a sharp angry flat-handed blow to the cheek. He giggled, and Miss Mackenzie began to cry. I felt nauseated with the pair of them, and stormed out of the room. I went to my bedroom, shut out the light, and lay on my bed, utterly drained. My head began to ache, and suddenly I knew what for a time I had suspected. I was going to have another child. And this, I thought with exultation, this will be mine! There'll be no Miss Mackenzie this time. All mine! It will be a girl. I shall call her Veronica. Then I fell deeply asleep.

CHAPTER SEVENTEEN

I

I WAS not able to attend the wedding of Mervyn and Enid at St. George's, Hanover Square, for it was a winter wedding, and by that time I was not presentable in public. But I had been to see the Hanover Square house that Mervyn had bought and that Dr. Gotherson was to share with the young people. Thus Mervyn overcame Enid's scruples about leaving her father. The first lift I ever saw in a private house was installed, a clumsy thing, but it worked, and it took Dr. Gotherson without palpitations to the top floor where several attic rooms were turned into a suite for him, with all his pigeonholes in order and a bathroom attached to his bedroom. When I inspected the place with Enid she was speechless at what she considered the honor that had befallen her. That she would be the beloved of a man who could take this house and furnish it as we now saw it in process of being furnished, and drive a lift through it, and give her father such quarters as he had never had in his life: all this overcame her, and standing there in the fading light of the late autumn afternoon, she looked down from the high windows upon Chantrey's statue of Pitt and let a few happy tears fall.

Hanover Square, Mervyn said, was "handy for the office": he could walk into Oxford Street in two minutes. He liked to talk in this way as though he were a born man of business; but I sometimes asked myself what the charming creature would have made of things had he found himself confronting the sort of tasks that his adoptive father had grappled with. Did Enid, I wondered, realize that, so far as her material benefits went, she owed them not to Mervyn but to a ruthless, sentimental and sketchily educated little Welshman whom she had never seen? Most of all, perhaps, she owed them to fires which, in fairly quick succession, had destroyed two drapers' shops that Mostyn-Lloyd owned in South Wales. So obviously were these the work of incendiaries that Mostyn-Lloyd had advertised an offer of substantial rewards for the discovery of the culprits. But these rewards had never been claimed, and perhaps it was the inflammable nature of South Wales shop property that caused Mostyn-Lloyd soon thereafter to look for a fireproof shop in London.

However, Daniel, who had recently come upon these interesting facts, would have been annoyed had I prattled of them to this child so deeply in love at my side, or, indeed, to anyone at all. So I said nothing; and when we had stood for some moments longer watching the carriages and hansoms passing through the square and had tested a few of the new marvelous gaslights in the house, we wandered away and talked about wedding clothes in a teashop.

2

Lucy Evans appeared to be reconciled to the idea of losing Mervyn. There were no more vapors and she was charming to Enid. Aloysius Slinn did not come again to the Gothersons', but Mervyn told me that he called often enough at the house in Kensington. I wondered what excuse there had been for that; and Mervyn said that the first call was made to return some money. From his story I gathered that it had happened in this way. When Lucy and Slinn drove away together from the tea party, the colonel expressed his pleasure at the brightening look of the sky, for continued damp, he said, was apt to bring on the malaria that he had contracted abroad. Once on the subject of "abroad" he could chatter amusingly and without end, as Enid had told me. His service as military attaché in Constantinople led him to Turkish bank notes. "Charming things," he said to Lucy. "Let me show you a few specimens."

But, alas, the wallet containing the specimens was nowhere to be found. Colonel Slinn was in consternation. "Heavens!" he cried. "What a confounded nuisance! My ready money was in that wallet, and now the banks are shut." He clicked his tongue with annoyance. "It's not losing the money that annoys me. I can go to the bank tomorrow, though it'll be deuced awkward this evening. It's the wallet itself. It was a gift from a dear friend—a Turkish minister."

He went through all his pockets again, but the wallet was not to be found. "I shall have to advertise its loss," he said. "Damnation! Forgive me, Mrs. Evans. I was carried away. I'd give a hundred pounds to have the thing back."

Lucy delicately raised the question of his present necessities—"till the banks open tomorrow"—but he waved that aside. He wouldn't dream of accepting a loan of money from a woman who, however charming and generous, willing to trust a poor devil in a bit of a hole, was, after all, a stranger, to all intents and purposes. "What do you know of me, Mrs. Evans?" he asked with a smile, "or, for that matter, what do I know of you?"

"Well," said Lucy, "may we know one another well enough for me to lend you what I happen to have?" She opened her purse. "I'm afraid it's only three pounds. And may I say that I know you well enough, I think, to ask you to come and take tea with me some afternoon when you return the money?"

She gave him her card. The colonel accepted it, and, protestingly, the three pounds.

"I don't expect," I said to Mervyn, "that his advertisement for the wallet was successful?"

"Oh, it was found, you know," he assured me. "That night Mama's coachman brought it into the house. It had got jammed behind the cushions in the carriage. It was a handsome thing in red morocco leather with his monogram on it in gold. Mama showed it to me, and the Turkish bank notes. There were also two English notes of a fiver each. He was tremendously grateful when he brought back Mama's three pounds."

I must say that the wind was taken out of my sails when the story reached this unexpected end. I took it to Daniel for enlightenment. He supplied it tersely. "First," he said, "there's the question of the man's credibility. He says he's a colonel, but he's not in the Army List. He says he's a member of the Garrick, and I know he's a liar. Well, then, I look at anything concerning him with a lack of credulity, shall we say? Now if you wanted to establish yourself with some innocent person as a reliable character, what easier means than to plant an expensive wallet, which could be a useful property to flash in many circumstances, containing all the evidence to back up what you've been talking about? You've been in Turkey, and here are the Turkish notes. You're not a beggar, and here are two fivers. I'll bet that rich-looking wallet and a couple of bank notes have been his credentials often enough."

"But I still don't understand, my dear. If he wanted to establish his credentials with her by showing her the Turkish notes and the money, why couldn't he just *do* it?"

He ruffled his hair and looked at me compassionately. "You have no psychology, Sarah," he said. "Don't you see the value of shedding a little doubt in her mind? Is he bogus? Will I ever see my money back? Have I been a fool? Then the resolving of the doubt. Ah! He's straight. And so she looks forward to seeing him again, proud that what she has *wanted* to believe about him is right after all. Something is established between them. I think Mr. Slinn is pretty clever. He's probably had a lot of experience. Unlike you, he has psychology. Mind you," he added, "you must pay no attention whatever to what I've said. There's not a hap'orth of evidence in it—bar the man's lying. For the rest, consider it guesswork."

3

Mr. Bernard Cupples didn't come within my range till some time after this. The ramifications in the doings of people like that are beyond my understanding, and exactly what he had been up to I don't know. Whatever it was, Daniel defended him in the courts and he was acquitted. Necessarily, Daniel and he talked about many things, and it chanced that Mr. Cupples mentioned "our mutual acquaintance, Colonel Slinn." Daniel didn't pursue that matter, but when he spoke of it to me I was more than interested: I was excited.

Lucy Evans had by then been married to Colonel Slinn for about a year. The marriage, by registrar, with no fuss or ceremony, indeed with an almost furtive secrecy, followed soon upon the marriage of Mervyn and Enid. The pair went abroad and had but lately returned.

I may as well say frankly what was in my mind concerning Colonel Slinn. I believed that when he wrote to Dr. Gotherson about his book he was doing something that he was in the habit of doing: that is, using any means that came to mind of introducing himself into a family to see what advantage could be picked up there. I believed that he was capable of even such a petty meanness as stealing a couple of sovereigns from Enid's handbag, although the Gotherson family must have been a disappointment to him, especially after his encounter with the poverty-stricken peer, whose relations with the turf and the stock exchange had been prolonged and unfortunate. He was probably preparing to end the little adventure when the extraordinary consequences of his theft suggested that there were possibilities after all, and these became clear when he discovered the situation in which Lucy Evans found herself. Putting it down brutally, that is how I saw it; but I was puzzled by one thing. The man was obviously as poor as a church mouse, but after the affair of the Turkish bank notes it was equally obvious that he now had money. I could well believe Daniel's theory of the attic in Long Acre, but the fact remains that he was at once established in an attractive enough suite in Jermyn Street. 1 know that, because Maggie Whale met him one day walking down Piccadilly, dressed to the nines, swinging a cane, and looking, as they say, on top of the world.

"Good afternoon, Miss Whale!" he cried. "I am taking the air, recuperating after a tremendous upheaval. Even an old soldier tires of shifting from camp to camp, but it had to be done. I could stand the Albany no longer."

He explained that he had just moved from the Albany to new chambers, and he begged her to look in and see if she approved of his arrangements. It was not an invitation that most women would have accepted, but Maggie was uninterested in the reactions of most women. She was fascinated by Colonel Slinn. Her novelist's instinct ached to run him down at all points, and with gladness she accompanied him to Jermyn Street. "Just chambers where I sleep," the colonel explained. "I eat as a rule at the Garrick."

They went up a stairway and Slinn opened a door with a latch key. "And the odd thing was," said Maggie, "that there was someone already in the sitting room. A short dark man, who was looking round as if he were the proprietor. Now how did he get there? He must have had a key."

Slinn said, the words seeming to be jerked out of him involuntarily: "Why—Cupples!"

The other bowed to Maggie, said: "Sorry, Colonel. Just off," and went.

"My landlord's agent," Slinn explained, recovering himself. "I suppose he's been making sure everything's in order.

They were attractive rooms, Maggie said—"must have cost a pretty penny"—and there was the further fact that Slinn now seemed to have money to spend in all directions. He took Lucy Evans about to the most fashionable restaurants, and sometimes took Mervyn, too, and he always insisted on having the best and paying for it.

It was an odd situation. What Mervyn thought of this obvious courtship of his mother I did not know and could not ask. He was so deeply involved in his own happy affair that he seemed willing to bless the world and anything it might do.

My child was beginning to show, and I did not go about much, but Maggie came to me one evening and said: "I was lunching with Harry Rokeby today at the Café Royal. Guess who was there?"

"Good lord, Maggie, what a stupid question that always is! How on earth can I guess?"

"All right, all right. Don't let the coming event cast peevish shadows. It was the colonel. He was taking luncheon with that little man I met at the rooms in Jermyn Street. A proper pair of conspirators they looked, I must say. What was the man's name? D'you remember?"

"Cupples, wasn't it?"

"That's it—Cupples."

And now, with Colonel and Mrs. Slinn back from their prolonged honeymoon, and living in the house in Kensington that contained Lucy's alluring bed, here again, in circumstances that were on the shady and disreputable side, was this name—Cupples, Mr. Bernard Cupples.

4

Soon after my rumpus with Richard and Miss Mackenzie the Law Courts wilted and closed and the long holiday was before us. It was a good opportunity to do what should have been done before. Miss Mackenzie was told that she would not be wanted when the holiday was over, and Daniel promised to think of a school for Richard. "I'll talk it over with some people in Scotland," he said.

I would not be going with him to Scotland. In my condition I did not want either to tramp the heather or meet a lot of people, but the visit was important to Daniel. Balfour would be one of the house party for a time, as well as other politicians, and Daniel, I knew, hoped that Balfour would remember him. He had spoken at one of Balfour's meetings and had received a flattering letter from the great man.

I had had a long and earnest session with Daniel on the subject of Richard. I all but accused him of neglecting the boy, of allowing him to do as he pleased and grow up as he liked, and I was not to be deflected by the words "my career," which tended more and more to slip in as the reason, or excuse, for Daniel's increasing absorption in his own affairs. "If Richard isn't a part of your career I'd like to know what is," I cried angrily. "The boy is growing up selfish and self-satisfied, and it's time he was taken in hand. There are too many women around him, and he thinks he can do as he likes with them."

The upshot of it was that Daniel found a young parson, not long out of Oxford, and anxious enough to earn a pound or two as a tutor. He was curate of a parish on the Norfolk coast, and so that summer we split completely. Daniel went north, Richard east, and I west, to Tresant. However, I did not go alone. Maggie Whale agreed to come with me. She shut up her house, and Glory Jane traveled with us. There was a fourth member of the party—Tom Chadderton. Those who saw us depart from Paddington may well have wondered whether we had snatched Tom Chadderton from out of some appalling street accident. He was fourteen years old. His broken nose was strapped across with sticking plaster. Both of his eyes had been blacked and were now an ugly greenish yellow. From his right ear up to the crown of his head his hair had been shaved, and sticking plaster adhered to this pathway.

He carried various scars, the mementoes of past troubles, that now had healed but would be with him forever. He was thin and white, silent and furtive. His clothes were respectable, and he looked unhappy in them.

It was Sally who passed Tom Chadderton on to us. This was the first summer after her return from Andorra. Maggie and I had gone to see her and to ask her permission to use Tresant, for though she had told us to go there whenever we liked, we saw no reason to omit the courtesy of acknowledging her ownership. She was in a difficult situation. Put briefly, what she had decided to do was to become poor and live with poor people.

"What do you want to *do* for them?" I had asked her; and she said: "Do? I don't want to do anything, except become one of them and share their lives, if they will let me."

It was not easy for Sally to become poor. She could not sell Tresant or anything in it. The law had tied up all that long before she was born. The machinery of the Tresant estate went on working, whatever she chose to do. The income of it was hers, and this income was imposing. Sally arranged that large sums of it should be given to the helping of work that she believed in; but so far as she was concerned as a person living in the East End of London, she took no more than permitted her to exist. Even this she took reluctantly, feeling that it was a barrier between her and people who had to earn every penny they received. It was about three pounds a week—"and that's princely, my dear Sarah, compared with what my neighbors get. Most of them keep wives and families on less."

So there she was. "I just want to see how it works—what happens. I may not be able to stay."

She called herself Mary Brown. Everything would go wrong, she was sure, if it were known that, though she had renounced riches, she could be, if she chose, a rich woman. That would make her the target of all the spongers and cadgers in the district, and so destroy what she longed for: to be gradually accepted by her neighbors as one of themselves. It was for this reason that, when Maggie or I visited her, we left our cabs some way off and arrived on foot, wearing our dingiest clothes. Even so, our voices, and Sally's voice, too, were against us. A voice is far more personal and betraying than a suit of clothes, and in that first year of her adventure Mary Brown did not get far. She obviously did no work; her talk was "classy"; and she was watched with the inborn wariness of the poor.

She was now my only link with the East End of London. Daniel had sold, out of the many properties left him by his aunt, all save those that were beyond question respectable. He did this for what I thought a rather dingy reason. "We've got to watch these blasted

Radicals," he said. "I shall probably be asked before long to fight a seat. It won't do me any good if they start bleating that I'm an East End slum-owner."

"But, Daniel, you don't make anything out of that. You lose on it. You're an excellent landlord."

"It would give them a handle," he said obstinately. "I shall sell out." And sell out he did. Mr. Cogan and his wife went from the eyrie overlooking Graybird Court. The property left to Daniel by Mrs. Gemstone was extensive, and so there was still plenty for Mr. Cogan to do. He moved to a little suburban house at Willesden. So now, as I have said, Sally was our only link with the East End. I never saw Graybird Court again, but I was to get to know Robin Hood Road well enough. It was a romantically-minded speculative builder who created the region. There was Friar Tuck Street, and Little John Row, and Maid Marian Street, and Longbow Lane, and Sherwood Avenue: every one of these streets alike, every house in every street alike, all built long ago, all stewing in the summer days, all incomparably dank and dreary in the winter weather, nowhere a trunk, a twig, a bud or a leaf, or any other thing to catch the eye and lift up the heart. There was a street, with the doors opening straight off the pavement. Behind each house was a back yard in which you couldn't swing a cat, and in each of these yards was a door leading into a narrow lane. Facing you then across the lane was the back door of another yard, and beyond that yard was another house like yours; and this repetition went on and on. It was flat, gray, endless, with the river not far off, so that, in winter nights you could feel it seeping through every street and every house; you could see its exhalation hanging on the air like an ogre's frozen breath before the puny lights of corner shops and the more blaring illuminations of the pubs; you could hear its age-old melancholy whimper from ships feeling their way about the rising or falling tide.

This was the forest in which dwelt Robin Hood's merry men, and with them Mary Brown. You entered Sally's house off the pavement, observing that the end of the street was blocked by a high wall. The street was a cul-de-sac; and it always felt to me like a blocked corridor in a prison, with the wall forbidding escape. The doors were like doors into prisoners' cells. When you went in, you were in a stone-paved passage, and found, as you moved about, that all this ground floor was paved with stone. On your right was a door leading into the front room that looked upon the street. Then there was a stairway going up steeply to two bedrooms. It went up between walls, with no banister—not so much as a handrail—and it was dark even at noon. But we won't climb up there for the moment. We will open the door in front of us. This takes us into the stone-floored kitchen. There is an open fireplace here, with no oven alongside it. If you have any meat to cook, you must do as everyone else does: you must drive a nail into the front edge of the mantelpiece, fasten one end of a piece of string to this and the other end to the meat, and put a tin pan below to catch the fat. Then you must sit there and keep the meat revolving on this improvised spit till it is done.

A door leads out of the kitchen into a back kitchen a few yards square. It contains a tap which supplies cold water—the only water in the house. From here you go out into the back yard, and at the end of that is a shed containing a waterless closet. That is all. The two rooms at the head of the stairway are nothing but small square boxes, one looking on the street, one on the backyard. From whichever way you look, you are looking at someone else's back or front window. For light, you can choose between oil lamps and candles.

I have described the region and the house with some particularity because it was here that Sally remained for the rest of her life.

Visitors did not, as they did elsewhere, make polite calls upon newcomers to the leafless forest. For a long time Sally knew no one. She bought in second-hand shops the furniture she needed. She couldn't do otherwise, for from that moment she had no "capital." She had three pounds a week, and would have no more until she could accumulate out of this. And so she selected with care her bits and pieces: the few necessary things for her bedroom, which was the front room downstairs, and the pots and pans for her kitchen. These second-hand shops didn't deliver goods: the buyer had to shift them. Investigating the stratagems of the poor, she found that she need not pay for labor. She could hire a hand truck, and did so, and brought the stuff to her house in a couple of journeys. Her installation was watched from behind curtains and from doorsteps. When it came to the chest-of-drawers, her heaviest piece of furniture, she took out the drawers, and took them in one by one, and was then resolutely pulling the rest of the thing off the truck when a man lounged across the street and said: "Let's give you a 'and, Missus," and between them they carried it into the front room.

The idea was in Sally's mind that here she would stay and become known at last as a good neighbor. By what means this would happen she didn't know, but she decided that her two little upper rooms must serve a neighborly purpose. One must become a spare bedroom: you never knew what emergency might arise. The other became a place for storing what people might need. As her spare cash permitted, she picked up clothes in second-hand shops and hung them up in this bedroom. The kitchen was her living room. It was as sparsely furnished as her room had been at Andorra. The only indulgence she gave herself was a broken-bottomed wicker chair.

And now there was nothing to do but live and wait. Her appearance began to take on the outline that the years thereafter did nothing but confirm. Her clothes were always black and shabby. She pulled her hair back over her head and held it into a bun with a few hairpins. She had great strength, a reservoir that had been filled in her girlhood and youth; but her physically rather inactive life tended to make her fat, and, to look ahead through the years, she became not unlike a dowdier and dirtier Widow of Windsor, which was true even in this: that, try as she would to subdue such symptoms, there came, even to the end of her life, an occasional imperious flash, a hard stare of the eyes that warned the imprudent: "We are not amused."

The first week she was in Robin Hood Road she heard a kitten mewling outside her house. She went into the dusk of the summer evening and saw it cringing in the gutter. She stooped over it, and as she did so she heard a smack into the wall at the end of the street. Looking up, she saw a few boys fitting new stones into their catapults. They were bedraggled, barefoot and hard-faced. Her instinct was to advance upon them and give them a piece of her mind. But this would be, at the very outset, to stir up animosity, so she choked down her rage and merely stood there, facing the boys and interposing herself between them and the kitten. It would have worked anywhere around Porteven, but it didn't work in Bermondsey. A few more stones smacked into the wall behind her, and one hit her in the knee. She picked up the kitten and retreated into her house, and for some time thereafter she could hear stones thudding on her front door, like arrows from the modern longbows of the merry men.

The kitten, which was hardly old enough to leave its mother, was deplorable. In the light of the oil lamp in the kitchen she watched fleas gamboling upon it. A stone had glanced across its face, making a wound from which a little blood oozed. Its skin was mangy and its fur matted with dirt. It was black save for a white waistcoat and white extremities. Its feet, the tip of its tail and the tips of its ears were white. It lay in Sally's lap, and fleas hopped onto her skirt as she parted its fur with her fingers; then it rolled upon its back, looked up at her out of eyes as heavenly blue as Porteven sea water in summertime, opened a pink mouth and yawned.

"It was the first person in all Bermondsey," Sally said to me, "to come to me in friendliness and to trust me."

In her perambulations of the district Sally had noticed what had obviously once been a corner shop but was now a doctor's surgery. Cheap green serge curtains hung behind the glass, and on the door was a plate inscribed: WARWICK RUSSELL, M.D. (LOND.) L.R.C.P. SUR-GERY HOUR, 6 P.M. She had seen many people passing through the door in the evenings, and the next day she passed through it herself, carrying the kitten in a basket. The floor of what had been the shop was covered with oilcloth, and round the walls were hard chairs. There was nothing else except a lot of notices printed in large type and pasted to the walls. "Don't spit in here or I'll throw you out. Don't spit any-where or you may give someone else your consumption." "Wash before you eat, and clean your teeth after you've eaten." "I know you've got bugs, but fight 'em. Ten killed are ten less to bite you." "Stop talking this nonsense about the night air. Sleep with your bedroom windows open." "You won't have lice unless you first have nits. Look out for nits, and if you find 'em come to me for a hair wash." "I don't want you here. Fresh air and water will help you to leave me in peace."

There was much else of this sort, and the reading of it, to say nothing of the lively expectation of meeting Dr. Warwick Russell, helped to keep Sally's mind off the sore eyes, the scabby faces, the coughing and sneezing that surrounded her. The place was packed with men, women and children. A door leading to an inner room would occasionally open, a patient would come out, and another without invitation would go in. Sally took care to be last. She knew that her errand was unusual, and that, if any human patients remained, she would probably get short shrift.

At last she went in, and there in a room smelling of scrubbing and beeswax, furnished with shelves loaded with labeled bottles, with a sink, with a roll-top desk that had a swivel chair before it, she saw Warwick Russell. His back was to her. His coat was off, and with his sleeves rolled up he was vigorously washing his hands at the sink. The water was whooshing; he was whistling; the level light of the evening sun irradiated the red hairs on his arms and the red of his startling poll. Bent over the sink though he was, he nevertheless looked enormous, and when he straightened and turned round, rubbing a towel up and down his forearms, he seemed to be six feet six. He was, in fact, six feet four.

"Well," he said, still rubbing and glaring down at her with eyes as heavenly blue as the kitten's—they lit up his florid face—"well, what the devil do *you* want?"

Sally fumbled with the fastening of the basket, hiding her face, and said timidly: "I don't know where to find a vet. I wondered if you'd look at this kitten?"

He threw himself into the swivel chair. His long legs shot out in front of him halfway across the room, and he fanned himself with the towel. "Well, good God Almighty!" he roared. "A bloody kitten!"

He got up, opened another door than that by which Sally had entered and shouted up a stairway: "Polly! Come down here!"

Oh, God, thought Sally, what a fool I am! Some housekeeper, she was sure, would appear and show her out, and it would serve her right for being a stupid intruder upon an overworked man. Then Polly

Russell tripped down the stairs and into the room, wearing her golden crown—a glory of red hair like her husband's, and she had on a long green cool-looking smock of linen out of which she rose like a flower out of a bell. She didn't look more than twenty, and tall as she was she seemed small beside the doctor. She rested a hand on his arm and said: "What is it?"

"This woman's brought a bloody kitten. I slave my guts out morning, noon and night on scabies and rabies, goiter, gallstones, rickets, syphilis, cancer and constipation; and when I'm all set for a pipe and a moment's peace—behold, a bloody kitten. What do we do with a woman like this? She looks moderately sane."

"We examine the kitten," said Polly.

"All right," said Dr. Russell. "Let's see the damned thing. I suppose we'll be opening a branch for pet mice and canaries next."

A moment later the kitten was in his hands, "and, you know," said Sally, "you can't make a mistake about a thing like that. They were *loving* hands." He held the kitten with tenderness, and grinned at it, and said: "Well, what have *you* been up to, you silly little devil?"

"He washes before meals—and after," Sally said demurely.

He turned his radiant grin from the kitten to her. "I hope you do, too," he said. "I don't want you drifting in here. Quite enough to go on with. Who are you, anyway? You don't sound like one of the girls of the village."

"Mary Brown. I live in Robin Hood Road."

He shot her a shrewd look. "Oh, you do. Bloody fine place, I must say. Ah well . . . Polly, you'd better take this upstairs." He handed her the kitten, and said to Sally: "Call for him in a week. Good night."

5

Sally did not have to wait for a week. Five days later, a kitten that looked as though he had been spring-cleaned, French polished and newly upholstered arrived in Robin Hood Road. Polly Russell carried the basket, and Sally asked her in. She was willing to take the East End as she found it, but it was pleasing to know that she had such a neighbor as this living not far away. She had thought a good deal about the Russells. The doctor was not easily to be overlooked. Bicycles in those days were of the "penny-farthing" variety, and on one of these Dr. Russell was to be seen pedaling round what he spoke of as his parish. The people called him the penny-farthing doctor, and that would be about what he, in fact, received for each consultation, leveling out one against another and including the cases in which he received nothing at all. Theoretically, he was a "sixpenny doctor," but, as he was apt to declare, the name simply showed what a bloody optimist he was. Sally had noticed how, as soon as Dr. Russell had alighted at a house door, some urchin would dart out of concealment and post himself alongside the machine like a sentry guarding a royal carriage. Not that there was any need of protection. The bicycle was unmistakable, and anyone who had done it harm would have been in physical danger, but the instinctive wish to do something for the doctor could not be overcome. Sally had seen him enter pubs, which then were open from early in the morning till eleven at night, and haul out men who were drunk or on the way. "Come on, now. Get home and put your head in a bucket of cold water. You don't deserve the wife you've got. What you've wasted here this week would buy her a new dress, to say nothing of boots for the kids. And don't forget you owe me three-and-six. My belly needs filling, as well as your bladder." He would watch the shambling figure make off with a shamed grin, and then, swinging his vast frame onto the slender machine he would pedal away, whistling the latest tune from the music halls.

Polly Russell had been married to the doctor for only a year. Sitting in the kitchen with the cat purring on her knee and with the tea pot on the table, Sally listened to the enthusiastic girl who wanted to talk of nothing but her Warwick and his work. She learned that Warwick Russell was the son of a Norwood shopkeeper, an only child on whom his parents had lavished everything they had. They were touchily proud of him, and they had always seen to it that he was kept from contact with what they called "the lower classes." Warwick was to be a "gentle-man." All their sacrifices would then be justified. What the Russells lived for was to see the name "Warwick Russell" on a Harley Street doorplate, and a carriage with a caped cockaded coachman outside.

Their sacrifices were real, for the small Norwood shop earned a bare living, and their savings went. Then the old man, saying nothing to his son, began to borrow, assured that all would be well, for Warwick's progress as a student at Guy's was brilliant, both in medicine and surgery. But going to Guy's meant knowing Bermondsey, and the careful subterfuges that had separated the boy from poor people and their lives broke down. He was overwhelmed by what he saw day after day.

When he was qualified he began to write in the medical journals, and his articles attracted attention not only in England but on the Continent. He accepted several positions in specialist institutes, and his name began to be talked about. Then, ironically on the same day, two things happened. Old Russell, whose creditors had been pressing him for some time, was declared bankrupt, and Warwick resigned the position he then held in order to become a sixpenny doctor. There was a terrible scene between him and the old man. Warwick, who had known nothing of the financial struggle, was accused of being a vampire sucking the old people dry in order to fling away their substance on a pack of dirty loafers. It went on and on, and the young giant was so distraught and shattered, both by what he had unknowingly done, and by the painful discovery of his father's deep unacknowledged motives, that he broke down in health. But he would not give in. When he was strong enough, he went to the Cotswolds on a walking tour, "and there," said Polly with a laugh, "he met me." She was the daughter of a country parson. "And here we are," she said. "We manage to starve our way along reasonably well."

Sally let her talk, and was filled with a deep sense of satisfaction. I didn't *ask* her to bring the kitten, she thought. I didn't *ask* her to unmask everything in this way. It had just happened, and that was the sort of thing she had hoped for. If Polly Russell had come to her, perhaps others would do so, too.

"How much is the kitten?" she asked.

"Sixpence."

And Sixpence is what the kitten thereafter was called.

6

Tom Chadderton, who was traveling into Cornwall with me and Maggie Whale, was one of the boys who had thrown stones from their catapults at Sally and Sixpence. He was lounging in the cul-de-sac when Polly Russell brought the kitten home, and he ran up to her and asked: "Wot you got there, Mrs. Penny-Farthing?"

Polly lifted the lid and showed him the renovated kitten. Tom stroked the sleek fur and said: "Ain't it lovely?" He was really happy to handle the little creature: as happy as he was to sling stones at any moving thing.

"Where you takin' 'im, Mrs. Penny-Farthing?"

Polly told him, and explained that someone had injured the kitten's face and that her husband had been treating it.

The two incidents—this kitten being taken home and the kitten Sally had taken into her house—now connected themselves in his not bright mind. "I done that!" he said proudly. "First go!" He pulled out his catapult and showed it to Polly.

"So while my husband is trying to make things right, you're making them wrong."

Tom Chadderton puzzled over this, and Polly helped him.

"He made your jaw right, didn't he?"

"Yers."

"Well, then. Don't be such a silly fool."

Tom ambled away, and perhaps recalled the afternoon when he had been sitting in the gutter holding his face in his hands and groaning. Dr. Russell alighted from the penny-farthing, looked at him, and asked: "What have you been up to? Trying to swallow a cricket ball? Open your mouth."

Then he had marched Tom straight to the surgery, opened the cyst, and sent him home feeling happier. These various happenings must have worked to some sort of consequence in the boy's mind, for a few evenings after Sixpence had returned to Sally, Tom saw the kitten in the street and one of his "gang" drawing back the elastic of a catapult. Tom was a big lad, the leader of those he associated with, and now he asserted his leadership by knocking this boy flat onto the pavement. Then he picked up Sixpence, carried him to Sally's door, and gave the door a kick with his boot. "You better keep this kitten in," he said.

Sally thanked him, and he stood there shuffling. "You a friend of the doc?" he said.

"Yes."

"Wot's yer name?"

"Mary Brown. What's yours?"

"Tom Chadderton."

"Well, thank you, Tom, for bringing Sixpence back. Some boys hurt him last week."

"I done it."

"Why?"

"Gawd knows."

He was moving off when he said over his shoulder: "I'll tell the blokes not to do it no more. 'Cos you're a pal of the doc. See?"

"Thank you, Tom."

She stood for a moment, Sixpence in her arms, and he suddenly came back and roughly fondled the fur of the kitten's head. " 'E's a nice little bugger," he said; and Sally felt then that Sixpence was fairly safe, and that she, too, as a friend of the doc, had made some progress.

7

Robin Hood Road was a noisy place. On its corner was the Foresters pub, which was not a cozy Dickensian tavern but a hard-faced brassy drink shop, the property of a brewery company that owned a score like it. Tom and Haggie Chadderton had known the inside of the pub from babyhood, for so long as there was money to be spent the Chadderton parents would go to the Foresters to spend it. The twins for some time were left to yell their heads off in the box that was their cradle; but one winter night a coal from the kitchen fire shot onto the rag hearth-mat, which smoldered and filled the room with a suffocating fume. The children were barely alive when neighbors, warned by the smell, ran in and rescued them. The Chaddertons, being considerate parents, took no more risks. They carried the children with them to the pub and soothed their peevishness by giving them sips of beer or gin.

The Chaddertons were a main source of the noise in Robin Hood Road. Tom and Haggie were now grown up and need not be taken to the pub, but the parents would come home singing at eleven at night, and, as likely as not, the singing would end in fighting, and that would issue in Mrs. Chadderton's screams as her husband pounded her or hurled her into the street. The noisy intervention of neighbors would not help matters, and often enough it was past midnight before uneasy silence settled upon the forest.

In the morning, Mr. Chadderton would set out upon his day's work. From some factory or other he bought defective china: chipped cups, cracked saucers, basins a little out of true: and he hawked these things about the East End streets. They were piled into a large basket which he carried upon his head, one hand lightly steadying it. Beneath the basket was a black-and-white checked cap. Round the bullneck was a black-and-red checked muffler. The face between the two checks was brutal and congested, lit by small red eyes, and the body seemed to be all pressed down toward the shambling feet. Mr. Chadderton would set forth yodeling. The yodel was his trade advertisement. It had become known far and wide, and his coming needed no other announcement. There was no call for him to yodel in Robin Hood Road, where anyone who wanted a crock had only to go to the house of old Crackpot, as he was called, and buy it, but he was as proud of his voice as an Italian tenor, and as no birds sang in the forest he had it all his own way.

This transient morning noise was not much, but on Saturday nights there was the Salvation Army with its band outside the Foresters, the banging of its drum and the blaring of its brass; and from the dawn cries of milkmen to the apocalyptic evening shouts of the barefoot newsboys, furnished inexhaustibly with " 'Orrible murder," there was not much intermission, what with "Coal a shillin' a 'undred," "Want sweep," "Winders to mend," "Scissors to grind," "Rags, bones, bottles, jars," "Catsmeat!" the churning of hurdy-gurdies, and all the rest of it.

This was the wild wood in which Tom Chadderton and his sister Haggie flowered. It was odd, Sally thought, how much Haggie was a creature of the night. She was rarely seen in the daytime, but at night Sally often passed her in the streets, munching fish and chips under a gas lamp, staring into corner-shop windows, vanishing down back lanes: a child with flying dirty hair, torn black woolen stockings, wearing someone else's cast-off clothes, and always alone, and wanting to be alone, for she could no more be openly approached than a wild doe.

Tom was more approachable. One evening, which Sally regarded as a time of triumph, there was a knock at her door, and she found Tom standing there with that look he had of wanting to run but of making himself stay by a great effort of will. He held in his hand an unwrapped meat bone, and he announced: "That's for yer cat, see?"

"Oh, thank you, Tom," Sally said. "Would you like to come in and give it to him?"

Tom considered, and said "Yers," and entered the house.

In the kitchen Sally invited him to sit down, and he sat in the wicker chair and watched Sixpence worrying the bone on the hearthmat. From time to time he bent and stroked the cat's fur; and presently he said: "I've frowed away my sling."

Sally did not dare to ask why, and Tom, who would have died before admitting his reason, said: "That's 'cos I'm goin' ter work. Regler. Can't go on bein' a bleedin' kid."

Sally had learned enough about boys like Tom Chadderton to know that they were expected to earn almost as soon as they could stand; and she said: "I expect you've had a good many jobs in your time, Tom."

"Yers. I been everythink."

She gave him tea and buns, and he told her of his life till then. Neither he nor Haggie had been to any sort of school. They couldn't read or write. Haggie had been "in service" a good many times. "She allus runs away." As for Tom, he had been every sort of errand boy, newspaper seller, and what not. "Now I'm goin' ter start regler—on me own," he said with satisfaction. "Not workin' for no one else. Just on me own."

Mr. Chadderton, Sally gathered, had bought a shoe-black's outfit from a man too crippled with rheumatism to do the necessary bending; and Tom was to go forth, taking over this man's pitch, and make his fortune.

This conversation took place on a Saturday evening, and throughout the following week Sally saw nothing of Tom. But late on the next Saturday night he turned up and told her of his week's adventures. He had bought some cat's meat for Sixpence, and a sticky screw of paper containing cheap sweets, which evidently had been clutched in his hand for a long time. "That's fer you—see. I got something fer Haggie, too."

Tom crossed the road to his own house just before eleven o'clock, and then came the babble of talk and the singing and quarreling and Mr. Chadderton's elated yodeling, which announced that the Foresters had finished their woodland session. Now quiet might be expected gradually to descend, and Sally got into bed, in her front room downstairs. But the usual Saturday night row soon broke out across the street, and this time it rose to a great fury. So great that Sally was frightened and got up and put on her clothes and stood at the window, looking across at the Chaddertons' house which she could see by the light of a street lamp. So disturbing was the racket that other people, she saw, came to doors and windows, and presently some of them began to bang on the Chadderton door, with cries for a bit o' bloody quiet and the like. Thereupon Chadderton appeared at the door, his face livid and inflamed, looking like a bull about to charge. The people drew back, afraid, and he hastily stooped and picked up his loaded crockery basket, which stood in the passage, raised it above his head with both arms, and hurled it among them. They scattered, and the basket fell with an almighty crash, exploding in a shrapnel of china splinters. Chadderton banged the door and retired.

The rumpus within the house then broke out afresh, with the sound of more crockery smashing, and with, at one point, a chamberpot flying through the front window and bursting upon the lamp post. At that moment the lamplighter, now engaged in his second function as lamp extinguisher, walked along the road with his pole over his shoulder; and, standing with perfect composure amid the wreckage, put out the light. Whatever might be happening in the world, this, and this alone, was his duty. He did it, and went.

The lamp being out, it was not easy for Sally to see what was happening in the street, but it was evident that the neighbors had resigned themselves to letting the rumpus exhaust itself by its own violence and had retired to their houses. From the Chadderton house came a few more terrific thunderclaps, the last of which sounded as if cannon balls were being bowled downstairs; then the storm blew itself away in diminishing mutters that at last faded into blessed silence. Sally watched the lights go out over there, and then with a sigh that was half weeping and half joy she turned again toward her bed.

But she did not get into it. A new sound, timid, frightened, caught at her hearing. Her attention had been so powerfully drawn by the drama in the street that she had overlooked this, which came from the back. She listened intently and heard it again: more like a scratching than a knocking at the door that opened upon her back yard. She took up her candle, passed through the kitchen into the back kitchen, and opened the door. "Oh, my God!" she exclaimed; and then: "Come in quick."

Tom Chadderton staggered in, supported by his sister Haggie. Sally bolted the door behind them, took them into the kitchen, and, when she had drawn the curtain across the window, lit the paraffin lamp. This greater light confirmed the horror that the candle glimmer had shown. Tom Chadderton was reeking in blood. His face was a bloody mess; his hands were imbrued with the blood he had tried to wipe from his eyes; blood was still dripping off his chin, flowing down his ears.

305

Haggie was holding him up. He looked as though he would fall down dead should she let go. He was sobbing and whimpering, but the girl was stony. She looked at Sally with suspicion; she gave the impression that, having delivered her gruesome burden, she would escape, vanish into the night, into the labyrinth of alleys and back lanes that threaded the forest. Her own face was contused with weals. "He said to bring 'im," she explained briefly.

This was no moment for inquiries or for any delay. Sally put Tom to sit in the wicker chair, with a pillow snatched from her bed behind his bleeding skull. Then she wrote to Dr. Russell. It was now well past midnight. She hoped he would come. She knew he would come. She gave the note to Haggie, unbolted the back-kitchen door, and the girl, without a word, melted into the darkness. Sally felt that the child was at home in this silent darkness of stone as she herself had been in the whispering agitated darkness of the places about Tresant, and she thought about Tresant as she sat there and waited. There was nothing she could do for Tom Chadderton but hold his hand and listen to the groans sobbing out of him.

When half an hour had crawled eternally by, Warwick Russell came, and Polly with him. Haggie slunk in behind them. Five people seemed to crowd the little room. Polly gave one look round, took up a kettle, filled it at the back-kitchen tap, lit an oil stove, and put the kettle on. Sally was beginning to feel lightheaded. "Polly put the kettle on. We'll all have tea," she thought. And then: "Put the kettle on! I ought to have done that!" She was learning. Polly and Dr. Russell ignored her. They saw what had to be done and worked without words, a team of two. Polly swept the table clear, opened the doctor's bag, spread instruments upon a white cloth, snatched a basin from a shelf, poured in boiling water, and dropped the instruments into it.

"Look at this bloody nose!" said the doctor. "He'll look like poor old Thackeray for the rest of his life."

There was snipping of hair, plying of needle, strapping of the nose, swabbing, and Tom Chadderton emerged from the mask of blood, pale, wincing, weeping.

"Damn lucky that skull wasn't fractured," said the doctor. "What hit him?"

"Vorses an' a boot an' the Ole Man's buckle-end," Haggie chanted. "And then 'e frew 'im downstairs. Me, too."

"Yes, you too. Let's have a look at you."

She was a simpler job.

"I've got a spare bedroom," Sally said.

"He ought to go to hospital," the doctor objected. "I'll bet your spare bedroom's full of bugs, like every room in this God awful region. *Is it buggy?*"

306

"There are a few," Sally admitted forlornly; and the doctor said: "All right. Take him up."

So Tom was taken up, and Haggie threw herself across the foot of his bed; and when Sally and the doctor got back to the kitchen Polly had already cleared up the mess, put three cups and saucers on the table and the kettle on the oil stove. "We've earned a cup of tea," she said. "I hope you don't mind."

The doctor lit his pipe, and sat down with a happy sigh. "Now then, tell us. What was it all about?"

Sally didn't know, then: but she learned later that all this blood and battery had a simple cause. Tom Chadderton had explained with pride what he had done with a few shillings out of his first week's earnings as a shoe-black. He had spent nothing on himself except what was necessary to buy food at a coffee stall; but he had seen a bit of cheap jewelry—a tawdry little necklace—that had cost him a shilling from a hawker's barrow. All the rest of his money he handed to his mother, for he had been well trained in the doctrine that he "owed everything" to his parents and that he should turn in every copper. That he had failed to do this, that he had outrageously held back enough to buy Haggie a trinket: it was this that infuriated the drunken father. Even so, the affair might not have gone beyond the customary clout across the head or kick in the backside if Tom, overproud of his new status, had not sharply answered the old man. "More money fer yer bloody booze. Well, you ain't gettin' it outer *me*—see? I'll go orf on me bloody own—see?"

That was what started it. It was then that Chadderton, infuriated by the first sign he had ever had that some day his absolute rule must end, snatched a glass vase from the mantelpiece and smashed it upon Tom's head. Tom was foolish enough to retaliate—all the hurt and puzzle of his young mind boiling up at this unforeseen consequence of what he considered a good deed. He was pulling off his boots, ready to go to bed, when the vase hit him, and instinctively he hurled the boot, which smacked Crackpot in the eye. Then the battle raged through the house, with Haggie joining in on Tom's side, and it reached its all too certain end with those two children smarting in Sally's room upstairs.

Neither of the children went home again. Haggie went to the Russells' house, to see once more if being "in service" could be endured, and Tom remained in Sally's back bedroom, slowly recovering from the mental shock and physical hurt. Warwick Russell advised that nothing should be said to the Chadderton parents. He considered them the worst pair in his parish. "If they find out where the children are, and start any trouble, I'll damn well have 'em up for assault and battery and make 'em smart," he promised. But the Chaddertons gave no trouble.

Perhaps they had had enough of the children, as the children had had enough of them. Anyway, a few days later, in the precipitate and unpredictable fashion of their sort, they did a moonlight flit, bilking their landlord of a few months' rent; so now there was no home for Tom and Haggie to return to, even had they wished to return.

It was about a week after this that Maggie Whale and I called on Sally to ask permission to spend a holiday at Tresant. We found Tom Chadderton recuperating in the kitchen, and it was Whaley, when we had heard his story, who said: "Wouldn't it be a good idea to take him with us and give him a good holiday?"

So there we were, pulling out of Paddington, with Tom Chadderton sitting on the seat between us.

8

I had worry enough of my own at the time. Richard, as I have said, was gone away to a coach, and I had it on my mind that things were not as well with the boy as they should be. Daniel had left for Scotland, and I wished him joy of his meeting with Mr. Balfour, without any personal enthusiasm for the idea that the better the meeting went off the greater was my chance that the course of Daniel's life would diverge from mine, for never was there a less politically-minded being than myself. And there was my preoccupation with the child I was to bear.

What with one thing and another, Tom Chadderton was left to Maggie, and I loafed about the place, sunning myself on the cliffs, taking an occasional timid bathe, and nostalgically visiting the spots associated with my mother and Lord Burnage, Sally and Eddy Rodda. It was disturbing to find myself already old and experienced enough for nostalgia.

I saw Tom at meals and was glad to notice the improvement in his appearance. We were away for a month, and before the time was up the sticking plaster was gone from his skull and nose, his hair had grown again, his bruises had turned to sun-browned skin, he was putting on weight and, perhaps for the first time in his life, he was not lousy. The fiction was kept up, lest Sally's position in Bermondsey be compromised, that this house belonged to a rich friend of Maggie's and that we were permitted to use it because he was abroad.

Tom's manners were as atrocious as one would expect, and a month was far too short a time for mending them. What seemed to excite him more than anything else was the abundance of moving life: the birds on the wing, the rabbits scuttling about the gorsy headlands, the restive curlews and the imperturbable slow-drifting swans. It was all too much for him, and Maggie found that he had assembled a new catapult. She discovered him down at the lakeside, loosing pebbles at the swans. There was an airgun in the house, and she taught him to use that, firing at a target; and this worked for a day or two. But it was the moving thing that fascinated him, and one day, without her knowing, he deserted the target and took the airgun down to the lakeside. He came back to the house carrying a dead seagull, enormously impressed by the possibilities of his weapon. After this, Maggie paid a Porteven fisherman to take Tom out in his boat, and this kept him occupied for much of what remained of the holiday. He was happier with the fishermen than with us, but he gave up going with them after one voyage that encountered enough wind to blow spray inboard. They told us that he had been terrified and very sick. We found that he was terrified, too, of the country dark, and slept with his window tight shut and the curtain drawn because of the noise of owls and curlews and herons.

I knew that Maggie was disappointed by what she had been able to do for him. "I should like to have him down here for a year," she said, "but I'm getting too old for that sort of thing."

When the holiday ended, it was with obvious relief that he accompanied us to the train. He looked very well, but his desire for London was unconcealed. When we got to Paddington there was the usual to-do with porters, which occupied us for a moment, and in that moment Tom Chadderton disappeared. We couldn't find him high or low, and we had to go home without him.

We learned later that he had turned up in Bermondsey that night and proudly presented Sally with the seagull, which, unknown to us, he had had stuffed by an amateur taxidermist at Porteven. The thing was standing on Sally's mantelpiece when next I called on her: the cruel yellow red-tipped beak, the cold arrogant inhuman eye, the heavenly grace of the plumage. This was all he had brought back from Tresant: something he had killed: but of himself, once he had handed Sally his gift and quickly gone, nothing at all was known.

CHAPTER EIGHTEEN

I

VERONICA was born at our house in Chelsea in December of 1885, and her existence gave me reason enough for not accompanying Daniel to Steignhampton when he fought his first parliamentary battle in the following summer. Steignhampton was a reasonably respectable seat now, but it had a bad history. It had been among

309

the rottenest of rotten boroughs, and in the eighteenth century the lord of the manor, finding opposition to his political views among his tenants, overcame this by the simple method of having the opposers' houses pulled down. Only those voters were left who were pledged to return whomsoever the lord of the manor desired. Steignhampton at that time returned two members—a useful contribution in any moment of parliamentary stress or uncertainty; and whatever else might be said of the corrruption of the times, at least Prime Ministers were not so corrupt that they forgot to pay their debts. Consequently, the two seats were worth £5,000 a year in sinecures to the lord of the manor and his son. Since then, a railway had gone through the district, a certain amount of heavy industry had developed, and the village had become a township that was still growing. Daniel did not win the seat, though Mr. Balfour went down to speak for him.

I remember some talk about this among the guests at a dinner party we gave: the first to which we invited the new sort of men with whom Daniel was associating. They couldn't understand why Daniel had had Balfour down there, or why in general he attached importance to Balfour's good will. One of them said Balfour had as much personality as an eel balancing on its tail, and all save Daniel agreed that he was a weakling with no hope of a political future.

"All the same," said Daniel, raising his glass with a smile, "here's to A. J. Balfour—the Prime Minister's nephew."

A babel of protest broke out at that, for the men in those circles ever protested the complete honesty of political life, the lack of nepotism or of any other vice. "You don't mean to say that Salisbury would allow such a consideration . . . ?"

The beaming smile did not leave Daniel's face. "No, no," he said. "Of course he wouldn't. But in time he will recognize what hasn't yet occurred to many people. But I'm sure of it."

"And what's that?"

"That A.J. is one of the most obstinate, wily and dependable politicians in the country. Don't be deceived by his appearance and his superficial manners. Let's discuss it again in five years' time and see who's right."

They passed over the subject with a shrugging of shoulders; and when Lord Salisbury formed his government, making Balfour Secretary for Scotland, they doubtless smiled, thinking that whatever might be the opinion of Daniel Undridge, Salisbury knew where his nephew belonged.

But a year later, when Michael Hicks Beach resigned, Balfour was made Secretary for Ireland, which even I knew was a very different matter; and a year after that, the death of the sitting member caused a by-election at Steignhampton, and Daniel entered Parliament.

310

I did not take Veronica down to Tresant till the summer of 1890. There was a party of us: myself and Veronica, whose name had transformed itself, in the way names do, to Nika; Richard, who was then twelve years old; Mervyn and Enid Mostyn-Lloyd with their little son Edward, who would be four years old that September; and Mrs. Aloysius Slinn. The absentees from this party, you will see, are Daniel and Colonel Slinn. The long summer holiday was not a restful time for Daniel. He liked to spend it in his constituency among people with votes, and at house parties among people with influence. He would have liked to arrange a party of that sort at Tresant, but being at Tresant in those days meant taking pot luck and doing a good deal of the work oneself. It wouldn't have done for his purpose. He thought it might be possible to slip down and join us toward the end of the holiday.

Colonel Slinn, I learned from Mervyn, had gone abroad with a friend of his named Bernard Cupples; and this was all I learned. Mervyn called upon me, really distressed, and asked if I had seen his mother lately, and, on my saying that I had, he wanted to know what I thought of her. I told him I thought she looked very ill.

I had not seen much of Lucy since her marriage, but, shortly before Mervyn's call on me, I had paid her a visit in Kensington. I went home deeply disturbed. It was as though I had gone to a gallery to see a beautiful picture that I had long known, and had found it cracked and soiled, deteriorated beyond measure. There was no longer any doubt that Lucy was older than I. She looked haggard, and, what was worse than her physical symptoms, she looked frightened. I didn't know what to do. When a woman has long been famous for her beauty you can't say: "My dear, how dreadful you look!" It was the suddenness of this disintegration that startled me, and the sense of something almost sinister. For, clearly, Lucy had not declined. She had, by whatever means, been overthrown.

And so this is the point at which I must look back through the years and show what it was that had overthrown Lucy Evans. We can begin with that moment at Enid's tea party when Colonel Slinn and I stood at the window watching the falling rain, and he talked to me about his childhood. There was some truth in the hints he had dropped. He was an only child, the son of a blacksmith in an English village. The smith loathed the slip of a stag-eyed boy who was all he ever begot, and the boy loathed him, and feared him, and nestled to his mother like a chick under a hen's wing. He lived an unhappy life, and grew up with a great distrust of men, a tendency to seek out the maternal comfort of women.

He was eighteen, working in the village grocer's shop, when his mother died. Nearly all the customers were women and he was not ill content. His father had died the year before from the kick of a horse that had been brought to the smithy for shoeing; and the year following that was the happiest he was ever to know, gossiping with the old women in the daytime, staying in the cottage with his mother in the evening. He might have gone on forever, after his mother's death, enjoying the daily chatter of the shop and the evening solitude of the cottage, which he kept as neat as it had ever been, if a forward young woman had not knocked him off his perch. He liked the old women who would bring him a few eggs, or a basket of vegetables, or offer to darn his socks; but this young one, though she was but recently married, left him in no doubt that a woman could want other men than her husband. Such an idea had never occurred to him, and this girl's bold eyes frightened him out of his wits. Knowing this, it became her pleasure to torment him with what seemed to be accidental touching of hands and brushing of thighs. He dealt with his problem by forthright flight. He vanished; no one in the village knew whither.

In the next glimpse we have of him he is driving a trap along the country roads in another county. He had found lodgings in the county town and employment with a high-class firm of provision merchants. They supplied the village shops far and wide, and there is Allan Semple, who was to become our Colonel Slinn, as happy as a lark, clicking to his horse, driving between the flowery hedges, picking up orders for his firm.

He was sent one day with a message to the office of Mr. Bernard Cupples, a young solicitor recently arrived in the village—a dark stoutish young man with sleasy eyes, superbly dressed.

It is unlikely that Allan Semple ever forgot that summer morning when he saw Mr. Bernard Cupples for the first time, standing in his office in a slant of sunshine, one hand jingling coins in his pocket, the other playing with the seals dangling from the thick golden watch chain that passed across his already rotund stomach like a rope fender round a boat's bows. The sun gleams would catch the high polish of the shoes upon his tiny feet and the pomade upon his slicked black hair.

Mr. Cupples could not resist trying to find the ins and outs of everybody's business, though he never dashed at people: he nibbled cautiously round and round, always on the alert to dart back into the depths of his pool; but he had a friendly chat that morning with Allan, who went away feeling that here at last was a man one need not fear.

The secret dream of Allan Semple, as of many a man, was to be what he was not. He would have loved to be a self-confident man of the world, one who traveled to foreign parts, mixed in cosmopolitan society, was brusque with men and irresistible with women. Maps of foreign lands, plans of foreign cities, fascinated him; and he spent all his spare time globe-trotting between the covers of books. He knew his way about London, though he had never been there, and once set Cupples right about the topography of Paris. Driving the trap through the blue-gold autumn weather, he transformed it now into a gondola, now a caïque, now a palanquin, and was happily dreaming in Venice, on the Golden Horn, or amid the splendid squalor of ruined cities of the East.

"You know," said Cupples, "you ought to go abroad for your holiday next year. Come with me to France."

Allan looked at him breathless. France! With Mr. Cupples.

"I've got no money," he said.

"Money! You'll never have money the way you're going on. Anybody who wants money can have it. And then he can have what money can buy. You don't want to spend your life looking at pictures in books. Why not the real thing?"

He sat down and twiddled the seals on his watch chain and said: "Let's have a game of cards."

Allan discovered that more things could be done with cards than he had suspected when playing simple games with his mother on winter evenings.

"See what I mean?" said Cupples. "Suppose we'd been playing for money. Where would you have been?"

"Broke," said Allan ruefully.

"Exactly." Cupples allowed the pack to fall in a graceful concertina from hand to hand.

They went to France the next summer. Allan had learned a lot about cards in the meantime. He would have been a dangerous opponent for most people, but Cupples still considered him a greenhorn. It was a long journey to London, and Allan played the part of the innocent traveler who diffidently tries his luck and is surprised to find himself a winner, thereupon retiring from the game. He began his first fatal reflections on the accessibility of easy money.

When they reached their hotel, Cupples said: "Now look, Allan. That was just to show you. If you thought I was going to pay for your holiday, you were mistaken. What I want you to understand is that other people can be made to pay for anything you want." He handed him the winnings, which were considerable.

"Why are you doing this for me, Mr. Cupples?"

"For you, Allan? Who said I am doing it for you? Have you ever heard of a missionary, Allan? A missionary is not much interested in his converts, you know. He simply finds a deep joy in making others like himself. It helps to dispel his loneliness."

"I don't understand you."

313

"Well, well. I should hate to be understood as easily as all that. You must give yourself time, Allan. After all, I'm ten years older than you. Perhaps we shall understand one another better in ten years' time."

3

In ten years' time Bernard Cupples had served his five years for the misappropriation of clients' money, and a good deal had happened to Allan Semple. On returning from Paris he had given up his job at the grocers' and worked for Cupples in various secret ways. Always, flush or broke, he was dependent upon, fascinated by, his elder, cutting such a dash as a well-known professional man, but living behind this mask a life that seemed to Allan, whose early scruples were soon overcome, so romantically and successfully lawless. It tickled him to think of the louts in his native village who had made his life a burden. If they could see him now! He had found a man—such a man!—who treated him as an equal.

That was his fond belief till one summer day when he and Cupples were making holiday in the South of France. A few of Cupples's cronies were in the town, and Allan, coming back to the hotel where he and Cupples shared a sitting room, paused outside the door, hearing voices within.

"Have you got Simple Semple with you this time?"

"You bet. We're still hand in glove."

"I know. You're the hand and he's the glove that hides it. Most useful. I wish I had someone like him."

"You can have him if you like. I'm getting rather tired of him."

Allan did not enter the room. He walked away and avoided Cupples till the evening. Each was in a bad mood when they met again: Allan because his pitiable self-respect had been destroyed; Cupples because he had received news, though Allan did not know this, that a stock exchange gamble, which he had counted on to double his fortune, had left him for the moment almost penniless. Neither referred to what was in his mind; but each was so on edge that they quarreled bitterly; and Allan did what he had done when the girl frightened him in his native village: saying nothing, he fled. Running away—from the hooting boys, from the ardent girl, from the picture of himself which he now perceived—was ever his only recourse.

4

When he ran away from Cupples, or from the knowledge of his own insignificance that Cupples had made him perceive, Allan was a

314

distraught and empty creature, badly in need of comfort. He would have liked to be a boy again, with his father dead, and his mother knitting by the fire as he sat under the lamp reading about Rio or Famagusta. He found that, without a directing mind, he was not much good even as a criminal or in those shady activities where crime and legality are divided by a gray hair. He found honest work from time to time, and considered this the measure of his failure. Always he longed for a strong man whom he could respect or a woman in whose company he could relax like a child with its mother.

It is not surprising that in his loneliness and depression he married. The surprise is that he found the courage to do it. Probably Maud Skirrow left him no option. He lodged at her mother's house, in a region half suburb, already half slum. When he went there, he didn't know of Maud's existence. The widow seemed a comfortable body. She never asked questions about his comings and goings, his occasional disappearances. She even addressed him as "Sir," and that confirmed his vanity in his appearance and in his manner of speech. "I can see you've known better days, sir," she said once; and Allan began at once to tell her of his better days. It was now that he discovered his gift for romancing. Many a cozy evening he spent at Mrs. Skirrow's fireside, giving her the convincing mixture of fact and fancy of which he was to become a master. He had by now seen many places and from his reading and his looking at pictures he was able to imagine many more. Mrs. Skirrow was enchanted. She began to darn his socks and iron his shirts.

One day she told him that "our Maud" was coming home, and that was the first he heard of her. Our Maud was working in a big provincial draper's shop, where the girls lived in, and you wouldn't believe, sir, the life it was: slaving till nine every night except Saturday, and on that day till eleven; and their doings watched, and fines imposed for every little slip; and as for the food! "Well, sir, if I knew our Maud could get something like *that* into her at breakfasttime, I'd sleep happier in my bed." Mrs. Skirrow put the bacon and kidneys down on the table, and their fragrance mingled with the fragrance of coffee. There was crisp bread, and the snap of early frost made a man all alive; but nevertheless Allan Semple felt his heart quake. Always—always, he thought—some damned girl comes and spoils it.

Mrs. Skirrow chattered on, stirring in his heart the old urge to fly to safety. "A bit of home. That's what she wants. She's a home girl, and so I've always told her. She didn't never oughter've stood it so long. It's not as though I haven't got a bit put aside, and as if there wasn't plenty here for her to do. The things girls have to put up with! You'd never believe, Mr. Semple. I'd give him Mr. Mathieson, if it had been me! 'You may be a shopwalker, Mr. Mathieson, but I'm not a streetwalker, and that's flat!' That's what I'd have said."

315

5

Allan made up his mind. He told Mrs. Skirrow that evening that he had to go to Brussels for his legendary firm. There was a mess that had to be cleared up at once. He would leave the next day, and he couldn't say when he'd be back. He packed a bag with the intention of finding new lodgings. After a time he would write to Mrs. Skirrow, inventing some excuse—"must live nearer the job" would do—and asking her to send on his things.

They parted in the morning with genuine regret. "Well," said Mrs. Skirrow, "when you *do* get back our Maud'll be here. She's due in a few days."

To her great surprise, he bent down suddenly and kissed her. Then he hurried to the gate where a hansom cab was waiting. She watched him go with pride. It wasn't often you saw a cab in *that* street, she thought, unless for a wedding or a funeral.

Semple decided to call on one of his shady friends and beg hospitality till he could find new lodgings. The friend had a job on hand that night, and Semple was easily persuaded to join the enterprise. It was at about ten o'clock, with a head reeling from the blow of a policeman's truncheon, that he found himself dodging through the back alleys of Soho, blotting himself into dark doorways, sneaking in spurts and dashes gradually to what he hoped was safety. By the time he reached a main thoroughfare he had shaken off pursuit. His head was aching terribly. He felt that he was going to drop and that he had better be in a bed. His own bed and comfortable Mrs. Skirrow rose powerfully upon his imagination. He could almost feel her tucking the sheets round him, and decided to go back at once.

Maud Skirrow opened the door. "Why, Mr. Semple!" she cried, knowing at once who this must be; and as he lurched past her and supported himself with one hand on the passage wall, she giggled. He sat down heavily on a chair. Maud shut and bolted the door. "Oo!" she said, "you haven't half been going it!"

He tried to rise, and all the cymbals in his head gave a great clash. He sank down again and said with dignity: "I am sober. Call your mother."

"You better get to bed," she said. "Come on. Give us your arm."

He was too far gone to resist, or to explain or to ask for explanations. She had to put an arm right round him and boost him up the stairs. She allowed him to flop onto his bed, heaved his feet up, and threw a rug over him.

She took him no breakfast in the morning, nothing but strong coffee. She ran up the blind, but the access of light did not wake him. He lay

316

where he had fallen, and looked as if he might be dead rather than sleeping. She began to be puzzled. She would have expected him to be sick, but he had not been, and there was no smell of drink about him. Then she noticed the bruise, high up on his forehead, almost hidden by hair. She decided not to wake him. She pulled down the blind and tiptoed out of the darkened room. Perhaps Ma was right. Ma said he was a proper gent and that he never touched a drop.

She was preparing her own midday meal in the kitchen when she heard a scuffling of feet, and there was Semple, holding himself up with a hand on either side of the doorway. "I apologize for being a nuisance last night," he said in a precise voice. "Where is Mrs. Skirrow?"

"Look, Mr. Semple," she said, "never mind Ma for the moment. I'll explain all that by and by. I'm Maud. Now take my advice. Get back to your room and get your clothes off and get into bed proper. You look as if you need a lot of rest."

He turned and went away without a word. She heard him climbing the stairs. An hour later, when she had finished her own meal, she took up a bowl of soup and some dry toast. He had followed her advice and was between the sheets, but awake. She raised him up, put pillows behind his back, and rested the tray on his knees. He ate hungrily. Then she brought water, sponged his hands and face, comforted the bruise by pressing the hot sponge gently upon it again and again, and said: "You ought to feel the better for that. Now try to go to sleep again. I'll nip up to have another look at you this evening."

She pulled down the blind, and the quiet dusk was comforting. The bed was warm, his stomach was glad of the soup, and the hot water had soothed his head. He fell asleep, thinking with wonder that a young woman could bring peace like a mother.

When Semple woke again, the short autumn dusk had faded. The blind was down, and now the red curtains were pulled across in front of it, and, what he had never seen in that room before, a fire was burning in the grate. Maud was sitting in an easy chair at the fireside. A lamp burned on the table. She was knitting, and the lamplight fell on the profile of her face.

Drowsy and comfortable, filled with a sense of well-being and deliverance, and, above all, of being looked after, Semple lay still, considering Maud. Presently, her busy fingers ceased their work and fell into her lap. Her eyes closed. There was something inexpressibly touching to Semple in the sight of the girl fallen asleep over her work. She had worn herself out, he thought, thinking of him, tending him.

A coal fell into the ash pan, and Maud opened her eyes. She came to the bed and stood looking down at him. She placed her hand on his forehead, and he liked the feel of it there. "You've had a lovely long sleep," she said. "I think you look better. You feel cool."

317

She went away and came back with a simple meal.

"It's funny the way this happened," she said. "Ma didn't expect me for a few days. I was working out my notice, and they was horrid to me. You know: just because I was going, which was sort of telling 'em I could get on without 'em, thank you very much, they started taking it out of me, picking on everything I did. So I says to myself 'Notice my foot!' and I packs up and clears out without a word to anybody. I caught a night train, and was Ma surprised! I must've arrived just after you'd gone, sort of. Well, you can guess the fine old palaver there was, and as if that wasn't enough excitement for one day, in the midst of it all comes a telegram for Ma: 'Minnie not expected to live. Come at once.' So there we was, and what with packing for Ma and getting her a cab and one thing and another—laugh! 'It's a good thing Mr. Semple's out of the way, any road,' says Ma. 'You'll have to look after things. I don't expect him back for a week an' I'll be back meself by then, choose 'ow.' And off she goes to Hunslet. And then that night, in comes you! Laugh!"

She put some coals on to the fire, and for a moment was silent. A footstep went by in the street, then the quiet came back and he could hear the small friendly purr of the burning lamp. The fire, the quietness, the lamp, a woman knitting: these seemed to him the very essence of the happiest times he had known.

"I'm afraid there'll be trouble when I get back to the office," he said. "I ought to be in Brussels now, straightening things out."

"There'll be no office for you for a few days, my lad," she said firmly. "Let 'em do what they like. We're all too anxious about what our bosses think. A man like you could get a good job anywhere. What happened?"

He had made up his tale by now. "Well, when everyone else was gone, I stayed in the office with Jenkinson, so as to go thoroughly into this rotten mess-up. There was a lot to be sorted out if I was to have the thing at my finger ends, and we made the mistake of going out to have a bit of supper. We ought to have stuck to what we were doing. When we got back, it meant rushing things, and then I found that if I was to catch my train I'd have to make a dash. And dash I did, believe me! Fortunately, Jenkinson came to the station with me. The train was starting, and I think I could have caught it if a fool of a porter hadn't tried to hold me back. I struggled with him and got loose, and even then I think I could have done it if he hadn't made another grab at me. Then I fell, and that finished it. I got this smack on the head on the edge of a porter's barrow. When I came round I was in a waiting room. They wanted to take me to hospital, but I wouldn't go. I said I'd find my way home. I told Jenkinson to keep my bag, because all the papers were in it. I can get it back with my own stuff any time."

He paused, not displeased with the story, then added: "I'm sorry it turned out like that. I wanted to go. I love foreign lands. . . ." And he was soon off on his blend of fact and fancy. She found it entrancing. For the first time, the scope of his journeys widened to embrace Turkey and Persia. "Ispahan! Now there's a place! The rose gardens in the moonlight of a Persian night!"

"I never seen the sea, except at Margate," said Maud. "I could've. Mr. Mathieson would have took me anywhere. He wanted to take me to Bridlington. And 'im a Sunday-school teacher with a wife and four boys! What I told him!"

She sponged his hands and face, and he slept like a log. In the morning he got up and shaved, and surprised in himself a wish that this would make him seem more attractive to Maud. There were two letters on the breakfast table: one for Maud from her mother, saying briefly: "Your Aunt Min was a goner when I got there. Funeral to-morrow. Returning next day. Mum. P.S. She left you five hundred pounds, which isn't as much as I expected, but lately she went religious, and a lot went on altar cloths and things like that. Mum."

The other letter was for Semple. It was from a man to whom he owed money, and it began: "Dear Sir—Unless . . ."

Semple read the letter with a gloomy face, got up, and walked to the fireplace. He threw letter and envelope on to the flames and watched them disappear. Then he sat down again at the table and said: "Well, that, I fear, is that."

"Not bad news, I hope, Mr. Semple?"

"Not bad and not good. As you said last night. I should have no difficulty in finding another post."

"You don't mean they've had the nerve to sack you?"

He nodded. He had come to a startling resolution. He was going to be a Good Man. He was going to Go Straight. If his past was to be wiped out, he must wipe out his mythical employers.

6

"I don't see why you shouldn't stay where you are," Mrs. Skirrow said. "What's the sense of wasting money when you've got a good home here?"

Maud didn't like the idea: she wanted a place of her own: but Semple was attracted by the notion of having two women to look after him instead of one. He sided with Mrs. Skirrow: he would always side with Mrs. Skirrow. There was some justice in Maud's outburst, only a month after the marriage: "I'm getting sick of it—you two sitting there like Darby and Joan an' me waiting on the pair of you like a skivvy."

No doubt, he would not have married her at all if he had not married her at once. He was in a warm glow of satisfaction. He had had a narrow shave, and, running from it, he had found himself in a haven more desirable than any he had expected to know again. The glow would pass, but Mrs. Skirrow and Maud kept it warm long enough for the marriage to take place first.

Semple found a job of sorts. He didn't tell them much about it, and excused his miserable pay on the ground that it would lead to important things. "I didn't jump at the first offer. I could have had twice what I'm getting now, and I'd have gone on getting twice, and no more than twice. What I wanted was a job with opportunity, and believe me I've got that. If I can put in a little money, there may be a partnership in it."

He never took Maud out. Once home, he liked to stay there, and Mrs. Skirrow took his part when Maud grumbled. "Allan's a home boy, and you should be thankful for that, my girl. You'll find plenty of gallivanters, but you'll go a long way before finding a man who knows that home is home."

And so life simmered along through the winter, placidly enough save for an occasional flash; and it was not till the turn of the year that disaster broke. Allan came home through a raw aguish evening to find Maud out and Mrs. Skirrow in high good temper. He was hardly in the house before her arms were round him and she cried: "Well—father!"

It took some time for this to sink into Allan's mind; and when at last he saw what she meant he started back and almost involuntarily exclaimed: "But—I can't!"

She laughed at him fatuously. "You may think you can't. But believe me, you've done it!"

He recoiled from her aghast, and shouted: "I can't, I tell you. Maud knows that as well as I do." He ran up to his bedroom and locked the door and wept.

7

A month of misery followed, a month in which Allan thought of nothing but escape, and Maud endured in sullen silence all that her outraged mother could pour upon her. In the bedroom one night the proud defiance that she had maintained to Allan broke down. She was abject, and that made him fear and hate her. She confessed that Mr. Mathieson had had her; "but honest, Allan, I never knew it was this. Honest. It was a bit of fun, sort of." He felt sick.

"Your mother's treating you something shameful," he said. "You're not the first girl to make a mistake, and you won't be the last."

She clung to him, weeping with joy at his clemency. She snuggled her nose into his shoulder and murmured: "Take me away from her, Allan."

"I want to," he said. "I'm *going* to. I'm trying to think of the best way."

They ought to have a house of their own, he said. "I don't mean a place like this—not a rented place. We ought to *buy* a house. Why should we pour money every week into a landlord's pocket? Let's start all over again, and start proper."

She stopped sniveling and listened. "You'll have to put that five hundred into my name at the bank. It won't disappear, believe me. It'll be there in solid property. I reckon three hundred'll get us a neat little place, and another hundred'll go a long way toward furnishing it. That leaves a hundred. Now if you don't like what I'm going to say, tell me so. But we've got to think of the future. I think that hundred pounds'll make all the difference to my prospects at the office. I'm not saying it's going to shoot me up into the millionaire class in a month, or a year. But a man with capital in a business is in a different position from a mere employee. But if you don't like the sound of it, say so."

Maud loved the sound of it. "Mind you," said Allan, "not a word to your mother."

She began to blub again. "You're so wise," she said.

"Well, someone's got to do the thinking for both of us."

"For all three of us," she ventured to say.

"All right, then. For all three of us. Now go to sleep."

He kissed her, concealing his loathing, and she slept happier than she had done for a long time. Semple lay awake thinking of boat trains and continental journeys. A week later he landed in France with five hundred pounds in his pocket.

8

A long time passed during which Semple is a dim figure. The one thing clear is that he spent much of it abroad. He had some talent with languages and had not wasted the opportunities furnished by his journeys with Cupples. He found work as a travel agency courier, and for aught I know he may have been in Constantinople and the other places he spoke of. He was out of work and living in London precariously on his wits when he and Cupples met again. The encounter took place on top of an omnibus in Oxford Street. When Semple climbed up and took his place, there was but one other passenger. He sat behind him, and could not resist the allurement of the tail of a frock coat spread defenselessly in his direction. He abstracted a wallet, and Cupples then turned round and, speaking quietly so that the driver could not hear, and speaking, too, with a laughing reproach, said: "Allan, Allan! You must do better than that! Will you never learn?"

It was clear at once to Semple that Cupples had watched him board the bus and had laid this simple trap. He had always feared Cupples as much as he admired him. Cupples was the last person he wanted to see again, for he knew that, if he were once drawn into the man's orbit, he would not have the strength to swing clear. Useless now to think of protesting that he was living an honest life: he had delivered himself.

Cupples held out his hand, and Semple sheepishly gave him the wallet. Cupples weighed it for a moment in one hand, thoughtfully slapping with it the other; then he took some papers from it and put them into his pocket and handed the wallet back to Semple, who saw that some folded bank notes were left inside. "It's a nice wallet, Allan," he said. "I'd like you to have it. You'll find my card inside. I shall expect you at six o'clock." He went down the bus steps without another word, leaving Semple cold with fear.

He wanted to wrap up wallet, notes and all, and post them to the address on the card; and at six o'clock he was climbing the stairs to Cupples's flat in Jermyn Street.

"Ah, my dear Allan! Despite your many failings, you understand the value of punctuality. Always bear that in mind. Never keep me waiting. Come in. Come in."

Allan had often in all those years thought of Cupples, and he had always thought of broad arrows and a cowed and cringing person with whom, should they ever have the bad luck to meet again, he would have no difficulty in keeping the upper hand. But this was the old Cupples, well-dressed, with cared-for hands, with all the remembered suavity, and with something formidable added: the craft and wariness of the egoist who has once been knocked down flat, and is now on his feet again, with some dangerous lessons learned.

It was a winter night. The fire was burning and the curtains were drawn, and Allan was put into a comfortable chair with cigarettes at his elbow. Not an intrusive sound came from anywhere. Allan had an uneasy sense that the place was padded. But what call was there for uneasiness? Cupples, an old friend who had helped him out of a rut, was joviality itself. "Well, Allan, you've improved, you know. You've improved out of all recognition. You need a little attention, but the general outline's fine. I think I could put things in your way. We could make something of you. Now, what have you been up to? How have you been treating the world?"

Allan had learned to drink. Cupples replenished his guest's whiskey, and his own. The fire purred. Allan began to feel happier than he had been for a long time. His tongue rattled through the years. He told everything, except the story of his marriage.

"Well, Allan, that's quite a saga. I think something could be made of it. Now look at me, my dear boy. No false modesty now. How do you think I keep my head above water, eh? How do I get all this?"—

waving his cigar to embrace the curtains, the carpets, the fire, the decanter. "Well, I'm not a very active person nowadays. I keep in the background. You are a man of intelligence. You see the necessity of that. But my—er—sojourn *elsewhere* made me acquainted with many people with many aptitudes. Now, my—er—shall we say my *specialty*, is in recognizing aptitudes, seeing how they can best be employed, and indeed arranging occasions for their employment. Now you, Allan. You have an attractive appearance. You have had the advantage of travel. We must let our minds play round that idea. Something may come of it. At the moment I just throw it out as a proposition . . . Eeles!"

Allan had imagined that they were alone in the flat, but now the door opened, and a man in the formal clothes of a gentleman's gentleman came in. It was these formal clothes that, more than anything else, made him sinister to Allan, for never did clothes and the man they contained seem more at variance. Eeles was short and thick. His hands were immense and they were folded into fists, from which Allan's imagination the more hastily revolted because the fists were like those of his father, the village blacksmith, that had at times pounded him black and blue. Eeles seemed to be all gathered into powerful muscular knots. His forehead was low, the bridge of his nose was smashed, and at the bottom of his face his chin stuck forward to balance the recession at the top.

"Eeles," said Cupples. "Colonel Slinn and I are ready."

The man went, and Cupples said: "You'd better start with a clean sheet, Allan. I think Colonel Slinn will do, don't you?"

A moment later Eeles wheeled in a delicious supper.

9

Cupples was patient with his new creation, Colonel Slinn. He provided him with enough money to clothe himself well and to be beyond the reach of any pressing anxiety, but not with enough to play the fool. He gave him orders—they were gentle, unobtrusive, but unquestionable—about his conduct. "You know, Slinn, you're not really a criminal type. You must have seen now for yourself that along those lines you'd get nowhere. You've been in a good deal of danger, you know. You could easily have fallen into the hands of some bungler who would have used you wrongly, and where would you have been then, eh? You're a weak character. I'm afraid if you'd never met me you'd have gone on like the dull millions who take what life sends them. Now turn this over in your mind. You must not commit any act outside the law. If you are to be of use to me it must be as a law-abiding citizen. Your weakness can be turned into strength as charm. You must get to know people. I mean, inside their own homes. You talk well. You've been about. A lot of people would like you. Let me know what you find out about them: anything—their characters, their history, their homes. Just leave anything else to me. You'd be surprised what an odd hint may lead to. When we were at luncheon today, I could have pointed out to you a man who at this moment has five thousand in his pocket because, when he was staying with the McCartnys, he put two and two together and rightly concluded that a certain person was Mrs. McCartny's lover."

To Slinn it seemed too good to be true. He had nothing to do but be charming and law-abiding. He was anxious to please Bernard Cupples, and glowed like a praised child when Cupples approved his idea. It was lawful to write to an author expressing pleasure in his work, or in hers, and asking to be allowed the honor of making a little call. "Of course, I'd choose well-to-do or well-connected people. How do you like it?"

Cupples did not overpraise, but he liked it well enough and took Slinn out to dinner and gave him the money to add evening clothes to his wardrobe.

Slinn who, as a tourist courier, had learned something about pictures, was able to give Cupples the tip about a house that contained a few worth picking up, and about a lady novelist's mania for putting all her savings into good jewelry. There were dry patches that made him despondent. "Don't worry, Ally. Just keep moving along. The big thing will come some day."

Slinn's mind was uninventive, and the "big thing" to him, after having heard Cupples's story of blackmail, was always some hint which might lead to a similar opportunity. So much of his work was shooting in the dark without result, and none of it seemed more unprofitable than the intrusion into the Gotherson household. He went there simply as a step to Lord Avonmere, who had almost thrown him out. Lord Avonmere was far more interested in the winner of the 2:30 at Sandown Park next Wednesday than in Persian rose gardens.

And then, quite suddenly, the Gotherson try-out turned into the "big thing" that Cupples was always looking for. Slinn disobeyed orders. He stole a few pounds, and so Mervyn Mostyn-Lloyd swam into the picture. Soon after him appeared Lucy Evans. The thing was then big enough for Cupples to provide Slinn with plentiful money and to go into a hotel so that Slinn might occupy the flat.

In the flat Slinn had time to think, and he thought of Maud Skirrow, who was Maud Semple. Whether she was alive or dead he did not know. It was a long time ago: getting on for ten years. The thought that she might be alive made his heart quake. Once more the temptation to run assailed him. Having concealed his marriage from Cupples, he now dared not tell of it. He simply said that the plan to marry Lucy

324

Evans seemed to him beyond reason. "Surely," he hedged weakly, "we can get the money some other way?"

Cupples had called late at the flat. He sat with one plump leg rocking over the other, his plump hand clasped round a whiskey glass. He was in his most benign mood. He sipped his drink, and asked reasonably: "You're not weakening? Surely you're not weakening, dear boy?"

"I don't like it."

"My dear chap, who's asking you to like it? Eeles!"

Eeles slid his knotty bulk round the door.

"Oh, Eeles, I just want to be certain about the fit of those things. Slip them on and come back here."

Eeles was quickly back, and held out his sledge-hammer right fist for inspection. The fingers were furnished with murderous-looking knuckle-dusters. Cupples took the hand and held it in his doughy paw which glittered with rings of a different order. "Yes," he approved. "I think they'll do."

Eeles, withdrawing a pace, did a few sharp dancing steps, ending with a vicious uppercut into the air.

"How d'you like them, Ally?" Cupples asked. "D'you think they're all right?"

Slinn answered with a dry throat: "I don't know anything about such things."

"Well, then," said Cupples, "you are more fortunate than those who do. All right, Eeles, thank you."

Cupples sipped again at his whiskey and then drew a wallet from his pocket. He took some papers from it. "Ally," he said, "I want you to be more prudent in future. I never could understand why you insisted on *writing* reports to me about houses that might repay attention. You've even signed them. Simple word of mouth is all you need. What is the point in accumulating evidence against yourself in this way? Supposing these things fell into the wrong hands?" He folded the papers into his wallet, which he replaced in his pocket. "Well, now. I must be off. It's getting late. I shall be glad when you're married, my dear chap. I dislike hotel life very much."

10

Cupples was a patient man. During the prolonged honeymoon of Colonel and Mrs. Slinn he did no more than remind Ally of his existence by sending him a letter or two every month. He did not like the answers: they seemed to him rather the contented cooing of a dove than anything else, and there were times when he chuckled to think that Slinn might now consider himself in a position to snap his fingers.

He lost no time in calling on the pair upon their return. They were in excellent health. Slinn, Cupples thought, had never looked better. After dinner they sat over their coffee in the drawing room. You couldn't imagine, Cupples reflected, a more peaceful and unthreatening moment. Danger, to those two, must have seemed impossible. It was rather a chilly autumn night and the fire was burning. He was given a cigar to smoke, good brandy to drink. There was free-and-easy talk of the places they had been to; and Cupples said: "I hope, Slinn, you had some luck in the casinos?"

"Oh, no!" Lucy answered. "We went now and then for fun. I wanted to see what such places were like, because I hadn't done much traveling before. We risked a few guineas now and then, but soon stopped even that."

"That is wise of you, ma'am," Cupples said. "I wish I were in Slinn's position, with a prudent woman to look after me."

He drew on his cigar, and said: "I find the little place in Jermyn Street most convenient, Slinn. Did you know, ma'am, that I took it over after Colonel Slinn left it?" He added with a smile: "I found nothing compromising."

"I should think not!" said Lucy primly.

"Well, of course, with Colonel Slinn, one wouldn't expect anything of that sort. But really, ma'am, most humans are far from impeccable, and sometimes criminally careless. I myself have a failing that you will no doubt think contemptible. I can't resist nosing into other people's business. You see—I'm frank."

"Oh, well," Lucy conceded agreeably, "curiosity comes naturally enough to most of us."

"There was a case not long ago," said Cupples. "I was living in another flat then, and I lent it to a young friend named Semple— Allan Semple. Did you ever come across Semple, Slinn?"

Slinn had got up to replenish the coffee cups. His head was bowed over the table, and he stood there for a moment, his face concealed, and presently said: "Semple? No."

"Oh, well, that doesn't matter. This man and I both had keys to the flat. I was living in a hotel, but I used to look in now and then. One day I came when he was out, and d'you know, ma'am, I *could not* resist rummaging through the papers he had in a dispatch case. Among them I found a marriage certificate. Nothing remarkable in that, except that Semple passed as a single man! And there he was—married to a girl with the extraordinary name of Skirrow—Maud Skirrow."

"Really, Mr. Cupples," Lucy said with mock seriousness, "you shouldn't give away your wickedness. You're positively chuckling over the poor man's folly."

"Folly? You're right, ma'am: that's the word. Of course, this Maud

Skirrow may have been dead. There are plenty of ifs in such a case. But supposing she were still alive—what criminal carelessness not to have burned the marriage lines! Keeping them like that—for ten years it was! What a situation for a novelist, ma'am!"

"Well, let's forget your wickedness," cried Lucy gaily, "and turn it into a game. You have given us the situation to date. Now let's see what we would make of it if we *were* novelists. You first, Mr. Cupples."

Cupples sipped his brandy, considered the glowing end of his cigar. "I'm not much good at this, I'm afraid, ma'am. I'm happier with facts than fancies. But let's see now. What about this? Cupples—forget I'm Cupples. Cupples is just the villain in the story at the moment— Cupples says: 'Oh ho, Allan Semple! Married, eh? I wonder if that girl's still alive?' Being a man of devouring curiosity, he can't rest till he has the answer. The marriage certificate tells him the church where the marriage took place. He wanders down there and finds it rather a depressing slummy sort of region. He makes discreet inquiries of the shopkeepers and so on, and finds that Mr. Semple had deserted Maud, who had a child. The child died, and Maud remained in the district, spending a cat-and-dog life with her mother, earning her living by working in small shops and so forth. Cupples finds that she has become an unpleasant sort of person, and that's not to be wondered at, con- sidering her desertion and the years spent with a resentful mother. However, all things end in time, and the resentful mother dies. Then Maud vanishes. . . . Am I boring you?"

"Oh, no, Mr. Cupples. I'm afraid I shan't make up half as good a tale."

"Well, let's see now. We've got to keep in touch with Maud some- how. How will this do? The daughter of one of the local tradesmen has been her friend. She still writes occasionally to this girl, and from her Cupples is able to obtain Maud's address. For, remember," he said, grinning into Lucy's face, "Cupples is a double-dyed villain, capable of anything. Let's go the whole hog and say he's an old convict who has known the inside of Dartmoor."

"Oh, come," Lucy protested. "Keep your tale within reason or Ally and I may as well give up."

"No, no, ma'am! Now you've set me off, you must allow me every license. Cupples, I insist, is capable of anything. And what does he find now? Allan Semple is as great a villain as he is himself, for he proposes to commit bigamy."

"Desertion—bigamy— Why, sir, there'll be murder in the tale next!"

"Who knows?" said Cupples placidly. "Semple marries bigamously a rich girl, and this, of course, is Cupples's great opportunity. He knows that Semple is in the hollow of his hand. Isn't that how we novelists put it? Yes—in the hollow of his hand. It has become as simple as this.

327

Cupples can produce Maud Skirrow if Semple doesn't produce his wife's money."

"You have certainly put the poor fellow in a desperate position. What if he refuses?"

"Well, he has, of course, changed his name. He is not now known as Allan Semple. But day after day letters reach him addressed to Allan Semple. His wife is first amused, then inquisitive, then—well, what would she become then? It would be so odd. Imagine it—day after day —Allan Semple, Allan Semple, Allan Semple. It would become like a toothache that would soon tear you to pieces. What would *you* do if it chanced that Ally here began to receive letters addressed to Allan Semple? But I'm afraid, after my tale, *even one* would make you jump."

"Well, continue, sir. How does it go now?"

Cupples smiled. "It's a serial. To be continued in our next. How would *you* have told the story, ma'am?"

"I'm afraid, Mr. Cupples, your version has become so vivid that there's no going back to the beginning. It will have to develop now from the point you have brought it to. How would you go on with it, Ally?"

She turned to her husband, whose chair was behind hers, and became aware of what Cupples had for some time perceived. Slinn looked like a dead man. She ran to him at once. "Ally! What is it? You are trembling."

"It's the change of climate. I'd got too used to the sunshine. I only hope it's not my malaria coming back."

The amusing game was forgotten. Cupples remained for a few moments, admiring her pretty concern and the way in which wealth could ring bells and call up servants to scurry around like jinn, warming beds, lighting fires, bringing hot drinks. The master was indisposed! And so the house was in a sort of orderly turmoil, everything at Lucy's command being done quickly and efficiently for the master's well-being. Cupples made his condolences and excuses and took himself off. He must have been not displeased. He had satisfied himself that a touch of the spur could make the nag wince.

11

Slinn remained in bed, shaken by the revelation of Cupples's implacable intention. On the evening of the day after Cupples had told his story Lucy was in the drawing room alone when her butler brought her two letters. "Do you know a Mr. Allan Semple, madam?" he asked. "Or is this a mistake?"

328

Lucy's heart shook. She managed to say: "Leave it. I'll ask Colonel Slinn about it."

When she was alone, she sat with the letter in her hand, and her hand trembled. After a long time she tore open the envelope. It contained a folded sheet of notepaper, blank. Somehow, that was more terrifying than the most villainous letter would have been. It screamed at her that there was no need for words. She dropped the page and the envelope into the fire, and as the flame turned to a red crust, and the red crackled to gray, her heart with it burned into a moment of passionate resentment at what had happened to her and then died into desolation.

But she had to be sure. Or rather she had to have evidence that what she was sure of was so. She knew where Slinn's keys lay in his dressing room, and she went there and brought them down and tried them till she found the one that fitted a bureau here in the drawing room. She soon had what she wanted. The man was not only a deceiver but a fool. There was a bundle of letters, tied with blue ribbon, and she read them without shame. They were years and years old, all from his mother, written when he was little more than a child. They were addressed to Allan Semple at a lodging in a seaside town, where obviously he was taking his first holiday away from home. They had reached him daily, and some thanked him for his dear letters. "Mother is longing to see you again." And these were the things he had chosen to harbor through what she now guessed to have been a lifetime of mean transgression—the things that he clung to even now! She put them back, tied in their ribbon, a crushed pansy in one of them, and she who had known so skillfully to slip and slide advantageously through the chinks and cracks of life could have wept at what she had on her hands.

She took up the second letter, which she had left, forgotten, on the fireside table till now. It was addressed to herself. "My dear Mrs. Slinn —I should like to be permitted to call on you tomorrow afternoon to inquire about Colonel Slinn's health. Could you make it convenient to send your carriage for me? If it were here at about three in the afternoon, that would be excellent. With all good wishes, ma'am, I am your obedient servant, Bernard Cupples."

Lucy flushed at the insolence of this letter, this scarcely veiled command. She knew that Cupples was not asking her to oblige him: he was daring her to disoblige him. She understood fully now the disproportionate misery into which Slinn's slight indisposition had thrown him. This was the moment—now at the beginning—to call on her friends; but her pride revolted at the notion of confessing herself no married woman, a fool and a dupe. The next afternoon Cupples arrived in her carriage. She took him into the drawing room.

"I trust, ma'am," he began, "that Colonel Slinn's health—"

"Stop it!" she said, so sharply that he looked up, surprised; then shrugged his shoulders.

"I have a checkbook here. How much money do you want?"

"I see that we understand one another. But I fear, ma'am, that you do not understand *fully*."

He waited, and she waited, too. She would not give him another word. He was obliged to continue. "You see, ma'am, in an affair of this sort it is not a question of a hasty composition. It is a matter of what may be necessary from time to time as circumstances dictate. At the moment the barometer is set fair. I assure you, you may sleep without one single uneasy thought troubling your head. Put your checkbook back in the drawer."

"I have no doubt," she said, "that it pleases you not to exercise your power. It might be a good idea to take what you can get when you can get it, for I can step out of your power very simply. I have only to see to it that the fool upstairs is shown up for what he is."

"Yes," Cupples said, "that is all you have to do. But doing is not the only thing in life. There is also taking the consequences. You, no doubt, have weighed up the situation in which you find yourself: a discredited old fool, a woman who snatched at a husband a good deal younger than herself: and you have also considered, I imagine, the pleasure of Mr. Mostyn-Lloyd at finding himself in the limelight. . . ."

There was silence for a time; and then Cupples said: "I think I shall change my mind. Will you please make me out a blank check? I give you my word of honor not to fill it in for more than five hundred pounds."

Lucy hesitated for a long time, then took up her pen, and the landslide began. Cupples folded the little piece of paper carefully into his wallet. "Don't bother about the carriage," he said. "I delight in walking in this late autumn air."

She found a few days later that the check had been filled in for half a guinea; and this terrified her, like the piece of blank paper addressed to Allan Semple.

CHAPTER NINETEEN

I

CUPPLES and Slinn were abroad during that summer of 1890 when Lucy Evans accompanied us to Tresant. They were often abroad, and it was this, I suppose, that made life possible for Lucy. Moreover, she had gradually come to realize that she was lucky: more lucky at any rate than she might have been. She had imagined that a blackmailer's tactics never varied, that the victim was seized and sucked dry as quickly as possible; that the time would speedily come when she would have to sell her carriage and horses, dismiss her staff, perhaps find herself struggling along in a cheap lodging. But none of this happened. The Kensington façade remained intact.

Cupples was often about the house when he and Slinn were not abroad, and she had to put up with the bantering familiarity that he permitted himself. "Well," he would say, "how is our golden goose today?" This, she saw, defined her position. She knew well enough that there were geese whom Cupples slaughtered without mercy, but she herself was preserved to produce golden eggs. All that she had, she had on sufferance, but she still had it. Her capital remained, on the condition that the income was freely at Cupples's disposal. He used the carriage whenever he wanted it; to show his overlordship, he would occasionally stay in the house for a day or two; and whatever money he needed, whether for holidays abroad or any other purpose, he asked for without compunction. He was preserving her as a stable point in his rickety world, but she was without illusion. Let that world begin to totter, and he would snatch all she had.

Meantime, if she lived quietly, she could live. At the end of the second year, she even made the odd discovery that her capital had appreciably increased. From time to time Cupples would order her: "Tell your man to buy me so and so" or to "sell so and so." She disobeyed once or twice, and, watching the market reports as Mostyn-Lloyd had taught her to do, she saw that Cupples was right every time. So now she always obeyed, even though she knew that the increased size of the golden eggs was for his benefit, not hers.

As for Slinn, he might as well have been dead, so far as she was concerned, but he had to be preserved for the sake of face. On the evening of the day when the letter came addressed to Allan Semple, she went up to his bedroom and said: "Get up to breakfast in the morning. I want to talk to you." She walked out of the bedroom and never entered it again. She had discovered him to be sexually impotent and hadn't minded that, for she herself was sexually as warm as a mermaid; but this that she had now discovered was another sort of weakness, and she had no mercy on it.

When the two men were in England, the Kensington house became the most extraordinary triangle establishment. What sympathy and human feeling there was, and what conversation took place, was between Lucy and Cupples. She had an admiration, probably unrecognized even by herself, for his ruthlessness. He admired her acceptance of the situation and her contempt for both himself and Slinn. Slinn fetched and carried, both at home and abroad. He was still, to Cupples,

331

a tourist agent, with a useful turn for languages and for handling the tedious details of hotels, railway tickets and so forth. And he had to be preserved, of course, for his incomparable importance as a bigamist. One evening the three were taking coffee together after dinner, and Cupples said: "Would you mind pouring me another cup, Lucy?" She was no longer "Ma'am." She got up and walked out of the room, pausing at the door to say: "My job is to provide the coffee, not to pour it. Tell your valet to do it."

Cupples grinned with appreciation. "Yes," he said, "you pour it out, Ally, there's a good chap," and Slinn did so.

2

There were many people under Cupples's observation, for one reason or another, and Maud Semple was one of them. She did not know that she was being observed, and Tom Chadderton did not know why he was observing her. He knew only that it was pleasant to be talked to so agreeably by a gentleman like Mr. Cupples and to receive a shining sovereign now and then for nothing at all.

There was a house in Villiers Street that may have been anything. A few men whom Cupples took to be lodgers went in and out; there were a few girls who made brief suspicious sojourns; there was this woman, who called herself Maud Skirrow, working as a general drudge; and there was an ancient parchment-and-bone creature, dressed always in violet silk, whom he took to be the owner or lessee, and who occasionally emerged to take the air up and down the street, and sometimes for a stretch along the Embankment. An odd, dubious establishment that might have repaid study; but it was only Maud Skirrow who interested him at the moment. She was now a woman in her middle thirties, rough and coarse. She always left the house on Thursday nights at six o'clock, walked down the street as far as the Embankment, and turned right toward Westminster.

Cupples had observed the shoe-black who had a pitch at the bottom of Villiers Street. He stopped often to have his shoes shined and always paid the boy excessively. But it was not easy to make Tom Chadderton talk. He was *farouche* and reserved. But Tom came to know his good-tempered and generous client by name, to look forward to his laughing banter, and to open up in his presence. Nothing could have suited Cupples better, for he found that Tom not only worked in Villiers Street but lived there, in a basement room.

Just before six o'clock on a Thursday night Cupples sat on the shoe-black's throne, with Tom kneeling in ministration before his small feet,

332

when Maud Skirrow came along, tossed a "Wotcher!" in Tom's direction, and passed on toward Westminster.

"You know the lady?" Cupples asked.

"Sort of. She goes by."

"H'm! How odd! How odd!" Cupples murmured.

"Why? Wot's odd about that, Mr. Cupples?"

"Well, I'm almost certain. . . . But, no. If you know the lady, you can't be expected to do it. Friendship is sacred."

"Wot you gettin' at, Mr. Cupples? I don't know the lady—see. It's just sort of. We just says wotcher—see. She comes out'erve an 'ouse up the street. That's all I know."

"Well, so long as you're not friends," Cupples mused. "I'd hate to ask friend to watch friend. So long as she *continues* to be in the house up the street—that's all I want to be sure of. Suppose she were to leave, and go to live somewhere else—could you get to know that, Tom?"

"Wot you gettin' at?" Tom repeated. "I ain't no nark, Mr. Cupples. I don't want nothing to do with narkin'—see."

"I'm glad to hear it, Tom. We'd better leave the whole thing alone."

"But wot you gettin' at?"

"I can't explain it to you, Tom. You've been honest with me, and I'll be honest with you and tell you frankly I can't explain it. I just want to be sure where that lady is. That's all. If she suddenly decides to leave this place, I want to know where she goes to. Don't ask me why. I can't tell you. But I can tell you this. I'm not concerned in anything that can ever harm the lady. Indeed, she might hear something to her advantage some day. Now don't say another word about it. I can see you're suspicious of me, so let's leave it all alone. I hate to have people suspicious of me."

Poor Tom's forehead creased with worry. Cheerful friendly people were rare enough. "But I *like* you, Mr. Cupples. I don't *want* you to think I'm suspicious. You treat me right, you do. You don't treat me like dirt."

"I treat you, Tom, as I treat everybody else, I hope: as a human being like myself. We all have our faults, and we all have our good qualities. When I see a good quality in a man, I respect it. The mere thought that I might want to use you as a—a—"

"A nark."

"As a nark," said Cupples, smiling at the quaint word, "that mere thought makes you suspicious. Well, that's to your credit, Tom. Here's my appreciation of an honest man." He handed Tom a sovereign. "Now say no more about it."

Tom pocketed the sovereign readily enough, and watched the unsullied dignity of Cupples's departure. That, he thought, is the last I shall see of the best customer I ever had.

But a few days later Cupples was on the throne again, debonair and agreeable as usual.

"She's still about, Mr. Cupples," Tom volunteered.

"Who, Tom? Who is about what or where?"

"The lady as says wotcher."

"Tom, Tom," Cupples reproved him, "you're not becoming a nark?"

"No, sir."

"I'm pleased to hear it. I should hate to lose my good opinion of you."

"I been thinkin' it out, Mr. Cupples. You wouldn't 'urt a fly."

"I'm afraid I give myself away too easily, Tom. You've found my weakness. And you're not the only one. Sooner or later, all my friends say the same thing. 'Cupples, you're too soft-hearted. You'd give your head away if it wasn't screwed on.' Well, there it is. I suppose I'm as God made me."

3

"Laugh!" Maud Skirrow used to say in the days when she first met Allan Semple; but she didn't find much to laugh at now. She was a wide-awake and realistic woman, inclined to ask "Why?" if she found a human being acting charitably. That sort of thing, Maud was certain, didn't happen without a motive, and she began to wonder what motive was behind the occasional sovereign that Bernard Cupples slipped to Tom Chadderton. She found Tom a simple creature. Her casual greeting to him developed into a friendly talk, into a shared cup of coffee at a stall on the Embankment, even into a night at a music hall, followed by tripe and onions behind the steamy windows of an eating house. They were both lonely, but even when such an occasion came to break the loneliness down, Maud was cautious, a listener rather than a talker. Tom talked readily enough, and as he grandly paid for the supper with a golden sovereign he told her where it had come from.

Maud was enormously interested when she learned of Mr. Cupples's concern with herself, but she did not allow Tom to see this. She often wondered what had become of Allan Semple and her five hundred pounds. It was an immense sum to her, and as she pondered this mysterious espionage she convinced herself that it was in some way connected with her vanished fortune. If Mr. Cupples was keeping an eye on her, it would be worth while, she decided, to keep an eye upon him. A few shillings paid to one of her down-and-out friends gave her the information she wanted: Mr. Cupples shared his time between a flat in Jermyn Street and a house in Kensington. Observing the house in Kensington, she had the pleasure of seeing her husband and Mr. Cupples drive away from the door in an open victoria.

Maud was almost knocked over by the speed with which things had happened. She took a turn through the streets to decide on her course, and she was quick-witted enough to realize that it would not do to knock at the door and ask for Mr. Semple. This new Mr. Semple, resplendent in his clothes, languid in prosperity, driving in a carriage from a stylish house, was almost certainly Mr. Semple no longer.

She at last approached the house, her heart beating madly, but composed in her appearance, and asked for Mr. Cupples. Fortune told her the name she wanted to know. "He is not at home. He's just gone out with Colonel Slinn."

Maud took a chance and asked: "Is Mrs. Slinn at home?"

The servant looked her up and down. Her worn hands, her flash clothes, were no commendation at that door. "Is Mrs. Slinn expecting you?"

No, by God, she's not—far from it, Maud thought wildly, but here I am, and if she's ever heard the name Semple that'll fetch her. "She's not expecting me," she said deferentially, "but if you would be so kind as to say that Mrs. Semple is asking for her, perhaps she'll see me."

She was left outside the door, but a moment later she was in the drawing room. Laugh!

Lucy Evans was standing. She remained standing, and kept Maud standing, too. She said: "What do you want?"

Maud did not want Allan Semple. She would have paid to keep him out of her life. Nor did she want to be a blackmailer. All she wanted was the money that had been stolen from her long ago. And so she answered promptly: "Five hundred pounds."

Once she had got what she considered her "rights" she was ready to disappear. But Lucy knew nothing of Semple's theft, and this cool demand seemed to her, naturally enough, the large first bite at what this woman would take for an unexhaustible meal. She walked up and down the room, wondering what to do. This would not be the case of Cupples over again. This would not be someone who cherished the golden goose. Semple's wife would be all dead loss, and, she feared from this beginning, loss on a large scale. The thing was getting beyond her, and she was more and more tempted to let façade go hang, to take back her freedom by allowing Semple's bigamy to be denounced. Then she would be clear of him, of Cupples, and of creatures like this woman, too. She stopped her pacing and turned on Maud and said: "Don't you think it a strange thing to walk like this into the house of a woman you don't know and say 'I want five hundred pounds'? Why on earth should I give you five hundred pounds?"

"I must say you didn't seem surprised just now," Maud answered. "I'm asking for nothing but my rights, and you know why. You're married to my husband."

"I know nothing of the sort. I have only your word for that. If you say that Colonel Slinn is your husband, not mine, all you have to do is prove it in the proper quarters. Bigamy is a serious offense. He'll go to jail, and then neither of us will have him. That might be an excellent thing," she added wearily.

Maud looked baffled at this turn of the affair. She didn't want a husband, especially a husband in jail. She did want her "fortune" back. She sat down, uninvited, and licked her lips, feeling the mastery of the situation slipping away. "Well . . ." she began; when the door opened and Cupples marched unceremoniously in. He didn't see who this was sitting in a chair with her back to him; and he said rudely: "Damn careless servants you've got, Lucy. The horse had a loose shoe, and shed it. We've had to give up our drive."

Maud got up, and he looked at her with eyes that did not admit recognition, but with a mind that leaped instantly to the implications of her presence. Maud was flabbergasted, caught between that cold stare and the gathering hostility that she sensed in Lucy. Lucy said: "I've given you the only advice I can give you. Please yourself whether you act on it." She rang a bell, and Maud was led out, feeling that life was not so simple as it had seemed when she sent in her name as a trump card.

"Sit down," Cupples said when they were alone. "What advice is this you're talking about? What did you tell her?"

"You know her?"

"Of course I know her. What did you tell her?"

"I told her that if she wanted to give information that would cause a charge of bigamy to be brought against her husband, she had better do it. I've put up with you and him for a long time, but this is too much. You understand how this game is played, and so long as it suits you, I shall be comfortable enough. But I cannot be bothered with amateurs. That would make life altogether too ragged."

Cupples considered his polished nails for a moment, and then got up. "Yes," he said, "amateurs are a nuisance. They ruin any profession."

He said no more about it.

Whether Lucy really had come to believe that a scandal didn't matter, or whether this was a pretense aimed at keeping him in his place, he could not be sure. But he was not prepared to test the matter at once. Perhaps the moment would come for that. In the meantime, Maud Skirrow's intervention was full of disastrous possibilities. It might give to a situation that had become delicate just the tilt which would cause Lucy to send them all packing, bag and baggage.

4

A few days after this, Cupples and Slinn set off for their usual continental holiday. Lucy Evans turned from the reading of the stock-market news to the other items in her newspaper and came upon this paragraph:

A woman was killed and a youth savagely assaulted on Hampstead Heath on the night of Bank Holiday. The youth, whose name is Thomas Chadderton, is now in hospital, where he gave the following account of the affair to the police. He says that the woman's name is Maud Skirrow and that she has for some time been employed as a general servant at a lodging house in Villiers Street. He and the woman had been friendly for some months, and they arranged to visit the fair on the Heath in the evening of Bank Holiday. They enjoyed themselves there in the customary way for some hours, and late in the evening were joined by a man whom neither of them knew, but whose company they accepted, and who stood treat freely to all the amusements. Later, the three of them went to a public-house where they drank a good deal. The dusk was coming on when they left, and they strolled along arm-in-arm, singing, till they found themselves in a remote part of the Heath where no one was about. They sat down among some bushes, and the youth told the police that the stranger then became amorous and put his arm round the woman Skirrow and said: "Push off, Tommy." The boy Chadderton withdrew to some distance and sat down, feeling sleepy from the beer he had drunk; but presently he got up and returned to the others. He found the stranger standing erect. The woman was lying on the ground. It was dark, but the youth was frightened by her immobility. He said to the man: "Wot you done to 'er?" and the man at once began to run away. The boy stumbled in pursuit, whereupon the man turned and battered him savagely about the head. He lost consciousness and was found some time later by passers-by, who revived him and whom he led to the spot where the woman was lying. The police were called. The youth was taken to hospital and the woman's body to the mortuary where examination showed that she had been strangled. Marks upon the neck suggest the use of a thin rope, and the boy's injuries lead the police to the conclusion that the assailant wore knuckle-dusters.

When Lucy Evans read this paragraph she remembered where she had heard that word knuckle-dusters. She recalled an autumn afternoon

337

when she and Slinn and Cupples were driving in Hyde Park, and the trees were golden, and the air had the tempered warmth of the season, full of indolence and relaxation, and, for a wonder, all three of them were at the same time in an amiable mood. She often wondered exactly what Cupples's extracurricular activities amounted to, and this was a moment when she could not believe that they were much more than such things as would suggest themselves to a restless, clever and shady mind. The oily-brown sliding eyes gave all that away, but with the gray topper on his head, the white spats, the dark carnation in his button-hole, he made up a figure impossible to associate with anything that she could think of as really desperate. And then, right there in the midst of all that silken urbanity of gleaming horses and smart carriages and lolling parasols, there were two policemen closing upon a man who began to run, but, seeing that way cut off, stopped, turned, and faced his pursuers, and suddenly swiped viciously at one of them who went down before a crack on the jaw that could be heard even above the civilized *brouhaha* of the moment.

Lucy winced and closed her eyes; the carriage swept on; and when she looked up again the whole violent intrusion was ended; it might never have happened; but Slinn was saying: "By God! What a smacker! He must have been wearing knuckle-dusters."

"What are knuckle-dusters?" she asked; and Slinn laughed and said: "Ask Bernard. He's an expert." And thereupon their accord was torn to pieces, with Cupples saying in a calm icy voice: "One of these days, Ally, you will say one word too much"; and Slinn wilting before that threat; and a sense that the moment of violence, which they had seemed to leave behind, was, after all, with them still, in everything: in the blue shadows that were beginning to stain the vistas of the park; in soured faces that swam up and vanished, soured envious faces outside this suave pageant in which they had their part; and in the hearts of these two men who meant so little and yet so much in her life.

When Cupples was gone that night she said to Slinn: "Now you'd better answer my question. What are knuckle-dusters?" and Slinn told her of that moment in the Jermyn Street flat when Mr. Eeles had danced on his toes, slashing through the air with his armored fists. And now Maud Skirrow was dead; and Maud Skirrow had been obnoxious to Bernard Cupples; and the man who killed her had been wearing knuckle-dusters.

5

It was soon after this that I called upon Lucy Evans and was so disturbed by the change in her appearance that I had a sense, as I have said, that she had not declined but been overthrown. I had been seeing little enough of her. I did not like Colonel Slinn or the man Cupples who was so often in the house; and Daniel would not go to the place at all.

There was no difficulty about persuading Lucy to join the party that went down to Tresant. She was anxious for company. She had a dependence that was new for her, and she attached herself to me with an eagerness that surprised me. She would say in the morning: "Sarah, let us spend the day together," and I could find no excuse for refusing. Mervyn and Enid enjoyed having children about them in a way that I never had done. They would be off with their Edward and my Veronica through all the happy hours God sent, with Richard, who was now twelve, half a help and half a hindrance. The five of them would come back at the day's end roasted, disheveled, satisfied, and Mervyn would cry: "Why don't you come with us some day, Mama? It would do you all the good in the world"; and the small Edward would show his grandmama the shells and pebbles and wilted flowers that were the day's record of adventure. And, as I looked at Lucy, it was possible for the first time to hear without wonder a child calling her grandmama. Whatever had passed over her had furrowed her deeply.

She and I didn't stir far from the house during that holiday. Occasionally we would carry a luncheon basket to the lawn bordering the lake outside the cottage where Maggie Whale had lived with Lucy as her companion during Mervyn's growing time. This, I found, was a favorite place of hers; and certainly if the beauty of a natural scene and the recollection of tranquil profitable hours have any peace to bestow, this was the place to find it. More and more I had the sense that Lucy was seeking peace, release from some memory, or fear, or experience, that was torturing her; and I knew that I could do no more than follow the wisdom with which Sally Gaylord was living in Bermondsey: I could only be at hand and wait for the troubling of the waters.

We were there one day, with our simple meal ended, and for a time we watched the others who had set off earlier in the punt. Their voices came across the water, and the sun sparkled on the drops that fell from the paddle Mervyn was plying; and as they passed slowly out of sight Lucy's heart, like mine, was doubtless full of sweet but oppressive memory of days when we were the young ones out there, with endless life, it seemed, before us; yet now already, in no more than a wink of time's eye, here we were, sitting on the shore, spectators, with experience rather than expectation for our lot.

Lucy stretched herself on the warm grass, and I remained sitting upright, looking at the water and the clouds and the hills, when I felt her hand steal into mine and lie there as if to find some reassurance. I pressed it warmly, and she said: "Why don't you hate me?" I didn't answer that except with another pressure of her hand, and then she sat up suddenly and said: "You should. I have murdered two people."

Again there seemed nothing to say. Something was going to pour out: I was certain of that: certain, too, that the sooner the better for Lucy's health. "There was Eddy Rodda," she said. "I drove him to his death as surely as we are sitting here."

It was a good thing that she should realize and confess the heartlessness of her conduct toward Eddy; but I could not leave it sticking in her mind like a stark knife. I said what could be said about that. Eddy, after all, had his share in that old guilt, and I made her see it. I really could not believe that a recent awakening to the consequences of her part in that affair had caused the crumbling of her personality that I now beheld.

"What else is there, Lucy?" I asked her; and thereupon she took from a pocket the newspaper paragraph which I have written about and handed it to me. I had not seen it before, and what at once caught my attention was the name Tom Chadderton. Who Maud Skirrow was I did not know; and Lucy did not know who the boy was.

We had begun to question one another excitedly when a man whom neither of us had seen before walked across the lawn toward us and asked with calm politeness: "Is either of you ladies Mrs. Slinn?"

We both got to our feet, and Lucy said: "Yes. I am."

I liked the look of this man, but I cannot recall what his looks then were. He had the anonymity so valuable in his profession. "I apologize for intruding on you, Mrs. Slinn," he said, "but I wonder whether you'd care to answer a few questions? I hope you will," he added with a smile, "because I've traveled all the way from London to ask them—from Scotland Yard."

Somehow I had been sure of that all along, and I think Lucy had, too. "Still," said the man, "you can please yourself, of course."

"I'll answer anything I can," Lucy said. "Shall we go into the cottage?"

"Thank you, ma'am. We wouldn't be bothering you at all, except that we've drawn a blank elsewhere. We're trying to find a man named Bernard Cupples, and we wondered if you could help. Ever heard of him?"

We sat down in Whaley's old writing room, and the detective looked across at me. "Who is this lady?" he asked. "I don't mind her being here, if you don't, Mrs. Slinn; but as a matter of form it might be as well for me to know who is present."

"I am the wife of Mr. Daniel Undridge, Q.C.," I said.

He appeared unimpressed. "Daniel Undridge, eh? Oh—ah—yes. I know about him, of course."

No pen, no pencil, no papers; a most unfrightening, informal, average sort of friendly man; but we didn't escape the flavor of something

340

formidable. I suppose it was the atmosphere of the great institution whence he came. "Ought we to know *your* name?" I asked.

"Oh, yes, yes—of course. Smith. Henry Smith." As anonymous as all the rest of him.

"Well, now," he said, leaning back in his chair with one leg over the other and twiddling a button on his waistcoat, "perhaps you've seen in the papers something about that woman named Maud Skirrow who was killed on Hampstead Heath?"

"Yes," said Lucy. "I saw a newspaper paragraph about it."

"There was a boy Chadderton—remember?" She nodded. "Well, naturally, we've had a lot of talks with him. D'you know him?"

"No."

"Never set eyes on him?"

"Never in my life."

"But you know a man named Bernard Cupples?"

"I know him very well indeed."

"I thought perhaps you might have heard of the boy Chadderton through him. From what the boy tells us, he and Cupples were acquainted."

"No," said Lucy. "I never heard of the boy."

"Well, I suppose there's no harm in telling you something about him. He says Cupples scraped an acquaintance with him, gave him pretty big tips, and asked him to keep an eye on this woman Skirrow. Then the woman Skirrow gets killed. Makes you think—'m?"

"Yes. I suppose it does."

"So we'd like to ask Mr. Cupples one or two questions. We know he had a flat in Jermyn Street, but there's no one there. We know a good deal about him one way and another. He has interested us for years. We know, for example, that he used to spend a lot of time in your house in Kensington. Almost a second home, wasn't it?"

"Yes. You could call it that. He was a great friend of my husband, Colonel Slinn."

"Colonel Slinn doesn't appear to be at home?"

"No. He and Mr. Cupples go to the Continent for a long holiday every year. This time, they left a few days before the—the—"

"The murder."

Lucy nodded.

"It would be a great help to us if you cared to give us their address."

"I haven't their address."

"Don't you hear from your husband during these prolonged holidays?"

"Will you allow me to be perfectly frank with you."

"Yes, indeed. I hoped you were being frank all along."

"I have been. I have answered your questions truthfully."

341

"Thank you, Mrs. Slinn. I think you have. What did you want to say to me?"

"Simply this. That my husband, when away, never sends me so much as a line, because he is as pleased to be quit of me for a time as I am to be quit of him. We detest one another. All I can tell you about him and Mr. Cupples is that they did what they do each year. They left London for Paris. I know it is their habit to stay there for a few days. Then they go where fancy takes them. They are never in one place for long, and where those places are, or what they do in them, is more than I can say. All I know is that at last—maybe in two months, maybe in three—they come back, and I am sorry to see them."

There was a moment's silence, Smith looking at Lucy with sympathetic interest. "Then you can't help us?" he said.

"Not in the way you want. I would if I could."

"Would you?" I looked suddenly from Lucy to Smith, so sharp was the tone of this question. "If you knew where your husband and Cupples were, would you tell me?"

For the first time, Lucy hesitated. Then she asked: "Why shouldn't I?"

"No, no, Mrs. Slinn; I am asking the questions, though you can please yourself whether you answer them. If you knew, would you tell?"

"I don't know. I can't answer a question which depends on a supposition."

"I see."

There was another pause. Mr. Smith got up and walked to the window and gazed for a time on the innocent beauty of lawn and lake. Then he turned and, leaning against the window sill, asked: "Did you know that your husband's name was not Slinn, but Semple?"

This question for the first time opened my eyes to what this haggard, undermined woman had been through. I looked at her, and she was trembling. She said faintly: "Yes."

"Did Cupples know?"

"Yes."

"Was Cupples blackmailing you?"

"Yes."

"Did you know that the woman who was killed on Hampstead Heath was Semple's wife?"

"Yes."

"Have you ever met her?"

"Once."

"Was *she* blackmailing you?"

"She asked for five hundred pounds."

"Did Cupples know that?"

"Yes."

"Doesn't it seem likely that one blackmailer would try to eliminate another?"

"This is supposition again. I will answer anything to do with the facts."

I admired the way in which, even in so desperate a moment, she had recovered some control of herself and pulled Mr. Smith up sharp. He seemed to admire her, too. The quick volley of questions ended. He came from the window, sat down again, and said: "Do you mind if I smoke?"

When his pipe was drawing, he wiped his forehead with his handkerchief. "That's all," he said. "Anything I say now is unofficial. When I asked you, Mrs. Slinn, whether you would tell us where Cupples was, supposing you knew, I must say I thought you wouldn't. Because, once we had laid hands on him, all that we know would necessarily have become public property. I don't think you would have liked that. You might have wanted Slinn and Cupples to have a chance of getting clear. Still, as you say, all that is a matter of supposition. I am satisfied that you don't know where they are."

"Thank you. I assure you I have answered everything truthfully. It hasn't been easy."

"It was fortunate," Smith said, "fortunate, that is, for you, that when the inquest was held we hadn't yet found out that Maud Skirrow was Maud Semple, and that Colonel Slinn was Allan Semple. Otherwise, I'm afraid that would already be public property. Unless someone appears on the charge of murdering this woman, or of being an accessory before the fact, these things will remain our secrets." He smiled and got up. "We have many secrets, you know. There are some I pray heaven we may make public some day, and there are others I'm prepared to keep where no one will see them." He took Lucy by the hand. "We'll do our best, Mrs. Slinn," he said, "to lay hold of Cupples. I hope we'll fail. I hope you never see him or Allan Semple again."

6

Lucy never did see Cupples or Semple again. Nothing more appeared in the newspapers about the Hampstead Heath murder, but that one paragraph, no one can doubt, came into Cupples's hands. If the boy Chadderton had not got involved, Cupples would perhaps have risked a return to London; but once the boy was in a hospital where he would be questioned by the police, the game was up. Cupples had good reason to know the resources of the police when their noses were on the trail. They wouldn't be long in finding that Maud Skirrow was Mrs. Semple and that Mr. Semple was Colonel Slinn, and that, through payments to Chadderton, Mr. Cupples was concerned in their fortunes. Eeles would have vanished, but the Jermyn Street flat couldn't vanish, and what the police would find there goodness knows.

It was many years after this—twenty years it must have been—that I was spending a week end with a friend in the country, and among the guests was Sir Henry Smith who was Chief Constable of the county police. I had some long talks with Sir Henry, who told me that they had never caught up with Cupples till it was too late to do anything about it. He had shot himself at Monte Carlo not long before. I asked if anything were known of Colonel Slinn, and he said: "Oh, yes. He's still alive, you know. I saw him last summer."

Slinn and Cupples had parted soon after Maud Skirrow's death. "So far as I know," Sir Henry said, "they never met again. Slinn was an excellent linguist, you know. He was always happier in some other country than his own. He stayed in France and moved about a bit doing small jobs here and there. Finally, he took French nationality, and a few years ago he married a French widow."

I exclaimed with surprise at this, and Sir Henry said: "Well, it was an intelligent thing to do. He was a poor weak wretch who always had to be under someone's thumb. And he took his shape from the thumb, like a pot in a potter's hands. If he'd never met Cupples, who was a far worse man than I imagine you ever guessed, he would have spent his life as a contented nonentity. Madame is the best thing that could have happened to him. She's immense—a vast old hen under whose wing he nestles. A friend of mine in the French Sûreté kept me in touch with his doings, and I went to have a look at him last summer when I happened to be in Amiens. I motored over to Doullens. D'you motor yet?"

I shook my head. "You'll come to it," he said. "Marvelous. Well, there I found him. They have a little shop. 'Semple. Tabac.' He's back to his real name. I went in and bought some tobacco. Horrible stuff. He looks as old as Methuselah—thin, withered, with a white mustache. He was sitting on a chair, reading of all things a weekly paper published in the West of England. He had steel spectacles on the end of a bleak nose. I said to him: 'Vous lisez les journaux anglais, m'sieur?' and he said: 'I was born in England, m'sieur, though I am now French. I was born in the village where this paper comes from.'"

Sir Henry said that Slinn pointed out to him a smudgy photograph of a local worthy. "He is dead," Slinn said with satisfaction, "dead as a doornail, and here am I, alive and kicking. Would you believe, m'sieur, when we were boys this fellow used to throw stones at me and hoot after me in the street. And here he is—dead as a doornail. Now and then they die—they appear in this paper—and I cut them out and

344

paste them in my book—I, who am still alive and kicking. Would you care to see my book, *m'sieur?*"

He produced the book, which had pictures of a few corn chandlers and ironmongers and such-like people stuck to its pages, and a few "In memoriam" lines cut from the "Births, Marriages and Deaths" column. It was a pathetic little graveyard, and he gloried in it. "He seemed as daft as a coot and as happy as a sandboy," said Sir Henry. "Now it's my turn, Mrs. Undridge. Tell me, what became of that woman who thought she was his wife?"

"Oh, she's dead. Been dead these ten years. She's buried down there at Tresant where you saw us that day."

"Forgive my curiosity. What name is on her gravestone?"

"Why, Slinn. She went on calling herself that."

On a day like this, I thought, the sun will be falling in bright dapples there: falling through the leaves and the beards of moss: and, oh, already I have too many tombs there, and plaques, and gravestones; for inside the gray oaken door with its massive hinges, inside the damp-smelling building where the light is always bat-light and where once I watched Richard scraping the mold from the tombs, there already is Richard's plaque not far from Justin's, and there is the tomb where Mama and Lord Burnage lie; and in the grass without, the long grass where the sorrel and the dog daisies will now be still in the windlessness that is always there, is the headstone of "Lucy Slinn, widow of Colonel Aloysius Slinn," and on one side of that is the headstone of "Edward Rodda, master mariner," and on the other that of Wesley Rodda, all three of them lying so close that if bones could work like moles in the clay they could stretch out and she could hold a hand of each. And of all that was between those three and tore them asunder, though now they lie so snugly, nothing remains but the little Merlin who has conspired with Enid Gotherson to produce this boy Edward—how odd that unthinkingly they had chosen Captain Rodda's name!—this boy Edward who, if I could read things aright, wanted to introduce Rodda blood into my own family.

CHAPTER TWENTY

I

YOU may well believe that when the holiday was over and we were all back in town, Lucy and I watched the newspapers with a passion of interest; but not so much as a ripple appeared again on the surface of that dark pool. I often called on her during that winter.

We had drawn closer together than we had ever been. Her experience had purged her character of much foolishness; she was gentler, less self-centered; and I was not surprised when she said to me in the spring: "What sense is there in my keeping on this place? I wonder whether Sally would rent me the cottage by the lake? Some place like that is all I need, and I should like to live there more than in any other place I know."

"Would Mervyn care for you to be so far away?"

"Do you really think it will matter to him? I used to be able to persuade myself that it would, but after all he has Enid and little Edward, and now there's another on the way. No; I think he'll get on all right without me."

It was a charming day. The portrait of her that Mr. Mostyn Lloyd had paid Millais to paint hung over the mantelpiece in the room where we were sitting, and I looked at this image of her, fresh as morning, pictured against a background that was the essence and epitome of just such a day as this. It was a Primavera. It was what had shattered and overthrown Eddy Rodda, and chained Mostyn Lloyd to her in devotion, and set Justin's heart whirling.

Lucy followed the direction of my glance, and for a time looked silently at this representation of the beauty that once was hers. "She thought the world was made for her, that woman," she said. "I may not have learned much in my life; but at least I've learned that she was wrong. Could *she* ever have imagined that anyone could get along without her? Well, I can."

"All the same," I said, "she was very lovely."

"You speak as if she were dead. Well, leave it at that. Will you come with me to see Sally?"

2

We called on Sally a few days later. We had made no arrangements, because she would not allow arrangements to be made. "I don't know what I shall be doing," she used to say. "You must come and take your chance with me as other people have to do."

The stuffed seagull that Tom Chadderton had brought from Tresant a few years before was still on the mantelpiece in the kitchen. I had asked Sally why she kept this lamentable relic which can have given her no pleasure, and she had answered: "Because some day Tom Chadderton may come back to see me, and I'd like him to know that I had kept his present."

And now Tom Chadderton had come back. When he was discharged from hospital he was asked if he had anywhere to go, and he had

346

replied: "Yers. Miss Brown in Bermondsey," and that was enough, for the repute of Miss Brown in Bermondsey had by now spread, especially as it was associated with the repute of Warwick Russell of Bermondsey.

It was afternoon, and Tom Chadderton was in bed. The hospital had done what it could. His head had been sewn up till it must have had as many stitches as the leather case of a football bladder. Mr. Eeles had not left much undone that could be done. To the already considerable geographical markings of Tom's face a few more had been added that would last his life. But this was not the worst. Hideous as they might leave Tom for evermore, these scars would heal; but his mind seemed beyond healing. He had been near to murder and to being murdered, and, more than this, he was afflicted with the sense that the money he had taken from Cupples associated him with Maud Skirrow's death. He had led her to the slaughter, and this was something he would never wipe from his mind. And so Tom was in bed. When he came to her, Sally simply took him in. Much was said and something was written in after days about "Mary Brown" and her influence among the wretched, but there was never any more in it than that: when they came to her she took them in, and all she was and all she had was theirs. It did not take her long to discover that, though Tom's body had been mended, his mind was flawed. He did not even remember the seagull over the mantelpiece, but he remembered the cat Sixpence and spent his first evening with Sally sitting in a chair, nursing the cat. Sally did not know what could be done, if anything, with Tom Chadderton, but for a beginning, she told him that he must be responsible for Sixpence. He must buy his food and see that he was fed and regularly dusted with flea powder and combed. Tom did all this with solemn concentration. It was his one hold on human responsibility. In the afternoons Sally sent him to bed, and he was in bed now, with Sixpence curled up at his feet.

This was Lucy's first visit to Bermondsey, and she was not prepared for what she found. She had known Tresant and all that it meant of ease and elegance and withdrawal from the world. And Tresant was Sally's. She had but to speak the word, and all that was slumbering there would wake again to life, with herself its center. I remembered how, on that day when Maggie Whale and I had found Lucy in the silken shell of her bed, she had petulantly burst forth: "Tresant could have been mine—not that crazy woman's." But I was sure she had never realized quite what the crazy woman was up to. She must have pictured her living in an oasis of ease in Bermondsey's desert of penury, doling out largess with an easy hand. And here she was, in this slum kitchen whose window looked on nothing but sooty brick and gray slate, and when we came in she was rising from her knees and wiping her hands on a sacking apron and saying: "Excuse the floor. It'll soon be dry. It was overdue for a scrub." She took up the bucket of scummy water in which a cloth and brush wallowed and went out to pour it down the drain in the back yard. Lucy gave me a look almost of dismay, for she had been unprepared not only for Sally's occupation but also for her appearance. It was years since the two had met, and dumpy little Sally, with boots on her feet—not shoes—with this sacking apron over her plain black worn clothes, with gray hair uncared for, with her hands red from soda, and her face beginning to be deeply wrinkled so that the eyes looked out with a twinkle from a radiation of fans: this Sally was certainly not a "lady" playing at being a charwoman.

We heard the clang of the bucket as Sally dumped it in the scullery, and then she came in, hung her apron behind the door, and gave Lucy a probing look from those deep-set eyes. "I wonder if you find me as changed as I find you?" she said. "What's come over you?"

We had agreed that neither Sally nor anyone else was to know what had come over Lucy, and I replied for her: "Lucy hasn't been at all well. Perhaps you know that her husband's left her? At any rate, nothing's been heard of him since last autumn when he went onto the Continent for a holiday."

"She looks all the better for it," Sally said in the brusque way that was to become increasingly her habit. "When I said she looked changed, I didn't mean she looked worse. She looks better than I've ever seen her —less taken up with herself. Well, I must get you some tea. How is that boy of yours, Sarah?" She put some heavy china mugs onto the table and smiled. "These horrified him," she said, "when he paid me his one and only visit. He had difficulty in drinking at all. He wanted to talk about nothing but Justin and Tresant, and he found this an inappropriate place for doing it. It didn't surprise me that he never came back. I was a great disappointment to him and he was to me. What are you going to do with him?"

"It's rather early days for talking about that," I hedged, for the truth was I had no idea what we were going to do with Richard. "He'll have to go through the usual mill," I said, "and then we shall see."

"Well, here you are," said Sally, and poured out the tea. She had cut bread-and-butter, and the slices lay solidly on our plates.

"Do you remember," she said, "how Tom Chadderton came to me after a row with his father a few years ago? You and Whaley were kind enough to take him off for a holiday. I think I told you at the time that a sister came with him—a girl with the odd name of Haggie. I believe her name is really Hagar. Anyway, Warwick Russell and his wife took an interest in her, and she's been living with them ever since—half servant, half companion. The words don't matter. They're all servants to one another in that house. They've made a wonderful job of her— you'll see: I expect she and Mrs. Russell will be looking in soon—and that's something, because Haggie seemed as elusive as a wild cat when I first came here."

"You did mention her. It was a trinket Tom had bought for her that started the row."

"Yes. Well, she couldn't read or write then, and now she can do both. She can cook, which is more than I can do, and she's altogether a nice person. But she ought to get out of Bermondsey. This place is all right for tough old hens like me, but Warwick Russell, I know, is worried about Haggie. There's no active sign of tuberculosis yet, but she seems to be heading that way."

There was a sound of footsteps in the passage and Sally shouted: "Leave the baby there in the pram and come on in." To us she said: "Don't forget that Sally Gaylord is dead. Mary Brown lives here."

I had not met Mrs. Russell before, but from what Sally had told me I had expected this startling red hair, this extraordinary aliveness and vigor that invaded the room. Haggie Chadderton seemed dim in the light of that sunburst personality, like some unassuming plant growing near a sunflower, yet Mrs. Russell did not oppress me as I am, I confess, oppressed by most exuberant people. You could no more be oppressed by her warmth than by the warmth of a summer day, so spontaneous and healthful it was. It was not difficult to understand how Warwick Russell, wandering disconsolate in the Cotswolds after his illness, found consolation here.

"Come and see my cockney," she invited me and Lucy, and we went into the passage to see the morsel called Robin Russell lying in his pram. He was asleep, and had the pathos of all newborn children, lambs on these cold pastures. Haggie Chadderton looked adoringly at the mother, adoringly at the child. I wondered whether adoration was the best atmosphere to breathe. For a time, no doubt. I had had my own phases of adoration. I had adored Lord Burnage and Maggie Whale, but I had grown out of both. Here in Bermondsey, and living with her under the same roof, it would be difficult for Haggie to grow out of Mrs. Russell. She was, I suppose, seventeen or eighteen years old, dark, slim and delicate. Her quietness was as notable as Mrs. Russell's incandescence. She spoke only when she was spoken to, and she spoke well, without a trace of Tom's unreformed cockney. I imagined that for the last three or four years there had been a quiet but passionate assimilation of the habits of a beloved model.

When Lucy and I left, I said: "Well, we never got to the subject of our visit, after all. I mean your renting the cottage."

"What did you think of that girl, Haggie Chadderton?"

"I thought she was well enough," I said, for I disliked coming in too heavily on first impressions.

"I liked her immensely. I think she and I could be happy together."

I looked at Lucy with surprise. "What's in your head now?"

"Well, if the girl's health makes it necessary for her to get out of Bermondsey, why shouldn't she come with me down into Cornwall?"

"For a holiday?"

"No. For good. That is, if she would care to, and if Sally would let me have the cottage. The last thing I want down there is the sort of servants I have about me in Kensington."

It came to pass as Lucy proposed. By the summer of that year she had sold the house which she entered so long ago as a dubious waif, and she and Haggie Chadderton were living in the cottage by the lake.

3

May the first was an agreeable day for a birthday. The weather was usually good; and I remember its glitter and sparkle on the day when I was forty-five. There were daffodils in a cut crystal bowl on the breakfast table in Chelsea, and the sunshine fell through the window and the facets of the bowl flashed blue and red under the pale gold of the flowers. I don't like birthdays now, but I was fool enough then to be excited by what friends had to say and to send me as I stepped past another of the too few milestones.

Birthday or not, Daniel was busy opening his own letters. He had got in late last night from some political occasion or other, and I had already gone to bed. This morning he had shouted from his dressing room: "Many happies, Sarah!" and I could confidently expect that among these letters and small packets by my plate there would be one from him. He never forgot such things. His secretary kept a list of birthdays to be remembered, as of so many other matters; and I didn't doubt that mine was safely recorded with those of his political leaders, the bigwigs down in the constituency, and the doubtful voters there whose partisanship might be tilted the right way by small personal attentions. Here it was: a cabochon emerald mounted in silver to make a brooch.

"Oh, thank you, Daniel. It's lovely."

"Like it?"

"I love it."

"Good." He reached out and patted my hand, his eye still hovering over the letter he held. And that, I knew, was that.

In the general election of the year before, Gladstone's Home Rule for Ireland people had been successful; but Daniel had nevertheless kept his seat at Steignhampton and even increased his majority. He had attracted attention in the new House by his anti-Home Rule speeches, and had earned the distinction of a personal castigation from

350

Gladstone. It looked as though, once his party was back, he could expect some junior ministerial post.

I went on turning over my letters. Lucy Evans wrote from Cornwall and sent a box of camellias. "These were gathered by Haggie. You will be surprised when you see her again. Dr. Russell would not worry about her health now. She's as brown as a nut, and full of energy. You know how anxious I was at first, wondering how a girl brought up as she was would take to this lonely country life. I needn't have worried. She loves it more and more. Every week a box of flowers goes off to Tom in Bermondsey. They must be a cheerful sight to the people who visit his surgery."

That was a surprising thing if you like: Tom Chadderton's surgery. It began with the affair of Sixpence who had his times and seasons for lording it over the roofs and in the back yards of Bermondsey, and was apt to return bedraggled and sometimes injured from the lists of love. One day he came home with an ear bloody and torn, and Sally was impressed by Tom's concern and devotion and by the cat's submission to his care. Till Tom's arrival she had herself treated Sixpence, when he needed treatment, and the cat had been unruly and difficult. She soon saw that Tom had an affinity with animals, and when he brought in a sparrow that had been shot by a catapult and began with match sticks to make splints, her heart was full of hope that here might be the thing she was looking for: the cure for his twisted mind. Tom never became a vet with orthodox degrees, but he was sent off for a year to live with a vet, and he returned with his natural aptitude strengthened by some knowledge. He did not put up a plate, though Warwick Russell would call him "my young colleague Chadderton," but it became known that he was there, that he would look after sick and injured birds and animals, and the sad pets of poor people kept him busy. He continued to live in Sally's house, but set up his "surgery" in a rented room in the same street, and there he would be found, knocking together cages and kennels, all his doings followed by the sharp eyes of canaries, and the wistful eyes of dogs, and the slitted watchful eyes of cats. He was patient and successful with the poor creatures, happier with them than with humans, to whom he remained a little wanting. But this increased the respect in which poor people held him. There seemed to linger among them the belief that the simple are God's children. Anyway, there Tom was, and Sally rightly felt that she could have done nothing better for him. He earned a few shillings and enormous self-respect.

Daniel got up and wiped his lips with his napkin. "I must be off. I don't expect I shall be in to dinner. Have a look at this and let me know what you think of it."

He went, dropping a letter by my plate and kissing the back of my

351

neck. I put the letter aside and went on reading through my own. One from Whaley, one from Richard. This was his birthday as well as mine. He was fifteen. He wrote from Rugby where he was now at school. "Dear Mama—This is to wish you many happy returns of your birthday. I expect by the time you get this I shall have the new cricket bat you promised me. Things are going on fairly well here, but you know without my saying it again that school isn't my idea of heaven. When are you going to persuade Father to let me join the cavalry? I haven't sent you anything because it's not easy to find the right sort of thing here, but something will come in time, you may depend. My love to you and Nika. Your loving son, Richard."

I put the letter down, feeling that it was rather like Daniel's kiss on the back of the neck, and read the others, from Whaley, Mervyn and Enid. Then at last I took up the letter Daniel had left for me, and which was addressed, I saw, in the handwriting of his sister, Marie Rimmel.

"My dear Daniel—I dislike entrusting to you the sorrows of our family, but Sebastien and I are in great distress about Julian. He is now nearly sixteen years old, and we both detect in him a lack of seriousness that seems to increase rather than grow less. As you know, poor Sebastien has worked his fingers to the bone. He took great financial risks in order to establish himself, incurring debts that called for long sacrifice; but all this he did without hesitation so that the family might have a sound bottom upon which Julian could build. We have suggested to him many professions: the law, medicine, the army, but he treats all these suggestions without seriousness, and on the idea being proposed that he should follow his father in the shipping business he was rude enough to say that nothing would induce him to do so. He said he would not mind being a seaman who sailed in ships, but he could never sit in an office and grow fat on the hard life these poor devils lived. (Excuse this expression, my dear Daniel. It is Julian's, not mine.)

"Sebastien and I, need I say? have been following with great interest the serious direction of your own life, and it is this which makes us think you will understand our distress. For what are we to do with a boy who has no direction? He neglects his studies and fills his room with trifles: old books for whose contents he has no concern at all, but is pleased with their binding or type or engravings; old prints and carved picture frames and bits of moth-eaten lace and brocade. Nor must I touch any of this, and who else should touch it but I, seeing that to employ a servant in so small a family would be a wicked waste? But no—it must not be touched—a whole roomful of such moldy nonsense—it must all be left to gather moth and dust, and this sort of thing, believe you, is the great concern of his life!

"It is Sebastien's belief that a complete change of circumstance may mean a change of outlook, and he thinks that as you yourself left France at an early age and studied in England, this might be also the salvation of your poor nephew. It will be a financial sacrifice for Sebastien to keep Julian in England, but he is prepared to do this. We cannot ask you to take the boy into your own house"—["You are doing so, but I won't have him," Daniel here wrote in pencil]—"but could you arrange something with a serious family who would be reasonable in terms?

"Well, that is the situation, and we await your reply with anxiety. The transport would cost little in one of the ships of Sebastien's company. Your loving sister, Marie."

Somehow, this depressing letter cheered me enormously, and I went upstairs to see Veronica, whose name had now become Nika, and who was eight years old.

4

I had made up my mind that Nika should not grow up as I had done, a young person cut off by several flights of stairs and by a deep psychological gulf from her parents. I could never forget the night when Mercy Kite had sneaked me down to see the fountains of roses rising out of the epergnes on the dining-room table; or the morning when, as a concession, I had been permitted to take breakfast with Papa and Mama and had dared to handle the letters and disarrange the *Times*; or the evenings when Mama would come dressed in white and kiss me before going off to some affair that I imagined as incomparably splendid. Not that this last experience was likely in any case to happen to Nika, for I went to few affairs that could be called splendid and I could never look like Mama. I hoped that my presence might be comforting to Nika: I knew it could never be exciting.

And so, on that morning, as on others, Nika would have had breakfast with me and would have chattered as usual if she had not been recovering from measles. She was all right now: today I would be able to take her out.

You know, I was thinking to myself as I climbed the stairs, that you are feeling gay now not because it is your birthday but because Nika will remember that it is as no one else has remembered. She will kiss you as no one else has kissed you today, and she will be as happy about your birthday as if it were her own. It won't be a date on the calendar for her: it will be a fiesta. I paused on the landing to relish my happiness. Through the window I could see the spring-flowering trees that never become trite and usual but are always the miracle of resurrection: the cherries of pink and white, the laburnum dripping

353

with golden rain. Oh, be careful, I thought, or you will suffer for this some day. It isn't wise to love anyone so much, to try, as you are doing, to recreate for someone else the childhood you would like to have had. And what can there be in common between your childhood, even had it been as you would have liked it, and Nika's, for Nika is all you never were. Certainly it was not from me that Nika got her beauty. Perhaps it was from my Mama.

I ran up the last flight and opened the door upon the white room full of morning light. She was not there. She could not be far off, of that I was certain; but my silly heart missed a beat and I cried: "Nika! Nika darling! Where are you?"

Then she leapt upon my back from some concealment, and the corn gold of her long hair fell upon my shoulders, and her warm little mouth was kissing me on the neck and the ear, and she struggled higher up so that she was able to put her head right over my shoulder and our faces met and we kissed for a long time.

"You are giving me all your kisses," she said. "You will have none left for anyone else."

She dropped to the floor and gave me a grave little curtsy, which was none the less dignified because she was wearing her nightdress. "Many happy, happy, happy returns of this auspicious occasion, my darling Mama," she said.

"Good gracious, Nika, wherever did you get that grand word from?"

"From the dictionary," she said. "I intend to astound you by learning one grand word every day."

She took me by the hand and led me to a cupboard in a corner of the room. A piece of string passed through the keyhole and hung down the front of the cupboard. "Now you must pull the string gently," she instructed me. I did so, and a tiny crystal clatter reached me ears. I pulled again. It was an enchanting sound.

"Open the door," she said.

Inside, the string was attached to a silver bangle hung all round with minute silver bells. Nika cut the string with a pair of scissors and slipped the bangle over my wrist. "Now you will always be able to hear little Sarah Rainborough at the Crystal Palace. Wobble your hand."

I wobbled my hand and the little bells rang and Nika clapped her hands and cried with delight: "There! Do you hear little Sarah Rainborough?"

"But how, Nika darling?"

"You told me, you told me again and again, how your Papa and Mama took you to the Crystal Palace. You were only three."

"Yes . . ."

"Well, then," she logically explained, "it was a great day for you—an auspicious occasion. Then, when I went into the shop with Uncle

Mervyn, the bangle was hanging on a little bar, and the wind came into the shop with us and the bells rang, because the bangle was near the door. And Uncle Mervyn said: 'What a lovely little noise—like crystal.' And so that is the noise of the Crystal Palace heard from a long way off. Now you're Mrs. Undridge, Q.C., M.P., but when you wobble your hand you can hear little Sarah Rainborough, aged three."

"Yes. I see. Thank you, darling. It's a beautiful notion."

Beautiful and sad and strange. The little bells rang again, and I wondered if I could bear to hear that music now that my child had explained its meaning to me. Sarah Rainborough, aged three, amid the flowers and the music and the springing fountains, seemed a long way off; and the thought of peace on earth, good will to men, that had filled her young heart, seemed even farther. I found that I was keeping my hand very still.

"And the strange thing is," Nika said, "that today we are *going* to the Crystal Palace."

"Darling—I didn't know that."

"No. It was Uncle Mervyn's secret. He said I could tell you on your birthday morning. He is taking us in his new motorcar. Have you ever ridden in a motorcar, Mama?"

"No."

"Then," she said, producing another grand dictionary word, "on this auspicious occasion you will have an unprecedented experience."

She began to dance in her nightdress, and I thought of the child of three dancing with impatience as Kitey tugged at her rebellious hair. That was on a birthday, too.

5

There was not much about Mervyn that Enid didn't like, but she didn't like this motorcar. Mervyn had bought it in France, and had so far done no more than crawl through one or two streets in the quiet hours of the early morning or late evening. These tremendous exploits had caused comment in the newspapers, which noted that Mr. Mervyn Mostyn-Lloyd, "the proprietor of the famous West End emporium of Mostyn-Lloyd," was among the most forward-looking men of his time. The "emporium" was lighted by electricity and it could be "communicated with telephonically," and so could the proprietor's house in Hanover Square.

Well, for that matter, so could our house in Chelsea. We had been "on the telephone" since the opening of the year, and indeed no sooner had I left Nika to dress and gone downstairs than the bell rang and there was Mervyn to speak to me. He was crestfallen, full of apologies. We could not go out in the motorcar after all. He had "got stuck," he said, in a street near Hanover Square the night before, and there the car still was, surrounded by an admiring crowd, with a mechanic underneath it and a policeman keeping order. Would it be all right if we went to the Crystal Palace in a cab? Then he could bring Edward. Enid would never allow Edward to go in the car. It was a great pity. He had been looking forward to his first really important run.

"Of course," he explained, when he arrived soon after luncheon, "Enid has the laugh. As soon as the car arrived I sold the horses."

"That was a great act of faith," I said.

"Not at all. Just a matter of common sense. The thing's here. We're bound to run into a few small troubles at the beginning, but in five years' time they'll be ended, and in ten a horse will be a curiosity that you'll see only in the zoo."

He was always tremendously taken up like this with new things, but they had to be new things that someone else had started. He had a mechanical but not an inventive mind. Once someone had explained a mechanical principle to him he could understand it perfectly, but he could never work it out for himself. He could answer all the little Edward's questions about how steamships and locomotives went along, and how pumps worked, and anything else of that sort; and he had a great faith in the future of all these machines that fascinated him.

"You wait, my dear Aunt Sarah. These motor engines are allowing us now to crawl rather painfully about the earth. It won't be long before they're taking us gaily through the sky. Stands to reason. Someone will do it."

But it wouldn't be Mervyn. Still, he would always be there to encourage with his belief that it "stands to reason." That might almost be called his life's motto. There was nothing reason couldn't do. Except, as we now know, use its own inventions reasonably. But that was a thought that did not then occur either to me or Mervyn.

We jogged out to Sydenham in a four-wheeler, and Nika, who was nine months older than Edward, took a matronly charge of him for their first visit to the Crystal Palace. We had tea there, and watched a troupe of acrobats on a high wire doing things that made me sick to look at them; and the children insisted on staying till dusk came and the fireworks flared up into the blackening gulf of the sky. It ended with a "set piece" depicting a battle scene, with a lot of banging and blazing that made my head reel. I didn't feel that this was "my" Crystal Palace at all. It was in a new place and it was of a different shape and it seemed altogether more like a vulgar fun fair than anything else. There was no Queen and no Duke; no sparrows disported themselves in majestic imprisoned elms near the vaulting glitter of fountains, under the marrow-moving surge of organ music. No one talked of peace on earth, and the machines which, somehow, were miraculously to bring it

356

had emerged from the crystal showcase and were beginning to creep among us here and there, like Mervyn's maimed motorcar that would not be maimed for long.

As I sat there with Edward and Nika, wide-eyed at these flaming wonders, each holding one of my hands in a close excited grip, my head began to ache and I began to understand that for me, from then on, *this* would not be the Crystal Palace. My palace was gone except as a dream, a shining bubble, floating now farther and farther back down the stream of memory, which, no doubt, would distort it more and more as the years went by, so that all I should have to treasure would be a figment of something which possibly had never been, at any rate as that child had seen it in her romantic innocence.

The fiery battle blazed and exploded to an end, and then I was glad to go.

"We'll have to find another cab," Mervyn said. "How annoying! But you wait, Aunt Sarah! In a year or two I shall be able to whizz you home from here in no time at all."

Oh no you won't, I thought, not from here, because I shan't ever see this place again. And I never did.

Daniel had telephoned to say that he would not be in to dinner. I took Nika straight to bed and kissed her good night. She was wilting with tiredness. I sat by the bedside, holding her hand till she should fall off, and she said sleepily: "Don't be unhappy, darling Mama."

"Sweetheart, what makes you think I'm unhappy?" I asked, startled.

She opened her eyes and didn't answer my question but said: "You mustn't be." Then she was asleep.

The telephone bell was ringing when I went downstairs, and I hastened to answer it, for the servants were afraid of it, as of something infernal. A woman's voice asked: "Is Mr. Daniel Undridge there?"

"No."

Rather imperiously she said: "Will you take this message for him, please." She clearly thought she was speaking to a servant.

"This is Mrs. Undridge."

"Oh." The voice faltered. It was a very beautiful voice, and I was sure it belonged to a very beautiful woman. "Oh. I beg your pardon. It doesn't matter."

I hung up the instrument and stood there gazing at it for a moment. Well, I thought, it doesn't matter. Not all that much. I've been expecting it, and now I know.

6

I ate my dinner alone—not a pleasant thing to do on my birthday. I should have gone out with Maggie Whale, or had her in, but she

357

was not in town. After dinner I went into the drawing room where a fire had been lit, for the evening had turned cold. This was now almost exclusively my room, for when Daniel was at home he liked to work in his study after dinner unless we were entertaining. We didn't entertain much. He knew I disliked assemblies got together not for friendliness but in pursuit of interests, and so he did most of his entertaining out. Perhaps I had failed him. Certainly I was unmoved by what had become the chief concern of his life.

It was good to relax in a chair by the fire. The headache that the banging fireworks had given me was passing away. And that was strange. I should have expected the short telephone conversation to make it worse, but it was better. It was odd to feel this sense almost of relief. For a long time I had known that what existed between me and Daniel was no more than a courteous association. I had wondered whether, elsewhere, he had found company, and now I knew that he had. Of course, no lawyer would call that voice on the telephone evidence confirming what I suspected; but it was evidence to me. And I took note, almost with amusement, that after a moment's brief shock I was unperturbed.

I knew that, whatever the lady with the beautiful voice might think, Daniel's master bias was political. He would allow nothing—not even you, dear lady—to interfere with his pursuit of office. In these days in which I am writing, appearance in a divorce case would not affect a man's prospects; but things were different then. The recent scandal over Sir Charles Dilke was there as a warning. I heard it discussed at one of our few political dinner parties; Daniel thought Sir Charles Dilke had been a fool. I was sure that Daniel and his lady would act with discretion. I was necessary as façade. I didn't mind that. There had been little but façade between me and Daniel for a long time.

The thoughts that had come to me at the Crystal Palace slid back into my mind, displacing these other thoughts as though they were of lesser importance.

Long, long ago, after Mama was dead, there had arrived at Tresant the portrait of her that Lord Burnage had commissioned from G. F. Watts. He could not bear to look at it. He had never opened the case that contained it, but had asked Whaley to keep it in her cottage. When Justin renovated Tresant, this picture of his mother and mine was hung in the drawing room; and now it was here in the room in which I was sitting. Sally had given it to me.

The fireshine was on the face whose enigmatic beauty looked at me out of the shadows. She had never been near to me, never dear and familiar as I was to Nika, but she had been with me on that far-off morning that was now so insistently recreating its shining moments. I felt like Moses on Pisgah, but looking backward, not forward, to a promised land. She had been with me, and she was dead, and the Duke was dead, and the Prince who had walked among the fountains with the Queen was dead: and Papa, who had stood on my other side, holding my hand, was dead, too.

There was no light in the room save firelight, and when I moved my arm, which carried the bracelet Nika had given me, the sound of the silver bells was so far off, seeming to speak through so many lost and foundered years, that it was hardly heard above the whickering of the flames.

It was strange that death had been necessary to bring me again into touch with my father. The hurt to his self-esteem when my mother left him must have been profound. I was now of an age to understand such a thing. He had never sought even the slightest association with me or her again, and I did not know of his death till a firm of solicitors wrote to me, asking me to call upon them, and I was given a copy of his will. A Miss Ella Costello was bequeathed, for the duration of her life, the interest upon ten thousand pounds and the freehold of the house she lived in, and a John Costello, whom I supposed to be her son and his, received an outright gift of five thousand pounds. There were bequests to servants. These few trivial details were the only light I ever had to help me to see the sort of life my father had lived in all those sundered years. Miss Costello's house was at Pinner: easy to get at, but sufficiently removed for discretion.

Apart from these sums, which were an insignificant bite out of a large fortune, Richard and I were the only beneficiaries. My father must have known of my marriage, for I appeared as Sarah Undridge, but he hadn't known about Richard. He put him in, merely in case he was there, as "the eldest male issue of the aforementioned Sarah Undridge," and made provision about what should happen "should there be no male issue of the aforementioned Sarah Undridge." It all seemed to me odd and pathetic, this man sitting down to dispose of his money to a daughter who can have meant literally nothing to him and a grandson of whose existence he was uncertain. But he was a man who believed that a principal object of life was to accumulate money and to pass it on within the family. Even the disruptive blow at his conception of "the family" had not been strong enough to change this outlook characteristic of his time.

I had had little money of my own till now. I had worked for a salary with Whaley and had been glad to get it; and then I had married a well-to-do man whose success in his profession made him richer. Now I was rich "in my own right," as they say, richer than Daniel; and it made no difference whatever to my life. And when Richard came of age he would be rich, too. He was old enough now to understand such things, and I had told him about it here in this room.

Sitting there that night before the fire, I recalled the moment: the tall handsome boy listening with grave attention to the news that a man he had never seen, and scarcely heard of, had, because of some bizarre preoccupation with family "continuity," though his own family life had been made so abruptly discontinuous, ensured that Richard, when he was twenty-one, could look forward to a life in clover. All the time I was speaking to him, Richard's eye was on his grandmother's portrait, and I did not need to be told what he was thinking. When I had finished he asked: "Would that be enough money to buy Tresant?"

"My dear Richard! Whatever put that idea into your head?"

"You know very well, Mama," he said, "that the idea has always been in my head—not the idea of *buying* Tresant, for I never knew I should have any money, but the idea of having it."

That was true enough.

"I don't see," he said, "that it's of any use to my aunt; she never goes to the place: and my Grandmamma was Lady Burnage. The Gaylords are my ancestors."

"If they were, my dear," I said gently, "you wouldn't need to *buy* the place. You would inherit it. As for its being sold, I've no doubt that if your Aunt Gaylord"—I could never bring myself to speak of Aunt Sally!—"wished to sell she would have sold long ago. The person who owns a place like that, you know, can't always please himself. An estate gets tied up by all sorts of legal conditions, and one of these may well forbid selling. But as to that, I don't know, so far as Tresant is concerned."

"There is no male heir but me," he said obstinately.

We left it at that, as we so often did, and sitting in the drawing room on that night of my visit to the Crystal Palace, it came to me with a sudden shock of surprise that perhaps Richard would have Tresant by inheritance after all. It had been Justin's, and now it was Sally's, who was Justin's half sister; but so was I his half sister; and I supposed that if Sally died the place would be mine. And if I had died before her, then would it not be my son's? However, all this was based on contingencies remote and unpleasant. I dismissed them from my mind, resolved on no account to put ideas into Richard's head. For the trouble with Richard was that he was not interested in Tresant as a responsibility, but only as a place that would help to gratify notions of grandeur.

7

I sat up unusually late. I was still up when Daniel came in at half past eleven. He went into the dining room to get some whiskey, and brought it in and sat sipping it opposite me at the fireside. "Had a good birthday, my dear?"

I was wearing the cabochon emerald brooch. "Yes, thank you, Daniel, but rather noisy and tiring at the end. Mervyn came along with Edward and took me and Nika to the Crystal Palace. It wasn't bad as birthdays go. Nika gave me this lovely bracelet"—I tinkled the bells—"but I lost one more illusion. I suppose that's what growing up is: losing illusions one by one."

He looked up sharply, but managed a smile as he asked: "And what's gone overboard this time?"

"I don't believe the Crystal Palace ever existed."

"Oh, that!" He sipped his whiskey happily. "But you've been there today, you tell me."

"Not to *my* Crystal Palace. I've decided that that was a dream."

"You were born romantic."

"Do you remember the night at Tresant when we listened to the tumbrils and knew that Justin was going away in the morning?"

"I do indeed. I warned you then that the notions talked about when the Crystal Palace was opened were stuff and nonsense."

Yes, I thought; but you warned me gently, and all night long you comforted me.

"I remember," he said, "that I explained the causes of the trouble that called Justin away. The black men obnoxious to both the Dutch and the British. The certainty that when the black men were put in their place—for the time being—the Dutch and British would be at each other's throats. Remember?"

"I remember."

"Well, you watch Cecil Rhodes and his friend Jameson. They'll brew something up before long."

"Who is Cecil Rhodes?"

He finished the whiskey, put down the glass and got up. "You know, Sarah, you really ought to concern yourself more with the world you live in. You despise politics, don't you?"

"I wouldn't say that. But I think they spend too much time on the wrong things."

"They spend time on things as they are, not on crystal dreams. Well, Rhodes is part of politics, and it would be profitable to keep an eye on his doings. It's not wise to be unaware of what is happening under your nose. I'm for bed. Good night, my dear."

He took my hand, raised it to his lips, and kissed it. It was a habitual good-night gesture that he had got into. As he dropped my hand Nika's little bells tinkled forlornly, and I noticed that the fire was out on the hearth.

361

CHAPTER TWENTY-ONE

1

DANIEL was an important enough man to be able to say in 1897: "If you'd like a seat in the Mall I think I can manage it."

"What about Richard and Nika?" I asked. "They'd love to be there."

At Richard's name Daniel's face went shut. Doing so little (as I thought) for Richard, he had always, nevertheless, felt aggrieved that Richard was not the sort of son he ought to have. Richard had not ceased to be a boy of silly romantic dreams: an ordinary, good-mannered, selfish, uninspiring boy, with nothing picking him out from other boys except the vehemence of his desire to be in a shining position. He would never, I knew, do a hand's turn toward making such a position for himself, unless perhaps his persistent wish to join a cavalry regiment indicated a line of talent. I had even urged Daniel to consider this, but he was not sympathetic. He snorted. "I wonder," he said, "whether he knows what it was like in the Crimea? They *ate* their horses. Take it from me, my dear, all my lord has in mind is riding down the Mall with polished boots and a shining breastplate and some of those funny colored horsehairs waving in his hat. A nursemaid's delight."

He would never forgive Richard for not being a studious follower in his own footsteps. I was annoyed, and I said: "You know, Daniel, you're remarkably like that dull, obstinate and pig-headed bourgeoise, your sister Marie."

As usual, he was giving his correspondence a first glance at the breakfast table. He looked at me in consternation and put down the letter he was reading. "Nika," he said—she always breakfasted with us —"if you've finished breakfast, would you mind going to your room?"

She went, and he said: "If you wish to quarrel with me, I don't want Nika present."

I could see that he was deeply hurt by what I had said—the more so as I had never said anything like that to him before. I preferred to let him go his way and to lead my own life as I wished to do, but this time I persisted.

"I'm sorry if I hurt you, Daniel."

"Hurt me? Do you think I can be hurt by a remark utterly preposterous and without foundation?" His face was red, and he began to ruffle his hair.

"All I meant to say was that your attitude to Richard is just like Marie's attitude to Julian. There was one thing Julian wanted to do, one thing that might be his line, and that was the one thing she was determined to turn him away from. Possibly Richard would make a good soldier."

He sidetracked the last sentence by saying: "Julian! Your concern with that boy amounts to mania."

"Well, it looks as though he was right and his mother wrong, and possibly you are wrong about Richard," I said, dragging the argument back to where I wanted it to be. "I'm terribly afraid," I added, "that if he goes on feeling that what he wants is unreasonably thwarted, he'll kick over the traces when he's twenty-one. He'll be a rich man then."

"He should never have known it," Daniel said, rightly enough, I thought. I often regretted not having kept that to myself. "As for his being thwarted, believe me, there are plenty of young men who would like to be thwarted by a public school and university education."

"Shall we keep to the case before the court?" I asked with a smile. "We are not discussing plenty of young men. We are discussing Richard."

He got up and swept the letters into his hand. "I find my work difficult enough," he said, "without having my thoughts utterly disarranged and torn to pieces first thing in the morning."

"I'm sorry. I wouldn't for worlds willingly throw sand into the Westminster works."

This was the nearest we ever came to a quarrel. I left the matter alone after that; but I was not surprised when, this question of the seats in the Mall arising some time later, Daniel did not look happy when I suggested taking Richard. Still, I should have liked him to be with me when I saw the Queen again—him and Nika. The occasion was her diamond jubilee, and this would be the fourth time in my life that I had seen her. I had seen her in pink and silver with the Prince at her side, walking in my palace among the trees and the fountains and the flowers while the air was full of music and, looking up, I watched the clouds moving over the blue sky till it seemed that the crystal ship was itself moving on the celestial voyage to paradise that its building figured; as if we were all bound for glory to the strains of the Halleluiah Chorus: Queen and Prince, the Duke and the sparrows, and even little Sarah Rainborough. I had seen her at Sydenham when the Palace was opened there, and ten years ago with thousands of others I had risen, and the movement of our rustled uprising created a hush and an awe, through which she came slowly up the nave of the Abbey, whose dark roof allowed no glimpse of sky for the play of foolish fancy, and she passed so close to me, a small, old lady, wearing black satin with a white front and a white bonnet with a black velvet band: she passed so close that I heard the tap of her stick on the floor and the sound of her breathing; and the shrunken blackness of her seemed to join her heart to mine in mourning for that morning, now so long ago, when all had seemed possible that now was buried deep and deep and deep.

That was the third time—the jubilee; and now here was this diamond jubilee that would be the fourth time, and Daniel was saying: "It seems to me that Richard would be much better employed where he is. Now that he's at Balliol, let him stick to it. Breaking up his work on any and every excuse is no good for him."

"I don't imagine," I said, "that Oxford, on Diamond Jubilee Day, will notify its loyalty by a passionate addiction to the dons," but Daniel would have none of it. "I have four seats to dispose of," he said, "and I'm lucky to have so many. I've already disposed of two. You can have the others. I should like Nika to go."

2

We were up early. There was still dew on the morning that soon would be parched by the mid-June sun, and thinking this as I ran upstairs to see that Nika was ready, I fell into an old fault of reading my own words as parables. But it was true enough: I felt parched and dry as I hastened to my dewy child.

"Nika! You must have been up at dawn, child, to be ready so soon!"

"I was not up half so early as Miss Whale used to get up."

Whaley loved her and they spent hours in talk. I could not have been much older than Nika is now, I thought, when Whaley was watching my antics at Tresant, my silly little tricks with the spectacles. There would be no need for Nika to use silly tricks in order to draw attention to herself. She was twelve, losing her baby fat, a long-legged filly. She had brushed her hair till it shone like gold wire round the oval of her face. Her eyes were gray and serious. She was wearing a dress of smoky gray gauze that had a hint of blue in it, and the ribbons of a dark blue sash round her waist fell behind her almost to her feet. Her shoes were silver.

"Miss Whale sometimes got up at four in the morning. She was living in the country with her father and she could go through the back door straight into the fields. She walked through the cold dew on the grass without any shoes on her feet and gathered mushrooms. Sometimes she gathered blackberries and made jam for her father, and sometimes elderberries and made wine. She must have been practical. I want to grow up a practical woman with no nonsense about me, like Miss Whale."

"Well, let's go and get a practical breakfast into us. We shall be sitting about for a long time."

"You haven't kissed me."

"I was trying to be practical. I didn't want to disarrange your dress."

She ran to me and I crushed her into my arms, and she said: "Never mind the dress. The Queen won't see *me*. I wonder what she *will* see? Mustn't it be terrible when you're the thing to *be* seen? There'll be soldiers and bands and princes and princesses, and nobody will very much want to see them. They'll all want to see the Queen—thousands and thousands and thousands of people. She'll be the cynosure of all eyes. Miss Whale says that's a cliché. But when everyone's there to see *you*, what do *you* see?"

"I expect she'll see the Duke and the Prince Consort who was her husband, and the sparrows in the crystal cage, and the Indian Mutiny and the dead soldiers in the Crimean war who were too many to bury, so they threw them with the dead horses into the harbor. Oh, she'll have plenty to see."

"Yes," said Nika, "I expect when you're old you're like the National Gallery that Miss Whale took me to—so much that you don't know *what* to look at. How old is she?"

"Seventy-eight."

"I'm twelve already, and six twelves are seventy-two. Only six times as long as I've had and I'll be catching her up." She sighed: "Life is not long, is it?"

"It's long enough for most people. Let's have breakfast."

It was only six o'clock and we breakfasted alone. Daniel was not interested in the occasion. The leader of his party was more to him than the Queen, and no doubt he would get up at seven as usual and do a good day's work. "I don't want any worries that will prevent me from doing a good day's work," he used to say. At seven we set out, and by eight we were on our stand in the Mall. It was a glorious day: the sun was warm, the trees had their summer beauty, and the world—the little world of London on Diamond Jubilee Day—was full of joy and animation. This was to be an occasion "featuring," as they say nowadays, the Empire; and the crowds stretching away on either hand, toward the Palace and toward Carlton House Terrace, were shouting and singing with a boisterous cockney self-confidence that would have led one to suppose that every one of them had made the Empire by his own exertions. Sitting there, with Nika at my side taking everything in with calm enjoyment, I thought about the Empire, and especially about Cecil Rhodes and his friend Dr. Jameson whom Daniel not long since had told me to watch. Just a year ago Dr. Jameson had been sent to jail for his little bit of empire-building; but nobody, I was sure, was remembering that now. And why on earth should they? I asked myself. Give over your everlasting internal doubts and questions, and enjoy this day.

"Mummy," Nika said, "don't they look funny when you see them together in hundreds and hundreds?"

365

She plucked at the leg-of-mutton sleeve of my blouse, for I was wearing what almost everyone else did: those sleeves puffed above the elbows, close-fitting on the forearms down to the wrists, the belt that waisted me like a wasp, and the skirt that flared out to fullness round my feet. On my head was a jaunty straw hat with a few feathers sticking up from the band.

I can see the woman now, walking up the steps of the stand, for our seats were at the top; and I suppose it is because she was wearing clothes just like this that I remember the fashion of the moment. The handle of a lilac-colored parasol was hung upon her left forearm and with her right hand she held her full skirt clear of the ground, revealing a pretty foot.

"May I trouble you?" she said, and smiled at me and Nika. We rose to allow her to pass. An older woman who was with her went first, and they took the seats next to ours, so that she was on my right hand and Nika on my left. She had a fan suspended from a long silver chain that went round her neck, and as soon as she was seated she flicked it open and began to fan herself vigorously. "What a day," she said, turning to me; "and what a crush!"

Oh, he can't, I thought, he can't have been so treacherous as to tell her I shall be here. He can't have done *that*! And I am sure he didn't. I am sure she never knew who I was; but from the moment she took the seat next to mine I never doubted who she was. She was in maturity of beauty: a woman, she looked, in her mid-thirties, dark, handsome and vivacious. She was forever smiling, or laughing outright, and this revealed her perfect teeth, so white against the cherry of her lips. It was a captivating mouth. Altogether, she was captivating.

From time to time, ever since she had spoken to me on the telephone, I had thought about her, I had tried to picture her. I had hoped against hope that my imagination of her as a beautiful woman was ill founded. But I was able not to be disturbed by her too deeply. Whether she was indeed beautiful, or one of the bloomered hoydens one saw riding bicycles in the park, or one of the new women with foreheads full of brains and mouths full of teeth that shelved out like low-tide reefs, I could keep her at arm's length in my imagination because I did not know *what* she was. But she was not at arm's length now. Her arm was touching mine and I felt my whole body flush with indignant heat, and I thought of changing places with Nika, but I could not do that either, because the idea of her touching Nika revolted me. And with it all, I knew that I was doing her wrong. She was no leper—no indeed she was not! Gaiety and graciousness palpably surrounded her; and perhaps she loved him as I once had done, though never again could I feel for him anything but compassion.

But thinking all this with my head made no difference to what I was feeling in my nerves and bones. My nerves tingled with revulsion and I knew the meaning of the words: "My bones are water."

The air was full of the music of regimental bands, of sunshine, of the crowd's gay and careless emotions; and stretching down in front of us, from here where we sat at the top of the stand, was a declivity of feathered hats and silks of blue and white and green and mauve, and men's tall shining hats, and all this was in agitation and livened by incessant chatter, and this chatter rose up, too, from the Mall itself, filling the long smooth sanded distance to the Palace. For she was "Sixty years a Queen." Sixty years from "I will be good" and putting Mama Kent in her place to this hot and sunny moment when she would come, doubtless in black as usual, with so much of good and so much of ill swirling in the memories that filled her gray old head.

Suddenly all the chatter died, so completely that you could for the first time hear the shrill calling of the swifts that darted over the Mall, and then there was music again and someone shouted: "They're coming!" On our stand a man's clear voice said: "May we have the parasols down, ladies, please?" and like those flowers that fold themselves when night comes the parasols drew in their gauzy petals and sank from sight.

She turned to me and said with a smile: "We're fortunate. We can keep ours open up here at the top. We interfere with nobody's view." She spoke to the elderly woman on her other side: "You have the parasol, Mama. You must be finding it very hot."

"No, thank you, Pearl darling. I'm very well as I am. Don't fuss about me."

She was determined to be amiable. "What about your little girl?" she asked me; and leaning across me to Nika she said: "Are you comfortable, darling? Would you like to borrow my parasol?"

"No, thank you, ma'am," Nika said. "I can see them! I can see them! They're coming! A soldier on a gray horse!"

It was Lord Roberts, carrying his field marshal's baton. And then there was no end to it, the men and the beautiful horses; and the man with the clear voice, one of those Englishmen whose function it is in life to enlighten people, kept up a calm brief commentary. Canadian Hussars . . . Canadian Dragoons . . . This is the Canadian Prime Minister in the carriage. . . . New South Wales . . . Maoris, these dark chaps . . . Cape Mounted Rifles . . .

So it went; clip-clop of hooves, throb of music, color, movement, burning sun, the excited shouts and cheers down there on the ground; the decorous interest here on the stand, punctuated by the decorous omniscient voice. It was royalty now; and the voice knew the Almanach de Gotha as familiarly as the Army List. That is the little Princess Ena . . . Denmark . . . Hanover . . . Teck . . . Bulgaria.

Landaus, horses with tossing heads and spume-whitened bits; and the procession of the Forty Princes.

"I'll never get through it," I thought. "How much longer? How much longer?"

She was smelling a bottle of some reviving salts, and offered them to me. I shook my head. "The poor things," she said. "It's a hot day for them. Royalty *do* have to work hard, I think—don't you?"

The *Times* said that her Majesty wore a black silk dress trimmed with lace and a bonnet to match, and carried a parasol in her hand. "Opposite her sat the Princess of Wales and her Royal Highness the Princess Christian. Beside the Royal carriage the Prince of Wales and the Duke of Connaught rode on the right and the Duke of Cambridge on the left. It was preceded by Viscount Wolseley as Commander-in-Chief, and immediately after it the Royal Standard was borne on high by a trooper of the Household Cavalry."

It must have been a good sight, and I suppose I saw something of it, but I have no recollection of it. None whatever. This was the culmination of the British Empire on its way to church; and what did the British Empire mean then to me? In her excitement at that supreme moment she allowed her parasol to tilt across my line of vision; and I was too exhausted to ask her to move it. And then, when a great sigh at the climax of glory went up from the crowd, Nika fainted.

Everywhere there was sudden relaxation. Below us the crowd broke ranks and surged forward like a ragged tide upon the yellow sand. On the stand men got up and stretched their cramped bones, women thrust away the beating sunlight with reopened parasols.

"Pearl, darling, put your parasol over the child. This heat is beyond endurance."

We both stood over Nika, I with my arms round her, she shading her from the sun, and I could smell a subtle scent that rose from her, but it was soon overpowered by the smell of the bottle that she held under Nika's nose. The elderly woman took the parasol, and this woman named Pearl with one hand held the smelling bottle and with the other flung open the fan that hung from the silver chain and agitated it in front of Nika's face. "The poor little darling," she said. "How sweet she looks! I hope she saw the Queen before she fainted. How old is she?"

She didn't seem to expect an answer, and I gave none, and she stroked Nika's forehead with long fingers. "There! She's opening her eyes!"

Nika soon pulled herself together, sat up, and passed a hand over her face. "You fainted, darling," said this woman named Pearl. "Did you see the Queen?"

Nika nodded, but did not speak. She looked shaky, but she was obviously on the mend, and a few sympathetic or inquisitive people who had lingered near us began to move away. The stand was emptying, and I said: "Thank you for helping. She'll be all right now. I'll take her down into the shade of the trees."

Nika got to her feet and smiled at this woman. She held out her hand and the woman took it and pressed it for a long moment as the two stood smiling into one another's eyes. "Thank you, ma'am," Nika said. "I really did see the Queen."

Then this woman whose name (as I should never forget) was Pearl turned and held out her hand to me, too. I looked for the first time fully into her candid merry eyes and saw the darkening in them of a faint surprise as she realized that, for some reason that she could not know, I was meeting her advance reluctantly. But her hand remained there, and I took it, and forced a smile to my lips and said: "Thank you. Please don't bother any more about us. We shall be all right."

Then she and the other woman went, and with Nika's slender weight upon my arm I moved slowly down the steps and into the shadow of the trees. Nika said: "Wasn't she lovely? I hope that when I grow up I shall be a lovely lady like that."

"Do you mean the Queen?"

"Oh, no! I didn't see the Queen. But that lady so much wanted me to have seen her. I wouldn't like to have disappointed that lady."

"No," I said. "She is obviously a lady one would not want to disappoint."

3

I could see the silver chain hanging from her neck and the fan at the end of it. That was an unusual thing: to wear a fan at the end of a chain. I had never seen anyone do it before. It would not be difficult to get a chain like that: the design, though attractive, was commonplace. Any silversmith would supply one.

But should I do it? Was there any sense, any point, in upsetting the courteous equilibrium in which Daniel and I managed our affairs? If in his presence I wore a fan on just that sort of chain it would be saying to him: You see. I not only know she is there. I know who she is.

I hated to fuss and coddle Nika, because I had been brought up to know alternate coddling and neglect. I didn't want either for the child. But I sent her to bed when we got back to Chelsea, and this was not out of concern for her health but because she would chatter about this woman Pearl. I couldn't stand it. Though Daniel, I was sure, had not told her of me and Nika, I felt outraged that he should have run the slightest risk—and the risk was *not* slight—of our falling unexpectedly upon discovery. This sense of his boldness, of his having dared to take a chance of putting me in an intolerable position, worried me like a maggot all through the afternoon as I sat in the drawing room with the blinds down to keep out the heat.

The next morning I went to Bond Street and bought the chain and had it fastened to a fan. Daniel had been morose at breakfast, and I put this down to the effect upon him of a paragraph in a newspaper which he handed me across the table. There had been a lot of rough horseplay and merrymaking in the West End on Jubilee night, and bands of undergraduates from Oxford had done their share. There were arrests, and among those listed as having been taken to Vine Street police station was Richard Undridge. I could not resist saying: "So he didn't stay in Oxford after all! Perhaps it would have been better if you had given him one of your four tickets."

I was surprised at the effect this had on Daniel. His face darkened suddenly, not with annoyance but with a sharp pain, and he said: "I wish to God I had." Then, leaving untouched the breakfast which had just been placed before him, he went from the room.

That evening I wore the fan on the chain, but Daniel did not see it. He did not come home till after I was in bed. The next morning at breakfast we read of Richard's being discharged, the magistrate even permitting himself a joke of the boys will be boys sort, and saying that high spirits carried to excess at such a moment could almost be interpreted as an ebullience of desirable patriotism. "The old fool!" Daniel growled, and said no more about it, sitting there with a stony face, leaving even his letters unopened.

I was surprised and disturbed. "Are you well, Daniel? Is anything the matter?"

"What on earth should be the matter?" he asked roughly. "Can't I turn my own thoughts over in my own head?"

"They seem to be excessively gloomy ones."

He glared at me, and through that look of animosity I was again aware of mortal pain. I could not understand him. He was shut from me. He said as he went out: "I shall be in to dinner tonight."

"But, of course, Daniel. We have the Hemings . . . "

"I have asked them not to come."

It was a strange day—this day I shall never forget. I did all the normal things, but about everything there was a sense of abnormality, of crisis. I did lessons with Nika in the morning, took her for a walk in the afternoon, left her at her music master's, called for her and walked home with her. It was a lovely day. Whaley came in to tea. After tea she and Nika went up to Nika's room for one of their long talks, and when they came down Whaley asked: "May I bear Nika away for a day or two? We'll go into the country tomorrow."

Nothing remarkable in any of this. Whaley often took the child to a cottage she now had in Hertfordshire; but when they were gone and the time for Daniel's return drew near I thought, with a nervous laugh: "We seem to be clearing the decks for action. The Hemings . . . Nika . . ." The house, this house where old Mrs. Gemstone had died almost in my arms, where Daniel and I had loved one another, seemed curiously quiet, as if listening. I heard Daniel come in, and when the dinner gong sounded I waited for him to go into the dining room before me. It was an excessively hot night, and I had ordered a cold meal which should be left on the sideboard. With a sense of crisis in my heart, I wanted the maids out of the way. I slipped the silver chain over my head, and when I entered the room I was flirting my fan. I shut the door quietly behind me.

Daniel was standing with his back to me, looking out of the window, a glass of sherry in his hand. His back had a bowed forlorn look, and when he turned my heart was smitten by his ashen face. I had intended that, whatever was to pass between us, I would leave the first word to him, but I could not help taking a step toward him, putting a hand on his shoulder, and saying: "You really do not look well. What is the matter?"

There was a feverish tic in his cheek and his eyes were hollow. He stared strangely at the chain and the fan, then asked: "How do *you* come to possess this?" Without waiting for an answer, he reached out and took hold of the chain, pulling it so roughly that one of the delicate links snapped. The fan fell to the floor; the chain remained in his fingers. He looked at it, seeming to forget me, the pain in his eyes deepening.

"What is the matter with you?" I asked. "What is wrong with my wearing a silver chain? It is mine. I bought it."

He dripped the links from one hand to the other, then threw the thing onto the table. "All right," he said. "I understand."

"I wonder whether you do?"

"I understand," he repeated emphatically. "But you've chosen a bitter moment to stab me." Then, after a long pause: "She is dead."

I had not known what to expect, but, of all things, not this . . . not this. "Oh, Daniel! Oh, my dear!"

He sat down on one of the chairs at the table in this very room, at this very table, where so long ago Mrs. Gemstone had fussed and fluttered because he was coming down from Oxford, and Whaley and I had tried to make things go smoothly, though we were excited, too, because he was coming, and he was so young and so gay. And now, I thought, he looks sixty and as if his life were ending.

I sat near him. His elbow was on the table and his head in his hand. His elbow was grinding into the snapped silver chain. "Tell me, Daniel. Tell me what happened."

"What is the use? It is finished."

She is finished, the woman named Pearl, so candid, full of laughter.

371

Cut down in a moment. I was appalled. "Tell me. It will be better for you."

"How can I talk about her to *you*? What *right* have I to talk about her to you?"

"Tell me."

"She was going home—she and her mother. They took a hansom. There were crowds everywhere. Noisy boisterous fools, roaming the streets, blowing horns, whirling rattles, throwing things. It was something thrown—I don't know—something—startled the horse and it bolted. Crashed into a lamp post."

He couldn't finish it for some moments. Then he said: "Her neck was broken. She died at once."

I ventured then to put a hand on his, but he got up, and a moment later I heard his footsteps pacing the floor in his room overhead. I picked up the chain from the table, the double of the one she had worn. It was probable that Daniel had given it to her, and this thought gave me no hurt. The chain was broken. Her neck was broken. Well, I thought, things *do* get broken. My love for Daniel was broken long ago, but, God knows how, I have got over that; and he will get over this. It is very strange that I am no longer in love with Daniel, but I am not. If I were, I should feel differently about this and about his anguish. My heart is full of compassion for him and for that lovely woman who must have known terror before the final wrench. But compassion is not love. The poets, I thought, made up a lot of things that I had not found to be true. "Love is not love that alters where it alteration finds." I had loved Daniel if ever man was loved, and I loved him no longer. Whaley had given Nika a copy of *The Golden Treasury* and we had been reading it together. We had been reading about the "last gasp of love's latest breath" and

> Now if thou would'st, when all have given him over,
> From death to life thou might'st him yet recover!

But I knew that this was not so, for now surely was such a moment as Drayton had in mind, a moment when the bitterness and sudden terror of human life had brought us close together, but there had been no magnetic flash, no quick flowering of the cold field that I still found to lie between us. I can give him compassion, I repeated in my heart, and even loving-kindness, but that, too, is not love as the poets talk about it. As for forgiveness: well, who was I, either to forgive or to ask to be forgiven? That was altogether too big a matter for me.

I listened to him walking up there over my head, and presently I went up and joined him. I said: "Is there anything I can do, my dear, to help you now?"

He looked at me strangely for a long time, and then said: "I should

372

like to tell you how it began, what it meant to me. You have a right to know. For some time I have felt that you knew. . . ."

"Yes."

"And yet you have put up with me, you haven't reproached me. . . ."

This did not move me. I stood at the window, looking down at the midsummer dusk creeping slowly through the street, and I knew that it was not any regard he had for me, or for the way I had taken this thing: it was not any of that that had held him to me. It was simply his ambition, his fear that a scandal would tarnish his worldly hopes. But for that, he would have left me.

"And so," he said, "you have earned a right to know something about it."

It is magnanimous of you, Daniel, I thought, to concede that your wife has acted with a propriety that entitles her to be told of your mistress; but I felt a pity for him and I did not say this. I said: "No, Daniel. Please don't tell me about it. I can accept it so long as you don't explain it. When is she to be buried?"

"Tomorrow." The words dragged out of him.

"Would you like me to come with you? Would that help? Nika is away. She has gone to visit Whaley."

The old lady who had been with her on the stand was not at the cemetery. Few people were, and I did not know any of them. I had put on an old black dress that seemed incongruous with the warmth and light of the afternoon, with the birds and butterflies that filled the place. There was a wreath on which I saw something written in Daniel's hand, but I did not wish to decipher it. This wreath and a few others were placed to one side to be put upon the grave when it was filled in, but the small bouquet that I carried, and to which I attached no writing, I threw in upon the coffin as the shovelfuls of earth began to fall. We had stood there in the great heat during a brief service, and a peacock butterfly alighted upon these few flowers and was still there when I threw them. It fluttered up out of the grave, and I thought how easy it would be to let imagination play with ideas suggested by this small happening. But this seemed to me a moment not for fancies but of brutal endings. The woman who had sparkled at my side a few days before was dead, and these flowers were already smashed into the heavy clay, and this butterfly would find the night cold and life brief.

Oh, I said, you are an old callous woman, incapable of feeling, with eyes too dry for tears. And it was this thought more than any, this thought that once I had been more sensitive to the world's anguish, that brought the tears streaming to my eyes. I took Daniel's arm, and through the river of my tears I saw that his eyes were dry, though his face was still twisted with pain. We walked out of the cemetery arm-in-arm, with not a word to say to one another, and went home.

CHAPTER TWENTY-TWO

I

RICHARD should have ended his course at Oxford in the summer of 1899; but toward the end of April he said in a letter to me: "Expect me in for a birthday breakfast on May the first." He would be twenty-one on that day.

"If he's coming at all," Daniel said testily, looking at his watch, "I wish he'd come promptly. He knows that breakfast is at eight o'clock. Not that he should be here at all. When I was at Oxford I stayed there—and worked."

His hair was white. He was now more politician than lawyer. In his constituency they liked him and were faithful to him. He had sat for Steignhampton without a break since the first time of election. He was round and rather pompous; pince-nez on watered silk swung on his chest. His ambition was to be Solicitor-General and eventually Attorney-General. He had come round to talking to me of his daily work and of his ambitions. Without sharing the ambitions, I listened sympathetically to the words. I even, more and more, allowed myself to be a political hostess. Once, Joseph Chamberlain was among the guests. Daniel hired a butler for that night. He was continually making such small investments. Not once since we walked arm-in-arm out of the cemetery following the burial of the woman named Pearl had we spoken of her or of that happening. I supposed he would always have stings of memory; but such stings become less vivid and hurtful; and for the commerce of day-by-day he turned to me, and I was glad. He never did succeed in getting high office, though his wit and persuasiveness as a speaker made him prized as a promoter of other people's enterprises. He was now Under Secretary of the Board of Public Communications.

Nika was standing at the window, hugging a parcel under her arm. At fourteen, she found it exciting to have a brother of twenty-one. She cried: "Good gracious! What a way to arrive! And with Cousin Julian, too!"

Daniel and I joined her at the window. A brougham with a cockaded coachman had drawn up. Richard and Julian got out: a pair of peacocks. Each wore a tall hat and carried a cane; but Julian's negligently-tied full bow of silk contrasted with Richard's tight-waisted gray tie, in which a large pearl was stuck. A square flat parcel dangled from Julian's hand.

374

Daniel turned from the window. "Well, I'm damned!" he said, but Nika clapped her hands.

There was a confusion of greetings— Many happy returns!—from us all to Richard and from them to me. "Now come and see my brougham before it drives away," Richard said excitedly, and Daniel said: "*Your* brougham! I thought it was something you'd hired."

"No, sir. It's mine."

We looked at it, dutifully and a little incredulously, and Richard said: "All right, Johnson. Be back in about an hour and a half."

A place for Julian was set at the table, and Daniel, shaking out his napkin as though he were shaking Richard, said: "Your mother and I never squandered money on a brougham!"

Richard was in high good temper. He smiled and said: "Use mine whenever you want it."

"How did you come by it?" Daniel demanded, still, it seemed, not having tumbled to the truth that Richard was intent on making an impudent gesture of independence. "You have hardly a penny to bless yourself with." He added: "Till today."

"That's it. Till today. And with such a day dawning, it wasn't difficult to raise money on account. I've been up and down from Oxford for the last few weeks getting things into order."

"I should call it getting them into disorder," said Daniel. "I know what the moneylenders charge for such services. It's a poor way to start an independent life, my boy. If that's what you intend to do?"

"Yes, that's what I intend to do. I've got chambers near Park Lane. Julian stayed there with me last night. What did you think of them, Julian?"

Julian laughed. "Their affluence terrified me. Their taste dismayed me."

"Oh, taste be hanged. I don't know what this taste is that you talk about."

"*Ça se voit, mon cher.*"

"Well, there they are, anyway. And I've got the brougham and Johnson to drive it. And a good manservant. His name is Trimmer. It has just that odd touch . . . I like an odd touch in a manservant's name. Don't you?"

Daniel looked at me across the table in dismay. The completeness of the declaration of independence had shaken him. It didn't surprise me. How odd, I thought, that a dead grandfather, whom one has never seen, who wasn't certain of one's existence, can do a thing like this!

"When do you return to Oxford?" Daniel asked.

"I am not returning to Oxford—and Oxford won't notice the difference."

"Then what do you propose to do with yourself?"

"Enjoy a year's freedom about the town, and then join a cavalry regiment."

"There is nothing I can do to stop you?"

"No. Nothing."

A look passed between them—of ironical satisfaction on Richard's part, of frustration on Daniel's. Then Richard said: "Well, all this now being understood, let's be happy. Mama, I've made up for all the miserable birthdays when I could buy you nothing."

He handed a small package across the table. "Open it now. I hope you'll like it."

It was wonderful. It lay there nested in blue tissue paper within the box, and I hardly dared take it out. It was about six inches high, a pigeon in white translucent jade, and its eyes were rubies. I thought of the hands, long dead, that had lovingly shaped this precious stuff into this precious thing; of the far foreign sky beneath which they had worked, the tip-tilted roofs of colored tile standing over pillars of lacquered teak, and of all beautiful inanimate things surviving the animation of human genius that made them. I was touched to the heart, and I went round the table and kissed Richard. "Darling! I can't say how much I love it. No one has ever given me a more splendid thing."

"You must thank Julian as much as me. He found it. I know nothing about such matters."

"Chi'en Lung," Julian murmured. "You won't see a better piece in a hurry. Now, may I give Richard my present?"

He unwrapped the flat parcel he had been carrying and leaned a framed picture against the wall, where the sunlight fell on it. "I hope you will like it, Richard. Hang it on some wall where there is nothing else."

There was utter silence. Julian looked anxiously from one to another of us, but he did not speak. The picture struck us dumb. No one there, except Julian, had ever seen anything like it before. It looked as though you could scoop the rich crude colors—red, green, yellow—in handfuls off the canvas. What it showed was simply a worn-looking woman sitting at a kitchen table, peeling an onion.

The jade pigeon with the ruby eyes was on the table. I looked from it to the picture. Serene, tranquil, almost celestial in its repose, it seemed to condemn the writhing emotional extravagance of the picture. As if divining my thoughts, Julian said: "This also has great beauty, you know, *ma chère tante*. Some day you will see it."

Daniel, with a gesture well known on platforms, had put on the pince-nez and stood looking at the picture. "Vincent," he said. "Never heard of any Vincent."

"His name," said Julian, "was Vincent van Gogh. He was a Dutchman who went mad in the sunshine of Southern France. I have met

376

in Paris many people who knew him. He was poor and he died young. Just nine years ago he shot himself."

"Not a moment too soon," said Richard.

Julian sighed. "You do not like it. Let me keep it. I shall give you something else."

"No, no. Don't be a damned fool. I will hang it because you gave it to me. But I doubt if Trimmer will stay."

Nika said: "She is a very sad woman and she has much to put up with."

Julian smiled with sudden relief and kissed Nika. "You are a disciple," he said. "I salute you."

Nika blushed. "I like her," she said. "There is no nonsense about her. She is a practical woman."

"I have seen many of Vincent's pictures," Julian said, "and I dearly wanted one. So when I was last in France I went down to Arles. I could have bought, of course, from a dealer, but I am myself too intelligent a dealer to do that. If you go to a place where an artist has been poor and has lived not too long ago you may find something. I found this in a back room behind a café. I expect it paid for a few drinks. I secured it for one thousand francs, and then I called on Papa and offered it to him for fifteen hundred. He prefers engravings of Meissonier—field marshals on nice horses looking at nice battles—and nearly chased me out of the house."

"You gave a thousand francs for that!" Daniel exclaimed.

"Yes, uncle, and now it is Richard's, and I make you a prophecy. Let him keep it, and he will in time get not less than a thousand pounds for it."

"A thousand pounds! There's not a picture in this house worth that."

"No, indeed," Julian agreed, smiling. "Some might pay it for the Watts portrait of Lady Burnage, but I would not."

Daniel looked as if he did not understand the world he was living in. He raised my hand to his lips, kissed Nika, and said good-by to the others. "I must come and see these rooms of yours, Richard."

"I shall be delighted, sir. I have remembered your favorite sherry."

"And don't fritter your money away on nonsense."

Richard did not answer, and Daniel went. Then other presents were produced, but nothing equaled the sensation of the jade pigeon and this picture for which I could feel no enthusiasm.

Richard's brougham came, and the two young men went off gaily, taking the Vincent with them. At the door Nika said: "May I see her again before you go?"

She was given another look and said with a sigh: "She's lovely."

But Julian did not kiss her again, and I caught myself wondering whether that disappointed her.

377

Julian, like Richard, was twenty-one; he had been twenty-one for five months. One would have thought the difference between them greater, for Julian already had a maturity that made Richard seem—what, indeed, he never ceased to be—a boy. No doubt, I thought, when I was alone and I sat considering Richard's beautiful present that nestled in my cupped hands, this gesture of independence seems to him manly, but it has the precipitate and hasty touch of a boy badly in need of reassurance. There was so little that he knew about anything. If he had seen this jade bird in a shop window he wouldn't have known what jade was, and he would probably have imagined that the rubies were glass beads. If he had taken a fancy to it and had asked the price, he would have expected to be told five pounds or thereabouts; and on the other hand when he *was* told the price he would have parted with whatever the dealer had asked. Julian, no doubt, had saved him money. I didn't think Richard saw how lovely the thing was: he had given it to me because it was very costly, and he wanted to show that an independent man of the world could give a costly present.

Julian's present to him wasn't costly, nor did any of us think it lovely. But he said it was, and it is odd, I said to myself, that I am persuaded he is right, that the lack of perception is in me. That present to Richard came out of something deep in Julian, but this present to me comes out of nothing deeper than Richard's purse.

It is difficult at this distance of time to be sure that I recapture correctly what my feelings then were for the two young men. We look back through the years and glibly say it was thus and thus; but the backward glimpse can be as distorting as summer haze or the bloom of an autumn evening that rubs the contours of things into a false tenderness. I can only put things down as they come back to me, and try to do it without sentimentality; and it seems to me that I loved them both but wished that Richard had more of Julian's qualities. I disliked a lot that went to make up Richard: his idleness, his delusions of grandeur: but there was not much that I disliked about Julian—perhaps not anything.

How old Cogan—Zealous Zebedee!—would love this pigeon! I must make a call there, I thought, and show it to him. His addiction to the Chinese had to satisfy itself in a less costly way than this, but he would love to see it and handle it. When Julian's mother had written asking Daniel to find rooms for the boy I thought of the Cogans. It was long since I had seen Julian, but, as I remembered him, he seemed to me the sort of person who would be at home with the quirks and idiosyncrasies of that household. And so it proved. What fun they had together! I took Nika with me—it was the first time she and Julian met—when I called at the small house in Willesden not long after Julian had gone there. It was a pleasant summer afternoon, and we found all three of them in the little back garden, Mr. Cogan's Precious Freight sitting in the rickshaw watching the other two. They had arrived at the great moment of an enterprise that had been going forward for weeks: the translation into actuality of the fancy that had pleased Mr. Cogan in the days when he lived over the entrance to Graybird Court. There, on the window ledge, he had had his minute Chinese garden, with water lilies carved by the Young Lady and goldfish made of painted wooden slivers swimming beneath the pigmy bridges that spanned the lake of glass. Now here it was, constructed in the garden by the busy hands of Julian and Mr. Cogan: a real wooden bridge, lacquered red, arching a ditch that was, when we arrived, cold-looking concrete; but in the bottom of it were two baskets containing water-lilies—one would be red and one cream, Mr. Cogan explained, his eyes shining—and a hose attached to the kitchen tap was ready to start the inundation.

It was pleasant to arrive at so important a moment, and Nika was permitted to turn the tap, while Mr. Cogan, Precious Freight and Julian watched the end of the rubber pipe that entered the concrete basin with an anxious concentration that suggested a doubt whether a municipal water supply could be trusted to rise to this occasion. They sighed with relief when the flow began; and Julian ran in to bring tea into the garden.

Yes, indeed; what fun they had had! The chairs and small wooden tables were lacquered in gay colors, the cups and plates were willow pattern, and Mr. Cogan, who had disappeared into the house, came out wearing his kimono rich with golden dragons, and would, I believe, have gladly given us opium to smoke instead of tea to drink if his appearance had not already proved sufficiently exciting to the neighbors, who leaned over the fence and were not tranquilized by Julian's shout: "Ha! Nous epatons les bourgeois!" As it was, the cups were without handles, and the tea had a smoky Chinese flavor and no milk, so that I drank it with loathing cloaked by a gusto that deceived no one. In a deep tranquillity we watched the water rise, and Mr. Cogan explained that the depressed-looking twig on one side was a willow which he visioned with lavish hair stroking the water, and that the saplings now standing upright with the help of poles were white cherries which would reflect their beauty in the pool.

We stayed till the pond was full, and then Nika was given a can from which with great care she released goldfish into the pond. This was the climax. Julian and Mr. Cogan stood upon the bridge, which

379

would hardly accommodate, much less support, more than two, leaned over breathless as the fleet of golden submarines in line ahead sailed under the bridge, and then they simultaneously turned to watch them come out on the other side.

That was the end of the small adventure, which I was happy to have shared; but it was by no means the end of the fun that Julian and the Cogans had together. For it was Julian who insisted that what Mrs. Cogan must do was model in clay, and that was the beginning of her small but durable reputation. Julian nursed it from the beginning. He arranged for the firing of these six-inch terra-cottas and for the sale of those that pleased him. The time was to come when all of them pleased him and none could be bought except in his own gallery. Nothing was repeated: they were unique pieces, for Julian believed in what he called scarcity value. I have a few of the things myself, and certainly they are beautiful.

3

On that morning of Richard's twenty-first birthday (and my fifty-third) Julian had left the Cogans (whose willow by now hung over the pool and whose cherry trees bloomed in the spring) and had taken a room in Clarges Street. He had no manservant, no brougham, very little of anything. He looked after himself. He had found employment with a Bond Street dealer, had left him and gone to work with a dealer in Paris, and was now back and working for another Bond Street dealer. And as regularly as the first day of a month came round Marie Rimmel would write to her brother Daniel deploring the inconsequent life of her son Julian. "Here we have now five years passed and still nothing responsible, no foundation. Admittedly he costs us nothing unless it be sorrow, but he is accumulating no defense against what life may bring." Marie saw life as a howling wind that might break in at any moment unless the chinks were well stuffed with sous. Daniel, with a brotherly solicitude which was formal, for Marie irritated him excessively, visited Bordeaux occasionally, but I had seen Marie and Sebastien only once since the time they stayed with us at Tresant. It was just a year ago, when Julian was settling into his room in Clarges Street, that they visited us in Chelsea. They were both fat and gray, and Sebastien was unbearably pompous. Nothing had ever made me aware of time's passing so startlingly as to see him and Daniel sitting at breakfast together and to remember that these were the two gay young sparks whose boat had crashed into the one in which Whaley and I had been rowed out to see the iron ship—that wonder whose progeny now belched over all the oceans: Daniel fidgeting to be up and away upon his own affairs; Sebastien, with a napkin tucked into his collar,

drooling on about some happening in the Conseil Municipal of
Bordeaux which he had long adorned and where he would before now
have been mayor but for intrigues which Marie, intervening, would
record with an interminable garrulity and sense of grievance. There was
the question, I remember, of a ship belonging to Sebastien's company.
She had gone down with all hands, overinsured and not notably sea-
worthy according to the Radicals who were always throwing this into
Sebastien's teeth—as if he would be a party to such a happening! She
recurred to it again and again. It seemed a worm of sin gnawing her
heart. At last Daniel would slip dexterously into a chink of silence,
rise and take up his brief case. "Well, duty, you know . . ." and they
would be left to me and Nika.

When finally they were gone, Nika, who had not seen them before
and never saw them again, asked gravely: "Are those really Cousin
Julian's father and mother?"

"Yes, darling."

And, still gravely, she murmured: "How odd! As if two hippo-
potamuses produced a gazelle."

"That is rather rude, darling. What did you expect—a pair of
archangels?"

"Well, naturally, a pair of gazelles."

And at the thought of Sebastien and Marie as a pair of gazelles we
both broke down into laughter that dissolved the boredom we had
endured. Nika ran up to her room where I heard her singing:

> Mam'selle,
> Une gazelle
> Ne s'interesse pas
> Dans des affaires municipaux
> De Bordeaux.

4

Throughout the year that had passed since then, Julian had come
often to see us, and he never came without bringing a trifling present
for Nika: some attractive but not expensive thing in porcelain or glass
or silver, or it might be a print or a fragment of carved ivory. In her
room which was sitting room and bedroom she cleared some of her
books from the bookcase and stored her treasures on the shelves. She
was a gay child and took these possessions lightly. They did not obsess
her, as Richard was obsessed by his relics of Justin Gaylord. He still
had these, still driveled about them like some incurable Jacobite drivel-
ing over a lock of Charlie's hair or a few moldy threads from his tartan,

but now they were not in the "Uncle Justin box": they were promoted to a small expensive showcase which Richard no doubt hoped would add to their appearance of authenticity. I was sure that in these chambers that he had taken this showcase would be well displayed and that this manservant Trimmer would be instructed to treat the relics with reverence. I wished Richard would grow up. But here was new evidence that he would not. I took up the box in which the jade pigeon had lain and saw that beneath the blue tissue was a sheet of writing paper. I unfolded it, and read "To my dear Mama, with love and good wishes from Richard." That was all right, but what horrified me was that the paper was embossed with the Gaylord crest and with the defiant motto that long ago I had scribbled on a torn-off corner of the *Times* and asked Whaley to translate: *Fiat voluntas mea*. I couldn't any longer be angry about such a thing. What was the use? I could only sigh.

I dropped the sheet of paper into the fire and was gathering my presents together when Nika came into the room. "Mummy, Quirky is worse. He won't eat a thing. Will you come and see him?"

We had rescued Quirky some months ago from that odious pet shop near Graybird Court. We had to pass there when visiting Sally in Robin Hood Road, and we had seen this ball of red fur rolled into a tiny box fit to hold nothing bigger than a mouse. Nika looked aghast at the pitiful puppies and kittens, the joyless birds, the goldfish toilfully trudging through the water like Channel swimmers exhausted on the last lap of their meaningless enterprise, and at this red furry ball withdrawn into miserable immobility. "Oh!" she cried. "It's a squirrel! The poor darling! It should be swinging through trees."

We took it home and soon it was leaping about in Nika's room. She made a nest for it in a box that was never closed except when the window was open. In a few weeks we took a risk and opened the window and went away, leaving Quirky to do as he pleased. We watched him joyfully exploring the trees of the garden and went for a walk. When we got back he was curled up, asleep, in his box. We never needed to bother about the window after that.

Quirky now was as miserably unlively as on the day we bought him. "We'd better take him along to Tom Chadderton," I said. "It's a long time since we've been to Bermondsey."

We did not bother to put on old clothes, and we took a cab to Robin Hood Road. There was no need any longer for disguise where Sally was concerned. Rich people had discovered her and her work, and a cab containing the well-intentioned who wanted to do a bit of "slumming" was now not unusual at her door. They got short measure from Sally. "You can do nothing for poor people—nothing at all," she would tell them, "except become one of them and share their miserable lives, without pretending that they're anything *but* miserable. Half a pound of tea and your left-off drawers don't help." She would treat them to the fierce cackle she had developed and the unyielding scrutiny of eyes that stripped naked their half-intentions. And yet, abashed as they were, she fascinated them, and some came again and again. "One of them always with a footman!" Sally said with immense relish. "Can't you imagine the conversation in Park Lane? 'But, darling, is it *safe* to venture among such people?' 'Jesus tells us to.' 'Jesus was different, darling. Jesus was a man.' 'Well . . . what if I took Roberts with me? And there'd be Jones on the box, within call.' 'That might be all right. See that the carriage is washed down when you return. Take those dress shirts of mine that are frayed at the cuffs. Now I must be off to Threadneedle Street. I'll have a word with Roberts. He ought to have a truncheon up his sleeve.' "

Sally's eyes twinkled. She was a good mimic, and her tales tended of late to have a ribald edge. But she would turn to a sudden seriousness. "Of course, they're doing what they think the religious part of their lives demands. I wonder when they'll see that religion can never be a *part* of anybody's life, and that God isn't much interested in religion—only in lives?"

So we took Quirky, nestled inside a fur muff, in a cab, and I dropped Nika at Tom Chadderton's door and went on to Sally's. There was a bicycle propped on the curbstone, and I guessed from this that Dr. Warwick Russell was with her. I hoped he was: I had never met the famous man. He was there all right! The kitchen was full of him and full of his anger. He was walking up and down, so far as the minute room allowed him, and this movement within restriction gave to his red immensity the look of a caged tiger. I was introduced, but sensed that Dr. Russell and Sally both thought my arrival inopportune. They ignored me and went on with their quarrel.

"Then why do you stay in the bloody place yourself?" the doctor was shouting.

"Because I'm a sane adult and decided of my own free will to do so."

"I sometimes doubt whether you're either sane or adult. You're grown up, but that's not necessarily being adult, and sometimes I think you're certifiable."

"You can think what you like. Anyway, we're not discussing me, so don't try to dodge the issue. We're discussing Robin, and whether you and Polly are justified in keeping him in this Godforsaken hole. You know as well as I do—you know better than I do, the pair of you—all about the stinking drains and the flies and bugs and lice and the way kids go down with fevers like ninepins. And don't get up, either, most of 'em, for all your high and mighty medical science. And you think it all right for Robin to stay here, go to school here, see nothing but this, know no one but the poor little devils who have to stay here whether they want to or not. Well, I think you're a couple of criminals, and mark my words: one of these days you and Polly will curse yourselves for what you're doing."

"Don't you believe it," Dr. Russell said hotly. "If there's to be any cursing, we'll curse this so-called God of yours. Look at it! Look through that window! Look at his beautiful world! All things bright and beautiful, the Lord God made them all!"

"If he's only so-called, He doesn't come into it—He's a figment. If, on the other hand, he's really a god, really there, and, according to your damned nonsensical reasoning, really responsible for all this, then you can throw your hand in. Because you can't fight against a god. You can't beat him anyway. Not even you. So you can pack up and go and sell constipation powders in Harley Street. It's only because all this filth is man-made and nothing to do with God—it's only that that makes any sense in your being here at all. And there's no sense in Robin's being here. He's had typhoid once. Next time you may not be so lucky."

"What the hell d'you mean by lucky? D'you think I just go pobbling round trusting to luck? I live in the light of science, I work in the light of science, you old witch doctor, and I'll die in the light of science."

"So may Robin."

I did not think that he could become angrier; but Sally's quiet insistence on that name seemed to make him swell till I thought he would explode. He stopped pacing; his fists clenched; and then he pulled himself together, and said with a smile: "Bad for my blood pressure. I must stop it." He sat down on one of the hard wooden chairs. "It's no good, Miss Mary Brown," he said quietly. "Like you, I've thrown in my lot here, with these filthy streets, with these filthy people. I don't love 'em, as I believe you do. Sometimes I hate 'em, their greed and dirtiness and apathy. But, by God, I'll not give up till I've cleaned this place, and seen grass growing in it, and clean healthy men and women walking in the streets. Then, perhaps, I'll walk out of it, but not till then; and so long as I stay, *all* of me will stay—every last damned thread and stitch of me. And that includes Robin."

The storm rumbled out. His hand lay on the scrubbed deal of the table, and Sally patted it with a gesture infinitely tender. "All right," she said. "All right, all right."

"You almost make me think it is," he said. "How d'you do it? What's the secret? Stroke my hand again."

He closed his eyes, that red colossus, and unself-consciously she stroked his hand. "Virtue comes out of you," he said. "The poor devils that I can do nothing for fly to you like birds to a lighthouse."

"What do you know about lighthouses? The poor birds dash themselves to death against the glass."

384

"Well, like a moth to a flame."

"They burn their wings."

"Oh, hell! What is it then? What d'you do down here? You seem to me to do nothing. I often wonder about you. What's it all about? What are you after?"

"It's difficult to tell you. It's difficult to tell anybody, even myself."

"Have a shot at it."

"Well, this grass in the streets that you talk about. It'll come, you know. Nothing can stop it. Perhaps it'll be good grass, green pastures, that men can walk on. Perhaps it'll be evil grass that's there because there are no more men to walk on it or on anything else. But one way or another the grass will come. Oh, I know the importance of drains and baths and schools and libraries, a good roof over your head and a decent suit on your back. Don't think I don't know that. But in the meantime, whichever way it goes with this grass, there's a lot of enduring to be done. You talk about virtue. There's no virtue in enduring this because one has to. There's no virtue in any sort of poverty that isn't embraced voluntarily by someone who knew riches. 'He was rich, yet for your sakes he became poor.' If these people come to me it's because they know that I'm one of them, asking nothing they haven't got, able to give them very little because I haven't got it to give, and yet able to give them something they wouldn't have without me, like poor Tom Chadderton with a broken sparrow."

"And what is that?"

"I don't quite know. But it's whatever you get when you see the importance of having nothing, when you don't struggle to have anything any more except the power to endure and say: 'Thy will be done.'"

Fiat voluntas mea. Fiat voluntas tua.

Sally had spoken quietly, slowly, as if trying to make her native language intelligible to a foreigner; and now I was moved to see a blush come to her withered cheek as she again put her hand on Dr. Russell's and said: "Does it make any sense, or am I talking like a fool? Do forgive me, my dear, for talking about it at all. It's not really a thing to put into words, and I'm afraid that for valiant people like you and Polly it must sound unconvincing."

He got up and left us abruptly. "God be with you," he said at the door.

I told Sally about Richard and the Gaylord motto. She was neither annoyed nor amused. "Such silliness," she said with a sigh. "Such silliness."

Nika came in, young and fresh as I had once known Sally to be, the Sally who had got drunk with me in Eddy Rodda's cave and walked on the cliffs with me and rode and swam. As her arms went round the child's neck I noticed the stubbed fingernails, the red puffiness of hands much in hot soda and water, and was afflicted by a sense of her endless struggle here to maintain even a semblance of decency. I was glad to see the warmth with which Nika embraced her. "Oh, Auntie," she said, "what a clever young man you've turned Tom Chadderton into! He says he'll have Quirky better in no time. And what d'you think he's doing now? Training performing fleas!"

"Oh, he is, is he?" Sally grinned. "Mine perform well enough without any training."

5

There is not much left of the West End that I knew as a girl and that was intact at this time of which I write and for long after. Dorchester House was still standing, and its gardens made a *plaisance* into which you could look from the windows of Richard's rooms on the first floor of the house in South Street. Julian Rimmel was there on a day in June when I called with Nika. We had spent the morning shopping and had looked in on the chance of finding Richard at home. Julian had done the same, but Richard was not at home. The man Trimmer said that Mr. Undridge would not be in for luncheon and he brought sherry which Julian and I sipped as I looked around to see what had come to my son from the chance of being the grandson of my father. It was something pretty downy, something that Sir Richard Rainborough, I was sure, would approve. This was such a room as I had stifled in when a child. We had shed a lot of this sort of thing in Chelsea, taken to a greater simplicity of furniture and decoration, but Richard had reeled back to the utmost amplitude of damasks, brocades and velvets, for chairs, cushions, curtains and tablecloths; and I felt that he would need, to do the room justice, a tasseled smoking cap and a meerschaum pipe. Rich-looking footstools were in front of the chairs; there was a thick silken bell pull; the arms of his college were on a wooden plaque over the mantelpiece and on a tobacco jar; and it was difficult to see the wallpaper for prints and miniatures, a trophy of arms, and skulls that pricked forward with a menace of horns and antlers. The only books I saw were Ouida's *Under Two Flags*, George du Maurier's *Trilby* and Marion Crawford's *A Cigarette Maker's Romance*. On a table the current *Strand Magazine* lay open at the latest adventure of Mr. Sherlock Holmes. The floor was mossy with inches of florid carpet.

Julian looked at the light through his sherry glass. "Excellent sherry," he said, "and beautiful glass." This exclusion of comment on everything else told me all I wanted to know of his opinion.

"Where is the woman," Nika asked, "the sad woman peeling the onion?"

386

"She's in a cupboard. Richard and I had a long conference about her, but we could find no place where she would fit."

"Let me see her again," said Nika, "if you know where she is."

Julian produced her from a cupboard and stood her against the leg of a chair, and still she puzzled me and I could not get the hang of her. "I like her, Julian," Nika said, "but I don't know why. Some day you must explain her to me."

"I think," Julian smiled, "you are a person who might hear what Van Gogh has to say. We have more of him at the gallery, but we're keeping them dark, for they still alarm people. You must come and see them. And there is much else to show you there. What do you say, *ma tante*? Shall I take *la petite* with me now? I will give her luncheon and bring her back afterward."

"You must not call me *la petite*," Nika reproved him. "You must call me Cousin Nika, or just Nika. I would prefer just Nika."

"Very well, Nika. Let's pretend you are grown up. What do you say, Aunt? Could you come, too?"

No, I could not come; I was expecting a luncheon visitor at home; and I watched them go, and was aware of Nika's extraordinary alacrity as Julian took her hand and led her from the room. I lingered there for a while, looking from the overdressed room to the coolness of the gardens of Dorchester House, and, unexpectedly, Richard soon afterward came in.

"Oh, Mama! How pleasant to see you here. Has Trimmer been looking after you?"

"Yes, thank you, darling. He thought you would not be back. I was just about to go."

"Oh, but you must have luncheon with me. Let's go to Romano's. I had an engagement that's broken down."

I had to decline, and he asked with genuine anxiety: "Well, do you think this is all right?"

"Charming, my dear."

He looked round appraisingly. "There's one thing I'd like. I hardly dare to ask you, Mama. You'll think I've got an awful cheek. But could you let me have—I don't mean as a gift, of course, but a sort of perpetual loan—that Watts portrait of Grandmama?"

Not Grandmama, I thought. Lady Burnage. That's my grandmother, Lady Burnage. I'm the only male descendant.

"I could clear some stuff from over the mantelpiece."

"I'm afraid not, darling," I said gently. "I'm very fond of it, and it's the only picture I have of my mother."

"Oh, well . . . Forgive me for asking, won't you?"

"But of course, Richard."

"You're sure you can't join me at Romano's?"

"Not today. Do ask me again."

He kissed me and I went.

6

We began soon after this to hear of A. B. Wibsey. Now that he could please himself whether he came or went, Richard came often enough to see us in Chelsea, and whether there or at luncheon, to which he delighted to take me and Nika out, A. B. Wibsey was ever on his lips. It was never Wibsey or Mr. Wibsey: it was always A. B. Wibsey or A.B. When Richard said "A.B.," he spoke proudly, as one permitted intimacy with the great, and when he said "A. B. Wibsey" the name was uttered as though everyone should know it, as though it ranked with H. G. Wells or G. B. Shaw. A. B. Wibsey was a writer. One couldn't yet call him a novelist because he hadn't written a novel. He had written nothing but short stories that had appeared in magazines like the *Strand*. Richard was so full of him that I imagined A. B. Wibsey was full of himself, that he had the contagious egotism by which some people can make others believe in their coming greatness before it has come. How Richard had made so unlikely an acquaintance I did not know. "I met him with a chap from the club and they came in for a drink." Well, that could be understood, but how had it developed? I was puzzled until one day, when Nika and I had called at Richard's rooms and were waiting for him to come and take us to luncheon, I picked up a book and a slip of paper fell from between the pages. As I put it back I could not help reading: "I.O.U. £20. A.B.W." Well, of course, if that was happening often it could explain a lot.

When I met Mr. Wibsey I did not like him, and I met him soon enough. "Mama, I want to give a dinner party at my rooms," Richard said. "I do hope you and Father will be able to come."

"I'll speak to him tonight, but I'm afraid he's very busy. It's a bad summer for anyone in the government. All this trouble with the Transvaal people . . . "

Richard laughed. "I don't understand these so-called statesmen," he said. "Trouble—what a word to use about a pack of Boer farmers! One doesn't allow people like that to cause trouble. One just wipes them out and takes over."

"Yes, darling," I said. "I suppose that's what it'll come to, but there's all the business of getting things down on paper first, so that it won't look like that."

"Well, let's leave it alone for the moment. I'm sick of it. The papers babble about nothing else. I shan't become interested till the Army takes over. Meantime, what about this dinner. Whom shall I ask? I'd like you and Father and Nika."

"Nika's rather young for going out to dinner."

"Well, you're always brought her up older than she is. She never meets people of her own age, except the Mostyn-Lloyd infants now and then. Anyway, I'd like her there."

We discussed the guests to be invited, and I suggested Julian and Whaley. "Good," he said. "It'll be fun for A. B. to meet old Whaley."

"You're asking Mr. Wibsey?"

"Oh, rather! I've done that already, and he'll bring someone along to be the fourth lady. So if Father can come, that'll be the lot—eight of us."

And those were the eight who met on a stifling July night in 1899. Daniel, Richard and Julian: Whaley, Nika and I, all dressed up to the nines, for Richard wanted this to be a stylish occasion, awaited the arrival of Mr. Wibsey and his lady.

Daniel was in a good mood. He had come to accept Richard as he was, not to yearn for a Richard who simply wasn't there, and, not surprisingly, this permitted a much happier relationship between them. Richard produced for him his favorite Amontillado sherry, and Daniel, enabled by years of practice among constituents, kept their conversation on cricket and the methods of Sherlock Holmes and such harmless matters. I was happy to see them so amiably engaged, while Whaley, who had not been here before, pottered about the room, resting a hand on my arm. She was not in the habit of doing that, and I was a little concerned for her. After all, she was getting on. I thought, "Whaley must be in her mid-sixties," and that was near enough to seventy, which sounded like the end of everything. She was an institution now. She had been young when she began to write, and she had lived an industrious life. There was a new book every year without fail, and the new books were being read by a new generation. She was fortunate in that. I asked her if she was feeling well, and she said: "I find the heat trying. What a nice pair Nika and Julian look."

They had moved away from the rest of us and were sitting in the window-seat, gazing across into the Dorchester House garden. Nika looked happy. With her hair made up in rather an adult fashion and an evening dress that permitted a peep of her ripening breasts, she seemed to carry more than her fourteen years, I couldn't hear what they were talking about. Whatever it was, it animated their faces, and I remembered that she had thought Julian's parents should be a pair of gazelles. I knew how much she liked and admired him, how she looked forward to the occasions, which became more frequent, when he would take her out to lunch and talk about the things that interested them both; and I wondered whether he ever thought of her as more than a pretty and intelligent little cousin who made a pleasant companion.

We were to dine at eight, and at eight-fifteen Trimmer disapprovingly announced: "Mr. Wibsey and Miss Monk."

Mr. Wibsey was wearing a pipe that smelled like a bloater, and a Norfolk jacket and knickerbockers. His plump calves swelled into brown woolen stockings. We were all a little disconcerted by his appearance: all, that is, save himself.

"Zoë and I came along on our bike," he announced, removing a tweed cap and throwing it onto a chair. Trimmer took it up and carried it out, as though he had arrested it charged with some offense against decency. Zoë was wearing cycling bloomers and a white blouse and a boater hat. She removed the hat at Richard's suggestion.

Mr. Wibsey, a glass of sherry in his hand, and his pipe, under the influence of several deep sucks, beginning to steam as though the anchor were up and he would presently put to sea, looked round upon us all and forbade Richard's attempt at introduction. "Never mind all that, Dick. We'll soon pick one another up. Don't give any drink to Zoë. She can't carry it. Fill this up."

I suppose he was then about twenty-five. His roundness was pallid, unhealthy-looking. He was round everywhere: his face was round, his calves were round, a round chubby fist held his glass. A straggle of fair mustache was ragged on his lip. I was surprised to find myself aware of power in this repulsive figure. His small gray eyes had startling penetration. They looked as if he could pick locks with them; and his nonchalance was not assumed. He stared upon us all in our silks and starched shirts as though we were on parade especially for his amused delectation. He knocked his pipe into the fireplace, put down his glass, and said: "Well, I'm hungry. So's Zoë. We've been on the road all the afternoon."

Richard took my arm and led the way into the dining room. Daniel followed with Whaley. Then came Julian with Miss Zoë Monk, and finally A. B. Wibsey with Nika. "What's *your* name?" I heard him ask.

"Oh, you'll soon pick it up," said Nika, who was annoyed, I guessed, at being separated from Julian.

"Now then," said Mr. Wibsey, "don't be cheeky."

I looked round at them, and Mr. Wibsey was taking a sideways peep down at Nika's breasts. I wished she hadn't come.

7

The food we ate and the wine we drank made the hot evening seem hotter. We sat at the littered table with the candle flames motionless. Not a puff came through the open window.

"Now stay where you all are," Mr. Wibsey said. "We're comfortable.

Let's have a talk. It's all nonsense, this withdrawing of the ladies. We men don't want to sit here for a bit of mucky chat, and the women don't want to go out and talk about antimacassars."

"Well, I want to go out, anyway," said Whaley, and went. Nika and I followed her. "Come back," Mr. Wibsey shouted; "we'll stay here. It's comfortable." And we obediently went back and found that he had removed his Norfolk jacket and hung it over his chair. He leaned back with his thumbs tautening purple braces that he allowed now and then to snap onto his chest with a soft *plop*, as though they impacted upon dough.

"If that chap of yours wants to clear this up, Dick, let him," Mr. Wibsey conceded magnanimously. "He can leave the port and the nuts."

Trimmer began to clear the table, wincing with pain. The candles gleamed into the revealed mahogany, lit up the rubies in the port. "Now, Zoë, go and give that chap a hand," Mr. Wibsey commanded. "Washing and wiping for eight is no joke. You can't talk, so you might as well be useful."

Zoë went, but what passed between her and Trimmer I never knew.

Richard offered cigars, but Mr. Wibsey lit his pipe from a candle flame and sipped his port. "So you're the celebrated Margaret Whale," he said. "Pleased to meet you. We're overdue for a talk, you and I. I've got a bone to pick with you, you know."

"I'm sorry to hear that. I try to be harmless."

"Well, you succeed. And that's my grievance. Now don't take this personally. I'm talking to you as a representative sort of successful novelist. I'm talking to the whole lot of 'em. And I say: You've all been at it too long. You said all you had to say in the first book you ever wrote, and you go on saying it again and again. You're blocking up the road. There are people with something to say, something that's not harmless pulp, and they can't get a word in. Why do you do it?"

"Well, I like doing it," Whaley said reasonably, "and it keeps body and soul together."

"Never mind soul for the moment. The existence of soul has never been proved. But we'll come to that later. . . ."

"Need we?" Whaley demurred.

"Well, leave it out altogether then. I respectfully suggest that there's at least a score of you old stagers who must have put by a potful and who could go on living on the fat of the land without blocking up the road for people with something new to say. I respectfully suggest that if you all took a holiday—say for ten years—it would be healthy for English literature."

"The great thing about your suggestion, I admit," said Whaley, "is its respectfulness. But I've never pretended to have anything to do with English literature."

"Well, I do so pretend. It's time we novelists concerned ourselves with this world full of wonderful changes. Look at all that's happening! Telephones, telegraphs, electricity, motorcars! Woman! Look at Woman!"

"We should be delighted to do so, sir," Julian said from behind his cigar, "if you would bring her from the kitchen."

"It'll be your turn in a minute," Mr. Wibsey promised him with menace. "In the meantime, I'll only say this: If Zoë is in the kitchen, it's because women and kitchens are what your boasted civilization has made them: women without minds, kitchens without technique. A few bits of machinery, and kitchens would do most of the work by themselves, and women could come out and use their heads."

"Leave the drains and use your brains," Julian murmured.

"Leave the sinks and play tiddley-winks," said Nika.

"Leave the plumbing appliances and study the natural sciences."

"Leave the baby o' nights and go out and shout for woman's rights."

"Now then, you two, don't be cheeky," Mr. Wibsey reproved them. "I'll deal with you in a minute. Woman," he said expansively, "Education, Man's future in the Air, a World Parliament—why, gosh! our thinking's got to be cosmic! This one little world's nothing—a spot of star dust. Thinking animals, given the right direction, could clear up its problems in a couple of generations, and then go on to consider this earth's relationship with the cosmos. And with all this to think about and write about, the minds of people are deflected and debauched by the sort of piddling stuff I'm talking about! It beats me—the sheer, damned, crass stupidity of the human mind."

"It's beaten a lot of people," Daniel said. "That's a fact to be reckoned with."

Mr. Wibsey reached behind him into his jacket, produced a new pipe, and lit it. "And you politicians," he said between puffs, glaring at Daniel through the smoke, "you politicians! What are you doing about it? Come on now, don't be shy. Address the class."

"Well," said Daniel, "we try, you know, to deal with things as they arise."

"Exactly," said Mr. Wibsey. "Do you ever stop things from arising? Do you ever try to make the right sort of things arise? Look at this muck-up in South Africa. Have you politicians been doing anything? No. You've been leaving it all to Rhodes and Jameson and the Jews who've got their grip on the gold mines. They're the people who are doing things, not you. Between them they've made it impossible for you to do anything but what you will do—and that's land the country in war within the next few months."

"Have you ever heard of the brutal way the Boers of the Transvaal treat the blacks?" Daniel asked.

Mr. Wibsey look at him with contempt. "Is that going to be the line?" he asked. "Well, it's a damned poor one. Can you see the British Empire going to war to stop a few Dutchmen from flogging a few niggers? Come off it. Don't make me laugh."

He gave Daniel no time to reply, but swerved round on his chair toward Julian. "Now, you, Mr. Rimmel," he said. "I've heard about you from your cousin Dick."

"I hope he gave me a reasonably unblemished character," Julian laughed.

"You're a Perpetuator," Mr. Wibsey flung out, with a denunciatory violence which made us all glance at Julian as though Perpetuation were worse than rape, arson and high treason.

"You perpetuate what's past and done with," Mr. Wibsey said. "You don't concern yourself with the milestone round the next corner. You dig out the milestones that humanity has left behind on its march, stick 'em in a museum, and charge for admission. You're nothing but a Backward Glancer."

"Don't you think," Julian asked, "that some things mean as much now as ever they did? Aren't there such things as Truth and Beauty that don't change?"

"What d'you take me for—someone in Standard One of the Board School? Not that I haven't been in Standard One of the Board School. I have. That's the sort of start you've got to make when your mother tries to keep a family by selling boots in a corner shop. And come to that, she sold more blacking and bootlaces than boots, and a family doesn't get very fat on a diet of bootlaces. But I'm not in Standard One now. I know all about Truth and Beauty. I know all about what you call Unchanging Values. But let me tell you this: there's new wine about; it's bubbling up everywhere; and you've got to find new bottles to put it in. That's the real job—not showing us how other people did it. Gosh! Can't you feel the bubbling? The world's full of it, and it's going to bubble all sorts of things out of existence: war, monarchy, the hereditary principle in legislation—all that muck. It's going—and what are we to put in its place? That's the question."

"And what's the answer?" Daniel asked.

"The answer," said Mr. Wibsey magnificently, "is the Spirit of Man. Everything is possible to the Spirit of Man, provided it doesn't get bogged down in traditional muck."

Whaley asked: "Is the Spirit of Man one of these new things that are bubbling up? Hasn't it more or less always been about?"

"It's never been alive to its own power as it is today," Mr. Wibsey answered. "And it's never before had the weapons that modern science is putting into its hands. Prospero is teaching his secrets to poor old Caliban, and it's my faith that Caliban can learn 'em and use 'em."

393

He got up and went to the door leading to Trimmer's quarters and shouted: "Zoë! Come on! We must be moving."

"Mr. Wibsey," I said, "I feel rather disappointed. You've read everybody's palm but mine. Why leave me out?"

He pulled on his jacket, considering me and Nika. "It's not much good," he said cruelly, "talking to the middle-aged. They're round the bend and heading for whatever they've been making for themselves so far. There's not much to be done about 'em. All you can do is look after that daughter of yours. Don't coddle her. Let her learn what life's about. Send her to London University. Let her learn something about science and economics." He waved his pudgy hand in a wild semi-circle. "Throw her to the Winds."

As if to emphasize his words, the curtains slowly lifted into the room like huge wings. A puff through the open window made the flames of the almost burned-out candles strain and stagger. Through the heat that had been growing for hours we heard the sharp smack of large raindrops on roofs. "I'm afraid, sir," said Trimmer, "a thunderstorm is beginning."

Lightning jagged and sizzled beyond the window and thunder rolled. "You'd better wait till this is over, A. B.," Richard said.

"No," said Mr. Wibsey, "I like it. Grand. Elemental. Come on, Zoë."

He gave a general good night and went. I followed Richard down the stairs. Trimmer opened the door and Mr. Wibsey pushed out the tandem bicycle that had been blocking the hall. In the roadway the straight rods of rain were striking, breaking, and hissing up in spray. Mr. Wibsey got onto the front seat and Miss Monk, whose white muslin blouse immediately shrank to a dishcloth about her, onto the back. "You'll get soaked to the skin, Zoë," Mr. Wibsey shouted gaily. "Never mind. It's not far, and we'll soon have your wet clothes off."

He waved his hand, rang his bell, and off they went, pedaling madly, heads down, the tires hissing, through the silver whips and scourges. We watched them till the bell sent a valedictory tinkle as they turned the corner.

Richard asked: "Was Miss Monk useful in the kitchen, Trimmer?"

"Yes, sir: as to the manner born."

CHAPTER TWENTY-THREE

I

I OFTEN think of that dinner party in Richard's rooms as the midmost point of my life. I have spent my years almost equally between two centuries, and that was the last year of the first of them. People are apt to see this twentieth century in which humanity now weeps and mourns as a time of cataclysm. We are living in the loft over the stable; the floor is desperately thin; and we can hear the beasts stirring beneath us. And we know that they are not the good chained comfortable beasts that come at our call and work in our service. Sometimes our hair stands on end as we listen, in a night's dark loneliness, to their unchained prowling, the scuffle of great pads, the rasp of breath coming out of hot red throats, and we picture the eyes lifted to their ceiling, which is our frail floor: the light green or golden pitiless eyes shining over the jaws that drip hungrily. Sometimes in dream the floor dissolves, and we are the beasts and the beasts are we, and all is chaos. And those who have known only this latter half of what has been my life think with envy of that first half, seeing it as green pastures and tranquil waters and talking of the long opulent Victorian afternoon and golden evening.

It wasn't so. The beasts were there then. The beasts are always there. Always our loft is perched between them and the stars, that seem to look implacably down on them and us, as if serenely and indifferently expecting the moment when the fools in the loft will become so heavily embroiled that they will smash the floor beneath their feet.

They were always embroiled, but they go on adding to the weight of their embroilment; and the only question is whether they will stop or whether the weight will become too much.

They were always embroiled. I have lived long enough to have no illusions about that. I am nearing my ninetieth year as I write this. I was born in a time when my living eyes could look at the Dook who had been at Waterloo. And then I watched the great glass bubble go up and heard the talk of peace on earth. And then I saw the Crimean men, legless and armless and eyeless and hopeless, sitting under the railings of Hyde Park, holding out their tin mugs for coppers, as we rode inside the Park and Mama bowed or did not bow, and Papa became a knight because he had helped to win the war. And I loved Lord Burnage who had ridden in the desperate moment of that war, and I had stroked the flank of the lovely beast that helped Tennyson to make the poem that moved us all to pride and wonder. And there had been the savage horror of mutiny in India; and I had watched my half brother Justin drive away, through the soft airs of a Cornish morning, because they were still embroiled, and he had never come back, and already that was so long ago that the moment when the path was empty and we turned back into the renovated house seemed, as the century ended, a moment lost in the mists of dream.

There had been embroilment in China, and Gordon had died at Khartoum, and the Boers had swept us off the hill at Majuba; and I had seen wooden ships with sails become ironclads with boilers, and rifles become machine guns, and cannon balls become explosive shells; and finally, at the turn of the century, the little soldier on the gray horse whom Nika had excitedly watched leading the grand parade to St. Paul's on Diamond Jubilee day had led a grand parade to Oom Paul, and many who went with him did not come back, and among them were Richard and Trimmer and poor Tom Chadderton.

And this was the long Victorian afternoon and golden evening.

2

As I think about it, it seems to me that we are now what we were then. We have not gone forward or back. We are what Cain was when he lifted a stone and smashed his brother. We are men who use for their murders whatever means are to hand. Only the means change, become more terrible, and now they become more terrible at so accelerated a pace that the floor of the loft is worn to a membrane trembling over chaos. It is thinner—oh, much thinner—than the walls of crystal that enclosed my childhood dream.

3

They were the C.I.V.s. I think that meant City Imperial Volunteers, but some, and A. B. Wibsey among them, called them Chamberlain's Innocent Victims. Their slouch hats and khaki uniforms and puttees gave them a romantic look that stirred the excited enthusiasm of all who saw them, and Caton Woodville was to draw a picture of one of them, with a bloody bandage round his head, a bayoneted rifle in his hand, and a wild look in his eye, that became in the popular imagination the very embodiment of Kipling's Absent-Minded Beggar— the "gentleman in khaki ordered south."

I was torn in two. I was proud of Richard. There is a terrible irrationality in a mother's heart that makes her proud to see her son in the panoply of war. And, also, I was afraid. He talked like a child. He talked of going out to help complete what his Uncle Justin had begun, as though there is any completion, any ending, along that road. He had not, after all, joined a cavalry regiment. He and Trimmer had rushed off and enlisted as privates. I was told nothing until they had acquired their panoply, and then they called upon me. Nika was out, and I gave them tea. I was glad to see how Richard had the art of making people comfortable in his presence. Trimmer was not disconcerted at sitting down to tea with us, as he well might have been. He was much older than Richard. In his wisdom and knowledge of the world he might have been the boy's father. He knew the ropes. He was a time-expired soldier; it was but a couple of years since he had been engaged at Omdurman. I had not known any of these things about Trimmer, and I am sure I never should have known them in other circumstances. I felt that there was a delicacy in the allusive way he introduced these reminiscences now. He was telling me to be of good cheer. My son would be in experienced hands.

"There's no need to worry about Mr. Richard, ma'am. This is only a little bit of a war. I've seen worse. I expect when we get out there Mr. Richard'll get his commission in no time, an' I'll be his batman. I'll look after him."

We tried to talk then of indifferent matters, and Richard gave me a book. "I thought you'd like to read this," he said. "It's A.B.'s first."

I wasn't much interested at that moment in A.B.'s first—the first of so many—and I laid it on the table. "Has he paid you what he owed you?" I asked rather brutally.

"How on earth did you know that? But, yes—he has. I often lent him a bit and he always paid back. He's very honorable about things like that, but a bit lax with women."

I said I had assumed that, as Mr. Wibsey was a bachelor with a tandem bicycle, and Richard told me: "Poor Zoë's gone. There's a new one now, and Zoë wasn't the first. However," he added, "I haven't seen him lately. He's a pro-Boer, and we had quite a row."

"A bit of no good, that chap," Trimmer said; and Richard demurred. "He's a bit of good and a bit of bad like the rest of us. Of course, he's a cad, but a cad of genius. You'll all hear of A.B. He'll make his mark."

"Well, sir," said Trimmer, already the officer's servant, "we'd better be moving. There's a bit of clearing up to be done."

I went to the door and watched them move away, looking romantic and brigandish in those felt hats with one side pinned up, and there was no premonition in my heart, as there somehow had been when I watched Justin drive away, that this look was the last one. But so it was. It was Daniel who had to do the clearing up—selling the brougham, disposing of the lease, storing the furniture, and all the rest of it. A telephone call told me that they had suddenly been moved to another part of the country, and soon after that they were ordered overseas.

4

I have never in all my life felt so hopelessly sad as I did on that May afternoon in 1900 when I drove to Bermondsey to see Sally. I have been sad enough often enough. Daniel had made me sad and Richard had made me sad; and there were times in childhood when I was alone at Tresant by the lake or the sea and a vast terrible sadness inexplicably possessed me, even though spring was there with resurrection or summer with a fullness of lusty life. But it didn't last. Out of myself, in all these circumstances, something would arise, something that transcended the feeling that the very world was weeping in an agony of being lost and abandoned, and I would come to the surface like Lazarus, aware of the tomb and never again to forget it, but alive in the sunlight.

What was terrible to me that day was the fever that took itself for joy. I had found a four-wheeler cab drawn by a poor old life-beaten horse and with a cabby who held the reins in knotted hands and looked down at me, as I explained where I wanted to go, with eyes red and sorrowful as an old bloodhound's. I knew that Mafeking, long invested, was now relieved, but I did not think the news would have these consequences. The scenes were terrifying. It looked as though no one was working anywhere. The crowds in the streets became denser as we advanced. Men and women alike marched in columns or, ten or a dozen arm-in-arm, stretched across the road; and all were singing and shouting, exchanging hats, whirling rattles, throwing confetti, playing upon mouth organs and concertinas; and there were organized bands with drums and fifes, and barrel organs grinding out "The Soldiers of the Queen" and "Good-bye, Dolly, I Must Leave You." People danced and shouted, and a girl in flowing skirts was doing cartwheel turns alongside my cab, to the delight of male eyes. There were innumerable ties being worn of khaki and red, and buttonholes were decorated with rosettes of red, white and blue and with enamel buttons bearing the portraits of Roberts and Kitchener, Baden-Powell, Gatacre, White, and all the others raised by the moment's madness to the status of gods.

People began to climb upon the cab. The horse in any case moved so slowly that this would have been easy, and, as it was, it did no more than walk, for the road was as crowded as the pavements. There were men with rattles on the roof, and presently the door opened and people came inside. Among them was the cartwheel lady, pursued by a youth inflamed by his vision of forbidden territory. They flopped down opposite me, and, taking no notice of me, he pulled her on to his knee, kissed her, and began taking outrageous liberties. There were also men sitting on either side of me, drunk both with the moment and with liquor. What with the jumping and banging on the roof, and the vigorous tussling and touseling opposite me, and the sheer weight of inertia on either hand, I expected the cab to collapse at any moment. I was terrified, and at the same time afflicted by a depth of sadness greater than any I had ever known; but there was nothing I could do, literally nothing at all. To get out would be to pass from a few caged beasts into the teeming and maddened population of the jungle, so I sat there and trembled.

Saturnalia and bacchanalia joined hands, and I was filled with fear and disgust at the thought that I would be compelled to witness even the last rites. But presently the struggling pair opposite me opened the door, got out, and, entwined like two vines each using the other for support, clove a way through the crowds toward a side street. We were passing now through a quieter and dingier part of the town, with narrower streets, and the crowd thinned. The men from the top of the cab leapt down, and I moved to the other side, leaving my remaining passengers to nod on one another's shoulders, not on mine. They were still there when I reached Sally's door. I paid the old cabby with mad generosity in my relief, and told him to take those two back and throw them where he liked into the maelstrom of a proud nation's rejoicing.

Even here, even in this poor and wretched trench of a street, flags and bunting stretched from side to side and disheveled old women were throwing up their knees in grotesque untutored dancing. Small boys, dressed in replicas of military uniform, were proudly marching up and down singing

> *Lord Roberts and Kitchener,*
> *Generals Buller and White,*
> *All brave British soldiers,*
> *All ready to fight.*
> *And when we catch Kruger*
> *How happy we'll be!*
> *We'll bring him over to England*
> *And all have a jolly good spree!*

In Sally's kitchen I collapsed, and I stayed with her through that night. For the night was worse than the day, and I dared not face it: full of the howling that took itself for joy, and was a release from a life more terrible than people could bear. How terrible 't was a phrase of Daniel's made me see. I was distraught when I returned the next afternoon from Sally's and wished for company, I asked my cabby to

399

drive to the House of Commons and sent a message in to Daniel. He came out and took me on to the terrace to have tea. "Well," he cried in high good humor, "we ought to be celebrating, Sarah. We ought to be ordering champagne, not tea."

I looked at him dumbly, this little boy I had met at Montreuil so long ago. Sometimes he seemed more a stranger to me now than he had been on that first day by the pond in the tranquil French garden. Certainly at this moment oceans divided his mood from mine. I poured out the tea and drank gladly, looking at the mild May sun glistering the incoming tide that ruckled against a contrary breeze. "I don't feel like celebrating," I said. "I saw enough celebration yesterday to last me a long time."

"It was a very heartening demonstration of public feeling. It showed that the country is behind the government."

I had nothing to say to that, for I didn't feel then, and still don't feel, that the most wonderful thing a people can do is be behind a government, and he said: "There's good reason to rejoice. We're turning the corner. It'll be a smack in the eye for the Kaiser, anyway."

"What's the Kaiser got to do with it?"

He looked at me with that surprise on his red plump face that was so often his reaction to things I said: a look which wondered how anyone could live in the world and be so ignorant of what was happening in it.

"You don't think he's pleased with this, do you? Have you forgotten already the open telegram he sent to Kruger when Jameson had to throw in his hand? He congratulated him that 'without appealing to the help of friendly powers'—those were the words, 'without appealing to the help of friendly powers'—he had squashed the raid. Well, that was pretty straight, don't you think? And he the son of the Queen's daughter! But he doesn't love us, my dear, and one of these days, mark my words, we'll have to deal with him."

A cloud went over the sun; the breeze that opposed the tide seemed suddenly colder and the tide itself lost its sparkle and was black and sullen. It came pouring up from the wide estuary, and it was pouring into that estuary from the North Sea or German Ocean, as the maps said; and "Yes," Daniel was saying, "a thing like that telegram can't be considered in isolation. It's got to be considered in relation to the general trend of things. Well, after all, there are the French. I don't suppose they've forgotten 1870."

No, I thought, as I made my way home, I don't suppose they have. No one ever seems to forget anything. It all goes into the general trend of things. And a vision of the general trend of things suddenly seared my imagination and showed me yesterday's revelers as a horde of benighted savages howling and dancing on the slopes of a volcano that shakes already with terrible laughter at what is to come.

5

"It's worrying about Richard," Daniel said, when he got home very late that night. In this strange placid companionship into which our lives had developed some new habits had sprung up, and one was that, however late it was when he got home, he would look into my room and, if I were awake, sit on the chair at my bedside, drinking the whiskey he liked for a nightcap and talking to me for ten minutes or so before going to his own room. That night, following our tea on the terrace, he found me hot and bright-eyed with a touch of fever. No doubt worrying about Richard was part of it, but I was worrying about more than that.

"You must have a doctor," he said. It was one in the morning and I cried: "For goodness sake! The poor man's probably been on his feet all day and just getting a bit of sleep. If there must be a doctor, wait till the morning."

But he got up, resolved to go, and I put out my hand to detain him. He took hold of it and said: "You're feeling terribly hot. I shall go." He stood there for a moment, still holding my hand and looking down at me with compassion in his eyes. "You worry about too many things," he said. And then, after a moment: "You're good, you know. Good . . . I . . ." He dropped my hand and kissed my lips, then went quickly away, saying: "I'll go at once."

Our doctor lived only a few doors away, and I lay there awaiting him, thinking of Daniel's goodheartedness and concern for me. I felt grateful to him. It was agreeable to have someone looking after me when I felt like a martyr on a grill. In the curious lightheadedness that possessed me my mind was clear, and I knew that this gratitude for his attention was such as I would give to a stranger who might help me should I find myself in a railway accident. This reflection made me feel terribly alone and a wave of heat washed over me from my toes to my forehead.

Dr. Linskill said it was influenza. He gave me a sedative and promised to call in the morning.

6

Through Whaley, I have known many writers, and, though they may be classified on other grounds, they may also be classified as those who love being in the swim and those who fly from any sort of "swim" as from the plague. The first sort are always anxious to respond for

"Literature" at public assemblies, to address meetings, attend committees, congresses and convocations, to be seen on occasions when the more elderly and eminent of their own sort sit in periodic pomp and receive the homage of those who hope someday themselves to occupy the throne.

Whaley had always detested these gaggles of gregarious geese, and it was not without irony that she herself now, as she put it, fell into celebrity. Her fiftieth book had been published, and a critic made that the occasion to write not so much about the book as about Margaret Whale and her career. It was a just and intelligent article, and people were made aware that behind the well-known popular work there was a seriousness, a consistent point of view—if you care to have it that way, a philosophy of life—that would probably give this author a permanent, though hardly a notable, place in English letters.

Then the *Daily Mail* sent a reporter to interview her, and it was discovered that here was someone who had been a guest of Dickens at Gad's Hill, and had talked with Tennyson and Carlyle and many others whose seats among the gods had not yet been seriously shaken.

Every week end now Whaley went down to her cottage in Hertfordshire, and there was an understanding that Nika should always go with her. And one Sunday afternoon a couple of aspiring writers called on her there and she gave them tea and talked to them. Such news is soon spread, and others came; and presently it was known that Miss Whale received visitors every Sunday afternoon from three to five, and you would find up to twenty people, eminent, or hoping to be, or persuaded that they were so, drinking her tea and eating her cake. Whatever Whaley may have thought of it all—and I imagine ironical amusement was deeply stirred into her weekly séance—Nika enjoyed it immensely, and this lovely young Hebe, who assisted the aging Glory Jane with the teapots and cups and plates, was an expected ingredient of the occasions.

When I was able to totter after my influenza, Whaley asked me to use the cottage for my recuperation. This was in June. Nika stayed there after the week end to receive me on the Monday and to remain with me. I had not been there before and was charmed with the place. The cottage might have been created from a drawing by Birket Foster. It fronted a village green which was traditionally wandered upon by geese, and there were ducks who quacked across a pond in front of an inn and stood on their heads to find their dinner in the slime. It had the supernal quiet of an English village of those days when petrol had not arrived to shatter the peace of the land and infernally stain the skies. The cottage front, with its windows leaded, was embowered—I *must* use that word, it was embowered—with jasmine, honeysuckle and roses that hid the flints and climbed to the mossy tiles of the roof.

The sitting room at the back was big, for several small rooms had here been knocked into one, and the French windows opened upon a noble prospect. The cottage was on a slight rise of land. Before you was the garden, which was nothing but a large lawn, beautifully kept. There must have been an acre of it, with a walnut tree clouding the middle with shade, and round this acre the yew hedges were clipped to the regularity and density of black battlemented walls. Beyond the garden, pasture sloped gently to a stream, and on the further side of that the land rose with abrupt vigor to a ridge along which marched the long line of a wood of beech trees.

It was very beautiful. I stood at the open window, supporting myself with one hand on a chair, for I still felt weak, looking at the rooks drifting through the air above the beeches, my most loved of trees, when Nika said: "And this is the throne, darling."

I turned to look at her where she stood indicating the fat lap of a chair in whose embraces I could imagine Whaley being regal. But it was not Whaley I saw: it was Nika, and it was my mother. The sun had moved across the roof and was sloping toward the beeches and its light came through the French window, and young though the child was, it was my mother, so rarely remembered, who flashed upon my vision, remembered now as she had been in a moment of extreme felicity. I was younger than Nika was now when I saw her in this semblance that annihilated so many years and gave her to me again as she was on a day soon after I had for the first time arrived at Tresant, and, being down on the bar, with the sea on my right hand pouring its great rollers upon the shore, I had seen her and Lord Burnage galloping on their horses toward me, as yet small figures, but becoming larger, until the thud of hooves on sand was heard even over the noise of ocean, and, passing me, they reined up, and my mother dismounted and stood there, her eyes sparkling, her cheeks whipped by the wind, and looking, I thought, the most beautiful woman I had ever seen, as she was. I could imagine now, as I could not then, what was in her heart, what wild glad blood was beating in her veins, as she asked: "Are you happy, darling?" and I, a glum young creature, made no answer, not knowing whether I was happy or not, in the utter disruption of my life.

I was glad now that I had never done anything to disrupt Nika's life, as I well might have done; and, looking at the tall girl, taller than her years warranted, and at her beauty so powerful as to have recreated that great beauty in one of its magical moments, I stepped to her and put my arm round her, and asked: "Are you happy, darling?"

"How does one be happy?" she asked. "I sometimes wish I knew."

She didn't say it with bitterness. She even smiled as she said it. Then she began to put the tea things on the table, and said: "I do think it's too bad of Cousin Julian not to come and see Whaley. He hasn't been down here once."

A. B. Wibsey's shrill voice could be heard above everybody's, and he was, obviously, out to shock some of these sobersides as he had tried to shock us at Richard's dinner party. "Woman. Take Woman. Free her from the shackles that Man has been binding on her for centuries and you'll get a surprise. Take chastity belts . . . "

"Take a rest," someone suggested in a tired voice.

"Don't be cheeky," A. B. Wibsey went on. "Let me finish. Take chastity belts. You think they've been abolished. Well, they haven't. Everything Man does in his legislation and his social conventions regarding Woman is simply putting a new lock on the chastity belt. She's locked up in the home like an Indian purdah woman. Give her freedom. Give her the vote, give her the professions, give her the universities, and you'll be surprised. Man is by nature polygamous. Remove the shackles, and you'll find Woman is by nature polyandrous."

"All A.B. wants," said the same tired voice, "is that Woman should exchange purdah for the harem."

"Take Me," A. B. Wibsey burst in, and that at last produced a general laugh.

"Now, then," he said, "the whole lot of you, don't be cheeky. Take Me. I intend to have a child by a woman of every English social class, from a scullery maid to a Duchess."

"Take oysters and stout," someone suggested, and even A. B. Wibsey didn't have an answer to that.

I had read A. B. Wibsey's first novel that Richard had given me, and I had been surprised and impressed. He wrote with extraordinary verve, if without much grace. Once you had begun to read, you were at his mercy. He swept you along. This one book had been enough to convince me that Richard was right when he said that people would hear of A.B. The man interested and puzzled me. I couldn't reconcile him with his writing. I wondered how far his vulgar garrulity was a compensation for the repressions of his childhood, or whether, perhaps, it was an attempt to be dancing always in the limelight. He won't need that, I thought. I wish he would realize that his books will be enough. I wish he would have some grace and restraint. There's no need for the little cock sparrow to be forever beating the gutter dust with his wings.

Whaley, in regal purple, in which she looked over-hot on that brilliant afternoon, was sitting on the throne placed between the leaves of the open French window. Her guests were walking on the lawn, or sitting in groups on chairs out there. Wibsey, in his Norfolk jacket and knickerbockers, was sprawled on the grass under the walnut tree, his shoes white with dust. He had come on his tandem machine, accompanied by a girl whose name I never learned. She sat against the trunk of the tree, as dumb as Zoë had been. Glory Jane, carrying a tray loaded with tea cups, and Nika carrying cake, went up to the group that had gathered round the pair, and Wibsey, sitting up, began again: "Now take these two women . . ."

"Oh, take a piece of cake," said Glory Jane, turning toward Nika, lifting a slab of Dundee, and slapping it down on Wibsey's plate. "Stop your gob for two minutes with that. One of these days, young man, your hot air is going to blow you up, and that'll be a nasty mess. It's a pity your mother never learned why the good God put canes and backsides into the same world."

Glory Jane had become immense. Her sleeves were rolled up over vast red arms. Her once glorious Titian hair was an untidy ashen heap that intruded ends into her eyes. Shaking her head at this annoyance, she looked doubly formidable. Wibsey sat there, surprised by her assault, and some of those standing round began to laugh. Wibsey had to do something about this laughter, and he said: "Now that is a typical tantrum of an unfulfilled woman. An unfulfilled woman has to let off steam in other directions. She becomes edgy and excitable. . . ."

There were no more cups on Glory Jane's tray, and she lifted it as though to smack him on the head. He ducked at the threat, and the abrupt movement caused him to spill full into his lap the cup of tea he held in his hand.

Certainly this situation was passing beyond a joke. People from other parts of the lawn began to crowd round, and Whaley with slow dignity dragged her purple to the scene. Glory Jane had dropped her tray and, with hands on hips, was shaking with laughter. Nika, however, was horrified. "Oh, Glory Jane!" she cried. "How could you!"

She took a napkin from the tray she was carrying and, kneeling down, began mopping at Mr. Wibsey's soaked garments.

It was at this moment that Whaley reached the scene. She snatched the napkin from Nika's hand and said sharply: "No, Nika! Go in, please." Then she threw the napkin to Wibsey's lady friend, who was pale and frightened. "Finish him off," she said, as if commanding an execution.

"Of all the termagants . . ." Wibsey began; but Whaley cut him short. "I don't *invite* people here," she said. "Anyone who likes can come, but these occasions would be pleasanter if those who came brought some manners. I know that's an old-fashioned idea, but Mr. Wibsey knows that I'm an old-fashioned and out-dated woman. Perhaps manners won't be wanted in the changed world that Mr. Wibsey is seeking. I'd like to suggest to him, at the outset of a career that will doubtless be brilliant, that the only thing one can really change is oneself. I'm sorry I can't help him to change his trousers. We haven't such garments in this house of unfulfilled women. Perhaps vigorous cycling in the warm sunshine would help. I suggest that the treatment should begin *immediately*."

"We better go," Mr. Wibsey's lady friend said. She looked unhappy, daunted by the ring of inquisitive and amused eyes. Perhaps it was out of consideration for her; but, for whatever reason, A. B. Wibsey, staying only to light his pipe with a touch of bravado, pushed the bicycle through the gate and rode away.

8

The new century came, and the Queen lived through its first three weeks. It was a strange day—that January day when we read of her death. First of all, there was the thing itself, which was moving enough, however one looked at it. I did not think her life had been a happy one, but hard work had helped her to carry it through. She had lost a beloved husband, and though there had been a lot of talk and some cruel jesting about her extravagant mourning, at any rate, I thought, it was clear that he had meant more to her than most men mean to most women. And then she had been unhappy about her eldest son. Everybody knew that, and perhaps this was one of the disadvantages of her exclusive love of her husband. No son could ever have pleased her who was not like him. But there it was: the boy who had written an essay about Thugs instead of about machines and pieces of carved marble was now our stout and guttural king. And she must have been unhappy too in this way the century ended. Perhaps, like the little Sarah Rainborough, she had had a vision as she watched the fountains springing in the crystal caverns fifty years ago. Well, this was the end of it for her: a bloody and desolate end enough. It had been a blood-stained century all through, like every other: in America, in France, in China, in Africa: oh, everywhere. But now it was over. We passed from one century into another: from the "Victorian golden evening" into the Edwardian dawn.

The second thing that happened on that day was that we kept an appointment, Nika and I, to visit the Rimmel Gallery in Brook Street. Julian called upon us early in Chelsea to ask whether we would wish to postpone the affair. The West End, he told us, was dead. Hardly a shop or office was open, and certainly he would not open his own gallery to the public, as he had intended to do. But if we cared to see the place he would take us.

I decided to go. I knew that this moment had for a long time been much in his heart. The opportunity had come to take a lease of the ground floor of these Brook Street premises, and he had gone at once to Bordeaux. He got only half the money he needed at an extravagant rate of interest, and when he came to me with this news I was shocked and outraged. There were times when I hated Sebastien and Marie Rimmel, and this was one of them; but, after all, they had known poverty and grinding anxiety, while to me, and everyone connected with me, money had poured in like water, without our having to raise a hand to do more than sign checks. However, at that moment the sou-splitting hard meanness of the document poor Julian brought back made me flame. I often felt degraded by the position I was in, of having more money than I knew what to do with, and that through no virtue of my own, not even the virtue of working; though I could never be bold enough to divest myself of it as Sally had done, seeking a holy poverty. No, I had no difficulty in crushing back any scruples that arose. I liked having money, and I liked doing what money permitted me to do; and I liked being able to say to Julian that, if he wished, he could tear up the document he had signed and I would finance the Rimmel Gallery and ask no interest at all until he was on his feet, and then a much lower one than his father demanded. And that is how the thing was done. It was the begining of an alliance between me and Julian that has lasted through all these years.

We took a cab to Piccadilly Circus, and from there we walked, in order to flavor the peculiar taste of the mourning town. It was different from the Sunday desolation, which is depressing enough. To my own heart, at any rate, the sense that it was *not* Sunday was strongly present, the sense one has when darkness comes not from the day's ineluctable close but from eclipse bringing the shadows untimely. In side streets our footsteps echoed between the shuttered fronts of shops, and the wings of the pigeons could be heard as they rose from their strutting, startled by our approach. A winter wind was blowing about us, rustling the garbage in the gutters, and what disturbed my heart more than all else was a sense not of something that was ended but of something that was beginning. This was the new year, the new reign, the new century, and we were walking in it through desolation: we three alone, not another soul in sight at this moment: only the wind in the gutters, and rats creeping behind dust bins, and pigeons of slate with jeweled eyes.

Nika was fifteen; Julian was twenty-three. In five years' time, I was thinking, the difference in their ages will not seem great.

"You see," Julian said, "my shutters are up like everyone else's. But my lighting inside is good. Let us go in and see."

The shutters were up; but this did not hide the fascia. It was of light green, with just one word on it in attractive lettering: *Rimmel.* From across the road Julian looked at this name with an abashed smile. "It looks assertive and defiant, *n'est-ce pas?* But in here"—laying his hand on his chest—"is a flutter, and I feel a little sick with both hope and fear. Nika, will you take the key and open the door?"

"Why me?" she asked, giving him a sidelong glance.

"Because I would like it so. You are my beautiful and gracious young cousin. Mr. Wibsey does not approve of my old things. As a counter-charm, we shall begin with something young and lovely."

Nika opened the door, and when it was shut behind us the passage we stood in was dark. "Now please to wait here till I call you," Julian said, and he passed through a door on the right.

This had once been a dwelling house, and, like most houses of its time and place, it had folding doors between two rooms on the ground floor. When Julian called us, we went in and found that these doors had been removed and that the one long room thus created was full of tender light. There is no need for me to say what was in it: an antique dealer's shop is a familiar enough object. This was an excellent thing of its sort, charmingly carpeted, not crowded, looking, even, as though it might be lived in, so well was everything displayed. The light fell through a number of crystal chandeliers, gleaming on ancient oak and mahogany, on jade, porcelain, glass and silver, on tapestried seats and brocade curtains: lovely materials, lovely shapes: salvage of beauty from many countries, many years. To go into such a place even from the roar of modern Bond Street is to enter into the peace of a tabernacle. That day, with the town mute about us, with the door locked behind us, there was a serenity that I found to be blessed, calming to my apprehensive heart. More than ever, I was glad that I had made this possible for Julian.

The warmth of a fire burning in a basket grate surrounded by Adam marble made the place seem more than ever like a charming private room. Over this fireplace was a framed tile, shimmering like peacock feathers with metallic luster. "There!" Julian said. "That is it! That is the beginning. Already, my dear Aunt, you have forgotten."

I had, but I soon remembered: the boy, joyous as a bird, the *qu'est-ce c'est's?* and *pourquoi's?* that he had rattled round the heads of his plodding parents, the treasures of Tresant lighting the powder train of his imagination. I felt warm to him, responsible for his well-being. I thought of him almost as of a son. He was a man I could love. He was a man I did love.

"Thank you, Julian, for making the place so charming for us. This fire and all the rest of it."

"Oh, that is old Zeb," he explained, and shouted: "Zeb! Come and show yourself!"

And now to my amazement Zebedee Cogan appeared from a small side room, looking his ageless self, the wrinkled lids of his eyes giving him the air of a wise old bird.

"My good Uncle Daniel, I fear, has lost an excellent rent collector and I have gained an assistant," Julian explained. "I cannot be here always, and who better than Zeb to hold the fort? He loves old things—that is the main point. Already he knows much of the Chinese. The rest he can learn."

In this lighted room behind the closed shutters the day was becoming more and more dreamlike. On a monkish refectory table sandwiches and fruit appeared on Worcester plates, and Julian poured champagne into Jacobite glasses. "To Rimmel's," he said. "To the new year. To the new century."

We drank, and when the little meal was done he washed the glasses, and one remained with each of us four as a memento of that occasion. Out of my very heart I wished him good fortune, and soon afterward, leaving him and Cogan busy about the place, Nika and I went out into the winter streets, doubly bitter after that core of light and beauty, and found a cab to take us home.

9

The third thing to happen that day was the coming of a letter from Richard. It was there when we reached Chelsea. Richard had not been granted the commission that Trimmer promised, nor, should he ever do so, would Trimmer be his batman. Trimmer was dead.

"I shan't go on about Trimmer," Richard wrote, when he had gone on for a long time. "It takes a job like this to teach you things about men, and I've learned a lot about him that I shan't soon forget. It's not going to be easy getting along without him, but at any rate he taught me some ways of doing so, and perhaps that's as much as one man can do for another.

"I was wounded in the engagement that finished him. Don't worry. It was nothing much, a clean flesh wound, but it meant my being sent down to Capetown, and I thought about a good many things while I was there, and one was that I didn't make a will before leaving England. If I died without having done so, I suppose everything would automatically go to Father. I don't want that to happen; I want it to go to Nika, but it wouldn't be a good idea for a child like her to have a lot of money. As soon as I could get about I went to a Capetown lawyer and had the thing put in order. Nika would have the money when she was twenty-one, and I have named you and Miss Whale— will she mind?—as trustees till then. Nika would have the right to ask the trustees to advance up to £500 a year in any year till she is twenty-one, when, as I say, the trustees pack up and Nika takes over.

"Well, enough of that morbid subject. It's just a matter of form.

409

I'm afraid Nika's never going to see that money, and, of course, you won't say a word to her unless and until. . . . I'm feeling very well now, and I'm more than ever convinced that the Army's the life for me. If I don't get a commission while this war's on, I'll get one when peace returns.

"Don't think too anxiously of me. Don't think of me as I used to think of Uncle Justin and of Lord Burnage in the Crimea—what a child I was!—that is, don't think of someone perpetually blasting into an enemy, 'living mid shot and shell.' The life can be boring enough. There were plenty of quiet times out under the stars with Trimmer, and he was a good one at talking about all sorts of things. He pointed out, what had never occurred to me, that this is the *first* war in which you've got every sort of English chap—cook's son, Duke's son, as Kipling says—throwing up his job to join the army. It wasn't so in the Crimea or India or the other African wars. All those jobs were done by the regular pros, but Trimmer says it'll never be like that again. He says every war will be a civilian war from now on, and that England may even have armies of conscripts! I must say I find that a bit hard to swallow! But he's right about this one, isn't he?" And so on, and so on.

And yes, I thought, sitting on that winter day in the first month of the century, while Nika was upstairs arranging her shelves to take the Jacobite glass, sitting there before the fire with Richard's letter in my hand, yes, I thought, that certainly is something new, something this young century has that no century has had before. I got up and walked to the window, looked out into the somber afternoon, at the misty street, the level roof of cloud that pressed down almost to the chimney pots. The weather sounded in my ears, like a roll of muffled drums.

CHAPTER TWENTY-FOUR

I

IT SEEMED odd to me to be ringing up Nika in her own rooms, which were in Bloomsbury. What advantage could there be, I asked myself for the thousandth time, in her being there? If she had belonged to a large family crowded into a small house that made privacy impossible, that would have been another matter. But here was this big house where she had always had her own place and where her wishes had been given fair attention. It wouldn't do for her. "It's something— oh, something psychological, I suppose. It's difficult to explain. It's— well, it's getting out of the nest and using my own wings. The very

410

fact that I used to keep a squirrel there makes me feel such a child in that place." She laughed at the memory of poor Quirky. "And all those bits of stuff Julian used to give me," she added with a flush and a hint of defiance. "I don't want to be reminded of it all. It's like being compelled all my life to drink out of my doll's tea cups."

"Aren't you taking those things with you? They're *good*, and I thought you liked them."

"I don't like being a jackdaw, especially when the baubles dropped into my nest represent someone else's taste, not mine."

"Very well," I sighed. "Don't overwork."

"You do see, don't you, that I've got to *educate* myself? What do I know about the things that really matter? History, science, economics. Take the condition of the working people . . ."

"No," I said, shuddering at so reminiscent a phrase. "I won't take that just now, thank you, Nika. Come and see us often. And I'm so glad your rooms have a telephone."

"Yes, but you won't *worry* me, will you? You won't ring up *needlessly?*"

"Very well. I'll just telephone if there's a death in the family or anything like that."

"Oh, Mummy! Don't take it badly. Let me be happy."

"I don't think you'll find, darling, that happiness depends on being in one room rather than another, or in Bloomsbury rather than Chelsea."

Her movement of sympathy toward me ended abruptly. "Oh, don't *moralize!*" she cried, and ran up to her room.

2

That was two years ago, and I felt more confidence in ringing her up now. A bit of the gloss had gone off her adventure. I explained about the party that was going down to Tresant, and she said she would come. That would make seven of us: Daniel and myself and Nika, Mervyn Mostyn-Lloyd with Enid and their son Edward, and Whaley. It would wake the place up, I thought. It was a long time since there had been so many at Tresant, and it would be good for Nika to meet some people different from the ones she had been with recently.

It seemed a long way back to the time when she was sixteen and Rimmel's had been in existence for about a year and one evening Julian had called on us in Chelsea cock-a-hoop about a deal he had made, securing for a client who was collecting pictures by the Sienese Primitives some examples that older and more famous galleries had been unable to obtain. It was teatime and he was very gay. He had left old Cogan in charge and come away, he said, to celebrate. It was only a small victory, but one of his first, and his joyous sparkle reminded me of the child I had met for the first time at Tresant. He could be a fascinating talker when in this mood, and he delighted us now with a story of how he had been wandering round Christie's and had found an old canvas that was to go into the morrow's sale: a dark and time-stained mediocre thing it looked, lost in a corner. "But I couldn't pass it by. You know, *ma chère tante*, there is something—what is it?—that speaks to you when you have in here"—with his characteristic laying of hand on breast—"the thing that can be spoken to. It was just one corner of that picture, just a tiny flaking, and I *knew* from what I saw that there was something under all that mud and varnish."

He had bought the picture for a few pounds the next day, "and old Dunstable, who boasts that he's never let a bargain pass him yet, said: 'Well, Mr. Rimmel, are you setting up as a marine store dealer?' and I laughed and said: 'When I have done with it I will offer it to you for five hundred pounds.' And I did. And he bought it. Under all the muck was a nice little Rembrandt—oh, not important, but a nice little picture."

He took Nika out to dinner that night, and this became a habit. From time to time there was something to "celebrate," and the celebration was always a dinner with Nika. She would be flushed and happy when he brought her home, all his gaiety added to all her beauty, and Rimmel's became for her, as for him, the first thing in life.

When she was sixteen she went to work there, and she remained there for two years, keeping his books, writing his letters, and what was more, I could not help thinking, being a most attractive asset to the establishment. She was happy in those two years, but there were times when Julian's very courtesy and kindliness to her disturbed my heart. Oh, I thought, there must be more than this, or less. But there was nothing I could do, nothing at all.

Julian was often abroad, and it was toward the end of Nika's second year at Rimmel's that he went to France to collect Impressionist pictures. He was one of the first people in this country to realize their importance, and he intended, he said, to try and assemble a collection "in pickle." "Oh, I expect I shall keep them for years. I will not horrify the public yet. But now is the time to buy them."

It was late autumn when he went, and he was away longer than usual. He wrote to Nika almost every day, sending instructions and suggestions, and always she brought these letters home at night and showed them to me, proud as Punch that he treated her as a responsible person, and also, I was sure, convinced that, apart from the business of the matter, he found pleasure in writing the letters to her, as she so clearly did in receiving them from him. I read them, seeking a gleam, a hope, but they were business letters, touched here and there with a cousinly affection: nothing more. I was sad for her, sad and apprehensive.

On a Saturday afternoon in November, when Nika was at home, the gallery being closed, he rang up as we were sitting down to tea. "Ah, my dear Aunt! Your little nephew is back, and in the highest spirits."

"You have been successful? You have found something good?"

"Many things. And one supreme treasure. May I call on you tonight? At about seven? We shall celebrate!"

"But certainly. Nika is looking forward to seeing you."

"Oh yes! The little Nika! She has done well. And she will love this treasure I bring."

Nika was at my side, tiptoe with excitement, during this conversation, her fingers itching to take the telephone receiver out of my hands, and now, when I put it down, she cried: "Well, how is he?"

"He seems to be in excellent spirits. He's found some good things and he's calling at seven. He wants to celebrate. He's found one especial treasure."

"It'll be the Goya!" she cried excitely. "I know he thought he'd get it this time." But I wondered. I did not think we should see a Goya.

I had just poured out the tea as the telephone rang, and now returned to the fireside table. But Nika would not eat. "I must go and sleep. Forgive me, won't you, Mummy? I must be rested for tonight. Call me at six, darling." She flew away. A "celebration" had never meant anything but dinner out with Julian. It couldn't mean anything else now.

Daniel was away. The house was very quiet, and just before six the quiet was broken by the sound of her voice, singing. There had been no need to call her. She was up, and I heard the water running into the bath.

She was an exceptionally long time getting ready; and when she came she had never, I thought, looked lovelier. I was startled by her beauty. My mother, as I have said, when going out at nights, almost always wore white with a red rose. And that is what Nika was wearing. She was ready for love, and this gave her a maturity, so that, sitting brooding by the fire, faraway in my thoughts, and then, looking up startled by the click of the latch and seeing this young beauty with rich white velvet falling down her in sumptuous folds and the red rose at her breast, I stayed where I was, spellbound. The likeness had struck me in Whaley's cottage, but then Nika was in country clothes. Also, time had passed; she had grown, she loved; and now it was as though, for a fancy-dress ball, she had tried consciously to reproduce the young bloom and grace of her grandmother.

She came toward me, stood over me sitting in my chair as my mother had stood to look down at me in bed, and there came from her the same subtle scent that then excited and disturbed me. She was so certain, so triumphant, as if waiting to move forward when the fanfare sounded, and it was she who embraced me, not I her. But I put my arms round her and she withdrew with a light laugh. "No, please, darling. Don't rumple me." Which, too, was something my mother used to say.

"Well, is it lovely, darling?"

"Yes, Nika. Very beautiful."

"I didn't tell you. I wanted it to be a secret. I bought it especially for the first celebration on Julian's return."

I could have wept, looking at her garlanded for the sacrifice. The front door bell pealed suddenly through the house, and a few seconds later it was all over. Julian had come in, excited, radiant, and with him this small girl snuggling cozily in furs, so that she had a sense of bringing with her cold woods and brilliant winter stars. Her eyes twinkled like stars from under a close-fitting hat of brown beaver. There was altogether about her a healthy crackle and sparkle. She stood there smiling, a small brunette, a little pretty nut-brown woman who had stabbed Nika to the heart.

"Ah, my good Aunt!" Julian cried. "Here is my treasure from France that I promised to bring. And Nika. But how lovely you look, my little cousin! Marthe, this is my invaluable assistant. You will love her. And you, Nika, will love Marthe."

The girl kissed me on both cheeks and then embraced Nika, crushing the rose on her breast. She looked like an affectionate little bear putting its paws round an icicle. I could almost feel the instantaneous and terrible moment in which Nika's excited pulsing blood turned to ice.

The front door bell rang again, and one of the maids came in to say: "The cab, Miss Veronica."

"Thank you," Nika said, and her voice was small out of a desert of loss and hopelessness. "Tell him to wait a moment."

She said to Julian: "You must excuse me. I have to go out to dinner. The arrangement was made before I knew you were coming. I must get my cloak."

I went out and lingered in the hall till she came slowly trailing down the stairs, wearing her white cloak, her gloves in her hand. "I told Annie," she said, "to order the cab. I thought he and I would be going out together in it. Fortunate, wasn't it? It gives me a getaway." She smiled desperately.

"What are you going to do, darling?"

"Oh, you needn't worry about me. I shall just drive round till they're gone. Get rid of them as soon as you can."

"Yes, darling." I pulled the cloak close round her. "It's very cold."

"Yes."

Her teeth began to chatter, and I came to a sudden resolution. "Go

414

up to bed," I said, "and stay there. They won't know that you haven't gone out."

"What a wonderful idea! I'm so dazed and dead that such a simple ruse is beyond me. Thank you."

She went back up the stairs as slowly as she had come down, holding hard onto the banisters. I gave the cabman a half sovereign and told him he would not be wanted, and then went into the drawing room to address myself to the terrible business of courtesy.

They were gone half an hour later, evidently anxious to be alone together, and I ran at once up to Nika's room. The light was on and she was sitting up in bed laughing and laughing. The sumptuous white velvet was thrown carelessly over a chair and the red rose bled upon it like a wound.

"To think," Nika cried, "that I might have been trotting round and round, and round and round, and I hadn't a penny to pay him! And I needn't have gone at all! Don't you think that's funny? Trotting round and round in a stinking old cab when I needn't have gone at all!"

She began to laugh again, hysterically, and I stayed there, stroking her forehead, till at last she fell asleep.

3

Sylvestre Gronnet kept one of the lesser known art galleries of Paris. Julian had often spoken of him to me and Nika, but he had never spoken of Gronnet's daughter Marthe. She had been brought up in her father's shop; she learned the business inside out. During his frequent visits to Paris Julian stayed with the Gronnets. "I shall be staying with the Gronnets." We had heard it often and had pictured the Gronnets as being a nice old married couple. But Gronnet had been a widower for years. He had been kind to Julian: he had given the young man the benefit of a long experience, and now Julian had married his daughter. It was an unexceptionable happening, one that looked like being in many ways advantageous to Julian. But it had broken Nika's heart. That was all.

She was up the next day, which was Sunday, and on Monday she went as usual to the Rimmel Gallery. When she came home she said that she would be going there no more. "Julian's wife was there. She's going to be there every day."

In the short talk I had had with Marthe and Julian on the Saturday night I had learned of Marthe's association with Gronnet's, of her expert knowledge of the trade, and I was not surprised to find that she intended to use this for Julian's benefit, as she had done for her father's. I had told Nika so, but she had said obstinately: "It will be different now she's married. She'll have a house to look after."

It was not a pleasant idea to me: this idea of Marthe at home and Nika expanding a hopeless devotion upon Julian in the shop; and I was not sorry the break had come at once.

"Did anything happen? Were things unpleasant?"

"Oh, they will never be pleasant again," she cried desperately. "I might as well die."

One does not die, my darling, I thought. One goes on, and the wound slowly heals, and the heart is a little harder, but one has learned that life is not all a matter of seeing every frantic desire fulfilled.

"Tell me about it, darling."

"Oh, what's the use of telling you? Small things happen, and they would be nothing but small things if it were not for what your heart is saying while they happen. You wouldn't understand that. You have had a happy life."

"I have had a lot to be thankful for. What happened?"

"They spent all day yesterday at the gallery. I didn't know that. There was a shelf of little porcelain figures that I had arranged. She changed them all, and when I got there this morning I saw that they had been changed, but I didn't know she'd done it. I liked my way best, and I was putting them all back the way they were. Then they arrived. She was onto me before she'd got her hat off, terribly excited. Her way was the right way. She understood such matters; I didn't. Wouldn't it be a good idea if all that sort of thing were left to her and I did the letters and answered the telephone? And so on and so on. I was put in my place. I'm the office girl. 'Vois-tu, Julian. C'est meilleur comme ca, n'est-ce pas?' as she twiddles the things this way and that. And he says yes—of course—they look much better that way. Well, that's how it's always going to be. And so . . . What's the good . . . ?"

It was soon after this that Nika spoke for the first time of Richard's will. When I had told her about it, soon after the news came of Richard's death, she had shuddered and begged me "Don't, don't, please"; and she had not again mentioned the matter till now. She said she would like to have the five hundred pounds a year to which she was entitled.

"But, darling, you have all you need. Your father and I see to that. You have a home, and a place in it where you can be alone if you want to."

"I don't want to be dependent."

"But you don't become independent by using Richard's money instead of ours."

That, I saw at once, was not an intelligent thing to say. It infuriated her, but, even though I knew how deeply she was suffering and how

416

her nerves were raw and tingling, I was not prepared for the vehemence of her outburst.

"Oh, I know," she cried, "that I'm good for nothing and to nobody. I know what a ghoul you think me, anxious to get my claws on a dead man's money. But I'm going to have it. It's mine, and there's nothing you can do to stop me. It's time I made something of myself. I'm tired of being a nobody who knows nothing and can do nothing. Everybody either despises me or treats me as an agreeable creature to fill in the time till a real person comes along. That's what I want. I want to be a real person, standing on my own feet, and if this money will help me to do it, then I'll have the money."

I asked Whaley to dine with me and Daniel, and we talked the matter over. Whaley said: "Cast your mind back to yourself at Nika's age. What were you doing?"

"I was your secretary."

"Very well. Nika has at least as much sense as you had then."

Daniel, who took little enough interest in his children except in moments of crisis, was not prepared to let it go so easily. "I don't see that the two cases have a thing in common. You and Sarah had been together since she was a child. There was a special and unusual relationship between you, and she was living in your house, under your care. Nika wants to fly off into what she calls independence, and that's altogether another matter. She'll have no supervision of any sort."

"What supervision has she now?" Whaley wanted to know. "If she wishes to go into town tomorrow, she will do it, won't she? No one will go with her."

"She's under our roof at nights," said Daniel.

"Well, children can be begotten in the daytime," said Whaley. "There's no closed season for that. And that's all you're afraid of at bottom, isn't it?"

She looked across the table at him with a comfortable grin on her face, and he was disconcerted. He pierced a cigar and lit it. "I'd like to wring that young Julian's neck," he said. "Upsetting us all like this."

"That would hardly put the apples back into the cart," said Whaley. "No. Let Nika do what she wants to. That will be an act of faith in yourselves as well as in her. I know Nika, and I know what you've made of her. Now believe in that. Believe that it's something good enough to see her through this crisis. I think it is. She isn't disgusted with you. She's not trying to run away from you, though it looks like it. It's her own self-esteem that's wounded. Believe me, she won't try to build that up by running wild."

She sounded so confident, so calm, that she did us both good. "Come upstairs to my study," Daniel said. "Let's have coffee there. It's a long time since I've sat down to a talk by my own fireside."

417

"The more fool you," Whaley answered bluntly, heaving her heavy body out of the chair. "It was on this very spot," she said, pointing to a corner of the room, "that your old aunt, Mrs. Gemstone, died. Sarah and I were with her, waiting for you to come home from Oxford. I wonder whether she'd be pleased with what you've made of yourself?"

Daniel gave her an arm to help her up the stairs. "Are you?" he asked.

"Not altogether," she answered, puffing a little as she went up. "You've given yourself too much to all this political blather."

"Someone's got to do the dirty work," Daniel laughed, putting her into his own big red leather chair by the fireside.

"Well, I'm sorry it had to be you. Don't let's have any of it tonight. And anyway, there won't be much more of it for you. The Boer War finished your lot for a long time. You look out, my boy. The Liberals are going to have you on the street in no time, and when you're there you'll stay there for a bit."

"Now, now," Daniel reproved her, "who's starting the political blather?" He poured out the coffee, and brandy for himself.

"I'll have one of those, too," said Whaley. "And you might offer me a cigar."

"A cigar!"

"Male prerogatives are falling like autumn leaves. Yes—a cigar. I took to smoking one each Sunday afternoon, to bolster up this legend that's growing about me, and I found that I liked 'em."

She swung her balloon glass under her nose and took a sip. She drew with satisfaction on the cigar.

"You look like a Sybil," Daniel laughed. I had not known him in such happy temper for a long time.

"Well, you know, I'm getting an old woman, and I've seen a thing or two in my time. One day I shall write my reminiscences. D'you know what Dickens *really* thought of Thackeray? It was down at Gad's Hill, and I was sitting in the garden reading Thackeray's latest when the great man came striding out of the tunnel. You know, some one who admired him had given him a Swiss chalet. He had it put up on a bit of land he owned on the other side of the road from Gad's Hill. Then he had a tunnel made under the road, and he used to go through there and write in the chalet. Well, that day along he came and took Thackeray's book out of my hand, and said: 'Oh, you're reading *that*! Let me tell you, Miss Whale . . . '"

She was happily away. I knew there would be no stopping her now.

4

It was two years after this evening that I was ringing up my twenty-year-old daughter and asking her to join the party going to Tresant.

I gave her the names, and she said: "I'm glad Father's coming. Poor old dear! What does he do with himself nowadays?"

A few months had passed since the great Liberal victory had swept Daniel's party almost out of existence. He was not even in the House. Steignhampton, faithful for so long, had done with him at last, and while it was swinging it decided to swing completely. It returned a Labour member. There were still not many of them, but this man from Steignhampton and Dr. Warwick Russell and a few others sat round Keir Hardie in the House of Commons. Daniel knew now that he had gone as far as he would ever go, and that had not been far. I hoped he would settle down to something in time. Now he was a restless wanderer between his house, his chambers and his clubs. He spent most evenings at home in his study, where he was translating Mark Twain's *Huckleberry Finn* into Greek verse. I thought there would be more sense in it if he took to jigsaw puzzles.

"Well, then," I said to Nika, "we'll all travel down together next Thursday—all except Mervyn and Enid with Edward, that is. They'll be motoring. How are you, darling?"

"Oh, in apple-pie order, as usual," she said cheerfully. "When are you coming to see me? It's weeks since you were here."

"I don't like to be intrusive."

"What rubbish you talk, Mummy! How could you be intrusive?"

"Well, there was a time, you know . . ."

"Oh, don't hark back," she cried. "*I* don't."

"All right. Expect me tomorrow."

I put down the receiver and wallowed in my happiness. A vase with a golden fountain of forsythia springing from it was on the table, and the May sun was warm, and Nika was anxious to see me. I rang for the coffee I liked to drink at this time of morning, and then young Edward Mostyn-Lloyd called and was able to join me. He was carrying a great bouquet of yellow tulips, and he presented them shyly. He was a nice boy, shy in everything, and he never came without bringing me a bouquet. His tie was to one side and his plentiful rough black hair was, as usual, all anyhow. He had no idea how to dress, and always contrived to look dusty. But the deep blue of his eyes, which the shy smile lighted like violets in a sun gleam behind the thick fringe of his lashes, was enchanting.

"Look at this hair, Edward," I said, putting him into a seat, and trying with my hand to smooth it into order. "Why don't you carry a comb?"

"There's no doing anything with it," he said. "Leave it alone. It's Celtic. It comes from my Welsh grandfather."

But your grandfather wasn't Welsh, I thought. Your grandfather was a reprehensible old buccaneer named Eddy Rodda. But I don't suppose you'll ever know that.

"And how come you to be taking your ease in London in May? Doesn't Oxford feel lonely without you?"

"Oh, I'll be back there tonight. Father's going to run me down in the car. At least, I hope I'll be there. You can never be sure with Father and his car. May I smoke?"

He lit a curved pipe, which looked odd stuck into his young ingenuous face. "It doesn't much matter whether I'm there or not," he said. "I shall be going into the shop in a few years' time, and I don't suppose Oxford will help me with that. Father's thinking of starting an antique department. That's why he asked me to come down and talk things over. He wants me to specialize on that side. We've been along to see Mr. Rimmel. If you ask me, it's a bit of cool cheek on the Guv'nor's part. The idea is that I should spend the vacations at Rimmel's, picking up ideas, instead of gallivanting about as I do now. Still, it's a bit hard on a chap—don't you think?—to ask him to take someone into his show so that the said someone can start a rival show and try to cut his throat."

"How did you find Mr. Rimmel?"

"Like death. White, and thin as a lath. So brittle-looking you'd think you could snap him with your fingers. Well, I shall be seeing you at Tresant soon? Father talks of a party down there. He treats the Oxford authorities pretty lightly, I must say. I suppose they look upon me and him leniently because of his huge donation last year. Give my love to Nika. How is she?"

"I've just been speaking to her on the telephone. She says she's in apple-pie order."

"She always is. Well, I look forward to seeing her. *Au revoir*."

Off he went, wearing his bowler hat and smoking his pipe, and I sat there for a long time thinking of Julian Rimmel looking like death.

5

Nika had never roughed it. Five hundred a year could make you pretty cozy in those days, and when at last she had found her rooms and arranged them and invited me to come and see them, I thought her comfortable enough. The rooms were in Russell Square: a fine big sitting room and a little bedroom. She furnished them herself, and there was nothing in them to remind her of Chelsea or of Julian. On a table under the sitting-room window was a typewriter—a thing unusual enough to surprise me. She was still in an edgy *farouche* condition, and I hardly dared ask her any questions. I hoped she would volunteer something about her way of life. But she didn't, and so I stood there, gently pressing the caps of the machine, and asked: "What do you do with this?"

"Not much yet. But I hope to earn my living with it."

We sat down to tea, and I was stricken so dumb with nervousness that she took pity on me and explained: "I'm attending a commercial college. I want to be someone's secretary. Miss Whale thought that would be a good idea."

"Oh. Has she been here?"

"No. I went to her for a long talk."

"It's odd. Whenever anyone wants 'a long talk' they go to Whaley.

"I don't think it odd. It's natural."

I looked round the room that was bare and severe, and took comfort from the thought that it didn't look flighty. Over the mantelpiece was the Van Gogh picture that had become Nika's when Richard died. I wondered whom she thought of when she looked at it: Richard or Julian?

She caught my glance, and said: "I've at last found someone besides myself who really likes that picture. Of all people, Mrs. Mostyn-Lloyd called here. Did you tell her where I was?"

"Yes. Did I do wrong?"

"Oh, no. She's a nice old thing and I hadn't seen her for years. I suppose she thought a girl living alone would be aching for company. I'm not, you know. Anyhow, she came, and brought Master Edward."

For the first time she laughed. "What a little oddity he is! His mother kept on smoothing his hair and saying: 'Darling, can't you do anything about this?' 'No,' he said. 'I'm afraid, Mama, it's a prenatal disaster. Were you startled by a maid carrying a mop?' But he *did* like the picture. He said nothing about it—just stood and looked at it with his hands in his pockets, whistling quietly through his teeth. When he was going, he nodded back at it and said: 'Any time you want to part with that, Nika, I'll chance ten bob on it.'"

Now she laughed really heartily. "How old is Edward?"

"Just about a year younger than you."

"Good heavens! I felt quite maternal to him."

"Well, now. Can I help you to wash up?"

"No. Don't fuss. I can do it in two minutes in the sink on the landing. And then I must put in some practice on the typewriter."

It was my signal to go.

6

The winter was just coming on then, and by the time it was ending, Nika had her job as a secretary. Daniel found it for her. Sir Charles Carey had been a friend of his for years. They had sat in the House together, and Sir Charles was one of the forlorn band of Conservatives to survive the last election. I had met him once or twice—a white-haired old man, more apt with his pen than with his tongue. He was an incurable pamphleteer: nothing that had ever happened in politics or that was happening now was safe from his obfuscation. It kept him busy and happy. He was wealthy and paid for the publication of his own pamphlets, and not one appeared without the sight of his name on the cover inflating his chest, which I had seen at public dinners scintillating with orders and decorations, as if it were a hoarding advertising his eminence. He was, in sober fact, a dear old thing, harmless and ineffective. Increasing rheumatism in the fingers prevented his writing, and this seemed to him to threaten the world with such darkness that public spirit compelled him to dictate.

And so Nika found something to do. Sir Charles, like her, lived in Russell Square, but, unlike her, he had a whole house to himself. She had only to cross the Square in the mornings to be dictated to, and then she could go back and type in her own place. There were the pamphlets, and letters to the *Times,* and letters to constituents, and speeches; and now that he could sit back and talk instead of sit up and write, Sir Charles became more than ever garrulous in correcting the world's follies. Nika was kept busy, and Daniel and I began to accept her situation with tranquillity. She liked Sir Charles and his wife, who was an earl's daughter, very *grande dame,* and they liked her. They were childless. Occasionally they took her out in the evenings, to dinner, the theater, the opera; and the foolish thoughts that had shaken me—thoughts of lively if not licentious company taking up a lot of Nika's time—dissolved before the reality of this almost spectral companionship with a male and female pillar of society.

In November, exactly a year after Julian had come back from France with his bride, and six months after Nika had begun to take a hand in preparing these pamphlets that I had heard A. B. Wibsey call "Mother Carey's Chickens," Wibsey's play was put on in the West End. He had justified with a vengeance Richard's belief in his future. His rise as a novelist had been both quick and complete. His name was heard everywhere. He had known how to capitalize his cockney cheek and ebullience; and his notorious and evanescent affairs with women added a sinister and piquant flavor to his reputation. They were not scullery maids on the back seat of a bicycle any longer.

Daniel and I went to the first night of this play. "Thought you'd like to see what this feller Wibsey's up to," he said. "I managed to get four tickets for the stalls. Ring up Nika and see if she'd care to come and bring someone."

Nika said that Sir Charles and his lady had already arranged to take her, and so Daniel sent the tickets to Julian Rimmel and said we would be pleased to see him and his wife at the theater that night. "I don't want Julian to think I'm annoyed with him," he said. "This'll give us a chance to meet in a friendly way again. We'll go and have supper somewhere after the show."

You dressed for the theater in those days. I remember the audience rather than the play, which was not a success, for Wibsey was a novelist, not a dramatist, and he left the theater alone after that. I remember the silks and velvets and diamonds, the rods, poles and perches of starched shirt front. I remember looking up and seeing Charles Carey in his box, an amiable old billy goat peering over a white-washed wall, and his wife coruscating beside him, and Nika very simple and lovely in dark blue silk with a sash of silver tissue and a red rose in her hair. I remember Julian coming in, looking as distinguished as any man there, tall and handsome, with that *aura* some men have that makes you look twice and think: "I wonder who *he* is," and Marthe, small beside him—a woman I hadn't seen much of, but who struck me now as warm and sensual, so dark, and seeming to exhale secrecy like a twilight wood. I shouldn't like, I thought, to have to fathom *you*. On her short rounded neck, which seemed to be pulsing with excited blood, she wore a collar of diamonds in an antique setting, something, I imagined, that Julian had borrowed from the stock of Rimmel's for this occasion. He couldn't afford to give her that sort of thing yet. Dusky, in an unlighted box facing across toward Nika, I glimpsed A. B. Wibsey, alone and anxious-looking. And so we were all there: the actors in this play that was about to begin.

When the lights went on for the first interval, Daniel said: "Charles Carey is beckoning us up. We'd better go and have a word with him."

I was surprised, as we pushed out of our seats, that Julian and Marthe followed. They must have seen that Nika was with the Careys, and they had not met her since the day a year ago when Marthe had rearranged the porcelain and Nika had left Rimmel's in despair. Julian would wonder what on earth was the matter with his little cousin, but Marthe would know. She would not leave him in doubt. Well, I thought, they'll have to meet again some time. They can't go on in this nonsensical fashion, and Nika has had a year to take hold of herself.

When we reached the Careys' box, Nika was not there. She could not face this meeting, I learned afterward, and she had fled. Charles Carey, who knew nothing of the situation, said: "Oh, she was here a moment ago. I expect she's cramped—stretching her legs in the corridor."

Marthe said: "I shall look—no? I shall find her for you—you see."

She went bustling out of the box, and presently found Nika, wandering forlornly. She embraced her, put an arm through hers, and tried to lead her back. At that moment A. B. Wibsey came along.

"Well," he said, "I saw you across the theater and was taking the liberty of coming to have a word. How's the old Whale floundering these days?"

Nika wanted nothing more than to be rid of both of them. "Oh, this is Mrs. Julian Rimmel," she said hastily. "Marthe, this is Mr. Wibsey, the author of the play. You know Mrs. Rimmel's husband, Mr. Wibsey. You met him—do you remember?—at dinner once, at my brother's."

Marthe said: "You are the *author*? Oh, but what an exciting night for you!" and Wibsey, whose methods were notoriously direct, answered: "I don't think the play's exciting. It's as dull as ditchwater. But what exciting diamonds you are wearing. And what an exciting neck they embrace. They say that these creases in the flesh are a sign of sensuality."

Nika waited for Marthe to fly, but she did not. She caressed her neck, looked into a mirror on the wall to examine the creases that attracted Mr. Wibsey, and turned to him with a smile. "I have always had them," she said.

Nika said in panic: "Are you coming to the box, Mr. Wibsey? My parents are there. They would like to meet you."

Mr. Wibsey turned his fair fat face to her and said: "No. Give them my compliments. And when you meet her, shake the old Whale's flipper with my affectionate contempt."

Nika left them. We almost collided with her returning to the box as we were going out. We found Marthe in the corridor talking to Wibsey. "Oh, Julian," she cried, "you know Mr. Wibsey, Nika tells me."

Julian shook Wibsey's hand, and Marthe said: "Mr. Wibsey invites us to his box in the next interval."

When the next interval came, Daniel and I remained in our seats. Julian and Marthe pushed their way out, and no sooner were they in the gangway than Julian was buttonholed by Mr. Dunstable, a famous connoisseur and collector with whom he had had dealings. Marthe hovered there with them for a moment, looking impatient and occasionally giving Julian's sleeve a twitch, then she left them, and presently I saw her arrive in Wibsey's box. Julian and Mr. Dunstable moved slowly up the center gangway together, talking earnestly, and just as the curtain went up they returned. It was obvious that Julian had not joined his wife. Probably he and Dunstable, immersed in whatever the point had been, had had a drink together and then come back. But Marthe did not come back. I looked up once or twice during this last act, and there she was in Wibsey's box. I said nothing to Julian, who was sitting next to me, but I could feel him stiff with annoyance.

During the fuss and general nonsense that ends a first night—the calls for "Author!" who was, that time, coldly received, the bowing alone, the bowing with leading actress affectionately held by the hand, and all the rest of it—Marthe slipped in beside Julian and took his hand.

"Where did you get to, darling?" she asked.

"Sorry. I was unable to leave Mr. Dunstable. Where did *you* get to?"

"Oh, it was so stupid! I waited and waited for you to come and take me back. And then it was too late. It was time for the curtain to go up, and I hadn't the courage to disturb people. So Mr. Wibsey let me stay."

"That was kind of him."

"Oh, Julian! You are not annoyed?"

"No, darling. I am naturally delighted."

Then she quite deliberately put his hand, which she had been holding, back onto his knee, like something she had done with. "With you it is always Mr. Dunstable, or Joseph Duveen, or this one or that. Even in Paris, when you stay with me and Papa, it is always the trade you talk of—nothing else."

There was silence for a moment, then she said: "Mr. Wibsey would like us to go to supper with him when all this is over"—waving her hand toward the stage.

"But you know we are already engaged to take supper with my uncle and aunt?"

"Don't bother about that," said Daniel, "if you'd rather—" but Julian broke in quite crossly. "Of course we'll come with you. It's a matter both of manners and inclination."

"Then how can we let Mr. Wibsey know?"

"He'll know when he finds us gone," said Julian firmly.

7

Lady Constance Carey was pleased to consider herself a patron of the arts. She had liked Julian when he was presented to her in her box at the theater, and a few days later she said to Nika: "Let us call at the gallery of that nice cousin of yours."

Sir Charles was not at the moment being delivered of a pamphlet; it was a fine clear wintry morning; they got into the brougham and were driven to Brook Street.

Nika was in a fever of unhappiness. She knew what none other of us knew at that time. She had seen Marthe's complaisant acceptance of Wibsey's opening moves, and then she had seen her sitting throughout the last act alone with Wibsey in his box. She had realized with a sudden intuition that made her feel sick that this hot-looking little dark woman was, potentially at any rate, unfaithful to Julian.

To Julian!

She had borne, and to some extent overcome, the stresses of the last year supported by one thought: she had stepped out of the way so that Julian might have his happiness. And now, she was sure, it had all meant nothing. Given the mood and the moment, this woman would betray him: with Wibsey, with anyone who appealed to her senses.

This was the worst thing life had done to Nika: it was worse than losing Julian. All the love for him that she had crushed down and tried to tear to pieces rose up again in a terrible entirety and beat about alive in her heart. And side by side with it was something she had never known before, something whose vehemence frightened her: a burning hate. "Oh, I would have flayed that woman alive if she had been at my mercy!" she said to me afterward.

"It would be nice," said Lady Constance, "to buy a pair of antique salt cellars or something like that, don't you think? The well-to-do should encourage the arts, don't you think? I have always regarded that as a social obligation."

Nika jerked herself out of a savage abstraction. "What have these places to do with the arts?" she asked. "They're concerned with trade. The man who made the salt cellars was the artist, and he's probably been dead for centuries."

"Well, the people in these places are always so nice—don't you think? So well-dressed and quiet-mannered. I always think of them as *priests* of art. I suppose God himself might be difficult to deal with if approached directly. Priests smooth things out so. They understand both sides. So we'll look for some nice salt cellars."

They got out of the brougham and Nika gave Lady Constance an arm up the steps. "It's so tiresome, my dear. My legs used to be so wonderful. I could skate for hours on end. I remember the lake at Trentham. There were wonderful Christmas parties there. And in Holland I once skated on the canals—all the way from Dordrecht to Utrecht. Or can you do that? I'm not sure. Anyway, it was from one place to another. And now that wretched man in Harley Street can't do a thing for me. Well, this is very nice—very nice indeed." She stood with both hands firmly planted on her stick, looking round the gallery.

And it *was* very nice, Nika thought. She had not seen it for a year, and it had matured, taken on character and patina. But there was one thing that she thought not very nice. A. B. Wibsey was there. He and Marthe Rimmel were the only people in sight.

Lady Constance announced in her clear authoritative voice: "I have come to see Mr. Rimmel."

Nika said: "This is Mrs. Rimmel. Marthe, this is Lady Constance Carey. Is Julian about?"

"I am sorry, my lady," Marthe said. "My husband has gone to Paris. He is away for perhaps some weeks. Will you not be seated?"

Nika supported Lady Constance to the chair by the fire, and, once she was seated, the old lady raised her ebony cane and pointed it at Mr. Wibsey. "Get on with your customer," she said to Marthe. "I shall wait."

"It is not a customer, my lady," Marthe explained. "It is a friend who looked in"; and Nika added: "This is Mr. A. B. Wibsey." Lady Constance looked unenlightened, and Nika said: "The novelist."

Lady Constance said: "Oh, do you write novels, young man? I always think that is an impertinence since Charles Dickens died."

"You saw Mr. Wibsey the other night," Nika reminded her. "He is the author of the play we went to. You must remember him taking the call."

"Taking the count, you mean." And the old lady permitted herself a secret trembling of the corsage which was her idea of a laugh. "Take it from me, Mr. Wibsey, that play won't run. It's an impertinence to write plays since Shakespeare died—don't you think?"

"Possibly," said Mr. Wibsey, "it's an impertinence of people to have got born since Adam and Eve."

"Very likely. A lot of good we've done, I must say. Now run along. I want to talk to Mrs. Rimmel about salt cellars. Perhaps I'll send you an invitation for some evening. You ought to meet people. Nothing like it for taking off the rough edges."

Mr. Wibsey was annoyed. He was beginning to be used to fame, and to like it. He was becoming accustomed to deference. He said rudely: "What do people do at these evenings?—sit round and listen to your husband reading his pamphlets?"

"Ah! You know Sir Charles's pamphlets?"

"I wipe my bottom with them."

Mr. Wibsey waited for the thunder to roll and the lightning to flash, but all that came was again that secret trembling of Lady Constance's upper works. "Now," she said, wagging a finger at him when she could speak, "if you write as badly as you talk, you are not much good. Charles Lamb referred to the danger of his works being used for post-culinary purposes. That's better—don't you think? You must not try to shock *me* with talk of bottoms. I know all about bottoms, young man. It may surprise you to know that I was *born* with one. Now off you go."

He went, and she said: "What an odd man! He is not socially sure of himself. Now, Mrs. Rimmel . . ."

While they were busy Nika wandered round the gallery and peeped

427

into the back premises where Mr. Cogan had his being. Mr. Cogan was not there. As she was supporting Lady Constance to the door she said to Marthe: "I have a message for Mr. Cogan. Is he about?"

"No. There were some things to be delivered this morning. He is gone with them."

She was holding the door open for them to go. "I didn't know that Mr. Cogan had become a messenger."

"I'm sorry," Marthe said pertly. "I must keep you informed of how we conduct our affairs."

Old Lady Constance had gone hobbling down the steps toward the brougham. Nika said: "Don't bother, Marthe. I shall keep myself informed of how you conduct your affairs," and hurried after her.

8

In the afternoon of that day Nika called on me in Chelsea and said: "Let us go together to have tea with Whaley." She had of late recovered so much of her calm that I was disturbed to find her once more as deeply agitated as when she left home. Nor was I surprised at this when she told me and Maggie of Wibsey's encounter with Marthe in the corridor of the theater, of Marthe's complaisance, and of what had happened in the gallery at Brook Street.

"*Julian's* wife!" Nika said, and the whole sad story of her sorrow and hatred was in that emphasis.

We sat in the changeless room that I had known now for so many years: the room where once we had been surrounded by "sacred cows and Budders," where I had wept over Daniel's cheerful and pointless visits, where Maggie had already, to me, seemed old when I was young. Now I felt old myself, as old as she was. I felt that I was catching up on life's sad wisdom. Looking through the window, I saw the mulberry tree bare, and there was a crinkle of ice on the pond in which stood the nude lady, looking down at the spot where Captain Grimshaw had ended his troubles. A smear of gray snow lay under the wall, and the gray sky leaned close. I turned to the cheerful hearth, by which Whaley and Nika sat with the tea tray between them. But the child was eating nothing.

"When you told Marthe that you would keep yourself informed of her affairs, what did you mean?" Whaley asked.

"Well, I thought perhaps it would startle her or frighten her. I couldn't *do* anything, could I? I couldn't *spy*." She shuddered at the thought. "So I suppose I didn't mean anything."

"Exactly," said Whaley. "And when you don't mean anything, it's just as well to know it. I'm glad you didn't mean anything."

428

She chewed steadily at a muffin and drank her tea. Then she asked: "Why don't you go down to Tresant for a while?"

"But, good gracious, Aunt Maggie, what would Sir Charles do?"

Maggie grinned. "It won't turn the world upside down if he does nothing at all for a few weeks. Believe me, no one will notice it. And that applies to you, too, Nika, and to most of us. Go and stay with Lucy Evans."

"But why?"

"Well, what you've told us doesn't prove anything. Your father would laugh at it as any sort of *evidence*. But all the same, I don't like the sound of it. If Wibsey and Julian's wife are having an affair, I don't see what any one of us three can do about it. So far as you are concerned, I'd like you to be as far away from it as possible, and Tresant's the farthest place I can think of. I know a lot about Wibsey and about Julian. I know that Wibsey *boasts* of his conquests. He doesn't hush them up, and so, if there's anything going on, Julian will learn about it. And what I know about Julian tells me that that will be the end of it with him. Julian is very fond of you." Nika winced at that. "That's why, if there's going to be any smirching, I should like him to know that you were nowhere near the affair. And I think that in time you, too, will be glad you were away." She took Nika's hand. "I know how you feel, my dear: how you love Julian and how you hate Marthe. Those two things together might lead you to interfere in a way you'd regret later."

"You are right," Nika said out of a stony face. "I couldn't trust myself near her."

"No. That's what I'm afraid of, my dear. You might try to force an issue, and perhaps Julian would never forgive you."

"Julian doesn't think of me one way or another."

"Now that is nonsense. There are all sorts of love in the world. Love is not always passionate. In the way of love, we must take what we can get, and be thankful. And we must give what we can. Go and give something to Lucy Evans. She will be glad to see you. She sees few people. Go in the morning. Your father will explain to Sir Charles. Do you think this is all sensible?"

"Yes. But very hard."

I saw her off in the morning at Paddington, and when Julian's marriage came to its unhappy crash I was glad she had taken Whaley's advice. She found, as it happened, plenty to occupy her mind, for Lucy Evans was ailing when she arrived and rapidly became worse. Mervyn reached Tresant only in time to see his mother die.

CHAPTER TWENTY-FIVE

I

WELL, these things were all behind us when we made our
journey to Tresant in May of 1906. It is from the time of this
visit that I date my resolution to make Tresant my home. I had sometimes wondered whether, some day, Sally would find the pull of the
place too much and leave her Bermondsey lair, but now it was clear
that that would never happen. Not this, but the house in Robin Hood
Road, was her home, her place. It had been permissible at one time to
think of that adventure as an aberration, something that she would come
through to another point, but now I saw it as the end of the true line
of her destiny.

I went to see her before we left for Cornwall. She was looking old;
she would be sixty in a year's time; but she was in good health and
tranquil. She made the ritual cup of tea and put a tin of biscuits on
a corner of the kitchen table. I suppose it would be agreeable to write
that everything about her, though poor, was spotless, just as novelists
like to speak of tweeds that "though old and worn, had evidently been
cut by a first-class tailor." The only thing about Sally that had been cut
by a first-class tailor was her face. The years of her life, and the way
of those years, had given it a serenity that was moving. I recalled the
phrase: "The shadow of a rock in a weary land." I had sometimes worried myself with thoughts of her, but I never did so after that day. She
so obviously had, here in this pig-sty, what few people find anywhere.
The oilcloth on the table was cracked and stained; there were no curtains to the windows. "Every bit of fabric, no matter what, is just so
much more to be washed," she once explained. "Everything gets filthy
here, so the only thing is to eliminate." That day, it was obvious that
she was not physically very clean. A faint disagreeable smell came from
her and her clothing, and I saw a louse on her neck. "Oh, well," I
thought, "I don't suppose Queen Elizabeth smelled very sweet, and
eighteenth century wigs and bigwigs were notoriously lousy." Even
without such excusing reflections, I would have loved her—just as she
was.

She laid a hand on my arm and smiled at me; and if her face in
tranquillity was moving, when she smiled it was something that
searched my heart. The girl she had been looked through the window
of the woman she had become, as though, miraculously, a Rembrandt
picture of wise age had taken light from a Romney of mischievous
girlhood. "Last week," she said, "I had a most extraordinary experience.

Here I've been, all these years: I've lost count: and I thought I'd better go and see what the grand world was doing. It would be rather like St. Anthony assisting at the bath of Venus, I thought, just to be sure he was proof against temptation. Imagine it, I walked down Bond Street! I dillied and dallied and looked in all the shop windows. Oh, the things! Gainsboroughs and meerschaum pipes and great fat hams and pies! And the dress shops and hat shops, and all the gold and glitter in Asprey's! There were riding habits such as I used to wear and the most gorgeous saddles and riding crops; and all of a sudden it came over me that I could buy anything I wanted—even a diamond coronet! I'd become so used to being poor old me that the thought was quite a shock; and then the idea of wanting any of it became so comic that I laughed and laughed. I was wearing that old bonnet and shawl that you see there hanging behind the door, and these great boots"—she pushed out her feet to show me—"and a policeman said: 'Now, Ma, what's the matter?' So I thought I'd better push on. And then I saw something that I *did* want, and that was violets. There was an old man sitting on a corner with a basketful, and they made me think of Cornwall. I thought of a morning—oh, even before I knew you—when I was wandering alone and I came by a place where violets grew. They were all over the ground outside an old church. I'd ridden there on my pony, and I got off and stood there holding the reins, and the violets were white and every shade of blue, and down on the water, on a mud bank, curlews were bubbling. D'you know that extraordinary bubbling note they have in spring . . . ? You know, there are moments—oh, perhaps half a dozen in a lifetime—when everything is perfect. Of course you know. You've told me of your own perfect moment at the Crystal Palace. Well, that was one of mine. Everything flowed together—it was harmony—the spring morning, and the scent of the violets, and the feel of the pony's neck under my hand, and the curlews bubbling, and the utter aloneness. And all that suddenly was *there*, in Bond Street, when I smelled those violets. So I bought three bunches and walked on. And then the extraordinary thing happened—I met my mother!"

She paused and squeezed herself another cup of tea off the leaves. "You saw her once," she said. "D'you remember?"

And I remembered the Derby morning in Hyde Park when my heart was sore as I watched Lord Burnage drive away, and then that lovely woman had spoken to Sally and Sally had not answered. But she had said to me and Whaley: "That is my Mama. She is the Duchess of Fallowshire."

"There was a dress shop," Sally said, "and standing outside it was a carriage, and I knew the uniform of the coachman sitting up aloft and of the footman standing at the curb. And I knew the coat of arms on the panel. And but for those things I shouldn't have known her at all.

She must be over eighty, and she came out of the shop with such a flutter of ceremony, the footman opening the door, the shopman bowing, the very horses tossing their heads with a sort of 'Here she comes.' And she was a painted old image that I should never have known from any other painted old image, and, oh dear! she certainly would never have known me! But I couldn't resist it. I stepped forward as she crossed the pavement and held out my little bunches, and I said: 'Vi'lets, lady? Sweet-smelling vi'lets?' The footman took me by the arm and pushed me back and she looked full at me and a smile broke her old mask, and she said: 'Don't be rough, Jackson.' So Jackson gave me a dirty look because he had been reproved, and she climbed in, and off they went. And that, I suppose, was fare ye well to Mama."

She raised the cup again to her lips, and I noticed a rather dirty bit of bandaging on one of her fingers.

"Doctor Russell wouldn't approve of that," I said.

"No. I don't suppose he would. There are lots of things about me that he wouldn't approve of. I'd better change it."

She unwrapped the bandage and the bit of pink lint under it and threw them into the fire. The cut was inflamed and septic-looking. "This comes of scrubbing the floor for Jinny Griffiths," she explained, as casually as though scrubbing floors for Jinny Griffiths was the thing she had been born to do. Perhaps it was. How do I know?

"Poor Jinny is nineteen," she said, "and about to have her first baby, and she's ill and terrified. Her husband's a hulking brute of twenty-five, a dock laborer, so violent that no one but me and Warwick Russell will go near the house. At the moment he's out of work, too."

"Then he could scrub the floors."

She shook some boracic powder out of a packet into a basin of hot water and stuck her finger into it.

"The world is full of people, my dear Sarah," she said, "who have made up their minds about what other people should do. Men should allow women to vote. The rich should part with their money to the poor. The poor should be sober and industrious. My old friend Dolly Dewhirst was full of such notions. They make up the bed-rock of party politics. But while that is being worked for—and I suppose it should be worked for—there remains the fact that the world is also full of people who do those things that they ought not to do, and leave undone those things that they ought to do. Jinny's husband ought not to scare the neighbors and undoubtedly he ought to scrub the floors. But he doesn't scrub the floors, and so I do. I just go round filling in time with odd jobs till the millennium comes to make me out of date."

She laughed and took her finger out of the basin. "Look at all this blasted pus," she said. "I must prick it out with a needle."

She did it efficiently, boiling the needle first, and packed her finger up in a new dressing. "Just a splinter," she said, "out of a very dirty floor. D'you know what that old fool Warwick Russell calls me now? God's charwoman. A bit too flattering, if you ask me. Still, I'm vain enough to like it. I've always thought my work down here had earned a title of some sort, and now I've got it."

I asked how Dr. Russell was, and she said: "Since Robin died . . .'

"Is Robin *dead*?"

"Dead as a doornail," she said. She never wasted emotion on what was done with. "Typhoid. I warned Warwick, but you can't argue with that man. And Polly can never have another child."

We sat in silence for a moment, with the stark fact between us, and she said: "It's given him a sort of inhuman energy. He's an odd creature. There's no memorial on the boy's grave—just a mound of grass. 'By God!' he said to me, 'I'll work now till every street and house in this place is his monument. I'll work till he's sleeping in the midst of paradise.' That's what's driven him to the House of Commons. I love that man. He's got Dolly Dewhirst's head and my heart all rolled into one. He makes me feel a self-indulgent old fool—sitting here, getting more and more like a decrepit spider in this filthy web."

She pondered for a moment, and then said simply: "But there. Somehow my road led to it. I couldn't help it."

I told her of the excursion we planned to Tresant, and asked her if she ever felt a wish to go there again. "No," she said thoughtfully, "no wish that I can't easily overcome, anyway. All that Tresant could do for me it did, and it's here." She laid her bandaged hand on her breast. "And I'm glad it's here. It's very precious to me. It's like good bread that I ate in childhood. It helped to make me, and it's digested into me; but I don't want to go back and sweep up crumbs. Be happy down there, my dear. Stay there as long as you like, whenever you like. It'll be yours when I'm gone. That's fixed in my will."

"Sally—darling—!"

She got up, dismissing me. "Now! No arguments, please, and no sentimentality. I must be off to have a peep at Jinny Griffiths, so you must go—unless you'd like to look in there, too?"

"No."

"I thought not." And the disarming lovely grin came back. "Well, off you go and look after your own. Kiss Nika for me."

"I must kiss *you* for Nika."

And I did so; and we clung to one another for a long moment, before she drew herself away and took down the bonnet and shawl from behind the door.

There was a double purpose in this visit to Tresant. We all needed a holiday, and there were mortuary matters also to be attended to. Daniel and I wanted to see the memorial plaque to Richard that had been set in the wall of the chapel alongside Justin's; and Mervyn wanted to see that the headstone had been put up on his mother's grave. So we went, all seven of us, from the house on the morning after our arrival: a morning sweet with bird song and gentle airs and new greenness, a resurrection morning for the commemoration of our dead. And I thought of others who were dead besides these two. How old I felt! Whaley and I alone of the seven could go back in memory to the day when things started for me here, the day when I landed, very sick, at Porteven and was driven to the house. My mother and Lord Burnage, Eddy Rodda and his son Wesley and his scolding long-suffering wife, Justin, Lucy's mother, and many others that I had known not so well as these, and many good kind animals, too: they were all gone; and now Lucy and Richard were gone. Only Whaley and I had known all these, and we two, in the churchyard where the grass was wet and the dew lay in the broad leaves of the winter heliotrope as if in saucers, and the daffodils abundantly grew among the graves: we two stood a little apart, like soldiers separated by their memories from people who had not shared the triumphs and disasters of their warfare.

We stood apart looking at them as they were grouped round the piece of granite which recorded simply the name and the years of "Lucy Slinn, the beloved wife of Colonel Aloysius Slinn." Well, leave it at that, I thought; it's all one now; and there she is, whom Millais found so lovely, with Eddy Rodda's bones at last within reach of her hand. She won't excite him now, poor ghost.

Maggie moved away and joined them: the son of Lucy and of Eddy Rodda, and their grandson, this bare-headed rough-haired boy Edward whose arm, I saw, was linked with Nika's. And the humor of life's unexpectedness took a grim hold of me. No, Eddy, I thought, it would certainly never have occurred to me, standing on that quay at Brest, a little child overwhelmed by the swift change of her life, and watching you and the two French whores saying your good-bys: it would never have occurred to me that I should live to see your grandson and my daughter arm-in-arm, and be pleased about it.

Stealing quietly away from them, I went to the leper's squint in the wall of the chapel, and I remembered the only other time I had looked through that hole bored to give a sight of God's mercy to the wretched. I had seen, that time, Richard, lost in his dream of grandeur, scraping up reliquary dust as something to be treasured, and my heart had been alarmed, thinking what life could do to such a vain concern. And now his own dust was part of the sun-baked lion-tawny veldt where, they tell me, after rain the flowers awake sudden and innumerable. But here, where nature goes about her affairs with less of drama, and the miracles are too slow to be seen for what they are, here was his memorial, a piece of marble that I could see shining like a bleached skull in the dark chapel, with the trees pressing round it dressed in young leaves that hid for a season the gray mossy tresses and writhen limbs of their antiquity.

I pushed open the slab of oak that was the door and shut it behind me, wishing to be alone, and walked through the crumble of tombs, over the paving which itself was tombstones, beneath the frayed webs of banners which would never again go with the trumpets valiant and undulate in the wind; went amid the smell of imprisoned years and the sense of so many lives come to an end in this disintegrating box of stone, and I stood by the brazen wings of the lectern-eagle which seemed a flame in the gloom. Standing there, I read the tablet next to Justin's, which I remembered white and was now old ivory:

Sacred to the Memory
of RICHARD UNDRIDGE
1878—1901
Who gave his Life in the
South African War.

His Grandmother was the Wife
of Charles Ormiston Gaylord,
Tenth Baron Burnage.

The golden evening brightens in the West,
Soon, soon, to faithful warriors cometh rest.

I had written it myself. I thought Richard would like the relationship to the Gaylords to be remembered there, and I did not grudge it to him. I hardly saw those words. The words I saw were "1878–1901. Soon . . . Soon . . ."

How soon it had been! I stole back and sat in a pew just inside the door, thinking of Justin and Richard and Trimmer, and poor Tom Chadderton, who had tried to mend broken creatures, and been himself broken beyond repair; and when, presently, the others came in, speaking in quiet voices, and moved up the aisle, I slipped out and began to walk home alone. But after a time Daniel, hurrying, overtook me. He put his arm through mine, looking down in a shy apologetic fashion as he asked: "Do you mind?"

Oh, God! I thought. Do you mind! What things life does to us! And I couldn't see the day for weeping.

435

3

I should not, I was sure, go often to the graveyard and the chapel
to see the headstones and the tombs. "Why seek ye the living among
the dead?" They live in our hearts, or they are dead indeed. But
in the evening of that day I went once more, so that I might go quite
alone, not wishing for the company even of Whaley.

The day had been as warm as one of June. The dew had gone
back out of the earth into the sky, to come again as dew or gentle rain
or blasting hail; the grass was dry, and a coolness came with the
green lucent evening. A star was shining, and amid so many trees
the light was dusky. Bats blundered about, and, this being the season
of high chorus for the birds, they were filling the air with gay roulades,
with cadenzas and cascades of melody; but one by one they were
tiring of a day that had been all encores, and, as the songs slowly died
away into half-heard twitters, imagination filled the trees and hedges
with wings gladly folded to rest and bright eyes looking out for a while
over the parapets of nests before closing with confidence in the friendliness of the dark.

I was not alone after all. A girl was standing by Lucy's grave, and
I knew that this was Haggie Chadderton. I remembered Sally's
description of her as she had been in those days, now long enough
ago, when she and Tom had lived in terror of old Crackpot Chadderton: a dusky slip of a thing, wild-haired, vanishing like a shadow into
the slum lanes at the approach of a stranger. She still looked a shadow.
She was thin and straight and dark, and had, for all her stillness at
this moment, an air of swiftness, as though a casual word might make
her look over her shoulder—her back was to me now—and streak
away into invisibility. The time she had spent with the Warwick
Russells and, later, with Lucy, had made her, I knew, a different
thing from the shy creature, fugitive amid the urban glades and
avenues of stone. Lucy had come to love her and to rely upon her;
and Nika, during that sad moment of her withdrawal from Julian's
tragedy, had been greatly taken with the young woman.

Once again, looking at her standing by Lucy's grave, the tragi-
comedy of life's unexpected tricks and stratagems came over me, for
Haggie was now a well-to-do-girl. Lucy Evans had not forgotten how
much she owed her for the comfort of her last years. The considerable fortune that she had inherited from her old protector Mostyn-
Lloyd had gone mainly to her grandson Edward, but a slice of it found
its way to Haggie, who now, if she wanted to, could be what they call
independent.

I was more and more fascinated by the power and persistence of

436

money in shaping destiny. How odd it was that of all the people I intimately knew Maggie Whale alone earned what she lived on! My father's "war work" during the disasters of the Crimea, and the fact that he owned iron-bearing land at the time when someone else's genius was causing railways to web the world, had made me rich, and had made Richard rich, and, through Richard's will, would, in a year's time now, make Nika rich. And my father himself, I was sure, would never have had money in this fat and opulent fashion but for the chance of an ancestor reputed to have been not overscrupulous, who, by luck, bought an estate stiff with unguessed riches. And so, too, with Lucy Evans and the present generation of Mostyn-Lloyds, and so, through Lucy, with this girl Haggie Chadderton. It all flowed, for them, from the impetuous, unscrupulous and hard-working Welshman who certainly never dreamed, during the early days of his assault on fortune, that the unfathomable ways of life would turn the stream of his wealth to a handsome girl he had never seen and her son by a Cornish brigand, and an old scholar's daughter, and their son, and to this girl standing now by Lucy Evans's grave! And there was Daniel and Mrs. Gemstone, and, if it came to that, there was the Rimmel Gallery, for Julian would have had a harder start but for the flow of money I had directed toward him: money coming from a beginning so far off and so odd, smirched at the source with legends of Eastern jewels dubiously come by. And, knowing so many people, myself among them, who unquestioningly accepted these benefits of mysterious fortune, I knew then only one, and never in all my life knew another, who had looked at this and put it aside to embrace poverty. That was Sally; and but for Sally I should not have known Haggie Chadderton; and not to have known Haggie would have made my life the poorer.

4

She looked over her shoulder with a start as I drew near, but did not vanish. I held out my hand. "I suppose you are Haggie Chadderton?"

Her warm dry brown hand took mine, and I said: "I'm Mrs. Undridge. Thank you for looking so well after my Nika."

"She was very nice to look after. So was Mrs. Slinn."

I made a note that to her Lucy was Mrs. Slinn, and we both turned away from Lucy's grave, on which were some flowers that I supposed she had put there. I felt that I did not, after all, want to linger with the dead. There was a quality of vibrant life about this thin dark girl that I turned to gratefully. The light was gone out of the sky, and we were at the dead of the moon. In the darkness

437

Haggie moved with the confidence of one who knew every step of the way, as I did myself. A white owl almost brushed our faces, moving in a silent sweep from darkness to darkness across our track, and she was undisturbed. She's a countrywoman now, I thought.

"It will be sad for me to leave this place," she said. "We were very happy here, Mrs. Slinn and I."

"What did you do with yourselves?"

"Oh, very little. Do you know all about me?"

"Yes. Mary Brown is my stepsister, and I see a good deal of her. She often speaks to me about you."

"Well, then: you will know about my bringing-up. I used to think a lot about being happy in those days, and about the sort of things that would *make* me happy. I suppose the way I thought was not different from any other girl's who might be fixed as I was—just Cinderella fancies, all ending up with being rich and having anything I took a mind to. Sometimes I used to wander as far as the West End, and watch the carriages arriving at the big houses where a ball was on, and the girls getting out and walking under the awnings up to the front door. And you'd see the footmen inside, and the flowers and the lights."

"Did you feel jealous?"

"No. I don't think I ever did. They didn't seem to belong to the same world. There would have been as much sense in being jealous of the angels singing in heaven. I was envious, but not jealous; and then other nights when I was wandering about the streets in our own part of the town I'd play at being one of those girls. Oh, there's many a back door in Bermondsey, with the ash-can outside, where I've arrived in state, and sat haughtily waiting for the carriage door to be opened, and then stepped out in silken shoes and walked into the splendor!"

She laughed, and it was a frank happy laugh that certainly had no bitterness or memory of bitterness.

"Let me put that shawl round your shoulders," she said, and she took the shawl that was hanging over my arm and draped it round me. "It's getting rather cold."

"Well," she said as we walked on through the darkness full of small wild scurrying creatures, "I was saying that Mrs. Slinn and I were very happy here. I learned how happy you could be without any of that sort of thing. Indeed, I learned *that* when I was staying with Dr. Russell and his wife."

"How did you and Mrs. Slinn fill the time?"

"Lord! There's no difficulty about that—what with the house-work and the bit of garden and walking and reading and sometimes just doing nothing at all! I tell you, Mrs. Undridge, there's a lot to be said for enjoying life by *not* doing things. It can be very com-

438

forting. So much better than inventing all sorts of duties and works that mean nothing and make the day all a scuffle and chatter. We *never* paid social calls. Fancy the rabbits combing their tails and setting out to eat a social dandelion with a few friends! They know better!"

The lights of Tresant were shining ahead of us, but I found myself in no hurry to be there. I was enjoying my company.

"A favorite walk of Mrs. Slinn's," Haggie said, "was through the woods along the lake, and then by the cliff path to Porteven. We'd go through the village and up the hill, and she'd sit there on a little canvas stool I used to carry for her, just looking over the top of the village away out to sea."

Yes, I thought, I can see the exact spot, and the hut that used to stand there, and the bath that Captain Rodda dug more than fifty years ago among the cress and burdocks and watermint. Certainly, sitting there, she would have plenty to think about as she looked at the summer sun shining on the water.

"But the best of all, I think, was the long winter nights. We burned nothing but logs, and we'd read by lamplight. Sometimes we'd have a book each, and sometimes I'd read to her. Her sight became bad."

Her words called up a familiar scene. How many nights, in that same room, Whaley and I had spent in that same satisfying way!

The gravel was now crunching under our feet. "So you see," Haggie said, "this place has come to mean a lot to me, and I shall be sorry to go."

"But need you go, Haggie?"

"What can I do? The cottage isn't mine, and it was only lent to Mrs. Slinn."

"Possibly," I said, "some day it will be mine, and in the meantime I'm sure I can promise you that if you want to stay there's nothing to stop you. I'm going to make the house itself a better place for living in. It'll be more used from now on. I shall be here a lot. I shall need a companion. Would you care to take that on?"

"Oh, Mrs. Undridge!"

"I see you would."

"The thought of going from here has been breaking my heart."

"Then stay and have it mended," I said, feeling mean and scheming, a creature with an eye always on her own comfort. "Now you mustn't cross these dark fields to the cottage alone. Come inside. I'll find Nika and Edward. They'll be company for you, and company for one another on the way back."

Scheming again! I saw with pleasure that they were not reluctant to do as I asked.

No, they were not at all reluctant, during that holiday, to be about together. In all that beauty, Daniel spent hours indoors, toiling over his translations into Greek: a labor that I was sure Haggie would have classed among the invented and meaningless. I myself was busy with schemes for Tresant. During years past it had had no one in control but an aged couple who had done little but make themselves snug in the kitchen and flick an occasional duster elsewhere. They would have to be pensioned and a few good servants brought in, with Haggie in charge of them. I chose two pleasant rooms for Haggie's private quarters and decided also which rooms to keep open for my own purposes. There was an enormous amount of stuff in the house— furniture, pictures, porcelain—that museums and art galleries would be glad to have as loans. I spent days going through the shrouded musty rooms making inventories: what should be kept, what should be loaned: and concerning all this I would get Sally's approval when I returned to town. What I wanted was a clean sweep of most of the rooms, which would then need no more attention than airing, and a few sitting rooms and bedrooms furnished with the best things out of the house. And I may as well say now that, before the year was out, that is how it was done. My place at Tresant, even after it became my own, was a pleasant camp among empty rooms. As for the estate and its agricultural affairs, they had been looked after, ever since Justin's death, by an excellent agent whom I left to do as he pleased. Haggie came into the house, and the ancient bodies removed themselves to her cottage.

While I was busy with all this, and Daniel with his Greek, and Whaley with a novel, Mervyn and Enid returned to town, for Mervyn, though he knew as well as I did that his departmental managers could run Mostyn-Lloyd's without him, liked the feeling of indispensability and would never stay long away from the premises. So off they went, stinking and spluttering through the May morning in Mervyn's latest car, both wearing goggles and Enid with a picture hat held to her head by cloudy chiffon that made a great blue butterfly under her chin. Thank God, I thought, standing at the front door with Nika and Edward to see them go, there is one marriage that is in no danger of disaster. They seemed glad to be leaving us behind—even their beloved Edward—and to have no company but their own.

And so there was no one left with the young people but three old fogies who were all busy with their own affairs. Nika was twenty. How deep her feeling for her cousin Julian had gone I had no means of knowing, for now that the disaster had fallen and time had begun to smooth the commotion of it, she did not speak of him any more and she had recovered, on the surface of her life at all events, a calm which, if I suspected it at times of being enigmatic and perhaps deceptive, was at all events maintained before watching eyes.

Edward, at nineteen, seemed to me a delightful creature, unspoiled by fortune, phlegmatic and four-square. How different from the volatile boy that Julian had been! Physically, his four-squareness was almost literal: he seemed carved out of a block of oak. "That square boy," Whaley called him. To the darkness of his father was added the rolling and rotund solidity of his grandfather, old Dr. Gotherson, who, at some incredible age, was defying all the fears and predictions of forthcoming death, and in his loft over Mervyn's house in Hanover Square still brooded and toiled among his red tape and pigeonholes.

There were no riding horses except the agent's hack in the Tresant stables now, but we managed to hire a couple, for Nika and Edward had both learned to amble about in Hyde Park, to the amusement of Mervyn, who considered horses to be anachronisms. It was good to see the pair of them riding forth in the lovely weather that persisted through all that holiday, or embarking in a punt on the lake, or, with their luncheon in a haversack, going off on foot in the morning to make a day of it. "I suppose," said Whaley, standing at my side as we watched them swinging away one morning, "after an unwise indulgence in champagne a sedative is welcome."

"Oh, Maggie, what a way to put it!"

"I don't know. Bubble, bubble, usually means toil and trouble. Nika won't be the first poor battered swimmer who thinks there's something to be said for the municipal baths."

"If you're going to be horrid, Maggie, I won't ask you to the wedding."

"It'll have to be pretty quick if I'm to attend it."

"Maggie! What on earth do you mean?"

"Never mind what I mean. I'm seventy years old, and I'm still a working woman. I must get to my desk."

She went up the steps into the house, and she went slowly, and, watching her, I was aware not for the first time of the burden of her years. She was stout and heavy and unhandy, and I walked the gravel in the morning sunshine with a tooth of misery in my heart. She had her book and Daniel had his Greek and Nika and Edward had one another. I alone had nothing to do but lie open to fear and apprehension. I thought of Whaley at seventy, the still famous woman, if in many minds her fame was now tinged with a rather amused affection; and I thought of her coming into the schoolroom in Portman Square on that morning so long ago, refusing to be put off by my hurt and injured reception, spreading out her warmth, her loving-kindness, for me to take if I wanted it, and being, ever after that, till this very present day, something I could count on to respond to my needs without stint or calculation. She had become somebody, and I was never anybody, and there was no reason why she should not have thown me off as she climbed to the top of her own hill. But she had never done so. She had been utterly and in all circumstances faithful and wise.

As I stood there pondering these things the gravel gave sound of an approach, and I turned, and there she was. "I can't work," she said. "It doesn't often happen. I've got myself through all these years into the routine of a dependable hack. But I suppose even a cab horse sometimes thinks: 'Oh, to the devil with it!' And that's how I feel this morning."

She put an arm through mine and breathed deeply the soft warm air. "We're standing on the very spot," she said with a laugh, "where you crushed your spectacles into the ground with your foot. D'you remember doing that?"

"I do indeed. I must have been a great trial to you. How did you put up with that horrid little girl with spots and spectacles?"

"Even spots and spectacles have their part in the scheme of things. Don't forget that because of them we went to London, so that the doctors might have a look at you; and so Lucy Evans met Mostyn Lloyd, and so, in the long run, Nika met Edward."

We walked toward the beautiful but now empty stables, and I said: "You were engaged to be with me till my character was formed. You hang onto me so closely that you must still have grave doubts about me."

"Oh, you're not so bad," she said lightly. "I think I can now safely turn you loose in the world." After a moment she added: "Anyway, I shall have to."

There was something so grave in her tone that I looked at her sharply, and she said: "Let's sit down here under the trees. These great roots make a good seat."

She lowered herself carefully, and I sat beside her under the opening green of the beech trees, with the land sloping down to the lake. It was all as we had known it unchanged through so many years: the swans, with sails hoisted amid the flat burgundy-stained dark green leaves of the lilies, like frigates in some lovely Sargasso, the curlews calling, the cottage across the sunny water sending up a blue feather into the air. It was incredibly beautiful on such a day, dear and familiar, and I could see Haggie Chadderton standing on the lawn in front of the cottage where Maggie and I had been so happy and sometimes Lord Burnage had come to see us, sitting in the donkey carriage, with Eddy Rodda leading the Sudden Sneezer. And there was, amid all this loveliness, black misery in my heart, because I knew why Whaley had brought me here: she had to tell me that she was about to die.

"Would you mind very much," she asked, "if I don't come back with you when you return to London?"

"Yes, I *shall* mind. The years have given me a positive crust of selfishness. Without any shame I *use* all my friends and you are the one I like to have handy above all others for running to when things take a bad turn."

She laid her fat yellowish hand on mine, and I went on: "We all do it, don't we? Sally ran to you before her pilgrimage to Andorra, and Nika has always rested on you. But if you want to stay here, my darling Whaley, I must try to get on without you. Do you want to tell me what it's all about?"

"I don't want to, but I suppose I'd better; and anyway there's not much to tell. I haven't been well, you know, for some time. My friend Harry Bates, the Harley Street man, has been doing what he could, and just before I came down here he had some X-ray photographs taken. He said that when they'd been examined he would communicate the results to the doctor in Porteven. That's odd, too. They were students together at Guy's. One ends up with a knighthood and a Harley Street practice, and the other in a village at the end of the earth. They've remained close friends through it all. But that's by the way. The thing is that now I have the verdict."

I didn't ask her to tell me what the verdict was. There was no need to do that. I asked: "How long will it be?"

"Oh," she said, "I may see the summer through. Anyway, I hope to finish my book. Don't worry, and don't say anything to the others. I find this a quiet place for work. That's all they need know. It's just a fancy I have for writing my last book here where I wrote the first."

A rounded time-worn shoulder of granite thrust itself through the grass a little way off down the field: a bit of the body of the earth lying unchanged and uncommunicating beneath the changing vesture of tree and grass. A pair of chaffinches were flirting upon it, uttering their glad little cry, *spink, spink, spink,* the busy transient creatures, wearing out their brief living upon that fragment of the huge underlying inertia that had seen and would see so many of their kind come and go.

As if divining my meditation, Whaley said: "Look at Haggie Chadderton! What a beautiful picture it all makes over there!"

You couldn't see that it was Haggie. All you could see was, across the glister of the sunny water, the green level landing place, and a girl in blue standing upon it, and around her a joy of flowers: the golden

443

forsythia, and pyrus of red and pink and white, and rhododendrons so heavily flowered that they seemed solid bastions of rosy stone. Rising above it all was the young spring green of the trees leaning against a sky of milky blue.

"It goes on," Whaley said. "Once it was my turn over there. Now it's Haggie's."

"Oh," I cried rebelliously, "don't try to comfort me with softness and call it philosophy. You say it goes on. I say it ends. And anyway, what a false picture it is of life for the most part. By luck, Haggie is over there; but how few people today are stepping onto a stage set like that! Ask Haggie herself. Ask Sally or Warwick Russell. Even the brief life most people have is mean and sordid: in the forecastles of ships and in mines and mills and foundries and slums and squalor. And the odd thing is that they think the way out of it is more mines and mills, more iron wheels going round faster and faster."

"Yes," she said, "life is brief. That has been observed, you know, from time to time. For most people it is pretty hard, for many it is grim, and for all it soon ends. I don't need you to tell me that there are plenty of people whose surroundings are not so attractive as Haggie's. Credit me with a bit of sense. But what you're really worrying about is yourself, not Haggie. What have *you* done to deserve preferential treatment on earth? That's been grizzling you for some time, hasn't it?"

I nodded mutely, and she went on: "For goodness sake don't grizzle—about that or anything else. Make up your mind. If you think your way of life is wrong, then go and do what Sally is doing. If you don't, then live as happily and beneficently as you can and as you are."

"That's only half the case. I may be troubled about my way of life and wish to alter it and yet not have the courage to do it. What then?"

"Well, I suppose you could either drive through the slums now and then in a carriage-and-pair, dishing out jelly and shirts and drawers, or you could accept the fact that you're like most other people: an imperfect creature, troubled by visions, but incapable of wrestling with the angel. I prefer the latter sort, so long as they're honest and understand their own limitations. And whatever you do, be happy. A poor man miserable through envy and a rich man miserable through fear are alike curses on the earth. Whatever way of life you choose, live it happily. Only courage will allow you to do that, and courage is the thing."

She got up and stood with one hand resting on the beech trunk as she looked over the shining water. "I'm a bright one to talk," she said. "I've had an easy life because I was born with a gift that could

444

be turned into a lot of money. We hear people say that So-and-so is gifted. Well, don't let us forget what a gift is. It's just something handed to us from outside. I had no more to do with the coming of my profitable gift than you had to do with the coming of your money. I hope I haven't used it too badly. One thing I can't stand is pretentiousness in gifted people. They should be the most humble and grateful people in the world."

I got up too, and we watched Haggie go into the cottage, and then slowly walked along the path through the wood.

"Forgive my going on about this," Maggie said, "but I'm sorry to find you worrying about your money. We all attach too much importance to money. If all the money in the world were leveled out tomorrow, I don't think it would make much difference. Cain and Abel were brothers, economically on a level, I suppose, but that didn't prevent Cain from murdering Abel, nor are hatred and bitterness any less in families where all are rich or all are poor. So long as *things* don't matter overmuch, you needn't worry about them. I'm sorry. I get tired so soon now. Let us sit down again."

We sat with an azure sea of bluebells at our backs and splinters of light pricking the lake water through the trees before us.

"Let me tell you of something that happened years and years ago," Whaley said. "It was when I was just getting on my feet as a writer. I had a few hundred pounds in the bank. One day I received a letter telling me that my father's brother, who was a cashier, had been arrested on a charge of embezzlement. Could I find the money to provide counsel for his defense? I'd never met him. I never did meet him. It wasn't an easy decision. I didn't know whether I could go on writing or, if I could, whether my books would sell. There was a chance that I was sinking all the money I would ever have. I took the chance. He was acquitted, and I know that he afterward became wealthy in Australia, but he never sent me back a penny and I never asked him to. Well, one lesson to be drawn from that was: never lend. But I drew another lesson: Give and be damned. Don't let money *worry* you one way or another. Thinking about it is one thing, worrying another."

We rested a lot that morning, but we came out at last to the lodge that had been Eddy Rodda's and to the yellow sweep of the bar and the wide shining of the sea. Maggie sat down on a bank of thyme and sea pinks, panting a little. "You're rebellious about a lot of things this morning, aren't you?" she said. "You think it hard that life should end. Well, all your thinking won't alter *that*. What a one my old friend Charles Dickens was for deathbeds! And, bless me, it'll be thirty-six years next month since he was on his own. I always have a day of remembrance for him on the ninth of June. But there isn't much to be said about it all, really. Even St. Paul was pretty

445

noncommittal. 'It doth not yet appear what we shall be.' It doth not yet appear. . . . No, indeed. Well, I'm prepared to wait and see. Let's leave it at that. And now I've nothing more to say about your problems or mine. There isn't much to be said worth listening to, anyway, so let's be quiet and look at the view."

So we were quiet and looked at the view—at the sea and the majestic sweep of sand whereon I had seen many things happen: where I had seen the horses pounding and the dead men from the wreck lying in the red flare of the burning driftwood and where, in a dream, I had seen Justin, a child, walk into the water, and where, now, under this May sun, I saw Nika and Edward, far-off moving spots, approaching the cliff to which the level sand rose up on the east. They climbed, he giving her a hand, and for a moment they stood side by side, looking out to sea. Then they turned and walked away, disappearing in the sunny haze of the morning.

CHAPTER TWENTY-SIX

I

EDWARD came down from Oxford in the autumn of 1909, and he and Nika were married in May of 1910. In October of 1911 my first grandchild, Nicolas Mostyn-Lloyd, was born at the house in St. John's Wood that Maggie Whale had bequeathed, together with her country cottage, to Nika. Vera, my second grandchild, was born in March, 1913. This second child came sooner than was expected. If I had known that it was to be born that night I certainly should not have gone out, as I did, to the dinner of the Anglo-German Society. This society was something Daniel had been persuaded to join. He had tired of his aimless existence. He knew that there was nothing more for him in politics, and he was not disposed to go back to the hard work of the bar: it was not fiancially necessary and he was feeling his years. With the diminution of such real importance, or at any rate public-eyeness, as he once had had, he became restlessly pompous, hating to be obscure, and so he tended to associate himself as president or vice-president or committee member, or even as a simple member, with all sorts of societies and councils and organizations of one kind and another that provided an opportunity for appearing and talking in public. At sixty-five, he was very stout and florid and short of breath. He was as proud as a woman of his hair, which was plentiful and shiningly white. It would have paid any cabinet, I thought, to keep him for his looks.

His endless public talking tired him as once it used not to do, and I wished he would tranquillize himself and cut down, or cut out altogether, these activities that were at once so fatiguing and so meaningless. I even sighed for the inane placidity of his days of Greek translation. As it was, his study was a litter of bluebooks, pamphlets and brochures, and I think he saw himself as a kingpin in a complicated and essential structure that would, without him, disintegrate with disastrous consequences far-reaching. He had constituted himself Minister of Omnibus Affairs, without portfolio. And it was a sad thing for me to understand this. It is always a sad thing to understand those who once were obscured by the mystery and intangibility of the thoughtlessly loved. But, so far as Daniel was concerned, it gave me a tenderness and solicitude that made almost a little Indian summer for us, the sun, that had once been heartening and life-giving, now lighting wistfully sere leaves that had ceased to grow and soon must fall.

For this reason, we were about together now more than we had ever been. This life he was leading involved a lot of dining out; and he liked me to go with him, and I felt I owed him my support. It was all very well for my dear dead Whaley to have urged me not to worry, but I did worry, and I worried now as I wondered whether I had been all to Daniel that I might have been, whether his turning to that beautiful girl so long ago was something that need have surprised and outraged me. I often thought of the one brief moment when her life touched mine, and a shame would fill me at remembrance of my hard self-righteous turning from her. Down the long retrospect of the years I could recall nothing but a sweet voice and a lovely face and a gracious manner; and I would be hurt by the knowledge of my own deficiencies. God knows, I had never been lovely, but there was so much that I could have been and had not been.

All this is not to say that dead love revived. It has been my experience that even friendship, once severed, cannot be mended; and certainly dead love never lives again. But I found a humility toward Daniel, based on an understanding of the failure on all levels that his life had been, and a readiness to help his rather fussy efforts to put a surface of seeming success on what was left to him. This was not pity from some height of arrogance. It was an understanding that we were on a rather forlorn voyage in the same boat.

So there we were, on that March night in 1913 at this dinner of the Anglo-German Society. The Germans were a bogey. Novelists were giving us disturbing tales of sudden descent upon our unsuspecting shores. Politicians were chanting: "We want eight and we won't wait," the eight being ships of war; and in my own mind that night, as we stood amid the laughing, chattering crowd under the chandeliers in the anteroom of the dining chamber, I recalled how, on Mafeking day, I had been unhappy and had visited the House to find Daniel, and he had spoken darkly of the danger from over the water. When I look back now, through the dense, discouraging tangle of all that has happened since, it is this day in March, 1913, not the day in August of the next year, that stands like a chasm between two worlds. All the details of it are clear in my mind, as if, unknowingly, I had absorbed its significance. We motored to the hotel. Daniel and I had never bothered to own a carriage, but now Mervyn had persuaded Daniel to buy a motorcar. It meant having a chauffeur, and buying an old stable near the house which was turned into a garage and the loft over it into a chauffeur's flat. So Daniel was able to go briskly about from one of his engagements to the next, and this way of doing it gave to his movements, merely because of their speed, a sense of importance and urgency that they did not in fact possess, just as today, because they fly to them in a hurry, statesmen see their doings through a mechanized glamour which is a bitter enemy of the reflective and spiritual mood in which great affairs should be approached. Daniel at this late stage of his career began to talk of keeping abreast of the times, and for him, as for so many other people, this did not mean, so far as I could see, anything more than being in an unfruitful hurry.

I remember, then, the dark green uniformed back of Henry Shape the chauffeur, and the bitter cold, and the snow falling, and the lights of the West End, and the blast of warmth that struck us inside the hotel. It was one of those occasions on which, as the invitation card said, "orders and decorations will be worn," and we were soon among the orders and decorations, the sashes across white shirt fronts, the long tails, the whispering skirts, the jeweled bosoms of many lovely women. It was a de luxe assembly. A world which, for a hundred years, had been piling its wealth higher and higher, concentrated it, in such moments as these, in a little space for all to behold. This, I thought, smiling and bowing as one after another came up and was presented to me by Daniel, is the Crystal Palace as it has, in fact, come into being. I had put on the odd silver bracelet with the silver bells that Nika gave me on a far-off birthday, and as I moved my hand to shake this hand and that I could hear the little Sarah Rainborough and recreate her childish belief that she was standing on the threshold of joy and equity. This, I thought, is what it has *really* come to, that moment of the glorification of industry and trade. It has come to this ability to sweep enormous treasure into a few moments for a few people; and I had, as I say, a feeling that even 1914 did not deepen that this summit on which we stood was as precarious as a rocking stone poised on the edge of an abyss.

The chandeliers coruscated above our heads, and the hotel footmen in white silk stockings and gaudy uniforms and powdered hair moved with impassive faces among us, offering drinks on ornate trays. I was in a mood in which things took on the proportions of fantasy, and these men looked like creatures of another world, so unresponsive were they to all that was going on about them, so mute and alien. I tried the effect of a smile upon one of them, and he met it with a blank unchanging demeanor that I found disconcerting, even frightening.

Then a gavel sounded on wood, and a hush fell, and through it a powerful voice called upon my lords, my ladies, my lord bishops, ladies and gentlemen to take their places.

They were incredible, those banquets of the vanished world. I see before my mind's eye the menu printed in embossed gold on parchment, with a majestic succession of dishes, each accompanied by a separate appropriate wine. I see the break in the middle for the absorption of a sorbet and a slender pasteboard-tubed Russian cigarette, so that the appetite might be at once rested and whipped to fresh endeavors. It went relentlessly on to the lavish placing before each gentleman not of an offered cigar box but of a bundle containing a dozen Corona cigars, tied felicitously with red, white and blue and with the colors of Germany. A military attaché from the German Embassy, wearing a superb uniform, was sitting on my right and Daniel on my left at the head table. The attaché pulled open the two little bows of ribbon, deftly plaited them together, and handed them to me. "Symbolic, I hope, Mrs. Undridge," he said. "We are all anxious to hear your distinguished husband. He is unwearied in the cause of understanding between our two nations."

I sat there twining the two pieces of colored silk round my fingers, and in the humming dynamo of conversation the fairy tinkle of the bells on my bracelet could not be heard. I glanced up and down the tables, where the waiters were pouring brandy into balloon glasses, and it looked as though the gardens and orchards of the world had been ransacked for the blooms that flourished and the pyramids of rare and costly fruit. Waiters with cigar piercers were solicitously leaning over shoulders, and the gavel sounded again, and Daniel, who was president of the society, proposed the loyal toasts of the two countries.

Then it went on and on. Speeches and toasts and the singing of *Lieder* that brought tears to German eyes, and I shall not say anything about all that except to recall one phrase of Daniel's speech proposing the toast "Germany." There had been an article in a popular news-paper, urging men to enlist in the still-new Territorial Army, and headed "The Germans Are Coming." Daniel referred to this, and you could feel the uneasiness moving through the room like a fog coming through Chelsea on a still winter night; and then, after one of his impressive pauses, Daniel said: "They are not coming. They are here. Look at them. What do you think of them?" And at that the fog blew away, and my lords and my lord bishops and all the ladies and gentlemen cheered so wildly that they could not remain seated to do it. They stood up and clapped and waved menu cards and the little pieces of colored ribbon, and the Germans, who were half of the assembly, remained seated and the eyes of many of them, I saw, were wet with tears.

I had been thinking about Nika. Even that occasion could not keep my mind off her for long, and I dodged a bishop's speech in order to go out and telephone for news. Edward answered the call, and was cock-a-hoop. "Oh, you're late, late, all behind the fair, dear madam. You have a granddaughter."

We talked for a while, and he said that Nika was remarkably well. "Of course, it wasn't expected today at all. Otherwise I should have stayed at home this afternoon. As it was, I was otherwise engaged. You won't guess what I've been up to."

"Something foolish, no doubt," I chaffed him.

"Well, that's a matter of how you see it. I've joined the Territorial Army. What d'you think of that?"

I had twined the two little bits of ribbon in and out of Nika's bracelet. Somehow they looked terrifying. I couldn't answer him, and he said: "Hallo! Are you there? Are you there, Mama?"

And still I couldn't answer him. I dropped the receiver, and stole back to the banqueting room, pausing in the doorway so as not to intrude till the bishop had finished. I was just in time for his closing words. "After all, we and you have one great salutary bond: we are Christian nations. In that fact is the surety that we shall see what in our hearts we all desire: peace on earth, good will to men."

2

In March of 1914 I saw Edward's car draw up outside the house and Edward and Nika climb out. It was a clumsy-looking car compared with the things that glide about the world today, but still, cars were now becoming manageable and reliable. Edward drove his own.

I turned to Julian, who had called to take lunch with me and had lingered late, and said: "It's Nika and Edward."

"I'd better be off then."

He and Nika were still uneasy and constrained in one another's company; but I persuaded him to stay.

"Very well, my dear Aunt," he said. "I must try and get over my nonsense. And so must Nika. Anyway, after what we've been discussing, there will perhaps not be many meetings for any of us."

"My dear Julian! What a thing to say!"

But I knew it had to be said, all the same. There was an announcement in the newspapers that morning that Mr. Asquith, while remaining Prime Minister, would become also Secretary for War. "What on earth is all this now, Daniel?" I asked at breakfast; and he read the paragraph and shook his head gravely. "Goodness knows," he said. "I shall be lunching at the Athenæum. Perhaps I'll pick up something there."

He hated being out of the swim, to have to pick things up, instead of being one of those entitled to know.

The news and his reaction to it left me unhappy, and I was glad when Julian rang up to ask whether he might come and take lunch with me. We talked of this and that till the coffee was served, and then he asked, lighting a cigarette: "What's all this about Asquith? What does Uncle Daniel make of it?"

"I don't know, my dear. He knows no more than you or I. But he doesn't like it."

"Who does? I thought we ought to discuss what happens to Rimmel's if the worst comes to the worst. After all, I'm not an Englishman. I'm a French subject, and in France we have national service. I should be called up."

"Oh, my dear," I cried, falsely diminishing my own heart's apprehensions, "just because there's been perhaps a row in the Cabinet and a shuffle of jobs . . . !"

"No, no. Let us be serious. I say again, I am a Frenchman. My father and mother were in France in 1870. Well, they are dead and out of this, but I inherit their memories."

"You take the news heavily."

"I don't want to be caught napping, that's all. I'm thinking of your side of it, too. You're pretty heavily involved in Rimmel's, and we ought to have a plan of action. Even if Cogan had stayed we couldn't have left him in charge. He'd become a pretty knowing old bird, but not so good as all that. Now that he's retired we must find someone to look after the place if I have to go. That's all it'll come to: just holding the place together till I come back."

"You talk as if you were gone already."

"Well, these scares, these warnings, come and go. But they show that the ground's shaky. If not this time, then some other time, there'll be a blow-up. Better be ready for it."

"I can't see you as a soldier, my dear."

He laughed, and nowadays he didn't often laugh. "Can't you, my

451

dear Aunt? Oddly enough, I can. One of the dashing type, unpredictable but ever ready."

I looked at him with speculation. The laugh had been rather bitter. His thin cheeks were afflicted by a tic.

"Do you ever hear anything of Marthe?"

"Only from your questions." And then: "Sorry, my dear. That was unpardonable. No. No, I hear nothing."

We discussed arrangements for Rimmel's. He knew a young man, he said, Robert Fournier, working with one of the best antique firms in Paris. "He really does know a lot and he has a flair. Also, he has only one leg, and so he'll never be called up. I know he'd come. He's anxious to spend a few years in London, and after that in New York. If we think of the future, that may be an attraction. It is one of my dreams to have a branch, or at any rate an agent, in New York. When I come back perhaps it would be possible to send Fournier out there. Still . . . the future. Better not think so far ahead. In many ways, my dear Aunt, I have learned not to count on tomorrow."

He was so young—well, he seemed young to me: he was thirty-six—and he had suffered so much. He was an odd combination of an artist's enthusiasm and a businessman's caution. "That mule, that bastard," he had called himself, "with beauty for a mother, and a father who was willing to put her on the streets."

"Julian, suppose the worst came to the worst, why should you fight? With your French and English, you would be useful in Intelligence. Don't countries have missions with one another's armies? You could be with the French mission at British Headquarters, or something like that."

"The French, my dear, have a brief decisive word of contempt. I shall not use it to you, but, so far as *embusqués* go, I am using it now in my heart. May I have some more brandy?"

I pushed the decanter to him, and he said: "In 1870 my great-grandmama, a lady who had reached many years, had a little house in the outskirts of Paris. The Prussians ordered her out and gave the place to a few of their officers. When that affair was over, she went back. I met her only once, but remember her clearly. She came to Bordeaux for a visit when I was a child. She was small and fragile, with rosy cheeks and she always wore a little lace cap. And so I can imagine this tiny lady going back to her house. I can imagine her finding the works of her clocks smashed with a poker. I can imagine her pictures torn to ribbons and the frames used for firewood, and the legs smashed off her tables and the sofas cut open with knives. Her books had been hurled pell mell and trampled with big boots. Her lovely china had been set up on the mantelpiece and shot at with revolvers, and her bed—her bed, *ma chère tante!*—had been used

452

as a w.c. No. I do not think I should be happy in Intelligence. Allow me to say that I am above all fastidious. There is a bad taste in my mouth that I may want to wash out."

He had risen to go, when I saw Edward and Nika coming to the front door. Marriage had suited Nika. Now, at twenty-eight, her beauty had found richness and fulfillment. She had been overslender, but she had put on substance; her breasts had ripened; she looked a young Demeter, crowned with corn gold over her broad white brow and violet eyes. Edward followed her, looking, as he always did, absurdly protective—"rather like a Scotland Yard man guarding the Crown jewels," said Julian on one of the few occasions when he had observed them together.

"It's too absurd," he said now, standing beside me at the window. "Nika should be accompanied wherever she goes at least by St. Michael or St. George. As it is, she has this nice old English sheep dog."

"Well," I said rather crossly and crudely, "at any rate he's given her a couple of whelps, and I'm not sorry if that keeps her mind off mythology."

Nika came in and kissed me and shook hands calmly enough with Julian. It was in this room that she had seen him so proudly producing Marthe on that disastrous night, but she looked now too well-ballasted for the memory of that sudden and unforeseen puff to agitate her. Julian had seemed then the conqueror with the world at his feet; but now he had learned, as he said, not to count on tomorrow. In looks, he had fined down and become rarefied as she had grown into an almost regal opulence.

It was just a casual call that they had made. The gravity of my conversation with Julian evaporated, and we merely chatted—about Nika's children, and friends, and this and that. Julian did not stay long. As he rose to go, Edward said: "If you can wait a moment, Nika and I are going into town. We could take you along."

"No, thank you. I shall walk for a bit and then take a bus. You should walk, too. You're getting too fat. You should keep fit. Remember you're a lieutenant of infantry."

"Only spare time." Edward grinned. "It's good fun."

Julian looked at him speculatively, and he seemed an old man looking at a boy. "Well," he said, "let's hope the fun lasts."

He said it gravely, and Nika cried: "What on earth do you mean, Julian? You don't take the Territorials seriously, do you?"

"No. No," he said hastily. "Take no notice of me. Well, *au revoir*."

"He gave me quite a turn," Nika exclaimed when he was gone. "He seemed so serious about something or other."

"Well," Edward said cheerfully, "there's a lot of war talk about, of course; but I think it's all bosh. I don't see that war is inevitable.

453

And even if it came, we wouldn't be there for a bit, would we? It stands to reason the French would be in it first." He laughed heartily. "Looking at it that way, it gives old Julian something to pull a long face about. He'd be in up to the neck before I was paddling."

"*Julian* would?"

"Of course. He's never been naturalized."

"I'd never thought of that. I seem to have known him always, and always I've thought of him as an Englishman. When that dreadful wife of his ran away, the first idea that came into my head was: 'That's what comes of marrying a foreigner.'"

I had not heard her speak of Marthe since the disaster. She added: "Well, he may be a Frenchman, but he's too old to be a soldier."

"Don't you believe it," Edward said. "Certainly he can give me a few years, but he's fighting fit." He looked ruefully down at his heavy body. "Don't you wish your poor old husband had a figure like a gazelle?"

"Thank you very much, but I'm quite satisfied with my husband," Nika said with some asperity.

3

Robert Fournier came to England on the first of June, a dark man of thirty, whose artificial leg you would hardly guess at, so cheerfully he got about with the help of a stick. His coming remains in my mind as the first of the swift series of events that overwhelmed us. On the day after he came, I went to Brook Street in order to make his acquaintance. Julian gave us tea in the sitting room behind the gallery, and, looking at this eager and enthusiastic young man, whom from the beginning I liked very much, I could not, nevertheless, see him without a feeling of something sinister that attached to his being there. For Julian had brought him solely because he thought dire possibilities lay ahead; and consequently that little meal in the charming room, with the silver teapot on the table, and the spirit lamp alight under the hot water, and these lovely chairs we sat on, and the walls displaying some of Rimmel's choicest pictures: all had for me a feeling of the macabre, of our assisting at some sort of unnerving last supper.

Julian made no pretense that it was a common social occasion. He was a man whose almost excessive sensitivity flourished over a bedrock of realism, which is what made him so successful an art dealer. And so he took it for granted that day that we all accepted the situation as it was and did not wish to gloss it. He was not lugubrious, so far as his own outlook was concerned. He never once said: "If I come back . . ." but always: "When I come back . . ." and the theme of his conversation was that then would be the time when Rimmel's, having spent these early years in getting roots into the ground, would shoot up and flourish.

He spoke with what, in the sad event, turned out to be extraordinary foresight. "This war that is coming sooner or later," he said, "will be the first war to be run on wheels, that is, the first war in which great fully industrialized nations will be engaged. After other wars, men went back and began again to dig their fields, which is the sensible thing to do; but industrialized nations will not do that. They will go back to mend their wheels. Their wheels will be strained and broken by the war, and though you can't eat wheels, and though mending them is more expensive than digging fields, nevertheless that is what they will do. That will need a lot of money, and a lot of money will mean a lot of taxation, and a lot of taxation will mean that a lot of people who have been rich will become poor. They will sell what they have in order to go on living at all. They will sell estates, and that doesn't concern me. They will also sell the art treasures their families have been accumulating for generations, and that concerns Rimmel's very closely."

Fournier said: "No doubt there will be much selling. Who is going to do the buying?"

"America," said Julian decisively. "Once the world begins to creep back into some sort of shape, we shall see a stream of Europe's treasures headed for America. It is possible that events will compel America to come into the war. But obviously she can never take the blows that Europe will take, and obviously, too, there will be a long time when she will have nothing to do but get rich on the tragic follies of us over here. When the war ends, there will be a lot of money in America, and there will be a lot of lovely stuff in Europe looking for a market. And so the firm of Rimmel will grow rich."

"It may be so," I said heavily. "But it seems a pity."

"Nonsense, my dear Aunt," Julian chided me. "A great artist produces for the world. Great art never stays still. It flows about. Look at the Louvre. Look at the National Gallery. And I know plenty of lovely stuff in this country that doesn't mean tuppence to the owners, who are the only people who ever see it. I could name you peers in plenty whose walls are covered with Rembrandts, Gainsboroughs and Constables, and who might as well have Marcus Stones for all they know or care about it."

"Well," said Fournier, "let's hope for peace and small profits."

"Yes," Julian agreed, "let's hope. There's no harm in that."

On the twenty-ninth of that June there was the garden party. Henry Shape motored us to the house where it was held—a beautiful house with cedars sweeping their dark wings across lawns running down to the Thames. The affair was in connection with another of Daniel's societies, and I can see him now in his tailed coat and sponge-bag check trousers, his gray topper and lavender tie, coming out of the house to join me where I sat already in the car in flowery chiffon. How gay we must have looked on that superb summer afternoon! And I wondered if his heart was as fearful as mine. For that was the day when news had come of the assassination of the heir to the Austrian throne. Daniel stood for a moment talking to Henry Shape about the route to be followed, and I heard their words and even spoke words myself; but in my head were the only words which I should hear that day to the full depth of my being: these words from the morning newspaper: "The crime may have a profound effect on the destinies of all Europe."

Tomorrow would be the last day of June, the turn of the year, and I was heavy with the knowledge that this was more than the turn of the year: it was the turn of everything I had ever known: the final unveiling of reality to the eyes of that child who, on a May morning sixty-three years ago, had listened with an eager heart to deceptive words and seen the phantom of peace dwelling in a house so frail that a handful of thrown pebbles could let in a draft. And now we were in for more than a handful of pebbles.

Daniel was wearing a pale flesh-pink carnation. With an oratorical gesture perfected on a thousand platforms, he drew the beribboned pince-nez from his pocket and began to read his notes. Even at a garden party, he would be expected to speak. Well, what is there to be said now? I wondered.

I left him to it and looked about me from the open car. Even then, at that moment so near to the utter change soon to be upon us, the immemorial English things lived on. We bowled smoothly over roads that were still dusty, between whitened hedges, past fields where the hay harvests were being turned by hand. The elms dreamed over slumbrous villages and cooled the doors of old inns. On the greens cricketers were at play, and in gardens one glimpsed the flash of young men and women in white on tennis lawns. Fishermen drowsed on little stools by canals along whose banks horses plodded ahead of barges gay with paint and twinkling with brass.

We turned in between a pair of gate posts bearing heraldic beasts rampant on their tops, drove for half a mile with rhododendrons flowering on either hand, and swept round to the graveled front of the house that stood on an eminence looking down over lawns to the gleam of the Thames. I had been there before and knew that it was normally a scene of serenity, with the beeches rising behind the house and the grass stretching before in unbroken green to the embanked edge of the water upon which the slow drift of a punt or a swan did no more than emphasize the sense of arrest and cessation, of an achievement beyond which there was nothing. But now a band was braying through the hot air, and here and there striped awnings protected tea tables from the sun, and there were shouts of people running cock shies and shooting galleries and hoopla stalls and all the rest of it, and gray toppers and swishing silk and chiffon and flowerlike parasols filled the lawns between the house and the river.

I spoke to our host and hostess, and then left them and Daniel discussing the arrangements for the talking that these gay ones on the lawn would soon have to endure, and passed the red perspiring necks of the uniformed band passionately devoted to Sullivan's popular airs, and engaged myself in the moving shimmer of summer frocks. And I asked myself: "What is coming over you? Who are you to think you can see farther and deeper than anyone else?" For here was, or seemed, no apprehension, no ear that heard the sound of tramping feet, no nerve that felt a cold wind stirring through the down-pouring heat of this summer day. The well-bred voices were concerned with invitations to take an ice or a cup of tea, or with the hard luck it was that Tony had broken his leg when that horse threw him, or with the wonderful show of sweet peas that Millicent's new gardener had raised for the flower show last week. Such colors! They really had to be seen to be believed.

Well, so have you, so have you, I comprehensively thought, as, having done my duty to Daniel by talking to a few of them, I wandered farther and farther down the lawns, escaping toward the river. And there, sitting on the embankment near a boathouse, was a young man in an officer's khaki, the Sam Browne belt shining, the tunic looking dreadfully hot, and he, in abstraction, throwing twigs and pebbles into the water. He sensed my approach, and as he turned his head I saw that it was Edward. He leapt up with a grin of pleasure on his dark young face and gave me a rather perfunctory kiss.

"You seemed deep in thought, Edward, my dear."

The smile faded, and I felt that at last, after all that surface shimmer either of imbecile ignorance or stupid pretense, I was facing reality. I sat myself down on the grass, and he sat there beside me, and we watched the shallow water glinting by and the white-blazed coots thrusting themselves through the nenuphars.

"Yes," said Edward. "I was thinking about Nika, to tell you the truth."

"How come you to be here at all? And in that rig?"

"Didn't you know? We're in camp about a mile away. I knew that you and Nika's father were expected, so I persuaded the colonel to give me a few hours' leave. You were rather late, and I got sick of wandering round among the fluff up there, so here I am—throwing stones into the river and thinking of Nika. Plenty to think about, isn't there?"

"Yes. I'm afraid there is."

"The colonel's no fool—one of the best. He knows what this news means. Of course, he's said nothing to the men, but he called a conference of officers and put it all pretty straight to us. I like a chap who seems to know what he's talking about and tells you the truth."

There didn't seem much to say, and we didn't say much, until presently he asked: "Are we being dreadfully impolite? I hear a bell tolling, and I suppose that means the talking's going to start. Oughtn't we to drift up?"

There was a punt tied up to this landing stage, and I said: "You had plenty of practice on the Cherwell. Let's get aboard."

The smile came back to his face. "Grand idea!" he said. "I expect you've had enough talking in your time."

I stepped into the punt. "I must confess that I'm a bit blasé about it and rather distrust it."

Edward untied the punt, took off his tunic and tie, and got in. "If the colonel sees me it'll be too bad. But we'll punt away from the direction of the camp."

He rolled up his sleeves, lifted the pole, and we were off. The heat and burden of the day had tired me. I took off my hat and lay full length in the forward part of the punt, my head on a pile of cushions, a parasol shading my face. Motor launches with gramophones had not yet come to trouble the stripling river, and the afternoon was blessedly quiet. Even the birds, in this great heat, had ceased to sing. Sullivan had given place to the National Anthem, but it came faintly and I hoped that when it was done the hot bandsmen would find some beer. I could imagine Daniel, gray topper in hand, standing reverently on the sun-baked terrace, giving the King his due, but glad that his own turn was coming. Under my head the sound of the water was sweet and lulling. I could see Edward's khaki slacks and chestnut-gleaming shoes, and, shifting the angle of my parasol, I looked up at his grave young face.

"It is sweet of you to take this trouble to give pleasure to an old woman, Edward."

458

"It's a pleasure to me, and you're not so old as all that. I always think of you as what is charmingly called a well-preserved woman."

"I don't think it charming. It sounds like a mermaid in alcohol. And anyway I'm sixty-six."

He didn't answer, but poled slowly on over the sunny water, and keeping pace with us, along the opposite bank, was a swan who had arched her wings till they made a snowy tent that she was carrying on her back and from which a cygnet peeped out like some passenger from a gondola. It was an absurd, endearing sight.

We met nothing whatever on the water, but proceeded through utter peace that smelled of mint and of sun-warmed hay, for the grass was down in many meadows.

"D'you know, I've never taken Nika out in a punt on the river. I must do that. There are so many things that Nika and I have never done, and that we must do. Of course, we've been in the punt on the lake at Tresant. But this is another thing. This going on and on . . . And that reminds me. How much farther do we go? I don't want you absent too long without leave."

I sat up and looked about me. We were coming to a rough landing stage behind which was a garden set with a few tables. "Let's stop here, Edward. This looks a pleasant destination. Your labor has earned refreshment."

"You are in a truant mood," he chaffed me. "The talking must have been over long ago."

"My husband can hardly go home without me," I assured him. "It will be a good thing for him to rest in the shade."

A girl came out of the cottage, carrying a red and white checked tablecloth. She threw it over the table and took our order, and we sat there among the hollyhocks and sweet peas and the straw beehives, within a corridor of shade drawn by a hazel hedge, and we watched the swifts, indefatigably energetic despite the heat, hurtling across the sky.

"We have been taught in any new bit of landscape to observe things that might be important," Edward said, lighting a cigarette, "and I observe that, against all probability, this cottage is on the telephone. I think it would be a good idea, while we are waiting for tea, if I rang up old Fortescue and asked him to let your husband know where you are and that you'll be delivered in good order fairly soon. This has been a charming adventure for you and me, but I'm afraid people may be getting anxious about you."

He went into the cottage, and I was so tired that, as soon as I was alone, I drowsed and nodded a little, and then there he was before me again, and seeing the shocked look on his face I was instantly wide awake and on my feet. "Edward! Whatever is the matter?"

459

"Will you come to the telephone? Colonel Fortescue is anxious to speak to you."

He took my arm and led me into the house, and then Colonel Fortescue was saying: "Oh, Mrs. Undridge! We've been searching for you high and low. Can we send a car anywhere for you? Mr. Undridge is unwell. Seriously unwell."

"Why! Whatever is the matter? He was perfectly fit . . ."

"You must come at once. He collapsed while speaking. The heat . . ."

I handed the receiver to Edward. "Tell him, my dear. Give him directions."

I went out, dazed, to gather my possessions from the garden seat, and then we waited, and from Edward's air I knew that he had been told more than I, and, sitting with his arm through mine behind Henry Shape's broad back, I knew well enough what it was that neither he nor Colonel Fortescue would tell me. We sped down the drive, passing a horse brake carrying away the bandsmen and their instruments, and it was a doctor who led me into a room where Daniel's body lay on a sofa. The blinds had been pulled down, and for a few moments they left me there alone with him and with the pink carnation and the pince-nez that dropped down the side of the sofa and were still fastened to his neck with ribbon. I hoped it had been swift and sudden, instantaneous, that he had not at the last moment known me a truant.

5

Henry Shape drove me and Edward to the place where Edward's Territorial battalion was in camp, and Edward asked his colonel's permission to see me back to town. It was refused; and as I went back alone I found an odd comfort in the thought that Edward was serving with a man who saw what were the first things and put them first.

Back in Chelsea, I had to ring up a number of people: Nika and Mervyn, and finally Julian Rimmel. Fournier answered the telephone. He said that Julian was not there. He had left for France. "Mr. Rimmel takes things seriously—perhaps too seriously, don't you think, Mrs. Undridge?"

I said No, I didn't think so, and put down the receiver and turned into the hot quiet house. Daniel and I and Richard and Nika had all been here together. Now I alone was here. Nika had said that she would come over at once to be with me, but that would be for a night or two only, and there would be a lot of nights and a lot of days. Somehow I knew that. I would go on living for a long time, but increasingly the time would be lonely. Already enough of my comrades had fallen out on the march to show me this.

There was not much about Daniel's death in the papers the next day. Other matters occupied the pages, though even yet these matters did not seem seriously to occupy the public mind.

Colonel Fortescue called to see me that morning. He must have got up very early, for Nika and I were still dallying over a late breakfast when he arrived, a tall rigid old man with a white mustache and pale blue eyes that had looked, fifty-seven years ago, on the massacre at Cawnpore and on many odd sights since that. He had come to ask me to allow him the honor, as he put it, of taking all the cares of this moment off my shoulders. Unless I wanted it so, there was no reason, he said, why Daniel's body should be brought back to town. The burial could take place in the country churchyard near his house, and everything could be left in his hands. And so it was arranged, and a few days later, in the continuing splendor of that summer, I stood in the graveyard of a country church on a small rise of land which permitted me to look down into the tea garden, upon the very seat, where Edward and I had been sitting while Daniel was being carried for the last time into a house. Edward in uniform stood on one side of me and Mervyn, in all the trappings of silk hat and the rest of it, on the other. And how little, I thought, this moment means outside the minds of one or two of the many standing here. I saw a punt arrive at the landing stage and a youth and his girl get out and walk into the garden, and the check tablecloth flicked over the table. The youth lit a cigarette, and I thought: "Good luck to you, whoever you are. Have a good time with your girl while you may." The swans were drifting with a little wind in their uplifted sails, and the swifts shrilled; and then the parson's voice was raised, and the youth in the garden suddenly understood its import, taking off his hat and crushing out his cigarette, carefully preserving it behind his ear. Don't bother, I thought, don't bother about us. You're not going to be allowed much time with your girl.

The Anglo-German Society had sent a few representatives, and I found myself looking across the grave at the military attaché who had sat at my side at the banquet. When it was all over, he came up to me, clicked his heels, took my hand and bowed over it very low, so that I saw the sun glinting on the hairs of his cropped fat neck.

"This is my son-in-law, Edward Mostyn-Lloyd," I said. "I think you should know one another."

The two uniformed young men did not shake hands or speak. They looked at one another briefly, appraisingly, then turned away, and I felt that I had seen the first encounter of the war that I knew would come, for when in all my now long years had I known anything but war, or the fear of it, or the making ready for it?

Old Fortescue, with those odd drained blue eyes, came to my side

461

and took my arm. He led me to his sumptuous car and we were driven back to his house for some refreshment. Then Edward went off to his camp and Mervyn motored me to town.

6

This, Mervyn's house in Hanover Square, was now to be my home. Old Gotherson had been dead for some years, and I was pleased when Mervyn suggested that if I cared to use his flat at the top of the house I could have it. I had said to him that the big house in Chelsea was wasteful and unnecessary, and so here I was. It had not been difficult for Mervyn, with all the resources of Mostyn-Lloyd's, to get the place ready in the few days since Daniel's death. The rooms had been cleaned and distempered, the woodwork repainted, the floors recarpeted, and new curtains hung at the windows. The house was electrically lit, which was a comfort I had not known in Chelsea, and even the lift to the flat had been electrified. Mervyn had put a minimum of temporary furniture into the rooms. In time, I would bring from Chelsea such few things of my own as I wanted to have about me.

When it came to the point, I was surprised to find how few they were. There was G. F. Watt's portrait of my mother, and Millais's portrait of Lucy Evans that Lucy had bequeathed to Maggie Whale and she to me. There was a portrait of Maggie herself—an early work by Augustus John; and, of all the odd things, there was the picture that old Undridge had painted of his son Daniel gazing into the pond in the Montreuil garden: the picture that had made the child wrathful but was highly esteemed by the man the child became. How Daniel got hold of it I don't know, but there it was, as deeply dripping with sentimentality as Daniel was dripping with water that day when Maggie tipped him into the pond; but it called many things back to my mind, and so I liked to have it there. I brought also my favorite easy chair and the desk I had used ever since I became, in my childish way, Maggie's secretary in the cottage at Tresant. This occupation amused Lord Burnage immensely. It was he who had the desk sent to the cottage from the house. It was a beautiful piece of work by Sheraton himself, as a receipt testified, and Julian often looked at it covetously. These few reminiscent things were all I needed to make me feel at home.

The summer faded into autumn, and the autumn prolonged itself with the fabulous beauty that all can remember whose memories go back to 1914: prolonged itself as though aware that once it was dead there was so much that could never be resurrected; and the winter came, with many fools saying: "It will be over by Christmas."

I did not see much of Edward's two sisters, Kathy and Sophia Mostyn-Lloyd. Mervyn had a country house called Coppocks on the fringes of Epping Forest, and as soon as the war began he sent the girls there. His mind was full of the possibilities of air warfare. All his opinions were accurate but premature. He was certain that London would endure concentrated bombing, as, indeed, it did, but not then. And so Kathy and Sophia were not much in Hanover Square.

They were a pair of tall striking girls in their middle twenties. All their appearance came from Mervyn's mother, Lucy Evans. They looked like twins, though Kathy was a little more than a year older than her sister. They had golden skins and long legs and blue eyes. They had done all the correct things. They had been presented at Court; they bought their clothes in Paris; they holidayed on the Riviera; pictures of them sprawling brown-legged on the sands there appeared in the *Tatler* and such papers. THE BEAUTIFUL MISSES MOSTYN-LLOYD. Back in town, they went to all the right dances and restaurants, first nights and other gala occasions. I often used to wonder with amusement what Captain Eddy Rodda would make of his granddaughters, and what their beaux would make of Captain Eddy Rodda. But by the winter of 1915 their beaux were otherwise engaged.

Although their father had grown up with me and my daughter was their sister-in-law, these girls were almost strangers to me. Whenever I had called at Hanover Square in the past, they were at Ascot or Cowes, or gone to France, or gone to Scotland for the shooting or to some great house for a Christmas house party. The fact that their mother had some relationship with the peerage gave them a social *cachet*, and their father's immense wealth made them desirable as wives. The beautiful Misses Mostyn-Lloyd were not likely to find themselves, as their mother Enid Gotherson had once been, stumped for small change.

I remembered the pair of them radiant at their brother's marriage to Nika, and transient as radiant, for from the very reception they disappeared, off to some affair in a distant shire; and it was after their return from that visit that I began to hear of Chester Wills. I even met him, and it was rare for me to meet any of the young men that Kathy and Sophia knew. Daniel and I were at a party that Mervyn gave for him, and I thought that if Kathy's evident infatuation with him came to a happy end she would be a lucky girl. He was a Virginian whose family had lived since the eighteenth century in one of those lovely houses that saw Georgian architecture at perfection on the other side of the Atlantic. If I use a word that is disliked now and say that he was an aristocrat, I have said all that I want to say about him.

In the summer after that, Mervyn and Enid and the two girls went to America and stayed with the Wills family. The old man was a Senator, the mother a Northerner who had enriched the family. I expected on their return to be told that Kathy was engaged to Chester Wills; but I was told nothing except that the visit had been most pleasant. Something evidently had gone wrong, and the beautiful Misses Mostyn-Lloyd continued their pictured career in Europe.

Of the two, I preferred Sophia, the younger. I thought her better ballasted than her sister. I could talk to her without having the impression that I was boring her, which is the impression Kathy always gave me. It was in March of 1915, when I had been for some months installed over Mervyn's house, that she came up one night to see me. My privacy was respected. If I wished to take meals with the family I was at liberty to do so. Otherwise, a maid brought them up in the lift. There was a house telephone connected with my sitting room, and no one ever disturbed me without first ringing and asking permission to come up.

On that March night Sophia rang, the first time either of the girls had done so. When she came up I thought she looked tired. I led her to the sofa by the fire and said: "Sit down, my dear."

But she did not. She stood for a moment looking about my large sparsely furnished room. "How quiet and peaceful!" she said.

Indeed, not a sound reached us here. The curtains were drawn, the fire purred. I had been greatly enjoying my solitude. She sat down with a sigh as if of relief, and I took the chair on the other side of the fireplace where I could look at her. She lit a cigarette and lay back for a moment lazily watching the smoke. "I motored in from Coppocks with Kathy this afternoon," she said. "We were to dine with some people at a restaurant tonight, but I invented a headache. I haven't one really, but oh! I do sigh occasionally for five minutes to myself. Especially in Kathy's present mood. So I came along here in a taxi and found a house of the dead. Father and Mother have gone off somewhere together. I asked them downstairs to send some sandwiches up here. Do you mind?"

"Indeed I don't," I said, pleased to have her to myself for once. "What is the matter with Kathy's present mood?"

She waited till her supper appeared, and I noticed that she had ordered a bottle of Chablis. She stubbed out the cigarette and began to eat hungrily. I suspected the pair of them of half starving in order to keep their figures.

"There's still some silly intrigue or other between her and Chester Wills. He's coming to Europe soon, and she's all on edge about it."

"Well, I know nothing about that. I've hardly heard his name mentioned since you all got back from America."

"Oh, that was a dreadful fiasco!" she cried. "Kathy's incapable of moderation. She likes one silly intrigue after another."

Intrigue was evidently her word of the moment. I said nothing. She was so clearly anxious to talk.

It had been a wonderful adventure, riding and river picnics in the day, dancing at night, hospitality on a scale they had not expected. But behind it all, I gathered from Sophia's artless narrative, there had been a propriety, a decorum, that Kathy had been too dense to perceive. Into the society that she had frequented in Europe a good deal of riff-raff had penetrated. It was becoming rather soiled. But no riff-raff penetrated the Wills home, and the beautiful Miss Katharine Mostyn-Lloyd, accustomed to seeing walls go down before the flutter of her eye-lashes, used her eyelashes altogether too freely. Sophia herself was unable to feel the nuance of that social situation. She had understood only its outline. "On her very wedding day," she cried desperately, "I believe she'd try for an intrigue with the parson or the best man."

I gathered that the atmosphere remained formally impeccable, but it was as if a slight frost had touched the glory of an autumn day. Here and there a smile was missing, as if another leaf had fallen; and an indefinable feeling entered poor Sophia's heart that she and Kathy were considered "not quite."

"Oh, well," she exclaimed with a sort of angry puzzlement, "nothing came of it and we came home."

"What do you mean, my dear," I asked her, "when you say that there's still some sort of intrigue between Kathy and Mr. Wills?"

"Well, the silly thing is that they're mad about one another. If she hadn't gone out there, with a lot of relatives littering the ground . . ."

"Yes, I see that."

"Well, they've been writing to one another ever since. Not often, but a letter now and then. And now that he's coming to Europe she'll try and start up the whole intrigue again. Meanwhile she's impossible to live with."

"Perhaps," I said, "if Mr. Wills really wants her for a wife, this time he'll see that it's a matter for him, not for his family."

"I wonder. She's rushing about worse than ever. What with the war and this and that. I wonder what he'll make of her?"

We never knew what he would have made of her. Two months later he left America on the *Lusitania*. The *Daily Mirror* said: "The boat was full of wealthy and important people." That was after she had been tor-pedoed and sunk. Chester Wills was among the many who were drowned.

Nothing happened to justify Mervyn's fear of heavy bombing, and the girls came back to town from Coppocks. I took my meals downstairs more often in order to see something of them. They interested me. They were girls of a kind I had never known intimately. If my father and mother had remained together, I myself, I reflected, would no doubt have been edged into this sort of life. I had escaped it, and Sally had escaped it because Lord Burnage had been at odds with society and because he loved Tresant so much. As for Nika, Daniel and I had never even dreamed of having her "presented" and going through the customary rigmarole of parties and dances for her. Her picture had appeared in the *Tatler* only once, and that was over the inscription: "The lovely Mostyn-Lloyd girls at their brother's wedding."

I reached the opinion that Kathy, dazzled by the fatuous publicity her doings and her beauty attracted, considered her way of life to have importance and significance, but that Sophia was in doubt and perplexity, especially as the horror of the times we were living in revealed itself to her. The summer of 1915 dragged by, and no one talked now of a war that would end in a few months, and the newspapers had the habit of publishing daily lists of the dead. It will always remain in my heart as one of the most dreadful things of that war: the columns that had to be printed in small type so that all the names could be squeezed in. Bairnsfather invented Old Bill and Young Alf, and we discovered therefrom what an amusing thing the war was, full of humorous cracks and comic sallies, and it was a pity to learn from these printed lists that so many men had been stopped short in their enjoyment of the hilarious outing.

I do not know what would have happened to Kathy if the *Lusitania* had managed to make the last few miles into Queenstown. As it was, her whole being became enameled. The gaiety that had always surrounded her doing sharpened and hardened, became an impermeable casing through which, I felt, the real woman did not appear. What the real woman may have been I never discovered: she was from that time forever hidden behind a glitter of devil-may-care and what-does-it-matter. There was amusement in plenty for those who wanted it, and Kathy wanted it badly and had it. The young men began to come back, or some of them did; and the fact that some of them did not gave an urgency to the visits of those who did. There were lavish shows in the theaters, and there were dancing and dining, and there was the sensation of being out with the doomed. I had begun by now my own work in Waterloo Station, where we provided refreshments for the tired hordes pouring off the leave trains; and I remember how, when we were nearing midwinter of 1915, I got back, weary to death, late on a night of bitter cold, and sat for a moment on a chair in the hall. I was so exhausted that I felt indisposed even to walk the few yards to the lift. I just sat there, pulling my coat about me, and heard the clock strike midnight. I dozed, and presently was awakened by the sound of a taxi stopping outside and a key in the door. At the same moment there was a rustle on the stairs and I saw Sophia coming down, her fair hair falling in a cloud outside her dressing gown. Kathy came in, threw her coat onto a chair, switched on all the lights, and stood there with her glazed look and in the glazed shine of white satin.

"Why the reception committee?" she asked with an unsteady laugh.

I explained myself, and Sophia, going forward and putting an arm round Kathy, said: "I've been listening for you, darling. I couldn't go to sleep till you came."

"My God," said Kathy, "you won't get much sleep if you do things like that."

Sophia tried to draw her toward the stairs, but she resisted and said: "I want a drink."

"No, darling. You don't really. Come to bed," Sophia urged.

"I want a drink, and I'm going to have a drink."

She broke away from her sister's arms and went into the dining room. She came out holding a glass. "Well—happy days," she said and drank.

We were all standing, and for a time we were all silent. Kathy, sipping her drink, seemed to be in a profound abstraction. Presently she said: "I have now seen *Chu Chin Chow* with four dead men. I wonder whether that will be the fifth."

She suddenly put the glass down jarringly on a table and ran upstairs, snatching up her cloak which trailed behind her. Sophia, who, I could see, was not far from tears, went after her, overtaking her and putting an arm round her.

I stood there for a moment with my heart almost frozen by what Kathy had said; then I put out the lights and dragged myself wearily to the lift.

9

By the spring of 1916 Sophia was gone. She was nursing in a base hospital at Etaples. Kathy continued to go her way, haggard and strained in the morning light, recreated every evening. Nika worked with me at Waterloo Station, a grave, preoccupied Nika, who would never, I was sure, forget the night when we stood in a bitter wind whistling and driving straight into the station from the black void of the

467

night, shaping itself under the glassy arches into knives and spears that came mercilessly upon us. Nika looked up at the great spans of glass, opaque and mysterious, and suddenly said: "Have you still got that bracelet I gave you—the one with the little silver bells?"

"Yes, darling. Why do you ask that?"

She laughed. "What a thing to give you! I was a romantic child! I wanted it to remind you of the Crystal Palace. Well, when you come to look at it, this is a Crystal Palace, too. Look at the roofs. An appropriate one, I think, don't you?"

Well, yes, it was a Crystal Palace of a sort; but there were no fountains or elm trees, no flowers or choirs or bishops in gee-gaw clothes.

"I mean the name is appropriate," Nika said. "Waterloo. It used to be just the name of a station to me, and the other night it suddenly struck me that it must have been named after the battle. When I got home, I read all about it. I can remember bits of what I read. 'So desperate was the fighting that some 45,000 killed and wounded lay on an area of roughly three miles. The position that the British infantry held was plainly marked by the red line of dead and wounded.' And that says nothing about horses. I shudder to think of the horses, poor brutes. Altogether, this is something like a Crystal Palace. I think you should always wear your bracelet here and listen to the joy-bells tinkling."

"You'd better come in out of the cold," I said. "The train will be here any minute."

And what a sight they were when they came, the boys of that war! I often thought of the summer day when Daniel died and Edward stood in the punt and from under my parasol I had a sight of shoes polished like chestnuts and of khaki slacks, stainless and impeccably pressed. But, oh dear! no one looked like that now, except Kathy's young men when they had had time to wash off the graveyard mud and climb for a few moments back into the light of day. What a pell-mell horde it was that now came surging upon us like a brown muddied tide! The train had clanked to a standstill, and stood hissing vehemently and filling the place with billowing steam. It was like a vast dragon, and down its length the dimly lit windows shone like scales. The scales ripped off, and out they poured, the concourse that was always the same, though made up of fresh particulars: the caking mud and the ringing boots, the shouting and laughing ones in groups, with song and mouth organ, the silent ones who walked alone, each in his own shadow, and all monstrously burdened with packs and rifles, and gas masks and entrenching tools, clinging and clattering about them, some in long overcoats and some in short British warms, some in lousy-looking sheepskins, some in caps and some—Canadians and Australians these—in hats with cocky turned-up brims that sent my heart racing back to

468

"Chamberlain's Innocent Victims" and Richard and Trimmer. Their legs were swathed in puttees and their necks in mufflers; and if I could have got inside their hearts I should have found them to be rogues and villains, heroes and simple men, boys scared out of their wits and needing their mothers, and hardened toughs whose need, which they intended to assuage within the next half hour, was a woman of any sort.

But I did not get within their hearts, nor, then, was any of this in my mind. There was one thing to do, and that was stand by the bubbling urns and the baskets of buns and feed them, whoever or whatever they might be. And as I did so, with Nika and the rest of them helping me, I thought of Sally and of something she had once said to me. "Doing? I'm not *doing* anything, unless you call it doing to be putting myself where anyone who needs me can pick me up and use me, and then put me down again and walk on."

And the faces! They will haunt me as long as I live—the faces that appeared, and looked for a few seconds into our cubicle, and were then gone forever. Some were too old for that game and some too young. There were faces of startling innocence, and faces seamed and scarred with sin. Frightened and calm, cynical and dedicated, inquiring faces and leering faces, faces that, even here, were looking at death, and faces that were coolly appraising us as women. They moved by, night after night, an unending film, rushing, for the most part, out of the station as quickly as they could go, for already they were in Blighty, already the clock was ticking off the moments of this respite, and there was so much to do, so much to do. Never was so small a cup handed to men with so quenchless a thirst.

And that night a hand came to take a cup from Nika, who was so busy passing out the tea that she was not seeing faces, she was seeing nothing but hands; and when she saw that hand she did not put the cup into it. She put the cup down and trembled; and then she looked up, and Edward said: "I didn't tell you. I wanted to surprise you," and she said: "Surprise me! Oh, my God, you've nearly killed me."

She was holding her hand to her heart; and then she ran out of the cubicle.

He had not even spoken to me. His face disappeared, and the film continued to unroll. "Christ!" I heard someone say. "He was quick on the mark!"

10

"My dear Aunt," Julian wrote, "I have never in my life done any shooting for sport. My imagination is too lively. There is a pheasant, so beautiful a bird, sailing along the edge of a wood, over the red and yellow trees, under the pale blue sky of autumn. Some gentleman

469

in tweeds has nothing to do but point a metal tube at him, squeeze a trigger, and there he is, staggering like a drunkard of the air, the flesh of his body full of bits of lead. And I, who have been so considerate to the pheasants, am treated in this way! Most unfair! And it wasn't a shotgun, either, dear Aunt, and they were not pellets of lead. Fortunately for me, I got only the whiff on the outskirts of the explosion, but enough to plug me with bits of metal in arms, legs, body and head. I have not written before this because the doctors have been too busy mining in my anatomy. They have now exhausted the chief veins and have only a few odd pockets to clear up. I am near Paris for these final operations. It is much, much nicer than Verdun. Indeed, I shall not tell you how very little Verdun is nice. The Somme, I imagine, is no nicer. I think of Edward. If he gets leave, embrace him for me. My love to you and Nika. Shake Fournier by the hand. Tell him I have become a colander in defense of our country."

11

This was in the early autumn of 1916. Throughout the summer there had been a change in Kathy. It began when she received a letter from Nigel Lancaster who was in a convalescent hospital at Hampstead. I had not heard of him, and when Kathy read his letter at the breakfast table, Mervyn and Enid, too, did not recall him. The letter asked Kathy to visit him at the hospital.

"Who is he, darling?" Enid asked.

Kathy looked, as was usual in the morning, very tired. "Oh, I must have met him somewhere," she said vaguely. "I suppose I shall recall him when I see him. If I see him."

Mervyn was reading the *Daily Mail*, and he said: "Well, good lord! That's a coincidence! This must be the chap!"

There was a photograph, which didn't mean much, and a paragraph headed: "Boy V.C." It told how Nigel Lancaster had passed straight from the O.T.C. of his public school into the army as a second lieutenant, had been drafted immediately to France, and how, on his first night in the trenches, the enemy had attacked. The attack had been bloody, and this child of eighteen had been the only officer left alive in a long stretch of the trench system. He had pulled his men together, driven out the enemy, pursued them to their trenches, and with his own hands taken a machine gun that was playing havoc. He had then split his men into two parties, and these, advancing along the enemy trench in opposite directions, had bombed out the Germans and were holding a hundred yards of their line when reinforcements arrived, and Nigel Lancaster, shot through the leg, was carried on a stretcher back to his own trench. "Sir Nigel," the account ended, "is the tenth baronet. He succeeded his father when ten years old."

After breakfast, Kathy rang up the hospital and was able to speak to Nigel Lancaster. She asked him where they had met and was answered by a burst of laughter. "Good lord," he said, "we haven't met. I write to all the pretty girls I see in the *Tatler*. I found your address in the telephone book. D'you mind?"

It was a new approach to Kathy. She was intrigued. No, she said, she didn't mind. When might she call?

That was how it began on an April day in 1916. During the next month Kathy saw Nigel every day, and she went out in the evenings but little. She was nearly ten years older than the boy. At the end of the month, the damaging wound in his leg was sufficiently improved to allow him to leave the hospital occasionally. Kathy brought him to lunch at Hanover Square. She had motored out to Hampstead, and I chanced to be at the window when she got back. Watching her help the boy from the car told me all I wanted to know. Mervyn's butler had gone out to lend a hand, and Kathy waved him aside impatiently. No one but she was to touch this precious cargo. The boy put his hands on her shoulders and eased himself out, then hung onto her, standing on one leg, while she reached in and got out the crutches. Once supported by these, he swung forward gaily, laughing.

He was short and slight, and there was an infectious impudence about him. He looked an impudent Ariel. It was evident that all through his life he had been used to getting what he wanted by using his charm. I could imagine his nurse, his governess, his Mama, all enchanted. At school he would be in more danger, but he would know how to enroll at any rate a trusty cohort as a barrier against charm-proof barbarians. His small body looked tough and well exercised; his features were irregular but mobile and vivacious. As I got to know him better, I saw him as a man for sudden stratagems. He had known nothing of war. I didn't count the strange savage episode in which he had been engaged. That had done nothing but lift him for a moment out of war. War, to me, was that which was printed on some of the faces filing past my cubicle at Waterloo. I had got to know them well, these old hands, with the long months of pounding and battering written on their brows, and, seared into their eyes, the remembrance of many men now become ghosts haunting the parapet and firing step. Edward was one of them.

There was an afternoon when I had young Lancaster to myself for

471

half an hour, and I talked to him about his famous exploit. He made no pretenses. He said: "Well, it was all very odd, you know. So swift. They were into our trench before you could say Jack Robinson. I was in a dugout with a few other officers, and before we could get out they were there. They lobbed a couple of bombs down among us. The lamp was blown out, and in the darkness I began calling on the others. I soon realized that they were all dead. Well, then I saw red. I mean *I did. I saw red*. And then, just as swift as the red, came the black. I blacked out. I remember rushing up the steps, shouting to our men and using the most horrible language. I remember that clearly. And then nothing. I suppose I acted instinctively, but I can't tell you about that. I knew nothing till they were putting me on a stretcher."

He sat there considering his small hand, and it was very quiet and tranquillizing, and there was no one to praise or flatter him. Certainly not I. I was too deeply acquainted with my vast anonymous film of war's splendor and misery to be much moved. And so I said nothing for a time, and the quietness ticked over, and then I asked: "Has it ever happened before—this seeing red and blacking out?"

I felt him begin to withdraw, like a snail whose horns have been touched, but I didn't move or speak or look at him; and presently he said: "Well, as a matter of fact it has—twice."

And he told me how, he being then a child of six or seven, he had returned from a riding lesson and was walking with a crop in his hand when he came upon a boy of his own age, the son of his father's gardener, and this boy had caught a rabbit in the kitchen garden. He was carrying it by the ears, a frightened struggling creature, and he said to Master Nigel: "This is how they kill 'em." And thereupon, with a swift down-stroke of the edge of the hand, he smote the rabbit's neck, and it was limp. Nigel remembered nothing of what happened then, but he was told. A passer-by hauled him off the gardener's boy who was lying with a head bloodied by blows from the crop.

The other thing was at school. It isn't often a boy is killed at cricket, but it happened. Nigel's dearest friend was batting, and a swift ball glanced up from a hard pitch and struck him on the temple. He died at once. The boys and masters crowded round, and Nigel once more did not know, till he was told, that he snatched a wicket out of the ground and rushed with it upraised toward the boy who had bowled the fatal ball, but that time he was restrained before blows had fallen.

So there it is, I thought. This child who is revolted by death, whose very consciousness fails him when death strikes—the death of a rabbit, the death of a boy in white, the death of the officers in the dugout: this boy is doomed to see much death; and in the days that followed, when this dark side was hidden and Nigel was the gay, impudent well-beloved, I felt very tender toward him, and full of fear.

472

He was soon walking with a stick, and at last, showing no more than a slight limp, with no help at all. He was a popular young man, and, as there was no family to claim him, for he was an only child and both father and mother were dead, many friends sought him. But he seemed to want no one but Kathy, and she wanted only him. Infant though he was, he swept her off her feet, as he could sweep almost anyone he wished. His love of life and joy was tremendous. I began to find Kathy more likable and considerate. Her glazed synthetic crust was cracking as a veneer of ice cracks in the sunshine. There was a luncheon party at Hanover Square in August to celebrate Nigel's nineteenth birthday, and, replying to Mervyn's toast of his health, he told us, in a characteristic impudent speech, that he and Kathy had become engaged to be married. More gravely, he added—and this was something that Kathy evidently had not known—that a medical board had passed him fit for service. "And that," he said, "means any day now." It meant the following week, the last week of August; and in the first week of September Edward came home on leave.

13

The Somme battle had then been raging for two months, and Edward had endured much before that began. During his earliest leaves he had been like most soldiers returning from the wars, and had swept Nika into gaiety. But he had become more and more preoccupied, and as much as any of the faces I studied his had the look of one who had known too long the deathy smell of no-man's-land. The last time he was at home, he had refused to have anything to do with London. It was in early spring, but the weather chanced to be warm, and he had taken Nika to that cottage by the Thames where he and I had dallied as Daniel died. They spent the whole time, Nika told me, lazing about in a punt; and one afternoon Edward drove the pole down into the mud at the edge of a field and stood up, looking over the new green of the grass where cows were grazing, and said: "That's where our camp was in 1914. Seems a long time ago. I wonder why I'm the only one left? I am, you know. Every one of the chaps who officered here with me is dead. Most of the men, too, I expect." He tied the punt's rope to a willow and stepped out into the field. "Let's have lunch here," he said.

Nika protested. "Should we, darling? Won't that be rather morbid for you?"

"I don't call it morbid to remember the men I knew here. Why am I left? Is there something I am supposed to do?"

He was puzzled, frowning and earnest when we saw him off at the end of that leave, and his letters, especially since the Somme battle

473

had begun, would certainly have annoyed the censor if they had been submitted to him. Nika used to bring them to me, cut to the heart, and there was not much that I could do to comfort her.

"Well, my dear, there's just time to write this, and then once more to our gentle task. I shall have trouble, I know, with the carpenter's son. He joined us with a draft last week, and he weeps and weeps. Good God, what is there to weep about when you're crusading in a holy cause? But the carpenter's son is very troublesome. I feel it in my bones that tonight I shall have to push him over the top with my own hands. 'Up and over, you carpenter's son of a bitch. Forward to your duty.' And if he's still troublesome perhaps I'll shoot the daylights out of him as a good example. After all, that might be the best way with the carpenter's son, don't you think?"

Nika folded the letter and put it into her handbag and began to cry quietly. "I'm afraid for him," she said. "I'm afraid, afraid."

So was I, and I was very tired. I realized that suddenly as I sat there thinking of Edward. You could reach the breaking point. After all, I was sixty-eight, and for a long time I had been working full stretch. I welcomed it when Nika said: "When his next leave comes, will you be a darling and take on the children? Let me have him all to myself."

"How would you like it," I asked, "if I took them right away—down to Cornwall? I think I could arrange to leave someone else in charge at Waterloo. After all, I haven't had a day off since I began work there."

And so it was that, as August was ending, I went with Kathy and Mervyn and Enid to say good-by to Nigel, dapper and almost childish-looking in a new fawn-colored British warm; and a week later I was at Tresant with Nicolas and Vera, who were full of excitement, for they had not been to Tresant before. Never had I made the lovely journey with a heavier heart, and while the children exclaimed with joy as we rushed along the Devonshire seacoast, in and out of tunnels through the red crumbling cliffs, now in sight of sparkling water and blue sky and the white gulls sailing, now in fetid darkness, I thought how this was like a woman's life in these days we were enduring; and I hoped that for Nika the spell now opening, with Edward in her arms, would be flood-tide happiness, enjoyed for a moment with an intensity that could forget the inevitable ebb.

Edward was due in England on this very day of our journey. The next day I took the children to see all the things that were so deeply a part of me. Haggie Chadderton came with us—a grave and beautiful character, I thought her, and glad I was that she was there, rather silent but with a sense about her of reliable depths—and, starting our explorations after luncheon, we took food with us, intending to be out till sunset. Nicolas was five, Vera only three, and they should have been

474

early to bed, but this was a special moment in their lives, and, as the day was warm and pleasant, I set aside all rules.

So we dawdled along through the woods, beside the lake, toward the bar, those three ingredients of Tresant that life had fluxed into my being, so that they were the three loveliest things in the world to me, and at the same time the three most pregnant with mortality. Here I could never fail to know the beauty and the brevity of life. And so, as Haggie went ahead, a child clinging to each of her hands, I loitered, following at my own pace and resting now and then; and I was oppressed by a sense of the generations: Eddy Rodda and his son Mervyn, and Mervyn's son Edward, and Edward's children toddling before me, their young shrill laughter coming back through the still autumn air among the moveless trees that had taken here and there a gentle smolder of red and yellow.

I let them go on, and when I reached the eminence from which I could see the bar, they were already halfway along it, scampering like foals, shouting to one another at marvels they picked up from the sand, charging down toward the sea and coming to an awed halt before the water climbing, and curling inward, and toppling with a crash into a smash and seethe and hiss of white foam that ran to their feet and then ran back carrying the pebbles that clattered together to make the undertone of the greater roaring.

I knew they would be tired out before the expedition was ended, and I didn't mind that, for this was to be a day they would remember. Tired out they certainly were, and we returned in the last light with little Nicolas on Haggie's back and Vera clinging to my hand and stumbling along the path. And as we went thus, rounding a bend in the woods, I saw Nika and Edward walking toward us. My heart gave a thump, and I came to a stand as they approached, Edward in an old tweed coat and flannel trousers, and I feared this apparition and waited for him to speak. "I am a family man, you know," he said. "I ought to be with my children. We caught the first train down."

But he didn't see much of the children or of Nika or of me. Across the lake was the cottage where I had lived with Whaley, and where, much later, Lucy Evans had lived, and Haggie after that. Now that Tresant was mine to do with as I pleased, I kept this cottage, scantily furnished, as a guest house. It was used by such friends of mine as were prepared to look after themselves. On the morning after his arrival Edward asked if he might use the cottage. "I have some writing to do," he said, "rather a lot, and I want to be alone to concentrate."

"But, darling," Nika cried. "Do you have to shut yourself up *now?* Your time is so short."

"Yes," he said. "I must use it well."

He was quiet and gentle, but there was an obstinate resolution about him. He kissed her and the children and went off carrying a dispatch case and swinging the key of the cottage. "Don't worry about me," he shouted. "I don't expect I shall be back to lunch. Have a good day."

The children had a good day, but Nika and I had a bad one. Haggie packed up luncheon for Nicolas and Vera and took them off in a punt; and we two stayed at home and wondered. There was little that we could say to one another, for we were in the dark. With Edward's unexplained departure, which, we were sure, portended more than he had cared to say, a tension settled upon us and sharpened as the morning went by with dreadful slowness.

Luncheon was a miserable meal, and when it was over Nika said: "Go and lie down, darling. You look worn out."

It was good advice, and I took it. I did not wake till four o'clock, and then I ran down eagerly to see if Edward had returned. He had not, and Nika had disappeared. I was told that she had gone for a walk, and, following the directions I was given, I went in search of her, and found her sitting under the beech trees on the spot where I had sat with Maggie on the day when I knew she was going to die. That day, we had looked across the lake and seen Haggie standing on the lawn outside the cottage, and now Nika was gazing in that direction too. Her knees were up, her elbows resting on them, and with her chin in her hands she seemed to be concentrating her longing, her very life, into annihilating the distance between herself and Edward. I remembered that, sitting here with Maggie, I had heard her speak of Nika's flight to Edward as a descent from the ocean into the municipal baths. It may have been that in the beginning; how do I know? But, looking at her now, I was aware, from the longing that seemed incarnate in her immobile figure, that she and Edward had found the real thing of marriage, the thing that, God help them, made them one, not two. As I approached without her hearing me, I saw Edward come out of the cottage and take a turn or two on the lawn, smoking a pipe, and, without seeing it, I could *feel* that her face lit up. Her hands dropped, pressed palm downward to the grass on either side of her, seeming to urge her whole body forward in longing toward him. Then he went in, and her face went dejectedly down again into the cups of her hands, and it was sorrowful to see her sitting there and the water between.

I let my old bones down stiffly beside the lithe and lovely figure of my daughter and put my arm round her and drew her to me. Her eyes were glittering with hard tears that could not fall. "He must be hungry," she said.

476

We sat together for a long time watching the cottage, then walked slowly back to the house.

The children were in bed and we were walking with Haggie on the gravel in front of the house when Edward came back through the early dusk and bat flight. He seemed in good spirits, and said as he approached: "It went well—better than I hoped for. Another day will finish it. Can you spare me for another day, darling?"

Nika kissed him. "Do what you have to do," she said briefly.

The next day passed as this one had done, and when Edward returned he was almost gay, like someone who feels a disease blessedly leaving his system. "Now," he cried, "you can know what it's all about. I should like to read something to you after dinner."

Life piles up its memorable pictures, and one I have forever is of Edward reading to us after dinner. In revulsion from uniform, he was wearing his oldest flannel trousers and tweed coat, tattered at the elbows and burned through here and there with hot droppings from his pipe. The coat was thrown open to show a bright blue shirt gaping at the neck. So he sat, one leg thrown over the other, under the light of a standard lamp, the pages of manuscript in his hand. His face had aged in the last two years. Here and there in his rough black hair was a strand of gray and a black clipped mustache was on his lip. Nika sat facing him, a few feet away, on a low stool, her attitude that in which I had found her by the lake. The lamp lit up both the faces, and I was removed in a corner, in the shadow.

"Well, it's not overlong," Edward said, knocking out his pipe. "It's to be printed as a pamphlet. It's called *Is Not This the Carpenter's Son?* After all, we are all," he said shyly, "in a sort of way the sons of God. However, you'd better hear it." And he began to read.

What he had to say he had said well. It was concise, unemotional, irrefutable if men pretended to live according to the doctrines of the religion they professed.

There was silence for a long time when he had finished; and Edward himself broke it. "A copy," he said, "will be posted to every member of both Houses and to all the influential people I can think of. And, of course, having taken this attitude, there's one thing I must do to back it up. I shall refuse to return to the butchery. I shall, no doubt, be sent by a medical board for observation by a psychiatrist. He will find that I am mentally deranged. In these days, the dawn of reason must be dismissed as the night of madness."

He looked anxiously at Nika, whose attitude had not changed all through the reading. She was still looking at him with an odd intensity. Her silence disturbed him, and he picked up the manuscript from the table where he had laid it. "There's only one person who could stop me now," he said to her, and he held the pages in the manner of one about to tear them across. "What do you say?"

Then Nika got up and took the pages from his hand and put them back on the table. She kissed him and said what she had said the night before. "My darling, do what you have to do."

He, too, got up then, and they held one another for a moment before he said: "We must return to London tomorrow."

15

Nika and Edward were taking it calmly enough; but you can't say, I thought, what will come of a thing like this. I had no doubt that, since Edward felt as he did, he was right to express himself as he did; but the consequences would be unpredictable. It was a moment when we must keep together. Edward, after all, was the son of Mervyn and Enid as well as Nika's husband, and so I suggested to them that while he was doing whatever he wanted to do we should all stay in Hanover Square. They agreed to this, and we rang up Mervyn that evening and told him that we were returning in the morning. The children would be left behind in Haggie's care.

Our wartime journey the next day was slow; it was late when we reached London, and we did not sit down to dinner in Hanover Square till nine o'clock. Kathy was in a bad mood. She was a girl with no self-control. Whatever she was feeling appeared on the surface, sometimes to cheer and sometimes to bedevil her companions. Now she was in the deepest depression. No letter had reached her from Nigel Lancaster since his departure. Deprived of his company, and wishing for no other, she was a restless ghost at our meal, her fingers crumbling bread, twitching the cloth, shredding a flower that she took from a vase on the table. Her mood, as she intended it to do, conveyed itself to all of us, left us aware of her sorrows. Looking at her angry, rebellious face, I dreaded the moment when Edward would explain, as I knew he intended to do this night, what it was that he had in mind.

We had hardly moved into the drawing room when Kathy rose abruptly and said: "Excuse me, everybody. I think I'll go to bed."

Edward said: "Could you spare just a few moments? There's something I want to say to the family. I've told Nika and her mother, but the rest of you should hear it, too."

Kathy sat down again, none too graciously, and Edward, taking his pipe from his mouth and looking thoughtfully at the bowl, said: "I hope none of you will think that I'm being precipitate and rushing in without thought. Believe me, I've thought a great deal about what I'm going to do. It's been growing in me for months. I'm not a reckless sort

478

of chap. Never have been. I'm acting now in cold blood. Well, to cut it short, I don't intend to return to the front, and I shall publish a protest against the war's continuance."

There was a silence. Nobody spoke or moved till Nika crossed the room, sat on the edge of Edward's chair, and put her arm round his neck.

Presently Kathy got up and walked toward the door. "I think, more than ever," she said, "that I shall go to bed. I shall need quiet to decide how I shall face my friends whose husbands and brothers are doing their duty." Then she went.

Poor Enid burst into tears. Whether they were tears of shame for her daughter or tears of perplexed anguish over the straits in which her son found himself I do not know. She, too, got up, and Nika went to her and with an arm about her accompanied her from the room. But when she was in the hall Enid ran back and embraced Edward and sobbed: "You have suffered too much, too much." Then she and Nika went up to her bedroom.

Mervyn had risen and was standing with his back to the fire, looking down at his son. His face was drawn and grave, but, looking up at him, this very handsome man with the gray hair and troubled eyes, I had no fears. I had known that face a long time, and I could read it. There was bravery in it now. He took a step forward and put a hand on his son's shoulder. "I can well imagine how you feel," he said. "The bloody business seems endless. Let's talk it over, Eddie."

I went up to my own room and left them there.

16

Kathy did not come down to breakfast. When the meal was over Edward said: "Could you come with me to Bermondsey this morning, Mama?"

They always go to Sally, I thought. Sooner or later, they always go to Sally. We went in a car over which an odd balloon of gas sagged and surged in the autumn breeze. Edward was still wearing tweeds. "I shall never put on uniform again," he said. "Not to go before a board or anything else. They'll have to strip me and forcibly put it on me if they want me in it."

He smiled at the thought of that tussle, and I was glad that he could smile. His face had lost the strain that I had seen on it during the leave before this. He was his old, normal, rather prosy and dependable self. Perhaps, as he said, they would call him mad; but undoubtedly he was saner than he had been for a long time. The taking of his decision seemed to have rocked his mind back onto the rails from which, as his

479

recent letters had shown, it had been jerked. He was capable of a long view, which I take to be the essence of sanity.

He knew what was the matter with Kathy: Nika had told him about Nigel Lancaster. He asked me questions about the boy, and I told him all I knew, except that story of the red-and-black that Nigel had confided to me. I never told that to anybody. "Poor Kathy!" he said. "She has always brought such suffering on her own head."

We met Sally in the street. Edward would not have known her. I don't suppose he had seen her more than two or three times in his life, but she was enshrined in his father's heart. None of Mervyn's children could fail to know about Sally.

I stopped the cab, and she had strolled by, an old shawl round her hair and pinned beneath her chin, her large hobnailed boots clattering on the pavement, a shopping basket over her arm. I called after her and she came back, and we walked to her house. "I was going to see if the butcher had a few scraps," she said, "but that can wait. I'm afraid they would be scraps indeed, for the butcher doesn't like me at the moment."

She had shaken Edward's hand when I introduced him, but said nothing to him: merely accepted him as she accepted everybody. If the king had come to Bermondsey, interested in her work, this is the way she would have strolled with him to her cottage.

We went through the wide-open front door and sat down in her kitchen. "How have you offended the butcher, Sally?" I asked.

"It was the scrap with Warwick Russell last week," she said. "I don't suppose you've heard of it. Too many scraps going on for that one to make much noise."

I knew that Warwick Russell, when the war broke out, had made his protest in the House of Commons and had not again entered the House whose business he was unable to abet. I knew, too, that in the hysteria of the times he had been turned upon by many of the people to whom he had given his life, but that he had remained here working nevertheless for those who wanted him.

Now, it seemed from what Sally told us, he had appeared at a public meeting and forced his way onto the platform and said vehemently what everybody knew him to think about the war. He had been howled at and abused, and a crowd had followed him to his house. "I was told of the racket," Sally said, "and went along to see what it was all about, and there he was standing on the doorstep facing them, saying nothing, just standing there, with the windows smashing all round him. I went and stood alongside him and put an arm through his. A pretty pair of fools we must have looked, Mr. and Mrs. St. Sebastien, knowing well that no one would loose an arrow at *us*. Still, it was pretty unnerving, especially when a brick went through the fanlight over our heads."

I could see that Edward's heart was too full for him to speak. He had heard much of Sally Gaylord—perhaps so much that he had come prepared for disillusion; and he had found what matched his own mood.

The glass still littered the pavement outside Warwick Russell's house, and soon we were crunching through it and making our way into the bleak room where, so long ago, Sally had first met him when she brought the cat that Tom Chadderton had injured with a catapult. We sat down while Warwick Russell read what Edward had written, and then he said simply: "Good! That says it all. Are you prepared to go through with this? I'm not interested in wobblers."

"Yes," said Edward.

"All right. You've come to a lucky shop. You'd walk a long way, you know, before you'd find a printer for this. But I know the man. Leave the stuff with me."

It was very brief and unemotional. Warwick came with us to the door, carrying a large hard broom. "At last," he said, "I suppose I'd better sweep up this bloody mess or I'll have some of the poor barefoot little devils coming to me with septic feet. Well, so long, Mary."

"So you're still Mary," I said as we walked away.

"What does it matter what I am? Poor Russell! He has to come to me now for his meals. There's not a woman who'll go in to do a hand's turn for him. A good many of them would like to, but they're afraid of what the others will do to them. There's a woman here whose son has won the Military Medal. A proper young scoundrel who was heading for Dartmoor when the war began and will probably arrive there when it's over. In his sacred name, his mother is keeping us all up to scratch. If she dared, she'd put Warwick's eyes out. So I have to do what I can for him."

"Why! Where's Polly?" I asked in surprise.

"Gone," she said briefly. "Who can blame her? A woman can stand so much and no more. Saints shouldn't marry. You seem shocked."

"Well . . ."

"Yes—well—. Life's like that, you know."

17

In the course of that day a letter from Nigel reached Kathy. She read parts of it at dinner, and from the glow in her eyes I was sure that the endearing parts which she did not read were satisfactory. What she read was what one would expect from an enthusiastic boy who knew nothing of war. We had all received such letters from Edward in the early days. Edward made no comment on it. As an officer who had to censor letters, he probably knew it by heart. The coming of the letter did not make Kathy any kinder to him, but it took some of the strain out of her face.

Edward now was more restless than she. He had finished the first part of what he intended to do, and while waiting for Warwick Russell to deliver the printed pamphlet he was at a loose end. Once or twice he and Kathy jarred. A word on one side or the other drew a sharp answer; and so we all moved uneasily to the day on which Edward's leave expired. He was due to catch a train early the next morning. In the course of the day the bundle of printed pamphlets was delivered in Hanover Square. Edward brought a handful to the table at lunchtime. "You might like to have one each," he said simply. "When I'm in clink or a madhouse, or wherever they decide to send me, you may care to know what constitutes crime and insanity in these days."

We all took one except Kathy. She said nothing. She simply kept her eyes on her plate and did not take the pamphlet that Edward held toward her.

In the afternoon I invited her to take tea with me in my room. I tried a last effort to make her see what Edward was doing. I reminded her of the long and terrible experience he had had, and she said: "I suppose it's driven him crazy"; and I knew drearily that there was the answer of the ninety-nine out of every hundred. I went on trying; and at last she ended it all with the remark: "Oh, for God's sake let's face it: he's funked. There's no more than that to be said. Once he publishes this precious document—if he dares to—I shall never be able to hold up my head again."

I knew then that there was no use in going on; and my heart was sick for the girl. All through her life she had grasped at so much, and she had so little. The beautiful Miss Mostyn-Lloyd was one of the most poverty-stricken creatures I had ever known, and because she had so little her emotions gripped tenaciously round whatever was the hoped-for thing of the moment. Now it was young Lancaster; and it had been enough to make one weep to see her snatch up the *Times* each morning since the boy had gone away and look with a glitter in her eyes down the columns of dead men's names. We were moving on: the *Times* was no longer, as I had to my cost once known it to be, an academic concern of Papa at the breakfast table. It was most bitterly the business of daughters now.

But it was not through the *Times* that we learned the news. A parlormaid came up with the letter as we sat there at the end of all we had to say to one another. It was from France, and I watched the look of joy on her face and the swift shadow chase the joy away as she saw that the writing was not his. When she had read it she got up—she was very tall—and stood, with the letter in her hand, looking icily out upon the London roofs and chimneys, and what she was seeing I don't know, but certainly not those. The letter fell to the carpet, and without saying a word to me she went.

It was some time before I picked the letter up and read it. There was no need to read it: I knew already what it said. Nigel had given Kathy's address to this Major Eliot and asked him to write if "anything happened." And now it had happened, and here was the letter, That was all. The next day I noticed Major Eliot's name among the dead; and that is what our life was like in those days: the dead writing to announce their fellow ghosts.

But this was not the next day: this was four o'clock on that afternoon, the last day of Edward's leave; and I went down and told what had happened. Edward set off to let his father know. Enid and Nika went up to Kathy's room and found the door locked. There was no sound, of crying or of anything else; but there was no response to the knocking and they came away, both of them weeping. Oh, there were tears in those days, rivers to make the fields of life fruitful, but like the fountains of the Crystal Palace they all went down the drain.

Mervyn returned, white and shaken, and Edward was not with him. Mervyn hardly seemed to know that he was alone. He ran two steps at a time upstairs and called to Kathy, and presently he came down again slowly, and for a few hours the silence in her room remained unbroken. It was our custom to dine at eight, and it was not till half past seven that Edward came back. The resolution—almost the serenity —that had come to his face was gone. He looked hag-ridden. "I have been walking," was all he said. He, too, went up to the silent room and knocked. "Kathy," he called. "Kathy, are you coming down to dinner, or shall we send something up?"

"I shall be there," she said.

She came down, carefully dressed as none other of us was. Our love reached out to her. The air was full of the solicitude that surrounded her, but she was ice. This blow that had melted us had frozen her. No one mentioned what was in our hearts, and there was no need to mention it. We were all there for her to lean on, and you could feel the terrible tension of her rejection of us. It was a ghastly pretense of a meal; and when it was over and the parlormaid gone Edward filled his pipe and struck a match and sucked at the stem and the pipe would not draw. On the mantelpiece was a vase full of pipe cleaners, little bundles of feathers held in paper bands. Kathy got up and brought a bundle to the table. She broke off the paper and spread out the feathers by her plate. They were of many colors. She set aside some that were speckled and some that were brown and some that were black. Then, with deliberation, she picked up one that was white and handed it to Edward.

Edward was sitting between Nika and Kathy. Nika, with her face flaming, sprang to her feet and reached across Edward to strike Kathy. Edward caught her hand. "No," he said. "No."

He got up and went out of the room, and tears began to flow again. All four of us women cried, and poor Mervyn uttered clucking noises of comfort. What else could he do? What could anybody do then but let the insanity run its course?

Edward returned wearing his uniform. Kathy alone spoke. "Thank you," she said.

A week later Nika received the telegram announcing Edward's death.

CHAPTER TWENTY-SEVEN

I

IN THE summer of 1924 I had done what I hated doing: I had taken my grandson, Nicolas, to the zoo. I detested this enormous prison, but the boy had wanted to go. It was the beginning of his school holiday; he would be off to Tresant in a day or two. Nika had already gone there with her daughter, Vera, who had had some childish ailment and was taken away to recuperate. I would follow with Nicolas soon. The St. John's Wood house was closed and the boy was staying with me and Mervyn in Hanover Square. Literally, with me and Mervyn: there was no one else. I did not know where Kathy was; no one did. We knew only where she had been or where she was going to. We would receive a postcard from somewhere in the South of France saying: "Freddie Loughborough has arrived with his steam yacht. Floss and I are going on with him to the Ægean." We had never before heard of Floss, and were not likely to hear of her again. By the time another card came from Luxor or some such place it would be Connie or Jill. Sophia was in the North of England, a sister in a large urban hospital. Enid had been dead for some years. She had not really been alive since Edward's death. The tension between her and Kathy thereafter had been terrible, the more terrible because each tried so desperately to avoid the utter break which I saw must come. It came after Kathy had wildly declared: "You should thank me. I saved him from dishonor." From that day on, Enid did not speak to her daughter. The misery of those few years for all of us is something I want to pass over briefly. It ended with the influenza scourge that fell upon the wretched world as the war came to its close. There was no fight in Enid: she was gone in a few days.

So there I was with this boy who would be thirteen in the autumn, a small copy of his father, dark and stocky, wearing a red jersey and flannel shorts. We were watching a polar bear drearily padding out its prison path: a few paces one way, a toss of the head, a few paces the other way; on and on endlessly, maddeningly. A voice behind us said: "That's more or less how I used to feel at the end of a day: dizzy with senseless repetition." I turned, and the man added: "Excuse me for speaking to you, Mrs. Undridge. Perhaps you don't remember me?"

I did and I didn't. As I scanned his face he said: "I'm Henry Shape." Of course it was! But older, more tired, and looking down and out. His clothes were thin and shabby, his heels down-trodden, his coat cuffs whiskered. He had been little to me but a broad back in a good serviceable coat, a reserved young man who said no more than his job required. I held out my hand to him, and he took it, looking a little surprised that it had been offered. His hesitation gave me the feeling that he was not accustomed to finding the world a welcoming place. Long, long ago—God! I thought, what a crone you must be to remember such a thing!—I had walked, a child, holding Whaley's hand, and I had given pennies to men sitting under the railings of Hyde Park—men without arms, without legs, with black patches hiding the empty sockets of their eyes—men back from the Crimean War. Men back from the wars . . . !

"Are you hungry?" I asked.

He said simply: "Yes."

"So am I," Nicolas said; and Henry Shape's wry grin at that was heart-breaking. So I took the hungry heir apparent of Mostyn-Lloyd's and the hungry Henry Shape to the tea room. Nicolas might be hungry, but he was good-mannered and looked after our guest. When we had done eating and drinking Henry Shape asked: "Do you mind if I smoke?" and, being given permission, he took a pouch from his pocket, carefully tipped a thimbleful of dust into the palm of his hand, and dropped this into the pipe.

"My grandfather smokes John Cotton," Nicolas said. "What is that?"

We were in the open air again now. We found a seat. "I'm not sure," Henry Shape said. "But it's good."

It did not take him long to smoke that dusty stuff, and when he had knocked out the pipe he got up and said: "Thank you, Mrs. Undridge. That was welcome. I must be off."

But I wasn't having that. I wanted to know what had happened to Henry Shape in the years since we had last met. It was clear to me that things were not well with him, clear also that he was not a self-pitying sort who would spill his song every time a penny was dropped into the slot. He had not said that his tobacco was the fag-ends of cigarettes, which I guessed it to be.

485

"I should be glad, Mr. Shape," I said, "if you could take lunch with me some day soon. Tomorrow, if you could manage it?"

He said that he could, and I gave him my address, and there he was the next day in my confessional over Mervyn's house. That is what Sophia and Kathy had taken to calling it, though little enough Kathy ever confessed. Henry was wearing a different suit, a gray herringbone, and his shoes were not bad. The job-hunting outfit, I said to myself. Oh, I was becoming well used to all the shifts and stratagems of the heroes who were already national nuisances and bores. "If only they wouldn't wear their medals!" I had heard. "Some of them come to the door wearing not only the ribbons but the medals themselves. I do think it's so lacking in self-respect to try and cash in like that on having done one's duty."

We had finished our meal, and I pushed across to him the tobacco jar that I had lifted from Mervyn's room. "Supposing you were wearing your medals," I asked, "what would they be?"

He looked at me warily. He was noncommittal today. At last he said: "Well, the usual couple, you know—general service and victory—and then there's the M.C. and D.S.O." He added: "Of course, you *can* win the D.S.O. in an office. I didn't."

I found him a tough oyster to open, but peace and quiet did their work, as I usually found them to do; and when the afternoon had worn on to four o'clock and tea was brought up, he was in a relaxed state and I knew all about it. There was Susie, to begin with. Already when Henry Shape was working for me and Daniel there had been Susie, and there had been Henry's dream of Susie sharing the flat with him over the garage. Susie had managed to be faithful till 1916, and by then she had discovered that any girl who wanted it could have one good time after another with relays of life-hungry men. Susie and two illegitimate children were now with her mother in Leicester, and that ended Henry's cozy dream of starting a garage of his own on the Great North Road.

He had been, I gathered, an intelligent, reliable soldier and he was given a commission in the field before 1915 was out. By 1917 he was a major, and in the late spring of that year he was taken prisoner. He spent eighteen months in Germany and was not, he said, such a fool as to try to escape. "It was a pretty lousy life, but one could put up with it, and I knew I was never likely again to have such a chance to study."

I asked him what he had studied, and he said it had mainly been mathematics and mechanics. "I've been fiddling about with motorcar engines ever since I was a child," he said. "I could do most things with 'em by rule of thumb, but I wanted to know it all scientifically. I found I had a natural aptitude for those things," he added modestly. "I got onto airplane engines at the end, and the general principles of airplane

486

construction. There's a lot to be done there. And, of course, I picked up a working knowledge of German from the Boches."

I noted that "of course," and said: "You didn't waste your time."

"I wonder. I don't find it much use in selling vacuum cleaners and notepaper."

I glanced at him over the tea cups: a medium-sized brown-haired man, about thirty-one or two, with a good nose and a jutting chin: an unimaginative, factual-looking face. At the moment it was oppressed by anxiety that could in time become fear. He was asking for nothing: he was not the sort of man who would ask for anything. He was one of thousands who had done a job, and now that the job was done had been discarded, like the Crimean veterans littering the pavements of my childhood. He would go slowly down; or, given the chance, he would, I felt, go slowly up, and perhaps not so slowly as all that. I felt a responsibility that I could not dodge weighing heavily on my shoulders.

"Next week," I said, "I shall be going to Cornwall with my grandson—the boy who was with me yesterday. Would you care to drive us down? It would be a change for you. A holiday wouldn't hurt you. You could stay down there till we came back. About a month, I should think."

He did not hesitate. He accepted it as simply as he would have accepted going out again into his wasteland.

"I should like that. I should like to be driving you again, Mrs. Undridge. It's a long time since I've had my hands on the wheel of a car."

2

When he was gone I took down the invitation card from the mantelpiece. "Cocktails 6-8 P.M." We had entered the age of gin. I didn't like the age, and I wasn't going to pretend that I did, and I thought it altogether appropriate that charwomen's tipple should be its symbolic drink. Gin was gin. It didn't need knowledge or taste or experience, as wine did. You just grabbed it and drank it. And you gave a gin party, called a cocktail party, instead of entertaining friends as you used to. You shrilled and chattered instead of conversing; and if you were a guest you did your host the honor of not concealing that you were on edge to "go on" somewhere else.

Well, well! Even Julian had come to it, for this invitation was to a party marking the opening of the Rimmel Gallery in Bond Street. As the financier of the concern, I had had to find more money for this, and I thought with a smile that no doubt I was even paying for the gin. It would all come back. The flow of Europe's treasures to America had begun, and, though we didn't know it at the time, there were now just four years of El Dorado fun for Rimmel's before the cold wind hit America and froze the golden stream. Fournier was already there, and impressive young men, looking like the offspring of peers, had been recruited for Bond Street. Another symptom of the times we lived in was that Kathy Mostyn-Lloyd was forever passing on tips to Julian Rimmel about her friends' possessions. Did he know that Teddy Teesdale had a fine Hobbema, and that, what with the death duties he had had to find when his father died and one thing and another, he was anxious to sell it? And Kathy would get her check—commission on her enterprising insight into the dissolution of her friends.

I didn't go to Bond Street till there was a chance that the riot would be ending. I talked to a few people and lingered till everyone was gone, and then Julian and I went up to his flat above the premises. Here he had a sitting room, a bedroom, a bathroom and a small kitchen. He was his own valet and his own cook. Cooking was his only recreation, and he was an artist. He led me to a chair and settled me down and said: "Exist for a few moments, and then we will eat."

It was a sparsely furnished lovely room containing things that Julian would not sell. The walls were shell-pink, the paintwork was white, and floor carpeted in the gray of a herring-gull's wing. The chairs were Georgian, upholstered in beautiful contemporary stuffs embroidered in *petit point*. His pictures were all fairly recent French things: some racehorses by Degas, a village street by Utrillo, trees and water by Monet, one of Modigliani's elongated women: things of that sort. There were a few small bronzes by Rodin and one by Epstein. A cabinet was full of Bow and Chelsea figures, and over the marble mantelpiece was a fantastic Chippendale mirror in the Chinese style.

He gave me breast of chicken and crisp strawed potatoes, and crepes that came to the table bubbling with blue flame, and a bottle of Chateau Larose. There was Wensleydale cheese and coffee and Armagnac. He was a tidy man and went back to the kitchen to wash up before joining me again in the sitting room. We stayed there talking till eleven o'clock. It was very peaceful. The only light was from the shaded tubes fixed over some of the pictures. "What do you think of my pictures?" he asked.

"I like them very well."

"You are a remarkable woman. You have no right to like this sort of thing at seventy-six."

"Who told you I'm seventy-six?"

"Oh, I know all about you! Your taste should have hardened round Sir Lawrence Alma Tadema. Still! Even these, I suppose, are now old-fashioned. However, there comes a point where one refuses to march, and these about mark it for me. It's time you were in bed."

488

We went down into the street and a girl dressed with tarnished smartness, leading a Pekinese in a red leather harness, strolled by with swaying hips as we stood there waiting for a cruising taxi. "A perfect Toulouse-Lautrec," he said.

I wondered about him. I wondered whether he always saw women as pictures. He put me down at my door and said he would walk back. He held my hand for a long time. "I think it's going to be all right," he said then. "I'm *sure* it's going to be all right. Do you need my thanks?"

"Not particularly."

"You know they are always yours. God bless."

3

In March of this year, 1924, I had taken breakfast with Mervyn on his birthday morning. He was sixty-seven, tall, thin, and his hair was quite white. When I came into the room he was standing before the fire, reading the *Times*. He wore a dressing gown and slippers. "You look very informal for a merchant-prince with his living to earn," I said.

"On his birthday," he answered, "even a merchant-prince is entitled to relax. Mostyn-Lloyd's can take care of itself for a day."

He walked to the window and looked out on the black bare trees. There was frost in the air. A foggy London sun was visible. Mervyn turned back into the room and threw down the paper. "I feel lonely," he said. "What a damned big house this is just for the two of us! And, even so, we live in separate parts of it."

Breakfast was brought in and we sat down to the table. "I know how you feel," I said. "After sixty, one should forget birthdays."

"When I was at Eton I used to mark the days off on my calendar, gloating on the approach of the holiday. Edward once told me that in France he did the same thing, as soon as a date had been fixed for leave. But that was ticking off the steps toward fruition. All the steps now are leaves stripping away. One feels that the bare tree is beginning to show through."

"Don't be morbid," I said. "I've got some cuff links for you."

"I want more than cuff links out of you. I want a good long talk about my beginnings. I feel in a reminiscent mood. I've been thinking a lot lately about the oddest things: your brother Justin, and old Miss Whale, and Sally and that woman who ran the settlement where she used to live."

"That woman, indeed!" I chided him. "That's a nice way to speak of Dame Dorothy Dewhirst! Don't forget, she's one of the most distinguished denizens of the Empire. Did I tell you that I met her about a year ago?"

"No."

"I did. There was a reception in her honor after she'd been made a Dame, and I wangled an invitation so as to see what she's like nowadays. All the advanced thinkers were there—all the Webbsey-Wibsey people. Well, there she was—regal, my dear: there's no other word for it— utterly regal. Immense, white-haired, undoubtedly impressive. One felt one should kiss her hand if she would be so kind as to permit the liberty. I got a few moments with her, and it took most of them to make her realize who I was. She asked most kindly about Sally, and her large, fat, powdered face shook with sorrow. 'Such a waste,' she said. 'Such a waste.' Just that. Poor Sally! She's never been called to give evidence before a Royal Commission in all her life, and never written a blue-book. That woman looked such a self-satisfied galleon that I wondered whether to turn a broadside on her; but just then the rat Wibsey came along and she opened her rich deep contralto on him. 'Ah, Mr. Wibsey—' So I left them together."

"Well," Mervyn said, "she had reason to feel a bit uppish. It must have been a great occasion for her. Whatever you may think of her, she's reached the top of the thing she was after. That's something. And she did it on her own, which is more than I can say. Everything was handed to me on a plate. How did it all come about? I know so little about my own beginnings."

So then we talked about Tresant and the old days. I answered all the questions he asked me; and that night, up in my own rooms, my mind was still buzzing with what we had unearthed. It had become very vivid in the retelling, and I decided to put it down on paper once for all. That is how I began to write this book which I shall continue and leave some day for Julian Rimmel to do with as he likes.

4

That summer when Henry Shape drove me and young Nicolas down to Tresant I went for the first time as the owner of the place. I had for long been a favored tenant. Now Tresant was mine. Nicolas, I hoped, would have it someday. I hoped, too, that he would live in the house, not make it merely a place to be visited. There was no Gaylord blood in him, but I, his grandmother, was at any rate a half sister of the last of the Gaylord men. It was time Tresant had someone to do what had last been done by Justin's father, time the regime of agents came to an end.

Soon after that conversation with Mervyn in March, Warwick Russell had rung me up.

"It's a long time since you've been down here to see Sally," he said.

"Sally? You mean Mary."

"Don't quibble," he said testily. "In a few days, from the look of things, I shall mean nobody at all. You'd better come quickly."

I telephoned to Mervyn and he came at once with his car and took me to Bermondsey. We found Dr. Russell at Sally's house. "I've just fetched in a nurse," he said. "We are doing what we can."

We all three sat in the kitchen, and he said: "For God's sake make me a cup of tea."

I did so, and the simple task confronted me at once with all the small difficulties and annoyances that Sally had been meeting through so many years. No gas, let alone electricity, had, even yet, reached this house. The kitchen grate on which, when I had made my visits here, a kettle had usually been bubbling, however hot the weather, was a litter of dust and cinder. In the scullery I found an oil stove, and this was empty. I searched for paraffin, and presently found a tin of it and got the stove going. In a kitchen cupboard I found tea.

"If you're looking for milk," Warwick Russell said, "it's that stuff in a tin." It was a glutinous mess. I made the tea, and he alone wanted it. He was haggard and unshaven. "I was up with her all night," he said. "I hadn't seen her for three days and came to find out what she was up to. She was lying dressed on her bed, wet through. We had a thunderstorm over here two nights ago. Did you have it?"

Yes, we had had it; and somehow, as Dr. Russell told us what he thought had happened, there seemed to me, if Sally had to die, a comfort in the notion that something as elemental as a thunderstorm had had a hand in it. He didn't know where she had been, but it must have been late when she returned, for the storm had not opened till midnight. "She had a slight stroke," he said, "and, as I see it, she must then have been outside her own door. There she lay and was soaked to the skin, and then she seems to have recovered sufficiently to crawl to her bed, which you know is on the ground floor." And there she had been till he found her, the old shawl pinned beneath her chin, the hobnailed boots on her feet.

"I undressed her and put her into bed," he said, "and did what I could, and sent for a nurse. But don't have any hopes," he added savagely. "She's done for. Pneumonia following a stroke would finish a horse, and she's no horse. I haven't liked the look of her lately."

Well, I thought, if it comes to looks, it's a long time since she's looked anything to write home about, and she at any rate would not be worried by that. Was there any consciousness at all in her mind, I wondered, as she lay on her miserable doorstep in the slashing rain? Was Bermondsey washed away and Tresant brought back? On the mantelpiece, dusty and moth-eaten, was the only piece of decoration she had ever permitted in this house: the stuffed seagull that Tom Chadderton had brought back from Cornwall. Was it simply a souvenir of poor Tom?

Or sometimes, looking at it, did she think of the great birds lying on the wind, and the horses, and the waves pounding the bar, and the serene swans on the lake? If she did, I am sure it was with no regret.

"May we see her?" I asked.

"As you please," Warwick Russell said in his angry grief. "She's no picture."

He led the way into the front room that was her bedroom, and there, with the nurse sitting alongside, was Sally in her bed. She had for a long time had false teeth. These had been taken from her mouth. Her jaws had fallen in and her nose, chin and cheekbones were sharp. There was a dew of sweat on her forehead and her head was moving restlessly from side to side on the pillow. She was unrecognizable as Sally—as the Sally of any time I had known her. Her eyes opened in an uncomprehending stare, without focus. Dr. Russell twitched my sleeve and we tiptoed back to the kitchen. "Well," he said. "There she is. I hope you like the look of her."

"You go," I said to Mervyn. "I shall stay."

When he was gone, I walked to Warwick Russell's house and found that now, with the war's animosities so far behind us, he had a reasonably competent housekeeper. I told her of what had happened, trying to be as sane and practical as I was sure Sally would have been in such circumstances. I had a small appetizing meal prepared and then went and brought him home.

Sally did not speak again and died that night. Such papers as she had I found in the kitchen-table drawer. Among them was a letter addressed to me. "I don't want people in Bermondsey to make any fuss of me," it said, "or people at Tresant, either. But I wish to be buried with my family at Tresant. Have my body put into a coffin, and then remove it quietly to Paddington in time for the night train to Cornwall. At Tresant, let there be nothing public, just a burial in the presence of those who knew me."

There were myself and Mervyn and Warwick Russell, and in the wall of the chapel we put a simple plate of marble, recording that near it was buried the last to bear the name of Gaylord.

5

Henry Shape had left me his address and I had written to him, confirming the engagement to take him down to Cornwall as a chauffeur and enclosing a month's pay in advance. It seemed to me likely that, living as he was from hand to mouth, he would have some debts that he wished to settle before leaving London, and, moreover, I didn't want a chauffeur who fainted on the road. He hadn't looked well-nourished, and I would be glad to think that he had had a week's good feeding before joining us.

Mervyn saw us off. He was anxious to meet Henry Shape. He had met him in those few months when Henry worked for us before Daniel's death, but he had forgotten him: eleven years is a long time. Mervyn liked, to use his horrid expression, to check up on people, and he had checked up on Henry Shape. The name of Henry's regiment and the name of some of his fellow officers had come out in our conversation, and it chanced that Mervyn knew one of these officers. All that he learned from him was to Henry Shape's credit, and I was glad of that, because I did not wish this engagement as a chauffeur to be the end of my association with him. After all, I thought, as we left the horrible sprawl of outer London behind us and reached into open country, it was Henry who had driven me back to old Fortescue's house on the day Daniel died, and Edward had been with me, and here now was Edward's son. I could easily, I thought, become quite sentimentally attached to this young man. I had never had that complete detachment from those I employed that my father had had from Ducat and his like.

We took it easy, on my insistence. And I had to insist. I could almost feel Henry's itch to let the car all out, but I kept my eye on the speedometer needle, and if it passed thirty-five I prodded him in the back with my stick. This didn't please him or Nicolas either. "Can't we do sixty, just for a few miles, Grannie?" the boy pleaded. "I *have* done seventy with Grandfather."

"Grandfather always was mad where motorcars are concerned, but I'm not, and so long as I'm in this car we won't do more than thirty-five," I said firmly.

We broke our journey for a meal in Exeter, and when that was done Nicolas asked: "May I sit in the front when we potter on again?"

So he sat with Henry Shape, and I was glad to hear that they had plenty to talk about. I put my head back and went to sleep. When I woke we were hurtling over Bodmin Moor and a glance at the speedometer showed me sixty-five miles. I poked with my stick. "Sorry, Mrs. Undridge," Henry apologized. "I thought you were still asleep."

"I have said nothing," I reminded him, "about being asleep or awake. If I were dead and this were a hearse, you would still drive it at not more than thirty-five miles an hour."

"You'll be late for your own funeral," Nicolas twitted me.

"I certainly don't intend to be early for it," I said.

When we rolled up to the house, there was quite a reception committee awaiting us: Nika, holding little Vera by the hand, Haggie Chadderton, and, of all the unexpected people, Sophia Mostyn-Lloyd. It's becoming preposterous, I thought, as they all surged forward, anxious, apparently, to open doors and lend me their arms, and carry

493

this and that. They are beginning to treat me like some decrepit piece of royalty. "Out of my way, the whole lot of you," I cried, waving my stick at them. "I'm quite capable of putting my own feet to the ground and walking up a few steps. I'm not eighty yet by a long way, and I'll begin to ask for your help when I'm ninety."

But they all insisted on kissing me, and Haggie kept a hold on my arm and we went up the steps together. I heard Nicolas explaining to Vera: "This is Henry Shape. He says one ought to get seventy out of this bus."

I stopped and turned and looked down on them all, and especially at those two young ones, standing on the gravel, with the field stretching away behind them and the little stream bubbling through the field toward the lake; and it came over me with a shock that I had been younger than either of those two when I had first stood there with Sally Gaylord, and that my mother then was younger than Nika was now. I went on into the house and Haggie said: "Come on now. It's no good pretending you're not tired. It's been a long journey, and you'd better have an hour's sleep before dinner."

"All right," I said. "Have it your own way. See that the children don't shout under my window."

6

I was glad to see Sophia there. It was high time she had a rest. She had come back from the war a changed woman, or perhaps the war had revealed the woman she was. I had never seen Lucy Evans's mother, but I had heard enough about her to know that she had been a resolute and self-reliant person, and Lucy herself, for all her beauty and apparent softness, had always known what she wanted and how to get it. This granddaughter of Lucy, this great-granddaughter of that now legendary old woman, had discovered what she wanted and had not been deflected from getting it. She had known the horror of the hospital wards in France. She had known them bombed in winter and had helped to carry screaming men out into the night of falling snow, to the tents run up hastily under the pine trees. She had watched maimed men, who would hardly be men again, leaving for England to meet the girls they were engaged to marry. She had seen the fear in their eyes as the badinage fell from their lips.

"How do I look, nurse?"

"Grand."

"Think she'll still love me?"

"Oh, never fear."

"Ah well, it'll be a job for her, anyway—official custodian of an ancient monument."

"She'll be proud of you."

"I wonder. D'you know, nurse, sometimes I bloody well wonder."

I knew that she meant it literally when she said to me: "I can never forget it—never—never."

She had not tried to. She laughed when Mervyn spoke to her of "picking up the threads of life."

"My dear Father," she said. "I haven't been dropping stitches. You should address yourself to Kathy."

It was a pity: that house was disrupted for good. Sophia would never forgive Kathy—not for Edward or for anything else. And Edward was gone, and Enid was gone.

Soon Sophia was gone, too; and it was because Kathy was all that he had that Mervyn clung to the poor creature who was now obviously dissolute as well as foolish. There she was, when she was at home, waking up every morning middle-aged, going out every night looking like an artificial gardenia.

I remembered the last scene I had witnessed between Kathy and Sophia. It was in the late summer of 1919. Sophia's bag—just one small bag—was in the hall, and we were finishing breakfast. Then Mervyn was to drive her to King's Cross to catch a northern train. She was going to begin nursing again at the beginning, as a hospital probationer. Later that week Kathy was to leave for the south of France, and she was full of it.

"It will be just incredible," she cried. "France again after all these years! Nancy Noble has been, and she says it's absolutely like old times. *Everybody's* there. I can't understand you, Sophy. Why don't you give up this dreary idea and come with us? Can you resist France?"

Sophia was eating sturdily as her sister's brittle fingers crumbled a few rusks. She looked up and said: "You forget, I have the advantage of you. I've *been* to France."

"Oh, that! The north. You don't call that *France,* do you?"

Sophia's silence was so full of contempt that Kathy cried: "All right. Everybody knows there's a Nightingale in Hanover Square. Well, go and dress your lousy ulcers, if that's your idea of a good time."

"Send me a postcard," Sophia said, "a nice blue sea and yachts to remind me of *France.* Let's be off, Father."

When they were gone, Kathy looked at me across the table and said furiously: "I could have done with a morning in bed. I get up after an exhausting night especially to see her off, and all I get . . ."

She caught my eye and faltered, and said: "*You* don't like me, either. Be honest. You don't, do you?"

I went round and patted her shoulder and kissed her on the forehead. "Go and finish your sleep," I said. "You'll be feeling better this evening with Sophia out of the way."

On the summer morning after my arrival at Tresant Haggie brought breakfast up to my bedroom, and this annoyed me.

"Why didn't someone wake me up, so that I could have breakfast with the rest of you?" I asked. "Understand once for all, I *never* have breakfast in bed. I *get up*."

"It was Miss Sophia's idea."

"Well, she'll have to change her ideas so far as I'm concerned. Take it away. I'll have a bath and be down in a quarter of an hour."

"All right. In one of your tantrums, eh?"

"No tantrums at all. I'm never in a tantrum, whatever a tantrum is. I'm a reasonable healthy woman who expects to be treated as such. That's all."

"So you got up after all?" said Sophia, sitting opposite me at the breakfast table.

"What d'you mean—after all? Of course I got up. What are *you* doing up? You don't look well."

"I'm not well. That's why I inflicted myself on you. D'you mind?"

"Of course I don't mind. What have you been up to?"

"Oh, just my usual carelessness. I picked up some septic trouble from a patient, and as I was pretty run down to begin with, it didn't do me much good. I've been in bed for nearly a month. As it's the first time I've ever been laid up, I found it rather humiliating."

"And you can think of nothing better to do than send breakfast up to me," I grumbled. "Why didn't you go to London? Your father's dying to see you."

"Kathy's there."

I sighed. What was there to do but sigh? "Poor Kathy! She leads a hard life."

"So do I," Sophia said without mercy. "Kathy is thirty-eight. She ought to have more sense—going round like a tenth-rate circus."

I let it stay at that. "Where is everybody?"

"Nika's taken Vera for a walk. Nicolas is in the stables with that nice chauffeur. Just imagine! I must have met him once. He was in my hospital for a time. I don't remember him, but he says he remembers me."

"What a heavenly morning it is! Let's go and see what they are up to."

They were thinking of building a punt. There had always been punts on the lake, but it was a long time since anyone had used them, and they were a pair of derelict water-logged things. In a corner of the stables someone at some time had set up a carpenter's bench, and here we found Nicolas and Henry Shape clicking their tongues over the condition of the tools. It was clear that to Henry tools were sacred things. If a temple had been desecrated he could not have been more annoyed than he was over the condition of this carpenter's outfit. "Never saw anything like it," he grumbled. "Marvelous stuff! Everything you want. I've dreamed of an outfit like this, and look at it! Everything rusty and seized up."

Outside, it was a blazing day. In here the coolth was grateful. Sophia and I sat on a couple of boxes and watched them: Henry in blue jeans, Nicolas with the sleeves of his red jersey rolled up over his elbows. Henry filed the teeth of a few saws, oiled them and hung them up. He sharpened chisels on a whirling stone. He unscrewed planes and knocked out the blades and sharpened them. He oiled the threads of wrenches and the joints of pliers. He gave Nicolas an oiled rag and a pile of bits and bade him rub them all down and arrange them in order of size in holes provided for the purpose.

"Oh, the hours you waste," Henry groaned, "through not having things in order! Just a rub of oil and the thing hanging in the right place . . ."

"Yes," said Sophia, "our surgeons would be pretty livid if everything wasn't there to be handed up on the dot."

"Exactly," Henry said, looking at her with a smile. "You've got the idea."

"Aunt Sophy, have you ever cut a man's leg off?" Nicolas demanded.

"Now, now, Nicky," Henry said, "your aunt's on holiday, so give her a rest from professional matters. Get hold of this. Did you ever see such a mess?"

He handed the boy a great box of screws of all sorts and sizes. "Now sort them out on the bench there. All the steel screws in one pile, all the brass in another. And when that's done, arrange each pile in sizes. We'll have to get a lot of boxes to put 'em in. And when that's done, there's those bolts. All the nuts are seized. Screw 'em loose and put oil in the threads."

"When do we begin to build the punt?" Nicolas wanted to know.

"Perhaps tomorrow. It depends. We'll begin when the tools are ready. Not before. We'll draw some plans tonight. Have a look round for copper nails. We'll need hundreds."

8

Henry Shape ate his meals at our table, as Haggie had always done. It hadn't taken him and Nicolas long to become Henry and Nicky to one another, and Nika saw little enough of her son that holiday. He and Henry were out swimming in the lake before breakfast, and I made it my business to go down once and watch them, for Nicolas wasn't much of a swimmer. But I didn't need to go twice. Henry swam superbly: I felt that half a dozen boys would be safe with him, let alone one. They would come back, rosy from toweling and running, and eat like horses. Then off they would go to the now orderly carpenter's shop, and work would go forward on the punt.

One morning Nika said to me: "Sophy takes a deep-rooted interest in carpentry—don't you think?"

"Well," I said rather dishonestly, "it *is* interesting to see a thing like that done from the very beginning. I often look in myself."

"So do I. Looking in's one thing. Sophy's never out of the place."

"Do you think that's a bad idea, darling?"

"I shall express no opinion one way or the other. I just wondered whether you'd noticed—that's all."

"Doubtless," I said, "Sophy likes to be there because Nicky's enthusiasm is such a lovely thing. She's very fond of him."

"I don't doubt Nicky's enthusiasm. It was a business yesterday to get him to spend an afternoon with me and Vera for once. When we got back he went straight to the carpenter's shop. Henry Shape had been carrying on with the job, and Sophy was there as usual. So perhaps it's not Nicky."

"No. I admit that there could be another explanation."

The day came for the launching, and the hull, gleaming with varnish, was carried to the water, everyone bearing a hand: Henry and Nicolas, Nika and Sophia, Haggie and some boys from the garden. She was laid on the grass, her nose in the water, with a long rope attached to her, to hold her when she was afloat. Nothing to be done save the shove off. Henry turned to Sophia and asked: "Will you do the launch, Miss Sophia?" Sophia bent down to push, and Haggie said: "I hope she floats." Nicolas looked with contempt at such a doubter. "*Henry* made her," he said firmly.

"You did your bit, old son," said Henry.

Sophia pushed, and out she slid, moving slowly to the length of the rope and then coming to a stand, a neat, well-balanced craft with the sun twinkling on her varnish.

It was just before one o'clock. "Leave her there now. We'll paddle round a bit after lunch, Nicky," Henry said. "And we'd better haul out those water-logged wrecks and dry 'em, and get them in order, too."

We walked back to the house, Sophia and I some distance behind the others, and I said to her: "I had a letter from your father this morning. Kathy's on the wing again and he's feeling lonely."

"Oh, dear! D'you mean I ought to go to London?"

"Please yourself."

498

"It's so lovely here."

"There are times when it's lovely anywhere."

She looked at me sharply and said: "Sometimes I think you see too much."

"Well, I've seen a few odd things in my time, and no one would take me for a fool."

"I think I'd better go to London."

"How old are you, Sophia?"

"Thirty-five."

"Well, then, you're no chicken. You're old enough to know what you're doing."

"I'm not so old that I wouldn't value your advice."

"Have you ever been in love before?"

She thought for a moment, then said: "I don't think so. No. Not seriously. No, I certainly haven't been. Only full of pity."

I could well imagine that her mind was back in the wartime hospital and that she had had experience enough there.

"It's a compliment in a way that you should ask for my advice," I said. "All the same, I'm reluctant to give it. I've given advice before, and regretted it. Can't you settle this for yourself?"

We walked a few paces in silence: then she said: "Very well, I'll settle it for myself."

That was the loveliest day of the holiday. After dinner there was a moon coming up and the air was breathless, the trees, weighted with summer, standing like great ships becalmed with all sail set. We walked out of the house into the hush of the evening, and I felt it was with intention that Nika took the children, one by each hand, and walked them away from the lake. "Come and see the glow-worms," she said. "I know a hedge that should be full of them." So did I know it. It was in the churchyard, and always these little creatures shone there, a puny galaxy; and I had heard Eddy Rodda say that they were the spirits of the dead. Well they might be, I thought, so small a light we leave behind us, in so great a surrounding darkness.

So we stood there in the still-warm evening air outside the house, Henry and Sophia and I, and the moon was fully up now over the eastern land beyond the lake, a half moon, but giving light; and I could feel the uneasiness of them and their desire; and I said: "Why don't you two take the punt out onto the lake?"

"Thank you," Henry said simply; and they walked away, following the path that skirted the stables and led to the landing place. It went, beyond the stables, through trees, and as they entered the trees' shadow I saw Sophia take his arm.

I walked up and down there for a long time, feeling very lonely, very old; and then I myself went the way they had gone, went on

499

beyond the landing stage to the path through the wood along the lake. Oh, how it was in me, the very blood and bone of me, that stony track with the trees on the rising to the right, and on the left the water shining through the trees that grew there too! I could walk it blindfold. It is here my glow-worm will twinkle when the time comes.

Halfway to the bar, I sat down on a boulder that was still warm, at a spot where the black pines stood on either hand and between them the water stretched before my view. After a time, Nika, who had put the children to bed and followed me, came and sat without a word alongside me, and took my hand, and together we listened to the furtive night scurry of the undergrowth and the trembling whimper of owls and the heart-breaking loneliness of the curlews' crying. We saw the punt break through the sequins of the moon's path, moving slowly, as though unforgettable moments were to be savored and stored up, as though in a pathetic desire that the always fugitive instant of loveliness should endure; and Nika said quietly: "I must be getting very old, darling, when I can take such an interest in someone else's love affair. And, after all, I *am* forty."

I squeezed her hand, with my heart full of love and pity. He had been dead for eight years. Already, she had been robbed of all those years.

The punt had passed into darkness. It was a hardly discernible shadow, scarcely moving against the deeper shadows of the land. "I remember being out there with Edward. Often. On nights just like this."

And I with Daniel. The hungry generations tread us down.

"I am very glad for Sophy," Nika said.

"Yes," I agreed. "I am glad for both of them. They've waited a long time, and they are good people."

"Yes," said Nika, "they are." From under her hands pressed down to the ground the scent of bruised thyme rose up like the lost fragrance of her years. "I'm sure they are good people. But that doesn't always count, does it?"

CHAPTER TWENTY-EIGHT

I

I WAS glad that I might still go to the house in St. John's Wood when I wished to. It was as much part of me as Tresant. I was a foolish little girl when first I went to live there with Maggie Whale. I had become a woman there, and I had seen the house pass to my daughter, and my two grandchildren had been born in it. I had often talked there with Lucy Evans, and now the place was lived in by Lucy's granddaughter Sophia and her husband, Henry Shape. At the time of their marriage, Nika decided to give up this house and to live altogether in the country cottage that Maggie had left her. And so Sophia bought the St. John's Wood house, and I could go there occasionally and look at the nude lady standing in the pond and at the mulberry tree, and I could feel the days of my years flow round me. It was a happy house. Any ghosts I might encounter there would have no chains to clank. It had known the earthy laughter of Glory Jane and the warm sanity of Maggie, to whom, I often thought, I owed more than to anyone I had known. Nika had been happy here, and now Sophia had found happiness with Henry Shape.

It is small wonder, then, that in my gathering loneliness I was often there. And I *was* lonely. Life was closing, contracting, shutting me into a narrowing cell, from whose slit I looked back along my road and salved my moments and set them down. It had become my great consolation, doing this.

Six years had passed since Nika and I sat by the lake at Tresant and watched the punt. In the June of the first of those years—1925—we were with Sophia and her husband in Yorkshire. Henry, as he had reason to be, was proud of his bride, and he had gone north in order that she might meet some of his relatives. The Shapes hailed from Malton. Henry's uncle had a shop there in a back street where bicycles were sold, and cycling accessories, electric torches, and small mechanical bric-a-brac of one sort and another. It was in this shop, a growing boy, that Henry had made his first discoveries in mechanics.

The more I saw of Sophia the more I liked the girl, and I liked nothing better than her readiness, even her eagerness, to meet Henry's people. In accepting him, she accepted all that he was and all that he came from, which was sensible enough seeing what she had come from herself a generation or two back—a peer on the one hand and Eddy Rodda on the other!

But what I want to write about here is not Henry Shape's forebears but an experience that befell me and Nika. Mervyn proposed a holiday in the north, and we went in two motorcars, Henry driving one which carried himself and his wife and Nicolas, and Mervyn taking me and Nika and little Vera. We had a splendid time along the coast and among the moors inland from Whitby, and for the only time in my life I saw the Cleveland hills from which the iron had come to make the Rainborough fortune; and toward the end of that June we were all in Malton, ready for the journey home. I had never been in York Minster, and I wished to see it. There was but the morrow left: on the day after that we were to set out for the South. And on the morrow, I found, we would not see the Minster in its customary condition: a service was to be held at which the famous six-hundred-year-old Five Sisters window, cleaned and renovated, was to be unveiled as a memorial to the women of the British Empire who had died on active service during the war.

It was at this service of unveiling and dedication that Nika and I found ourselves the next day. I remember that soldiers, not vergers, showed us into our seats. I remember the huge congregation and the uniforms scattered among the civilian clothes, and the organ pealing, and my mind went back through the years and I was holding my mother's hand and we were waiting for the Queen as I dreamed of peace on earth. And now we were waiting for a woman who was to be a queen, though then it seemed unlikely; and she came dressed in gray, with a blue hat, and her husband, who was to be a king, was with her in a soldier's uniform. I remember the Duchess of York pulling a string and the tall white veil falling from the window and the light coming, as it had come six hundred years before, through the pearly subtlety of the glass. There it had been, I thought, for all those years, and throughout all those years men had fought in this land and in all other lands, and never once till now had women fought, but we had put that right. Now for the first time, not as inspired individuals like St. Joan, not in casual and accidental units, but as organized forces, women had fought, and here were commemorated 1,465 of them who had died; and this wonder of stained glass that for six hundred years had filtered a gentle light into the huge dusky building would have a new and terrible significance. It would remind us that the creative mother henceforth must bear a part in destroying her sons.

I had hardly noticed that the Archbishop of York was speaking, so far back and so far forward my thoughts had been ranging, but now Cosmo's ripe authoritative voice reached my ears, and it was saying that amid all the multitude of monuments in churches and streets and on village greens there had so far been none that specially and expressly commemorated the women who had given their lives to the Empire. Well, I thought, that bitter reproach is now removed: we have advanced to that point. The rotund voice went on, wrapping itself with sonorous affection around its own eloquence, assuring us that the old mother, the Minster, would now, as it were, adopt these women and girls as her own and enfold them with her silence and her peace.

We sat there, a silent and consenting congregation, and allowed the rounded blasphemies to go by undenied. Yes, the Minster would enfold in the silence and peace of death the names of those who had untimely died; and whose deaths, I thought with a shudder, would surely be, when the time came round again, not a warning of what must not be done but a precedent for what all women now must do. There would be no going back once the death dance had begun along that path. "The gates of pearl" the Archbishop called the window, but now, I said, you might as well write over it *Fanua mortis* and have done with it.

The sweet voices of choir boys were trilling, sending birdlike notes up into the roof—For all thy saints, who from their labor rest—and as I stood for the singing and felt Nika's hand hot in mine my heart was rebellious still; and I thought: Saints, indeed! That's one way of getting out of it. Put them all in haloes! But they were sinners like the rest of us, and why we should bless the name of Jesus because they rest from their labors I don't know. Their labors had hardly begun, poor young things, and they, at any rate, you may be sure, would have been well pleased to go on with them.

But the drums were the worst of it. "The Last Post" and "Reveille" were bad enough, the sad, lost notes of silver wandering through the caverns of stone; and then, while we stood in a great silence as they died away, there came the drums, a quiet rolling at first, coming from some hidden place, rising, rising, rising, till it was a tremendous sound like a wind rushing through every chink and cranny of the building. Four or five times the sound sank, rose again in that tremendous crescendo, and froze the marrow of my bones. The very walls that had withstood the centuries seemed to tremble, and in my hand Nika's hand was trembling like a captive bird, and Sleep well, little sisters, I thought. They've done you proud.

2

Mervyn had not belonged to all my life. He was not alive during those early years in Portman Square: the years of Papa and Mama, of Mercy Kite and old Ducat, of bowling through the Park at Mama's side; the years that came to an end when my thoughtless question about the plaster cherub's belly button loosed catastrophe—catastrophe from which emerged the salvation of Maggie Whale. It seemed no time at all, as I searched my memory of those old days, which I now so constantly did, scribbling away in my lonely room, no time at all after Maggie's coming that we were at Tresant, standing outside Eddy Rodda's lodge, watching the slip of a girl who was Lucy Evans run, crying, toward Porteven, carrying her child with her, pursued by Mrs. Rodda's angry voice. The child was Mervyn, nine years younger than I was, and ever after that day his life threaded in and out of mine with more or less emphasis. These children, Nicolas and Vera, were his grandchildren and mine. He was the nearest thing I had to a contemporary. At times, those who saw us together might well think him the elder. The years were heavy on him in the empty house. The shine of that fantastic moment when he had found Enid penniless in the shop and their young hearts had suddenly flowed together had not tarnished through all their married years. They were in love to the end; and it was the end of so much else, too. Edward was dead; Sophia was gone, and soon thereafter Kathy found herself a flat in a mews. She said she wanted to live her own life. Heaven knows, her occasional, her less and less frequent, sojourns in Hanover Square had not prevented her from living it, such as it was. It couldn't go on much longer, anyway, I reflected. The years themselves would see to that, as they saw to so much. Kathy couldn't go on being one of the bright young things, as the phrase was in that decade, with middle-age closing quickly about her, do what she would with rest homes and beauty-parlors and dressmakers. But she was rich. It would be some time before she had the shame of knowing that that was why she was tolerated.

And so Mervyn and I drew closer together. I always went down, at this time, to dine with him, and sometimes we would ring up Julian Rimmel and ask him to join us, and sometimes Julian would ask us to his flat and spread himself on one of his small superb meals. He was twenty years younger than Mervyn, nearly thirty years younger than I, but his life had matured him. "I have had a bit of being a married man and don't want any more of it," he said. "I have had a bit of being a soldier and don't want any more of that, either. I am learning how much one can do without, which is the art of living, as of cooking. Small perfection. I have even learned to do without being a Frenchman. Does the British nation approve, do you think, *ma chère tante*, now that I have taken out a life subscription?"

"Well, we absorbed the Normans, and I suppose we shall manage to digest you," I said. "I remember that years ago Maggie Whale talked to me about how languages grew, how we took in masses of French words with the Normans. . . ." And there we were, back at Maggie Whale, back at some old day or other. It was surprising how much of our talk now was reminiscence. And Mervyn and I would stroll back to Hanover Square, arm-in-arm, warm with Julian's coffee and old brandy.

When we didn't go out, his habit now was to come up to my room. It was the coziest, most intimate room in the house and we were without ceremony. He would sit by the fire in his old comfortable slippers, reading, smoking his pipe, and I would sit at my writing table and get on with the task that was absorbing me. It was useful to have him there. I consulted him about things that had eluded me. We pooled our memories.

One night he laid down his book and said: "I don't think, Sarah, that I want any more of London or of business. I've started things moving toward selling Mostyn-Lloyd's and this house, too. I'm past seventy. Time I had a rest. I shall go and live altogether at Coppocks. I may even sell that. I don't know yet. But something much smaller would suit me."

"My good man," I said, "you can't do that sort of thing. I've been here for ten years now."

"What's wrong with Tresant?"

"Nothing, as you well know. You know, too, that most of my time is spent in London and that I loathe hotels."

"You could go into a service flat."

"I could also learn this new stuff they call dancing and go out to night clubs. But I don't intend to."

He came to my table and took a long envelope from his pocket and opened the paper it contained. "Look at this," he said. "I didn't want to break the news till things had been arranged. When I said I was thinking of selling this place I meant that I had already sold it. It won't be a house any more. Well, it hasn't been a house for a long time, has it?— not to me. It's just a place that reminds me of things I had better forget. I feel like a bird hanging onto a nest in winter, when the singing's over and the young ones are gone. But birds don't. They have more sense."

"What are you up to? I feel suspicious when a prosy merchant prince tries out a tag of poetry." But I was sad for him even as I twitted him. It was not only the young ones who were gone.

"Well," he said, "these are the plans. The place will become offices. This thing here is an outside lift. It's fortunate that we've got an end wall. We build an up-ended brick tube here, at this point"—he indicated with the stem of his pipe—"put a lift in it, and break a way through at the top into this floor. It simply means that you don't have to come through the house, and no one in the house can get at you. It was a condition of the sale."

"You all think of the old woman, don't you?" I said, deeply touched.

"Well, this flat is almost historic. Old Gotherson worked here for years, happy as a mole. You can have his ghost to keep you company."

And it wasn't his ghost only. They were crowding in upon me, the many ghosts—I knew now more ghosts than living people—and in that room, when the alterations were done, I could go on with my task of calling them about me. I could no longer go down to the house for my meals, or ring a bell and have them brought up; and so from this time Haggie Chadderton became my companion whether I was in London or Cornwall. A box room was turned into a kitchen. For days on end I saw no one but Haggie, and if I wanted other company I would stroll along to Julian in Bond Street or go for a week end to Nika's cottage in the country.

3

I am still writing about the life before the Second World War, but the *time* of writing is when that war was over. Here I am at Tresant, and here I am likely to stay. My revels now are ended. I was never much of a traveler, except in time. So far as that goes I have had an exceptional allowance. But I did enjoy moving to and fro between here and London, and living in London. It gave me something to complain about. In London I could think of the peace of Tresant, and at Tresant I could long for the pulse of London's life. I always seemed to live the more truly in the one when I was in the other. It is the sort of weather we are having here this morning that especially makes me think of London, though thinking is as far as it will get this time. It is early spring. The air is warm and damp, and the camellias are blooming in their thousands. If I could transplant to this place some poor wretch who is at this moment tramping the pavement of Threadneedle Street or the Strand, he would think he had arrived in paradise; and all the thanks I can give is to feel in my heart a longing for an astringent London morning in autumn.

Well, I shall treat myself to one on paper: to an October morning in 1930. Haggie came down in the lift with me. She always did. She seemed to think there was a mystery in the manipulation of the thing that only she had mastered. Flinging open the bottom gate, she let me out into the street. "Here's your stick," she said. "Are you sure you ought to walk? I could call a taxi."

"Of course I ought to walk. What d'you take me for—a valetudinarian?"

"You're an octogenarian, anyway."

"That's more than you'll ever be if you don't use the legs God gave you."

"All right. You're in one of your moods. Mind how you cross the streets. Look out for the cars."

"The cars can look out for me."

"You'll be brought home on a shutter yet."

"Don't buoy yourself up with foolish hopes," I said, sniffing the keen air.

It was a lovely morning for a dodder and I doddered to Bond Street and had my morning coffee and a cream bun. Then I crossed the road to Rimmel's and looked at the Jacobean chairs in the window, heavy overcarved things that I detested, standing by a table whose legs had bulbs like a prize-fighter's biceps. I went in to tell Julian what I thought of them, and found Nika and Vera there.

"Oh, Mother!" Nika cried. "Are you out by yourself again?"

"You talk as though I had escaped from Bedlam. Of course I'm out by myself."

Vera giggled. "Mother is very maternal," she said. "She thinks everybody is either too young or too old to be out alone. I, of course, am too young."

"Well, so you are," I told her. "You're only sixteen."

"Seventeen."

"Well, seventeen. Don't try to impress *me* with your seventeen. I'm eighty-two. I hope," I said to Nika, "you're not thinking of spending any money here? They rob you right and left in this place."

"I'm looking for something nice for Nicolas. He's nineteen next week."

"Well, we'd better hound down Julian and get a reduction." I called one of the ambassadors who came gliding over the mossy carpet. "Is Mr. Rimmel in?"

"He's in his rooms, madam. I'll ring him."

We went up, and Julian was standing looking out of the window at the thin autumn sunshine on the roofs and chimneys. He did not turn as we entered, and I cried: "Come now! This is a fine time of day to be studying slate and brick."

He turned then, and I saw that something had deeply disturbed him, but, with Vera there, I let it go for the moment, and Nika bought what she wanted and soon she and her daughter went. We sat down then and he lit a cigarette, and I asked: "What is it?"

"What is what?"

"My dear Julian . . ."

"Oh, very well. You don't miss much, and you'd have had to know sooner or later. Poor Fournier has committed suicide."

The stark sudden words left me without words of my own. I waited for him to go on. "If he had only *told* me!" Julian said. "The poor fool! It was so unnecessary. Did he think me a monster?"

He had been talking for some time of bringing Fournier back from New York. In America the storm had burst during the year before this. Ruin was widespread, with banks in the dust and millionaires glad of any job that would keep body and soul together. Rimmel's branch in New York had been closed for some time. Fournier had stayed on merely as a watching agent. "This tells it all," Julian said, handing me a letter he had received from a New York lawyer.

In the halcyon years, few but golden, Rimmel's had reaped a fortune from America, and Robert Fournier had prospered like the rest of us. He had invested his money, every cent, in American securities, and the securities had proved insecure. He had found himself penniless save for his salary, which, after all, was something many Americans at that time would have liked to have. "In an endeavor to straighten out his situation," said the letter, "he played fast and loose with the Rimmel funds that were at his disposal and I have to advise you that a considerable loss must be expected in this direction." And then, with his own money gone, and unable to face the discovery of what he had done with the firm's money, poor

Fournier had joined the procession of suicides, who were plentiful enough in New York, God knows, to provide a contagious example. The loss of a few thousand pounds would not make all that difference to Rimmel's. What was hurting Julian was the loss of his friend, and, more even than that, the thought that in extremity his friend had not turned to him. To me, wandering home, it was the opening of another door upon this disastrous world. What was wrong—what was the matter with us all—that, having torn millions of young lives to bloody ribbons in the name of sanity, we still, ten years later, were in an asylum like this?

4

This breakdown of the economic life of a great nation was called a "depression," as though one were dealing with a person who was a bit off color at breakfast but could be put right with a pick-me-up by noon. What the "depression" really amounted to I had learned from letters that Mervyn sent me. He had passed through the United States to the West Coast and thence gone on toward the islands and Australia. I didn't know what he was looking for—something he would never find, I suspected—but, having sold Mostyn-Lloyd's and his houses, he was like a ship whose moorings have been pulled up. He had to keep moving. He was still away. He had wanted Kathy to go with him, but she had refused. They had, at the same moment, reached opposite desires. Mervyn had not traveled much, and now he persuaded himself, not wisely I think, that this had been a great loss and that the one thing necessary to him was to be on the move. Kathy had been on the move for years, though always with the same stupid people, and now, at the age of forty-three, she had come to rest and couldn't be budged. Toward the end, she had not even bothered to let us know where she was, but an odd cat or two would occasionally drop a hint that she had done with one man and had taken up with another, or that she was "taking a rest" somewhere in the country.

It was from one of the discreet "nursing homes" to which she resorted that Mervyn had received a letter, and had in consequence asked me to go down there with him; and there we had been told by the doctor who ran the place that Kathy was once more "cured," but that, for her health and sanity's sake, she had better avoid the necessity of being "cured" again. We had a talk with Kathy, walking among the roses in a charming garden, the old house dreaming in the sun behind us. I couldn't believe it. I couldn't believe that I had walked here before, down these sloping lawns to the river, and that I had found Edward there, wearing uniform and dreaming of Nika. But this was it. This was old Fortescue's place, and he was dead, and death duties had been paid, and his son had inherited, already an aging man, and he had died, too, and more death duties had been paid, and that was the end of the Fortescues in that place. So now it was more nobly employed in the salvage of wealthy wrecks. Kathy must have been a *Golden Hind*.

She knew nothing of the associations of this place in my mind, nothing of my meeting here with her brother whom she had sentenced to death; and this was as well, or her "cure" would perhaps not have gone so smoothly. You may be sure that I said nothing of it to her as she hung onto my arm, walking there in that haunted place. She didn't hang heavily. I felt as though I were supporting a few clothed bones, the specter of the beautiful Miss Mostyn-Lloyd.

Mervyn and I might have been trained in the most suave and evasive school of diplomacy. We spoke of her "illness" as of a child's on the mend after measles, and poor Mervyn told her of his prolonged world tour and wondered whether going with him wasn't the thing to put her back on her feet again. But Kathy wasn't having diplomacy, and, little as there was about her that I had ever had reason to admire, I admired her frankness in this crisis. "It's the last thing in the world I should want," she said to her father, without even a word of thanks. "Here I am. Look at me!" She detached herself from my arm and confronted us, a gaunt middle-aged woman with sunken features and withered hair. "Do I look as if I'm up to hurtling round the earth? Leave me alone. I know where I stand, and if it gives you any consolation to hear me say it, I'll say I know what a fool I am to be standing there. I always thought I could do without the lot of you, and I'm not going to start barging in now. I'll do without you still. And without everybody else. You can believe that. I've done with them all. I shall find a hole and stay there."

It sounded valiant, but it was self-deceiving, for the fact obviously was that they had done with her.

We had wandered right down to the water. I stood looking at a forlorn punt there, and wondered whether it was the one in which Edward had punted me, and after me, Nika. You are going to be very lonely, Kathy, I thought. Nika will never forgive you, never see you again, or Sophia either.

"Well," said Mervyn, jingling the coins in his pocket as we all stood watching the sun-bright water glance by, "we'd better get back, eh?"

There's no getting back, my dear. Here, where I had frivolously been a truant as Daniel died; here, where Edward had been young and troubled; here, of all places, I know that there's no getting back.

I was thinking of these things as I strolled slowly along Bond Street on leaving Julian. They brought Kathy back to my mind, which had jumbled from Fournier's death to Mervyn's letters from the States, and from that to his offer to take Kathy with him. That was now nearly two years ago, and I was glad Kathy had not gone. "I'll do without everybody," she had said: a silly boast, because she could never do without the cunning little Welsh draper whose money was still pouring into her pockets. And, as it happened, she had found some human company. It was still not twelve o'clock and I resolved on an impulse to call on her and Bob Seagrim. I liked Bob Seagrim, and I was sure he was good for Kathy. He had been in and out of her life as long as I could remember. He was older than she—he couldn't be far off fifty now—and in the days before the war he seemed to turn up wherever she was, and, like herself, he was what they call a "must" for the society photographers. How often I had seen the list ended with the words "and the Honorable 'Bob' Seagrim." He was the younger brother of a peer who had beaten him to the title and a ruinous poverty-stricken estate by half an hour—"the most profitable half hour of my life," he would say. "Though, come to think of it, it *wasn't* my life, was it? I wasn't there—what? Hanging back at the tape, to let old Charles get away to the thorns and ditches—what?"

However, if not in a metaphorical way, at any rate in fact, he was always to be found among the thorns and ditches, always riding someone else's horse, putting up in someone else's house, fitted up with someone else's guns for shooting, and invited to someone else's yacht or villa on the Riviera. He had won the National Hunt Cup at Cheltenham and ridden twice in the Grand National. In that formidable race he had been thrown at the first obstacle with an immense field thundering about him. "Just rolled myself under the hedge. Only thing to do—what? Looked up and saw 'em all flashing over my head. Extraordinary sight. All those bellies—what."

He had broken most of his bones and many hearts, but he wouldn't marry a girl without a fortune, and the fathers of girls with fortunes were not impressed by the Honorable Bob Seagrim. I don't imagine that he worried much about it one way or the other. They were happy days for him: horses, guns and fishing rods were always at his disposal, and his mind didn't really exist outside these things and their use.

He had proposed to Kathy with great regularity, small seriousness, and no hope. "There it is, Kath. Not a bean. Never have had. Never will have—what. Still, what d'you say?"

I knew there was a deep fondness between them; but I had lost sight of Bob Seagrim and didn't know that as Kathy's stock fell in the circles she frequented—"Poor old thing! Why doesn't she face it? She'd had it"—Seagrim was always about, touched with the same despair that was now hastening its footstep behind her in the quiet of every night. The war had done him no good. One leg was gone and one eye. He hid the socket behind a black patch. Gas had touched his lungs and bursts of coughing shook him. Horses to lend were not so common and he couldn't ride them, anyway. With his usual valor he learned to get round a dance floor on his wooden leg, but who wanted to gaze into that black shutter which might open on so much better forgotten? And too many of those who had liked to have Bob Seagrim about were not about themselves: they had made their last appearance in print, not in the society columns but in the casualty lists.

In a night club Kathy had been accompanied by a boy half her age, and Seagrim, sitting at a table near theirs, had watched Kathy literally sag into her seat at the end of a dance. He had heard the youth say: "Look, darling, why don't you go home? Get to bed. You're not up to this sort of thing, you know."

It had been suggested before. This was the first time it had been directly and brutally said, with a smile and a warm pressure of the hand. She said to the young man: "Get me my cloak." The night was young—for a night club. People watched, curious, amused, as the boy brought the cloak and put it round her. "Excuse me, darling, won't you, if I stay?"

Seagrim saw Kathy take a note from her bag, but before it reached the boy's hand he moved between them. "If the little sod doesn't fulfill his contract, he can pay for his own fun—what?" he said loudly. He gave Kathy his arm out of the room, collected his coat and hat, and took her in a taxi to the ridiculous flat in a mews that she had then. A few days later he drove her to the nursing home in the Fortescue house. He was a faithful visitor there, and when Kathy came out and began reassembling what was left of her life he was at hand. She bought and furnished a house in South Audley Street, and that was her address ever after. She no longer lived at addresses on winged post-cards. She became her age—and worn and haggard she was for her age. She did not go out or ask people in. Except Bob Seagrim. He came in and stayed in. I don't for a moment suppose they ever went to bed together. They lived like married people who had separate bedrooms. They were old friends who had met occasionally on a road leading to nothing, but now they were there, and they took what comfort they could in one another. Neither of them cared a button what anyone thought of the arrangement. Bob Seagrim became well-dressed and had a good motorcar with a special arrangement of the works to suit his one-leggedness. He was a member of some good clubs and spent a lot of time in them. But he never failed to be home for the evening meal and he never went out after it, unless to a theater with Kathy. She paid for it all, and was certainly getting the best value her money had ever brought her.

And so on that autumn morning I looked them up in South Audley Street. "I was telling Kath about the widgeon," Bob Seagrim said. "You never saw such a thing. I was staying with the Forbes-Fenwicks in Norfolk. You know Percy Forbes-Fenwick—what? Well, the widgeon were on some mudflats near their place. Four acres of 'em. I've told this to people before and they don't believe it. One acre is common enough—even two. But four acres—that's something. They were so close not another could have got down among 'em. I suppose you know widgeon, Mrs. Undridge?"

"Only a nodding acquaintance. I've never been properly introduced to them with a gun."

"I call it a pretty bird to watch on the water—what? Well, we put a few shot into that lot."

"I should have thought in the circumstances machine guns would have been more scientific."

Major Seagrim looked puzzled. "Machine guns? Oh, no. You couldn't do that with widgeon! Pretty barbarous—what?"

"Yes, I suppose it would be—with widgeon."

"Rather."

"Bob," Kathy said, "you trot along to the club now."

"Oh, is it time? Right. Well, see you this evening, Kath."

We watched him go, and I said: "I like your Bob."

"So do I," she answered. "It's as good as having twenty years of the *Tatler*'s files in the house. What more can I ask?"

6

They were an endless source of amusement and interest to me, the two men who had finally landed the beautiful Misses Mostyn-Lloyd. My brief acquaintance with Henry Shape before the war and during the holiday when he found Sophia in Cornwall made me wonder what his reaction would be to marriage with a rich woman. They had been married now for five years and I had the answer. Henry had taken an engineering degree at Cambridge and had then joined the research staff of an airplane construction company. His one idea of how to use Sophia's money had been to fit himself to earn his own. "If the worst comes to the worst now," he said, "Sophy won't starve," and I smiled at the thought of the worst coming to the worst with

Mostyn-Lloyd money. I knew something of its spread over all sorts of profit-bearing concerns, so that even if some of them went—and they were not likely to—Sophia would not feel much of a draft. She had fallen in happily with Henry's wishes, encouraged them, even, for the last thing she wanted was a household parasite. She poured out money for Henry, but always in the direction of his personal ambition and ultimate independence. She wouldn't live in rooms at Cambridge but rented a house there, and she bought a Rolls Royce car in which at the week ends they would come home to St. John's Wood. And now that Henry was working in Buckinghamshire she bought a cottage there. They were as happy as I had expected them to be, with a quiet happiness that made me think of a fire that had begun with a glowing established heart and had never known the fierce crackle and skyward rush when the young flame strikes. Their love could warm them, but never consume them. They loved one another's qualities, but they were not in love with one another for better or worse. It would be a bad lookout for them, I sometimes thought, if either fell below a certain standard that the other obviously had in mind. But I was sure that this would not happen. They were now just in their forties: old enough for their qualities to be established. After five years of marriage they had no children. Vera and Nicolas were the only members of a new generation.

Nicolas was waiting for me when I got back from Kathy's house that morning. I knew he would be there, for his car was in the street, and you could not mistake Nicolas's car, a scarlet wasp of a thing, open to all the winds of heaven, that buzzed angrily for a moment when he got into it, and then shot away like a bullet. "No thirty-five an hour for me, Grandmama."

Nicolas would be going up to Oxford in a few days' time, He kissed me, and Haggie said: "Don't be rough with her."

"You'd better put me in a case and have done with it, my girl," I said.

"Well, you've been wambling about all the morning. I expect you're exhausted."

"I haven't been wambling: I've been walking, as I always do. And I'm as fresh as a daisy. Well, Nicolas, what's brought you here?"

"I'm going to take you to the Café Royal," he said. "And you jolly nearly missed it. Fortunately, I've got a table booked, but we'll have to rush all the same."

"That's the last thing she ought to do, Mr. Nicolas," Haggie said. "She ought to lie down for ten minutes, and then eat her lunch here. You ring up and cancel the table and eat with us."

"Nonsense!" I said. "Nicolas, we'll go in your car. And step on the gas!"

But he was a sensible boy, and didn't. "Where d'you think I could park this thing?" he asked. "We must leave it here and take a taxi."

"Let me sit down here a moment," I said when we were in the vestibule.

"Sorry, Grandmama. Have I tired you?"

"No. I'm never tired—except of being coddled. I want to have a look at a few ghosts."

"Oh, is that all? Right you are, then. Tell me about them when we get inside, will you?"

I saw them very clearly, and I told him about them.

"They're a pretty antique collection of spooks," he said. "You wouldn't have to go much farther back to have 'em gibbering in gyves."

"Well, there they were. Your great-grandmother was waiting for her son, your grandfather. She was getting on in years then, but she was looking her loveliest. And women dressed then to help their loveliness. That day she really was superb. But look at women now! God help us—look at that pair!"

"They don't look bad to me," he grinned. "Especially the little 'un with the tip-up nose. Look at her leg."

"Ah well, I suppose every generation must see with its own eyes. I'll have onion soup, dry toast and nothing else. Your grandfather came in dressed up to the nines, too. They could carry it in those days."

"I've seen photographs of 'em. I must say they were a sight for sore eyes. But give me flannel bags with a collar that doesn't cut your throat. What about a bit of cold chicken?"

"Very well then. And a lettuce heart. Positively nothing else. That was the first day I ever saw your grandmother. There she was, a slip of a thing in dusky red, looking shy and very sweet."

"Talking of sweets. While the waiter's here let's order and have done with it. The crème caramel's pretty good as a rule."

"All right. But I positively must have no more than that. I keep my health by eating very little. I'll just follow that with coffee and brandy. Nothing else. Your grandmother was sitting over there. And I was sitting here with Maggie Whale. Just away there on our right was her publisher. And who d'you think was with him?"

"No idea. Chaucer? Some old ghost with his head under his arm?"

"George Meredith."

"Oh. That's a new one. Who was he? I know the family saga pretty well. Where does George come in?"

"Good God, boy! What do you read?"

"Nothing, if I can help it."

"What are you going to Oxford for?"

514

"Oh, I don't know. What does one go to Oxford for? I mean except for the ultimate purpose of having gone to Oxford?"

"What are you going to do when you come down? And what's that you're pouring into my glass?"

"Hock, darling."

"I never drink anything but water at lunchtime. But you'd better let it stay. Tell the waiter I'd like a little more of that chicken. The tiniest bit. Well, what are you going to do?"

"I don't know. Something to do with Henry's show, I hope. They keep on evolving new types. I'd like to be in on trying 'em out. I'd like to be a test pilot."

"You'd probably be as sick as a dog."

"Oh, no. I've had a go, and I'm all right. I've been up occasionally with Henry."

"So *he* flies, does he?"

"Not much. But you know what Henry is. If he's doing a thing at all he likes to do it from A to Z. And so, as he's in on designing planes, he likes to know something about conditions in the air. So he took his pilot's certificate."

"What's Vera going to do?"

"Oh, she's crazy. She has an affinity with all four-footed things. I'm surprised she doesn't go about on all fours herself."

"Well, I must say my grandchildren have the most extraordinary tastes."

"Yes. My tastes are so extraordinary that I'm going to eat Camembert on top of crème caramel. Will you join me?"

"No."

"Not just the tiniest . . . ?"

"Well . . ."

"That's the spirit. Your brandy'll settle everything down into a most harmonious understanding."

"I must say you're learning young to do yourself proud."

"Well," he said with a sudden gravity, "one has to start young nowadays—don't you think?—if one is to start at all."

"And what may you mean by that?"

"Well—ah, here's the brandy. Let us leave philosophy alone and give ourselves to Bacchus. As a Bacchante, Grandmama, I find you fascinating. Here's to you and your ghosts."

7

With our women, beauty seemed to go hoppity-skip, missing one generation and landing on the next. My mother was a beauty, but no head had ever turned to look at me. Nika was a lovely child and, after her marriage to Edward, had a season of wonderful richness, but this faded when he died. She was still an attractive woman, but that is another matter. Her eyes too often looked puzzled, and when we were alone, reading perhaps by her fireside on a winter's evening, I would see how slack her attention was, how she would forget what she was reading and sit there watching the flames till a word of mine brought her back with a start.

And now here was Vera, seventeen years old and as plain as bread-pudding. She was short and dark; she wore her hair in a bob round her homely features, and she had an excellent healthy complexion. I sometimes wondered whether she slept in jodhpurs, she seemed so often to be wearing them. These garments, a tweed coat, a shirt and tie, were her favorite dress. In Whaley's day there had been no stable at this cottage where Nika now lived, but a stable and much else had appeared. There was a garage for Nika's car and Nicolas's; a stable for Vera's Arab horse, and kennels for her dogs. These were two Irish wolf hounds, creatures of great dignity with blue-gray coats, named Finn and Seumas, and a very wonderful sight it was, I thought, to see Vera riding forth on that horse, his tail streaming, and the hounds padding behind or laying themselves out on the hillside, racing among the racing shadows of the clouds.

Vera was a reserved child. There was a hunt in the district, but it didn't interest her. There was a local horse show at which she never appeared. She seemed to have no friends nor to want any. Sometimes she would take food with her and be off all day. "Where have you been, darling? What have you done?" Nika would ask; and she would say: "Oh, I tethered Firdausi, and then just sat down and watched Finn and Seumas running."

Even when she was in the house little was seen of her. She would go to her own room, and I often wondered what she did there. Sometimes when she came back glowing from a ride, I would be impressed by a spark in her dark blue eye, something deep down behind the plainness of her, and this, I would think, shines out of the real Vera, if only we could get at it. Nicolas had said he wondered she did not go on all fours. To me, it seemed not unlikely that, unseen to any of us, in her own secret places, she flew.

I went down there the week after Nicolas had gone to Oxford. Nika had bought a good deal of land round the cottage, and the cottage itself had been doubled in size. The old well from which Whaley and I had drawn our water was now surmounted by an ornamental wrought-iron well head and was merely decorative. There was water inside the house, even in all the bedrooms, and electric light. It was no longer the simple place in which Maggie used to receive her Sunday afternoon homage, to which the young people would come cycling through the white dust. The roads were tarred; there were motorcars everywhere; as you walked in the garden airplanes droned over you; and the pub across the green had a cocktail bar where you sat on strips of red leather stretched over tubular steel. It was easy now to get to the village from London, and consequently many new houses had been built and barns turned into studios. Old ponds, dredged and cemented, had become swimming pools. One of them, I was told, was electrically heated. Young women, who looked as if on week-end vacation from a musical comedy chorus, walked in blue or purple slacks upon the green, waiting for the cocktail bar to open.

But the place was still quiet enough, apart from week-end incursions, for all these rather overvivid young people had their livings to earn in one way or another, which was more than I had ever had to do. I neither wanted their world nor begrudged them their own way of enjoying themselves in it. After all, I could stay behind Nika's walls, and they, poor things, had not, I imagined, much private stockade for the shutting out of a very pressing world. They would probably be willing enough to swop their lives for Vera's.

Vera had been for a time at a very fashionable girls' school, but had come home before her course was ended. I never knew why. There was so little I knew about the child. I was not sorry when Nika said to me one evening during that visit: "Could you bear to be alone with Vera, darling—just for a day?"

"Oh, yes. I could put up with it. Why?"

"I'm going to Oxford to see Nicolas."

"But he's only just got there!"

"I know. But I'd like to go. I'll take the car. I've rung up the Mitre, and I shall stay there tomorrow night and come back the next day."

She set off in a wonderful mellow autumn morning, and it was quiet when she was gone. It was mid-week, and in mid-week, once the city men had left in the morning, the village was slumbrous. Vera vanished after breakfast. She was down in the stables, polishing her horse and dogs. Presently she came back and said: "I shall be off all day, Grandmama. D'you mind?"

I spent the day pottering about in the garden. Nika had made it a wonderful place. In the midst of all else was a flower garden, enclosed in gray stone walls, a secret place where never a murmur came to tell of the changes in the village without. There were stone seats, and in the middle of the lawn was a lily pond, and under the walls were the herbaceous borders. Michaelmas daisies, helenium, phlox of all colors, a few late delphiniums, were blooming motionless in the soft weather, and the air was full of the drone of bees, the flash of dragonflies, and the dart and hover of furry humming-bird hawk-moths, prodding their long tongues deep into flower upon flower. The gray of the walls was almost hidden by roses and by many shrubs that had done with flowering and were jeweled with berries of yellow, ivory and red.

One end of the garden rose to a stone platform. You reached it by graceful steps down which a cascade of pink convolvulus, gray-leaved, poured its color. The platform was roofed with Cotswold slates and colonnaded. I let myself down there onto a long red-cushioned wicker seat. I could see nothing but the garden, and the blue sky, and the birds flying across it. How free they seemed! I wondered whether Nika, sitting in this beautiful prison that she had made, ever thought how free they were. Free to soar and sing, to fight, to starve, to die on a cold winter's day. But free. The oddest thoughts came into my mind. I thought of Nika walking here, and I thought of the polar bear I had watched at the zoo: the poor wretch who was condemned never to hunt and to raven and to hunger, never to stand gazing upon illimitable desolation and to feel the draft from frozen stars. I slept for a long time.

Vera and I dined together, and then, as usual, she retired up to her room. It had been an exceptionally warm day for late October, and even now, with the light fading, the warmth lingered. I waited for an hour, and then I went up and knocked at her door and she called to me to come in. She put down a book and got up.

"It's full moon tonight," I said, "and moonrise will be in half an hour. Shall we go and watch it?"

We went through the garden and into the fields beyond and began to climb slowly toward the circle of beech trees that crowned the rising land. It was a superb evening, with a velvet texture, full of plum bloom, and breathless. Rabbits scuttled away from us into their burrows on the fringes of the wood, and, when we got there, not a sigh was shaking the noble trees. Vera had brought a cushion and a shawl. She made me sit upon the cushion and laid the shawl over my shoulders. Down below us we could see the lights of the village. They were warm and tender. The eastern horizon was full of light. A ridge of downs made a dark line there, and the line was cut very sharp, and presently the moon's forehead looked over, and slowly the whole sphere heaved itself up, smoky bronze. At the same moment in the wood behind us a nightingale tried over quietly its first opening notes, and soon was confidently launched, filling the air about us with song. Vera sat down beside me.

"Ah!" I said. "I'm glad to hear that. We have no nightingales in Cornwall. They don't go so far west."

"Well," said Vera, "the birds may be different, but I expect the people are the same. Do you like people?"

"My dear child! What an odd question! I've liked a lot of people in my time, and detested a lot."

"No. I don't mean that exactly." She struggled for expression. "Supposing the whole lot of them were one thing that you could look at as we're looking now at that moon—would you like the thing or loathe it?"

"I can't stand outside it like that. I'm part of it."

"I don't suppose I shall ever make anyone understand what I mean. But I detest people. They're barbarous."

She said it with finality, digging her nails into the turf. I guessed that more was coming and said nothing.

"Look at history," she said comprehensively. "We did the Crusades once at school, and that's why I left."

"I often wondered, my dear. Tell me. What happened?"

"Oh, you know it all, I expect—the way they stuff you up with holy men like Peter the Hermit and wonderful kings like Richard Cœur de Lion and all the rest of it. Well, we had to write an essay on it, and I said I thought them all a set of bloodthirsty rascals. Some talked of Allah and some of God, and I said that if their representatives were anything to go by, Allah and God put very odd ideas into people's heads. And then I went on to the European religious wars, which weren't supposed to be in it at all, and said that when Allah was right out of it men could still burn one another and cut another into four pieces in the name of God alone; so I supposed the trouble was that men were uncivilized beasts anyway, who got a sort of kick out of torture."

"H'm. And that wasn't well received?"

"It certainly was not. I was talked to with infinite tenderness by the headmistress. I would understand better when I grew up. I mustn't imagine that a child of my age could grasp what had troubled many great minds. And so forth. I said I understood very well. I understood that all these wars they drilled into me showed men to be bloodthirsty louts, and I didn't want to listen to any more of it or to read any more of it. But that wouldn't do, either. It was not for me to decide on the curriculum. We gradually got very heated. I told her I was surprised she could allow such things to be taught without pointing out the truth about them. I asked her what she thought the world had gained through my father being butchered, and one sharp word led to another. So Mama was asked to remove this disruptive influence."

As well as the spark that flashed occasionally in her eye, our little Vera had another taking quality: a gentle voice of great sweetness;

519

and it was strange amid the conventional beauties of nature—the moon, the bird song, the trees down there like protecting wings folded round the village—to hear this quiet voice dismissing it all as a deceptive back cloth for a bloody drama.

"There's more than war in human life," I said, not very enthusiastically, but with a wish not to let a canker ruin the young bud; and she said, sitting as I had seen Nika sit when she looked across the lake at Tresant toward the cottage where Edward had shut himself away, that is, with her elbows on her drawn-up knees and her chin cupped in her hands as she gazed at the indifferent moon; sitting thus, she said: "Oh, there's too much of it. It's disproportionate, because it's so destructive. It's like an earthquake. If there were only one in half a century, knocking down what has been built, that would be enough, wouldn't it? And it's not an earthquake: it's the builders themselves gone mad and bloody and smashing one another."

The nightingale had stopped singing, and Vera said with a laugh: "That bird doesn't like having his bluff called."

"No doubt," I said, "he would have preferred you to find beauty in his song, as Keats did."

"Poor Keats!" she said. "All he found was contrast: that world of song, and this world that he knew too well

> *Where youth grows pale, and spectre-thin, and dies,*
> *Where but to think is to be full of sorrow*
> *And leaden-eyed despairs."*

We sat then for a long time saying nothing, and the moon climbed sadly up the sky, and the rabbits came back and frisked in the pale light. Now and then the nightingale trilled quietly, as though about to start again, but didn't; and Vera said: "Poor dear! He's longing for an encore, and we're letting him down."

Far off in the valley a train went by. There was no sound of its wheels, but we heard the thin wail of its whistle and saw it pass like a necklace of rubies drawn through the darkness by an invisible hand.

"It looks very beautiful," Vera said; "but it's probably full of terrible people, like those houses down there in the village that glow so enchantingly. I shall never trust appearances. There is no beauty anywhere unless it's inside us."

She lit a cigarette. She so obviously did not want to talk that I said nothing. I just sat there on the shore of that sea of pale light, the moon throwing the shadows of the trees back into the heart of the wood, and I wondered how much of what was odd and aboriginal in Eddy Rodda had come through into his great-granddaughter sitting here at my side. When she had finished the cigarette I asked her: "Don't you think you ought to see more people? There are some nice girls in the village, aren't there?"

"I don't think so," she said. "I used to go riding with some of them. Then we had the annual gymkhana, and I competed in the jumping. I won everything I went in for. I couldn't help it with a horse like Firdausi. They were green with jealousy. It was then that I learned how wars start."

"Whatever has that to do with war?"

"Oh, everything—everything. Wars, like all else, begin in the heart. Wars are terrible only because hearts and minds are terrible, only because people are terrible. Everybody who is envious and jealous, rude and abrupt, is a warmaker. A person who is unfair or contemptuous to a servant is as much a warmaker as the great villains we are asked to admire in the history books. So I made up my mind that I would never compete again—not in anything. I would only love and admire and emulate."

"Tell me, child—what do you want to do?"

"I want to be lonely."

"What do you want to be?"

"A poet."

I got up with a creak of my old bones, and we stood side by side looking down the hill at the valley full of a thin milky opalescence. The moon had lost its flushed bronze; it was higher, smaller, a disc of pale shining gold. The lights down there were going out one by one. I was deeply moved with a sense of privilege. I felt that even Nika had never been nearer to her daughter than I had been permitted to be that night.

"Why do you tell me these things?" I asked.

"Because you are old and wise," she said. And when we were down the hill she asked shyly: "Would you like to see Firdausi before we go in?"

She let the hounds out of the kennels and they went with her into the stable. She switched on the light, and I stopped in the doorway and peeped in; and I was never to forget the moment when the girl who had learned to hate her kind stood with an arm round that lovely arch of neck and the two hounds walked quietly about. Love was here; and what is wrong with the world of men, I asked myself, that she can't love that, too? This love was right and beautiful, but it was not right or beautiful that so much had to be rejected. Oh, my dear child, you are a disquieting symptom. All's wrong with what love must despise and forego.

CHAPTER TWENTY-NINE

I

I DON'T have to look back so far now. When I began this book I was seeking a child who was a long way off. She has been getting nearer, and now I am looking at a woman who is recognizably myself, who will never change, and who will have little more to put up with.

I remember that just before my ninetieth birthday, which was in 1938, I decided to read through all that I had written till then. After this, it was not likely that I should turn the corner of another decade. I had to admit that at ninety I was no chicken. I was going a bit slower, sometimes spending days without leaving my room, and reading and writing were among the few consolations left to me. Haggie was another. She was only sixty, a spry and nimble creature, forbearing with my nonsense.

Well, I read all this stuff, and it left me chastened and ashamed of myself as a writer. How I had slopped and squandered without proportion! Digging my childhood and youth out of the rubble of the years fascinated me. There was so much that I had forgotten. It was like coming upon a cupboard full of childish toys. I put it all down without much rhyme or reason except that I, if no one else, was enchanted. I hope it will be forgiven me. But now, if I am ever to end, I must keep to the outline. I shall have to. My hand and my eyes tire quickly.

However, on my ninetieth birthday I did not, I am sure, look as old as Mervyn Mostyn-Lloyd, though I could give him nine years. It was he who thought it a good idea to make a splash of the ninetieth birthday. He was leading a very odd life, it seemed to me. His journeyings had stretched out into years. He was reluctant to come home, I think, because there was nothing to come home to. His work was gone, his houses were sold, his wife and son were dead, and his daughters had found their own oddly divergent directions. When at last he did come back, it was not vitalized by his experiences, but rather sucked dry. He had developed the habit, which he never got out of again, of wandering about in search of places that were oases in the desert lives of the aimless rich. He had picked up a manservant, a reliable middle-aged person who had been in the Royal Marines and who could drive a car. They wandered about together, but never now out of England, and never staying anywhere for more than a few weeks. The most slumbrous hotels knew them in Bournemouth and Bath, Falmouth and Penzance, Cheltenham, Leamington, Torquay. "I must go where the sun is," Mervyn used to say; and he would be found in some stewed "sun lounge," taking the sun through plate glass, with a rug over his knees and a detective novel in his hand. He had become pathetic.

When he was in London he would have a suite at Claridge's, and it was there that the ninetieth birthday party was held. Time had brought tolerance, if not liking, between Nika, Kathy and Sophia. It had seemed once as though Nika and Sophia would never again consent to sit down with Kathy, and it was Bob Seagrim who made it possible. It is difficult to know what to call such men. The word nonentity suggests itself but must be rejected, for he so emphatically existed. He had neither brains nor æsthetic feeling, and in so far as he could be considered a man of action, his action, save for the interlude of the war, had been directed to no end but self-indulgence. He was, perhaps, a man out of his time, who needed a Gloriana's court to which he could return from stirring doings, but God knows there had been no such court in my time or any exploratory doings except the discovery of markets. And there he was, beyond it all now, anyway, having about him an indefinable sense of tradition and rectitude. You could say, if you liked, that he had been living on Kathy, as, in a sense, he had; but he was giving value for money, if you wanted to look at it on that level. Spite and enmity seemed silly where he was.

Well, it was because of his healing work that all my old brigade was present. Mervyn and his two daughters, and with the daughters Bob Seagrim and Henry Shape. Haggie was there because I wouldn't go anywhere without her. Julian Rimmel, who was sixty-one and looking it, already traditional, a "character," with his thin uprightness, his air of Gallic breeding, his trim mustache and imperial and monocle. Nika came alone. Vera, looking very happy, brought young Roger Hazard, who wore a turtle-necked blue sweater, green corduroys, sandals and no socks. His hair was uncombed—looked positively matted—and there was dirt under his fingernails. A waiter in white silk stockings was handing round cocktails. "My good man," Roger said in his rather high well-bred voice, "why do you consent to do this sort of thing? Why don't you rebel? I don't like these. Ask someone to mix me a sidecar."

It was a long, charming room. The air, though this was May Day, had a blithe nip. Mervyn had caused a fire to be lit and lights were on behind parchment shades. No foot made a sound on the carpet. Mervyn and I were rather withdrawn from the others, standing near the fire, and he was looking at his watch in a fussy way he had, and I knew he was fidgeting because Nicolas, our grandson, had not come. Then he came, with a girl I had not seen before—what he himself, I

523

imagined, would have called a smasher. Nika, I was sure, had not seen her either. She looked at the girl with a long steady considering glance; and oh dear, I thought, here it all goes again. Well, this will be the last of it. I certainly shan't assist at the obsequies of another generation, as I now appear to be doing at Nika's.

"Look at Nika," I said quietly to Mervyn. "I've seen a face give a woman away like that before. It was the day you brought Enid to the Café Royal to meet your mother. Remember?"

I could see him in his beautiful coat and top hat, his gray silk tie and stylish cane. I looked at Roger Hazard, raising the sidecar to his lips with dirty fingers and at Nicolas's unpressed lounge suit and soft collar. The suitors today certainly didn't bother about trappings. But Vera looked happy, and this new girl had all that clothes and make-up could bestow. Nicolas was bringing her across the room to me. "Grandmama, this is Julia Marsh," he said. "Julia, this is the occasion of the feast. This venerable pile has withstood the tempests of ninety years, and, as you see, she will probably survive to watch you dandling grandchildren upon your knee."

The girl took my hand and smiled at me, shyly for one with such an air of sophistication. I guessed it was armor, not very thick. "What a charming bracelet," she said, retaining my hand to examine it. "All those little bells!"

"It sleeps," I exclaimed, "for three hundred and sixty-four days of the year. Nicolas's mother gave it to me on a birthday long ago, and I wear it always on my birthday."

Then Nicolas presented the girl to his grandfather, but Mervyn was absent, thinking, I believe, rather of that occasion when Lucy Evans had met Enid than of anything now about him. However, he recovered himself, looked at his watch again, and said: "We had better begin luncheon." He gave me his arm ceremoniously and led me to the top of the table, where I sat with him on my right and Julian on my left. In middle age Mervyn had rounded out into a full-bodied man; now he was shrunken. His cheeks had fallen in and his nose was pinched; and this emphasized the high bony brainbox which was wrapped in nothing but yellowish parchment drawn upon by the squiggles of a few blue-black veins. His voice had become querulous.

"What's all this nonsense about Vera publishing a book of poems?" he asked. "And who is this feller Hazard she goes about with?"

Julian answered the second question. "I was down at his father's place last week," he said. "He's got a lot of lovely stuff that he wants to sell—furniture, pictures, books—but I'm afraid he's a bit late in the day, unless I can find someone in America. They've been living in Somerset for centuries—one of those odd families that have never done anything except go on and on. Never been ennobled. Never had even a baronetcy. But down there to be Mr. Hazard is enough. It's still pretty feudal: immense mansion, immense deer park, with the pretty creatures twinkling among the trees. It's all utterly enchanting, and utterly doomed."

Mervyn glanced down the table at the heir to this splendor. "Looks like a rag-and-bone man to me," he grumbled. "Don't they wash down there?"

"There's a stone room in the basement, called the washhouse. The hardy Hazards go down there and tip buckets of cold water over themselves. The old man does it still, because that's how the Hazards have always washed. Effete visitors like myself have cans of hot water carried to their dressing rooms."

"Isn't Roger one of the boys who kicked up a row in the Oxford Union?" I asked. "The ones who carried the anti-King-and-Country resolution?"

"Yes. He's very left-wing and very vocal, which is a change for a Hazard. Calls himself a Communist. He was a Mosley Blackshirt for a time."

"These young fools keep chopping and changing. Don't know their own minds," Mervyn grumbled.

"Perhaps not," Julian agreed. "But they're trying to, and that's an agreeable change, don't you think? Young Hazard will get through to something in the end. He's had so much antiquity that I expect novelty seems new to him. Which, of course, it isn't. Not necessarily."

"What does his father think of him?" I asked.

"He regards him with utter unconcern. A Hazard can do no wrong. That is the family faith. A Hazard comes home in the end, like the cows at evening."

"Nika tells me he runs a bookshop in Charing Cross Road," I said. "I haven't been there. I don't go into those parts. But I sent Haggie Chadderton to spy round. She says the place is called the Future Bookshop, and that the window was full of this book of Vera's."

"She sent me a copy," Mervyn said. "I don't understand a word of it."

I wasn't surprised at that, but, for me, I thought I understood it well enough; understood, that is, the seething dislike of the follies of men that lay behind it. Eight years had passed since Vera and I had our talk in the moonlight, and I didn't see that much had happened since then to change her views. So when I found these views expressed in her poems they didn't surprise me. As poems, the things merely irritated me: I was old-fashioned enough to think they were not poems at all. There was one called "It's Logical, Isn't It?"

> Why is Johnnie Jones
> Selling rags and bones?
> So that Johnnie Jones
> Can wear rags upon his bones.

Another was called "Advance upon All Fronts."

> Boom goes the Bishop,
> Boom, boom go the Cannons,
> And the Stock Exchange goes boom, Boom, BOOM.
> But in the Inn there is No Room.
> All tickets have been sold out for the Last Dance of
> the Present Season.

Vera's odd book was a success. The people who were writing this sort of thing themselves reviewed it in their coterie journals with enthusiasm, and even in newspapers outside that narrow circle it was cautiously praised by reviewers who seemed to fear that they might be missing an important thing. One way and another, it "caught on" in a moderate fashion, and Vera found herself courted. She spoke, and was photographed, at a Foyle's Luncheon, organized to put the young poets of the day on review; and she was a guest at one of those select luncheons in Lady Sybil Colefax's house in North Street where the hostess gathered the fiery sparks of the moment to glow companionably. It was there that she met Roger Hazard, who was sitting in his sandals and sweater between an austere woman poet in black and ivory and a Cabinet minister's secretary, who, it was hoped, would be, within the limits of discretion, indiscreet about what was really happening in Germany.

"I must get back to my shop," Roger said as the company was breaking up, "I'm only a tradesman. You going my way? I've got a taxi here."

So Vera and Roger began their friendship; and she was soon thinking that one person at least might be considered an exception to her generally low view of human kind.

I certainly had plenty to think about at that ninetieth birthday party, and I hardly noticed what I was eating; but now here was coffee in front of me and Mervyn pouring brandy into an immense glass, and I said: "Good gracious! Is luncheon finished?"

"Yes," Julian laughed, "and, as usual, you've absent-mindedly done very well."

Mervyn knocked on the table with a spoon and got up, and I hauled on his coat-tail, crying: "Oh, dear! No nonsense, Mervyn. No talking," but he was not to be denied, and off he went, unaware that, compared with him, I looked a babe in arms. ". . . the health of this very remarkable old lady whom we all hold in affectionate honor. If I'm ever as old as she is, and I've got some way to go before I shall be that"—tentative laughter—"I hope people will be able to say of me what I can say of her. And what I can say is this. She has never done anything that appears on the face of it to be remarkable, but she has lived to this great age without making an enemy in the world, and that's remarkable enough. She was the friend of my mother, she has always been my friend, as she was, too, of my dear wife. All three of my children are here today. I am sure my loved son Edward is here, although you cannot see him, and the friendship she has given to the three of them is something I am deeply moved to think about but haven't any skill to express. My son-in-law Henry Shape, and my son outside the law Bob Seagrim, and my grandchildren Vera and Nicolas and my friend her nephew Julian Rimmel—she has been a friend to all of these; and what I am going to ask you to consider is this—that these people I have mentioned are of several generations and of hugely different sorts, but they have this one thing in common: that old Sarah has always been a shoulder they could cry on and a sympathetic ear into which they could speak their hopes. If I went on for another twenty minutes I couldn't say more than that. It's what I wanted to say and I've said it, so here's to this wonderful old lady, with all our love."

Well, there it is: the only testimonial I've received in my life, so I may as well write it down. I should have liked Maggie Whale and Sally Gaylord to hear it, for theirs were the brows that should wear any laurels handed to me.

People kept shouting for a reply, but there was nothing I could say but "Thank you," and I said it; and Haggie Chadderton stood up and said: "Please leave her alone. Don't tire her out," and then the clamor stopped and Vera and some of the others came round and kissed me, including, of all people, Bob Seagrim, whose black patch magnified itself, when his face pressed mine, into a great darkness within which I seemed to see all those who were not there: Justin and Richard, Tom Chadderton and Trimmer, Edward and that wayward boy Nigel who had broken Kathy's heart. Dear Bob Seagrim! He seemed to belong to those who had charged, like the Six Hundred, into the valley and not come out at the other end, rather than to the living about him. I knew nothing more pathetic than this association of his with Kathy, a clinging on both sides to a few embers, cherished the more because there was no more fuel, and when these were out all was done. That brother of his who had beaten him by half an hour had been dead these three years, and Bob was now Lord Cheveringham to anyone who cared to call him so. None of us did, and he even signed his letters Bob Seagrim. "Bit long in the tooth—what?—to don the purple. If Kath had wanted a title, another thing. But she doesn't, and she won't marry me. Don't blame her. Look a bit too much like a chunk of the old Menin Gate—what?"

So Cheveringham Castle was rented to someone who canned meat in Chicago, and that gave Bob some pocket money, and Kathy didn't have to go on paying into his account. He tried tipping the balance the other way with presents more lavish than he could afford till she told him to stop it.

He left me, and went to talk to Nika and Sophia and Henry Shape, and he drew Kathy into the group, and I rejoiced to see them all laughing together. But Nika's eyes strayed continually to Nicolas and this girl Julia Marsh, and that was something, I thought, that I should have to know more about soon. But here, in the meantime, was Vera, loitering with intent, I could see; and soon she approached and asked: "Are you going back now to Hanover Square? May I come along?" Yes, yes, I thought, come along and tell me how wonderful he is. That's what you want, isn't it?

She came in a taxi with me and Haggie, who was firm-minded, and took me into the bedroom and said: "Now down you get on that bed at once and shut your eyes for half an hour. If Miss Vera wants to talk, she can bottle it up till then. All this excitement at your age! Sheer murder I call it." She was fussing and bustling, and had me on the bed with my feet up, a pillow under my head and a rug over me. It was three o'clock. "All right," I said, "you're strong enough to bully me and push me down here, but, mark me, I shall be up as soon as your back's turned. So see that Vera stays."

She stayed and was there when my eyes opened two hours later. I wondered for a moment where I was, as I often did now, and I raised my arm, and the bracelet slipped almost to my elbow. And then I knew who I was and where I was and how old I was. I knew what a long journey I had made and how the flesh, my companion all the way, was deserting me. There was not enough of it for the bracelet to catch in. I kept my arm held up and looked at the withered stick, then turned it down, and the bracelet fell with its ringing of minute bells, but I caught only the faintest sound of the ringing, and that was the first time that had happened. Sarah Undridge couldn't hear her child-hood clearly any more. She was going deaf, poor old thing: deaf at any rate to such fairy music as that.

Well, I thought, there are worse things at sea than a bit of deafness; I threw off the rug and put my legs to the ground, and was sitting there rubbing my eyes when Vera peeped round the door. She ran in at once on seeing me up, and offered an arm to help me into the sitting room, but I wouldn't have that. "None of your Haggie nonsense," I said, and walked in on my own.

Haggie had gone off somewhere and Vera had put tea ready. The evening had turned a little cold and cheerless. "Draw the curtains," I said, "and switch on the fire," and we sat there with one lamp lit among the tea things. I was doing this more and more: impatiently shutting out the lingering day, reaching toward quietness and the dark. It was my best time: this time when once more I could feel that I had done with doing, and could sit down and think of what I and so many others had done. But tonight I couldn't do that. These young ones were still doing, and they would expect me to share the ardor of their forward looking.

"Well, child, what do you do with yourself all day?"

She was willing enough to talk. She was now among those who came in to town every morning from the village, but she didn't come on the businessmen's train. She arrived at the Future Bookshop at noon, and then Roger Hazard went out to lunch. He couldn't afford to pay an assistant and he didn't like shutting the shop between one and two, which was the time when people, free from their offices, tended to look in. He had been accustomed to eating a sandwich in the shop, and it was in the interests of his better feeding that Vera had volunteered to relieve him. When he got back she went to her own lunch, and then the pair of them stayed till five. "I do the letters and pack up any books that have to go by post, and so forth. We *had* to shut up today, to come to your party. So you see what an important person you are. I can't think of anyone else we'd have done it for."

"Have you met Mr. Hazard's people?"

"He hasn't got what you could call people—only a father. He lives somewhere down in Somerset. No, I haven't met him. What does that matter?"

"You know nothing about him?"

"Only a few things Roger has let drop. He's pretty old—Roger was born late—and he manages to get along without working."

So you know nothing, I thought, of the great house and the deer park and the Hazards going back and back—undistinguished but everlasting. Well, it's not for me to tell you.

"Are you thinking of marriage?"

"My dear Gran!"

"Well, oddly enough, there is such a thing as marriage."

"We're just very good friends. I'm not sure that Roger approves of marriage."

"What does he approve of?"

"The Future," she said with the superb naïveté of the young.

"Well, that is obliging of him, but I'm not sure that the future is

529

going to be any great shakes. There's only one thing we can bet on where the future is concerned, and that is that it will proceed like the past in weeks and months and years, and some of them will be tolerable and some intolerable. And the intolerable ones will have to be put up with all the same."

"Don't you think the world changes for the better?"

"It changes for the better and it changes for the worse, and a change for the worse could easily take us far, far below where we were when the last change for the better began, so that there'd be more than all to do again."

"I must say," Vera said with a smile, "that my Grandmama Undridge is a corrective to what I hear day by day."

"Then you must come and see me more often, child. Does this young man of yours think the millennium is round the corner?"

"Oh, it's not only Roger: it's so many of the people who come to the shop. It's that sort of shop, you see. They're all waiting for the withering away of the State."

I was glad to detect a gentle irony in her tone. "Well," I said, "you can tell them from Grandmama Undridge that when the State withers away their bellies won't. They will still have to be filled and their backs clothed and a roof put over their heads. And that will mean then, as it means now with the State gaily flourishing, work and nothing but work. And you can tell them, too, that judging from the way the population of the world is increasing, it looks as though there'll have to be more work than ever for less food, roof and clothes. That will create a situation that will take some handling, and whether you call the handlers the State or anything else, they will have precious little time for young men gassing in bookshops. So there's your Granny Undridge's guess for the future. Now let's leave it. Tell me, who is this girl Nicolas brought to luncheon?"

"Oh, Julia Marsh. She's a mannequin."

She looked at me with a sly smile, evidently waiting for an ex-pression of shock. I did not gratify her; and she went on: "You ought to be told that your grandson Nicolas is partial to a well-set-up young thing."

"Well," I said, "that's a sign of sense in him. Where and how did he meet her?"

"Human nature's very odd," she said, as though she were telling me something I didn't know. "Those who should be doing this are so often doing that. One of Nicolas's friends is a buyer of clothes, but he dreams of nothing but airplanes. He longs to be a test pilot like Nicolas, or thinks he does. One's never sure. Anyway, he'd do any-thing for Nicolas; wangling him a ticket for a display of new season's clothes was nothing. Can't you imagine it—the lovely lighting and the soft carpets and the little gilded chairs, and our Nicolas sitting there agog as the girls swayed by, twirling and posing. It's one of my favorite pictures. And that's how Nicolas first saw Julia. From what I gather, he'll have no surprises on the wedding night, if there is one. Julia was displaying the most intimate of ravishing intimacies—things I've never possessed."

"H'm."

"For once, I have left my Grandmama speechless."

"But full of thought."

"Well, they can be happy thoughts. She's a good girl, but a bit dumb, as they say. I've met her once or twice, and rather like her. She keeps a widowed mother. Well, I must dash for a taxi, or I'll miss the last train."

She got up and kissed me.

"Is this bookshop paying?" I asked.

"Not yet."

"Who guarantees the overdraft at the bank?"

"Mama."

I was sitting there alone, tickled by the thought that Daniel's daughter—Daniel's money, for that matter—was paying for the withering away of the State. And Vera wanted to tell *me* that human nature was odd!

2

I allowed a decent time to pass and then asked Roger Hazard to luncheon. Between his accepting the invitation and the date for its fulfillment there was a row in an East End street: a clash between marching Blackshirts and a gang of people attending an open-air meeting at which Roger was one of the speakers. The police had become involved, a few bobbies' helmets had rolled in the gutter, and there were some arrests. Roger was among those who appeared before the beak. It cost him a talking-to and a small fine. I wondered whether Daniel's money paid that!

"Well," I said, shaking his thin, well-formed and class-consciously dirty hand, "so you didn't get into jug? That must have been a disappointment."

"It would have helped," he laughed. "The blood of the martyrs is the seed of the Church, as you've probably heard."

I gave him sherry and a cigarette. His gray eyes looked at me consideringly through the smoke. "Do I get a copy of the report?" he asked.

I was pleased with his cheek, but pretended not to get him. "What report?"

"Well, I suppose I'm summoned before the matriarch of the clan for some other purpose than to eat cold mutton."

"You don't eat cold mutton here," I assured him. "And you needn't tell me that there are thousands who would be glad to eat it. I expect I know that rather better than you do. However, while you're here there'll be no harm in my having a look at you."

Haggie brought in the cold consommé, and there was iced hock. "Tell me," I said, "what does your father think of it all?"

He drew back a bit at that, and I said: "I know that Dr. Johnson laid it down that civilized conversation does not proceed by question and answer, so you may consider me uncivilized if you think Dr. Johnson said the last word about everything, which I don't."

Happily, he relished this. "Well, frankly," he said, "I think he was one of the world's great bores, dominated by an excess both of conscience and constipation. Eno's and a disbelief in hell fire would have made a different man of him. So just to spite him, ask away."

"Now," I said, "we shall have duckling and green peas and new potatoes. Rather conventional, but a convention is often the sustaining of an excellent thing."

"If that remark is intended as a parable, I reject it. There are lots of conventions I want to bust. However, as to what my father thinks of it all, the answer is simple. He doesn't think. So far as I have been able to discover, I am the first Hazard to have felt a crepitation between the eyebrows and the top of the head. Before the eighteenth century, they engaged largely in any wars that were knocking about. During the eighteenth century they went in for building in Somerset and gambling and seduction in London. During the nineteenth century they started a game book, and to read it is like looking at a poulterer's shop window at Christmas time. Exhausted by these three centuries of enterprise, in the twentieth century they have done nothing at all."

"Ancestors," I said, "are always difficult either to live up to or down from."

"Mine I revere, with a positively Chinese reverence. When I am at home I wander through the house and look at them: in the library which caused vast flocks and herds of innocent beasts to be slaughtered to provide the leather binding for books undisturbed by any impious hand since first they came from the craftsmen; in the study, where my father studies Edgar Wallace throughout the week and the *News of the World* on Sundays; in the dining room where twenty Chippendale chairs stand round a table at the head of which he sits down to a chop like a chairman of a large board of directors who fear the shareholders have rumbled them and have all failed to turn up; in the bedrooms, where the cold crinkles your bones even when you have withdrawn into the fastnesses of a four-poster looking like Sheba's tent. There they are, my ancestors. Those that were within a hundred miles of a battle are painted amid gunshot and fume, holding horses with distended nostrils, manifestly snorting 'Ha ha!' and with a few proletarian corpses making the foreground realistic. Those who ever shot a snipe appear with rows of their feathered friends laid in all friendship on the ground before them as they stand, gun in hand, a few assorted dogs looking reverentially into their eyes. The women are all incredibly beautiful, loitering upon terraces that reach for miles into the distance, and they, too, have dogs that are always noble and immense or idiotic and minute. There are also conversation pieces, containing collections of ancestors, who, apparently, are examining the color of one another's ties, the shape of one another's noses or bosoms, the hairdo's, or this or that, but never by any chance conversing. . . . Am I monopolizing the conversation?"

"You are catching up on your dumb ancestors, and your duckling is getting cold."

"Well, then, I'd better catch up on my dumb duckling and let my ancestors get cold."

I began to understand why Vera liked him.

"Happily," he said, "the Hazards always had the sense to be painted by the best people. I suspect that they caught them young, before they had enough reputation to demand high prices. Anyway, there are Gainsboroughs and Romneys and Reynoldses and what not, to say nothing of a few Canalettos and so forth that some of the boys brought back from their European wanderings. When I sell up, I shall be in clover."

"Sell up . . . I suppose that means repudiate. Selling your grandfather and great aunt—probably to America—is to be the sign that you've done with all they stood for?"

"Yes."

"A friend of mine has had some conversation with your father lately. Your father seemed unperturbed about—what shall we say?—your vagaries. He thinks that a Hazard at last always goes back where he belongs."

"He's quite right about that. Everybody at last goes back where he belongs. The trouble with the Hazards is that they've taken such a time to realize where they belong. God knows what put them where they were to begin with, but I've tried to make it clear to you that ever since there's any record of them, not one of them has ever, by the work of his head, his hands or his heart, done a thing that any Tom, Dick or Harry could not have done as well or better. Well then, tell me, where do they belong?"

He was now, for the first time, serious. His face flushed a little. He pushed his plate of half-finished food aside and said: "I want nothing else. Do you mind if I smoke?"

I nodded, and he lit a cigarette. Then he got up and began to pace the room. "Listen," he said. "I'm going to tell you something. When I was a boy my father had a shepherd named Tom Knowles, and Tom had a son named Jack. It was all in the order of things that I should be friendly with Jack Knowles. One was encouraged to be on good terms with the tenants. Jack was a bright boy, given to reading, and I used to pull his leg about it. But it was no good pulling Jack's leg: he knew what he wanted. Our place is very remote. You've got to walk miles to get to a public library, and Jack was always doing that walk. I'll tell you why. He came to me once when I was on holiday from Harrow and asked if a certain book was in our library. I hadn't the foggiest idea. I knew no more about the library than any other Hazard had known, but I asked Jack to come and have a look. My father was out. Jack was enraptured by what he found in the library—not only the book he had asked for, but all sorts of books that set his eyes sparkling. I told him to take what he wanted, and off he went with an armful—every one with the Hazard crest beautifully embossed in gold on the leather.

"Now I'm going to cut this part of it short. I'll just say that I got into a hell of a row from the old man. Jack is not a tidy reader. Some of the books came back dirty and some with the corners of pages turned down, and there were even passages underlined in red ink. I was out when Jack brought them back, but my father was in. If poor Jack had painted whiskers on a Romney picture of one of my sainted female ancestors there couldn't have been a worse hullaballoo. And the damned books were never looked at from generation to generation! Well, that is why Jack walked to the public library. What is worse is that he hadn't been very polite to my father, though I don't know what he said.

"Well, the next thing was this. The old man keeps up the charming custom of slaughtering birds in the autumn, and all hands are expected to report as beaters when he and his cronies sally forth. Jack was ordered to be there as usual, and he pointed out that on the opening day of the slaying he would be sitting for a scholarship in the neighboring town. This was badly received. It all linked up with the affair of the books, but the old man couldn't do anything. After all, he didn't employ Jack, only his father, but he informed me that the boy was getting above himself. Jack won the scholarship, and the week that this was known old Tom Knowles was sacked. He was getting beyond his work, and this and that. Certainly poor old Tom was prematurely decrepit and there wasn't much hope of his getting another job. His wife couldn't help, for she was crippled by rheumatism—a not uncommon complaint in Hazard cottages—and it looked as though Jack would have to drop

534

the scholarship and buckle to and keep his parents, which, I presume, was the salutary lesson he was intended to learn."

He stopped walking about and crushed out his cigarette on the messy plate of duckling. "Well," he said quietly, sitting down, "it was about that time that I began learning lessons, too."

"And what happened to Jack Knowles?"

"As if he were a Hazard, he has at last arrived where he belongs. Last week he was elected a Fellow of Merton. I should have been proud if my family had had a hand in that. But it was left to Mrs. Knowles's brother, who kept a back-street tobacconist's shop in the town where Jack began to attend the Grammar School. He was not a nice man. I knew him: a dirty old miser who'd been hoarding for years. But he had this odd idea that families must stick together—a regular Hazard notion—and he took them in, and Jack went to school, and old Tom had to earn his keep, chopping wood, lighting fires, and running errands. That old swob—he was a bachelor—made their lives a misery. But Jack lived through it. So you see, it's not a noble story for anyone concerned, and if you like beautifully ironical conclusions to stories, this one has even that. Jack is a light of the Conservative party! He writes me long letters about my foolish ways."

"I expect his parents are very proud of him."

"I don't know about that. His work would certainly be without meaning to them, and they probably think he's a stuck-up little swine. He sends 'em a bit of money but he never goes near them, and takes care that they don't come near him. I warned you that this was not a noble story. That day when I lent Jack the books, we both began to detest our families: he hated his for their poverty and ignorance, I hated mine for their ignorance and riches, and Jack and I will probably end by detesting one another. With equal incomes in a classless society, none of this hatred could arise."

"Does Vera ever talk to you about me?"

"Not much. She doesn't often get beyond Auden and T. S. Eliot. She has a severely limited mind. She should be educated."

"Well, then, I must tell you something about myself. My husband was a minor politician, but wealthy enough, and at one time promising enough, to entertain the bigwigs who had really arrived. I saw a lot of them at my dinner table. They all had equal incomes—or equal enough to make no difference. There was no reason why any one of them should struggle for an extra five hundred or thousand a year. But they were as jealous and egotistical as cats, and if a job was going, you can believe me the back-stairs work was worth watching. A bigger job meant more power; and when you can teach men to relinquish, or not to pursue, power—then you'll be getting somewhere. If you think equal incomes have anything to do with it, you're as naïve as Bernard

Shaw. You can give everybody five pounds a week, but by an odd dispensation of providence one here and there will be a Jack Knowles or an Adolf Hitler, and he'll not want more money, but he'll want a special house to do his important work in, and a special car to save his important time, and a special bodyguard to maintain his important privacy, and off you go again. . . . There was a nice soufflé, but we won't bother with that now. Would you like some coffee?"

"No, thank you. I must get back to the shop."

"You have convinced me," I said, "that there have been many fools in your family. Don't add to their number. For every Hazard who acted as idiotically as your father did to Jack Knowles I could produce a Hazard-like person who did the opposite thing."

"The whole system is wrong," he said savagely.

"You're telling me! But look out how you try to mend it. It may need a certain delicacy."

3

Well, this was in June of 1938, and later that year I did not go for a gas mask. I was getting too old for that sort of nonsense. Why should I seek to preserve my life in a world that had come to that? Nor did I go to Tresant, as Nika wanted me to: not till Mr. Chamberlain had come back from Munich and feverishly told us that, after all, it was peace on earth. I had heard it when I was three years old! I was hearing it now. I wondered whether that poor well-meaning fellow really believed it: really believed that, when the madhouse was soaked in petrol and the lunatics were striking matches all over the place, you could stop the blaze by signing a piece of paper! The world was full of covenants and agreements and pacts and charters, leagues, committees and conventions; but there was no communion, and without that, what did all the rest of it matter? I should feel very alarmed for the future of a street where the neighbors thought it necessary to have so many understandings about good behavior.

However, if I didn't go, Mervyn did: not to Tresant; he went out of the country, and took his money with him. He came to bid me good-by, and told me that England was no longer a possible place for him; his well-being demanded sun; he was off to California. I pretended to believe him, but I despised him. I was sorry it had come to that. The little Merlin whom Eddy Rodda begot, whom I had watched flailing his limbs about on the lawn by the lake when I was a child and Maggie was still young and Lucy Evans was a beautiful girl. He had been kind to me in many ways, and we shared a couple of grandchildren, but we had grown apart. I loved life—even at ninety, I loved life—too much to coddle it and dodge half its implications. No, life was not a thing to

536

be preserved: it was to be lived and endured. *Advienne que pourra!* I thought, watching Mervyn's thin, veined hand raising his wine glass and shaking a little. Henceforth, for the bit that's left to me, let that be my motto. *Advienne que pourra!* So Mervyn went, and took his money with him, and his Royal Mariner, and found plenty of sunshine and orange juice, and died before the Second World War came.

It was Bob Seagrim who came to see me about the gas mask. The old war-horse! His nostrils were positively sniffing what was to come. For years he had been useless, stumping between South Audley Street and his clubs, and now he saw the chance to be a man again. He was in charge of the distribution of the masks in our district and had brought a car to take me to the fitting. He had to make do with taking Haggie, and was deeply upset at my naughtiness. "If anything happened to you, I should have to explain myself—what?"

"Just tell 'em I'm an obstinate old woman," I said, laughing at the thought of Authority, in the midst of a gas-bomb raid, worrying about the fate of Sarah Undridge. "If you're going that way, drop me at the Rimmel Gallery."

"Well," Julian said, "here we are again! D'you remember coming to discuss the fate of the business in 1914? We solved it by bringing young Fournier over that time. This time it won't be so easy. Civilization has made some progress since then."

It was evening. Bond Street was quiet, and there is always something terrible and menacing in the quiet of a great city's streets, as there is not in country quiet. Just then, all the tensions of the world seemed to be sapping and mining at these miles of deceptive solidity that surrounded me. It was all deceptive, Crystal Palace glass or War Office ashlar. I had learned that much.

"So Mervyn's gone!" Julian exclaimed.

"Yes, and I'm not sorry to see the back of him. He was becoming a misery. I'd rather remember what he was than see what he is."

"Yes. Well, I don't want to follow him, but a lot of Rimmel property will have to do so. Not necessarily to America, but to somewhere safer than Bond Street. Neville is stroking the hyena's head at the moment, and we don't know what will come of that. He may persuade it to lie down for a bit, but it won't lie down for long, and so we'd better decide what we are to do."

As usual, he had got things arranged in his own mind. "I'm thinking of making use of that chap Hazard," he said. "The father of that boy who runs the bookshop. He's not too well off. I've sold a few pictures for him, but the times are a bit restless for much of that. Well, I thought we might rent his place for the duration of the war, when it comes. I'm afraid there's no *if* about it. It'd make a good warehouse. We'd have to spend a bit of money on it—put in a first-class central-heating system, for one thing. He'd welcome that, I imagine. The place is pretty moldy. All the pictures could be hung—the tapestries, too. There's plenty of wall space. Everything else could be stored in the rooms. We'd just keep a bit of token stuff here."

"Well, go ahead. You're evidently determined to, whatever I say. I think it's a good scheme."

"Most of the staff here would go, of course. One of them—someone over service age—will have to live down there with the stuff. The place is utterly remote. The chance of a bomb dropping on it is one in ten thousand. I've seen the insurance people about it."

The evening had faded to night. The chimney pots, seen through the window, were black upon the dirty zinc of the sky. I sat there listening to him, but hardly hearing him: bombs, insurance, service age: it all sounded at once fantastic and dreadfully real, as if one were wandering in a nightmare and knew that it was no use trying to wake up, because one was awake, and the nightmare was in one's waking heart. Julian switched on a table lamp, a pretty silk parasol held over a Meissen shepherdess, and the darkness fled, and there was only the softly lighted room, and Julian, and the rich friendliness of all our years together. That, at our age, we should be discussing such things! "Draw the curtains," I said, and he did so.

"Hold my hand." He took it in his.

"Now," I said, "let them drop their bloody bomb, all the half-wits and idiots of the world, and end it here. They make me sick."

He stroked my hand. "*Ma chére tante!*" he murmured.

"They make me spew," I repeated. "We are given over to cultured gorillas and the educated scum of the earth. Well, they'll end yet in the battered stumps of their trees and literally crawling amid the scum that spawned them. May they enjoy it!"

I withdrew my hand from his, feeling better for the outburst. "Forgive me. You see what we are coming to when an early Victorian can so forget decorum."

"I must see you home."

"You'll do that all right," I laughed. "At least, I hope so. One never knows in these days. And glad I shall be to get there."

It had happened once or twice of late, and it happened overwhelmingly now: I felt the full surge and weight of all my years. They clung upon me, hard to bear, and I wished they would let me go.

4

Well, they didn't. That war came, and I stayed through it in London, not leaving the town for one day or one night. I never carried a gas mask, because I never had one. I never carried an identity card because I put it in the fire. I had been used to being a person, not a number, and I didn't intend to have that changed now. When it was all over, I went down to Tresant, and that, I knew, was the last journey I should ever make. I shall not leave the place again. Here I am, adding the last pages to what I have to write, and a slow and weary business it is. There are moments when to raise my pen to the ink pot is too much, and my eyes suddenly fail to see the last words I have written.

There is no need for me to write anything about the war. I was going to say that those who wish to know about that will find plenty written, but I am not sure, for in the war's last days the atomic bomb was dropped, and so there may soon be nothing left for anyone to read about anything. These pages will go with the rest. It will be an ironic end to man's everlasting peeping and prying after knowledge: the destruction of all that knowledge has accumulated on the earth.

But writers are incorrigible, even such writers as I. On the brink of judgment, when the heavens roll up as a scroll, they will still be scratching their pens across paper; and I with the rest will tell the few personal things that happened to me and mine in those years that began apocalypse.

5

When the war ended and I felt that I could now with a clear conscience leave the exhausted and broken city that had endured so much, and I with it, I thought to slip quietly away with Haggie. The evening before this, I had gone to say good-by to Julian Rimmel. Leaning on Haggie's arm, I was able to walk the whole length of Bond Street, plastered over with "To Let" notices, having many shops whose once-opulent windows were reduced to the space of a square yard—mere frames containing pitiful small-scale pictures of an old splendor. And there were railings behind which the pits and caverns gaped, full of filth and rubble and springing flowers and cats that hunted mice in these patches of significant wilderness. I was sorry to say good-by to Bond Street in such circumstances, for the street was full of memories. Unbroken, but dingy with its tarnished paint and its small supplies, still stood the confectioner's shop into which, so long ago, Whaley and I had gone with Lord Burnage, before he had married my mother, before I had seen Montreuil and Daniel in the garden there, or Tresant and Sally. Still there, too, was the shop outside which, long afterward, a rather dirty old woman from the East End had stood in her big boots, a shopping basket on her arm, a shawl over her head, and seen the Duchess of Fallowshire come out and known her for her mother; and later still in that very shop had worked Julia Marsh, the beautiful nonentity who was married to my grandson, Nicolas. But, as Vera had once told me, Julia was a good girl. She and Nicolas were happy. They had already given me three great-grandchildren, but my mind had never fully comprehended them. There comes a time when interest in posterity wears thin. Let them knit their own breeches.

It was odd to think of my grandson as a knight, but he was, and Julia was Lady Mostyn-Lloyd. Odder still—what would Daniel have said?—to think that our old chauffeur was Sir Henry Shape. Henry had shown genius for airplane design, I learned; he had, too, with Sophia's money, become one of the most influential directors of his company. And it was Nicolas who tested the designs, gaily taking his life into his hands; and these two, it was felt, had deserved well of their country. I skip over it all: I shall not pretend to be elated. Cowering with Haggie in our flat, terrified to death, both of us, night after night, I was not ready to worship either airplane designers or test pilots. And walking along this street in the quiet evening, in the awed hush that had now fallen here and on all the world, a hush in which one felt with a sharp anguish the horror of what had been done, I was able to imagine, as I looked about me, the outcome of their labors.

We came to a stand opposite Rimmel's. Like so many other shops, it had only a "token" window, containing an object attractive enough but not of much value. The valuable stuff would be coming back soon; it was still in Somerset. However, old Mr. Timothy Hazard was no longer there to enjoy the new central heating system. He had turned out with a shotgun when the Local Defense Volunteers were formed, and had lived long enough to see them become an armed Home Guard, but not much longer. On a winter's night, with an aguish mist blanketing all that flat country, he had taken part in an exercise, fallen into a ditch, and still seen the thing through. A Hazard had to set an example to others, so he remained till dawn, soaked to the skin, took a cold bath in his stone bathroom when he got home, and died for his Spartan nonsense.

His son Roger needed to be a Spartan, too, and was. He remained obstinately, even clamorously, opposed to the war so long as Germany was in treaty with Russia; but once Russia was in it against Germany, he perceived the rightness of England's cause. He took an R.N.V.R. commission, and endured the anguish of service in destroyers convoying merchant ships to Murmansk. He was wounded by airplane fire, he was frozen to the marrow, and he lived through it uplifted by zeal for the messianic race whose cause he was serving. He made the voyage three times, and from the third voyage he did not at once come back. I never learned the truth of it: whether he missed his ship by accident, or whether of his own design he smuggled himself into the paradise he

540

wished to explore. All we knew was that he was missing, that questions from on high were addressed to Russia, that Russia knew nothing of any such person, was pained at the suggestion that she had anything to conceal in the matter of Lieut. Roger Hazard, R.N.V.R.

A long time later a motor launch, containing an armed guard, put him aboard a British destroyer at Murmansk, and immediately sheered off, with no explanation. What explanation Roger, on his part, gave to Authority, I do not know. To us, he was evasive. I met him before he joined another destroyer destined for warmer waters, and he gave me the impression of a frightened man. He was older, and, whatever had happened to him, wiser. I suppose the plunge into the icy water of knowledge is the more terrible when the imagination has been heated by fantasy. He was like a man who has been given a night by a long-desired beloved, and has found her embrace monstrous.

I do not expect or wish to see or hear anything more of Roger Hazard. He will now have to decide for himself what to do with his Somerset estates, how to excel in usefulness the ancestors he despised, and whether sandals and dirty fingernails will make a valuable contribution to the well-being of his tenants. Had Vera lived, it might have been otherwise, but she did not. It was now twenty years since Nika and I had heard the sound of the drums rushing like death's wind through the stony caves of York Minster, and had listened to the Archbishop complacently accepting the lives of women as the new and popular contribution to feeding Moloch. Well, both he and that cause had prospered since then. It was all in order now, nothing un-usual, nothing to make sermons about, for our daughters to join our sons among Christian soldiers, marching as to war. There is only one further advance to be made now. We must decide to use babies, too young to serve any other useful purpose, as rations for those who can fight; and the Archbishop's successor will then be able to dedicate a window in memory of the first ten thousand who thus give their lives for their country.

I can be bitter when I think of our little Vera. She was a child I especially loved, and who herself loved with a special intensity, even though she believed that she hated and despised mankind. It was because she loved and cared so much that her juvenile venom spouted at all that fell below her standards. It would in time, I think, have turned to the honey of wisdom. I had no fears for her. Better the venom in her mouth than the babble of love and brotherhood in the mouths of rogues and twisters. I remembered the light that sprang up in the stable, and the huge velvet eyes of the horse, and her arm round his neck as her cheek lay upon it, and the dogs padding softly. Love was there. If no wise men came to that stable, it was not her fault. It was in that moment that I knew her for a child of sorrow, because she was all compounded of love and would consequently be acquainted with grief. It was a summer's day in the Mediterranean Sea, and all the girls had for the first time put on their tropical whites, we were told by one who was saved. Vera had chosen the Wrens because Roger Hazard had chosen the Navy. There they were, then, making for some port where they were to be employed, in bridal white under the blue sky, when the torpedo hit them. "One of our destroyers got the submarine." Well, thank you, it all helps: that will be a few more widows, I suppose. What more can you ask?

About Kathy and poor Bob Seagrim I did not feel so badly. They were not the future, as Vera was. They were burned-out hulks that spurted into a final flame on the weltering sea of those days. They had never a moment's peace at the end. In such time as she could spare, Kathy called on me now more often than she had ever done. She looked terribly old, stringy and forlorn, without a lineament of peace or tranquillity in her face. Her brittle fingers were yellow with nicotine, and a cigarette was forever in her mouth, smoldering into her screwed-up eyes. She had a uniform of sorts, and dashed about driving a van through streets that were a horror of hissing water, and roaring flames, and crashing buildings, taking meals where they were wanted. She seemed to me to belong uniquely to all that she was doing: to those days of dread and nights of terror. She had gone through all her days without love, and seemed now a wild priestess, charioting through chaos, which is lovelessness.

Bob Seagrim was a fire warden. He had tried to be accepted into a rescue squad; but they wouldn't have him because of his leg. He, too, was often with me, Lord Cheveringham in a boiler suit and tin hat. Nothing could part him from either. He wore them to his club, which was blown to smithereens, and then to another club that took in the homeless. And then that one went, too, and the smashing-up of the clubs filled him with a terrible cold anger. "I mean, there'll be *nothing* left soon—what?"

Well, there was nothing left of Bob Seagrim or Kathy. They were together at the end, and I expect that is how they would have wanted it; and the end was a rocket that fell in a road they were crossing.

"Now do you really want to see Mr. Rimmel, or had we better get home?" Haggie asked. "You can't sit about in the streets like this."

I hadn't realized that I was sitting, but I was. There was a pile of cement blocks up against the frontage of the shop where Sally had recognized her mother, and I was sitting on that, looking at Rimmel's, miraculously preserved over the way, and my memories flooding about me.

"I have told you, Haggie my dear," I said, "how, outside this very shop, Sally Gaylord met her mother for the last time. Well, I've just

542

remembered something about that. Sally pretended to be a flower seller, and offered her mother some bunches of violets. She told me afterward that she had bought them because suddenly the sight and smell of them made her think of Tresant."

"It's time you began thinking of it, too," Haggie said. "You ought never to have stayed here all these years, and it's high time you were going."

I got up from my cold perch, and looked up and down the street that I should not see again after this day. "Yes, Haggie," I said. "It's high time I was going. Let us just say good-by to Mr. Rimmel."

So we crossed the road and said good-by to Julian and in the morning we were away.

6

As I have said, we thought to slip away quietly; but there was a deputation at Paddington: Sir Henry and Lady Shape, Sir Nicolas and Lady Mostyn-Lloyd, and Nika.

Poor Nika! She had lost everything. Nicolas was by her side, a hard-eyed looking man, but he was not holding her arm: he was holding Julia's. And that was right enough, I suppose: that was how it should be. Julia was certainly a wonderful-looking woman and they were still in love. I looked at Julia: as beautiful as Lucy Evans had ever been, but I was sure she had not Lucy's grim tenacity, her ability to strike a hard bargain with the world and see that the world kept it. She was a lovely husk, a gorgeous clothes-hanger. Well, even that was something.

I wished Nicolas would give a little attention to his mother. She was hanging behind the others, looking incredibly forlorn. Wars had taken from her a brother, a husband, a daughter. Life had denied her the one man to whom she could have given all she was. She had given Edward much, and he had deserved all she could give him; and I don't suppose she ever thought now of Julian Rimmel save as a distinguished-looking old man in whose company she could be at ease. But I knew there was much that she had never become that she could have become. There were empty rooms in her house whose doors she had learned not to open, and it is a pity to have to learn that.

But there it is, I thought. Life is not a fairy tale, with the prince and the glass coach arriving punctually at the door. At best it is an endless climb, with the peak for your aim and the foothills for your last bed if you are lucky.

I had tried to persuade Nika to come with me to Tresant, but she would not, and that was sensible. It was only selfishness that asked it. A creature as near to death as I was should crawl the last yards with as little disturbance as possible to other people. Nika's old house in St. John's Wood—the house she had sold to Sophia—was gone. The naked lady who had amused Glory Jane, the mulberry tree and the fine room where Mrs. Grimshaw had once displayed her sacred cows and Budders: all went in a flash and a flame, and there were now few corporeal things to link me with Maggie Whale. Time I was off. Nika lived now, alone save for one little maid, in the cottage where she would have nothing but memories: memories of Maggie "receiving" in her gorgeous purple; memories (I hoped) of my visits; memories of Vera riding Firdausi upon the lean downs, a plain-faced Diana forever outdistanced by the elusive quarry of her imagination.

Sir Henry Shape said: "Haggie, be sure Mrs. Undridge doesn't try to get to the luncheon car. She might fall in the swaying corridors. You'll find all you need in that basket." He smiled at me. "I'm afraid the train will go at more than thirty miles an hour. And you won't be able to poke the driver in the back with your stick."

Everything about him was perfect: his clothes, his manicured hands, his close-cropped glistening white hair, his strong white teeth. He smelled as though he used perfumed soap twice a day in his bath. The train, the station, most of the passengers, had that drear and shabby, unrepaired, uncared-for look that the long struggle had put upon the world: it had put this look into the world's eyes: the poor old ersatz, second-hand, down at heel, make-do-and-mend world. Mend? I wondered. There comes a time when all's past mending. But Sir Henry Shape was on top of all this. He looked like a new Rolls Royce consorting with the time-battered motor hulks that turn out for the annual run to Brighton.

And, of course, I thought, that is how it must be. Henry is the mechanic who will ride high over whatever it is that civilization is reaching for. He is one of the masters.

Sophia looked well pleased to have Henry as he was. After all, he was nothing much when she took up with him. There were plenty then who thought her a fool, and she had now the complacency of those who see faith justified. Henry had never given her a moment's anxiety; he had gone straight as a locomotive along a track. She looked, I thought, a little prim. I hoped humanity in general would have reason to be as well pleased with its Henry Shapes as she was. He was certainly, I said to myself, happy that at my age I could make my little private joke, the Shape of things to come. As for Nicolas, he would always be content to be a satellite of that planet.

"Now," I said, "off with you—all the lot of you. I don't like people hanging round till the train begins to move. And there's one thing certain: if you want to see me again you'll have to come to Cornwall. I shall never come back to London."

544

They all kissed me then. Julia was the last, and for some reason hers were the only eyes that had tears. She was so young and so lovely: perhaps, more than the others, she caught a whiff of life's tragedy, saw in a flash, in the greatness of my years and time's December ravages in my face, what all must tend to, even her April. I felt that I had remained too long in life as death's remembrancer.

"Good-by, my dear," I said. "Kiss the children for me," and when they were all gone I said to myself how false that was. For I was tired of the generations; Julia's children meant nothing to me. They would have to make such terms as they could with the world that time and change would spin beneath their feet.

CHAPTER THIRTY

I

YOU think you can stand anything. Even at my age you are foolish enough to think that—just like the fool-politicians and the fool-scientists who think they can go on forever monkeying about with human society and its physical environment. I don't know what they are going to discover soon: but I have discovered, since coming down here to Tresant, that my revels now are ended. Theirs well may be, too.

I have not been unwell, but after the tension of being in London through all the war years I am tired. I hardly stir out of the house. The year was well advanced when Haggie and I got here: winter was soon upon us; and I was glad to hibernate. Now and then, in a gleam of winter sunshine, I go out onto the gravel and move up and down for half an hour; then I am glad to come indoors and sit by the fire. I easily become cold in the feet and hands, even though I live in wool boots and wear mittens that Haggie industriously knits.

The times I like best are the mornings and the evenings. In the mornings I get up about ten, have breakfast by the fire in my bedroom, and then go on with this writing. This is the room my mother and Lord Burnage had, the room where they both died and where my little brother Justin was born. I am not disturbed by these ghosts, or by any others who must thickly throng this place. I am still in the land of the living, and it is in living shape that so many people come back to me. I am able to accept them all comfortably: here by the fire, sitting at the desk that Lord Burnage sent down to Whaley's cottage for me, that went with me to London, and is now back on the spot to which Mr. Sheraton first delivered it. Yes, I can accept all these who are long dead and gone, but living for me, far more comfortably than I can accept, say, the children of Nicolas and Julia Mostyn-Lloyd. That very name: Mostyn-Lloyd! When it drifts into my mind, it is never of great-grandchildren that I think, or of grandchildren either. It is of that gaunt woman, Lucy Evans's mother, pondering on her child's future and deciding to make what use she could of the sister who had married a Welsh draper. Of her, and of that sister herself whom Lucy so ruthlessly supplanted, and of Mostyn-Lloyd, that odd mixture of shrewdness and slippery guile, of downright roguery and generous impulse.

And once started on such a track as that, off my mind would go to wander among the beings that Lucy's bright presence had allured, as a shining spinner allures the deep-sea creatures out of their lairs. The loathsome Cupples and his henchman Eeles; that pathetic weakling Aloysius Slinn, and the wretched girl Skirrow he had married and run from. Already they, and their vibrations on the outskirts of my own life, seemed as far off as though they were creatures I had read about in some old tale.

So it went in my bedroom in the mornings, my mind sometimes seduced down those dark lanes and alleyways, sometimes pulling itself up to confront the necessity of adding new lines and bringing this record to a close. But it was very slow, this work at the growing end, slow and tiring. I was readier for musing than for even such light toil as taking the pen across the paper. It was not light to me, and for an hour at a time my cold hand would lie upon the paper, and I would be staring at its veins as if they were blue roads leading back over the hills and through the valleys of my years. It would be nice, I would think, to be able to make something neat and finished of it all, as though it were a work of art which, if it had nothing else, had the beauty of significance. But I could not do this. I had lost too many of the threads. I had lost even some of the characters in the play. They had just walked off the stage, without any telling last line, and were seen no more. The Cogans, for example. What had happened to Zealous Zebedee, to Conscientious Cogan, and the Young Lady of Graybird Court? I simply did not know. I did not know whether they were alive or dead. Dead, I supposed.

Haggie would come in to make up the fire, a brown, thin, aging woman, and she would glance at my feet, to make sure I was wearing my wool boots, and at my hands, and say: "You've left those mittens off again. You'll be perished. And ought you to be sitting there straining your eyes over that old writing? Hundreds and hundreds of pages. What's it all about?"

"Never you mind what it's all about, my girl."

And when she was gone her question would remain. What was it all about?—this story of a child of three who had skipped like a lamb

546

because the world was ringing with promise, and who was now squeezing the last drops out of an old dishclout amid ruins and lamentation. I would turn over the hundreds and hundreds of pages, beginning with a firm confident hand, weakening and wavering, ending in this unlovely scrawl, these blots and incertitudes. What was it all about? And I would give up for the day. I don't know. . . . I don't know. . . .

In the evenings we sat in a small paneled room downstairs. Haggie would read to me, for though my eyes were good enough for reading large print I was afraid to strain them. My senses were all there, but they were diminished: sight, smell and hearing were fading. There is a great bush of wintersweet outside the window. When I was a child, the bouquet of the yellow flowers could intoxicate a winter's day for me. Haggie loved it, and there were always a few sprays in this little room, but now I had to stick my nose into the heart of them to catch a faint odor. It grieved me, this dimming of the faculties by which animals are in contact with their physical world. My sight, above all, I clung to, and so Haggie read—old books. I was a lover of rereading: the sifted and the certain. There could be no new truth, no new beauty: only, at best, new forms for it; and I was too old to be chasing new forms. I would preserve my mind, like my body, with the food that experience had proved it to thrive on. A juicy Dickens steak suited me better than the fashionable vitamin pills. And if I went to sleep at the fireside and Haggie had to wake me up to ask: "Now do you want your game of dominoes, or are you going straight to bed?"—well, that was only to be expected at ninety-six.

2

And then I was ninety-seven. The winter was gone, and here was another May the first for Sarah Undridge, who was Sarah Rainborough.

Haggie came in and drew back the curtains. She had brought a great bunch of camellias—the superb ones we call *camellia reticulata*. Almost six inches across some of the flowers were, lovely pink things still wet with dew. She put them in a bowl by the bedside and then kissed me on the forehead. "Many happy returns of the day," she said. "Will you be getting up?"

"Of course I shall be getting up. Don't treat me as if I were an old woman."

"You *are* an old woman."

"I know I am. But don't treat me like one. I shall not only get up: I shall go out."

"It will be the death of you," she said, still twiddling with the flowers.

547

"What if it is? Something's got to be the death of us—all of us. You might bear that in mind. You're no chicken. And, anyway, it won't be the death of me. I shall live to be a hundred. I've set my mind on that. Boost up these pillows."

She raised me in the bed and arranged the pillows behind my back. "You're in a bad mood," she said.

"I have a right to be in any mood I like. It's my birthday. Not many people gave their first squeak ninety-seven years ago."

"If you go out, you mustn't go far."

"We'll see about that. I shall go this afternoon in the donkey cart. Now kiss me. And kiss me properly. I don't like this habit you have of pecking like a canary."

She kissed me properly and asked: "What would you like for breakfast?"

"Why do you insist every morning on asking that silly question? You remind me of a coachman we once had—a man named Ducat. He drove my father to the City every morning, and though he knew very well where they were going to, he always asked: 'Where to, sir?'"

"Yes. You've told me about that."

"All right. I know I'm an old bore. You needn't remind me. And you needn't ask me what I'll have for breakfast when you know full well that I never have anything but a cup of warm milk. I'll have coffee."

"Coffee! It'll be the death of you!"

"You seem to think that death and I are becoming very familiar. You're a cheerful soul on a birthday morning, I must say. Just put enough coffee into the milk to make it look like a birthday drink."

"There are lots of letters and telegrams."

"They can wait."

"Are you all right now? Shall I go and get the milk?"

"Of course I'm all right. I've never been better. You can go and get the coffee. And if you can recognize Mr. Rimmel's writing, bring me his letter. The others can wait."

I opened the drawer in my bedside table and took out the bracelet Nika had given me on a birthday morning in Chelsea long ago. It was always kept there. I put it on, and it slipped over my wrist more easily than it had done then. When it was on, I kept my hand still on the counterpane. I didn't want to think about it—not yet. I just wanted it to be there. I wore it always on my birthdays.

Haggie brought me the milky coffee and Julian's letter and went away. When I had drunk the coffee I read the letter and thought about Julian. It was here I had first seen him, a sprightly child, dancing beside his solid parents. I hoped he would not be disgusted with the mountain of manuscript I intended to lay upon him. It was beginning

548

to be burdensome to me, and I hated to see how the words shook and wavered on the page. The lines were so firm and resolute at the beginning, written in that hand that had proudly transcribed Whaley's books—dear, dear Whaley—and now they trembled like a candle flame that feels the draft and has little wax left to consume.

Well, I thought resolutely, make an end of it then. What happens to you henceforth can be nothing but a slow dying. Have done, you old ghost. You have finished with life.

So be it. Tonight, I said, if I feel up to it, I shall write *Nunc dimittis*, though I cannot pretend that I shall depart in peace, having seen salvation.

What *have* I seen? I wondered, looking out over the wide sea. The donkey had brought me in the wicker carriage that spared my old bones with its air-filled tires. Haggie walked at his head, but he needed no guiding. He knew the way well enough—past the lake where the lily leaves lay in rafts and the coots and moorhens bobbed ahead of the broad arrows that the sun caught and set glittering; into the path that hung over the water where the white swans sailed like ships convoying a fleet of downy cygnets, and on the right the pine boles' corrugations had the hardy and immemorial look of things that have seen and survived much coming and going of transient life, planting themselves deeper and deeper into the wisdom of the earth, though in the long run that will not avail them: they must go, also: there will be one storm too many.

The new foliage was green and gentle overhead, and the wood anemones starred the grass on the path's border. I knew it all: every yard, every inch, nid-nodding my way through it as if I were not seeing it but being it. Here now was the great revelation: the burst out from umbrage, out from the shadow of the leaves that were new every spring, to the unchanging deep of the salty sea.

"Now help me out," I said to Haggie, and she said: "Surely you're not going to get out!" and I said: "Do as you're told, girl, or I'll get out without you."

She laughed and said: "Girl, indeed!" and helped me out.

I tottered a little when my feet were on the rough ground, but her arm was about me; and I said: "Thank you, my dear. You are very good to me."

"You perplex me today," she said, and looked as if she were going to cry. "I don't know what's come over you."

But I knew very well what had come over me. I should never be here again: that was all. I lowered myself with her help onto a cushion of thyme in a spot where a lichened rock, warmed by the sun, gave me support. She pulled my cloak about me, and I said: "Now leave me. Come back for me in half an hour."

What have I seen? I wondered, looking out on the wide heave and swell, and down onto the bar, and away to Porteven whose gray roofs shone in the sunlight. Well, I have seen no salvation, no peace on earth, good will to men. I have seen courage, endurance and loyalty, dishonor, treachery and shame. I have seen what makes the life of men. It was so long ago since a child had been childishly uplifted by thoughts of Man, an animal advancing with one heart and mind toward a good goal. And now all that was gone; the crystal ship had sailed away and vanished over the horizon, as these majestic swans now came, with a heart-stirring noise of wings, beating up from the landlocked water and out into the blue over the sea till my eyes could follow them no longer. There were left for me only men and women—and not many of those now—good, and bad, and oddly mixed; and until enough of these separate bricks were good I did not see much hope of palace-building. There was so much that you could do—all those things that Dame Dolly Dewhirst had rightly been honored for having tried to get done—but all my weary years had not taught me to believe that the City of God was like a municipal bathhouse, or ever could be built so.

It seemed to me, sitting there against the warm rock, a poor conclusion to have drawn from so much living; but there had been the living itself, and the surprising versatility of God's creatures that I had known, and I was sorry that it was coming to an end. I would gladly live for another century, I thought, to see what will come out of it all; and I raised my hand to shelter my eyes from the sun, and the bells on Nika's bracelet rang faintly to remind me that it could not be. "There!" she had cried, putting it on to my arm. "Do you hear little Sarah Rainborough?" And backward now, not forward, was the course for me: backward through the memory of so many lost and foundered years.

Falmouth, January 19, 1949
January 11, 1951.